'The first two volumes of one of the greatest novels ever written'   Kim Stanley Robinson

'A masterpiece. Totally original, new, incomparable; the beginning of something great'   Ursula Le Guin

'One of the great science fantasy epics of all time'
                                                      George R.R. Martin

Also by Gene Wolfe

The Book of The New Sun

SHADOW AND CLAW

The Shadow of the Torturer
The Claw of the Conciliator

GENE WOLFE

Text copyright © Gene Wolfe 1980, 1981
Introduction copyright © Alastair Reynolds 2011
All rights reserved

The right of Gene Wolfe to be identified as the author of this work
and of Alastair Reynolds to be identified as the author of this
introduction has been asserted by them in accordance with the
Copyright, Designs and Patents Act 1988.

First published in Great Britain in 2000 by
Millennium
An imprint of Victor Gollancz

This edition published in Great Britain in 2011 by
Gollancz
An imprint of the Orion Publishing Group
Orion House, 5 Upper St Martin's Lane,
London WC2H 9EA
An Hachette UK Company

A CIP catalogue record for this book
is available from the British Library

Printed and bound by CPI Group (UK) Ltd, Croydon, CRO 4YY

The Orion Publishing Group's policy is to use papers that
are natural, renewable and recyclable products and made
from wood grown in sustainable forests. The logging and
manufacturing processes are expected to conform to the
environmental regulations of the country of origin.

www.orionbooks.co.uk

INTRODUCTION

The Book of the New Sun – the first two volumes of which constitute this omnibus edition – is that rare thing: a genuine classic of the field which was recognised as such immediately upon publication, and which has only gained in stature in the intervening decades. It remains as mysterious as it is influential, and there can be little doubt that, fifty or a hundred years from now – if books are still being read and discussed at all – it will be regarded as one of the central texts of late twentieth century science fiction. Its staunchest admirers, in fact, are content simply to rate it as a great work of fiction, irrespective of genre.

Although Wolfe had published novels before *The Book of the New Sun*, his reputation at that point rested largely on an astonishing and diverse body of short fiction, most of which had appeared in the preceding decade. Startlingly diverse in theme, many of these stories nonetheless foreshadowed the key obsessions that would occupy him through the writing of the New Sun novels and subsequent associated works. Puzzles of identity and memory, the nature of narrative itself, and a deep interest in religious motifs loom large in Wolfe's output. From the outset it has also been clear that Wolfe requires commitment from his readers; a willingness to interrogate the surface of his stories, alert to those off-hand details and seeming inconsistencies which may unlock vast layers of subterranean meaning. This was no more apparent than in *The Fifth Head of Cerberus*, Wolfe's previous science fiction novel, which in three masterful novellas illuminated a story of confused identity in a crumbling, gloom-saturated far future.

The Book of the New Sun is also unambiguously science fiction, although the inattentive reader could be forgiven for mistaking the furniture and tone for that of baroque fantasy. As in the 'Dying

Earth' tales of Wolfe's central inspiration, Jack Vance, there are swords, magicians, monsters and fabled relics. But the magic is almost entirely explicable in terms of forgotten science, and the setting – it is not giving too much away – is really our own post-technological Earth, countless thousands (even millions) of years in the future, after a period of galactic expansion and contraction. None of this is stated baldly, however. We explore 'Urth' through the only partially trustworthy eyes of Severian, formerly of the Guild of Torturers, now a disgraced executioner for hire. Wolfe's masterstroke, sustained for the entirety of the quartet, is to present to us the complexities of Urth and its associated cosmos in a manner entirely consistent with Severian's position, background and personal concerns, and at the same time convey to us all (or nearly all) that we need to make sense of this strange, dreamlike environment. It is a testament to the richness of the text, and Wolfe's complete inhabitation of Severian's state of mind, that an entire school of debate has accreted around the interpretation of the books' many colourful incidents and details.

If the above risks framing *The Book of the New Sun* as an exercise in impenetrable obscurantism, nothing could be further from the truth. The genius of the thing is that it operates on the level of ripping adventure story, replete with action, horror, romance and daring-do *while at the same time* offering ample reward for those prepared to read carefully, and to re-read and re-read.

The language is splendid, the characterisation marvellous, the set pieces guaranteed to haunt the mind for years. Trust me on this. I re-read *The Book of the New Sun* about once a decade, I hope to continue doing so for decades to come, and I doubt very much that I will ever exhaust its wonders.

Alastair Reynolds

Alastair Reynolds (www.alastairreynolds.com) is the author of, amongst others, the REVELATION SPACE trilogy (REVELATION SPACE, REDEMPTION ARK and ABSOLUTION GAP) as well as HOUSE OF SUNS and TERMINAL WORLD.

Alastair has donated his fee for this introduction to the Alzheimer's Society.

www.alzheimers.org.uk

THE SHADOW OF
THE TORTURER

A thousand ages in thy sight
  Are like an evening gone;
Short as the watch that ends the night
  Before the rising sun.

Resurrection and Death

IT IS POSSIBLE I already had some presentiment of my future. The locked and rusted gate that stood before us, with wisps of river fog threading its spikes like the mountain paths, remains in my mind now as the symbol of my exile. That is why I have begun this account of it with the aftermath of our swim, in which I, the torturer's apprentice Severian, had so nearly drowned.

"The guard has gone." Thus my friend Roche spoke to Drotte, who had already seen it for himself.

Doubtfully, the boy Eata suggested that we go around. A lift of his thin, freckled arm indicated the thousands of paces of wall stretching across the slum and sweeping up the hill until at last they met the high curtain wall of the Citadel. It was a walk I would take, much later.

"And try to get through the barbican without a safe-conduct? They'd send to Master Gurloes."

"But why would the guard leave?"

"It doesn't matter." Drotte rattled the gate. "Eata, see if you can slip between the bars."

Drotte was our captain, and Eata put an arm and a leg through the iron palings, but it was immediately clear that there was no hope of his getting his body to follow.

"Someone's coming," Roche whispered. Drotte jerked Eata out.

I looked down the street. Lanterns swung there among the fog-muffled sounds of feet and voices. I would have hidden, but Roche held me, saying, "Wait, I see pikes."

"Do you think it's the guard returning?"

He shook his head. "Too many."

"A dozen men at least," Drotte said.

Still wet from Gyoll we waited. In the recesses of my mind we stand shivering there even now. Just as all that appears imperishable tends toward its own destruction, those moments that at the time seem the most fleeting recreate themselves—not only in my memory (which in the final accounting loses nothing) but in the throbbing of my heart and the prickling of my hair, making themselves new just as our Commonwealth reconstitutes itself each morning in the shrill tones of its own clarions.

The men had no armor, as I could soon see by the sickly yellow light of the lanterns; but they had pikes, as Drotte had said, and staves and hatchets. Their leader wore a long, double-edged knife in his belt. What interested me more was the massive key threaded on a cord around his neck; it looked as if it might fit the lock of the gate.

Little Eata fidgeted with nervousness, and the leader saw us and lifted his lantern over his head. "We're waiting to get in, goodman," Drotte called. He was the taller, but he made his dark face humble and respectful.

"Not until dawn," the leader said gruffly. "You young fellows had better get home."

"Goodman, the guard was supposed to let us in, but he's not here."

"You won't be getting in tonight." The leader put his hand on the hilt of his knife before taking a step closer. For a moment I was afraid he knew who we were.

Drotte moved away, and the rest of us stayed behind him. "Who are you, goodman? You're not soldiers."

"We're the volunteers," one of the others said. "We come to protect our own dead."

"Then you can let us in."

The leader had turned away. "We let no one inside but ourselves." His key squealed in the lock, and the gate creaked back. Before anyone could stop him Eata darted through. Someone cursed, and the leader and two others sprinted after Eata, but he was too fleet for them. We saw his tow-colored hair and patched shirt zigzag among the sunken graves of paupers, then disappear in the thicket of statuary higher up. Drotte tried to pursue him, but two men grabbed his arms.

"We have to find him. We won't rob you of your dead."

"Why do you want to go in, then?" one volunteer asked.

"To gather herbs," Drotte told him. "We are physicians' gallipots. Don't you want the sick healed?"

The volunteer stared at him. The man with the key had dropped his lantern when he ran after Eata, and there were only two left. In their dim light the volunteer looked stupid and innocent; I suppose he was a laborer of some kind.

Drotte continued, "You must know that for certain simples to attain their highest virtues they must be pulled from grave soil by moonlight. It will frost soon and kill everything, but our masters require supplies for the winter. The three of them arranged for us to enter tonight, and I borrowed that lad from his father to help me."

"You don't have anything to put simples in."

I still admire Drotte for what he did next. He said, "We are to bind them in sheaves to dry," and without the least hesitation drew a length of common string from his pocket.

"I see," the volunteer said. It was plain he did not. Roche and I edged nearer the gate.

Drotte actually stepped back from it. "If you won't let us gather the herbs, we'd better go. I don't think we could ever find that boy in there now."

"No you don't. We have to get him out."

"All right," Drotte said reluctantly, and we stepped through, the volunteers following. Certain mystes aver that the real world has been constructed by the human mind, since our ways are governed by the artificial categories into which we place essentially undifferentiated things, things weaker than our words for them. I understood the principle intuitively that night as I heard the last volunteer swing the gate closed behind us.

A man who had not spoken before said, "I'm going to watch over my mother. We've wasted too much time already. They could have her a league off by now."

Several of the others muttered agreement, and the group began to scatter, one lantern moving to the left and the other to the right. We went up the center path (the one we always took in returning to the fallen section of the Citadel wall) with the remaining volunteers.

It is my nature, my joy and my curse, to forget nothing. Every rattling chain and whistling wind, every sight, smell, and taste, remains changeless in my mind, and though I know it is not so with everyone, I cannot imagine what it can mean to be otherwise, as if one had slept when in fact an experience is merely remote. Those few steps we took upon the whited path rise before me now: It was cold and growing colder; we had no light, and fog had begun to roll in from Gyoll in earnest. A few birds had come to roost in the pines and cypresses, and flapped uneasily from tree to tree. I remember the feel of my own hands as I rubbed my arms, and the lantern bobbing among the steles some distance off, and how the fog brought out the smell of the river water in my shirt, and the pungency of the new-turned earth. I had almost died that day, choking in the netted roots; the night was to mark the beginning of my manhood.

There was a shot, a thing I had never seen before, the bolt of violet energy splitting the darkness like a wedge, so that it closed with a thunderclap. Somewhere a monument fell with a crash. Silence then . . . in which everything around me seemed to dissolve. We began to run. Men were shouting, far off. I heard the ring of steel on stone, as if someone had struck one of the grave markers with a badelaire. I dashed along a path that was (or at least then seemed) completely unfamiliar, a ribbon of broken bone just wide enough for two to walk abreast that wound down into a little dale. In the fog I could see nothing but the dark bulk of the memorials to either side. Then, as suddenly as if it had been snatched away, the path was no longer beneath my feet—I suppose I must have failed to notice some turning. I swerved to dodge an oblesque that appeared to shoot up before me, and collided full tilt with a man in a black coat.

He was solid as a tree; the impact took me off my feet and knocked my breath away. I heard him muttering execrations, then a whispering sound as he swung some weapon. Another voice called, "What was that?"

"Somebody ran into me. Gone now, whoever he was."

I lay still.

A woman said, "Open the lamp." Her voice was like a dove's call, but there was urgency in it.

The man I had run against answered, "They would be on us like a pack of dholes, Madame."

"They will be soon in any case—Vodalus fired. You must have heard it."

"Be more likely to keep them off."

In an accent I was too inexperienced to recognize as an exultant's, the man who had spoken first said, "I wish I hadn't brought it. We shouldn't need it against this sort of people." He was much nearer now, and in a moment I could see him through the fog, very tall, slender, and hatless, standing near the heavier man I had run into. Muffled in black, a third figure was apparently the woman. In losing my wind I had also lost the strength of my limbs, but I managed to roll behind the base of a statue, and once secure there I peered out at them again.

My eyes had grown accustomed to the dark. I could distinguish the woman's heart-shaped face and note that she was nearly as tall as the slender man she had called Vodalus. The heavy man had disappeared, but I heard him say, "More rope." His voice indicated that he was no more than a step or two away from the spot where I crouched, but he seemed to have vanished like water cast into a well. Then I saw something dark (it must have been the crown of his hat) move near the slender man's feet, and understood that that was almost precisely what had become of him—there was a hole there, and he was in it.

The woman asked, "How is she?"

"Fresh as a flower, Madame. Hardly a breath of stink on her, and nothing to worry about." More agilely than I would have thought possible, he sprang out. "Now give me one end and you take the other, Liege, and we'll have her out like a carrot."

The woman said something I could not hear, and the slender man told her, "You didn't have to come, Thea. How would it look to the others if I took none of the risks?" He and the heavy man grunted as they pulled, and I saw something white appear at their feet. They bent to lift it. As though an amschaspand had touched them with his radiant wand, the fog swirled and parted to let a beam of green moonlight fall. They had the corpse of a woman. Her hair, which had been dark, was in some disorder now about her livid face; she wore a long gown of some pale fabric.

"You see," the heavy man said, "just as I told you, Liege, Madame, nineteen times of a score there's nothin' to it. We've only to get her over the wall now."

The words were no sooner out of his mouth than I heard someone shout. Three of the volunteers were coming down the path over the rim of the dale. "Hold them off, Liege," the heavy man growled, shouldering the corpse. "I'll take care of this, and get Madame to safety."

"Take it," Vodalus said. The pistol he handed over caught the moonlight like a mirror.

The heavy man gaped at it. "I've never used one, Liege . . ."

"Take it, you may need it." Vodalus stooped, then rose holding what appeared to be a dark stick. There was a rattle of metal on wood, and in place of the stick a bright and narrow blade. He called, "*Guard yourselves!*"

As if a dove had momentarily commanded an arctother, the

woman took the shining pistol from the heavy man's hand, and together they backed into the fog.

The three volunteers had hesitated. Now one moved to the right and another to the left, so as to attack from three sides. The man in the center (still on the white path of broken bones) had a pike, and one of the others an ax.

The third was the leader Drotte had spoken with outside the gate. "Who are you?" he called to Vodalus, "and what power of Erebus's gives you the right to come here and do something like this?"

Vodalus did not reply, but the point of his sword looked from one to another like an eye.

The leader grated, "All together now and we'll have him." But they advanced hesitantly, and before they could close Vodalus sprang forward. I saw his blade flash in the faint light and heard it scrape the head of the pike—a metallic slithering, as though a steel serpent glided across a log of iron. The pikeman yelled and jumped back; Vodalus leaped backward too (I think for fear the other two would get behind him), then seemed to lose his balance and fell.

All this took place in dark and fog. I saw it, but for the most part the men were no more than ambient shadows—as the woman with the heart-shaped face had been. Yet something touched me. Perhaps it was Vodalus's willingness to die to protect her that made the woman seem precious to me; certainly it was that willingness that kindled my admiration for him. Many times since then, when I have stood upon a shaky platform in some market-town square with *Terminus Est* at rest before me and a miserable vagrant kneeling at my feet, when I have heard in hissing whispers the hate of the crowd and sensed what was far less welcome, the admiration of those who find an unclean joy in pains and deaths not their own, I have recalled Vodalus at the graveside, and raised my own blade half pretending that when it fell I would be striking for him.

He stumbled, as I have said. In that instant I believe my whole life teetered in the scales with his.

The flanking volunteers ran toward him, but he had held onto his weapon. I saw the bright blade flash up, though its owner was still on the ground. I remember thinking what a fine thing it would have been to have had such a sword on the day Drotte became captain of apprentices, and then likening Vodalus to myself.

The axman, toward whom he had thrust, drew back; the other drove forward with his long knife. I was on my feet by then, watching the fight over the shoulder of a chalcedony angel, and I saw the knife come down, missing Vodalus by a thumb's width as he writhed away and burying itself to the hilt in the ground. Vodalus slashed at the leader then, but he was too near for the length of his blade. The leader, instead of backing off, released his weapon and clutched him like a wrestler. They were at the very edge of the opened grave—I suppose Vodalus had tripped over the soil excavated from it.

The second volunteer raised his ax, then hesitated. His leader was nearest him; he circled to get a clear stroke until he was less than a pace from where I hid. While he shited his ground I saw Vodalus wrench the knife free and drive it into the leader's throat. The ax rose to strike; I grasped the helve just below the head almost by reflex, and found myself at once in the struggle, kicking, then striking.

Quite suddenly it was over. The volunteer whose bloodied weapon I held was dead. The leader of the volunteers was writhing at our feet. The pikeman was gone; his pike lay harmlessly across the path. Vodalus retrieved a black wand from the grass nearby and sheathed his sword in it. "Who are you?"

"Severian. I am a torturer. Or rather, I am an apprentice of the torturers, Liege. Of the Order of the Seekers for Truth and Penitence." I drew a deep breath. "I am a Vodalarius. One of

the thousands of Vodalarii of whose existence you are unaware."
It was a term I had scarcely heard.

"Here." He laid something in my palm: a small coin so
smooth it seemed greased. I remained clutching it beside the
violated grave and watched him stride away. The fog swallowed
him long before he reached the rim, and a few moments later a
silver flier as sharp as a dart screamed overhead.

The knife had somehow fallen from the dead man's neck.
Perhaps he had pulled it out in his agony. When I bent to pick it
up, I discovered that the coin was still in my hand and thrust it
into my pocket.

We believe that we invent symbols. The truth is that they
invent us; we are their creatures, shaped by their hard, defining
edges. When soldiers take their oath they are given a coin, an
asimi stamped with the profile of the Autarch. Their acceptance
of that coin is their acceptance of the special duties and burdens
of military life—they are soldiers from that moment, though
they may know nothing of the management of arms. I did not
know that then, but it is a profound mistake to believe that we
must know of such things to be influenced by them, and in fact
to believe so is to believe in the most debased and superstitious
kind of magic. The would-be sorcerer alone has faith in the
efficacy of pure knowledge; rational people know that things act
of themselves or not at all.

Thus I knew nothing, as the coin dropped into my pocket, of
the dogmas of the movement Vodalus led, but I soon learned
them all, for they were in the air. With him I hated the
Autarchy, though I had no notion of what might replace it.
With him I despised the exultants who failed to rise against the
Autarch and bound the fairest of their daughters to him in
ceremonial concubinage. With him I detested the people for
their lack of discipline and a common purpose. Of those values
that Master Malrubius (who had been master of apprentices
when I was a boy) had tried to teach me, and that Master

Palaemon still tried to impart, I accepted only one: loyalty to the guild. In that I was quite correct—it was, as I sensed, perfectly feasible for me to serve Vodalus and remain a torturer. It was in this fashion that I began the long journey by which I have backed into the throne.

Severian

MEMORY OPPRESSES ME. Having been reared among the torturers, I have never known my father or my mother. No more did my brother apprentices know theirs. From time to time, but most particularly when winter draws on, poor wretches come clamoring to the Corpse Door, hoping to be admitted to our ancient guild. Often they regale Brother Porter with accounts of the torments they will willingly inflict in payment for warmth and food; occasionally they fetch animals as samples of their work.

All are turned away. Traditions from our days of glory, antedating the present degenerate age, and the one before it, and the one before that, an age whose name is hardly remembered now by scholars, forbid recruitment from such as they. Even at the time I write of, when the guild had shrunk to two masters and less than a score of journeymen, those traditions were honored.

From my earliest memory I remember all. That first recollection is of piling pebbles in the Old Yard. It lies south and west of the Witches' Keep, and is separated from the Grand Court. The curtain wall our guild was to help defend was ruinous even then, with a wide gap between the Red Tower and the Bear, where I used to climb the fallen slabs of unsmeltable gray metal to look out over the necropolis that descends that side of Citadel Hill.

When I was older, it became my playground. The winding paths were patrolled during daylight hours, but the sentries were largely concerned for the fresher graves on the lower ground, and knowing us to belong to the torturers, they seldom had much stomach for expelling us from our lurking places in the cypress groves.

Our necropolis is said to be the oldest in Nessus. That is certainly false, but the very existence of the error testifies to a real antiquity, though the autarchs were not buried there even when the Citadel was their stronghold, and the great families—then as now—preferred to inter their long-limbed dead in vaults on their own estates. But the armigers and optimates of the city favored the highest slopes, near the Citadel wall; and the poorer commons lay below them until the farthest reaches of the bottom lands, pressing against the tenements that came to line Gyoll, held potter's fields. As a boy I seldom went so far alone, or half so far.

There were always the three of us—Drotte, Roche, and I. Later Eata, the next oldest among the apprentices. None of us were born among the torturers, for none are. It is said that in ancient times there were both men and women in the guild, and that sons and daughters were born to them and brought up in the mystery, as is now the case among the lamp-makers and the goldsmiths and many other guilds. But Ymar the Almost Just, observing how cruel the women were and how often they exceeded the punishments he had decreed, ordered that there should be women among the torturers no more.

Since that time our numbers have been repaired solely from the children of those who fall into our hands. In our Matachin Tower, a certain bar of iron thrusts from a bulkhead at the height of a man's groin. Male children small enough to stand upright beneath it are nurtured as our own; and when a woman big with child is sent to us we open her and if the babe draws breath engage a wet-nurse if it be a boy. The females are rendered to the witches. So it has been since the days of Ymar, and those days are now by many hundreds of years forgotten.

Thus none of us knows our descent. Each would be an exultant if he could, and it is a fact that many persons of high lineage are given over to us. As boys each of us formed his own conjectures, and each attempted to question the older brothers among the journeymen, though they were locked in their own bitternesses and told us little. Eata, believing himself descended of that family, drew the arms of one of the great northern clans on the ceiling above his cot in the year of which I speak.

For my part, I had already adopted as my own the device graved in bronze above the door of a certain mausoleum. They were a fountain rising above waters, and a ship *volant*, and below these a rose. The door itself had been sprung long ago; two empty coffins lay on the floor. Three more, too heavy for me to shift and still intact, waited on the shelves along one wall. Neither the closed coffins nor the open ones constituted the attraction of the place, though I sometimes rested on what remained of the soft, fadded padding of the latter. Rather, it was the smallness of the room, the thick walls of masonry, and the single, narrow window with its one bar, together with the faithless door (so massively heavy) that remained eternally ajar.

Through window and door I could look out unseen on all the bright life of tree and shrub and grass outside. The linnets and rabbits that fled when I approached could neither hear nor scent me there. I watched the storm crow build her nest and rear her young two cubits from my face. I saw the fox trot by with upraised brush; and once that giant fox, taller than all but the tallest hounds, that men call the maned wolf, loped by at dusk on some unguessable errand from the ruined quarters of the south. The caracara coursed vipers for me, and the hawk lifted his wings to the wind from the top of a pine.

A moment suffices to describe these things, for which I watched so long. The decades of a saros would not be long enough for me to write all they meant to the ragged apprentice boy I was. Two thoughts (that were nearly dreams) obsessed me and made them infinitely precious. The first was that at some not-distant time, time itself would stop . . . the colored days that had so long been drawn forth like a chain of conjuror's scarves come to an end, the sullen sun wink out at last. The second was that there existed somewhere a miraculous light—which I sometimes conceived of as a candle, sometimes as a flambeau—that engendered life in whatever objects it fell upon, so that a leaf plucked from a bush grew slender legs and waving feelers, and a rough brown brush opened black eyes and scurried up a tree.

Yet sometimes, particularly in the sleepy hours around noon, there was little to watch. Then I turned again to the blazon over the door and wondered what a ship, a rose, and a fountain had to do with me, and stared at the funeral bronze I had found and cleaned and set up in a corner. The dead man lay at full length, his heavy-lidded eyes closed. In the light that pierced the little window I examined his face and meditated on my own as I saw it in the polished metal. My straight nose, deep-set eyes, and sunken cheeks were much like his, and I longed to know if he too had dark hair.

In the winter I seldom came to the necropolis, but in summer that violated mausoleum and others provided me with places of observation and cool repose. Drotte and Roche and Eata came too, though I never guided them to my favorite retreat, and they, I knew, had secret places of their own. When we were together we seldom crept into tombs at all. Instead we made swords of sticks and held running battles, or threw pinecones at the soldiers, or scratched boards on the soil of new graves and played draughts with stones, and ropes and snails, and high-toss-cockle.

We amused ourselves in the maze that was the Citadel too, and swam in the great cistern under the Bell Keep. It was cold and damp there even in summer, under its vaulted ceiling beside the circular pool of endlessly deep, dark water. But it was hardly worse in winter, and it had the supreme advantage of being forbidden, so we could slip down to it with delicious stealth when we were assumed to be elsewhere, and not kindle our torches until we had closed the barred hatch behind us. Then, when the flames shot up from the burning pitch, how our shadows danced up those clammy walls!

As I have already mentioned, our other swimming place was in Gyoll, which winds through Nessus like a great, weary snake. When warm weather came, we trooped through the necropolis on our way there—first past the old exalted sepulchers nearest the Citadel wall, then between the vainglorious death houses of the optimates, then through the stony forest of common monuments (we trying to appear highly respectable when we had to pass the burly guards leaning on their polearms). And at last across the plain, bare mounds that marked the interments of the poor, mounds that sank to puddles after the first rain.

At the lowest margin of the necropolis stood the iron gate I have already described. Through it the bodies intended for the potter's field were borne. When we passed those rusting portals we felt we were for the first time truly outside the Citadel, and thus in undeniable disobedience of the rules that were supposed to govern our comings and goings. We believed (or pretended to believe) we would be tortured if our older brothers discovered the violation; in actuality, we would have suffered nothing worse than a beating— such is the kindness of the torturers, whom I was subsequently to betray.

We were in greater danger from the inhabitants of the many-storied tenements that lined the filthy street down which we walked. I sometimes think the reason the guild has endured so long is that it serves as a focus for the hatred of the people, drawing it from the Autarch, the exultants, and the army, and even in some degree from the pale cacogens who sometimes visit Urth from the farther stars.

The same presentment that told the guards our identity often seemed to inform the residents of the tenements; slops were thrown at us from upper windows occasionally, and an angry mutter followed us. But the fear that engendered this hatred also protected us. No real violence was done to us, and once or twice, when it was known that some tyrannical wildgrave or venal burgess had been delivered to the mercy of the guild, we received shouted suggestions as to his disposal—most of them obscene and many impossible.

At the place where we swam, Gyoll had lost its natural banks hundreds of years ago. Here it was a two-chain-wide expanse of blue nenuphars penned between walls of stone. Steps intended for boat landings led down into the river at several points; on a warm day each flight would be held by a gang of ten or fifteen brawling youths. The four of us lacked the strength to displace these groups, but they could not (or at least would not) deny us admission, though whichever we chose to join would threaten us as we approached and taunt us when we were in their midst. Soon, however, all would drift away, leaving us in sole possession until the next swimming day.

I have chosen to describe all this now because I never went again after the day on which I saved Vodalus. Drotte and Roche believed it was because I was afraid we would be locked out. Eata guessed, I think—before they come too near to being men, boys often have an almost female insight. It was because of the nenuphars.

The necropolis has never seemed a city of death to me; I know its purple roses (which other people think so hideous) shelter hundreds of small animals and birds. The executions I have seen performed and have performed myself so often are no more than a trade, a butchery of human beings who are for the most part less innocent and less valuable than cattle. When I think of my own death, or of the death of someone who has been kind to me, or even of the death of the sun, the image that comes to my mind is that of the nenuphar, with its glossy, pale leaves and azure flower. Under flower and leaves are black roots as fine and strong as hair, reaching down into the dark waters.

As young men we thought nothing of these plants. We splashed and floated among them, pushed them aside, and ignored them. Their perfume countered to some degree the foul odor of the water. On the day I was to save Vodalus I dove beneath their crowded pads as I had done a thousand times.

I did not come up. Somehow I had entered a region where the roots seemed far thicker than I had ever encountered them before. I was caught in a hundred nets at once. My eyes were open, but I could see nothing—only the black web of the roots. I swam, and could feel that though my arms and legs moved among their millions of fine tendrils, my body did not. I grasped them by the handful and tore them apart, but when I had torn them I was immobilized as ever. My lungs seemed to rise in my throat to choke me, as if they would burst of themselves out into the water. The desire to draw breath, to suck in the dark, cold fluid around me, was overwhelming.

I no longer knew in what direction the surface lay, and I was no longer conscious of the water as water. The strength had left my limbs. I was no longer afraid, though I knew I was dying, or perhaps already dead. There was a loud and very unpleasant ringing in my ears, and I began to see visions.

Master Malrubius, who had died several years before, was waking us by drumming on the bulkhead with a spoon: that was the metallic din I heard. I lay in my cot unable to rise, though Drotte and Roche and the younger boys were all up, yawning and fumbling for their clothes. Master Malrubius's cloak was thrown back; I could see the loose skin of his chest and belly where the muscle and fat had been destroyed by time. There was a triangle of hair there, and it was as gray as mildew. I tried to call to him to tell him I was awake, but I could make no sound. He began to walk along the bulkhead, still striking it with his spoon. After what seemed a very long time he reached the port, stopped and leaned out. I knew he was looking for me in the Old Yard below.

Yet he could not see far enough. I was in one of the cells below the examination room. I lay there on my back, looking up at the gray ceiling. A woman cried but I could not see her, and I was less conscious of her sobs than of the ringing, ringing, ringing of the spoon. Darkness closed over me, but out of the darkness came the face of a woman, as immense as the green face of the moon. It was not she who wept—I could hear the sobs still, and this face was untroubled, and indeed filled with that kind of beauty that hardly admits of expression. Her hands reached toward me, and I at once became a fledgling I had taken from its nest the year before in the hope of taming it to perch on my finger, for her hands were each as long as the coffins in which I sometimes rested in my secret mausoleum. They grasped me, pulled me up, then flung me down, away from her face and from the sound of sobbing, down into the blackness until at last I struck what I took to be the bottom mud and burst through it into a world of light rimmed with black.

Still I could not breathe. I no longer wished to, and my chest no longer moved of itself. I was sliding through the water, though I did not know how. (Later I learned that Drotte had seized me by the hair.) At once I lay on the cold, slimy stones with Roche, then Drotte, then Roche again, breathing into my mouth. I was enveloped in eyes as one is enveloped in the repetitious patterns of a kaleidoscope, and thought that some defect in my own vision was multiplying Eata's eyes.

At last I pulled away from Roche and vomited great quantities of black water. After that I was better. I could sit up, and breathe again in a crippled way, and though I had no strength and my hands shook, I could move my arms. The eyes around me belonged to real people, the denizens of the riverside tenements. A woman brought a bowl of some hot drink—I could not be sure if it was soup or tea, only that it was scalding and somewhat salty, and smelled of smoke. I pretended to drink it, and afterward found that I had slight burns on my lips and tongue.

"Were you trying to do that?" Drotte asked. "How did you come up?"

I shook my head.

Someone in the crowd said, "He shot right out of the water!"

Roche helped me steady my hand. "We thought you'd come up somewhere else. That you were playing a joke on us."

I said, "I saw Malrubius."

An old man, a boatman from his tar-stained clothes, took Roche by the shoulder. "Who's that?"

"Used to be Master of Apprentices. He's dead."

"Not a woman?" The old man was holding Roche but looking at me.

"No, no," Roche told him. "There are no women in our guild."

Despite the hot drink and the warmth of the day, I was cold. One of the youths we sometimes fought brought a dusty blanket, and I wrapped myself in it; but it was so long before I was strong enough to walk again that by the time we reached the gate of the necropolis, the statue of Night atop the khan on the opposite bank was a minute scratch of black against the sun's field of flame, and the gate itself stood closed and locked.

III

The Autarch's Face

It was midmorning of the next day before I thought to look at the coin Vodalus had given me. After serving the journeymen in the refectory we had breakfasted as usual, met Master Palaemon in our classroom, and after a brief preparatory lecture followed him to the lower levels to view the work of the preceding night.

But perhaps before I write further I should explain something more of the nature of our Matachin Tower. It is situated toward the back of the Citadel, upon the western side. At ground level are the studies of our masters, where consultations with the officers of justice and the heads of other guilds are conducted. Our common room is above them, with its back to the kitchen. Above that is the refectory, which serves us as an assembly hall as well as an eating place. Above it are the private cabins of the masters, in better days much more numerous. Above these are the journeymen's cabins, and above them the apprentices' dormitory and classroom, and a series of attics and abandoned cubicles. Near the very top is the gun room, whose remaining pieces we of the guild are charged with serving should the Citadel suffer attack.

The real work of our guild is carried out below all this. Just underground lies the examination room; beneath it, and thus outside the tower proper (for the examination room was the propulsion chamber of the original structure) stretches the labyrinth of the oubliette. There are three usable levels, reached by a central stairwell. The cells are plain, dry, and clean, equipped with a small table, a chair, and narrow bed fixed in the center of the floor.

The lights of the oubliette are of that ancient kind that is said to burn forever, though some have now gone out. In the gloom of those corridors, my feelings that morning were not gloomy but joyous—here I would labor when I became a journeyman, here I would practice the ancient art and raise myself to the rank of master, here I would lay the foundation for the restoration of our guild to its former glory. The very air of the place seemed to wrap me like a blanket that had been warmed before some clean-scented fire.

We halted before the door of a cell, and the journeyman on duty rattled his key in the lock. Inside, the client lifted her head, opening dark eyes very wide. Master Palaemon wore the sable-trimmed cloak and velvet mask of his rank; I suppose that these, or the protruding optical device that permitted him to see, must have frightened her. She did not speak, and of course none of us spoke to her.

"Here," Master Palaemon began in his driest tone, "we have something outside the routine of judicial punishment and well illustrative of modern technique. The client was put to the question last night—perhaps some of you heard her. Twenty minims of tincture were given before the excruciation, and ten after. The dose was only partially effective in preventing shock and loss of consciousness, so the proceedings were terminated after flaying the right leg, as you will see." He gestured to Drotte, who began unwrapping the bandages.

"Half boot?" Roche asked.

"No, full boot. She has been a maidservant, and Master Gurloes says he has found them strong-skinned. In this instance he was proved correct. A simple circular incision was made below the knee, and its edge taken with eight clamps. Careful work by Master

Gurloes, Odo, Mennas, and Eigil permitted the removal of everything between the knee and the toes without further help from the knife."

We gathered around Drotte, the younger boys pushing in as they pretended they knew the points to look for. The arteries and major veins were all intact, but there was a slow, generalized welling of blood. I helped Drotte apply fresh dressings.

Just as we were about to leave the woman said, "I don't know. Only, oh, can't you believe I wouldn't tell you if I did? She's gone with Vodalus of the Wood, I don't know where." Outside, feigning ignorance, I asked Master Palaemon who Vodalus of the Wood was.

"How often have I explained that nothing said by a client under questioning is heard by you?"

"Many times, Master."

"But to no effect. Soon it will be masking day, and Drotte and Roche will be journeymen, and you captain of apprentices. Is this the example you'll set the boys?"

"No, Master."

Behind the old man's back, Drotte gave me a look that meant he knew much about Vodalus and would tell me at a convenient time.

"Once the journeymen of our guild were deafened. Would you have those days again? Take your hands from your pockets when I speak to you, Severian."

I had put them there because I knew it would distract his anger, but as I drew them out I realized I had been fumbling the coin Vodalus had given me the night before. In the remembered terror of the fight I had forgotten it; now I was in agony to look at it—and could not, with Master Palaemon's bright lens fixed on me.

"When a client speaks, Severian, you hear nothing. Nothing whatsoever. Think of mice, whose squeaking conveys no meaning to men."

I squinted to indicate that I was thinking of mice.

All the long, weary way up the stair to our classroom, I ached to look at the thin disc of metal I clutched; but I knew that if I were to do so the boy behind me (as it happened, one of the younger apprentices, Eusignius) would see it. In the classroom, where Master Palaemon droned over a ten-day corpse, the coin was like a coal of fire, and I dared not look.

It was afternoon before I found privacy, hiding myself in the ruins of the curtain wall among the shining mosses, then hesitating with my fist poised in a ray of sun because I was afraid that when I saw it at last the disappointment would be more than I could bear.

Not because I cared for its value. Though I was already a man, I had had so little money that any coin would have seemed a fortune to me. Rather it was that the coin (so mysterious now, but not likely to remain so) was my only link with the night before, my only connection with Vodalus and the beautiful, hooded woman and the heavy man who had struck at me with his shovel, my only booty from the fight at the opened grave. My life in the guild was the only life I had known, and it seemed as drab as my ragged shirt in comparison with the flash of the exultant's sword blade and the sound of the shot echoing among the stones. All that might be gone when I opened my hand.

In the end I looked, having drained the dregs of pleasant dread. The coin was a gold chrisos, and I closed my hand once more, fearing that I had only mistaken a brass orichalk, and waited until I found my courage again.

It was the first time I had ever touched a piece of gold. Orichalks I had seen in some plenty, and I had even possessed a few of my own. Silver asimi I had glimpsed once or twice. But chrisos I knew only in the same dim way I knew of the existence of a world outside our city of Nessus, and of continents other than our own to the north and east and west.

This one bore what I at first thought was a woman's face—a woman crowned, neither young nor old, but silent and perfect in the citrine metal. At last I turned my treasure over, and then indeed I caught my breath; stamped on the reverse was just such a flying ship as I had seen in the arms above the door of my secret mausoleum. It seemed beyond explanation—so much so that at the time I did not even trouble to speculate about it, so sure was I that any speculation would be fruitless. Instead, I thrust the coin back into my pocket and went, in a species of trance, to rejoin my fellow apprentices.

To carry the coin about with me was out of the question. As soon as there was an opportunity to do so, I slipped into the necropolis alone and sought out my mausoleum. The weather had turned that day—I pushed through drenching shrubbery and trudged over long, aged grass that had begun to flatten itself for winter. When I reached my retreat it was no longer the cool, inviting cave of summer but an icy trap where I sensed the nearness of enemies too vague for names, opponents of Vodalus who surely knew by now that I was his sworn supporter; as soon as I entered they would rush forward to swing the black door shut on newly oiled hinges. I knew that it was nonsense, of course. Yet I also knew there was truth in it, that it was a proximity in time I felt. In a few months or a few years I might reach the point at which those enemies waited for me; when I had swung the ax I had chosen to fight, a thing a torturer does not normally do.

There was a loose stone in the floor almost at the foot of my funeral bronze. I pried it up and put the chrisos under it, then muttered an incantation I had learned years before from Roche, a few lines of verse that would hold hidden objects safe:

> "Where I put you, there you lie,
> Never let a stranger spy,
> Like glass grow to any eye,
> Not of me.
>
> Here be safe, never leave it,
> Should a hand come, deceive it,
> Let strange eyes not believe it,
> Till I see."

For the charm to be really effective one had to walk around the spot at midnight carrying a corpse-candle, but I found myself laughing at the thought—which suggested Drotte's mummery about simples drawn at midnight from graves—and decided to rely on the verse alone, though I was somewhat astonished to discover that I was now old enough not to be ashamed of it.

Days passed, and the memory of my visit to the mausoleum remained vivid enough to dissuade me from making another to verify that my treasure was safe, though at times I longed to do so. Then came the first snow, turning the ruins of the curtain wall into an almost impassably slippery barrier, and the familiar necropolis into a strange wilderness of deceptive hummocks, in which monuments were suddenly too large under their coats of new snow, and the trees and bushes crushed to half size by theirs.

It is the nature of apprenticeship in our guild that, though easy at first, its burdens grow greater and greater as one comes to manhood. The smallest boys do no work at all. At the age of six, when work begins, it is at first no more than running up and down the stairs of the Matachin Tower with messages, and the little apprentice, proud of being entrusted with them, hardly feels the labor. As time progresses, however, his work becomes more and more onerous. His duties take him to other parts of the Citadel—to the soldiers in the barbican, where he learns that the military apprentices have drums and trumpets and ophicleides and boots and sometimes gilded cuirasses; to the Bear Tower, where he sees boys no older than himself learning to handle wonderful fighting animals of all kinds, mastiffs with heads as large as a lion's, diatrymae taller than a man, with beaks sheathed in steel; and to a hundred other such places where he discovers for the first time that his guild is hated and despised even by those (indeed, most of all by those) who make use of its services. Soon there is scrubbing and kitchen work. Brother Cook performs such cooking as might be interesting or pleasurable, and the apprentice is left to pare vegetables, serve the journeymen, and carry an endless succession of stacks of trays down the stairs to the oubliette.

I did not know it at the time, but soon this apprentice life of mine, which had been growing harder for as long as I could remember, would reverse its course and become less drudging and more pleasant. In the year before he is to become a journeyman, a senior apprentice does little but supervise the work of his juniors. His food and even his dress improve. The younger journeymen begin to treat him almost as an equal, and he has, above all, the elevating burden of responsibility and the pleasure of issuing and enforcing orders.

When his elevation comes, he is an adult. He does no work but that for which he has been trained; and he is free to leave the Citadel when his duties are over, for which recreation he is supplied with liberal funds. Should he eventually rise to mastership (an honor that requires the affirmative votes of all the living masters), he will be able to pick and choose such assignments as may interest or amuse him, and direct the affairs of the guild itself.

But you must understand that in the year I have been writing of, the year in which I saved the life of Vodalus, I was unconscious of all that. Winter (I was told) had ended the campaigning season in the north, and thus brought the Autarch and his chief officers and advisors back to the seats of justice. "And so," as Roche explained, "we have all these new clients. And more to come . . . dozens, maybe hundreds. We might have to reopen the fourth level." He waved a freckled hand to show that he at least was ready to do whatever might be necessary.

"Is he here?" I asked. "The Autarch? Here in the Citadel? In the Great Keep?"

"Of course not. If he ever came, you'd know it, wouldn't you? There'd be parades and inspections and all kinds of goings on. There's a suite for him there but the door hasn't been opened in a hundred years. He'll be in the hidden palace—the House Absolute—north of the city someplace."

"Don't you know where?"

Roche grew defensive. "You can't say where it is because there's nothing there except the House Absolute itself. It's where it is. To the north, on the other bank."

"Beyond the Wall?"

He smiled on my ignorance. "Far past it. Weeks, if you walked. Naturally the Autarch could get here by flier in an instant if he wanted to. The Flag Tower—that's where the flier would land."

But our new clients did not come in fliers. The less important arrived in coffles of ten to twenty men and women, chained one behind the other by the neck. They were guarded by dimarchi, hard-bitten troopers in armor that looked as if it had been made for use and used. Each client carried a copper cylinder supposedly containing his or her papers and thus his or her fate. All of them had broken the seals and read those papers, of course; and some had destroyed them or exchanged them for another's. Those who arrived without papers would be held until some further word concerning their disposition was received—probably for the remainder of their lives. Those who had exchanged papers with someone else had exchanged fates; they would be held or released, tortured or executed, in another's stead.

The more important arrived in armored carriages. The steel sides and barred windows of these vehicles were not intended to prevent escape so much as to thwart rescue, and no sooner had the first of them thundered around the east side of the Witches' Tower and entered the Old Yard than the whole guild was filled with rumors of daring raids contemplated or attempted by Vodalus. For all my fellow apprentices and most of the journeymen believed that many of these clients were his henchmen, confederates, and allies. I would not have released them for that reason—it would have brought disgrace on the guild, which for all my attachment to him and his movement I was unready to do, and would have been impossible anyway. But I hoped to provide those I considered my comrades-in-arms with such small comforts as lay within my power: extra food stolen from the trays of less deserving clients and occasionally a bit of meat smuggled from the kitchen.

One blustering day I was given the opportunity to learn who they were. I was scrubbing the floor in Master Gurloes's study when he was called away on some errand, leaving his table stacked with newly arrived dossiers. I hurried over as soon as the door had clanged behind him, and was able to skim most of them before I heard his heavy tread on the stair again. Not one—*not one*—of the prisoners whose papers I had read had been an adherent of Vodalus. There were merchants who had tried to make rich profits on supplies needed by the army, camp followers who had spied for the Ascians, and a sprinkling of sordid civil criminals. Nothing else.

When I carried my bucket out to empty in the stone sink in the Old Yard, I saw one of the armored carriages halted there with its long-maned team steaming and stamping, and the guards in their fur-trimmed helmets sheepishly accepting our smoking goblets of mulled wine. I caught the name Vodalus in the air; but at that moment it seemed I was the only one who heard it, and suddenly I felt Vodalus had been only an eidolon created by my imagination from the fog, and only the man I had slain with his own ax real. The dossiers I had fumbled through a moment before seemed blown like leaves against my face.

It was in this instant of confusion that I realized for the first time that I am in some degree insane. It could be argued that it was the most harrowing of my life. I had lied often to Master Gurloes and Master Palaemon, to Master Malrubius while he still lived, to Drotte because he was captain, to Roche because he was older and stronger than I, and to Eata and the other smaller apprentices because I hoped to make them respect me. Now I could no longer be sure my own mind was not lying to me; all my falsehoods were recoiling on me, and I who remembered everything could not be certain those memories were more than my own dreams. I recalled the moonlit face of Vodalus; but then, I had wanted to see it. I recalled his voice as he spoke to me, but I had desired to hear it, and the woman's voice too.

One freezing night, I crept back to the mausoleum and took out the chrisos again. The worn, serene, androgynous face on its obverse was not the face of Vodalus.

IV

Triskele

I HAD BEEN POKING A STICK up a frozen drain as punishment
for some petty infraction, and I found him where the keepers of
the Bear Tower throw their refuse, the bodies of the torn animals
killed in practice. Our guild buries its own dead beside the wall
and our clients in the lower reaches of the necropolis, but the
keepers of the Bear Tower leave theirs to be taken away by
others. He was the smallest of those dead.

There are encounters that change nothing. Urth turns her
aged face to the sun and he beams upon her snows; they
scintillate and coruscate until each little point of ice hanging
from the swelling sides of the towers seems the Claw of the
Conciliator, the most precious of gems. Then everyone except
the wisest believes that the snow must melt and give way to a
protracted summer beyond summer.

Nothing of the sort occurs. The paradise endures for a watch
or two, then shadows blue as watered milk lengthen on the
snow, which shifts and dances under the spur of an east wind.
Night comes, and all is as it was.

My finding Triskele was like that. I felt that it could have and
should have changed everything, but it was only the episode of a

few months, and when it was over and he was gone, it was only another winter passed and the Feast of Holy Katharine come again, and nothing had changed. I wish I could tell you how pitiful he looked when I touched him, and how cheerful.

He lay on his side, covered with blood. It was as hard as tar in the cold, and still bright red because the cold had preserved it. I went over and put my hand on his head—I don't know why. He seemed as dead as the rest, but he opened one eye then and rolled it at me, and there was a confidence in it that the worst was over now—I have carried my part, it seemed to say, and borne up, and done all I could do; now it is your turn to do your duty by me.

If it had been summer, I think I would have let him die. As it was I had not seen a living animal, not so much as a garbage-eating thylacodon, in some time. I stroked him again and he licked my hand, and I could not turn away after that.

I picked him up (surprised at how heavy he was) and looked about trying to decide what to do with him. He would be discovered in our dormitory before the candle had burned a finger's width, I knew. The Citadel is immense and immensely complicated, with little-visited rooms and passages in its towers, in the buildings that have been erected between the towers, and in the galleries delved under them. Yet I could not think of any such place that I could reach without being seen half a dozen times on the way, and in the end I carried the poor brute into the quarters of our own guild.

I then had to get him past the journeyman who stood guard at the head of the stair leading to the cell tiers. My first idea was to put him in the basket in which we took down the client's clean bedding. It was a laundry day, and it would have been easy enough to make one more trip than was actually required; the chance that the journeyman-guard would notice anything amiss seemed remote, but it would have involved waiting more than a watch for the scrubbed linen to dry and risking the questions of the brother on duty in the third tier, who would see me descending to the deserted fourth.

Instead I laid the dog in the examination room—he was too weak to move—and offered to take the guard's place at the head of the ramp. He was happy enough to seize the opportunity to relieve himself and handed over his wide-bladed carnificial sword (which I in theory was not supposed to touch) and his fuligin cloak (which I was forbidden to wear, though I was already taller than most of the journeymen) so that from a distance it would appear that there had been no substitution. I put on the cloak and as soon as he was gone stood the sword in a corner and got my dog. All our guild cloaks are voluminous, and this one was more so than most since the brother I had replaced was large of frame. Furthermore, the hue fuligin, which is darker than black, admirably erases all folds, bunchings, and gatherings so far as the eye is concerned, showing only a featureless dark. With the hood pulled up, I must have appeared to the journeymen at their tables in the tiers (if they looked toward the stair and saw me at all) as a brother somewhat more portly than most descending to the lower levels. Even the man on duty in the third, where the clients who had lost all reason howled and shook their chains, could have seen nothing unusual in another journeyman going down to the fourth when there were rumors that it was to be refurbished—or in an apprentice running down shortly after the journeyman went up again: no doubt he had forgotten something there and the apprentice had been sent to fetch it.

It was not a prepossessing place. About half of the old lights still burned, but mud had seeped into the corridors until it lay to the thickness of one's hand. A duty table stood where it had been left, perhaps, two hundred years before; the wood had rotted and the whole thing fell at a touch.

Yet the water had never been high here, and the farther end of the corridor I chose was free even of the mud. I laid my dog on a client's bed and cleaned him as well as I could with sponges I had carried down from the examination room.

Under the crusted blood his fur was short, stiff, and tawny. His tail had been cut so short that what remained was wider than it was long. His ears had been cut almost completely away, leaving only stiff points shorter than the first joint of my thumb. In his last fight his chest had been laid open. I could see the wide muscles like drowsy constrictors of pale red. His right foreleg was gone—the upper half crushed to a pulp. I cut it away after I had sutured up his chest as well as I could, and it began to bleed again. I found the artery and tied it, then folded the skin under (as Master Palaemon had taught us) to make a neat stump.

Triskele licked my hand from time to time as I worked, and when I had made the last stitch began slowly licking that, as if he were a bear and could lick a new leg into shape. His jaws were as big as an arctother's and his canines as long as my index finger, but his gums were white; there was no more strength in those jaws now than in a skeleton's hands. His eyes were yellow and held a certain clean madness.

That evening I traded tasks with the boy who was to bring the clients their meals. There were always extra trays because some clients would not eat, and now I carried two of these down to Triskele, wondering if he were still alive.

He was. He had somehow climbed out of the bed where I had laid him and crawled—he could not stand—to the edge of the mud, where a little water had gathered. That was where I found him. There was soup and dark bread and two carafes of water. He drank one bowl of soup, but when I tried to feed him the bread I found he could not chew it enough to swallow; I soaked it in the other bowl of soup for him, then filled the bowl again and again with water until both carafes were empty.

When I lay on my cot almost at the top of our tower, I thought that I could hear his labored breathing. Several times I sat up, listening; each time the sound faded away, only to return when I had lain flat for a time. Perhaps it was only the beating of my heart. If I had found him a year, two years, before, he would have been a divinity to me. I would have told Drotte and the rest, and he would have been a divinity to us all. Now I knew him for the poor animal he was, and yet I could not let him die because it would have been a breaking of faith with something in myself. I had been a man (if I was truly a man) such a short time; I could not endure to think that I had become a man so different from the boy I had been. I could remember each moment of my past, every vagrant thought and sight, every dream. How could I destroy that past? I held up my hands and tried to look at them—I knew the veins stood out on their backs now. It is when those veins stand out that one is a man.

In a dream I walked through the fourth level again, and found a huge friend there with dripping jaws. It spoke to me.

Next morning I served the clients again, and stole food to take down to the dog, though I hoped that he was dead. He was not. He lifted his muzzle and seemed to grin at me with a mouth so wide it appeared his head might fall in two halves, though he did not try to stand. I fed him and as I was about to leave was struck by the misery of his condition. He was dependent on me. Me! He had been valued; trainers had coached him as runners are coached for a race; he had walked in pride, his enormous chest, as wide as a man's, set on two legs like pillars. Now he lived like a ghost. His very name had been washed away in his own blood.

When I had time, I visited the Bear Tower and struck up such friendships as I could with the beast handlers there. They have their own guild, and though it is a lesser guild than ours, it has much strange lore. To a degree that astonished me, I found it to be the same lore, though I did not, of course, penetrate to their arcanum. In the elevation of their masters, the candidate stands under a metal grate trod by a bleeding bull; at some point in life each brother takes a lioness or bear-sow in marriage, after which he shuns human women.

All of which is only to say that there exists between them and the animals they bring to the pits a bond much like that between our clients and ourselves. Now I have traveled much farther from our tower, but I have found always that the pattern of our guild is repeated mindlessly (like the repetitions of Father Inire's mirrors in the House Absolute) in the societies of every trade, so that they are all of them torturers, just as we. His quarry stands to the hunter as our clients to us; those who buy to the tradesman; the enemies of the Commonwealth to the soldier; the governed to the governors; men to women. All love that which they destroy.

A week after I had carried him down, I found only Triskele's hobbling footprints in the mud. He was gone, but I set out after him, sure that one of the journeymen would have mentioned it to me if he had come up the ramp. Soon the footprints led to a narrow door that opened on a welter of lightless corridors of whose existence I had been utterly unaware. In the dark I could no longer track him, but I pressed on nevertheless, thinking that he might catch my scent in the stale air and come to me. Soon I was lost, and went forward only because I did not know how to go back.

I have no way of knowing how old those tunnels are. I suspect, though I can hardly say why, that they antedate the Citadel above them, ancient though it is. It comes to us from the very end of the age when the urge to flight, the outward urge that sought new suns not ours, remained, though the means to achieve that flight were sinking like dying fires. Remote as that time is, from which hardly one name is recalled, we still remember it. Before it there must have been another time, a time of burrowing, of the creation of dark galleries, that is now utterly forgotten.

However that may be, I was frightened there. I ran—and sometimes ran into walls—until at last I saw a spot of pale daylight and clambered out through a hole hardly big enough for my head and shoulders.

I found myself crawling onto the ice-covered pedestal of one of those old, faceted dials whose multitudinous faces give each a different time. No doubt because the frost of these latter ages entering the tunnel below had heaved its foundation, it had slipped sidewise until it stood at such an angle that it might have been one of its own gnomons, drawing the silent passage of the short winter day across the unmarked snow.

The space about it had been a garden in summer, but not such a one as our necropolis, with half-wild trees and rolling, meadowed lawns. Roses had blossomed here in kraters set upon a tessellated pavement. Statues of beasts stood with their backs to the four walls of the court, eyes turned to watch the canted dial: hulking barylambdas; arctothers, the monarchs of bears; glyptodons; smilodons with fangs like glaives. All were dusted now with snow. I looked for Triskele's tracks, but he had not come here.

The walls of the court held high, narrow windows. I could see no light through them, and no motion. The spear-towers of the Citadel rose on every side, so that I knew I had not left it— instead, I seemed to be somewhere near its heart, where I had never been. Shaking with cold I crossed to the nearest door and pounded on it. I had the feeling that I might wander forever in the tunnels below without ever finding another way to the surface, and I was resolved to smash one of the windows if need be rather than return that way. There was no sound within, though I beat my fist against the door panels again and again.

There is really no describing the sensation of being watched. I have heard it called a prickling at the back of the neck, and even a consciousness of eyes that seem to float in darkness, but it is neither—at least, not for me. It is something akin to a sourceless embarrassment, coupled with the feeling that I must not turn around, because to turn will be to appear a fool, answering the promptings of baseless intuition. Eventually, of course, one does. I turned with the vague impression that someone had followed me through the hole at the base of the dial.

Instead I saw a young woman wrapped in furs standing before a door at the opposite side of the court. I waved to her and began to walk toward her (hurriedly, because I was so cold). She advanced toward me then, and we met on the farther side of the dial. She asked who I was and what I was doing there, and I told her as well as I could. The face circled by her fur hood was exquisitely molded, and the hood itself, and her coat and fur-trimmed boots, were soft-looking and rich, so that I was miserably conscious as I spoke to her of my own patched shirt and trousers and my muddy feet.

Her name was Valeria. "We do not have your dog here," she said. "You may search, if you do not believe me."

"I never thought you did. I only want to go back where I belong, to the Matachin Tower, without having to go down there again."

"You're very brave. I have seen that hole since I was a little girl, but I never dared go in."

"I'd like to go in," I said. "I mean, inside there."

She opened the door through which she had come and led me into a tapestried room where stiff, ancient chairs seemed as fixed in their places as the statues in the frozen court. A diminutive fire smoked in a grate against one wall. We went to it, and she took off her coat while I spread my hands to the warmth.

"Wasn't it cold in the tunnels?"

"Not as cold as outside. Besides, I was running and there was no wind."

"I see. How strange that they should come up in the Atrium of Time." She looked younger than I, but there was an antique quality about her metal-trimmed dress and the shadow of her dark hair that made her seem older than Master Palaemon, a dweller in forgotten yesterdays.

"Is that what you call it? The Atrium of Time? Because of the dials, I suppose."

"No, the dials were put there because we call it that. Do you like the dead languages? They have mottoes. 'Lux dei vitae viam monstrat,' that's 'The beam of the New Sun lights the way of life.' 'Felicibus brevis, miseris hora longa.' 'Men wait long for happiness.' 'Aspice ut aspiciar.'"

I had to tell her with some shame that I knew no tongue beyond the one we spoke, and little of that.

Before I left we talked a sentry's watch or more. Her family occupied these towers. They had waited, at first, to leave Urth with the autarch of their era, then had waited because there was nothing left for them but waiting. They had given many castellans to the Citadel, but the last had died generations ago; they were poor now, and their towers were in ruins. Valeria had never gone above the lower floors.

"Some of the towers were built more strongly than others," I said. "The Witches' Keep is decayed inside too."

"Is there really such a place? My nurse told me of it when I was little—to frighten me—but I thought it was only a tale. There was supposed to be a Tower of Torment too, where all who enter die in agony."

I told her that, at least, was a fable.

"The great days of these towers are more fabulous to me," she said. "No one of my blood carries a sword now against the enemies of the Commonwealth, or stands hostage for us at the Well of Orchids."

"Perhaps one of your sisters will be summoned soon," I said, for I did not want, for some reason, to think of her going herself.

"I am all the sisters we breed," she answered. "And all the sons."

An old servant brought us tea and small, hard cakes. Not real tea, but the maté of the north, which we sometimes give our clients because it is so cheap.

Valeria smiled. "You see, you have found some comfort here. You are worried about your poor dog because he is lame. But he, too, may have found hospitality. You love him, so another may love him. You love him, so you may love another."

I agreed, but secretly thought that I would never have another dog, which has proved true.

I did not see Triskele again for almost a week. Then one day as

I was carrying a letter to the barbican, he came bounding up to me. He had learned to run on his single front leg, like an acrobat who does handstands on a gilded ball.

After that I saw him once or twice a month for as long as the snow lasted. I never knew whom he had found, who was feeding him and caring for him; but I like to think it was someone who took him away with him in the spring, perhaps north to the cities of tents and the campaigns among the mountains.

V

The Picture-Cleaner and Others

THE FEAST OF HOLY KATHARINE is the greatest of days for our guild, the festival by which we are recalled to our heritage, the time when journeymen become masters (if they ever do) and apprentices become journeymen. I will leave my description of the ceremonies of that day until I have occasion to tell of my own elevation; but in the year I am recounting, the year of the fight by the graveside, Drotte and Roche were elevated, leaving me captain of apprentices.

The full weight of that office did not impress itself on me until the ritual was nearly over. I was sitting in the ruined chapel enjoying the pageantry and only just conscious (in the same pleasant way I was anticipating the feast) that I would be senior to all the rest when the last of it was done.

By slow degrees, however, a feeling of disquiet seized me. I was miserable before I knew I was no longer happy, and bowed with responsibility when I did not yet fully understand I held it. I remembered how much difficulty Drotte had encountered in keeping us in order. I would have to do it now without his strength, and with no one to be to me what Roche had been to him—a lieutenant of his own age. When the final chant crashed to a close and Master Gurloes and Master Palaemon in their gold-traced masks had slow-stepped through the door, and the old journeymen had hoisted Drotte and Roche, the new journeymen, on their shoulders (already fumbling in the sabretaches at their belts for the fireworks they would set off outside), I had steeled myself and even formed a rudimentary plan.

We apprentices were to serve the feast, and before we did so were to doff the relatively new and clean clothes we had been given for the ceremony. After the last cracker had popped and the matrosses, in their annual gesture of amity, had torn the sky with the largest piece of ordinance in the Great Keep, I hustled my charges—already, or so I thought, beginning to look at me resentfully—back to our dormitory, closed the door, and pushed a cot against it.

Eata was the oldest except for myself, and fortunately for me I had been friendly enough in the past that he suspected nothing until it was too late to make effective resistance. I got him by the throat and banged his head half a dozen times against the bulkhead, then kicked his feet from under him. "Now," I said, "are you going to be my second? Answer!"

He could not speak, but he nodded.

"Good. I'll get Timon. You take the next biggest."

In the space of a hundred breaths (and very quick breaths they were) the boys had been kicked into submission. It was three weeks before any of them dared to disobey me, and then there was no mass rebellion, only individual malingering.

As captain of apprentices I had new functions, as well as more freedom than I had ever enjoyed before. It was I who saw that the journeymen on duty got their meals hot, and who supervised the boys who toiled under the stacks of trays intended for our clients. In the kitchen I drove my charges to their tasks, and in the classroom I coached them in their studies; I was employed to a much greater degree than previously in carrying messages to distant parts of the Citadel, and even in a small way in conducting the guild's business. Thus I became acquainted with all the thoroughfares and with many an unfrequented corner— granaries with lofty bins and demonic cats; wind-swept ramparts overlooking gangrenous slums; and the pinakotheken, with their great hallway topped by a vaulted roof of window-pierced brick, floored with flagstones strewn with carpets, and bound by walls from which dark arches opened to strings of chambers lined—as the hallway itself was—with innumerable pictures.

Many of these were so old and smoke-grimed that I could not discern their subjects, and there were others whose meaning I could not guess—a dancer whose wings seemed leeches, a silent-looking woman who gripped a double-bladed dagger and sat beneath a mortuary mask. After I had walked at least a league among these enigmatic paintings one day, I came upon an old man perched on a high ladder. I wanted to ask my way, but he seemed so absorbed in his work that I hesitated to disturb him.

The picture he was cleaning showed an armored figure standing in a desolate landscape. It had no weapon, but held a staff bearing a strange, stiff banner. The visor of this figure's helmet was entirely of gold, without eye slits or ventilation; in its polished surface the deathly desert could be seen in reflection, and nothing more.

This warrior of a dead world affected me deeply, though I could not say why or even just what emotion it was I felt. In some obscure way, I wanted to take down the picture and carry it—not into our necropolis but into one of those mountain forests of which our necropolis was (as I understood even then) an idealized but vitiated image. It should have stood among trees, the edge of its frame resting on young grass.

"—and so," a voice behind me said, "they all escaped. Vodalus had what he had come for, you see."

"You," snapped the other. "What are you doing here?"

I turned and saw two armigers dressed in bright clothes that came as near to exultants' as they dared have them. I said, "I have a communication for the archivist," and held up the envelope.

"Very well," said the armiger who had spoken to me. "Do you know the location of the archives?"

"I was about to ask, sieur."

"Then you are not the proper messenger to take the letter, are you? Give it to me and I'll give it to a page."

"I can't, sieur. It is my task to deliver it."

The other armiger said, "You needn't be so hard on this young man, Racho."

"You don't know what he is, do you?"

"And you do?"

The one called Racho nodded. "From what part of this Citadel are you, messenger?"

"From the Matachin Tower. Master Gurloes sends me to the archivist."

The other armiger's face tightened. "You are a torturer, then."

"Only an apprentice, sieur."

"I don't wonder then that my friend wants you out of his sight. Follow the gallery to the third door, make your turn and continue about a hundred paces, climb the stair to the second landing and take the corridor south to the double doors at the end."

"Thank you," I said, and took a step in the direction he had indicated.

"Wait a bit. If you go now, we'll have to look at you."

Racho said, "I'd as soon have him ahead of us as behind us."

I waited nonetheless, with one hand resting on the leg of the ladder, for the two of them to turn a corner.

Like one of those half-spiritual friends who in dreams address us from the clouds, the old man said, "So you're a torturer, are you? Do you know, I've never been to your place." He had a weak glance, reminding me of the turtles we sometimes frightened on the banks of Gyoll, and a nose and chin that nearly met.

"Grant I never see you there," I said politely.

"Nothing to fear now. What could you do with a man like me? My heart would stop like that!" He dropped his sponge into his bucket and attempted to snap his wet fingers, though no sound came: "Know where it is, though. Behind the Witches' Keep. Isn't that right?"

"Yes," I said, a trifle surprised that the witches were better known than we.

"Thought so. Nobody never talks about it, though. You're angry about those armigers and I don't blame you. But you ought to know how it is with them. They're supposed to be like exultants, only they're not. They're afraid to die, afraid to hurt, and afraid to act like it. It's hard on them."

"They should be done away with," I said. "Vodalus would set them quarrying. They're only a carryover from some past age— what possible help can they give the world?"

The old man cocked his head. "Why, what help was they to begin? Do you know?"

When I admitted I did not, he scrambled down from the ladder like an aged monkey, seeming all arms and legs and wrinkled neck; his hands were as long as my feet, the crooked fingers laced with blue veins. "I'm Rudesind the curator. You know old Ultan, I take it? No, course not. If you did, you'd know the way to the library."

I said, "I've never been in this part of the Citadel before."

"Never been here? Why, this is the best part. Art, music, and books. We've a Fechin here that shows three girls dressing another one with flowers that's so real you expect the bees to come out of it. A Quartillosa, too. Not popular anymore, Quartillosa isn't, or we wouldn't have him here. But the day he was born he was a better draughtsman than the drippers and spitters they're wild for today. We get what the House Absolute don't want, you see. That means we get the old ones, and they're the best, mostly. Come in here dirty from having hung so long, and I clean them up. Sometimes I clean them again, after they've hung here a time. We've got a Fechin here. It's the truth! Or you take this one now. Like it?"

It seemed safe to say I did.

"*Third* time for it. When I was new come, I was old Branwallader's apprentice and he taught me how to clean. This was the one he used, because he said it wasn't worth nothing. He begun down here in this corner. When he'd done about as much as you could cover with one hand, he turned it over to me and I did the rest. Back when my wife still lived I cleaned it again. That would be after our second girl was born. It wasn't all that dark, but I had things on my mind and wanted something to do. Today I took the notion to clean it again. And it needs it—see how nice it's brightening up? There's your blue Urth coming over his shoulder again, fresh as the Autarch's fish."

All this time the name of Vodalus was echoing in my mind. I felt certain the old man had come down from his ladder only because I had mentioned it, and I wanted to ask him about it. But try as I might, I could find no way to bring the conversation around to it. When I had been silent a moment too long and was afraid he was about to mount his ladder and begin cleaning again, I managed to say, "Is that the moon? I have been told it's more fertile."

"Now it is, yes. This was done before they got it irrigated. See that gray-brown? In those times, that's what you'd see if you looked up at her. Not green like she is now. Didn't seem so big either, because it wasn't so close in—that's what old Branwallader used to say. Now there's trees enough on it to hide Nilammon, as the saw goes."

I seized my opportunity. "Or Vodalus."

Rudesind cackled. "Or him, that's right enough. Your bunch must be rubbing their hands waiting to have him. Got something special planned?"

If the guild had particular excruciations reserved for specific individuals, I knew nothing of it; but I endeavored to look wise and said, "We'll think of something."

"I suppose you will. A bit ago, though, I thought you was for him. Still you'll have to wait if he's hiding in the Forests of Lune." Rudesind looked up at the picture with obvious appreciation before turning back to me. "I'm forgetting. You want to visit our Master Ultan. Go back to that arch you just come by—"

"I know the way," I said. "The armiger told me."

The old curator blew those directions to the winds with a puff of sour breath. "What he laid down would only get you to the Reading Room. From there it'd take you a watch to get to Ultan, if ever you did. No, step back to that arch. Go through and all the way to the end of the big room there, and down the stair. You'll come to a locked door—pound till somebody lets you in. That's the bottom of the stacks, and that's where Ultan has his study."

Since Rudesind was watching I followed his directions, though I had not liked the part about the locked door, and steps downward suggested I might be nearing those ancient tunnels where I had wandered looking for Triskele.

On the whole I felt far less confident than when I was in those parts of the Citadel that I knew. I have learned since that strangers who visit it are awed by its size; but it is only a mote in the city spread about it, and we who grew up within the gray curtain wall, and have learned the names and relationships of the hundred or so landmarks necessary to those who would find their way in it, are by that very knowledge discomfited when we find ourselves away from the familiar regions.

So it was with me as I walked through the arch the old man had indicated. Like the rest of that vaulted hall it was of dull, reddish brick, but it was upheld by two pillars whose capitals bore the faces of sleepers, and I found the silent lips and pale, closed eyes more terrible than the agonized masks painted on the metal of our own tower.

Each picture in the room beyond contained a book. Sometimes they were many, or prominent; some I had to study for some time before I saw the corner of a binding thrusting from the pocket of a woman's skirt or realized that some strangely wrought spool held words spun like thread.

The steps were narrow and steep and without railings; they twisted as they descended, so that I had not gone down more than thirty before the light of the room above was nearly cut off. At last I was forced to put my hands before me and feel my way for fear I would break my head on the door.

My questing fingers never encountered it. Instead the steps ended (and I nearly fell in stepping off a step that was not there), and I was left to grope across an uneven floor in total darkness.

"Who's there?" a voice called. It was a strangely resonant one, like the sound of a bell tolled inside a cave.

V I

The Master of the Curators

"WHO'S THERE?" echoed in the dark. As boldly as I could, I said, "Someone with a message."

"Let me hear it then."

My eyes were growing used to the dark at last, and I could just make out a dim and very lofty shape moving among dark, ragged shapes that were taller still. "It is a letter, sieur," I answered. "Are you Master Ultan the curator?"

"None other." He was standing before me now. What I had at first thought was a whitish garment now appeared to be a beard reaching nearly to his waist. I was as tall already as many men who are called so, but he was a head and a half taller than I, a true exultant.

"Then here you are, sieur," I said, and held out the letter.

He did not take it. "Whose apprentice are you?" Again I seemed to hear bronze, and quite suddenly I felt that he and I were dead, and that the darkness surrounding us was grave soil pressing in about our eyes, grave soil through which the bell called us to worship at whatever shrines may exist below ground. The livid woman I had seen dragged from her grave rose before me so vividly that I seemed to see her face in the almost luminous whiteness of the figure who spoke. "Whose apprentice?" he asked again.

"No one's. That is, I am an apprentice of our guild. Master Gurloes sent me, sieur. Master Palaemon teaches us apprentices, mostly."

"But not grammar." Very slowly the tall man's hand groped toward the letter.

"Oh yes, grammar too." I felt like a child talking to this man, who had already been old when I was born. "Master Palaemon says we must be able to read and write and calculate, because when we are masters in our time, we'll have to send letters and receive the instructions of the courts, and keep records and accounts."

"Like this," the dim figure before me intoned. "Letters such as this."

"Yes, sieur. Just so."

"And what does this say?"

"I don't know. It's sealed, sieur."

"If I open it—" (I heard the brittle wax snap under the pressure of his fingers) "—will you read it to me?"

"It's dark in here, sieur," I said doubtfully.

"Then we'll have to have Cyby. Excuse me." In the gloom I could barely see him turn away and raise his hands to form a trumpet. "Cy-by! Cy-by!" The name rang through the dark corridors I sensed all about me as the iron tongue struck the echoing bronze on one side, then the other.

There was an answering call from far off. For some time we waited in silence.

At last I saw light down a narrow alley bordered (as it seemed) by precipitous walls of uneven stone. It came nearer—a five-branched candlestick carried by a stocky, very erect man of forty or so with a flat, pale face. The bearded man beside me said, "There you are at last, Cyby. Have you brought a light?"

"Yes, Master. Who is this?"

"A messenger with a letter." In a more ceremonious tone, Master Ultan said to me, "This is my own apprentice, Cyby. We have a guild too, we curators, of whom the librarians are a division. I am the only master librarian here, and it is our custom to assign our apprentices to our senior members. Cyby has been mine for some years now."

I told Cyby that I was honored to meet him, and asked, somewhat timidly, what the feast day of the curators was—a question that must have been suggested by the thought that a great many of them must have gone by without Cyby's being elevated to journeyman.

"It is now passed," Master Ultan said. He looked toward me as he spoke, and in the candlelight I could see that his eyes were the color of watered milk. "In early spring. It is a beautiful day. The trees put out their new leaves then, in most years."

There were no trees in the Grand Court, but I nodded; then, realizing he could not see me, I said, "Yes, beautiful with soft breezes."

"Precisely. You are a young man after my own heart." He put his hand on my shoulder—I could not help noticing that his fingers were dark with dust. "Cyby, too, is a young man after my heart. He will be chief librarian here when I am gone. We have a procession, you know, we curators. Down Iubar Street. He walks beside me then, the two of us robed in gray. What is the tinct of your own guild?"

"Fuligin," I told him. "The color that is darker than black."

"There are trees—sycamores and oaks, rock maples and duckfoot trees said to be the oldest on Urth. The trees spread their shade on either side of Iubar Street, and there are more on the esplanades down the center. Shopkeepers come to their doors to see the quaint curators, you know, and of course the booksellers and antique dealers cheer us. I suppose we are one of the spring sights of Nessus, in our little way."

"It must be very impressive," I said.

"It is, it is. The cathedral is very fine too, once we reach it. There are banks of tapers, as though the sun were shining on the night sea. And candles in blue glass to symbolize the Claw.

Enfolded in light, we conduct our ceremonies before the high altar. Tell me, does your own guild go to the cathedral?"

I explained that we used the chapel here in the Citadel, and expressed surprise that the librarians and other curators left its walls.

"We are entitled to, you see. The library itself does—doesn't it, Cyby?"

"Indeed it does, Master." Cyby had a high, square forehead, from which his graying hair was in retreat. It made his face seem small and a trifle babyish; I could understand how Ultan, who must occasionally have run his fingers over it as Master Palaemon sometimes ran his over mine, could think him still almost a boy.

"You are in close contact, then, with your opposite numbers in the city," I said.

The old man stroked his beard. "The closest, for we are they. This library is the city library, and the library of the House Absolute too, for that matter. And many others."

"Do you mean that the rabble of the city is permitted to enter the Citadel to use your library?"

"No," said Ultan. "I mean that the library itself extends beyond the walls of the Citadel. Nor, I think, is it the only institution here that does so. It is thus that the contents of our fortress are so much larger than their container."

He took me by the shoulder as he spoke, and we began to walk down one of the long, narrow paths between the towering bookcases. Cyby followed us holding up his candelabrum—I suppose more for his benefit than mine, but it permitted me to see well enough to keep from colliding with the dark oak shelves we passed. "Your eyes have not yet failed you," Master Ultan said after a time. "Do you apprehend any termination to this aisle?"

"No, sieur," I said, and in fact I did not. As far as the candlelight flew there was only row upon row of books stretching from the floor to the high ceiling. Some of the shelves were disordered, some straight; once or twice I saw evidence that rats had been nesting among the books, rearranging them to make snug two- and three-level homes for themselves and smearing dung on the covers to form the rude characters of their speech.

But always there were books and more books: rows of spines in calf, morocco, binder's cloth, paper, and a hundred other substances I could not identify, some flashing with gilt, many lettered in black, a few with paper labels so old and yellowed that they were as brown as dead leaves.

"'Of the trail of ink there is no end,'" Master Ultan told me. "Or so a wise man said. He lived long ago—what would he say if he could see us now? Another said, 'A man will give his life to the turning over of a collection of books,' but I would like to meet the man who could turn over this one, on any topic."

"I was looking at the bindings," I answered, feeling rather foolish.

"How fortunate for you. Yet I am glad. I can no longer see them, but I remember the pleasure I once had in doing it. That would be just after I had become master librarian. I suppose I was about fifty. I had, you know, been an apprentice for many, many years."

"Is that so, sieur?"

"Indeed it is. My master was Gerbold, and for decades it appeared that he would never die. Year followed straggling year for me, and all that time I read—I suppose few have ever read so. I began, as most young people do, by reading the books I enjoyed. But I found that narrowed my pleasure, in time, until I spent most of my hours searching for such books. Then I devised a plan of study for myself, tracing obscure sciences, one after another, from the dawn of knowledge to the present. Eventually I exhausted even that, and beginning at the great ebony case that stands in the center of the room we of the library have maintained for three hundred years against the return of the Autarch Sulpicius (and into which, in consequence, no one ever comes) I read outward for a period of fifteen years, often finishing two books in one day."

Behind us, Cyby murmured, "Marvelous, sieur." I suspected that he had heard the story many times.

"Then the unlooked-for seized me by the coat. Master Gerbold died. Thirty years before I had been ideally suited by reason of predilection, education, experience, youth, family connections, and ambition to succeed him. At the time I actually did so, no one could have been less fit. I had waited so long that waiting was all I understood, and I possessed a mind suffocated beneath the weight of inutile facts. But I forced myself to take charge, and spent more hours than I could expect you to believe now in attempting to recall the plans and maxims I had laid down so many years ago for my eventual succession."

He paused, and I knew he was delving again in a mind larger and darker than even his great library. "But my old habit of reading dogged me still. I lost to books days and even weeks, during which I should have been considering the operations of the establishment that looked to me for leadership. Then, as suddenly as the striking of a clock, a new passion came to me, displacing the old. You will already have guessed what it was."

I told him I had not.

"I was reading—or so I thought—on the seat of that bow window on the forty-ninth floor that overlooks— I have forgotten, Cyby. What is it that it overlooks?"

"The upholsterers' garden, sieur."

"Yes, I recall it now—that little square of green and brown. I believe they dry rosemary there to put in pillows. I was sitting there, as I said, and had been for several watches, when it came to me that I was reading no longer. For some time I was hard put to say what I had been doing. When I tried, I could only think of certain odors and textures and colors that seemed to have no connection with anything discussed in the volume I held. At last I realized that instead of reading it, I had been observing it as a physical object. The red I recalled came from the ribbon sewn to the headband so that I might mark my place. The texture that tickled my fingers still was that of the paper on which the book was printed. The smell in my nostrils was old leather, still bearing the traces of birch oil. It was only then, when I saw the books themselves, that I began to understand their care."

His grip on my shoulder tightened. "We have books here bound in the hides of echidnes, krakens, and beasts so long extinct that those whose studies they are, are for the most part of the opinion that no trace of them survives unfossilized. We have books bound wholly in metals of unknown alloy, and books whose bindings are covered with thickset gems. We have books cased in perfumed woods shipped across the inconceivable gulf between creations—books doubly precious because no one on Urth can read them.

"We have books whose papers are matted of plants from which spring curious alkaloids, so that the reader, in turning their pages, is taken unaware by bizarre fantasies and chimeric dreams. Books whose pages are not paper at all, but delicate wafers of white jade, ivory, and shell; books too whose leaves are the desiccated leaves of unknown plants. Books we have also that are not books at all to the eye: scrolls and tablets and recordings on a hundred different substances. There is a cube of crystal here—though I can no longer tell you where—no larger than the ball of your thumb that contains more books than the library itself does. Though a harlot might dangle it from one ear for an ornament, there are not volumes enough in the world to counterweight the other. All these I came to know, and I made safeguarding them my life's devotion.

"For seven years I busied myself with that; and then, just when the pressing and superficial problems of preservation were disposed of, and we were on the point of beginning the first general survey of the library since its foundation, my eyes began to gutter in their sockets. He who had given all books into my keeping made me blind so that I should know in whose keeping the keepers stand."

"If you can't read the letter I brought, sieur," I said, "I will be glad to read it to you."

"You are right," Master Ultan muttered. "I had forgotten it. Cyby will read it—he reads well. Here, Cyby."

I held the candelabrum for him, and Cyby unfolded the crackling parchment, held it up like a proclamation, and began to read, the three of us standing in a little circle of candlelight while all the books crowded around.

"'From Master Gurloes of the Order of the Seekers for Truth and Penitence—'"

"What," said Master Ultan. "Are you a torturer, young man?"

I told him I was, and there occurred a silence so long that Cyby began to read the letter a second time: "'From Master Gurloes of the Order of the Seekers—'"

"Wait," Ultan said. Cyby paused again; I stood as I had, holding the light and feeling the blood mounting to my cheeks. At last Master Ultan spoke again, and his voice was as matter-of-fact as it had been in telling me Cyby read well. "I can hardly recall my own admission to our guild. You are familiar, I suppose, with the method by which we recruit our numbers?"

I admitted I was not.

"In every library, by ancient precept, is a room reserved for children. In it are kept bright picture books such as children delight in, and a few simple tales of wonder and adventure. Many children come to these rooms, and so long as they remain within their confines, no interest is taken in them."

He hesitated, and though I could discern no expression on his face, I received the impression that he feared what he was about to say might cause Cyby pain.

"From time to time, however, a librarian remarks a solitary child, still of tender years, who wanders from the children's room . . . and at last deserts it entirely. Such a child eventually discovers, on some low but obscure shelf, *The Book of Gold*. You have never seen this book, and you will never see it, being past the age at which it is met."

"It must be very beautiful," I said.

"It is indeed. Unless my memory betrays me, the cover is of black buckram, considerably faded at the spine. Several of the signatures are coming out, and certain of the plates have been taken. But it is a remarkably lovely book. I wish that I might find it again, though all books are shut to me now.

"The child, as I said, in time discovers *The Book of Gold*. Then the librarians come—like vampires, some say, but others say like the fairy godparents at a christening. They speak to the child, and the child joins them. Henceforth he is in the library wherever he may be, and soon his parents know him no more. I suppose it is much the same among the torturers."

"We take such children as fall into our hands," I said, "and are very young."

"We do the same," old Ultan muttered. "So we have little right to condemn you. Read on, Cyby."

"'From Master Gurloes of the Order of the Seekers for Truth and Penitence, to the Archivist of the Citadel: Greetings, Brother.

"'By the will of a court we have in our keeping the exulted person of the Chatelaine Thecla; and by its further will we would furnish to the Chatelaine Thecla in her confinement such comforts as lie not beyond reason and prudence. That she may while away the moments until her time with us is come—or rather, as she has instructed me to say, until the heart of the Autarch, whose forebearance knows not walls nor seas, is softened toward her, as she prays—she asks that you, consonant with your office, provide her with certain books, which books are—'"

"You may omit the titles, Cyby," Ultan said. "How many are there?"

"Four, sieur."

"No trouble then. Proceed."

"'For this, Archivist, we are much obliged to you.' Signed, 'Gurloes, Master of the Honorable Order commonly called the Guild of Torturers.'"

"Are you familiar with any of the titles on Master Gurloes's list, Cyby?"

"With three, sieur."

"Very good. Fetch them, please. What is the fourth?"

"The Book of the Wonders of Urth and Sky, sieur."

"Better and better—there is a copy not two chains from here. When you have your volumes, you may meet us at the door through which this young man, whom I fear we have already detained too long, entered the stacks."

I attempted to return the candelabrum to Cyby, but he indicated by a sign that I was to keep it and trotted off down a narrow aisle.

Ultan was stalking away in the opposite direction, moving as surely as if he possessed vision. "I recollect it well," he said. "The binding is of brown cordwain, all edges are gilt, and there are etchings by Gwinoc, hand-tinted. It is on the third shelf from the floor, and leans against a folio in green cloth—I believe it is Blaithmaic's *Lives of the Seventeen Megatherians*."

Largely to let him know I had not left him (though no doubt his sharp ears caught my footfalls behind him), I asked, "What is it, sieur? The Urth and sky book, I mean."

"Why," he said, "don't you know better than to ask that question of a librarian? Our concern, young man, is with the books themselves, not with their contents."

I caught the amusement in his tone. "I think you know the contents of every book here, sieur."

"Hardly. But *Wonders of Urth and Sky* was a standard work, three or four hundred years ago. It relates most of the familiar legends of ancient times. To me the most interesting is that of the Historians, which tells of a time in which every legend could be traced to half-forgotten fact. You see the paradox, I assume. Did that legend itself exist at that time? And if not, how came it into existence?"

"Aren't there any great serpents, sieur, or flying women?"

"Oh, yes," Master Ultan answered, stooping as he spoke. "But not in the legend of the Historians." Triumphantly, he held up a small volume bound in flaking leather. "Have a look at this, young man, and see if I've got the right one."

I had to set the candelabrum on the floor and crouch beside it. The book in my hands was so old and stiff and musty that it seemed impossible that it had been opened within the past century, but the title page confirmed the old man's boast. A subtitle announced: "Being a Collection from Printed Sources of Universal Secrets of Such Age That Their Meaning Has Become Obscured of Time."

"Well," asked Master Ultan, "was I right or no?"

I opened the book at random and read, ". . . by which means a picture might be graven with such skill that the whole of it, should it be destroyed, might be recreated from a small part, and that small part might be any part."

I suppose it was the word *graven* that suggested to me the events I had witnessed on the night I had received my chrisos. "Master," I answered, "you are phenomenal."

"No, but I am seldom mistaken."

"You, of all men, will excuse me when I tell you I tarried a moment to read a few lines of this book. Master, you know of the corpse-eaters, surely. I have heard it said that by devouring the flesh of the dead, together with a certain pharmacon, they are able to relive the lives of their victims."

"It is unwise to know too much about these practices," the archivist murmured, "though when I think of sharing the mind of a historian like Loman, or Hermas . . ." In his years of blindness he must have forgotten how nakedly our faces can betray our deepest feelings. By the light of the candles I saw his twisted in such an agony of desire that out of decency I turned away; his voice remained as calm as some solemn bell. "But from what I once read, you are correct, though I do not now recall that the book you hold treats of it."

"Master," I said, "I give you my word I would never suspect you of such a thing. But tell me this—suppose two collaborate in the robbing of a grave, and one takes the right hand for his share, and the other the left. Does he who ate the right hand have but half the dead man's life, and the other the rest? And if so, what if a third were to come and devour a foot?"

"It's a pity you are a torturer," Ultan said. "You might have been a philosopher. No, as I understand this noxious matter, each has the entire life."

"Then a man's whole life is in his right hand and in his left as well. Is it in each finger too?"

"I believe each participant must consume more than a

mouthful for the practice to be effective. But I suppose that in theory at least, what you say is correct. The entire life is in each finger."

We were already walking back in the direction we had come. Since the aisle was too narrow for us to pass one another, I now carried the candelabrum before him, and a stranger, seeing us, would surely have thought I lighted his way. "But Master," I said, "how can that be? By the same argument, the life must reside in each joint of every finger, and surely that is impossible."

"How big is a man's life?" asked Ultan.

"I have no way of knowing, but isn't it larger than that?"

"You see it from the beginning, and anticipate much. I, recollecting it from its termination, know how little there has been. I suppose that is why the depraved creatures who devour the bodies of the dead seek more. Let me ask you this—are you aware that a son often strikingly resembles his father?"

"I have heard it said, yes. And I believe it," I answered. I could not help thinking as I did of the parents I would never know.

"Then it is possible, you will agree, since each son may resemble his father, for a face to endure through many generations. That is, if the son resembles the father, and *his* son resembles him, and that son's son resembles him, then the fourth in line, the great-grandson, resembles his great-grandfather."

"Yes," I said.

"Yet the seed of all of them was contained in a drachm of sticky fluid. If they did not come from there, from where did they come?"

I could make no answer to that, and walked along in puzzlement until we reached the door through which I had entered this lowest level of the great library. Here we met Cyby carrying the other books mentioned in Master Gurloes's letter. I took them from him, bade goodbye to Master Ultan, and very gratefully left the stifling atmosphere of the library stacks. To the upper levels of that place I returned several times; but I never again entered that tomblike cellar, or ever wished to.

One of the three volumes Cyby had brought was as large as the top of a small table, a cubit in width and a scant ell in height; from the arms impressed upon its saffian cover, I supposed it to be the history of some old noble family. The others were much smaller. A green book hardly larger than my hand and no thicker than my index finger appeared to be a collection of devotions, full of enameled pictures of ascetic pantocrators and hypostases with black halos and gemlike robes. I stopped for a time to look at them, sharing a little, forgotten garden full of winter sunshine with a dry fountain.

Before I had so much as opened any of the other volumes, I felt that pressure of time that is perhaps the surest indication we have left childhood behind. I had already been two watches at least on a simple errand, and soon the light would fade. I gathered up the books and hurried along, though I did not know it, to meet my destiny and eventually myself in the Chatelaine Thecla.

VII

The Traitress

IT WAS ALREADY TIME for me to carry their meals to the journeymen on duty in the oubliette. Drotte was in charge of the first level, and I brought his last because I wanted to talk to him before I went up again. The truth was that my head was still swimming with thoughts engendered by my visit to the archivist, and I wanted to tell him about them.

He was nowhere to be seen. I put his tray and the four books on his table and shouted for him. A moment later I heard his answering call from a cell not far off. I ran there and looked through the grilled window set at eye level in the door; the client, a wasted-looking woman of middle age, was stretched on her cot. Drotte leaned over her, and there was blood on the floor.

He was too occupied to turn his head. "Is that you, Severian?"

"Yes. I've got your supper, and books for the Chatelaine Thecla. Can I do anything to help?"

"She'll be all right. Tore her dressings off and tried to bleed herself to death, but I got her in time. Leave my tray on my table, will you? And you might finish shoving their food at the rest for me, if you've got a moment."

I hesitated. Apprentices were not supposed to deal with those committed to the guild's care.

"Go ahead. All you have to do is poke the trays through the slots."

"I brought the books."

"Poke those through the slot too."

For a moment more I watched him as he bent over the livid woman on the cot; then I turned away, found the undistributed trays, and began to do as he had asked. Most of the clients in the cells were still strong enough to rise and take the food as I passed it through. A few were not, and I left their trays outside their doors for Drotte to carry in later. There were several aristocratic-looking women, but none who seemed likely to be the Chatelaine Thecla, a newly come exultant who was—at least for the time being—to be treated with deference.

As I should have guessed, she was in the last cell. It had been furnished with a carpet in addition to the usual bed, chair, and small table; in place of the customary rags she wore a white gown with wide sleeves. The ends of those sleeves and the hem of the skirt were sadly soiled now, but the gown still preserved an air of elegance as foreign to me as it was to the cell itself. When I first saw her, she was embroidering by the light of a candle brightened by a silver reflector; but she must have felt my eyes upon her. It would gratify me now to say there was no fear in her face, yet it would not be true. There was terror there, though controlled nearly to invisibility.

"It's all right," I said. "I've brought your food."

She nodded and thanked me, then rose and came to the door. She was taller even than I had expected, nearly too tall to stand upright in the cell. Her face, though it was triangular rather than heart-shaped, reminded me of the woman who had been with Vodalus in the necropolis. Perhaps it was her great violet eyes, with their lids shaded with blue, and the black hair that, forming a V far down her forehead, suggested the hood of a cloak. Whatever the reason, I loved her at once—loved her, at least, insofar as a stupid boy can love. But being only a stupid boy, I did not know it.

Her white hand, cold, slightly damp, and impossibly narrow,

touched mine as she took the tray from me. "That's ordinary food," I told her. "I think you can get some that's better if you ask."

"You're not wearing a mask," she said. "Yours is the first human face I've seen here."

"I'm only an apprentice. I won't be masked until next year."

She smiled, and I felt as I had when I had been in the Atrium of Time and had come inside to a warm room and food. She had narrow, very white teeth in a wide mouth; her eyes, each as deep as the cistern beneath the Bell Keep, shone when she smiled.

"I'm sorry," I said. "I didn't hear you."

The smile came again and she tilted her lovely head to one side. "I told you how happy I was to see your face, and asked if you would bring my meals in the future, and what this was you brought me."

"No. No, I won't be. Only today, because Drotte is occupied." I tried to recall what her meal had been (she had put the tray on her little table, where I could not see its contents through the grill). I could not, though I nearly burst my brain with the effort. At last I said lamely, "You'd probably better eat it. But I think you can get better food if you ask Drotte."

"Why, I intend to eat it. People have always complimented me on my slender figure, but believe me, I eat like a dire wolf." She picked up the tray and held it out to me, as though she knew I would need every help in unraveling the mystery of its contents.

"Those are leeks, Chatelaine," I said. "Those green things. The brown ones are lentils. And that's bread."

"'Chatelaine'? You needn't be so formal. You're my jailer, and can call me anything you choose." There was merriment in the deep eyes now.

"I have no wish to insult you," I told her. "Would you rather I called you something else?"

"Call me Thecla—that's my name. Titles are for formal occasions, names for informal ones, and this is that or nothing. I suppose it will be very formal though, when I receive my punishment?"

"It is, usually, for exultants."

"There will be an exarch, I should think, if you will let him in. All in scarlet patches. Several others too—perhaps the Starost Egino. Are you certain this is bread?" She poked it with one long finger, so white I thought for a moment that the bread might soil it.

"Yes," I said. "The Chatelaine has eaten bread before, surely?"

"Not like this." She picked the meager slice up and tore it with her teeth, quickly and cleanly. "It isn't bad, though. You say they'll bring me better food if I ask for it?"

"I think so, Chatelaine."

"Thecla. I asked for books—two days ago when I came. But I haven't got them."

"I have them," I told her. "Right here." I ran back to Drotte's table and got them, and passed the smallest through the slot.

"Oh, wonderful! Are there others?"

"Three more." The brown book went through the slot as well, but the other two, the green book and the folio volume with arms on its cover, were too wide. "Drotte will open your door later and give them to you," I said.

"Can't you? It's terrible to look though this and see them, and not be able to touch them."

"I'm not even supposed to feed you. Drotte should do it."

"But you did. Besides, you brought them. Weren't you supposed to give them to me?"

I could argue only weakly, knowing she was right in principle. The rule against apprentices working in the oubliette was intended to prevent escapes; and I knew that tall though she was, this slender woman could never overpower me, and that should she do so she would have no chance of making her way out without being challenged. I went to the door of the cell where Drotte still labored over the client who had tried to take her own life, and returned with his keys.

Standing before her, with her own cell door closed and locked behind me, I found myself unable to speak. I put the books on her table beside the candlestand and her food pan and carafe of water;

there was hardly room for them. When it was done I stood waiting, knowing I should leave and yet unable to go.

'Won't you sit down?'

I sat on her bed, leaving her the chair.

"If this were my suite in the House Absolute, I could offer you better cornfort. Unfortunately, you never called while I was there."

I shook my head.

"Here I have no refreshment to offer you but this. Do you like lentils?"

"I won't eat that, Chatelaine. I'll have my own supper soon, and there's hardly enough for you."

"True." She picked up a leek, and then as if she did not know what else to do with it dropped it down her throat like a mountebank swallowing a viper. "What will you have?"

"Leeks and lentils, bread and mutton."

"Ah, the torturers get mutton—that's the difference. What's your name, Master Torturer?"

"Severian. It won't help, Chatelaine. It won't make any difference."

She smiled. "What won't?"

"Making friends with me. I couldn't give you your freedom. And I wouldn't—not if I had no friend but you in all the world."

"I didn't think you could, Severian."

"Then why do you bother to talk to me?"

She sighed, and all the gladness went out of her face, as the sunlight leaves the stone where a beggar seeks to warm himself. "Who else have I to talk to, Severian? It may be that I will talk to you for a time, for a few days or a few weeks, and die. I know what you're thinking—that if I were back in my suite I would never spare a glance for you. But you're wrong. One can't talk to everyone because there are so many everyones, but the day before I was taken I talked for some time with the man who held my mount. I spoke to him because I had to wait, you see, and then he said something that interested me."

"You won't see me again. Drotte will bring your food."

"And not you? Ask him if he will let you do it." She took my hands in hers, and they were like ice.

"I'll try," I said.

"Do. Do try. Tell him I want better meals than this, and you to serve me—wait, I'll ask him myself. To whom does he answer?"

"Master Gurloes."

"I'll tell the other—is it Drotte?—that I want to speak to him. You're right, they'll have to do it. The Autarch might release me—they don't know." Her eyes flashed.

"I'll tell Drotte you want to see him when he's not busy," I said, and stood up.

"Wait. Aren't you going to ask me why I'm here?"

"I know why you're here," I said as I swung back the door. "To be tortured, eventually, like the others." It was a cruel thing to say, and I said it without reflection as young men do, only because it was what was in my mind. Yet it was true, and I was glad in some way, as I turned the key in the lock, that I had said it.

We had had exultants for clients often before. Most, when they arrived, had some understanding of their situation, as the Chatelaine Thecla did now. But when a few days had passed and they were not put to torment, their hope cast down their reason and they began to talk of release—how friends and family would maneuver to gain their freedom, and of what they would do when they were free.

One would withdraw to his estates and trouble the Autarch's court no more. Another would volunteer to lead a muster of lansquenets in the north. Then the journeymen on duty in the oubliette would hear tales of hunting dogs and remote heaths, and country games, unknown elsewhere, played beneath immemorial trees. The women were more realistic for the most part, but even they in time spoke of highly placed lovers (cast aside now for months or years) who would never abandon them, and then of bearing children or adopting waifs. One knew when these never-to-be-born children were given names that clothing would not be far behind: a new wardrobe on their release, the old clothes to be burned; they talked of colors, of inventing new fashions and reviving old ones.

At last the time would come, to men and women alike, when instead of a journeyman with food, Master Gurloes would appear trailing three or four journeymen and perhaps an examiner and a fulgurator. I wanted to preserve the Chatelaine Thecla from such hopes if I could. I hung Drotte's keys on their accustomed nail in the wall, and when I passed the cell in which he was now swabbing blood from the floor told him that the chatelaine desired to speak with him.

On the next day but one, I was summoned to Master Gurloes. I had expected to stand, as we apprentices usually did, with hands behind back before his table; but he told me to sit, and removing his gold-traced mask, leaned toward me in a way that implied a common cause and friendly footing.

"A week ago, or a little less, I sent you to the archivist," he said. I nodded.

"When you brought the books, I take it you delivered them to the client yourself. Is that right?"

I explained what had happened.

"Nothing wrong there. I don't want you to think I'm going to order extra fatigues for what you did, much less have you bent over a chair. You're nearly a journeyman yourself already—when I was your age, they had me cranking the alternator. The thing is, you see, Severian, the client is highly placed." His voice sank to a rough whisper. "Quite highly connected."

I said that I understood that.

"Not just an armiger family. High blood." He turned, and after searching the disorderly shelves behind his chair produced a squat book. "Have you any notion how many exulted families there are? This lists only the ones that are still going. A compendium of the extinguished ones would take an encyclopedia, I suppose. I've extinguished a few of them myself."

He laughed and I laughed with him.

"It gives about half a page to each. There are seven hundred and forty-six pages."

I nodded to show I understood.

"Most of them have nobody at court—can't afford it, or are afraid of it. Those are the small ones. The greater families must: the Autarch wants a concubine he can lay hands on if they start misbehaving. Now the Autarch can't play quadrille with five hundred women. There are maybe twenty. The rest talk to each other, and dance, and don't see him closer than a chain off once in a month."

I asked (trying to hold my voice steady) if the Autarch actually bedded these concubines.

Master Gurloes rolled his eyes and pulled at his jaw with one huge hand. "Well now, for decency's sake they have these khaibits, what they call the shadow women, that are common girls that look like the chatelaines. I don't know where they get them, but they're supposed to stand in place of the others. Of course they're not so tall." He chuckled. "I said stand in place, but when they're laying down the tallness probably doesn't make much difference. They do say, though, that oftentimes it works the other way than it's supposed to. Instead of those shadow girls doing duty for their mistresses, the mistresses do it for them. But the present Autarch, whose every deed, I may say, is sweeter than honey in the mouths of this honorable guild and don't you forget it—in his case, I may say, from what I understand it is more than somewhat doubtful if he has the pleasure of any of them."

Relief flooded my heart. "I never knew that. It's very interesting, Master."

Master Gurloes inclined his head to acknowledge that it was indeed, and laced his fingers over his belly. "Someday you may have the ordering of the guild yourself. You'll need to know these things. When I was your age—or a trifle younger, I suppose—I used to fancy I was of exulted blood. Some have been, you know."

It struck me, and not for the first time, that Master Gurloes and Master Palaemon too must have known whence all the apprentices and younger journeymen had come, having approved their admissions originally.

"Whether I am or no, I cannot say. I have the physique of a rider, I think, and I am somewhat over the average in height despite a hard boyhood. For it was harder, much harder, forty years ago, I'll tell you."

"So I have been told, Master."

He sighed, the kind of wheezing noise a leather pillow sometimes makes when one sits on it. "But with the passage of time I have come to understand that the Increate, in choosing for me a career in our guild, was acting for my benefit. Doubtless I had acquired merit in a previous life, as I hope I have in this one."

Master Gurloes fell silent, looking (it seemed to me) at the jumble of papers on his table, the instructions of jurists and the dossiers of clients. At last, when I was about to ask if he had anything further to tell me, he said, "In all my years, I have never known of a member of the guild put to torment. Of them, several hundred, I suppose."

I ventured the commonplace saying that it was better to be a toad hidden under a stone than a butterfly crushed beneath it.

"We of the guild are more than toads, I think. But I should have added that though I have seen five hundred or more exultants in our cells, I have never, until now, had charge of a member of that inner circle of concubines closest to the Autarch."

"The Chatelaine Thecla belonged to it? You implied that a moment ago, Master."

He nodded gloomily. "It wouldn't be so bad if she were to be put to torment at once, but that isn't to be. It may be years. It may be never."

"You believe she may be released, Master?"

"She's a pawn in the Autarch's game with Vodalus—even I know that much. Her sister, the Chatelaine Thea, has fled the House Absolute to become his leman. They will bargain with Thecla for a time at least, and while they do, we must give her good fare. Yet not too good."

"I see," I said. I was acutely uncomfortable not knowing what the Chatelaine Thecla had told Drotte, and what Drotte had told Master Gurloes.

"She's asked for better food, and I've made arrangements to supply it. She's asked for company as well, and when we told her visitors would not be permitted, she urged that one of us, at least, should keep her company sometimes."

Master Gurloes paused to wipe his shining face with the edge of his cloak. I said, "I understand." I was fairly certain that I indeed understood what was to come next.

"Because she had seen your face, she asked for you. I told her you'll sit with her while she eats. I don't ask your agreement—not only because you're subject to my instructions, but because I know you're loyal. What I do ask is that you be careful not to displease her, and not to please her too much."

"I will do my best." I was surprised to hear my own steady voice.

Master Gurloes smiled as if I had eased him. "You've a good head, Severian, though it's a young one yet. Have you been with a woman?"

When we apprentices talked, it was the custom to invent fables on this topic, but I was not among apprentices now, and I shook my head.

"You've never been to the witches? That may be for the best. They supplied my own instruction in the warm commerce, but I'm not sure I'd send them another such as I was. It's likely, though, that the Chatelaine wants her bed warmed. You're not to do it for her. Her pregnancy would be no ordinary one—it might force a delay in her torment and bring disgrace on the guild. You follow me?"

I nodded.

"Boys your age are troubled. I'll have somebody take you where such ills are speedily cured."

"As you wish, Master."

"What? You don't thank me?"

"Thank you, Master," I said.

Gurloes was one of the most complex men I have known, because he was a complex man trying to be simple. Not a simple, but a complex man's idea of simplicity. Just as a courtier forms himself into something brilliant and involved, midway between a dancing master and a diplomacist, with a touch of assassin if needed, so Master Gurloes had shaped himself to be the dull creature a pursuivant or bailiff expected to see when he summoned the head of our guild, and that is the only thing a real torturer cannot be. The strain showed; though every part of Gurloes was as it should have been, none of the parts fit. He drank heavily and suffered from nightmares, but he had the nightmares when he had been drinking, as if the wine, instead of bolting the doors of his mind, threw them open and left him staggering about in the last hours of the night, trying to catch a glimpse of a sun that had not yet appeared, a sun that would banish the phantoms from his big cabin and permit him to dress and send the journeymen to their business. Sometimes he went to the top of our tower, above the guns, and waited there talking to himself, peering through glass said to be harder than flint for the first beams. He was the only one in our guild—Master Palaemon not excepted—who was unafraid of the energies there and the unseen mouths that spoke sometimes to human beings and sometimes to other mouths in other towers and keeps. He loved music, but he thumped the arm of his chair to it and tapped his foot, and did so most vigorously to the kind he liked best, whose rhythms were too subtle for any regular cadence. He ate too much and too seldom, read when he thought no one knew of it, and visited certain of our clients, including one on the third level, to talk of things none of us eavesdropping in the corridor outside could understand. His eyes were refulgent, brighter than any woman's. He mispronounced quite common words: *urticate*, *salpinx*, *bordereau*. I cannot well tell you how bad he looked when I returned to the Citadel recently, how bad he looks now.

VIII

The Conversationalist

NEXT DAY, for the first time, I carried Thecla's supper to her. For a watch I remained with her, frequently observed through the slot in the cell door by Drotte. We played word games, at which she was far better than I, and after a while talked of those things those who have returned are said to say lie beyond death, she recounting what she had read in the smallest of the books I had brought her—not only the accepted views of the hierophants, but various eccentric and heretic theories.

"When I am free," she said, "I shall found my own sect. I will tell everyone that its wisdom was revealed to me during my sojourn among the torturers. They'll listen to that."

I asked what her teachings would be.

"That there is no agathodaemon or afterlife. That the mind is extinguished in death as in sleep, yet more so."

"But who will you say revealed that to you?"

She shook her head, then rested her pointed chin upon one hand, a pose that showed off the graceful line of her neck admirably. "I haven't decided yet. An angel of ice, perhaps. Or a ghost. Which do you think best?"

"Isn't there a contradiction in that?"

"Precisely." Her voice was rich with the pleasure the question gave her. "In that contradiction will reside the appeal of this new belief. One can't found a novel theology on Nothing, and nothing is so secure a foundation as a contradiction. Look at the great successes of the past—they say their deities are the masters of all the universes, and yet that they require grandmothers to defend them, as if they were children frightened by poultry. Or that the authority that punishes no one while there exists a chance for reformation will punish everyone when there is no possibility anyone will become the better for it."

I said, "These things are too complex for me."

"No they're not. You're as intelligent as most young men, I think. But I suppose you torturers have no religion. Do they make you swear to give it up?"

"Not at all. We've a celestial patroness and observances, just like any other guild."

"We don't," she said. For a moment she seemed to brood on that. "Only the guilds do, you know, and the army, which is a kind of guild. We'd be better off, I think, if we did. Still all the days of feast and nights of vigil have become shows, opportunities to wear new dresses. Do you like this?" She stood and extended her arms to show the soiled gown.

"It's very pretty," I ventured. "The embroidery, and the way the little pearls are sewed on."

"It's the only thing I have here—what I was wearing when I was taken. It's for dinner, really. After late afternoon and before early evening."

I said I was sure Master Gurloes would have others brought if she asked.

"I already have, and he says he sent some people to the House Absolute to fetch them for me, but they were unable to find it, which means that the House Absolute is trying to pretend I don't exist. Anyway, it's possible all my clothes have been sent to our chateau in the north, or one of the villas. He's going to have his secretary write them for me."

"Do you know who he sent?" I asked. "The House Absolute must be nearly as big as our Citadel, and I would think it would be impossible for anyone to miss."

"On the contrary, it's quite easy. Since it can't be seen, you can be there and never know it if you're not lucky. Besides, with the roads closed, all they have to do is alert their spies to give a particular party incorrect direction, and they have spies everywhere."

I started to ask how it was possible for the House Absolute (which I had always imagined a vast palace of gleaming towers and domed halls) to be invisible; but Thecla was already thinking of something else altogether, stroking a bracelet formed like a kraken, a kraken whose tentacles wrapped the white flesh of her arm; its eyes were cabochon emeralds. "They let me keep this, and it's quite valuable. Platinum, not silver. I was surprised."

"There's no one here who can be bribed."

"It might be sold in Nessus to buy clothing. Have any of my friends tried to see me? Do you know, Severian?"

I shook my head. "They would not be admitted."

"I understand, but someone might try. Do you know that most of the people in the House Absolute don't know this place exists? I see you don't believe me."

"You mean they don't know of the Citadel?"

"They're aware of that, of course. Parts of it are open to everyone, and anyway you can't miss seeing the spires if you get down into the southern end of the living city, no matter which side of Gyoll you're on." She slapped the metal wall of her cell with one hand. "They don't know of *this*—or at least, a great many of them would deny it still exists."

She was a great, great chatelaine, and I was something worse than a slave (I mean in the eyes of the common people, who do not really understand the functions of our guild). Yet when the time had passed and Drotte tapped the ringing door, it was I who rose and left the cell and soon climbed into the clean air of evening, and

Thecla who stayed behind to listen to the moans and screams of the others. (Though her cell was some distance from the stairwell, the laughter from the third level was audible still when there was no one there to talk with her.)

In our dormitory that night I asked if anyone knew the names of the journeymen Master Gurloes had sent in search of the House Absolute. No one did, but my question stirred an animated discussion. Although none of the boys had seen the place or so much as spoken with anyone who had, all had heard stories. Most were of fabled wealth—gold plates and silk saddle blankets and that sort of thing. More interesting were the descriptions of the Autarch, who would have had to be a kind of monster to fit them all; he was said to be tall when standing, of common size seated, aged, young, a woman dressed as a man, and so on. More fantastic still were the tales of his vizier, the famous Father Inire, who looked like a monkey and was the oldest man in the world.

We had just begun trading wonders in good earnest when there was a knock at the door. The youngest opened it, and I saw Roche—dressed not in the fuligin breeches and cloak the regulations of the guild decree, but in common, though new and fashionable, trousers, shirt, and coat. He motioned to me, and when I came to the door to speak to him, he indicated that I was to follow him.

After we had gone some way down the stair, he said, "I'm afraid I frightened the little fellow. He doesn't know who I am."

"Not in those clothes," I told him. "He'd recall you if he saw you dressed the way you used to be."

That pleased him and he laughed. "Do you know, it felt so strange, having to bang on that door. Today is what? The eighteenth—it's been under three weeks. How are things going for you?"

"Well enough."

"You seem to have the gang in hand. Eata's your second, isn't he? He won't make a journeyman for four years, so he'll be captain for three after you. It's good for him to have the experience, and I'm sorry now you didn't have more before you had to take the job on. I stood in your way, but I never thought about it at the time."

"Roche, where are we going?"

"Well, first we're going down to my cabin to get you dressed. Are you looking forward to becoming a journeyman yourself, Severian?"

These last words were thrown over his shoulder as he clattered down the steps ahead of me, and he did not wait for an answer.

My costume was much like his, though of different colors. There were overcoats and caps for us too. "You'll be glad for them," he said as I put mine on. "It's cold out and starting to snow." He handed me a scarf and told me to take off my worn shoes and put on a pair of boots.

"They're journeymen's boots," I protested. "I can't wear those."

"Go ahead. Everyone wears black boots. Nobody will notice. Do they fit?"

They were too large, so he made me draw a pair of his stockings on over my own.

"Now, I'm supposed to keep the purse, but since there's always a chance we may be separated, it would be better if you have a few asimi." He dropped coins into my palm. "Ready? Let's go. I'd like to be back in time for some sleep if we can."

We left the tower, and muffled in our strange clothing rounded the Witches' Keep to take the covered walk leading past the Martello to the court called Broken. Roche had been right: it was starting to snow, fluffy flakes as big as the end of my thumb sifting so slowly through the air that it seemed they must have been falling for years. There was no wind, and we could hear the creaking our boots made in breaking through the familiar world's new, thin disguise.

"You're in luck," Roche told me. "I don't know how you worked this, but thank you."

"Worked what?"

"A trip to the Echopraxia and a woman for each of us. I know you know—Master Gurloes told me he'd already notified you."

"I had forgotten, and anyway I wasn't sure he meant it. Are we going to walk? It must be a long way."

"Not as long as you probably think, but I told you we have funds. There will be fiacres at the Bitter Gate. There always are—people are continually coming and going, though you wouldn't think it back in our little corner."

To make conversation, I told him what the Chatelaine Thecla had said: that many people in the House Absolute did not know we existed.

"That's so, I'm sure. When you're brought up in the guild it seems like the center of the world. But when you're a little older—this is what I've found myself, and I know I can rely on you not to tell tales—something pops in your head, and you discover it isn't the linchpin of this universe after all, only a well-paid, unpopular business you happen to have fallen into."

As Roche had predicted there were coaches, three of them, waiting in the Broken Court. One was an exultant's with blazonings painted on the doors and palfreniers in fanciful liveries, but the other two were fiacres, small and plain. The drivers in their low fur caps were bending over a fire they had kindled on the cobbles. Seen at a distance through the falling snow it seemed no bigger than a spark.

Roche waved an arm and shouted, and a driver vaulted into the seat, cracked his whip, and came rattling to meet us. When we were inside, I asked Roche if he knew who we were, and he said, "We're two optimates who had business in the Citadel and are bound now for the Echopraxia and an evening of pleasure. That's all he knows and all he needs to know."

I wondered if Roche were much more experienced at such pleasures than I was myself. It seemed unlikely. In the hope of discovering whether he had visited our destination before, I asked where the Echopraxia lay.

"In the Algedonic Quarter. Have you heard of it?"

I nodded and said that Master Palaemon had once mentioned that it was one of the oldest parts of the city.

"Not really. There are parts farther south that are older still, a waste of stone where only omophagists live. The Citadel used to stand some distance north of Nessus, did you know that?"

I shook my head.

"The city keeps creeping upriver. The armigers and optimates want purer water—not that they drink it, but for their fishponds, and for bathing and boating. Then too, anyone living too near the sea is always somewhat suspect. So the lowest parts, where the water's the worst, are gradually given up. In the end the law goes, and those who stay behind are afraid to kindle a fire for fear of what the smoke may draw down on them."

I was looking out the window. We had already passed through a gate unknown to me, dashing by helmeted guards; but we were still within the Citadel, descending a narrow close between two rows of shuttered windows.

"When you are a journeyman you can go into the city any time you want, provided you're not on duty."

I knew that already, of course; but I asked Roche if he found it pleasant.

"Not pleasant, exactly . . . I've only gone twice, to tell you the truth. Not pleasant, but interesting. They know who you are, naturally."

"You said the driver didn't."

"Well, he probably doesn't. Those drivers go all over Nessus. He may live anywhere, and not get to the Citadel more than once a year. But the locals know. The soldiers tell. They always know, and they always tell, that's what everybody says. They can wear their uniforms when they go out."

"These windows are all dark. I don't think there's anyone in this part of the Citadel at all."

"Everything's getting smaller. Not much anybody can do about that. Less food means fewer people until the New Sun comes."

Despite the cold, I felt stifled in the fiacre. "Is it much farther?" I asked.

Roche chuckled. "You're bound to be nervous."

"No, I'm not."

"Certainly you are. Just don't let it bother you. It's natural. Don't be nervous about being nervous, if you see what I mean."

"I'm quite calm."

"It can be quick, if that's what you want. You don't have to talk to the woman if you don't want to. She doesn't care. Of course, she'll talk if that's what you like. You're paying—in this case I am, but the principle's the same. She'll do what you want, within reason. If you strike her or use a grip, they'll charge more."

"Do people do that?"

"You know, amateurs. I didn't think you'd want to, and I don't think anybody in the guild does it, unless perhaps they're drunk." He paused. "The women are breaking the law, so they can't complain."

With the fiacre sliding alarmingly, we wheeled out of the close and into a still narrower one that ran crookedly east.

The House Azure

OUR DESTINATION was one of those accretive structures seen in the older parts of the city (but so far as I know, only there) in which the accumulation and interconnection of what were originally separate buildings produce a confusion of jutting wings and architectural styles, with peaks and turrets where the first builders had intended nothing more than rooftops. The snow had fallen more heavily here—or perhaps had only been falling while we rode. It surrounded the high portico with shapeless mounds of white, softened and blurred the outlines of the entrance, made pillows of the window ledges, and masking and robing the wooden caryatids who supported the roof, seemed to promise silence, safety, and secrecy.

There were dim yellow lights in the lower windows. The upper stories were dark. In spite of the drifted snow, someone within must have heard our feet outside. The door, large and old and no longer in the best condition, swung back before Roche could knock. We entered and found ourselves in a narrow little room like a jewel box, in which the walls and ceiling were covered with blue satin quilting. The person who had admitted us wore thick-soled shoes and a yellow robe; his short, white hair was smoothed back from a wide but rounded brow above a beardless and unlined face. As I passed him in the doorway, I discovered that I was looking into his eyes as I might have looked into a window. Those eyes could truly have been of glass, so unveined and polished they seemed—like a sky of summer drought.

"You are in good fortune," he said, and handed us each a goblet. "There is no one here but yourselves."

Roche answered, "I'm sure the girls are lonesome."

"They are. You smile . . . I see you do not believe me, but it is so. They complain when too many attend their court, but they are sad, too, when no one comes. Each will try to fascinate you tonight. You'll see. They'll want to boast when you are gone that you chose them. Besides, you are both handsome young men." He paused, and though he did not stare, seemed to look at Roche more closely. "You have been here previously, have you not? I remember your red hair and high color. Far to the south, in the narrow lands, the savages paint a fire spirit much like you. And your friend has the face of an exultant . . . that is what my young women like best of all. I see why you brought him here." His voice might have been a man's tenor or a woman's contralto.

Another door opened. It had a stained-glass insert showing the Temptation. We went into a room that seemed (no doubt in part because of the constriction of the one we had just left) more spacious than the building could well contain. The high ceiling was festooned with what appeared to be white silk, giving it the air of a pavilion. Two walls were lined with colonnades—these were false, the pretended columns being only half-round pilasters pressed against their blue-painted surfaces, and the architrave no more than a molding; but so long as we remained near the center, the effect was impressive and nearly perfect.

At the farther end of this chamber, opposite the windows, was a high-backed chair like a throne. Our host seated himself in it, and almost at once I heard a chime somewhere in the interior of the house. In two lesser chairs, Roche and I waited in silence while its clear echoes died. There was no sound from outside, yet I could sense the falling snow. My wine promised to hold the cold at bay, and in a few swallows I saw the bottom of the cup. It was as though I were awaiting the beginning of some ceremony in the ruined chapel, but at once less real and more serious.

"The Chatelaine Barbea," our host announced.

A tall woman entered. So poised was she, and so beautifully and daringly dressed, that it was several moments before I realized she could be no more than seventeen. Her face was oval and perfect, with limpid eyes, a small, straight nose, and a tiny mouth painted to appear smaller still. Her hair was so near to burnished gold that it might have been a wig of golden wires.

She posed herself a step or two before us and slowly began to revolve, striking a hundred graceful attitudes. At the time I had never seen a professional dancer; even now I do not believe I have seen one so beautiful as she. I cannot convey what I felt then, watching her in that strange room.

"All the beauties of the court are here for you," our host said. "Here in the House Azure, by night flown here from the walls of gold to find their dissipation in your pleasure."

Half hypnotized as I was, I thought this fantastic assertion had been put forward seriously. I said, "Surely that's not true."

"You came for pleasure, did you not? If a dream adds to your enjoyment, why dispute it?" All this time the girl with the golden hair continued her slow, unaccompanied dance.

Moment flowed into moment.

"Do you like her?" Our host asked. "Do you choose her?"

I was about to say—to shout rather, feeling everything in me that had ever yearned for a woman yearning then—that I did. Before I could catch my breath, Roche said, "Let's see some of the others." The girl ended her dance at once, made an obeisance, and left the room.

"You may have more than one, you know. Separately or together. We have some very large beds." The door opened again. "The Chatelaine Gracia."

Though this girl seemed quite different, there was much about her that reminded me of the "Chatelaine Barbea" who had come before her. Her hair was as white as the flakes that floated past the windows, making her youthful face seem younger still, and her dark complexion darker. She had (or seemed to have) larger breasts and more generous hips. Yet I felt it was almost possible that it was the same woman after all, that she had changed clothing, changed wigs, dusked her face with cosmetics in the few seconds between the other's exit and her entrance. It was absurd, yet there was an element of truth in it, as in so many absurdities. There was something in the eyes of both women, in the expression of their mouths, their carriage and the fluidity of their gestures, that was one. It recalled something I had seen elsewhere (I could not remember where), and yet it was new, and I felt somehow that the other thing, that which I had known earlier, was to be preferred.

"That will do for me," Roche said. "Now we must find something for my friend here." The dark girl, who had not danced as the other had, but had only stood, smiling very slightly, curtsying and turning in the center of the room, now permitted her smile to widen a trifle, went to Roche, seated herself on the arm of his chair, and began whispering to him.

As the door opened a third time, our host said, "The Chatelaine Thecla."

It seemed really she, just as I had remembered her—how she had escaped I could not guess. In the end it was reason rather than observation that told me I was mistaken. What differences I could have detected with the two standing side by side I cannot say, though certainly this woman was somewhat shorter.

"It is she you wish, then," our host said. I could not recall speaking.

Roche stepped forward with a leather burse, announcing that he would pay for both of us. I watched the coins as he drew them out, waiting to see the gleam of a chrisos. It was not there—there were only a few asimi.

The "Chatelaine Thecla" touched my hand. The scent she wore was stronger than the faint perfume of the real Thecla; still it was the same scent, making me think of a rose burning. "Come," she said.

I followed her. There was a corridor, dimly lit and not clean, then a narrow stair. I asked how many of the court were here, and she paused, looking down at me obliquely. Something there was in her face that might have been vanity satisfied, love, or that more obscure emotion we feel when what had been a contest becomes a performance. "Tonight, very few. Because of the snow. I came in a sleigh with Gracia."

I nodded. I thought I knew well enough that she had come only from one of the mean lanes about the house in which we were that night, and most likely on foot, with a shawl over her hair and the cold striking through old shoes. Yet what she said I found more meaningful than reality: I could sense the sweating destriers leaping through the falling snow faster than any machine, the whistling wind, the young, beautiful, jaded women bundled inside in sable and lynx, dark against red velvet cushions.

"Aren't you coming?"

She had already reached the top of the stair, nearly out of sight. Someone spoke to her, calling her "my dearest sister," and when I had gone up a few steps more I saw it was a woman very like the one who had been with Vodalus, she of the heart-shaped face and black hood. This woman paid no heed to me, and as soon as I gave her room to do so hurried down the stair.

"You see now what you might have had if you'd only waited for one more to come out." A smile I had learned to know elsewhere lurked at one corner of my paphian's mouth.

"I would have chosen you still."

"Now *that* is truly amusing—come on, come with me, you don't want to stand in this drafty hall forever. You kept a perfectly straight face, but your eyes rolled like a calf's. She's pretty, isn't she."

The woman who looked like Thecla opened a door, and we were in a tiny bedroom with an immense bed. A cold thurible hung from the ceiling by a silver-gilt chain; a lampstand supporting a pink-tinted light stood in one corner. There was a tiny dressing table with a mirror, a narrow wardrobe, and hardly room enough for us to move.

"Would you like to undress me?"

I nodded and reached for her.

"Then I warn you, you must be careful of my clothes." She turned away from me. "This fastens at the back. Begin at the top, at the back of my neck. If you get excited and tear something, he'll make you pay for it—don't say you haven't been told."

My fingers found a tiny catch and loosed it. "I would think, Chatelaine Thecla, that you would have plenty of clothes."

"I do. But do you think I want to return to the House Absolute in a torn gown?"

"You must have others here."

"A few, but I can't keep much in this place. Someone takes things when I'm gone."

The stuff between my fingers, which had looked so bright and rich in the colonnaded blue room below, was thin and cheap. "No satins, I suppose," I said as I unfastened the next catch. "No sables and no diamonds."

"Of course not."

I took a step away from her. (It brought my back almost to the door.) There was nothing of Thecla about her. All that had been a chance resemblance, some gestures, a similarity in dress. I was standing in a small, cold room looking at the neck and bare shoulders of some poor young woman whose parents, perhaps, accepted their share of Roche's meager silver gratefully and pretended not to know where their daughter went at night.

"You are not the Chatelaine Thecla," I said. "What am I doing here with you?"

There was surely more in my voice than I had intended. She turned to face me, the thin cloth of her gown sliding away from her breasts. I saw fear flicker across her face as though directed by a mirror; she must have been in this situation before, and it must have turned out badly for her. "I am Thecla," she said. "If you want me to be."

I raised my hand and she added quickly, "There are people here to protect me. All I have to do is scream. You may hit me once, but you won't hit me twice."

"No," I told her.

"Yes there are. Three men."

"There is no one. This whole floor is empty and cold—don't you think I've noticed how quiet it is? Roche and his girl stayed below, and perhaps got a better room there because he paid. The woman we saw at the top of the stair was leaving and wanted to speak to you first. Look." I took her by the waist and lifted her into the air. "Scream. No one will come." She was silent. I dropped her on the bed, and after a moment sat down beside her.

"You are angry because I'm not Thecla. But I would have been Thecla for you. I will be still." She slipped the strange coat from my shoulders and let it fall. "You're very strong."

"No I'm not." I knew that some of the boys who were afraid of me were already stronger than I.

"Very strong. Aren't you strong enough to master reality, even for a little while?"

"What do you mean?"

"Weak people believe what is forced on them. Strong people what they wish to believe, forcing that to be real. What is the Autarch but a man who believes himself Autarch and makes others believe by the strength of it?"

"You are not the Chatelaine Thecla," I told her.

"But don't you see, neither is she. The Chatelaine Thecla, whom I doubt you've ever laid eyes on— No, I see I'm wrong. Have you been to the House Absolute?"

Her hands, small and warm, were on my own right hand, pressing. I shook my head.

"Sometimes clients say they have. I always find pleasure in hearing them."

"Have they been? Really?"

She shrugged. "I was saying that the Chatelaine Thecla is not the Chatelaine Thecla. Not the Chatelaine Thecla of your mind, which is the only Chatelaine Thecla you care about. Neither am I. What, then, is the difference between us?"

"None, I suppose."

While I was undressing I said, "Nevertheless, we all seek to discover what is real. Why is it? Perhaps we are drawn to the theocenter. That's what the hierophants say, that only that is true."

She kissed my thighs, knowing she had won. "Are you really ready to find it? You must be clothed in favor, remember. Otherwise you will be given over to the torturers. You wouldn't like that."

"No," I said, and took her head between my hands.

X

The Last Year

I THINK IT WAS Master Gurloes's intention that I should be
brought to that house often, so I would not become too much
attracted to Thecla. In actuality I permitted Roche to pocket the
money and never went there again. The pain had been too
pleasurable, the pleasure too painful; so that I feared that in time
my mind would no longer be the thing I knew.

Then too, before Roche and I had left the house, the white-
haired man (catching my eye) had drawn from the bosom of his
robe what I had at first thought was an icon but soon saw to be a
golden vial in the shape of a phallus. He had smiled, and because
there had been nothing but friendship in his smile it had frightened
me.

Some days passed before I could rid my thoughts of Thecla of
certain impressions belonging to the false Thecla who had initiated
me into the anacreontic diversions and fruitions of men and
women. Possibly this had an effect opposite to that Master Gurloes
intended, but I do not think so. I believe I was never less inclined to
love the unfortunate woman than when I carried in my memory
the recent impressions of having enjoyed her freely; it was as I saw it
more and more clearly for the untruth it was that I felt myself

drawn to redress the fact, and drawn through her (though I was hardly conscious of it at the time) to the world of ancient knowledge and privilege she represented.

The books I had carried to her became my university, she my oracle. I am not an educated man—from Master Palaemon I learned little more than to read, write, and cipher, with a few facts concerning the physical world and the requisites of our mystery. If educated men have sometimes thought me, if not their equal, at least one whose company did not shame them, that is owing solely to Thecla: the Thecla I remember, the Thecla who lives in me, and the four books.

What we read together and what we said of it to one another, I shall not tell; to recount the least of it would wear out this brief night. All that winter while snow whitened the Old Yard, I came up from the oubliette as if from sleep, and started to see the tracks my feet left behind me and my shadow on the snow. Thecla was sad that winter, yet she delighted in talking to me of the secrets of the past, of the conjectures formed of higher spheres, and of the arms and histories of heroes millennia dead.

Spring came, and with it the purple-striped and white-dotted lilies of the necropolis. I carried them to her, and she said my beard had shot up like them, and I should be bluer of cheek than the run of common men, and the next day begged my pardon for it, saying I was that already. With the warm weather and (I think) the blossoms I brought, her spirits lifted. When we traced the insignia of old houses, she talked of friends of her own station and the marriages they had made, good and bad, and how such and such a one had exchanged her future for a ruined stronghold because she had seen it in a dream; and how another, who had played at dolls with her when they were children, was the mistress now of so many thousands of leagues. "And there must be a new Autarch and perhaps an Autarchia sometime, you know, Severian. Things can go on as they have for a long while. But not forever."

"I know little of the court, Chatelaine."

"The less you know, the happier you will be." She paused, white teeth nibbling her delicately curved lower lip. "When my mother was in labor, she had the servants carry her to the Vatic Fountain, whose virtue is to reveal what is to come. It prophesied I should sit a throne. Thea has always envied me that. Still, the Autarch . . ."

"Yes?"

"It would be better if I didn't say too much. The Autarch is not like other people. No matter how I may talk sometimes, on all of Urth there is no one like him."

"I know that."

"Then that is enough for you. Look here," she held up the brown book. "Here it says, 'It was the thought of Thalelaeus the Great that the democracy'—that means the People—'desired to be ruled by some power superior to itself, and of Yrierix the Sage that the commonality would never permit one differing from themselves to hold high office. Notwithstanding this, each is called The Perfect Master.'"

I did not see what she meant, and said nothing.

"No one really knows what the Autarch will do. That's what it all comes down to. Or Father Inire either. When I first came to court I was told, as a great secret, that it was Father Inire who really determined the policy of the Commonwealth. When I had been there two years, a man very highly placed—I can't even tell you his name—said it was the Autarch who ruled, though to those in the House Absolute it might seem that it was Father Inire. And last year a woman whose judgment I trust more than any man's confided that it really made no difference, because they were both as unfathomable as the pelagic deeps, and if one decided things while the moon waxed and the other when the wind was in the east, no one could tell the difference anyway. I thought that was wise counsel until I realized she was only repeating something I had said to her myself half a year before." Thecla fell silent, reclining on the narrow bed, her dark hair spread on the pillow.

"At least," I said, "you were right to have confidence in that woman. She had taken her opinions from a trustworthy source."

As if she had not heard me, she murmured, "But it's all true, Severian. No one knows what they may do. I might be freed tomorrow. It's quite possible. They must know by now that I am here. Don't look at me like that. My friends will speak with Father Inire. Perhaps some may even mention me to the Autarch. You know why I was taken, don't you?"

"Something about your sister."

"My half-sister Thea is with Vodalus. They say she is his paramour, and I think it extremely likely."

I recalled the beautiful woman at the top of the stairs in the House Azure and said, "I think I saw your half-sister once. It was in the necropolis. There was an exultant with her who carried a cane-sword and was very handsome. He told me he was Vodalus. The woman had a heart-shaped face and a voice that made me think of doves. Was that she?"

"I suppose so. They want her to betray him to save me, and I know she won't. But when they discover that, why shouldn't they let me go?"

I spoke of something else until she laughed and said, "You are so intellectual, Severian. When you're made a journeyman, you'll be the most cerebral torturer in history—a frightful thought."

"I was under the impression you enjoyed such discussions, Chatelaine."

"Only now, because I can't get out. Though it may come as a shock to you, when I was free I seldom devoted time to metaphysics. I went dancing instead, and pursued the peccary with pardine limers. The learning you admire was acquired when I was a girl, and sat with my tutor under the threat of the stick."

"We need not talk of such things, Chatelaine, if you would rather we not."

She stood and thrust her face into the center of the bouquet I had picked for her. "Flowers are better theology than folios, Severian. Is it beautiful in the necropolis where you got these? You aren't bringing me the flowers from graves, are you? Cut flowers someone brought?"

"No. These were planted long ago. They come up every year."

At the slot in the door, Drotte said, "Time to go," and I stood up.

"Do you think you may see her again? The Chatelaine Thea, my sister?"

"I don't think so, Chatelaine."

"If you should, Severian, will you tell her about me? They may not have been able to communicate with her. There will be no treason in that—you'll be doing the Autarch's work."

"I will, Chatelaine." I was stepping through the doorway.

"She won't betray Vodalus, I know, but there may be some compromise."

Drotte closed the door and turned the key. It had not escaped me that Thecla had not asked how her sister and Vodalus had come to be in our ancient—and by such people as themselves, forgotten—necropolis. The corridor, with its lines of metal doors and cold-sweating walls, seemed dark after the lamp in the cell. Drotte began to talk of an expedition he and Roche had made to a lion pit across Gyoll; over the sound of his voice I heard Thecla calling faintly, "Remind her of the time we sewed Josepha's doll."

The lilies faded as lilies do, and the dark death roses came into bloom. I cut them and carried them to Thecla, nigrescent purple flecked with scarlet. She smiled and recited:

"Here Rose the Graced, not Rose the Chaste, reposes.
The scent that rises is no scent of roses."

"If their odor offends you, Chatelaine . . ."

"Not at all, it is very sweet. I was only quoting something my grandmother used to say. The woman was infamous when she was a girl, or so she told me, and all the children chanted that rhyme when she died. Actually I suspect it is much older, and lost in time, like the beginnings of all the good and bad things. Men are said to desire women, Severian. Why do they despise the women they obtain?"

"I don't believe all do, Chatelaine."

"That beautiful Rose gave herself, and suffered such mockery for it that I know of it, though her dreams long ago turned to dust with her smooth flesh. Come here and sit by me."

I did as I was told, and she slipped her hands under the frayed bottom of my shirt and drew it over my head. I protested, but found myself unable to resist.

"What are you ashamed of? You who have no breasts to hide. I've never seen such white skin coupled with dark hair . . . Do you think my own skin white?"

"Very white, Chatelaine."

"So do others, but it is dun next to yours. You must flee the sun when you're a torturer, Severian. You'll burn terribly."

Her hair, which she often let fall free, today was bound about her head in a dark aureole. She had never more closely resembled her half-sister Thea, and I felt such desire for her that I seemed to be spilling my blood upon the floor, growing weaker and fainter with each contraction of my heart.

"Why are you pounding on my door?" Her smile told me she knew.

"I must go."

"You'd better put your shirt back on before you leave—you wouldn't want your friend to see you like that."

That night, though I knew it was in vain, I went to the necropolis and spent several watches in wandering among the silent houses of the dead. The next night I returned, and the next, but on the fourth Roche took me into the city, and in a drinking den I heard someone who seemed to know say that Vodalus was far to the north, hiding among the frost-pinched forests and raiding kafilas.

Days passed. Thecla was certain now, since she had been held in safety so long, that she would never be put to torment, and had Drotte bring her materials for writing and drawing, with which she planned a villa she meant to build on the southern shore of Lake Diuturna, which is said to be the most remote part of the Commonwealth, as well as the most beautiful. I took parties of apprentices to swim, thinking that to be my duty, though I could never dive in deep water without fear.

Then, suddenly as it seemed, the weather was too cold for swimming; one morning there was sparkling frost on the worn flagstones of the Old Yard, and fresh pork appeared on our plates at dinner, a sure sign that the cold had reached the hills below the city. Master Gurloes and Master Palaemon summoned me.

Master Gurloes said, "From several quarters we have had good reports of you, Severian, and now your apprenticeship is nearly served."

Nearly whispering, Master Palaemon added, "Your boyhood is behind you, your manhood ahead of you." There was affection in his voice.

"Just so," Master Gurloes continued. "The feast of our patroness draws near. I suppose you have given thought to it?"

I nodded. "Eata will be captain after me."

"And you?"

I did not understand what was meant; Master Palaemon, seeing that, asked gently, "What will you be, Severian? A torturer? You may leave the guild, you know, if you prefer."

I told him firmly—and as though I were slightly shocked by the suggestion—that I had never considered it. It was a lie. I had known, as all the apprentices knew, that one was not firmly and finally a member of the guild until one consented as an adult to the connection. Furthermore, though I loved the guild I hated it too—not because of the pain it inflicted on clients who must sometimes have been innocent, and who must often have been punished beyond anything that could be justified by their offences; but because it seemed to me inefficient and ineffectual, serving a power that was not only ineffectual but remote. I do not know how better to express my feelings about it than by saying that I hated it for starving and humiliating me and loved it because it was my home, hated and loved it because it was the exemplar of old things, because it was weak, and because it seemed indestructible.

Naturally I expressed none of this to Master Palaemon, though I might have if Master Gurloes had not been present. Still, it seemed incredible that my profession of loyalty, made in rags, could be taken seriously; yet it was.

"Whether you have considered leaving us or not," Master Palaemon told me, "it is an option open to you. Many would say that only a fool would serve out the hard years of apprenticeship and refuse to become a journeyman of his guild when his apprenticeship was past. But you may do so if you wish."

"Where would I go?" That, though I could not tell them so, was the real reason I was staying. I knew that a vast world lay outside the walls of the Citadel—indeed, outside the walls of our tower. But I could not imagine that I could ever have any place in it. Faced with a choice between slavery and the emptiness of freedom, I added, "I have been reared in our guild," for fear they would answer my question.

"Yes," Master Gurloes said in his most formal manner. "But you are no torturer yet. You have not put on fuligin."

Master Palaemon's hand, dry and wrinkled as a mummy's, groped until it found mine. "Among the initiates of religion it is said, 'You are an epopt always.' The reference is not only to knowledge but to their chrism, whose mark, being invisible, is ineradicable. You know our chrism."

I nodded again.

"Less even than theirs can it be washed away. Should you leave now, men will only say, 'He was nurtured by the torturers.' But when you have been anointed they will say, 'He is a torturer.' You may follow the plow or the drum, but still you will hear, 'He is a torturer.' Do you understand that?"

"I wish to hear nothing else."

"That is well," Master Gurloes said, and suddenly they both smiled, Master Palaemon showing his few old crooked teeth, and

Master Gurloes his square yellow ones, like the teeth of a dead nag. "Then it is time that we explained to you the final secret." (I can hear the emphasis his voice gave the words even as I write.) "For it would be well for you to think upon it before the ceremony."

Then he and Master Palaemon expounded to me that secret which lies at the heart of the guild and is the more sacred because no liturgy celebrates it, and it lies naked in the lap of the Pancreator.

And they swore me never to reveal it save—as they did—to one about to enter upon the mysteries of the guild. I have since broken that oath, as I have many others.

XI

The Feast

THE DAY OF OUR PATRONESS falls in the fading of winter. Then do we make merry: the journeymen perform the sword dance in procession, leaping and fantastic; the masters light the ruined chapel in the Grand Court with a thousand perfumed candles, and we ready our feast.

In the guild, the annual observance is counted as *lofty* (in which a journeyman is elevated to mastership), *lesser* (in which one apprentice at least is created journeyman), or *least* (in which no elevation takes place). Since no journeyman rose to mastership in the year in which I was made a journeyman—which is not to be wondered at, since such occasions are rarer than the decades—the ceremony of my masking was a lesser feast.

Even so, weeks were spent in preparation. I have heard it said that no less than one hundred and thirty-five guilds have members laboring within the Citadel walls. Of these, some (as we have seen among the curators) are too few to keep their patron's feast in the chapel, but must join their brothers in the city. Those more numerous celebrate with such pomp as they may to raise the esteem in which they are held. Of this kind are the soldiers upon Hadrian's day, the matrosses on Barbara's, the witches on Mag's, and many others. By pageantry and wonders, and freely given food and drink, they seek to have as many as may be from outside their guilds attend their ceremonies.

Not so is it among the torturers. No one from without the guild has dined with us at Holy Katharine's feast for more than three hundred years, when a lieutenant of the guard (so it is said) dared to come for a wager. There are many idle tales of what befell him—as that we made him seat himself at our table upon a chair of glowing iron. None of them are true. By the lore of our guild, he was made welcome and well feasted; but because we did not, over our meat and Katharine cake, talk of the pain we had inflicted, or devise new modes of torment, or curse those whose flesh we had torn for dying too soon, he grew ever more anxious, imagining that we sought to lull his fears so we might entrap him subsequently. Thus thinking, he ate little and drank much, and returning to his own quarters fell and struck his head in such a way that he evermore upon occasion lost his wits and suffered great pain. In time he put the muzzle of his own weapon into his mouth, but it was none of our doing.

None but torturers, then, come to the chapel on Holy Katharine's day. Yet each year (knowing we are watched from high windows) we prepare as do all the rest, and more grandly. Outside the chapel our wines burn like gems in the light of a hundred flambeaux; our beeves steam and wallow in ponds of gravy, rolling baked-lemon eyes; capybaras and agoutis, posed in the stances of life and bearing fur in which toasted cocoanut mingles with their own flayed skin, clamber on logs of ham and scale boulders of new-baked bread.

Our masters, of whom, when I was made journeyman, there were only two, arrive in sedan chairs whose curtains are woven of blossoms, and tread carpets patterned of colored sands, carpets telling of the traditions of the guild and laid grain by grain by the journeymen in days of toil and destroyed at once by the feet of the masters.

Within the chapel wait a great spiked wheel, a maid, and a sword. That wheel I knew well, for as an apprentice I had several times assisted in setting it up and taking it down. It was stored in the topmost part of the tower, just under the gun room, when it was not in use. The sword—though it seemed a true headsman's blade from a pace or two away—was no more than a wooden batten provided with an old hilt and brightened with tinsel.

Of the maid I can tell you nothing. When I was very young, I did not even wonder about her; those are the earliest feasts I can remember. When I was a little older and Gildas (who was long since a journeyman at the time of which I write) was captain of apprentices, I thought her perhaps one of the witches. When I grew a year older, I knew such disrespect would not be tolerated.

Perhaps she was a servant from some remote part of the Citadel. Perhaps she was a resident of the city, who for gain or because of some old connection with our guild consented to play the part; I do not know. I only know that each feast found her in her place, and so far as I could judge, unchanged. She was tall and slender, though not so tall nor so slender as Thecla, dark of complexion, dark of eye, raven of hair. Hers was such a face as I have never seen elsewhere, like a pool of pure water found in the midst of a wood.

She stood between the wheel and the sword while Master Palaemon (as the older of our masters) told us of the founding of the guild, and of our precursors in the years before the ice came—this part was different each year, as his scholarship decided. Silent she stood too while we sang the Fearful Song, the hymn of the guild, which apprentices must get by heart but which is sung only on that one day of the year. Silent she stood too while we knelt among the broken pews and prayed.

Then Master Gurloes and Master Palaemon, aided by several of the older journeymen, began her legend. Sometimes one spoke alone. Sometimes all chanted together. Sometimes two spoke to different effect while the others played flutes they had carved of thighbones, or the three-stringed rebec that shrieks like a man.

When they reached that part of the narration at which our patroness is condemned by Maxentius, four masked journeymen rushed out to seize her. So silent and serene before, she resisted now, struggled and cried out. But as they bore her toward it, the wheel appeared to blur and change. In the light of the candles, it seemed at first that serpents, green pythons with jeweled heads of scarlet and citrine and white, writhed from it. Then it was seen that these were flowers, roses in the bud. When the maid was but a step away they bloomed (they were of paper, concealed, as I well knew, within the segments of the wheel). Feigning fear, the journeymen drew back; but the narrators, Gurloes, Palaemon, and the others, speaking together as Maxentius, urged them on.

Then I, still unmasked and in the dress of an apprentice, stepped forward and said: "Resistance avails nothing. You are to be broken on the wheel, but we would do you no further indignity."

The maid gave no answer but reached out and touched the wheel, which at once fell to pieces, collapsing with a clatter to the floor, all its roses gone.

"*Behead her,*" demanded Maxentius, and I took up the sword. It was very heavy.

She knelt before me. "You are a counselor of Omniscience," I said. "Though I must slay you, I beg you spare my life."

For the first time the maid spoke, saying, "Strike and fear not."

I lifted the sword. I remember that for a moment I feared it would overbalance me.

When I think back on that time, it is that moment I recall first; to remember more, I must work forward or backward from that. In memory it seems to me I stand always so, in gray shirt and ragged trousers, with the blade poised above my head. While I raised it, I was an apprentice; when it descended, I would be a journeyman of the Order of the Seekers for Truth and Penitence.

It is our rule that the executioner must stand between his victim and the light; the maid's head lay in shadow on the block. I knew that the sword in falling would do her no harm—I would direct it to one side, tripping an ingenious mechanism that would elevate a wax head smeared with blood while the maid draped her own with a fuligin cloth. Still I hesitated to give the blow.

She spoke again from the floor at my feet, and her voice seemed to ring in my ears. "Strike and fear not." With such strength as I was capable of, I sent the false blade down. For an instant it seemed to me that it met resistance; then it thudded into the block, which fell into two. The maid's head, all bloody, tumbled forward toward the watching brothers. Master Gurloes lifted it by the hair and Master Palaemon cupped his left hand to receive the blood.

"With this, our chrism," he said, "I anoint you, Severian, our brother forever." His index finger traced the mark upon my forehead.

"So be it," said Master Gurloes, and all the journeymen save I.

The maid stood. I knew even as I watched her that her head was only concealed in the cloth; but it seemed there was nothing there. I felt dizzy and tired.

She took the wax head from Master Gurloes and pretended to replace it on her shoulders, slipping it by some sleight into the fuligin cloth, then standing before us radiant and whole. I knelt before her, and the others withdrew.

She raised the sword with which I had so lately struck off her head; the blade was bloody now from some contact with the wax. "You are of the torturers," she said. I felt the sword touch either shoulder, and at once eager hands were drawing the head mask of the guild over my face and lifting me. Before I well knew what had occurred, I was on the shoulders of two journeymen—it was only afterward that I learned they were Drotte and Roche, though I should have guessed it. They were bearing me up the processional aisle through the center of the chapel, while everyone cheered and shouted.

We were no sooner outside than the fireworks began: crackers about our feet and even around our ears, torpedoes banging against the thousand-year-old walls of the chapel, rockets red and yellow and green leaping into the air. A gun from the Great Keep split the night.

All the brave meats I have described were on the tables in the court; I sat at the head between Master Palaemon and Master Gurloes, and drank too much (very little, for me, has always been too much), and was cheered and toasted. What became of the maid

I do not know. She disappeared as she has each Katharine's Day I can remember. I have not seen her again.

How I reached my bed I have no notion. Those who drink much have told me that they sometimes forget all that befell them in the latter part of the night, and perhaps it was so with me. But I think it more likely that I (who never forget anything, who, if I may for once confess the truth, though I seem to boast, do not truly understand what others mean when they say *forget*, for it seems to me that all experience becomes a part of my being) only slept and was carried there.

However it may be, I woke not in the familiar low room that was our dormitory, but in a cabin so small it was much higher than wide, a journeyman's cabin, and because I was the most junior of the journeymen, the least desirable in the tower, a portless cubbyhole no larger than a cell.

My bed seemed to toss beneath me. I gripped the sides and sat up and it was still, but as soon as my head touched the pillow once more the swaying began again. I felt I was wide awake—then that I was awake again but had been sleeping only a moment before. I was conscious that someone was in the tiny cabin with me, and for some reason I could not have explained I thought it was the young woman who had taken the part of our patroness.

I sat up in the tossing bed. Dim light filtered beneath the door; there was no one there.

When I lay down again, the room was filled with Thecla's perfume. The false Thecla from the House Azure had come, then. I got out of bed, and nearly falling opened the door. There was no one in the passage outside.

A chamber pot waited beneath the bed, and I pulled it out and filled it with my spew, rich meats swimming in wine mixed with bile. Somehow I felt what I had done was treason, as if by casting out all that the guild had given me that night I had cast out the guild itself. Coughing and sobbing I knelt beside the bed, and at last, after wiping my mouth clean, lay down again.

No doubt I slept. I saw the chapel, but it was not the ruin I knew. The roof was whole and high and straight, and from it there hung ruby lamps. The pews were whole and gleamed with polish; the ancient stone altar was swatched in cloth of gold. Behind the altar rose a wonderful mosaic of blue; but it was blank, as if a fragment of sky without cloud or star had been torn away and spread upon the curving wall.

I walked toward it down the aisle, and as I did so I was struck by how much lighter it was than the true sky, whose blue is nearly black even on the brightest day. Yet how much more beautiful this was! It thrilled me to look at it. I felt I was floating in air, borne up by the beauty of it, looking down upon the altar, down into the cup of crimson wine, down upon shewbread and antique knife. I smiled . . .

And woke. In my sleep I had heard footsteps in the passage outside, and I knew I had recognized them, though I could not just then recall whose steps they were. Struggling, I brought back the sound; it was no human tread, only the padding of soft feet, and an almost imperceptible scraping.

I heard it again, so faint that for a time I thought I had confused my memory with reality; but it was real, slowly coming up the passage, slowly going back. The mere lifting of my head brought a wave of nausea; I let it fall again, telling myself that whoever might pace back and forth, it was no affair of mine. The perfume had vanished, and sick though I was, I felt I needed to fear unreality no longer—I was back in the world of solid objects and plain light. My door opened a trifle and Master Malrubius looked in as though to make certain I was all right. I waved to him and he shut the door again. It was some time before I recalled that he had died while I was still a boy.

XII

The Traitor

THE NEXT DAY my head ached and I was ill. But as I was (by a long-standing tradition) spared from the cleaning of the Grand Court and the chapel, where most of the brothers were, I was needed in the oubliette. For a few moments at least the morning calm of the corridors soothed me. Then the apprentices came clattering down (the boy Eata, not quite so small now, with a puffed lip and the gleam of triumph in his eye), bringing the clients' breakfast—cold meats mostly, salvage from the ruins of the banquet. I had to explain to several clients that this was the only day of the year on which they would get meat, and went along assuring one after another that there would be no excruciations—the feast day itself and the day after are exempt, and even when a sentence demands torment on those days, it is postponed. The Chatelaine Thecla was still asleep. I did not wake her, but unlocked her cell and carried her food in and put it on her table.

About midmorning I again heard the echoes of footsteps. Coming to the landing, I saw two cataphracts, an anagnost reading prayers, Master Gurloes, and a young woman. Master Gurloes asked if I had an empty cell, and I began to describe those that were vacant.

"Then take this prisoner. I have already signed for her."

I nodded and grasped the woman by the arm; the cataphracts released her and turned away like silver automata.

The elaboration of her sateen costume (somewhat dirty and torn now) showed that she was an optimate. An armigette would have worn finer stuffs in simpler lines, and no one from the poorer classes could have dressed so well. The anagnost tried to follow us down the corridor, but Master Gurloes prevented him. I heard the soldiers' steel-shod feet on the steps.

"When am I . . .?" It had a rising, somehow terrorized inflection.

"To be taken to the examination room?"

She clung to my arm now as though I were her father or her lover. "Will I be?"

"Yes, Madame."

"How do you know?"

"All who are brought here are, Madame."

"Always? Isn't anybody ever released?"

"Occasionally."

"Then I might be too, mightn't I?" The hope in her voice now made me think of a flower growing in shadow.

"It's possible, but it's very unlikely."

"Don't you want to know what I've done?"

"No," I said. As it happened, the cell next to Thecla's was vacant; for a moment I wondered if I should put this woman there. She would be company (the two could speak through the slots in their doors), but her questions and the opening and closing of the cell might wake Thecla now. I decided to do it—the companionship, I felt, would more than compensate for a little lost sleep.

"I was affianced to an officer, and I found he was maintaining a jade. When he wouldn't give her up, I paid bravos to fire her thatch. She lost a featherbed, a few sticks of furniture, and some clothes. Is that a crime for which I should be tortured?"

"I don't know, Madame."

"My name is Marcellina. What is yours?"

I turned the key to her cell while I debated answering her. Thecla, whom I could hear stirring now, would doubtless tell her in any event. "Severian," I said.

"And you get your bread by breaking bones. It must give you good dreams by night."

Thecla's eyes, widely spaced and as deep as wells, were at the slot in her door. "Who is that with you, Severian?"

"A new prisoner, Chatelaine."

"A woman? I know she is—I heard her voice. From the House Absolute?"

"No, Chatelaine." Not knowing how long it might be before the two would be able to see each other again, I made Marcellina stand before Thecla's door.

"Another woman. Isn't that unusual? How many do you have, Severian?"

"Eight on this level now, Chatelaine."

"I would think you would often have more than that."

"We rarely have more than four, Chatelaine."

Marcellina asked, "How long will I have to stay here?"

"Not long. Few stay here long, Madame."

With an unhealthy seriousness, Thecla said, "I am about to be released, you understand. He knows."

Our guild's new client looked at what could be seen of her with increased interest. "Are you really about to be set free, Chatelaine?"

"He knows. He's mailed letters for me—haven't you, Severian? And he's been saying goodbye for these last few days. He's really rather a sweet boy in his way."

I said, "You must go in now, Madame. You may continue to talk, if you like."

I was relieved after I had served the clients their suppers. Drotte met me on the stair and suggested I go to bed.

"It's the mask," I told him. "You're not used to seeing me with it on."

"I can see your eyes, and that's all I need to see. Can't you recognize all the brothers by their eyes, and tell whether they're angry, or in the mood for a joke? You ought to go to bed."

I told him I had something to do first, and went to Master Gurloes's study. He was absent, as I had hoped he would be, and among the papers on his table I found what I had, in some fashion I cannot explain, known would be there: an order for Thecla's excruciation.

I could not sleep after that. Instead I went (for the last time, though I did not know it) to the tomb in which I had played as a boy. The funeral bronze of the old exultant was dull for lack of rubbing, and a few more leaves had drifted through the half-open door; otherwise it was unchanged. I had once told Thecla of the place, and now I imagined her with me. She had escaped by my aid, and I promised her that no one would find her here, and that I would bring her food, and when the hunt had cooled I would help her secure passage on a merchant dhow, by which she could make her way unnoticed down the winding coils of Gyoll to the delta and the sea.

Were I such a hero as we had read of together in old romances, I would have released her that very evening, overpowering or drugging the brothers on watch. I was not, and I possessed no drugs and no weapon more formidable than a knife taken from the kitchen.

And if the truth is to be known, between my inmost being and the desperate attempt there stood the words I had heard that morning—the morning after my elevation. The Chatelaine Thecla had said I was "rather a sweet boy," and some already mature part of me knew that even if I succeeded against all odds, I would still be *rather a sweet boy*. At the time I thought it mattered.

The next morning Master Gurloes ordered me to assist him in performing the excruciation. Roche came with us.

I unlocked her cell. She did not understand at first why we had come, and asked me if she had a visitor, or if she were to be discharged.

By the time we reached our destination she knew. Many men faint, but she did not. Courteously, Master Gurloes asked if she would like an explanation of the various mechanisms.

"Do you mean the ones you are going to employ?" There was a tremor in her voice, but it was not marked.

"No, no, I wouldn't do that. Just the curious machines you will be seeing as we pass through. Some are quite old, and most are hardly ever used."

Thecla looked about her before answering. The examination room—our workroom—is not divided into cells, but is a unified space, pillared with the tubes of the ancient engines and cluttered with the tools of our mystery. "The one to which I will be subjected—is that old too?"

"The most hallowed of all," Master Gurloes replied. He waited for her to say something more, and when she did not, proceeded with his descriptions. "The kite I'm certain you must be familiar with—everyone knows of it. Behind it there . . . if you'll take a step this way you'll be able to see it better . . . is what we call the apparatus. It is supposed to letter whatever slogan is demanded in the client's flesh, but it is seldom in working order. I see you're looking at the old post. It's no more than it seems, just a stake to immobilize the hands, and a thirteen-thonged scourge for correction. It used to stand in the Old Yard, but the witches complained, and the castellan made us move it down here. That was about a century ago."

"Who are the witches?"

"I'm afraid we don't have time to go into that now. Severian can tell you when you're back in your cell."

She looked at me as if to say "Am I really going back, eventually?" and I took advantage of my position on the side opposite Master Gurloes to clasp her icy hand.

"Beyond that—"

"Wait. Can I choose? Is there any way I can persuade you to . . .

do one thing instead of another?" Her voice was still brave, but weaker now.

Gurloes shook his head. "We have no say in the matter, Chatelaine. Nor do you. We carry out the sentences that are delivered to us, doing no more than we are told, and no less, and making no changes." Embarrassed, he cleared his throat. "The next one's interesting, I think. We call it Allowin's necklace. The client is strapped into that chair, and the pad is adjusted against his breastbone. Each breath he draws thereafter tightens the chain, so that the more he breathes, the less breath he can take. In theory it can go on forever, with very shallow breaths and very small tightenings."

"How horrible. What is that behind it? That tangle of wire, and the great glass globe over the table?"

"Ah," said Master Gurloes. "We call this the revolutionary. The subject lies here. Will you, Chatelaine?"

For a long moment Thecla stood poised. She was taller than any of us, but with that terrible fear in her face, her height was no longer imposing.

"If you do not," Master Gurloes continued, "our journeymen will have to force you. You would not like that, Chatelaine."

Thecla whispered, "I thought you were going to show me all of them."

"Only until we reached this spot, Chatelaine. It's better if the client's mind is occupied. Now lie down, please. I won't be asking again."

She lay down at once, quickly and gracefully, as I had often seen her stretch herself in her cell. The straps Roche and I buckled about her were so old and cracked that I wondered if they would hold.

There were cables to be wound from one part of the examination room to another, rheostats and magnetic amplifiers to be adjusted. Antique lights like blood-red eyes gleamed on the control panel, and a droning like the song of some huge insect filled the entire chamber. For a few moments, the ancient engine of the tower lived again. One cable was loose, and sparks as blue as burning brandy played about its bronze fittings.

"Lightning," Master Gurloes said as he rammed the loose cable home. "There's another word for it, but I forget. Anyway, the revolutionary here runs by lightning. It's not as if you were going to be struck, of course, Chatelaine. But lightning's the thing that makes it go.

"Severian, push up your handle there until this needle's here." A coil that had been as cold as a snake when I had touched it a moment before was warm now.

"What does it do?"

"I couldn't describe it, Chatelaine. Anyway, I've never had it done, you see." Gurloes's hand touched a knob on the control panel and Thecla was bathed in white light that stole the color from all it fell upon. She screamed; I have heard screaming all my life, but that was the worst, though not the loudest; it seemed to go on and on like the shrieking of a cartwheel.

She was not unconscious when the white light died. Her eyes were open, staring upward; but she did not appear to see my hand, or to feel it when I touched her. Her breathing was shallow and rapid.

Roche asked, "Shall we wait until she can walk?" I could see he was thinking how awkward so tall a woman would be to carry.

"Take her now," Master Gurloes said. We got out the travail.

When all my other work was complete, I came into her cell to see her. She was fully aware by then, though she could not stand. "I ought to hate you," she said.

I had to lean over her to catch the words. "It's all right," I said.

"But I don't. Not for your sake . . . if I hate my last friend, what would be left?"

There was nothing to say to that, so I said nothing.

"Do you know what it was like? It was a long time before I could think of it."

Her right hand was creeping upward, toward her eyes. I caught it and forced it back.

"I thought I saw my worst enemy, a kind of demon. And it was me."

Her scalp was bleeding. I put clean lint there and taped it down, though I knew it would soon be gone. Curling, dark hairs were entangled in her fingers.

"Since then, I can't control my hands . . . I can if I think about it, if I know what they're doing. But it is so hard, and I'm getting tired." She rolled her head away and spat blood. "I bite myself. Bite the lining of my cheeks, and my tongue and lips. Once my hands tried to strangle me, and I thought oh good, I will die now. But I only lost consciousness, and they must have lost their strength, because I woke. It's like that machine, isn't it?"

I said, "Allowin's necklace."

"But worse. My hands are trying to blind me now, to tear my eyelids away. Will I be blind?"

"Yes," I said.

"How long before I die?"

"A month, perhaps. The thing in you that hates you will weaken as you weaken. The revolutionary brought it to life, but its energy is your energy, and in the end you will die together."

"Severian . . ."

"Yes?"

"I see," she said. And then, "It is a thing from Erebus, from Abaia, a fit companion for me. Vodalus . . ."

I leaned closer, but I could not hear. At last I said, "I tried to save you. I wanted to. I stole a knife, and spent the night watching for a chance. But only a master can take a prisoner from a cell, and I would have had to kill—"

"Your friends."

"Yes, my friends."

Her hands were moving again, and blood trickled from her mouth. "Will you bring me the knife?"

"I have it here," I said, and drew it from under my cloak. It was a common cook's knife with a span or so of blade.

"It looks sharp."

"It is," I said. "I know how to treat an edge, and I sharpened it carefully." That was the last thing I said to her. I put the knife into her right hand and went out.

For a time, I knew, her will would hold it back. A thousand times one thought recurred: I could reenter her cell, take back the knife, and no one would know. I would be able to live out my life in the guild.

If her throat rattled, I did not hear it; but after I had stared at the door of her cell for a long while, a little crimson rivulet crept from under it. I went to Master Gurloes then, and told him what I had done.

XIII

The Lictor of Thrax

FOR THE NEXT TEN DAYS I lived the life of a client, in a cell of the topmost level (not far, in fact, from that which had been Thecla's). In order that the guild should not be accused of having detained me without legal process, the door was left unlocked; but there were two journeymen with swords outside my door, and I never stepped from it save for a brief time on the second day when I was brought to Master Palaemon to tell my story again. That was my trial, if you like. For the remainder of the time, the guild pondered my sentence.

It is said that it is the peculiar quality of time to conserve fact, and that it does so by rendering our past falsehoods true. So it was with me. I had lied in saying that I loved the guild—that I desired nothing but to remain in its embrace. Now I found those lies become truths. The life of a journeyman and even that of an apprentice seemed infinitely attractive. Not only because I was certain I was to die, but truly attractive in themselves, because I had lost them. I saw the brothers now from the viewpoint of a client, and so I saw them as powerful, the active principles of an inimical and nearly perfect machine.

Knowing that my case was hopeless, I learned in my own person what Master Malrubius had once impressed on me when I was a child: that hope is a psychological mechanism unaffected by external realities. I was young and adequately fed; I was permitted to sleep and therefore I hoped. Again and again, waking and sleeping, I dreamed that just as I was to die Vodalus would come. Not alone as I had seen him fight in the necropolis, but at the head of an army that would sweep the decay of centuries away and make us once more the masters of the stars. Often I thought to hear tread of that army ringing in the corridors; sometimes I carried my candle to the little slot in the door because I thought I had seen the face of Vodalus outside in the dark.

As I have said, I supposed I would be killed. The question that occupied my mind most during those slow days was that of means. I had learned all the arts of the torturer; now I thought of them—sometimes one by one, as we had been taught them, sometimes all together in a revelation of pain. To live day after day in a cell below ground, thinking of torment, is torment itself.

On the eleventh day I was summoned by Master Palaemon. I saw the red light of the sun again, and breathed that wet wind that tells in winter that spring is almost come. But, oh, how much it cost me to walk past the open tower door and looking out see the corpse door in the curtain wall, and old Brother Porter lounging there.

Master Palaemon's study seemed very large when I entered it and yet very precious to me—as though the dusty books and papers were my own. He asked me to sit. He was not masked and seemed older than I remembered him. "We have discussed your case," he said. "Master Gurloes and I. We have had to take the other journeymen into our confidence, and even the apprentices. It is better that they know the truth. Most agree that you are deserving of death."

He waited for me to comment, but I did not.

"And yet there was much said in your defense. Several of the journeymen urged in private meetings, to me and to Master Gurloes as well, that you be permitted to die without pain."

I cannot say why, but it became of central importance to me to know how many of these friends I had, and I asked.

"More than two, and more than three. The exact number does not matter. Do you not believe that you deserve to die painfully?"

"By the revolutionary," I said, hoping that if I asked that death as a favor it would not be granted.

"Yes, that would be fitting. But . . ."

And here he paused. The moment passed, then two. The first brass-backed fly of the new summer buzzed against the port. I wanted to crush it, to catch and release it, to shout at Master Palaemon to speak, to flee from the room; but I could do none of these things. I sat, instead, in the old wooden chair beside his table, feeling that I was already dead but still must die.

"We cannot kill you, you see. I have had a most difficult time convincing Gurloes of that, yet it is so. If we slay you without judicial order, we are no better than you: you have been false to us, but we will have been false to the law. Furthermore, we would be putting the guild in jeopardy forever—an Inquisitor would call it murder."

He waited for me to comment, and I said, "But for what I have done . . ."

"The sentence would be just. Yes. Still, we have no right in law to take life on our own authority. Those who have that right are properly jealous of it. If we were to go to them, the verdict would be sure. But were we to go, the repute of the guild would be publicly and irrevocably stained. Much of the trust now reposed in us would be gone, and permanently. We might confidently expect our affairs to be supervised by others in the future. Would you enjoy seeing our clients guarded by soldiers, Severian?"

The vision I had in Gyoll when I had so nearly drowned rose before me, and it possessed (as it had then) a sullen yet strong attraction. "I would rather take my own life," I said. "I will feign to swim, and die in mid-channel, far from help."

The shadow of a sour smile crossed Master Palaemon's ruined face. "I am glad you made that offer only to me. Master Gurloes would have taken far too much pleasure in pointing out that at least a month must pass before swimming can be made credible."

"I am sincere. I sought a painless death, but it was death I sought, and not an extension of life."

"Even if it were midsummer, what you propose could not be permitted. An Inquisitor might still conclude that we contrived your death. Fortunately for you, we have agreed upon a less incriminating solution. Do you know anything of the condition of our mystery in the provincial towns?"

I shook my head.

"It is but low. Nowhere but in Nessus—nowhere but here in the Citadel—is there a chapter of our guild. Lesser places have no more than a carnifex, who takes life and performs such excruciations as the judicators there decree. Such a man is universally hated and feared. Do you understand?"

"Such a position," I answered, "is too high for me." There was no falsehood in what I said; I despised myself, at that moment, far more than I did the guild. Since then I have recalled those words often, though they were but my own, and they have been a comfort to me in many troubles.

"There is a town called Thrax, the City of Windowless Rooms," Master Palaemon continued. "The archon there—his name is Abdiesus—has written the House Absolute. A marshall there has transmitted the letter to the Castellar, and from him I have it. They are in sore need in Thrax of the functionary I have described. In the past they have pardoned condemned men on the condition that they accept the post. Now the countryside is rotten with treachery, and since the position entails a certain degree of trust, they are reluctant to do so again."

I said, "I understand."

"Twice before members of the guild have been dispatched to outlying towns, though whether those were such cases as this the chronicles do not say. Nevertheless, they furnish a precedent now, and an escape from the maze. You are to go to Thrax, Severian. I have prepared a letter that will introduce you to the archon and his magistrates. It describes you as highly skilled in our mystery. For such a place, it will not be a falsehood."

I nodded, being already resigned to what I was to do. Yet while I sat there, maintaining the expressionless face of a journeyman whose only will is to obey, a new shame burned in me. Though it was not so hot as the one for the disgrace I had brought upon the guild, still it was fresher, and hurt the more because I had not yet grown accustomed to the sickness of it as I had the other. It was this: that I was glad to go—that my feet already longed for the feel of grass, my eyes for strange sights, my lungs for the new, clear air of far, unmanned places.

I asked Master Palaemon where the town of Thrax might be.

"Down Gyoll," he said. "Near the sea." Then he stopped as old men will, and said, "No, no, what am I thinking of? Up Gyoll, of course," and for me hundreds of leagues of marching waves, and the sand, and the seabirds' crying all faded away. Master Palaemon took a map from his cabinet and unrolled it for me, bending over it until the lens by which he saw such things nearly touched the parchment. "There," he said, and showed me a dot on the margin of the young river, at the lower cataracts. "If you had funds you might travel by boat. As it is, you must walk."

"I understand," I said, and though I remembered the thin piece of gold Vodalus had given me, safe in its hiding place, I knew I could not take advantage of whatever wealth it might represent. It was the guild's will to cast me out with no more money than a young journeyman might be expected to possess, and for prudence's sake as well as honor's, so I must go.

Yet I knew it was unfair. If I had not glimpsed the woman with the heart-shaped face and earned that small gold coin, it is more than possible I would never have carried the knife to Thecla and forfeited my place in the guild. In a sense, that coin had bought my life.

Very well—I would leave my old life behind me . . .

"Severian!" Master Palaemon exclaimed. "You are not listening to me. You were never an inattentive pupil in our classes."

"I'm sorry. I was thinking about a great many things."

"No doubt." For the first time he really smiled, and for an instant looked his old self, the Master Palaemon of my boyhood. "Yet I was giving you such good advice for your journey. Now you must do without it, but doubtless you would have forgotten everything anyway. You know of the roads?"

"I know they must not be used. Nothing more."

"The Autarch Maruthas closed them. That was when I was your age. Travel encouraged sedition, and he wished goods to enter and leave the city by the river, where they might be easily taxed. The law has remained in force since, and there is a redoubt, so I've heard, every fifty leagues. Still the roads remain. Though they are in poor repair, it is said some use them by night."

"I see," I said. Closed or not, the roads might make for an easier passage than traveling across the countryside as the law demanded.

"I doubt you do. I mean to warn you against them. They are patrolled by uhlans under orders to kill anyone found upon them, and since they have permission to loot the bodies of those they slay, they are not much inclined to ask excuses."

"I understand," I told him, and in private wondered how he came to know so much of travel.

"Good. The day is half spent now. If you like, you may sleep here tonight and depart in the morning."

"Sleep in my cell, you mean."

He nodded. Though I knew he could scarcely see my face, I felt that something in him was studying me.

"I will leave now, then." I tried to think of what I would have to do before I turned my back on our tower forever; nothing came to me, yet it seemed there must surely be something. "May I have a watch in which to prepare? When the time is up, I will go."

"That's easily granted. But before you leave, I want you to return here—I have something to give you. Will you do it?"

"Of course, Master, if you want me to."

"And Severian, be careful. There are many in the guild who are your friends—who wish this had never happened. But there are others who feel you have betrayed our trust and deserve agony and death."

"Thank you, Master," I said. "The second group is correct."

My few possessions were already in my cell. I bundled them together and found the whole bundle so small I could put it in the sabretache hanging from my belt. Moved by love, and regret for what had been, I went to Thecla's cell.

It was empty still. Her blood had been scrubbed from the floor, but a wide, dark spot of blood-rust had etched the metal. Her clothing was gone, and her cosmetics. The four books I had carried to her a year before remained, stacked with others on the little table. I could not resist the temptation to take one; there were so many in the library that they would never miss a single volume. My hand had stretched forth before I realized I did not know which to choose. The book of heraldry was the most beautiful, but it was too large by far to carry about the country. The book of theology was the smallest of all, but the brown book was hardly larger. In the end it was that I took, with its tales from vanished worlds.

I climbed the stair of our tower then, past the storeroom to the gun room where the siege pieces lounged in cradles of pure force. Then higher still to the room of the glass roof, with its gray screens and strangely contorted chairs, and up a slender ladder until I stood on the slippery panes themselves, where my presence scattered blackbirds across the sky like flecks of soot and our fuligin pennon streamed and snapped from the staff over my head.

Below me the Old Yard seemed small and even cramped, but infinitely comfortable and homey. The breach in the curtain wall was greater than I had ever realized, though to either side of it the Red Tower and the Bear Tower still stood proud and strong. Nearest our own, the witches' tower was slender, dark, and tall; for a moment the wind blew a snatch of their wild laughter to me and I felt the old fear, though we of the torturers have always been on the most friendly terms with the witches, our sisters.

Beyond the wall, the great necropolis rolled down the long slope toward Gyoll, whose waters I could glimpse between the half-rotted buildings on its banks. Across the flood of the river the rounded dome of the khan seemed no more than a pebble, the city about it an expanse of many-colored sand trodden by the master torturers of old.

I saw a caique, with high, sharp prow and stern, and a bellying sail, making south with the dark current; and against my will I followed it for a time—to the delta and the swamps, and at last to the flashing sea where that great beast Abaia, carried from the farther shores of the universe in anteglacial days, wallows until the moment comes for him and his kind to devour the continents.

Then I abandoned all thoughts of the south and her ice-choked sea and turned north to the mountains and the rising of the river. For a long time (I do not know how long, though the sun seemed in a new place when I took notice of its position again) I looked to the north. The mountains I could see with my mind's eye, but not with the body's: only the rolling expanse of the city with its million roofs. And to tell the truth, the great silver columns of the Keep and its surrounding spires blocked half my view. Yet I cared nothing for them, and indeed hardly saw them. North lay the House Absolute and the cataracts, and Thrax, City of Windowless Rooms. North lay the wide pampas, a hundred trackless forests, and the rotting jungles at the waist of the world.

When I had thought on all those things until I was half mad, I came down to Master Palaemon's study again and told him I was ready to depart.

XIV

Terminus Est

"I HAVE A GIFT for you," Master Palaemon said. "Considering your youth and strength, I don't believe you will find it too heavy."

"I am deserving of no gifts."

"That is so. But you must recall, Severian, that when a gift is deserved, it is not a gift but a payment. The only true gifts are such as you now receive. I cannot forgive you for what you have done, but I cannot forget what you were. Since Master Gurloes rose to journeyman, I have had no better scholar." He rose and walked stiffly to the alcove, where I heard him say, "Ah, she is not overburdensome for me yet."

He was lifting something so dark it was swallowed by the shadows. I said, "Let me assist you, Master."

"No need, no need. Light to raise, weighty to descend. Such is the mark of a good one."

Upon his table he laid a night-black case nearly long enough for a coffin, but much narrower. When he opened its silver catches, they rang like bells.

"I am not giving you the casket, which would only impede you. Here is the blade, her sheath to protect her when you are traveling, and a baldric."

It was in my hands before I fully understood what it was he gave me. The sheath of sable manskin covered it nearly to the pommel. I drew it off (it was soft as glove leather), and beheld the sword herself.

I shall not bore you with a catalog of her virtues and beauties; you would have to see her and hold her to judge her justly. Her bitter blade was an ell in length, straight and square-pointed as such a sword's should be. Man-edge and woman-edge could part a hair to within a span of the guard, which was of thick silver with a carven head at either end. Her grip was onyx bound with silver bands, two spans long and terminated with an opal. Art had been lavished upon her; but it is the function of art to render attractive and significant those things that without it would not be so, and so art had nothing to give her. The words *Terminus Est* had been engraved upon her blade in curious and beautiful letters, and I had learned enough of ancient languages since leaving the Atrium of Time to know that they meant *This Is the Line of Division*.

"She is well honed, I promise you," Master Palaemon said, seeing me test the man-edge with my thumb. "For the sake of those given over to you, see you keep her so. My question is whether she is not too ponderous a mate for you. Raise her and see."

I clasped *Terminus Est* as I had the false sword at my elevation, and lifted her above my head, taking care not to strike the ceiling. She shifted as though I wrestled a serpent.

"You have no difficulty?"

"No, Master. But she writhed when I poised her."

"There is a channel in the spine of her blade, and in it runs a river of hydrargyrum—a metal heavier than iron, though it flows like water. Thus the balance is shifted toward the hands when the blade is high, but to the tip when it falls. Often you will have to wait the completion of a final prayer, or a hand signal from the quaesitor. Your sword must not slack or tremble— But you know all that. I need not tell you to respect such an instrument. May the Moira favor you, Severian."

I took the whetstone from its pocket in the sheath and dropped it into my sabretache, folded the letter he had given me to the archon of Thrax, wrapped it in a scrap of oiled silk, and committed it to the sword's care. Then I took my leave of him.

With the broad blade slung behind my left shoulder, I made my way through the corpse door and out into the windy garden of the necropolis. The sentry at the lowest gate, nearest the river, allowed me to pass without challenge, though with many a strange look, and I threaded the narrow streets to the Water Way, that runs with Gyoll.

Now I must write something that still shames me, even after all that has occurred. The watches of that afternoon were the happiest of my life. All my old hatred of the guild had vanished, and my love for it, for Master Palaemon, my brothers, and even the apprentices, my love for its lore and usages, my love which had never wholly died, was all that remained. I was leaving all those things I loved, after having disgraced them utterly. I should have wept.

I did not. Something in me soared, and when the wind whipped my cloak out behind me like wings, I felt I might have flown. We are forbidden to smile in the presence of any but our masters, brothers, clients, and apprentices. I did not wish to wear my mask, but I had to pull up my hood and bow my head lest the passersby see my face. Wrongly I thought I would perish on the way. Wrongly I thought I should never return to the Citadel and our tower; but wrongly too I believed that there were many more such days to come, and I smiled.

In my ignorance, I had supposed that before dark I would have left the city behind me, and that I would be able to sleep in relative safety beneath some tree. In actuality, I had not so much as outwalked the older and poorer parts before the west was lifted to cover the sun. To ask hospitality in one of the tottering buildings that bordered the Water Way, or attempt to rest in some corner, would have been an invitation to death. And so I trudged along under stars brightened by the wind, no longer a torturer in the eyes of the few who passed me, but only a somberly clad traveler who shouldered a dark paterissa.

From time to time boats glided through the weed-choked water while the wind drew music from their rigging. The poorer sort showed no lights and seemed hardly more than floating debris; but several times I beheld rich thalamegii with bow and stern lamps to show off their gilding. These kept to the center of the channel for fear of attack, yet I could hear the song of their sweepsmen across the water:

> Row, brothers, row!
> The current is against us.
> Row, brothers, row!
> Yet God is for us.
> Row, brothers, row!
> The wind is against us.
> Row, brothers, row!
> Yet God is for us.

And so on. Even when the lamps were no more than sparks a league or more upriver, the sound came on the wind. As I was later to see, they pull the shaft with the refrain, and put it back again with the alternate phrases, and so make their way watch upon watch.

When it seemed that it must soon be day, I saw upon the broad, black ribbon of the river a line of sparks that were not the lights of vessels but fixed fires stretching from bank to bank. It was a bridge, and after tramping long through the dark I reached it. Leaving the lapping tongues of the river, I mounted a flight of broken steps from the Water Way to the more elevated street of the bridge, and at once found myself an actor in a new scene.

The bridge was as well lighted as the Water Way had been shadowed. There were flambeaux on staggering poles every ten strides or so, and at intervals of about a hundred strides, bartizans whose guardroom windows glared like fireworks clung to the bridge piers. Carriages with lanterns rattled along, and most of the people who thronged the walkway were accompanied by linkboys or carried lights themselves. There were vendors who shouted the wares they displayed in trays hung from their necks, externs who gabbled in rude tongues, and beggars who showed their sores, feigned to play flageolets and ophicleides, and pinched their children to make them weep.

I confess I was much interested by all this, though my training prohibited me from gawking at it. With my hood drawn well over my head, and my eyes resolutely to the front, I passed among the crowd as if indifferent to it; but for a short time at least I felt my fatigue melt away, and my strides were, I think, the longer and swifter because I wanted to remain where I was.

The guards in the bartizans were not city roundsmen but peltasts in half-armor, bearing transparent shields. I was almost at the western bank when two stepped forward to bar my way with their blazing spears. "It is a serious crime to wear the costume you affect. If you intend some jape or artifice, you endanger yourself for its sake."

I said, "I am entitled to the habit of my guild."

"You seriously claim you are a carnifex, then? Is that a sword you carry?"

"It is, but I am no such thing. I am a journeyman of the Order of the Seekers for Truth and Penitence."

There was a silence. A hundred people or so had surrounded us in the few moments required for them to ask, and me to answer, their question. I saw the peltast who had not spoken glance at the other as if to say *he means it*, and then at the crowd.

"Come inside. The lochage wishes to speak with you."

They waited while I preceded them through the narrow door. The interior boasted only one small room, with a table and a few chairs. I mounted a little stair much worn by booted feet. In the room above, a man in a cuirass was writing at a high desk. My captors had followed me up, and when we stood before him, the one who had spoken previously said, "This is the man."

"I am aware of that," the lochage answered without looking up.

"He calls himself a journeyman of the guild of torturers."

For a moment the quill, which had skated along steadily before, paused. "I had never thought to encounter such a thing outside the pages of some book, but I dare say he speaks no more than the truth."

"Ought we to release him then?" the soldier asked.

"Not quite yet."

Now the lochage wiped his quill, sanded the letter over which he had labored, and looked up at us. I said, "Your subordinates stopped me because they doubted my right to the cloak I wear."

"They stopped you because I ordered it, and I ordered it because you were creating a disturbance, according to the report of the eastern turrets. If you are of the guild of torturers—which to be honest I had supposed reformed out of existence long ago—you have spent your life in the— What do you call it?"

"The Matachin Tower."

He snapped his fingers, and looked as though he were both amused and chagrined. "I mean the place where your tower stands."

"The Citadel."

"Yes, the Old Citadel. It's east of the river, as I recall, and just at the northern edge of the Algedonic Quarter. I was taken there to see the Donjon when I was a cadet. How often have you gone out into the city?"

I thought of our swimming expeditions and said, "Often."

"Dressed as you are now?"

I shook my head.

"If you're going to do that, pull back that hood. I can only see the tip of your nose wiggle." The lochage slid from his stool and strode to a window overlooking the bridge. "How many people do you think there are in Nessus?"

"I have no idea."

"No more do I, Torturer. No more does anyone. Every attempt to count them has failed, as has every attempt to tax them systematically. The city grows and changes every night, like writing chalked on a wall. Houses are built in the streets by clever people who take up the cobbles in the dark and claim the ground—did you know that? The exultant Talarican, whose madness manifested itself as a consuming interest in the lowest aspects of human existence, claimed that the persons who live by devouring the garbage of others number two gross thousands. That there are ten thousand begging acrobats, of whom nearly half are women. That if a pauper were to leap from the parapet of this bridge each time we draw breath, we should live forever, because the city breeds and breaks men faster than we respire. Among such a throng, there is no alternative to peace. Disturbances cannot be tolerated, because disturbances cannot be extinguished. Do you follow me?"

"There is the alternative of order. But yes, until that is achieved, I understand."

The lochage sighed and turned to face me. "If you understand that at least, good. It will be necessary, then, for you to obtain more conventional clothing."

"I cannot return to the Citadel."

"Then get out of sight tonight and buy something tomorrow. Have you funds?"

"A trifle, yes."

"Good. Buy something. Or steal, or strip the clothes from the next unfortunate you shorten with that thing. I'd have one of my fellows take you to an inn, but that would mean more staring and whispering still. There's been some kind of trouble on the river, and they're telling each other too many ghost stories out there already. Now the wind's dying and a fog's coming in—that will make it worse. Where are you going?"

"I am appointed to the town of Thrax."

The peltast who had spoken before said, "Do you believe him, Lochage? He's shown no proof that he's what he claims."

The lochage was looking out the window again, and now I too saw the threads of ochre mist. "If you can't use your head, use your nose," he said. "What odors entered with him?"

The peltast smiled uncertainly.

"Rusting iron, cold sweat, putrescent blood. An impostor would smell of new cloth, or rags picked from a trunk. If you don't wake to your business soon, Petronax, you'll be north fighting the Ascians."

The peltast said, "But Lochage—" shooting such a look of hatred toward me that I thought he might attempt to do me some harm when I left the bartizan.

"Show this fellow you are indeed of the torturers' guild."

The peltast was relaxed, so there was no great difficulty. I knocked his shield aside with my right arm, putting my left foot on his right to pin him while I crushed that nerve in the neck that induces convulsions.

X V

Baldanders

THE CITY AT THE WESTERN END of the bridge was very different
from the one I had left. At first there were flambeaux at the corners,
and nearly as much coming and going of coaches and drays as there
had been on the bridge itself. Before quitting the bartizan, I had
asked the lochage's advice about a place to spend what remained of
the night; now, feeling the fatigue that had deserted me only briefly,
I plodded along watching for the inn sign.

After a time the dark seemed to thicken with each step I took,
and somewhere I must have taken the wrong turning. Unwilling to
retrace my way, I tried to maintain a generally northerly route,
comforting myself with the thought that though I might be lost,
each stride carried me nearer Thrax. At last I discovered a small
inn. I saw no sign and perhaps it had none, but I smelled cooking
and heard the clink of tumblers, and I went in, throwing open the
door and dropping into an old chair that stood near it without
paying much attention to where I had come or whose company I
had entered.

When I had been sitting there long enough to get my breath and
was wishing for a place where I could take off my boots (though I
was far from ready to get up to look for one), three men who had

been drinking in a corner got up and left; and an old man, seeing, I suppose, that I was going to be bad for his business, came over and asked what I wanted. I told him I required a room.

"We have none."

I said, "That's just as well—I have no money to pay anyway."

"Then you will have to leave."

I shook my head. "Not yet. I'm too tired." (Other journeymen had told me of playing this trick in the city.)

"You're the carnifex, ain't you? You take their heads off."

"Bring me two of those fish I smell and you won't have anything but the heads left."

"I can call the City Guard. They'll have you out."

I knew from his tone that he did not believe what he said, so I told him to call away, but to bring me the fish in the meantime, and he went off grumbling. I sat up straighter then, with *Terminus Est* (which I had had to take from my shoulder to sit down) upright between my knees. There were five men still in the room with me, but none of them would meet my eye, and two soon left.

The old man returned with a small fish that had expired upon a slice of coarse bread, and said, "Eat this and go."

He stood and watched me while I had my supper. When I had finished it, I asked where I could sleep.

"No rooms. I told you."

If a palace had stood with open doors half a chain away, I do not think I could have driven myself to leave that inn to go to it. I said, "I'll sleep in this chair, then. You're not likely to have more trade tonight anyway."

"Wait," he said, and left me. I heard him talking to a woman in another room.

When I woke, he was shaking me by the shoulder. "Will you sleep three in a bed?"

"With whom?"

"Two optimates, I swear to you. Very nice men, traveling together."

The woman in the kitchen shouted something I could not understand.

"Did you hear that?" the old man continued. "One of them's not even come in yet. This time of night, he probably won't come at all. There'll be just the two of you."

"If these men have rented a bedchamber—"

"They won't object, I promise. Truth is, Carnifex, they're behind. Three nights here, and only paid for the first."

So I was to be used as an eviction notice. That did not disturb me much, and in fact it seemed somewhat promising—if the man sleeping there tonight left, I would have the room to myself. I clambered to my feet and followed the old man up a crooked stair.

The room we entered was not locked, but it was as dark as a tomb. I could hear heavy breathing. "Goodman!" the old fellow bawled, forgetting he had said his tenant was an optimate. "What-do-you-call-yourself? Baldy? Baldanders? I brought company for you. If you won't pay your rate, you got to take in boarders."

There was no reply.

"Here, Master Carnifex," the old man said to me, "I'll make you a light." He puffed at a bit of punk until it was bright enough to ignite a stub of candle.

The room was small, and held no furniture but a bed. In it, asleep on his side (as it appeared) with his back toward us and his legs drawn up, was the largest man I had ever seen—a man who might fairly have been called a giant.

"Aren't you going to wake, Goodman Baldanders, and see who your lodgemate might be?"

I wanted to go to bed and told the old man to leave us. He objected, but I pushed him out of the room and as soon as he was gone sat down on the unoccupied side of the bed and pulled off my boots and stockings. The weak light of the candle confirmed that I had developed several blisters. I took off my cloak and spread it on the worn counterpane. For a moment I considered whether I should take off my belt and trousers or sleep in them; prudence and weariness together urged the latter, and I noticed that the giant seemed fully dressed. With a feeling of inexpressible fatigue and relief I blew out the candle and lay down to spend the first night outside the Matachin Tower that I could recall.

"Never."

The tone was so deep and resonant (almost like the lowest notes of an organ) that I was not certain at first what the meaning of the word had been, or even if it had been a word at all. I mumbled, "What did you say?"

"Baldanders."

"I know—the innkeeper told me. I'm Severian." I was lying on my back, with *Terminus Est* (which I had brought into the bed for safekeeping) between us. In the dark, I could not tell whether my companion had rolled to face me or not, yet I was certain I would have felt any motion of that enormous frame.

"You—strike off."

"You heard us when we came in then. I thought you were asleep." My lips shaped themselves to say I was no carnifex, but a journeyman of the torturers' guild. Then I recalled my disgrace, and that Thrax has sent for an executioner. I said, "Yes, I'm a headsman, but you need not fear me. I only do what I am feed to do."

"Tomorrow, then."

"Yes, tomorrow will be time enough for us to meet and talk."

And then I dreamed, though it may have been that Baldanders' words, too, were a dream. Yet I do not think so, and if they were, it was a different dream.

I bestrode a great, leather-winged being under a lowering sky. Just equipoised between the rack of cloud and a twilit land we slid down a hill of air. Hardly once, it seemed to me, the finger-winged soarer flapped her long pinions. The dying sun was before us, and it seemed we matched the speed of Urth, for it stood unmoving at the horizon, though we flew on and on.

At last I saw a change in the land, and at first I thought it a desert. Far off, no cities or farms or woods or fields appeared, but only a level waste, a blackened purple in color, featureless and nearly static. The leathern-winged one observed it as well, or perhaps snatched some odor from the air. I felt iron muscles beneath me grow tense, and there were three wing strokes together.

The purple waste showed flecks of white. After a time I became aware that its seeming stillness was a sham born of uniformity—it was the same everywhere, but everywhere in motion—the sea—the World-River Uroboros—cradling Urth.

Then for the first time I looked behind me, seeing all the country of humankind swallowed in the night.

When it was gone, and there was everywhere beneath us the waste of rolling water and nothing more, the beast turned her head to regard me. Her beak was the beak of an ibis, her face the face of a hag; on her head was a miter of bone. For an instant we regarded each other, and I seemed to know her thought: *You dream; but were you to wake from your waking, I would be there*.

Her motion changed as a lugger's does when the sailors make it to come about on the opposite tack. One pinion dipped, the other rose until it pointed toward the sky, and I scrabbled at the scaled hide and plummeted into the sea.

The shock of the impact woke me. I twitched in every joint, and heard the giant mutter in his sleep. In much the same way I murmured too, and groped to find if my sword still lay at my side, and slept again.

The water closed over me, yet I did not drown. I felt I might breathe water, yet I did not breathe. Everything was so clear that I felt I fell through an emptiness more translucent than air.

Far off loomed great shapes—things hundreds of times larger than a man. Some seemed ships, and some clouds; one was a living head without a body; one had a hundred heads. A blue haze obscured them, and I saw below me a country of sand, carved by the currents. A palace stood there that was greater than our Citadel, but it was ruinous, its halls as unroofed as its gardens; through it moved immense figures, white as leprosy.

Nearer I fell, and they turned up their faces to me, faces such as I had seen once beneath Gyoll; they were women, naked, with hair of sea-foam green and eyes of coral. Laughing, they watched me fall, and their laughter came bubbling up to me. Their teeth were white and pointed, each a finger's length.

I fell nearer. Their hands reached up to me and stroked me as a mother strokes her child. The gardens of the palace held sponges and sea anemones and countless other beauties to which I could put no name. The great women circled me round, and I was only a doll before them. "Who are you?" I asked. "And what do you do here?"

"We are the brides of Abaia. The sweethearts and playthings, the toys and valentines of Abaia. The land could not hold us. Our breasts are battering rams, our buttocks would break the backs of bulls. Here we feed, floating and growing, until we are great enough to mate with Abaia, who will one day devour the continents."

"And who am I?"

Then they laughed all together, and their laughter was like surf upon a beach of glass. "We will show you," they said. "We will show you!" One took me by each hand, as sisters take their sister's child, and lifted me up, and swam with me through the garden. Their fingers were webbed, and as long as my arm from shoulder to elbow.

They halted, settling through the water like carracks sinking, until their feet and mine touched the strand. There stood before us a low wall, and on it a little stage and curtain, such as are used for children's entertainments.

Our roiling of the water seemed to flutter the kerchief-sized cloth. It rippled and swayed, and began to draw back as though teased by an unseen hand. At once there appeared the tiny figure of a man of sticks. His limbs were twigs, still showing bark and green bud. His body was a quarter-span of branch, big through as my thumb, and his head a knot whose whorls formed his eyes and mouth. He carried a club (which he brandished at us) and moved as if he were alive.

When the wooden man had jumped for us, and struck the little stage with his weapon to show his ferocity, there appeared the figure of a boy armed with a sword. This marionette was as finely finished as the other was crude—it might have been a real child reduced to the size of a mouse.

After both had bowed to us, the tiny figures fought. The wooden man performed prodigious leaps and seemed to fill the stage with the blows of his cudgel; the boy danced like a dust mote in a sunbeam to avoid it, darting at the wooden man to slash with his pin-sized blade.

At last the wooden figure collapsed. The boy strode over as if to set his foot upon its chest; but before he could do so, the wooden figure floated from the stage, and turning limply and lazily rose until it vanished from sight, leaving behind the boy, and the cudgel and the sword—both broken. I seemed to hear (no doubt it was really the squeaking of cartwheels on the street outside) a flourish of toy trumpets.

I woke because a third person had come into the room. He was a small, brisk man with fiery red hair, well and even foppishly dressed. When he saw me awake, he threw back the shutters that had covered the window, bringing red sunlight streaming in.

"My partner," he said, "sleeps soundly always. His snoring didn't deafen you?"

"I slept well myself," I told him. "And if he snored, I didn't hear him."

That seemed to please the small man, who showed a good many gold teeth when he smiled. "He does. He snores to shake Urth, I assure you. Happy you got your rest anyway." He extended a delicate, well-cared-for hand. "I am Dr. Talos."

"The Journeyman Severian." I threw off the thin coverings and stood up to take it.

"You wear black, I see. What guild is that?"

"It is the fuligin of the torturers."

"Ah!" He cocked his head to one side like a thrush, and hopped about to look at me from various angles. "You're a tall fellow—that's a shame—but all that sooty stuff is very impressive."

"We find it practical," I said. "The oubliette is a dirty place, and fuligin doesn't show bloodstains."

"You have humor! That's excellent! There are few advantages, I'll tell you, that profit a man more than humor. Humor will draw a crowd. Humor will calm a mob or reassure a nursery school. Humor will get you on and get you off, and pull in asimis like a magnet."

I had only the vaguest idea of what he was saying, but seeing that he was in an affable mood, I ventured, "I hope I didn't discommode you? The landlord said I was to sleep here, and there was room for another person in the bed."

"No, no, not at all! I never came back—found a better place to pass the night. I sleep very little, I may as well tell you, and I'm a light sleeper too. But I had a good night of it, an excellent night. Where are you going this morning, optimate?"

I was fumbling under the bed for my boots. "First to look for some breakfast, I suppose. After that, out of the city, to the north."

"Excellent! No doubt my partner would appreciate a breakfast—it will do him a world of good. And we're traveling north. After a most successful tour of the city, you know. Going back home now. Played the east bank down, and playing the west up. Perhaps we'll stop at the House Absolute on our way north. That's the dream, you know, in the profession. Play the Autarch's palace. Or come back, if you've already played there. Chrisos by the hatful."

"I've met one other person, at least, who dreamed of going back."

"Don't put on that long face—you must tell me about him

sometime. But now, if we're to go to breakfast— *Baldanders!* Wake up! Come, Baldanders, come! Wake up!" He danced to the foot of the bed and grasped the giant by an ankle. "Baldanders! Don't take him by the shoulder, optimate!" (I had made no motion to do so.) "He thrashes about sometimes. BALDANDERS!"

The giant murmured and stirred.

"A new day, Baldanders! Still alive! Time to eat and defecate and make love—all that! Up now, or we'll never get home."

There was no sign that the giant had heard him. It was as if the murmur of the moment before had been only a protest voiced in a dream, or his death rattle. Dr. Talos seized the foul blankets with both hands and swept them back.

The monstrous shape of his partner lay revealed. He was even taller than I had supposed, nearly too tall for the bed, though he slept with his knees drawn almost to his chin. His shoulders were an ell across, high and hunched. His face I could not see; it lay buried in his pillow. There were strange scars about his neck and ears.

"Baldanders!"

His hair was grizzled, and despite the innkeeper's pretended error, very thick.

"Baldanders! Your pardon, optimate, but may I borrow that sword?"

"No," I said. "You may not."

"Oh, I'm not going to kill him, or anything of that sort. I only want to use the flat of it."

I shook my head, and when Dr. Talos saw I was still adamant, he began to rummage about the room. "Left my stick downstairs. Vile custom, they'll thieve it. I should learn to limp, I really should. There's nothing here at all."

He darted out the door, and was back in a moment carrying an ironwood walking stick with a gilt-brass knob. "Now then! *Baldanders!*" The strokes fell upon the giant's broad back like the big raindrops that precede a thunderstorm.

Quite suddenly, the giant sat up. "I'm awake, Doctor." His face was large and coarse, but sensitive and sad as well. "Have you decided to kill me at last?"

"What are you talking about, Baldanders? Oh, you mean the optimate here. He's not going to do you any hurt—he shared the bed with you, and now he's going to join us at breakfast."

"He slept here, Doctor?"

Dr. Talos and I both nodded.

"Then I know whence my dreams rose."

I was still saturated with the sight of the huge women beneath the monstered sea, and so I asked what his dreams had been, though I was somewhat in awe of him.

"Of caverns below, where stone teeth dripped blood . . . Of arms dismembered found on sanded paths, and things that shook chains in the dark." He sat at the edge of the bed, cleaning sparse and surprisingly small teeth with one great finger.

Dr. Talos said, "Come on, both of you. If we're to eat and talk and get anything done today—why, we must be at it. Much to say and much to do."

Baldanders spat into the corner.

XVI

The Rag Shop

IT WAS ON THAT WALK through the streets of still slumbering Nessus that my grief, which was to obsess me so often, first gripped me with all its force. When I had been imprisoned in our oubliette, the enormity of what I had done, and the enormity of the redress I felt sure I would make soon under Master Gurloes's hands, had dulled it. The day before, when I had swung down the Water Way, the joy of freedom and the poignancy of exile had driven it away. Now it seemed to me that there was no fact in all the world beyond the fact of Thecla's death. Each patch of darkness among the shadows reminded me of her hair; every glint of white recalled her skin. I could hardly restrain myself from rushing back to the Citadel to see if she might not still be sitting in her cell, reading by the light of the silver lamp.

We found a cafe whose tables were set along the margin of the street. It was still sufficiently early that there was very little traffic. A dead man (he had, I think, been suffocated with a lambrequin, there being those who practice that art) lay at the corner. Dr. Talos went through his pockets, but came back with empty hands.

"Now then," he said. "We must think. We must contrive a plan."

A waitress brought mugs of mocha, and Baldanders pushed one toward him. He stirred it with his forefinger.

"Friend Severian, perhaps I should elucidate our situation. Baldanders—he is my only patient—and I hail from the region about Lake Diuturna. Our home burned, and needing a trifle of money to set it right again we decided to venture abroad. My friend is a man of amazing strength. I assemble a crowd, he breaks some timbers and lifts ten men at once, and I sell my cures. Little enough, you will say. But there's more. I've a play, and we've assembled properties. When the situation is favorable, he and I enact certain scenes and even invite the participation of some of the audience. Now, friend, you say you are going north, and from your bed last night I take it you are not in funds. May I propose a joint venture?"

Baldanders, who appeared to have understood only the first part of his companion's speech, said slowly, "It is not entirely destroyed. The walls are stone, very thick. Some of the vaults escaped."

"Quite correct. We plan to restore the dear old place. But see our dilemma—we're now halfway on the return leg of our tour, and our accumulated capital is still far from sufficient. What I propose—"

The waitress, a thin young woman with straggling hair, came carrying a bowl of gruel for Baldanders, bread and fruit for me, and a pastry for Dr. Talos. "What an attractive girl!" he said.

She smiled at him.

"Can you sit down? We seem to be your only customers."

After glancing in the direction of the kitchen, she shrugged and pulled over a chair.

"You might enjoy a bit of this—I'll be too busy talking to eat such a dry concoction. And a sip of mocha, if you don't object to drinking after me."

She said, "You'd think he'd let us eat for nothing, wouldn't you? But he won't. Charges everything at full price."

"Ah! You're not the owner's daughter, then. I feared you were. Or his wife. How can he have allowed such a blossom to flourish unplucked?"

"I've only worked here about a month. The money they leave on the table's all I get. Take you three, now. If you don't give me anything, I will have served you for nothing."

"Quite so, quite so! But what about this? What if we attempt to render you a rich gift, and you refuse it?" Dr. Talos leaned toward her as he said this, and it struck me that his face was not only that of a fox (a comparison that was perhaps too easy to make because his bristling reddish eyebrows and sharp nose suggested it at once) but that of a stuffed fox. I have heard those who dig for their livelihood say there is no land anywhere in which they can trench without turning up the shards of the past. No matter where the spade turns the soil, it uncovers broken pavements and corroding metal; and scholars write that the kind of sand that artists call polychrome (because flecks of every color are mixed with its whiteness) is actually not sand at all, but the glass of the past, now pounded to powder by aeons of tumbling in the clamorous sea. If there are layers of reality beneath the reality we see, even as there are layers of history beneath the ground we walk upon, then in one of those more profound realities, Dr. Talos's face was a fox's mask on a wall, and I marveled to see it turn and bend now toward the woman, achieving by those motions, which made expression and thought appear to play across it with the shadows of the nose and brows, an amazing and realistic appearance of vivacity. "Would you refuse it?" he asked again, and I shook myself as though waking.

"What do you mean?" the woman wanted to know. "One of you is a carnifex. Are you talking about the gift of death? The Autarch, whose pores outshine the stars themselves, protects the lives of his subjects."

"The gift of death? Oh, no!" Dr. Talos laughed. "No, my dear, you've had that all your life. So has he. We wouldn't pretend to give you what is already yours. The gift we offer is beauty, with the fame and wealth that derive from it."

"If you're selling something, I haven't got any money."

"Selling? Not at all! Quite the contrary, we are offering you new employment. I am a thaumaturge, and these optimates are actors. Have you never wanted to go on the stage?"

"I thought you looked funny, the three of you."

"We stand in need of an ingenue. You may claim the position, if you wish. But you must come with us now—we've no time to waste, and we won't come this way again."

"Becoming an actress won't make me beautiful."

"I will make you beautiful because we require you as an actress. It is one of my powers." He stood up. "Now or not at all. Will you come?"

The waitress rose too, still looking at his face. "I have to go to my room . . ."

"What do you own but dross? I must cast the glamour and teach you your lines, all in a day. I will not wait."

"Give me the money for your breakfasts, and I'll tell him I'm leaving."

"Nonsense! As a member of our company, you must assist in conserving the funds we will require for your costumes. Not to mention that you ate my pastry. Pay for it yourself."

For an instant she hesitated. Baldanders said, "You may trust him. The doctor has his own way of looking at the world, but he lies less than people believe."

The deep, slow voice seemed to reassure her. "All right," she said, "I'll go."

In a few moments, the four of us were several streets away, walking past shops that were still for the most part shuttered. When we had gone some distance, Dr. Talos announced, "And now, my dear friends, we must separate. I will devote my time to the enhancement of this sylph. Baldanders, you must get our collapsing proscenium and the other properties from the inn where you and Severian spent the night—I trust that will present no difficulties. Severian, we will perform, I think, at Ctesiphon's Cross. Do you know the spot?"

I nodded, though I had no notion of where it might be. The truth was that I had no intention of rejoining them.

Now, as Dr. Talos quick-stepped away with the waitress trotting behind him, I found myself alone with Baldanders on the deserted street. Anxious that he leave too, I asked him where he meant to go. It was more like talking to a monument than speaking with a man.

"There is a park near the river where one may sleep by day, though not by night. When it is nearly dark, I will awaken and collect our belongings."

"I'm afraid I'm not sleepy. I'm going to look around the city."

"I will see you then, at Ctesiphon's Cross."

For some reason I felt he knew what was in my mind. "Yes," I said. "Of course."

His eyes were dull as an ox's as he turned away to lumber with long steps toward Gyoll. Since Baldanders's park lay east and Dr. Talos had taken the waitress west, I resolved to walk north and so continue my journey toward Thrax, the City of Windowless Rooms.

Meanwhile, Nessus, the City Imperishable (the city in which I had lived all my life, though I had seen so little of it), lay all about me. Along a wide, flint-paved avenue I walked, not knowing or caring whether it was a side street or the principal one of the quarter. There were raised paths for pedestrians at either side, and a third in the center, where it served to divide the northbound traffic from the southbound.

To the left and right, buildings seemed to spring from the ground like grain too closely planted, shouldering one another for a place; and what buildings they were—nothing so large as the Great Keep and nothing so old; none, I think, with walls like the metal walls of our tower, five paces through; yet the Citadel had nothing to compare with them in color or originality of conception, nothing so novel and fantastic as each of these structures was, though each stood among a hundred others. As is the fashion in some parts of the city, most of these buildings had shops in their lower levels, though they had not been built for the shops but as guildhalls, basilicas, arenas, conservatories, treasuries, oratories, artellos, asylums, manufactures, conventicles, hospices, lazarets, mills, refectories, deadhouses, abattoirs, and playhouses. Their architecture reflected these functions, and a thousand conflicting tastes.

Turrets and minarets bristled; lanterns, domes, and rotundas soothed; flights of steps as steep as ladders ascended sheer walls; and balconies wrapped facades and sheltered them in the par-terre privacies of citrons and pomegranates.

I was wondering at these hanging gardens amid the forest of pink and white marble, red sardonyx, blue-gray, and cream, and black bricks, and green and yellow and tyrian tiles, when the sight of a lansquenet guarding the entrance to a casern reminded me of the promise I had made the officer of the peltasts the night before. Since I had little money and was well aware that I would require the warmth of my guild cloak by night, the best plan seemed to be to buy a voluminous mantle of some cheap stuff that could be worn over it. Shops were opening, but those that sold clothing all appeared to sell what would not fit my purpose, and at prices greater than I could afford.

The idea of working at my profession before I reached Thrax had not yet occurred to me; if it had, I would have dismissed it, supposing that there would be so little call for a torturer's services that it would be impractical for me to seek out those who required them. I believed, in short, that the three asimis, and the orichalks and aes in my pocket would have to carry me all the way to Thrax; and I had no idea of the size of the rewards that would be proffered me. Thus I stared at balmacaans and surtouts, dolmans and jerkins of paduasoy, matelasse, and a hundred other costly fabrics without ever going into the places that displayed them, or even stopping to examine them.

Soon my attention was seduced by other goods. Though I knew nothing of it at the time, thousands of mercenaries were outfitting themselves for the summer campaign. There were bright military capes and saddle blankets, saddles with armored pommels to protect the loins, red forage caps, long-shafted khetens, fans of silver foil for signaling, bows curved and recurved for use by cavalry, arrows in matched sets of ten and twenty, bow cases of boiled leather decorated with gilt studs and mother-of-pearl, and archers' guards to protect the left wrist from the bowstring. When I saw all these, I remembered what Master Palaemon had said before my masking about following the drum; and although I had held the matrosses of the Citadel in some contempt, I seemed to hear the long rattle of the call to parade, and the bright challenge the trumpets sent from the battlements.

Just when I had been wholly distracted from my search, a slender woman of twenty or a little more came out of one of the dark shops to unfasten the gratings. She wore a pavonine brocade gown of amazing richness and raggedness, and as I watched her, the sun touched a rent just below her waist, turning the skin there to palest gold.

I cannot explain the desire I felt for her, then and afterward. Of the many women I have known, she was, perhaps, the least beautiful—less graceful than her I have loved most, less voluptuous than another, less reginal far than Thecla. She was of average height, with a short nose, wide cheekbones, and the elongated brown eyes that often accompany them. I saw her lift the grating, and I loved her with a love that was deadly and yet not serious.

Of course I went to her. I could no more have resisted her than I could have resisted the blind greed of Urth if I had tumbled over a cliff. I did not know what to say to her, and I was terrified that she would recoil in horror at the sight of my sword and fuligin cloak. But she smiled and actually seemed to admire my appearance. After a moment, when I said nothing, she asked what I wanted; and I asked if she knew where I might buy a mantle.

"Are you sure you need one?" Her voice was deeper than I had expected. "You've such a beautiful cloak now. May I touch it?"

"Please. If you wish to."

She took up the edge and rubbed the fabric gently between her palms. "I've never seen such a black—so dark you can't see folds in it. It makes my hand look as though it's disappeared. And that sword. Is that an opal?"

"Would you like to examine that too?"

"No, no. Not at all. But if you really want a mantle . . ." She gestured toward the window, and I saw that it was filled with articles of worn clothing of every kind, jelabs, capotes, smocks, cymars, and so on. "Very inexpensive. Really reasonable. If you'll just go in, I'm sure you'll find what you want." I entered through a jingling door, but the young woman did not (as I had so much hoped she would) follow me inside.

The interior was dim, yet as soon as I looked about I thought I understood why the woman had not been disturbed by my appearance. The man behind the counter was more frightening than any torturer. His face was a skeleton's or nearly so, a face with dark pits for eyes, shrunken cheeks, and a lipless mouth. If it had not moved and spoken, I would not have believed he was a living man at all, but a corpse left erect behind the counter in fulfilment of the morbid wish of some past owner.

XVII

The Challenge

YET IT DID MOVE, turning to look at me as I came in; and it did speak. "Very fine. Yes, very fine. Your cloak, optimate—may I see it?"

I walked across a floor of worn and uneven tiles to him. A slash of red sunshine alive with swarming dust stood stiff as a blade between us.

"Your garment, optimate." I caught up my cloak and extended my left hand, and he touched the fabric much as the young woman had outside. "Yes, very fine. Soft. Wool-like, yet softer, much softer. A blend of linen and vicuna? And wonderful color. A torturer's vesture. One doubts the real ones were half so fine, but who can argue with a textile like that?" He ducked beneath his counter and emerged with a handful of rags. "Might I examine the sword? I'll be extremely careful, I promise you."

I unsheathed *Terminus Est* and laid her on the rags. He bent over her, neither touching her nor speaking. By that time my eyes had become accustomed to the dimness of the shop, and I noticed a narrow black ribbon that stretched forward a finger's width from the hair above his ears. "You are wearing a mask," I said.

"Three chrisos. For the sword. Another for the cloak."

"I didn't come here to sell," I told him. "Take it off."

"If you like. All right, four chrisos for the sword." He lifted his hands and the death's-head fell into them. His real face, flat-cheeked and tanned, was remarkably like that of the young woman I had seen outside.

"I want to buy a mantle."

"Five chrisos for it. That's positively my last offer. You'll have to give me a day to raise the money."

"I told you, this sword is not for sale." I picked up *Terminus Est* and resheathed her.

"Six." Reaching across the counter, he took me by the arm. "That's more than it's worth. Listen, it's your last chance. I mean it. Six."

"I came in to buy a mantle. Your sister, as I would assume she was, said you would have one at a reasonable price."

He sighed. "All right, I'll sell you a mantle. Will you tell me first where you got that sword?"

"It was given me by a master of our guild." I saw an expression I could not quite identify flicker across his face, and I asked, "You don't believe me?"

"I do believe you, that's the trouble. Just what are you?"

"A journeyman of the torturers. We don't often get to this side of the river, or come this far north. But are you really so surprised?"

He nodded. "It's like encountering a psychopomp. Can I ask why you're in this quarter of the city?"

"You may, but it's the last question I'm going to answer. I'm on my way to Thrax, to take up an assignment there."

"Thank you," he said. "I won't pry any more. I don't have to, really. Now since you'll want to surprise your friends when you take off your mantle—am I right?—it ought to be of some color that will contrast with your vesture. White might be good, but it's a rather dramatic color itself, and terribly hard to keep clean. What about a dull brown?"

"The ribbons that held your mask," I said. "They're still there."

He was dragging down boxes from behind his counter and did

not reply. After a moment or two we were interrupted by the tinkling of the bell above the door. The new customer was a youth whose face was hidden in an inlaid close helmet, of which down-curving and intertwined horns formed the visor. He wore armor of lacquered leather; a golden chimera with the blank, staring face of a madwoman fluttered on his breastplate.

"Yes, hipparch." The shopkeeper dropped his boxes to make a servile bow. "How may I assist you?"

A gauntleted hand reached toward me, the fingers pinched as though to give me a coin.

"Take it," the shopkeeper said in a frightened whisper. "Whatever it is."

I extended my own hand, and received a shining black seed the size of a raisin. I heard the shopkeeper gasp; the armored figure turned and went out.

When he was gone, I laid the seed on the counter. The shopkeeper squeaked, "Don't try to pass it to me!" and backed away.

"What is it?"

"You don't know? The stone of the avern. What have you done to offend an officer of the Household Troops?"

"Nothing. Why did he give me this?"

"You've been challenged. You're called out."

"To monomachy? Impossible. I'm not of the contending class."

His shrug was more eloquent than words. "You'll have to fight, or they'll have you assassinated. The only question is whether you've really offended the hipparch, or if there's some highly placed official of the House Absolute behind this."

As clearly as I saw the shopkeeper, I saw Vodalus in the necropolis standing his ground against the three volunteer guards; and though all prudence told me to toss aside the avern stone and flee the city, I could not do it. Someone—perhaps the Autarch himself or shadowy Father Inire—had learned the truth about Thecla's death, and now sought to destroy me without disgracing the guild. Very well, I would fight. If I were victorious he might reconsider; if I were killed, that would be no more than just. Still thinking of Vodalus's slender blade, I said, "The only sword I understand is this one."

"You won't engage with swords—in fact, it would be best if you left that with me."

"Absolutely not."

He sighed again. "I see you know nothing about these matters, yet you are going to fight for your life at twilight. Very well, you are my customer, and I've never yet abandoned a customer. You wanted a mantle. Here." He strode to the back of his shop and came forward carrying a garment the color of dead leaves. "Try this one. It will be four orichalks if it fits."

A mantle so large and loose could not but fit unless it was grossly short or long. The price seemed excessive, but I paid, and in donning the mantle took one step further toward becoming the actor that day seemed to wish to force me to become. Indeed, I was already taking part in more dramas than I realized.

"Now then," the shopkeeper said, "I must stay here to look after things, but I'll send my sister to help you get your avern. She has often gone to the Sanguinary Field, so perhaps she can also teach you the rudiments of combat with it."

"Did someone speak of me?" The young woman I had met at the front of the shop now came from one of the dark storerooms at its rear. With her upturned nose and strangely tilted eyes, she looked so much like her brother I felt sure they were twins, but the slender figure and delicate features that seemed incongruent in him were compelling in her. Her brother must have explained what had befallen me. I do not know, because I did not hear it. I was looking only at her.

Now I begin again. It has been a long time (twice I have heard the guard changed outside my study door) since I wrote the lines you read only a moment before. I am not certain it is right to record these scenes, which perhaps are important only to me, in so much detail. I might easily have condensed everything: I saw a shop and went in; I was challenged by an officer of the Septentrions; the

shopkeeper sent his sister to help me pluck the poisoned flower. I
have spent weary days in reading the histories of my predecessors,
and they consist of little but such accounts. For example, of Ymar:

> Disguising himself, he ventured into the countryside, where he
> spied a muni meditating beneath a plane tree. The Autarch
> joined him and sat with his back to the trunk until Urth had
> begun to spurn the sun. Troopers bearing an oriflamme galloped
> past, a merchant drove a mule staggering under gold, a beautiful
> woman rode the shoulders of eunuchs, and at last a dog trotted
> through the dust. Ymar rose and followed the dog, laughing.

Supposing this anecdote to be true, how easy it is to explain: the
Autarch had demonstrated that he chose his active life by an act of
will, and not because of the seductions of the world.

But Thecla had had many teachers, each of whom would
explain the same fact in a different way. Here, then, a second
teacher might say that the Autarch was proof against those things
that attract common men, but powerless to control his love of the
hunt.

And a third, that the Autarch wished to show his contempt for
the muni, who had remained silent when he might have poured
forth enlightenment and received more. That he could not do by
leaving when there was none to share the road, since solitude has
great attractions for the wise. Nor could he when the soldiers
passed, nor the merchant with his wealth, nor the woman, for
unenlightened men desire all those things, and the muni would
have thought him one more such man.

And a fourth, that the Autarch accompanied the dog because it
went forth alone, the soldiers having other soldiers, the merchant
his mule and the mule his merchant, and the woman her slaves;
while the muni did not go forth.

Yet why did Ymar laugh? Who shall say? Did the merchant
follow the soldiers to buy their booty? Did the woman follow the
merchant to sell her kisses and her loins? Was the dog of the

hunting kind, or such a short-limbed one as women keep to bark lest someone fondle them while they sleep? Who now shall say? Ymar is dead, and such memories of his as lived for a time in the blood of his successors are long faded.

So mine in time shall fade too. Of this I feel sure: not one of the explanations for the behavior of Ymar was correct. The truth, whatever it may have been, was simpler and more subtle. Of me it might be asked why I accepted the shopkeeper's sister as my companion—I who in all my life had had no true companion. And who, reading only of "the shopkeeper's sister," would understand why I remained with her after what is, at this point in my own story, about to happen? No one, surely.

I have said that I cannot explain my desire for her, and it is true. I loved her with a love thirsty and desperate. I felt that we two might commit some act so atrocious that the world, seeing us, would find it irresistible.

No intellect is needed to see those figures who wait beyond the void of death—every child is aware of them, blazing with glories dark or bright, wrapped in authority older than the universe. They are the stuff of our earliest dreams, as of our dying visions. Rightly we feel our lives guided by them, and rightly too we feel how little we matter to them, the builders of the unimaginable, the fighters of wars beyond the totality of existence.

The difficulty lies in learning that we ourselves encompass forces equally great. We say, "I will," and "I will not," and imagine ourselves (though we obey the orders of some prosaic person every day) our own masters, when the truth is that our masters are sleeping. One wakes within us and we are ridden like beasts, though the rider is but some hitherto unguessed part of ourselves.

Perhaps, indeed, that is the explanation of the story of Ymar. Who can say?

However that may be, I let the shopkeeper's sister help me adjust the mantle. It could be drawn tightly about the neck, and when it was worn so, my fuligin guild cloak was invisible beneath it. Still without revealing myself, I could reach through the front or through slits at the sides. I unfastened *Terminus Est* from her baldric and carried her like a staff for as long as I wore that mantle, and because her sheath covered most of her guard and was tipped with dark iron, many of the people who saw me no doubt thought it was one.

It was the only time in my life when I have covered the habit of the guild with a disguise. I have heard it said that one always feels a fool in them, whether they succeed or not, and surely I felt a fool in that one. And yet it was hardly a disguise at all. Those wide, old-fashioned mantles originated with shepherds (who wear them still), and were passed from them to the military in the days when the fighting with the Ascians took place here in the cool south. From the army they were taken up by religious pilgrims, who no doubt found a garment that could be converted into a more-or-less-satisfactory little tent very practical. The decline of religion has no doubt done much to extinguish them in Nessus, where I never saw any other than the one I wore myself. If I had known more about them when I put on mine in the rag shop, I would have bought a soft, wide-brimmed hat to go with it; but I did not, and the shopkeeper's sister told me I looked a good palmer. No doubt she said it with that twinkle of mockery with which she said everything else, but I was concerned with my appearance and failed to notice it. I told her and her brother that I wished I knew more of religion.

Both smiled, and the brother said, "If you mention it first, no one will want to talk about it. Besides, you can get the reputation of being a good fellow by wearing that and *not* talking about it. When you meet someone you don't want to talk to at all, beg alms."

So I became, in appearance at least, a pilgrim bound for some vague northern shrine. Have I said that time turns our lies into truths?

XVIII

The Destruction of the Altar

THE HUSH OF EARLY MORNING had vanished while I was in the rag shop. Wains and drays rumbled by in an avalanche of beasts, wood, and iron; the shopkeeper's sister and I had no more than stepped out of the door than I heard a flier skimming among the towers of the city. I looked up in time to see it, sleek as a raindrop on a windowpane.

"That's probably the officer who called you out," she remarked. "He'll be on his way back to the House Absolute. A hipparch of the Septentrion Guard—isn't that what Agilus said?"

"Is that your brother? Yes, something like that. What is your own name?"

"Agia. And you know nothing of monomachy? And have me for an instructor? Well, high Hypogeon help you. We'll have to go to the Botanic Gardens to begin with and cut you an avern. Fortunately they're not too far from here. Do you have enough money for us to take a fiacre?"

"I suppose so. If it is necessary."

"Then you're really not an armiger in costume. You're a— whatever you are."

"A torturer. Yes. When am I supposed to meet the hipparch?"

"Not until late afternoon, when the fighting begins at the Sanguinary Field and the avern opens its flower. We've plenty of time, but I think we'd better use it in getting you one and teaching you how to fight with it." A fiacre drawn by a pair of onegars was dodging toward us, and she waved to it. "You're going to be killed, you know."

"From what you say, it seems very likely."

"It's practically certain, so don't worry about your money." Agia stepped out into the traffic, looking for a moment (so finely chiseled was that delicate face, so graceful the curve of her body as she lifted an arm) like a memorial statue to the unknown woman on foot. I thought she was certain to be killed herself. The fiacre drew up to her with the skittish animals dancing to one side as though she were a thyacine, and she vaulted in. Light as she was, her weight made the little vehicle rock. I climbed in beside her, where we sat with our hips pressed together. The driver glanced back at us, Agia said, "The landing for the Botanic Gardens," and we jolted off. "So dying doesn't bother you—that's refreshing."

I braced myself with a hand on the back of the driver's bench. "Surely that's not unusual. There must be thousands, and perhaps millions of people like me. People accustomed to death, who feel that the only part of their lives that really mattered is over."

The sun was now just above the tallest spires, and the flooding light that turned the dusty pavement to red gold made me feel philosophical. In the brown book in my sabretache there was the tale of an angel (perhaps actually one of the winged women warriors who are said to serve the Autarch) who, coming to Urth on some petty mission or other, was struck by a child's arrow and died. With her gleaming robes all dyed by her heart's blood even as the boulevards were stained by the expiring life of the sun, she encountered Gabriel himself. His sword blazed in one hand, his great two-headed ax swung in the other, and across his back, suspended on the rainbow, hung the very battle horn of Heaven. "Where wend you, little one," asked Gabriel, "with your breast more scarlet than the robin's?" "I am killed," the angel said, "and I

return to merge my substance once more with the Pancreator."
"Do not be absurd. You are an angel, a pure spirit, and cannot
die." "But I am dead," said the angel, "nevertheless. You have
observed the wasting of my blood—do you not observe also that it
no longer issues in straining spurtings, but only seeps sluggishly?
Note the pallor of my countenance. Is not the touch of an angel
warm and bright? Take my hand and you will imagine you hold a
horror new dragged from some stagnant pool. Taste my breath—is
it not fetid, foul, and nidorous?" Gabriel answered nothing, and at
last the angel said, "Brother and better, even if I have not
convinced you with all my proofs, I pray you stand aside. I would
rid the universe of my presence." "I am convinced indeed," Gabriel
said, stepping from the other's way. "It is only that I was thinking
that had I known we might perish, I would not at all times have
been so bold."

To Agia I said, "I feel like the archangel in the story—if I had
known I could spend my life so easily and so soon, I would not—
probably—have done it. Do you know the legend? But I have made
my decisions now, and there's nothing more to say or do. This
afternoon the Septentrion will kill me with what? A plant? A
flower? In some way I don't understand. A short time ago, I
thought I could go to a place called Thrax and live there whatever
life there was to be lived. Well, last night I roomed with a giant.
One is not more fantastical than the other."

She did not reply, and after a time I asked, "What is that
building over there? The one with the vermilion roof and the forked
columns? I think there's allspice pounded in the mortar. At least, I
smell something of that sort from it."

"The mensal of the monachs. Do you know you are a
frightening man? When you entered our shop, I thought you only
another young armiger in motley. Then when I found you really
were a torturer, I thought it couldn't really be so bad after all—that
you were only a young man like other young men."

"And you have known a great many young men, I imagine."
The truth was that I was hoping she had. I wanted her to be more

experienced than I; and though I did not for an instant think myself pure, I wished to think her less pure still.

"But there is something more to you after all. You have the face of someone who stands to inherit two palatinates and an isle somewhere I never heard of, and the manners of a shoemaker, and when you say you're not afraid to die, you think you mean it, and under that you believe you don't. But you do, at the very bottom. It wouldn't bother you a bit to chop off my head either, would it?"

Around us swirled traffic of every sort: machines, wheeled and wheelless vehicles pulled by animals and slaves, walkers, and riders on the backs of dromedaries, oxen, metamynodons, and hackneys. Now an open fiacre like our own drew up beside us. Agia leaned toward the couple it carried and shouted, "We'll distance you!"

"Where bound?" the man called back, and I recognized Sieur Racho, whom I had once met when I had been sent to Master Ultan for books.

I gripped Agia by the arm. "Are you mad, or is he?"

"The Garden Landing, for a chrisos!"

The other vehicle tore away with ours behind it. "Faster!" Agia shouted to our driver. Then to me: "Have you a dagger? It's best to put the point to his back, so he can say he drove under threat of annihilation if we're stopped."

"Why are you doing this?"

"As a test. No one will believe your disguise. But everyone will believe you're an armiger in fancy dress. I've just proved it." (We careened about a dray loaded with sand.) "Besides, we'll win. I know this driver and his team's fresh. The other's been carting that whore for half the night."

I realized then that I would be expected to give Agia the money if we won, and that the other woman would claim my (nonexistent) chrisos from Racho if they did. Yet how sweet to humble him! Speed and the nearness of death (for I felt certain I would indeed be slain by the hipparch) made me more reckless than I had ever been in my life. I drew *Terminus Est*, and thanks to the length of her blade I could reach the onegars easily. Their flanks were already soaked with sweat, and the shallow cuts I made there must have burned like flames. "That's better than any dagger," I told Agia.

The crowd parted like water before the drivers' whips, mothers clasping their children as they fled, soldiers vaulting on their spears to the safety of windowsills. The conditions of the race favored us: the fiacre ahead to some extent cleared our path, and it was more impeded by other vehicles than we. Still we gained only slowly, and to get a few ells' advantage, our driver, who no doubt anticipated a rich tip if he won, sent the onegars hurtling up a flight of broad chalcedony steps. Marbles and monuments, pillars and pilasters, seemed thrown at our faces. We crashed through the green wall of a hedge as high as a house, overturned a cartload of comfits, dove through an arch and down a stair wound in a half turn, and were in the street again without ever knowing whose patio we had violated.

A baker's barrow drawn by sheep ambled into the narrow space between our vehicle and the other, and our big rear wheel jolted it, sending a shower of fresh bread into the street and throwing Agia's slight body against mine so pleasantly that I put an arm about it and held it there. I had clasped women so before—Thecla often, and hired bodies in the town. There was new bittersweetness in this, born of the cruel attraction Agia held for me. "I'm glad you did that," she said in my ear. "I hate men who grab me," and covered my face with kisses.

The driver looked back with a grin of triumph, letting the maddened team choose its own path. "Gone down the Twisted Way—got them now—across the common and reach them by a hundred ells."

The fiacre reeled and plunged into a narrow gateway in a barrier of shrubbery. An immense building loomed before us. The driver tried to turn his animals, but it was too late. We hit its side; it gave like the fabric of a dream, and we were in a cavernous space, dimly lit and smelling of hay. Ahead was a stepped altar as large as a cottage and dotted with blue lights. I saw it and realized I was seeing it too well—our driver had been swept out of his seat or had jumped clear. Agia shrieked.

We crashed into the altar. There was a confusion of flying objects impossible to describe, the sense of everything whirling and tumbling and never colliding, as in the chaos before creation. The ground seemed to leap at me; it struck with an impact that set my ears humming.

I had been holding *Terminus Est*, I think, while I flew through the air, but she was no longer in my hand. When I tried to get up to look for her, I had no breath and no strength. Somewhere far off, a man shouted. I rolled on my side, then managed to get my lifeless legs beneath me.

We seemed to be near the center of the building, which was as big around as the Great Keep and yet completely empty: without interior walls, stairs, or furniture of any kind. Through the golden, dusty air I could see crooked pillars that seemed of painted wood. Lamps, mere points of light, hung a chain or more overhead. Far above them, a many-colored roof rippled and snapped in a wind I could not feel.

I stood on straw, and straw was spread everywhere in an endless yellow carpet, like the field of a titan after harvest. All about me were the battens of which the altar had been constructed: fragments of thin wood braved with gold leaf and set with turquoises and violet amethysts. With some vague idea of finding my sword, I began to walk, stumbling almost at once over the smashed body of the fiacre. One onegar lay not far from it; I recall thinking it must have broken its neck. Someone called, "Torturer!" and I looked around and saw Agia—standing erect, though shakily. I asked if she were all right.

"Alive, anyway, but we must leave this place at once. Is that animal dead?"

I nodded.

"I could have ridden on it. Now you'll have to carry me if you can. I don't think my right leg will bear my weight." She tottered as she spoke, and I had to spring to her and catch her to keep her from falling. "Now we have to go," she said. "Look around . . . can you see a door? Quickly!"

I could not. "Why is it so urgent that we leave?"

"Use your nose if you can't use your eyes to see this floor."

I sniffed. The odor in the air was no longer straw, but straw burning; at almost the same instant I saw the flames, bright in the gloom, but still so small that a few moments before they must have been mere sparks. I tried to run, but could manage nothing better than a limping walk. "Where are we?"

"It's the Cathedral of the Pelerines—some call it the Cathedral of the Claw. The Pelerines are a band of priestesses who travel the continent. They never—"

Agia broke off because we were approaching a cluster of scarlet-clad people. Or perhaps they were approaching us, for they seemed to me to have appeared in the middle distance without warning. The men had shaven heads and held gleaming scimitars curved like the young moon and blazing with gilding; a woman with the towering height of an exultant cradled a sheathed two-handed sword: my own *Terminus Est*. She wore a hood and a narrow cape that trailed long tassels.

Agia began, "Our animals ran wild, Holy Domnicellae . . ."

"That is of no moment," the woman who held my sword said. There was much beauty in her, but it was not the beauty of women who quench desire. "This belongs to the man carrying you. Tell him to set you on your feet and take it. You can walk."

"A little. Do as she says, Torturer."

"Don't you know his name?"

"He told me, but I've forgotten."

I said, "Severian," and steadied her with one hand while I accepted *Terminus Est* with the other.

"Use it to end quarrels," the woman in scarlet said. "Not to begin them."

"The straw floor of this great tent is on fire, Chatelaine. Do you know it?"

"It will be extinguished. The sisters and our servants are crushing the embers now." She paused, her gaze flickering from Agia to me and back to Agia again. "In the remains of our high altar, which your vehicle destroyed, we found only one thing that seemed yours, and likely to be of value to you—that sword. We have returned it. Will you now also return to us anything of value to us you may have found?"

I remembered the amethysts. "I found nothing of value, Chatelaine." Agia shook her head, and I continued, "There were splinters of wood set with precious stones, but I left them where they had fallen."

The men shifted the hilts of their weapons in the hands and sought good footing, but the tall woman stood motionless, staring at me, then at Agia, then at me once more. "Come to me, Severian."

I came forward, a matter of three or four paces. It was a great temptation to draw *Terminus Est* as a defense against the men's blades, but I resisted it. Their mistress took my wrists in her hands and looked into my eyes. Her own were calm, and in the strange light seemed hard as beryls. "There is no guilt in him," she said.

One of the men muttered, "You are mistaken, Domnicellae."

"No guilt, I say. Step back, Severian, and let the woman come forward."

I did as she told me, and Agia limped to within a long pace of her. When she would not come nearer, the tall woman came to her and took her wrists as she had mine. After a moment, she glanced toward the other women who had waited behind the swordsmen. Before I realized what was happening, two of them seized Agia's gown and drew it over her head and away. One said, "Nothing, Mother."

"I think this the day foretold."

Her hands crossed over her breasts, Agia whispered to me, "These Pelerines are insane. Everyone knows it, and if I had had more time I would have told you so."

The tall woman said, "Return her rags. The Claw has not vanished in living memory, but it does so at will and it would be neither possible nor permissible for us to stop it."

One of the women murmured, "We may find it in the wreckage still, Mother." A second added, "Should they not be made to pay?"

"Let us kill them," a man said.

The tall woman gave no indication that she had heard any of them. She was already leaving us, seeming to glide across the straw. The women followed her, looking at one another, and the men lowered their gleaming blades and backed away.

Agia was struggling into her gown. I asked her what she knew of the Claw, and who these Pelerines were.

"Get me out of here, Severian, and I'll tell you. It isn't lucky to talk of them in their own place. Is that a tear in the wall over there?"

We walked in the direction she had indicated, stumbling sometimes in the soft straw. There was no opening, but I was able to lift the edge of the silken wall enough for us to slip under.

XIX

The Botanic Gardens

THE SUNLIGHT WAS BLINDING; it seemed as if we had stepped from twilight into full day. Golden particles of straw swam in the crisp air about us.

"That's better," Agia said. "Wait a moment now and let me get my bearings. I think the Adamnian Steps will be to our right. Our driver wouldn't have gone down them—or perhaps he would, the fellow was mad—but they should take us to the landing by the shortest route. Give me your arm again, Severian. My leg's not quite recovered."

We were walking on grass now, and I saw that the tent-cathedral had been pitched on a champian surrounded by semifortified houses; its insubstantial belfries looked down upon their parapets. A wide, paved street bordered the open lawn, and when we reached it I asked again who the Pelerines were.

Agia looked sidelong at me. "You must forgive me, but I don't find it easy to talk of professional virgins to a man who's just seen me naked. Though under other circumstances it might be different." She drew a deep breath. "I don't really know a great deal about them, but we have some of their habits in the shop, and I asked my brother about them once, and after that paid attention to whatever I heard. It's a popular costume for masques—all that red.

"Anyway, they are an order of conventionals, as no doubt you've already discerned. The red is for the descending light of the New Sun, and they descend on landowners, traveling around the country with their cathedral and seizing enough to set it up. Their order claims to possess the most valuable relic in existence, the Claw of the Conciliator, so the red may be for the Wounds of the Claw as well."

Trying to be facetious I said, "I didn't know he had claws."

"It isn't a real claw—it's said to be a gem. You must have heard of it. I don't understand why it's called the Claw, and I doubt that those priestesses do themselves. But assuming it to have had some real association with the Conciliator, you can appreciate its importance. After all, our knowledge of him now is purely historical—meaning that we either confirm or deny that he was in contact with our race in the remote past. If the Claw is what the Pelerines represent it to be, then he once lived, though he may be dead now."

A startled glance from a woman carrying a dulcimer told me the mantle I had bought from Agia's brother was in disarray, permitting the fuligin of my guild cloak (which must have looked like mere empty darkness to the poor woman) to be seen through the opening. As I rearranged it and reclasped the fibula I said, "Like all these religious arguments, this one gets less significant as we continue. Supposing the Conciliator to have walked among us eons ago, and to be dead now, of what importance is he save to historians and fanatics? I value his legend as a part of the sacred past, but it seems to me that it is the legend that matters today, and not the Conciliator's dust."

Agia rubbed her hands, seeming to warm them in the sunlight. "Suppposing him—we turn at this corner, Severian, you may see the head of the stair, if you'll look, there where the statues of the eponyms stand—supposing him to have lived, he was by definition the Master of Power. Which means the transcendence of reality, and includes the negation of time. Isn't that correct?"

I nodded.

"Then there is nothing to prevent him, from a position, say, of thirty thousand years ago, coming into what we call the present. Dead or not, if he ever existed, he could be around the next bend of the street or the next turn of the week."

We had reached the beginning of the stair. The steps were of stone as white as salt, sometimes so gradual that several strides were needed to go from one descent to the next, sometimes almost as abrupt as a ladder. Confectioners, sellers of apes, and the like had set up their stands here and there. For whatever reason, it was very pleasant to discuss mysteries with Agia while descending these steps, and I said, "All this because those women say they possess one of his glittering fingernails. I suppose it performs miraculous cures?"

"On occasion, so they claim. It also forgives injuries, raises the dead, draws new races of beings from the soil, purifies lust, and so on. All the things he is supposed to have done himself."

"You're laughing at me now."

"No, only laughing at the sunshine—you know what it is supposed to do to women's faces."

"Make them brown."

"Make them ugly. To begin with, it dries the skin and creates wrinkles and so on. Then too, it shows up every little defect. Urvasi loved Pururavas, you know, before she saw him in a bright light. Anyway, I felt it on my face, and I was thinking, 'I don't care for *you*. I'm still too young to worry about you, and next year I'll get a wide hat from our stock.'"

Agia's face was far from perfect now in the clear sunshine, but she had nothing to fear from it. My hunger fed at least as ravenously upon her imperfections. She possessed the hopeful, hopeless courage of the poor, which is perhaps the most appealing of all human qualities; and I rejoiced in the flaws that made her more real to me.

"Anyway," she continued, squeezing my hand, "I have to admit I've never understood why people like the Pelerines always think ordinary people have to have their lust purified. In my experience, they control it well enough by themselves, and just about every day, too. What most of us need is to find someone we can unbottle it with."

"Then you care that I love you." I was only half joking.

"Every woman cares if she's loved, and the more men who love her, the better! But I don't choose to love you in return, if that's what you mean. It would be so easy today, going around the city with you like this. But then if you're killed this evening, I'll feel badly for a fortnight."

"So will I," I said.

"No you won't. You won't even care. Not about that or anything, not ever again. Being dead doesn't hurt, as you of all people should know."

"I'm almost inclined to think this whole affair is some trick of yours, or of your brother's. You were outside when the Septentrion came—did you tell him something to inflame him against me? Is he your lover?"

Agia laughed at that, her teeth flashing in the sun. "Look at me. I have a brocade gown, but you've seen what's beneath it. My feet are bare. Do you see rings or earrings? A silver lamia twined about my neck? Are my arms constricted with circlets of gold? If not, you may safely assume I have no officer of the Household Troops for my paramour. There's an old sailor, ugly and poor, who presses me to live with him. Other than that, well, Agilus and I own our shop. It was bequeathed to us by our mother, and it's free of debt only because we can find no one who's enough of a fool to lend anything on it. Sometimes we rip up something from our stock and sell it to the paper-makers so we can buy a bowl of lentils to divide between us."

"You should eat well tonight anyway," I told her. "I gave your brother a good price for this mantle."

"What?" Her good humor seemed to have returned. She took a step back and feigned astonishment with an open mouth. "You won't buy me a supper this evening? After I've spent the day counseling you and guiding you about?"

"Involving me in the destruction of the altar those Pelerines had erected."

"I'm sorry about that. I really am. I didn't want you to tire your legs—you'll need them when you fight. Then those others came up, and I thought I saw a chance for you to make some money."

Her look had left my face and come to rest on one of the brutal busts that flanked the stair. I asked, "Is that really all there was to it?"

"To confess the truth, I wanted them to go on thinking you might be an armiger. Armigers go about in fancy dress so much because they're always going to fetes and tournaments, and you have the face. That's why I thought so myself when I first saw you. And you see, if you were, then I was someone that somebody like that, an armiger and probably the bastard of an exultant, might care for. Even if it was only a kind of joke. I had no way of knowing what would happen."

"I understand," I said. Suddenly laughter overcame me. "What fools we must have looked, jolting along in the fiacre."

"If you understand, then kiss me."

I stared at her.

"Kiss me! How many chances have you left? I'll give you more, what you want—" She paused, then laughed too. "After supper, perhaps. If we can find a private spot, though it won't be good for your fighting." She threw herself into my arms then, rising on her toes to press my lips. Her breasts were firm and high, and I could feel the motion of her hips.

"There now." She pushed me away. "Look down there, Severian. Between the pylons. What do you see?"

Water glimmered like a mirror in the sun. "The river."

"Yes, Gyoll. Now to the left. Because there are so many nenuphars, the island is hard to see. But the lawn is a lighter, brighter green. Don't you see the glass? Where it catches the light?"

"I see something. Is the building all glass?"

She nodded. "That's the Botanic Gardens, where we're going. They'll let you cut your avern there—all you have to do is demand it as your right."

We made the rest of the descent in silence. The Adamnian Steps wind back and forth across a long hillside, and they are a favored place for strollers, who often hire a ride to the top and descend. I saw many couples finely dressed, men with the marks of old difficulties scarring their faces, and romping children. Saddening me more, I saw too from several points the dark towers of the Citadel on the opposite bank, and on the second or third such sighting it came to me that when I had swum from the eastern bank, diving from the water-stairs and fighting with the tenement children, I had once or twice noticed this narrow line of white on the other shore, so far upstream as to be nearly beyond sight.

The Botanic Gardens stood on an island near the bank, enclosed in a building of glass (a thing I had not seen before and did not know could exist). There were no towers or battlements: only the faceted tholus, climbing until it lost itself against the sky and its momentary brilliancies were confounded with the faint stars. I asked Agia if we would have time to see the gardens—and then, before she could reply, told her that I would see them whether there was time or not. The fact was that I had no compunction about arriving late for my death, and was beginning to have difficulty in taking seriously a combat fought with flowers.

"If you wish to spend your last afternoon visiting the gardens, so be it," she said. "I come here myself often. It's free, being maintained by the Autarch, and entertaining if you're not too squeamish."

We went up steps of glass, palely green. I asked Agia if the enormous building existed only to provide blooms and fruit.

She shook her head, laughing, and motioned toward the wide arch before us. "On either side of this corridor are chambers, and each chamber is a bioscape. I warn you though that because the corridor is shorter than the building itself, the chambers will widen as we go into them more deeply. Some people find that disconcerting."

We entered, and in so doing stepped into such silence as must have been in the morning of the world, before the fathers of men first hammered out brazen gongs, built squealing cartwheels, and splashed Gyoll with striding oars. The air was fragrant, damp, and a trifle warmer than it had been outside. The walls to either side of the tessellated floor were also of glass, but so thick that sight could scarcely penetrate them; leaves and flowers and even soaring trees seen through these walls wavered as though glimpsed through water. On one broad door I read:

THE GARDEN OF SLEEP

"You may enter whichever you like," an old man said, rising from his chair in a corner. "And as many as you like."

Agia shook her head. "We won't have time for more than one or two."

"Is it your first visit? Newcomers generally enjoy the Garden of Pantomime."

He wore a faded robe that reminded me of something I could not place. I asked if it were the habit of some guild.

"Indeed it is. We are the curators—have you never met one of our brotherhood previously?"

"Twice, I believe."

"There are only a few of us, but our charge is the most important that society boasts—the preservation of all that is gone. Have you seen the Garden of Antiquities?"

"Not yet," I said.

"You should! If this is your first visit, I would advise you to begin with the Garden of Antiquities. Hundreds and hundreds of extinct plants, including some that have not been seen for tens of millions of years."

Agia said, "That purple creeper you're so proud of—I met it growing wild on a hillside in Cobblers Common."

The curator shook his head sadly. "We lost spores, I'm afraid. We know about it . . . A roof pane broke, and they blew away." The unhappiness quickly left his lined face, draining away as the troubles of simple people do. He smiled. "It's likely to do well now. All its enemies are as dead as the disorders its leaves cured."

A rumbling made me turn. Two workmen were wheeling a cart through one of the doorways, and I asked what they were doing.

"That's the Sand Garden. They're rebuilding it. Cactuses and yucca—that kind of thing. I'm afraid there's not much to see there now."

I took Agia by the hand, saying, "Come on, I'd like to look at the work." She smiled at the curator and gave a half shrug, but followed docilely enough.

Sand there was, but no garden. We stepped into a seemingly unlimited space dotted with boulders. More stone rose in cliffs behind us, concealing the wall through which we had come. Just beside the doorway spread one large plant, half bush, half vine, with cruel, curved thorns; I assumed that it was the last of the old flora, not yet removed. There was no other vegetation, and no sign of the restocking the curator had implied except for the twin tracks of the workmen's cart, winding off among the rocks.

"This isn't much," Agia said. "Why don't you let me take you to the Garden of Delectation?"

"The door is open behind us—why is it I feel I can't leave this place?"

She looked at me sidelong. "Everyone feels like that in these gardens sooner or later, though usually not so quickly. It would be better for you if we stepped outside now." She said something else as well, something I could not catch. Far off, I seemed to hear surf pounding on the edge of the world.

"Wait . . ." I said. But Agia drew me out into the corridor again. Our feet carried away as much sand as a child might hold in the palm of one hand.

"We really don't have much time left now," Agia told me. "Let me show you the Garden of Delectation, then we'll pluck your avern and go."

"It can't be much later than midmorning."

"It's past noon. We were more than a watch just in the Sand Garden."

"Now I know you're lying to me."

For an instant I saw a flash of anger in her face. Then it was spread over with an unction of philosophical irony, the secretion of her injured self-esteem. I was far stronger than she, and poor though I was, richer; she told herself now (I felt I could almost hear her voice whispering in her own ear) that by accepting such insults she mastered me.

"Severian, you argued and argued, and in the end I had to drag you away. The gardens affect people like that—certain suggestible people. They say the Autarch wants some people to remain in each to accent the reality of the scene, and so his archimage, Father Inire, has invested them with a conjuration. But since you were so drawn to that one, it's not likely any of the others will affect you so much."

"I felt I belonged there," I said. "That I was to meet someone . . . and that a certain woman was there, nearby, but concealed from sight."

We were passing another door, on which was written:

THE JUNGLE GARDEN

When Agia did not answer me, I said, "You tell me the others won't affect me, so let's go in here."

"If we waste our time with that, we won't get to the Garden of Delectation at all."

"Only for a moment." Because she was so determined to take me into the garden she had selected, without seeing any of the others, I had grown frightened of what I might find there, or bring with me.

The heavy door of the Jungle Garden swung toward us, bringing a rush of steaming air. Beyond, the light was dim and green. Lianas half obscured the entrance, and a great tree, rotted to punk, had fallen across the path a few strides away. Its trunk still bore a small sign: *Caesalpinia sappan.*

"The real jungle is dying in the north as the sun cools," Agia said. "A man I know says it has been dying so for many centuries. Here, the old jungle stands preserved as it was when the sun was young. Come in. You wanted to see this place."

I stepped inside. Behind us the door swung shut and vanished.

X X

Father Inire's Mirrors

As Agia had said, the real jungles sickened far to the north. I had never seen them, yet the Jungle Garden made me feel I had. Even now, as I sit at my writing table in the House Absolute, some distant noise brings back to my ears the screams of the magenta-breasted, cynaeous-backed parrot that flapped from tree to tree, watching us with white-rimmed and disapproving eyes—though this is no doubt because my mind was already turned to that haunted place. Through its screaming, a new sound—a new voice—came from some red world still unconquered by thought.

"What is it?" I touched Agia's arm.

"A smilodon. But he's far away and only wants to frighten the deer so they'll blunder into his jaws. He'd run from you and your sword much faster than you could run from him." Her gown had been torn by a branch, exposing one breast. The incident had left her in no good mood.

"Where does the path lead? And how can the cat be so far off when all this is only one room of the building we saw from the top of the Adamnian Steps?"

"I've never gone so deeply into this garden. You were the one who wanted to come."

"Answer my questions," I said, and took her by the shoulder.

"If this path is like the others—I mean, in the other gardens—it runs in a wide loop that will eventually return us to the door by which we came in. There's no reason to be afraid."

"The door vanished when I shut it."

"Only trickery. Haven't you seen those pictures in which a pietist exhibits a meditating face when you're on one side of the room, but stares at you when you cross to the opposite wall? We'll see the door when we approach it from the other direction."

A snake with carnelian eyes came gliding onto the path, lifted a venomous head to look at us, then slipped away. I heard Agia's gasp and said, "Who's afraid now? Will that snake flee you as quickly as you would flee it? Now answer my question about the smilodon. Is it really far away? And if so, how can that be?"

"I don't know. Do you think there are answers to everything here? Is that true in the place you come from?"

I recalled the Citadel and the age-old usages of the guilds. "No," I said. "There are inexplicable offices and customs in my home, though in these decadent times they are falling out of use. There are towers no one has ever entered, too, and lost rooms, and tunnels whose entrances have not been seen."

"Then can't you understand that it's the same way here? When we were at the top of the steps and you looked down and saw these gardens, could you make out the entire building?"

"No," I admitted. "There were pylons and spires in the way, and the corner of the embankment."

"And even so, could you delimit what you saw?"

I shrugged. "The glass made it difficult to tell where the edges of the building were."

"Then how can you ask the questions you do? Or if you have to ask them, can't you understand that I don't necessarily have the answers? From the sound of the smilodon's roar, I knew he was far off. Perhaps he is not here at all, or perhaps the distance is of time."

"When I looked down on this building, I saw a faceted dome. Now when I look up, I see only the sky between the leaves and vines."

"The surfaces of the facets are large. It may be that their edges are concealed by the limbs," Agia said.

We walked on, wading a trickle of water in which a reptile with evil teeth and a finned back soaked himself. I unsheathed *Terminus Est*, fearing he would dart at our feet. "I grant," I told her, "that the trees grow too thickly here to permit me to see far to either side. But look here, through the opening where this freshet runs. Upstream I can see only more jungle. Downstream there is the gleam of water, as though it empties into a lake."

"I warned you that the rooms open out, and that you might find that disturbing. It is also said that the walls of these places are specula, whose reflective power creates the appearance of vast space."

"I once knew a woman who had met Father Inire. She told me a tale about him. Would you like to hear it?"

"Suit yourself."

Actually it was I who wanted to hear the story, and I did suit myself: I told it to myself in the recesses of my mind, hearing it there hardly less than I had heard it first when Thecla's hands, white and cold as lilies taken from a grave filled with rain, lay clasped between my own.

"I was thirteen, Severian, and I had a friend named Domnina. She was a pretty girl who looked several years younger than she really was. Perhaps that's why he took a fancy to her.

"I know you know nothing of the House Absolute. You must take my word for it that at one place in the Hall of Meaning there are two mirrors. Each is three or four ells wide, and each extends to the ceiling. There's nothing between the two except a few dozen strides of marble floor. In other words, anyone who walks down the Hall of Meaning sees himself infinitely multiplied there. Each mirror reflects the images in its twin.

"Naturally, it's an attractive spot when you're a girl and fancy yourself something of a beauty. Domnina and I were playing there one night, turning around and around to show off new camisias. We had moved a couple of big candelabra so one was on the left of one mirror and the other on the left of the facing one—at opposite corners if you see what I mean.

"We were so busy looking at ourselves that we didn't notice Father Inire until he was only a step away. Ordinarily, you understand, we would have run and hidden when we saw him coming, though he was scarcely taller than we. He wore iridescent robes that seemed to fade into gray when I looked at them, as if they had been dyed in mist. 'You must be wary, children, of looking at yourselves like that,' he said. 'There's an imp who waits in silvered glass and creeps into the eyes of those who look into it.'

"I knew what he meant, and blushed. But Domnina said, 'I think I've seen him. Is he shaped like a tear, all gleaming?'

"Father Inire did not hesitate before he answered her, or even blink—still, I understood that he was startled. He said, 'No, that is someone else, dulcinea. Can you see him plainly? No? Then come into my presence chamber tomorrow a little after Nones, and I'll show him to you.'

"We were frightened when he left. Domnina swore a hundred times that she would not go. I applauded her resolution and tried to strengthen her in it. More to the point, we arranged that she should stay with me that night and the next day.

"It was all for nothing. A little before the appointed time, a servant in a livery neither of us had ever seen came for poor Domnina.

"A few days before I had been given a set of paper figures. There were soubrettes, columbines, coryphees, harlequinas, figurantes, and so on—the usual thing. I remember that I waited on the window seat all afternoon for Domnina, toying with these little people, coloring their costumes with wax pencils, arranging them in various ways and inventing games she and I would play when she came back.

"At last my nurse called me to supper. By that time I thought Father Inire had killed Domnina, or that he had sent her back to her mother with an order that she must never visit us again. Just as I was finishing my soup there was a knock. I heard mother's servitrix go to answer the door, then Domnina burst in. I'll never forget her face—it was as white as the faces of the dolls. She cried and my nurse comforted her, and eventually we got the story out of her.

"The man who had been sent for her had taken her through halls she hadn't known existed. That, you understand, Severian, was frightening in itself. We both thought ourselves perfectly familiar with our wing of the House Absolute. Eventually he had led her into what must have been the presence chamber. She said it was a large room with hangings of a solid, dark red and almost no furniture except for vases taller than a man and wider than she could spread her arms.

"In the center was what she at first took to be a room within the room. The walls were octagonal and painted with labyrinths. Over it, just visible from where she stood at the entrance to the presence chamber, burned the brightest lamp she had ever seen. It was blue-white, she said, and so brilliant an eagle could not have kept his eyes on it.

"She had heard the click of the bolt when the door had been closed behind her. There was no other exit she could see. She ran to the curtains hoping to find another door behind them, but as soon as she pulled one aside, one of the eight walls painted with labyrinths opened and Father Inire stepped out. Behind him she saw what she called a bottomless hole filled with light.

"'There you are,' he said. 'You've come just in time. Child, the fish is nearly caught. You can watch the setting of the hook, and learn by what means his golden scales are to be meshed in our landing net.' He took her arm and led her into the octagonal enclosure."

At this point I was forced to interrupt my tale to help Agia through a section of the path almost completely overgrown. "You're talking to yourself," she said. "I can hear you muttering behind me."

"I'm telling myself the story I mentioned to you. You seemed to have no wish to hear it, and I wanted to listen to it again—besides, it concerns the specula of Father Inire, and may contain hints useful to us."

"Domnina drew away. In the center of the enclosure, just under the lamp, was a haze of yellow light. It was never still, she said. It moved up and down and from side to side with rapid flickerings, never leaving a space that might have been four spans high and four long. It did indeed remind her of a fish. Much more than the faint flagae she had glimpsed in the mirrors of the Hall of Meaning ever had—a fish swimming in air, confined to an invisible bowl. Father Inire drew the wall of the octagon closed behind them. It was a mirror in which she could see his face and hand and shining, indefinite robes reflected. Her own form too, and the fish's . . . but there seemed to be another girl—her own face peering over her shoulder; then another and another and another, each with a smaller face behind it. And so on *ad infinitum*, an endless chain of fainter Domnina-faces.

"She realized when she saw them that the wall of the octagonal enclosure through which she had passed faced another mirror. In fact, all the others were mirrors. The light of the blue-white lamp was caught by them all and reflected from one to another as boys might pass silver balls, interlacing and intertwining in an interminable dance. In the center, the fish flickered to and fro, a thing formed, as it seemed, by the convergence of the light.

"'Here you see him,' Father Inire said. 'The ancients, who knew this process at least as well as we and perhaps better, considered the Fish the least important and most common of the inhabitants of specula. With their false belief that the creatures they summoned were ever present in the depths of the glass, we need not concern ourselves. In time they turned to a more serious question: By what means may travel be effected when the point of departure is at an astronomical distance from the place of arrival?"

"'Can I put my hand through him?'

"'At this stage you may, child. Later I would not advise it.'

"She did so, and felt a sliding warmth. 'Is this how the cacogens come?'

"'Has your mother ever taken you riding in her flier?'

"'Of course.'

"'And you have seen the toy fliers older children make on the pleasance at night, with paper hulls and parchment lanterns. What you see here is to the means used to travel between suns as those toy fliers are to real ones. Yet we can call up the Fish with these, and perhaps other things too. And just as the boys' fliers sometimes set the roof of a pavilion ablaze, so our mirrors, though their concentration is not powerful, are not without danger.'

"'I thought that to travel to the stars you'd have to sit on the mirror.'

"Father Inire smiled. It was the first time she had seen him smile, and though she knew he meant only that she had amused and pleased him (perhaps more than a grown woman could have) it was not pleasant. 'No, no. Let me outline the problem to you. When something moves very, very fast—as fast as you see all the familiar things in your nursery when your governess lights your candle—it grows heavy. Not larger, you understand, but only heavier. It is attracted to Urth or any other world more strongly. If it were to move swiftly enough, it would become a world itself, pulling other things to it. Nothing ever does, but if something did, that is what would happen. Yet even the light from your candle does not move swiftly enough to travel between the suns.'

"(The Fish flickered up and down, forward and back.)

"'Couldn't you make a bigger candle?' I feel sure Domnina was thinking of the paschal candle she saw each spring, thicker than a man's thigh.

"'Such a candle could be made, but its light would fly no more swiftly. Yet even though light is so weightless we have given its name to that condition, it presses against what it falls on, just as wind, which we cannot see, pushes the arms of a mill. See now what happens when we provide light to mirrors set face to face: The image they reflect travels from one to the other and returns. Suppose it meets itself in returning—what do you suppose happens then?'

"Domnina laughed despite her fear, and said she could not guess.

"'Why it cancels itself. Think of two little girls running across a lawn without looking where they're going. When they meet, there are no more little girls running. But if the mirrors are well made and the distances between them are correct, the images do not meet. Instead, one comes behind the other. That has no effect when the light comes from a candle or a common star, because both the earlier light and the later light that would otherwise tend to drive it forward are only random white light, like the random waves a little girl might make by flinging a handful of pebbles into a lily pond. But if the light is from a coherent source, and forms the image reflected from an optically exact mirror, the orientation of the wave fronts is the same because the image is the same. Since nothing can exceed the speed of light in our universe, the accelerated light leaves it and enters another. When it slows again, it reenters ours—naturally at another place.'

"'Is it just a reflection?' Domnina asked. She was looking at the Fish.

"'Eventually it will be a real being, if we do not darken the lamp or shift the mirrors. For a reflected image to exist without an object to originate it violates the laws of our universe, and therefore an object will be brought into existence.'"

"Look," Agia said, "we're coming to something."

The shade of the tropical trees was so intense that spots of sunshine on the path seemed to blaze like molten gold. I squinted to peer beyond their burning shafts of light.

"A house set on stilts of yellow wood. It's thatched with palm fronds. Can't you see it?"

Something moved, and the hut seemed to spring at my eyes as it emerged from the pattern of greens, yellows, and blacks. A shadowed splotch became a doorway; two sloping lines, the angle of the roof. A man in light-colored clothes stood on a tiny veranda looking down the path at us. I straightened my mantle.

"You don't have to do that," Agia said. "It doesn't matter in here. If you're hot, take it off."

I removed the mantle and folded it over my left arm. The man on the veranda turned with an expression of unmistakable terror and went into the hut.

XXI

The Hut in the Jungle

A LADDER LED to the veranda. It was made of the same knobby-jointed wood as the hut, lashed together with vegetable fiber. "You're not going up that?" Agia protested.

"If we're going to see what's to be seen here we must," I said. "And recalling the state of your undergarments, I thought you might feel more comfortable if I preceded you."

She surprised me by blushing. "It will only lead to such a house as was used in the hot parts of the world in ancient days. You'll soon be bored, believe me."

"Then we can come down, and we will have lost very little time." I swung myself up the ladder. It sagged and creaked alarmingly, but I knew that in a public pleasureground it was impossible that it should be really dangerous. When I was halfway up, I felt Agia behind me.

The interior was hardly larger than one of our cells, but there all resemblance ceased. In our oubliette, the overwhelming impression was of solidity and mass. The metal plates of the walls echoed even the slightest sounds; the floors rang beneath the tread of the journeymen and gave not a hairsbreadth under the walker's weight; the ceiling could never fall—but if it should, it would crush everything below it.

If it is true that each of us has an antipolaric brother somewhere, a bright twin if we are dark, a dark twin if we are bright, then that hut was surely such a changeling to one of our cells. There were windows on all sides save the one through which we entered by the open door, and they had neither bars nor panes nor any other sort of closing. Floor and walls and window frames were of the branches of the yellow tree; branches not planed to boards but left in the round so that I could, in places, see sunlight through the walls, and if I had dropped a worn orichalk, it would very likely have come to rest on the ground below. There was no ceiling, only a triangular space beneath the roof where pans and food bags hung.

A woman was reading aloud in a corner, with a naked man crouched at her feet. The man we had seen from the path stood at the window opposite the door, looking out. I felt that he knew we had come (and even if he had not seen us a few moments before, he must certainly have felt the hut shake when we climbed the ladder), but that he wished to pretend he did not. There is something in the line of the back when a man turns so as not to see, and it was evident in his.

The woman read: "Then he went up from the plain to Mt. Nebo, the headland that faces the city, and the Compassionating showed him the whole country, all the land as far as the Western Sea. Then he said to him: 'This is the land I swore to your fathers I should give their sons. You have seen it, but you shall not set your feet upon it.' So there he died, and was buried in the ravine."

The naked man at her feet nodded. "It is even so with our own masters, Preceptress. With the smallest finger it is given. But the thumb is hooked into it, and a man has only to take the gift, and dig in the floor of his house, and cover all with a mat, than the thumb begins to pull and bit by bit the gift rises from the earth and ascends into the sky and is seen no more."

The woman seemed impatient with this, and began, "No, Isangoma—" But the man at the window interrupted her without turning around. "Be quiet, Marie. I want to hear what he has to say. You can explain later."

"A nephew of mine," the naked man continued, "a member of my own fire circle, had no fish. And so he took up his gowdalie and went to a certain pool. So quietly did he lean over the water he night have been a tree." The naked man leaped up as he said this, and posed his sinewy frame as though to spear the woman's feet with a shaft of air. "Long, long he stood . . . until the monkeys no longer feared him and returned to drop sticks in the water, and the hesperom fluttered to her nest. A big fish came out of his den in the sunken trunks. My nephew watched him circle, slowly, slowly. He swam near the surface, and then when my nephew was about to drive home the three-toothed spear, there was no longer a fish to be seen, but a lovely woman. At first my nephew thought the fish was the fish-king, who had changed his form that he might not be speared. Then he saw the fish moving beneath the woman's face, and knew that he saw a reflection. He looked up at once, but there was nothing to be seen but the whisk of the vines. The woman was gone!" The naked man looked up, mimicking very well the amazement of the fisherman. "That night my nephew went to the Numen, the Proud One, and slit the throat of a young oreodont, saying—"

Agia whispered to me, "In the name of the Theoanthropos, how long do you mean to stay here? This could go on all day."

"Let me look about the hut," I whispered back, "and we'll go."

"Mighty is the Proud One, sacred all his names. Everything found beneath leaves is his, the storms are carried in his arms, the poison holds no death unless his curse is pronounced over it!"

The woman said, "I don't think we need all these praises of your fetish, Isangoma. My husband wishes to hear your story. Very well, but tell it and spare us your litanies."

"The Proud One protects his supplicant! Would not he be shamed if one who adores him were to die?"

"Isangoma!"

From the window, the man said, "He's afraid, Marie. Can't you hear it in his voice?"

"There is no fear for those who wear the sign of the Proud One!

His breath is the mist that hides the infant uakaris from the claws of the margay!"

"Robert, if you won't do something about this, I will. Isangoma, be silent. Or leave and never return here again."

"The Proud One knows Isangoma loves the Preceptress. He would save her if he could."

"Save me from what? Do you think there's one of your dreadful beasts here? If there were, Robert would shoot it with his gun."

"The tokoloshe, Preceptress. The tokoloshe come. But the Proud One in his condensation will protect us. He is the mighty commander of all tokoloshe! When he roars, they hide beneath the fallen leaves."

"Robert, I think he's lost his mind."

"He has eyes, Marie, and you don't."

"What do you mean by that? And why do you keep looking out that window?"

Quite slowly, the man turned to face us. For a moment he looked at Agia and me, then he turned away. His expression was the one I have seen our clients wear when Master Gurloes showed them the instruments to be used in their anacrisis.

"Robert, for goodness' sake tell me what's wrong with you."

"As Isangoma says, the tokoloshe are here. Not his, I think, but ours. Death and the Lady. Have you heard of them, Marie?"

The woman shook her head. She had risen from her seat and opened the lid of a small chest.

"You wouldn't have, I suppose. It's a picture—an artistic theme, rather. Pictures by several artists. Isangoma, I don't think your Proud One has much authority over these tokoloshe. These come from Paris, where I used to be a student, to remonstrate with me for giving up art for this."

The woman said, "You have a fever, Robert. That's obvious. I'm going to give you something, and you'll feel better soon."

The man looked toward us again, at Agia's face and my own, as though he did not wish to do so but found himself unable to control the motion of his eyes. "If I am ill, Marie, then the diseased know things the well have overlooked. Isangoma knows they're here too, don't forget. Didn't you feel the floor tremble while you were reading to him? That was when they came in, I think."

"I've just poured you a glass of water so you can swallow your quinine. There are no ripples in it."

"What are they, Isangoma? Tokoloshe—but what are tokoloshe?"

"Bad spirits, Preceptor. When man think bad thought or woman do bad thing, there is another tokoloshe. He stay behind. Man think: *No one know, everyone dead.* But tokoloshe remain until end of world. Then everyone will see, know what that man did."

The woman said, "What a horrible idea."

Her husband's hands clenched the yellow stick of the windowsill. "Don't you see they are only the results of what we do? They are the spirits of the future, and we make them ourselves."

"They are a lot of pagan nonsense, that's what I see, Robert. Listen. Your vision is so sharp, can't you listen for a moment?"

"I am listening. What do you want to say?"

"Nothing. I only want you to listen. What do you hear?"

The hut fell silent. I listened too, and could not have not listened if I had wanted to. Outside the monkeys chattered, and the parrots screamed as before. Then I heard, over the jungle noises, a faint humming, as though an insect as large as a boat were flying far away.

"What is it?" the man asked.

"The mail plane. If you're lucky, you should be able to see it soon."

The man craned his neck out the window, and I, curious to see what he was looking for, went to the window on his left and looked out as well. The foliage was so thick that at first it seemed impossible to see anything, but he was staring almost straight up past the edge of the thatch, and I found a patch of blue there.

The humming grew louder. Into view came the strangest flier I have ever seen. It was winged, as if it had been built by some race that had not yet realized that since it would not flap wings like a bird in any case, there was no reason its lift, like a kite's, could not come from its hull. There was a bulbous swelling on each argent pinion, and a third at the front of the hull; the light seemed to glimmer before these swellings.

"In three days we could be at the landing strip, Robert. The next time it comes, we would be waiting."

"If the Lord has sent us here—"

"Yes, Preceptor, we must do what the Proud One wishes! There is none like he! Preceptress, let me dance to the Proud One, and sing his song. Then it may be the tokoloshe will depart."

The naked man snatched her book from the woman and began to beat it with the flat of his hand—rhythmic claps as though he played a tambour. His feet scraped the uneven floor, and his voice, beginning with a melodic stridulation, became the voice of a child:

> "In the night when all is silent,
>   Hear him screaming in the treetops!
>   See him dancing in the fire!
> He lives in the arrow poison,
>   Tiny as a yellow firefly!
>   Brighter than a falling star!
> Hairy men walk in the forest—"

Agia said, "Im leaving, Severian," and stepped through the doorway behind us. "If you want to stay and watch this, you can. But you'll have to get your avern yourself, and find your way to the Sanguinary Fields. Do you know what will happen if you fail to appear?"

"They'll employ assassins, you said."

"And the assassins will employ the snake called yellowbeard. Not on you, at first. On your family, if you have any, and your friends. Since I've been with you all over our quarter of the city, that probably means me."

> "He comes when the sun is setting,
>   See his feet upon the water!
>   Tracks of flame across the water!"

The chant continued, but the chanter knew we were going: his singsong held a note of triumph. I waited until Agia had reached the ground, then followed her.

She said, "I thought you'd never leave. Now that you're here, do you really like this place so much?" The metallic colors of her torn gown seemed as angry as she herself against the cool green of the unnaturally dark leaves.

"No," I said. "But I find it interesting. Did you see their flier?"

"When you and the inmate looked out the windows? I wasn't such a fool."

"It was like no other I've ever seen. I should have been looking at the roof facets of this building, but instead I saw the flier *he* expected to see. At least, that's what it seemed like. Something from somewhere else. A little while ago I wanted to tell you about a friend of a friend of mine who was caught in Father Inire's mirrors. She found herself in another world, and even when she returned to Thecla—that was my friend's name—she wasn't quite sure she had found her way back to her real point of origin. I wonder if we aren't still in the world those people left, instead of them in ours."

Agia had already started down the path. Flecks of sunlight seemed to turn her brown hair to dark gold as she looked over her shoulder to say, "I told you certain visitors are attracted to certain bioscapes."

I trotted to catch up with her.

"As time goes on, their minds bend to conform to their surroundings, and it may be they bend ours as well. It was probably an ordinary flier you saw."

"He saw us. So did the savage."

"From what I've heard, the further an inhabitant's consciousness must be warped, the more residual perceptions are likely to remain. When I meet monsters, wild men, and so forth in these gardens, I find they're a lot more likely to be at least partially aware of me than the others are."

"Explain the man," I said.

"I didn't build this place, Severian. All I know is that if you turn around on the path now, that last place we saw probably won't be there. Listen, I want you to promise me that when we get out of here, you'll let me take you straight to the Garden of Endless Sleep. We don't have time left for anything else, not even the Garden of Delectation. And you're not really the kind of person who ought to go sightseeing in here."

"Because I wanted to stay in the Sand Garden?"

"Partly, yes. You're going to make trouble for me here sooner or later, I think."

As she said that, we rounded one of the path's seemingly endless sinuosities. A log tagged with a small white rectangle that could only be a species sign lay across the path, and through the crowding leaves on our left I could see the wall, its greenish glass forming an unobtrusive backdrop for the foliage. Agia had already taken a step past the door when I shifted *Terminus Est* to the other hand and opened it for her.

XXII

Dorcas

WHEN I HAD FIRST heard of the flower, I had imagined averns would be grown on benches, in rows like those in the conservatory of the Citadel. Later, when Agia had told me more about the Botanic Gardens, I conceived of a place like the necropolis where I had frolicked as a boy, with trees and crumbling tombs, and walkways paved with bones.

The reality was very different—a dark lake in an infinite fen. Our feet sank in sedge, and a cold wind whistled past with nothing, as it seemed, to stop it before it reached the sea. Rushes grew beside the track on which we walked, and once or twice a water bird passed overhead, black against a misted sky.

I had been telling Agia about Thecla. Now she touched my arm. "You can see them from here, though we'll have to go half around the lake to pluck one. Look where I'm pointing . . . that smudge of white."

"They don't look dangerous from here."

"They've done for a great many people, I can assure you. Some of them are interred in this garden, I imagine."

So there were graves after all. I asked where the mausoleums stood.

"There aren't any. No coffins either, or mortuary urns, or any of that clutter. Look at the water slopping at your boots."

I did. It was as brown as tea.

"It has the property of preserving corpses. The bodies are weighed by forcing lead shot down their throats, then sunk here with their positions mapped so they can be fished up again later if anyone wants to look at them."

I would readily have sworn that there was no one within a league of where we stood. Or at least (if the segments of the glass building really confined the spaces they enclosed as they were supposed to do) within the borders of the Garden of Endless Sleep. But Agia had no sooner said what she did than the head and shoulders of an old man appeared over the top of some reeds a dozen paces off. "'Tis not true," he called. "I know they say so, but 'tisn't right."

Agia, who had allowed the torn bodice of her gown to hang as it would, quickly drew it up again. "I didn't know I was talking to anyone but my escort here."

The old man ignored the rebuke. No doubt his thoughts were already too involved with the remark he had overheard for him to pay much heed. "I've the figure here—would you like to see it? You, young sieur—you've an education, anyone can tell that. Will you look?" He appeared to be carrying a staff. I watched its head rise and fall several times before I understood that he was poling toward us.

"More trouble," Agia said. "We'd better go."

I asked if it might not be possible for the old man to ferry us across the lake, thus saving us the long walk around.

He shook his head. "Too heavy for my little boat. There's but room for Cas and me here. You great folk would capsize us."

The prow came into sight, and I saw that what he said was true: the skiff was so small it seemed almost too much to ask of it that it keep the old man himself afloat, though he was bowed and shrunken by age (he appeared older even than Master Palaemon) until he could hardly have weighed more than a boy of ten. There was no one in it with him.

"Your pardon, sieur," he said. "But I can't come no nearer. Wet she may be, but she gets too dry for me, or you couldn't walk upon it. Can you step here by the edge so's I can show you my figure?"

I was curious to see what it was he wanted of us, so I did as he asked, Agia following me reluctantly.

"Here now." Reaching into his tunic he pulled out a small scroll. "Here is the position. Have a look, young sieur."

The scroll was headed with some name and a long description of where this person had lived, whose wife she was, and what her husband had done for a living; all of which I only pretended to glance at, I am afraid. Below the description were a crude map and two numbers.

"Now you see, sieur, it ought to be easy enough. First number there, that's paces *over* from the Fulstrum. Second number's paces *up*. Now would you believe that for all these years I've been trying to find her, and never found her yet?" Looking at Agia, he drew himself up until he stood almost normally.

"I'd believe it," Agia said. "And if it will satisfy you, I'm sorry to hear it. But it has nothing to do with us."

She turned to go, but the old man thrust out his pole to prevent my following her. "Don't you heed what they say. They put them where the figure shows, but they don't stay there. Some has been see'd in the river, even." He looked vaguely toward the horizon. "Out there."

I told him I doubted that was possible.

"All the water here, where'd you think it come from? There's a conduit underground that brings it, and if it didn't this whole place'd dry out. When they get to moving about, what's to prevent one from swimming through? What's to prevent twenty? Can't be any current to speak of. You and her—you come to get a avern, did you? You know why they planted 'em here to begin with?"

I shook my head.

"For the manatees. They're in the river, and used to swim in through the conduit. It scared the kin to see their faces bobbing in the lake, so Father Inire had the gardeners plant the averns. I was here and saw it. Just a little man he is, with a wry neck and bow legs. If a manatee comes now, those flowers kill it in the night. One morning I come looking for Cas like I always do unless I've something else I have to take care of, and there was two curators on the shore with a harpoon. Dead manatee in the lake, they said. I went out with my hook and got it, and it wasn't no manatee, but a man. He'd spit up his lead, or they hadn't put enough in. Looked as good as you or her, and better than me."

"Had he been dead long?"

"No way of telling, for the water here pickles them. You'll hear it said it turns their skin to leather, and so it does. But don't think of the sole of your boot when you hear it. More like a woman's glove."

Agia was far ahead of us, and I began to walk after her. The old man followed us, poling his skiff parallel to the floating path of sedge.

"I told them I'd had better luck in one day for them than I've had in forty years for myself. Here's what I use." He held up an iron grapple on a length of rope. "Not that I haven't caught aplenty, all kinds. But not Cas. I started where the figure showed, year after she died. She wasn't there, so I kept working my way out. After five years of that I was a ways far away—that's what I thought then—from what it said. I got to be afraid she might be there after all, so I begun over. First where it said, then working out. Ten years of that. I got to be afraid again, so what I do now is start in the morning where it says, and make my first cast there. After that I go to where I stopped the last time, and circle out some more. She's not where it says—I know that, I know everyone that's there now, and some of them I've pulled up a hundred times. But she's wandering, and I keep thinking maybe she'll come home."

"She was your wife?"

The old man nodded, and to my surprise said nothing.

"Why do you want to recover her body?"

Still he said nothing. His pole made no sound as it slipped in and out of the water; the skiff left only the faintest of wakes behind it, tiny ripples that lapped the side of the sedge track like the tongues of kittens.

"Are you sure you would know her, after so long a time, if you found her?"

"Yes . . . yes." He nodded, slowly at first, then vigorously. "You're thinking I may have hooked her already. Drug her up, looked her in the face, and throwed her back in. Ain't you? It ain't possible. Not know Cas? You wondered why I want her back. One reason is the memory I have of her—the one that's strongest—is of this brown water closing over her face. Her eyes shut. Do you know about that?"

"I'm not certain I know what you mean."

"They've a cement they put on the lids. It's supposed to hold them down forever, but when the water hit them, they opened. Explain that. It's what I remember, what comes into my mind when I try to sleep. This brown water rolling over her face, and her eyes opening blue through the brown. I have to go to sleep five, six times every night, what with the waking up. Before I lie down here myself I'd like to have another picture there—her face coming back up, even if it's only on the end of my hook. You follow what I say?"

I thought of Thecla and the trickle of blood from beneath the door of her cell, and I nodded.

"Then there's the other thing. Cas and I, we had a little shop. Cloisonné-work, mostly. Her father and brother had the trade of making it, and they set us up on Signal Street, just past the middle, next to the auction house. The building's still there, though nobody lives in it. I'd go over to the inlaws and carry the boxes home on my back, and pull them open, and put the pieces on our shelves. Cas priced 'em, sold, and kept everything so clean! You know how long we did that? Run our little place?"

I shook my head.

"Four years, less a month and a week. Then she died. Cas died. It wasn't long before it was all gone, but it was the biggest part of my life. I've got a place to sleep in a loft now. A man I knew years before, though that was years after Cas was gone, he lets me sleep there. There isn't a piece of cloisonné in it, or a garment, or so much as a nail from the old shop. I tried to keep a locket and Cas's combs, but everything's gone. Tell me this, now. How am I to know it wasn't no dream?"

It seemed to me that the old man might be spell-caught, as the people in the house of yellow wood had been; so I said, "I have no way of knowing. Perhaps, as you say, it was a dream. I think you torment yourself too much."

His mood changed in an instant, as I have seen the moods of young children do, and he laughed. "It's easy to see, sieur, that despite the outfit under that mantle, you're no torturer. I do truly wish I could ferry you and your doxie. Since I can't, there's a fellow farther along that has a bigger boat. He comes here pretty often, and he talks to me sometimes like you did. Tell him I hope he'll take you across."

I thanked him and hurried after Agia, who by this time was a great distance ahead. She was limping, and I recalled how far she had walked today after wrenching her leg. As I was about to overtake her and give her my arm, I made one of those missteps that seem disastrous and enormously humiliating at the time, though one laughs at them afterward; and in so doing I set in motion one of the strangest incidents of my admittedly strange career. I began to run, and in running came too near the inner side of a curve in the track.

At one moment I was bounding along on the springy sedge—at the next I was floundering in icy brown water, much impeded by my mantle. For the space of a breath I knew again the terror of drowning; then I righted myself and got my face above water. The habits developed on all those summer swims in Gyoll reasserted themselves: I blew the water from my nose and mouth, took a deep breath, and pushed my sopping hood back from my face.

I was no sooner calm than I realized that I had dropped *Terminus Est*, and at that moment losing that blade seemed more terrible than the chance of death. I dove, not even troubling to kick off my boots, forcing my way through an umber fluid that was not water purely, but water laced and thickened with the fibrous stems of the reeds. These stems, though they multiplied the threat of drowning many times, saved *Terminus Est* for me—she would surely have outraced me to the bottom and buried herself in the mud there despite the meager air retained in her sheath, if her fall had not been obstructed. As it was, eight or ten cubits beneath the surface one frantically groping hand encountered the blessed, familiar shape of her onyx grip.

At the same instant, my other hand touched an object of a completely different kind. It was another human hand, and its grasp (for it had seized my own the moment I touched it) coincided so perfectly with the recovery of *Terminus Est* that it seemed the hand's owner was returning my property to me, like the tall mistress of the Pelerines. I felt a surge of lunatic gratitude, then fear returned tenfold: the hand was pulling my own, drawing me down.

XXIII

Hildegrin

WITH WHAT MUST surely have been the last strength I possessed, I managed to throw *Terminus Est* onto the floating track of sedge and grasp its ragged margin before I sank again.

Someone caught me by the wrist. I looked up expecting Agia; it was not she but a woman younger still, with streaming yellow hair. I strove to thank her, but water, not words, poured from my mouth. She tugged and I struggled, and at last I lay wholly supported on the sedge, so weak I could do nothing more.

I must have rested there at least as long as it takes to say the angelus, and perhaps longer. I was conscious of the cold, which grew worse, and of the sagging of the whole fabric of rotting plants, which bent beneath my weight until I was half submerged again. I breathed in great gasps that failed to satisfy my lungs, and coughed water; water trickled from my nostrils too. Someone (it was a man's voice, a loud one I seemed to have heard a long time before) said, "Pull him over or he'll sink." I was lifted by my belt. In a few moments more I was able to stand, though my legs trembled so I feared I would fall.

Agia was there, and the blond girl who had helped me onto the sedge, and a big, beef-faced man. Agia asked what had happened, and half-conscious though I was I noticed how pale she was.

"Give him time," the big man said. "He'll be all right soon enough." And then, "Who in Phlegethon are you?"

He was looking at the girl, who seemed as dazed as I felt. She made a stammering sound, "D-d-d-d," then hung her head and was silent. From hair to heels she was smeared with mud, and what clothing she had seemed no better than rags.

The big man asked Agia, "Where did that one come from?"

"I don't know. When I looked back to see what was keeping Severian, she was pulling him onto this floating path."

"Good thing she did, too. Good for him, anyway. Is she mad? Or chant-caught here, you think?"

I said, "Whatever she is, she saved me. Can't you give her something to cover herself with? She must be freezing." I was freezing myself, now that I was alive enough to notice it.

The big man shook his head, and seemed to draw his heavy coat about him more closely. "Not unless she gets clean I won't. And she won't unless she's put back in the water, and stirred around, too. But I've something here that's the next best thing, and maybe better." From one of his coat pockets he took a metal flask shaped like a dog, which he handed to me.

A bone in the dog's mouth proved to be the stopper. I offered the flask to the blond girl, who at first seemed not to know what to do with it. Agia took it from her and held it to her lips until she had taken several swallows, then handed it back to me. The contents seemed to be plum brandy; its fiery impact washed away the bitterness of the fen water very pleasantly. By the time I replaced the bone in the dog's mouth, his belly was, I think, better than half empty.

"Now then," said the big man, "I think you people ought to tell me who you are and what you're doing here—and don't none of you say you've just come to see the sights of the garden. I see enough gawkers these days to know them before they come in hailing distance." He looked at me. "That's a good big whittle you've got there, to begin with."

Agia said, "The armiger is in costume. He has been challenged, and has come to cut an avern."

"He's in costume and you aren't, I suppose. Do you think I don't know stage brocade? And bare feet too, when I see them?"

"I never said I was not in costume, nor that I was of his rank. As for my shoes, I left them outside so as not to ruin them in this water."

The big man nodded in a way that gave no clue as to whether he believed her or not. "Now you, goldy-hair. The embroidered baggage here has already said she don't know you. And from the look of him, I don't believe her fish—that you pulled out for her, and a good piece of work that was, too—knows any more than I do. Maybe not that much. So who are you?"

The blond girl swallowed. "Dorcas."

"And how'd you get here, Dorcas? And how'd you get in the water? For that's where you've been, plainly. You couldn't of got that wet just pulling out our young friend."

The brandy had brought a flush to the girl's cheeks, but her face was as vacant and bewildered as before, or nearly so. "I don't know," she whispered.

Agia asked, "You don't remember coming here?"

Dorcas shook her head.

"Then what's the last thing you do remember?"

There was a long silence. The wind seemed to be blowing harder than ever, and despite the drink, I was miserably cold. At last Dorcas murmured, "Sitting by a window . . . There were pretty things in the window. Trays and boxes, and a rood."

The big man said, "Pretty things? Well, if you was there, I'm assured there was."

"She's mad," Agia said. "Either someone's been taking care of her and she's wandered away, or no one is taking care of her, which seems more likely from the state of her clothes, and she wandered in here when the curators weren't looking."

"It may be somebody's cracked her over the head, took her things, and threw her in here thinking she was gone. There's more ways in, Mistress Slops, than the curator knows of. Or maybe somebody brought her in to be sunk when she was only sick and sleepin'. In a com'er, as they call it, and the water woke her up."

"Surely whoever brought her in would have seen her."

"They can stay under a long time in a com'er, so I've heard. But whichever way it was, it don't much matter now. Here she is, and it's up to her, I should say, to find out where she come from and who she is."

I had dropped the brown mantle and was trying to wring my guild cloak dry; but I looked up when Agia said, "You've been asking all of us who we are. Who are you?"

"You've every right to know," the big man said. "Every right in the world, and I'll give you better bona fides than any of you have given me. Only after I does so, I must be about my own business. I come because I saw the young armiger here drowning, like any good man would. But I've my own affairs to take care of, the same as the next."

With that he pulled off his tall hat, and reaching inside produced a greasy card about twice the size of the calling cards I had occasionally seen in the Citadel. He handed it to Agia, and I peered over her shoulder. In florid script, the legend read:

HILDEGRIN THE BADGER
Excavations of *all* kinds, by a single
digger or 20 score.
Stone is not too hard nor mud too soft.
Ask on *Argosy* Street at the sign of the
BLIND SHOVEL
Or inquire at the Alticamelus around
the corner on Velleity.

"And that's who I am, Mistress Slops and young sieur—which I hope you won't mind my calling you, firstly because you're younger nor me, and secondly because you're a sight younger than what she is, for all you was probably born only a couple years sooner. And I'll be on my way."

I stopped him. "Before I fell in, I met an old man in a skiff who told me there was someone farther down the track who could ferry us across the lake. I think you must be the man he referred to. Will you take us?"

"Ah, the one what's lookin' for his wife, poor soul. Well, he's been a good friend to me many a time, so if he recommends you, I suppose I'd better do it. My scow will hold four in a pinch."

He strode off motioning for us to follow; I noticed that his boots, which seemed to have been greased, sank in the sedge even deeper than my own. Agia said, "She's not coming with us." Still it was obvious that she (Dorcas) was, trailing along behind Agia and looking so forlorn that I dropped behind to try to comfort her. "I'd lend you my mantle," I whispered to her, "if it weren't so wet it would make you colder than you are already. But if you'll go along this track the other way, you'll come out of here altogether and into a corridor where it's warmer and drier. Then if you'll look for a door with *Jungle Garden* on it, that will let you into a place were the sun is warm and you'll be quite comfortable."

I had no sooner spoken than I remembered the pelycosaur we had seen in the jungle. Fortunately, perhaps, Dorcas showed no sign of having heard what I said. Something in her face conveyed that she was afraid of Agia, or at least aware, in a helpless way, of having displeased her; but there was no other indication she was any more alert to her surroundings than a somnambulist.

Conscious that I had failed to relieve her misery, I began again. "There's a man in the corridor, a curator. I'm sure he'll at least try to find some clothes and a fire for you."

The wind whipped Agia's chestnut hair as she looked back at us. "There are too many of these beggar girls for anyone to be worried about one, Severian. Including yourself."

At the sound of Agia's voice, Hildegrin glanced over his shoulder. "I know a woman might take her in. Yes, and clean her up and give her some clothes. There's a high-bred shape under that mud, thin though she is."

"What are you doing here, anyway?" Agia snapped. "You contract laborers, according to your card, but what's your business here?"

"Just what you said, Mistress. My business."

Dorcas had begun to shiver. "Honestly," I told her, "all you have to do is go back. It's much warmer in the corridor. Don't go in the Jungle Garden. You might go into the Sand Garden, it's sunny and dry in there."

Something in what I had said seemed to touch a chord in her. "Yes," she whispered. "Yes."

"The Sand Garden? You'd like that?"

Very softly: "Sun."

"Here's the old scow now," Hildegrin announced. "With so many, we're going to have to be particular about the seatin'. And there's to be no movin' about—she'll be low in the water. One of the women in the bow, please, and the other and the young armiger in the stern."

I said, "I'd be happy to take an oar."

"Ever rowed before? I thought not. No, you'd best sit in the stern like I told you. It ain't much harder pullin' two oars than one, and I've done it many a time, believe me, though there was half a dozen in her with me."

His boat was like himself, wide, rough, and heavy-looking. Bow and stern were square, so much so that there was hardly any horizontal taper from the waist, where the rowlocks were, though the hull was shallower at the ends. Hildegrin got in first, and standing with one leg to either side of the bench, used an oar to nudge the boat closer to shore for us.

"You," Agia said, taking Dorcas by the arm. "You sit up there in front."

Dorcas seemed willing to obey, but Hildegrin stopped her. "If you don't mind, Mistress," he said to Agia, "I'd sooner it was you in the bow. I won't be able to keep my eye on her, you see, when I'm rowin', unless she sits behind. She's not right, which even you and me can agree on, and low as we'll be I'd like to know if she starts friskin' around."

Dorcas surprised us all by saying, "I'm not mad. It's just . . . I feel as if I've just been wakened."

Hildegrin made her sit in the stern with me nonetheless. "Now this," he said as he pushed us off, "this is something you're not likely to forget if you've never done it before. Crossin' the Lake of Birds here in the middle of the Garden of Everlastin' Sleep." His oars dipping into the water made a dull and somehow melancholy sound.

I asked why it was called the Lake of Birds.

"Because so many's found dead in the water, is what some say. But it might only be that that's because there's so many here. There's a great deal said against Death. I mean by the people that has to die, drawin' her picture like a crone with a sack, and all that. But she's a good friend to birds, Death is. Wherever there's dead men and quiet, you'll find a good many birds, that's been my experience."

Recalling how the thrushes sang in our necropolis, I nodded.

"Now if you'll look past my shoulder, you'll have a clear view of the shore ahead of us and be able to see a lot of things you couldn't before, because of the rushes growin' all around you back there. You'll notice, if it's not too misty, that the land rises farther on. The bogginess stops there, and the trees begin. Can you see 'em?"

I nodded again, and beside me Dorcas nodded as well.

"That's because this whole peep show is meant to look like the mouth of a dead volcaner. The mouth of a dead man is what some say, but that's not really so. If it was, they'd of put in teeth. You'll remember, though, that when you come in here you come up through a pipe in the ground."

Once more, Dorcas and I nodded together. Though Agia was no more than two strides from us, she was nearly out of sight behind Hildegrin's broad shoulders and fearnought coat.

"Over there," he continued, jerking his square chin to show the direction, "you ought to be able to see a spot of black. Just about halfway up, it is, between the bog and the rim. Some sees it and thinks it's where they come out of, but that's behind you and lower down, and a whole lot smaller. This that you see now is the Cave of the Cumaean—the woman that knows the future and the past and everything else. There's some that say this whole place was built only for her, though I don't believe it."

Softly, Dorcas asked, "How could that be?" and Hildegrin misunderstood her, or at least pretended to do so.

"The Autarch wants her here, so they say, so he can come and talk without travelin' to the other side of the world. I wouldn't know about that, but sometimes I see somebody walkin' around up there, and metal or maybe a jewel or two flashin'. Who it is I wouldn't know, and since I don't want to know my future—and I know my past, I should think, better than her—I don't go near the cave. People come sometimes hopin' to know when they'll be married, or about success in trade. But I've observed they don't often come back."

We had nearly reached the center of the lake. The Garden of Endless Sleep rose around us like the sides of a vast bowl, mossy with pines toward the lip, scummed with rushes and sedge below. I was still very cold, more so because of the inactivity of sitting in the boat while another rowed; I was beginning to worry about what the immersion in water might do to the blade of *Terminus Est* if I did not dry and oil it soon, yet even so, the spell of the place held me. (A spell there was, surely, in this garden. I could almost hear it humming over the water, voices chanting in a language I did not know but understood.) I think it held everyone, even Hildegrin, even Agia. For some time we rowed in silence; I saw geese, alive and content for all I could tell, bobbing a long way off; and once, like something in a dream, the nearly human face of a manatee looking into my own through a few spans of brownish water.

XXIV

The Flower of Dissolution

BESIDE ME, Dorcas plucked a water hyacinth and put it in her hair. Except for the vague spot of white on the bank some distance ahead, it was the first flower I had seen in the Garden of Endless Sleep; I looked for others, but saw none.

Is it possible the flower came into being only because Dorcas reached for it? In daylight moments, I know as well as the next that such things are impossible; but I am writing by night, and then, when I sat in that boat with the hyacinth less than a cubit from my eyes, I wondered at the dim light and recalled Hildegrin's remark of a moment before, a remark that implied (though quite possibly he did not know it) that the seeress's cave, and thus this garden, was on the opposite side of the world. There, as Master Malrubius had taught us long ago, all was reversed: warmth to the south, cold to the north; light at night, dark by day; snow in summer. The chill I felt would be appropriate then, for it would be summer soon, with sleet riding the wind; the darkness that stood even between my eyes and the blue flowers of the water hyacinth would be appropriate then too, for it would soon be night, with light already in the sky.

The Increate maintains all things in order surely; and the theologicans say light is his shadow. Must it not be then that in darkness order grows ever less, flowers leaping from nothingness into a girl's fingers just as by light in spring they leap from mere filthiness into the air? Perhaps when night closes our eyes there is less order than we believe. Perhaps, indeed, it is this lack of order we perceive as darkness, a randomization of the waves of energy (like a sea), the fields of energy (like a farm) that appear to our deluded eyes—set by light in an order of which they themselves are incapable—to be the real world.

Mist was rising from the water, reminding me first of the swirling motes of straw in the insubstantial cathedral of the Pelerines, then of steam from the soup kettle when Brother Cook carried it into the refectory on a winter afternoon. The witches were said to stir such kettles; but I had never seen one, though their tower stood hardly a chain from ours. I remembered that we rowed across the crater of a volcano. Might it not have been the Cumaean's kettle? Urth's fires were long dead, as Master Malrubius had taught us; it was more than possible that they had cooled long before men had risen from the position of the beasts to cumber her face with their cities. But witches, it was said, raised the dead. Might not the Cumaean raise the dead fires to boil her pot? I dipped my fingers into the water; it was as cold as snow.

Hildegrin leaned toward me as he rowed, then drew away as he pulled his oars. "Goin' to your death," he said. "That's what you're thinkin'. I can see it in your face. To the Sanguin'ry Field, and he'll kill you, whoever he is."

"Are you?" Dorcas asked, and gripped my hand.

When I did not answer, Hildegrin nodded for me. "Don't have to, you know. There's them that doesn't follow the rules, and yet runs free."

"You're mistaken," I said. "I wasn't thinking about mono-machy—or dying either."

In my ear, too softly, I think, even for Hildegrin to hear, Dorcas said, "Yes, you were. Your face was full of beauty, of a kind of nobility. When the world is horrible, then thoughts are high, full of grace and greatness."

I looked at her, thinking she was mocking me, but she was not. "The world is filled half with evil and half with good. We can tilt it forward so that more good runs into our minds, or back, so that more runs into this." A movement of her eyes took in all the lake. "But the quantities are the same, we change only their proportion here or there."

"I would tilt it as far back as I can, until at last the evil runs out altogether," I said.

"It might be the good that would run out. But I am like you; I would bend time backward if I could."

"Nor do I believe that beautiful thoughts—or wise ones—are engendered by external troubles."

"I did not say beautiful thoughts, but thoughts of grace and greatness, though I suppose that is a kind of beauty. Let me show you." She lifted my hand and slipping it inside her rags pressed it to her right breast. I could feel the nipple, as firm as a cherry, and the warmth of the gentle mound beneath it, delicate, feather-soft and alive with racing blood. "Now," she said, "what are your thoughts? If I have made the external world sweet to you, aren't they less than they were?"

"Where did you learn all this?" I asked. Her face was drained of its wisdom, which condensed in crystal drops at the corners of her eyes.

The shore on which the averns grew was less marshy than the other. It seemed strange, after having walked on buoyant sedge and floated on water for so long, to set foot again on soil that was no worse than soft. We had landed at some distance from the plants; but we were near enough now that they were no longer a mere bank of white, but growths of definite color and shape, whose size could be readily estimated. I said, "They are not from here, are they? Not from our Urth." No one replied; I think I must have spoken too softly for any of the others (except perhaps Dorcas) to hear.

They had a stiffness, a geometrical precision, surely born under some other sun. The color of their leaves was that of a scarab's back, but infused with tints at once deeper and more translucent. It seemed to imply the existence of light somewhere, some inconceivable distance away, of a spectrum that would have withered or perhaps enobled the world.

As we walked nearer, Agia leading the way—I following her with Dorcas behind me, and Hildegrin following us—I saw that each leaf was like a dagger blade, stiff and pointed, with edges sharp enough to satisfy even Master Gurloes. Above these leaves, the half-closed white blossoms we had seen from across the lake seemed creations of pure beauty, virginal fantasies guarded by a hundred knives. They were wide and lush, and their petals curled in a way that should have seemed tousled if it had not formed a complex swirling pattern that drew the eye like a spiral limned on a revolving disc.

Agia said, "Good form requires that you pick the plant yourself, Severian. But I'll go with you and show you how. The trick is to put your arm under the lowest leaves, and snap the stem off at the ground."

Hildegrin caught her by the shoulder. "That you won't, Mistress," he said. And then to me, "You go forward since you're of a mind to, young sieur. I'll take the females to safety."

I was already several strides past him, but I stopped for an instant when he spoke. Luckily Dorcas called out, "Be careful!" at that moment, and I was able to pretend it was her warning that had halted me.

The truth was otherwise. From the time we had met Hildegrin, I had felt certain I had encountered him before, though the shock of recognition that had come so swiftly when I saw Sieur Racho again was in this instance long delayed. Now it had come at last, with paralyzing force.

As I have said, I remember everything; but often I can find a fact, face, or feeling only after a long search. I suppose that in this case, the problem was that from the moment he had bent over me on the sedge track I could see him clearly, and previously I had hardly seen him at all. It was only when he said, *"I'll take these females to safety,"* that my memory closed upon his voice.

"The leaves are poisoned," Agia called. "Twisting your mantle tight about your arm will give you some protection, but try not to touch them. And watch out—you are always closer to an avern than you think."

I nodded to show I understood.

Whether the avern is deadly to the life of its own world I have no way of knowing. It may be that it is not, that it is only dangerous to us by reason of a nature accidentally inimical to our own. Whether that is so or not, the ground between and beneath the plants was covered with short and very fine grass, grass quite different from the coarse growth elsewhere; and this short grass was littered with the curled bodies of bees and dotted with the white bones of birds.

When I was no more than a couple of paces from the plants, I stopped, suddenly aware of a problem I had given no thought to previously. The avern I selected would be my weapon in the contest to come—yet because I knew nothing as yet of the way it would be fought, I had no means of judging which plant might be best adapted to it. I could have gone back and questioned Agia, but I would have felt absurd examining a woman on such a matter, and in the end I decided to trust my judgment, since she would no doubt send me back for another if my first choice were wholly unsuitable.

The averns varied in height from seedlings of hardly more than a span to old plants of three cubits or a little less. These older plants had fewer, though larger, leaves. Those of the smaller ones were narrower, and so closely spaced that the stems were completely hidden; those of the big plants were much broader in proportion to their length, and somewhat separated on the fleshy-looking stems. If (as seemed likely) the Septentrion and I were to use our plants as maces, the largest possible plant with the longest possible stem and the stoutest possible leaves would be the best. But these all grew well away from the edges of the planting, so that it would be necessary to break down a number of smaller plants to reach them;

and to do that by the method Agia had advised was clearly impossible, because the leaves of many of the smaller plants grew nearly to the ground.

In the end I chose one about two cubits high. I had knelt beside it and was reaching toward it when as though a veil had been snatched away I realized that my hand, which I had thought still several spans from the needlelike point of the nearest leaf, was about to be impaled. I drew it back hurriedly; the plant seemed almost out of reach—indeed, I was not certain I could touch its stem even by lying prone. The temptation to use my sword was very great, but I felt it would disgrace me before Agia and Dorcas to do so, and I knew I would have to handle the plant during the combat in any case.

I advanced my hand again, cautiously, this time keeping my forearm in contact with the ground, and discovered that though I had to press my shoulder against the grass as well to prevent my upper arm from being stabbed by the lowest leaves, I could touch the stem quite readily. A point that appeared to be half a cubit from my face trembled with my breath.

It was while I was snapping off the stem—no easy task—that I saw the reason only the short, soft grass flourished beneath the averns. One of the leaves of the plant I was breaking had cut half through a blade of coarse marsh grass, and the entire grass plant, almost an ell across, had begun to wither.

Once picked, the plant was an enormous nuisance, as I ought to have anticipated. It would plainly have been impossible to carry it in Hildegrin's boat as it was without killing one or more of us, so before we reembarked I had to climb the slope and cut a sapling. When the twigs had been lopped, Agia and I bound the avern to one end of its spindly trunk, so that as we made our way through the city later, I appeared to be bearing some grotesque standard.

Then Agia explained the use of the plant as a weapon; and I broke a second plant (although she objected, and at even greater risk, I fear, than before, since I was somewhat too confident) and practiced what she had told me.

The avern is not, as I had assumed, merely a viper-toothed mace. Its leaves can be detached by twisting them between the thumb and forefinger in such a way that the hand does not contact the edges or the point. The leaf is then in effect a handleless blade, envenomed and razor-sharp, ready to throw. The fighter holds the plant in his left hand by the base of the stem and plucks the lower leaves to throw with his right. Agia cautioned me, however, to keep my own plant out of my opponent's reach, since as the leaves are removed an area of bare stem appears, and this he might grasp and use to wrest my plant from me.

When I flourished the second plant and practiced striking out with it and picking and throwing the leaves, I found that my own avern was likely to be almost as great a danger to me as the Septentrion's. If I held it near me, there was a grave risk of pricking my arm or chest with the long lower leaves; and the flower with its swirling pattern held my gaze whenever I glanced down to tear off a leaf, and with the dry lust of death sought to draw me to it. All this seemed unpleasant enough; but when I had learned to keep my eyes away from the half-closed blossom, I reflected that my opponent would be exposed to the same dangers.

Throwing the leaves was easier than I had supposed. Their surfaces were glossy, like the leaves of many of the plants I had seen in the Jungle Garden, so that they left the fingers readily, and they were heavy enough to fly far and true. They could be thrown point-foremost like any knife, or made to spin in flight to cut down anything in their path with their deadly edges.

I was eager, of course, to question Hildegrin about Vodalus; but no opportunity to do so came until he had rowed us back across the silent lake. Then for a moment Agia became so intent on driving Dorcas away that I was able to draw him to one side and whisper that I, too, was a friend to Vodalus.

"You've mistaken me, young sieur, for somebody else—do you refer to Vodalus the outlaw?"

"I never forget a voice," I told him, "or anything else." And then in my eagerness, I impulsively added what was perhaps the worst thing I could have said: "You tried to brain me with your shovel." His face became masklike at once, and he stepped back into his boat and rowed out onto the brown water.

When Agia and I left the Botanic Gardens, Dorcas was still with us. Agia was anxious to make her go away, and for a time I permitted her to try. I was moved in part by the fear that with Dorcas near it would be impossible for me to persuade Agia to lie with me; but even more by a vague appreciation of the pain Dorcas would feel, lost and dismayed as she was already, if she should see me die. Only a short time before, I had poured out to Agia all my sorrow at the death of Thecla. Now these new concerns had replaced it, and I found I had poured it out indeed, as a man might spill sour wine on the ground. By the use of the language of sorrow I had for the time being obliterated my sorrow—so powerful is the charm of words, which for us reduces to manageable entities all the passions that would otherwise madden and destroy us.

Whatever my motives may have been, and whatever Agia's may have been, and whatever Dorcas's may have been for following us, nothing Agia did succeeded. And in the end, I threatened to strike her if she did not desist, and called to Dorcas, who was then fifty paces or so behind us.

After that we three trudged along in silence, drawing many strange looks. I was soaked to soddenness, and no longer cared whether my mantle covered my fuligin torturer's cloak. Agia in her torn brocade must have looked nearly as strange as I. Dorcas was still smeared with mud—it dried on her in the warm spring wind that now wrapped the city, caking in her golden hair and leaving smears of powdery brown on her pale skin. Above us the avern brooded like a gonfalon; from it there drifted a myrrhic perfume. The half-closed flower still shone as white as bone, but its leaves looked nearly black in the sunlight.

XXV

The Inn of Lost Loves

IT HAS BEEN my good fortune—or evil fortune, as it may be—that the places with which my life has been largely associated have been, with very few exceptions, of the most permanent character. I might tomorrow, if I wished, return to the Citadel and (I think) to the very cot on which I slept as an apprentice. Gyoll still rolls past my city of Nessus; the Botanic Gardens still glitter in the sun, faceted with those strange enclosures wherein a single mood is preserved for all time. When I think of the ephemera of my life, they are likely to be men and women. But there are a few houses as well, and first among these stands the inn at the margin of the Sanguinary Field.

We had walked away the afternoon, down broad avenues and up narrow byways, and always the buildings that hemmed us round were of stone and brick. At last we came to grounds that seemed no grounds at all, for there was no exalted villa at their center. I remember I warned Agia that a storm was brewing—I could feel the closeness of the air, and I saw a line of bitter black along the horizon.

She laughed at me. "What you see and what you feel too is nothing more than the City Wall. It's always like this here. The Wall impedes the movement of the air."

"That line of dark? It goes halfway to the sky."

Agia laughed again, but Dorcas pressed herself against me. "I am afraid, Severian."

Agia heard her. "Of the Wall? It won't hurt you unless it falls on you, and it has stood through a dozen ages." I looked questioningly at her, and she added, "At least it looks that old, and it may be older. Who knows?"

"It could wall out the world. Does it stretch completely around the city?"

"By definition. The city is what is enclosed, though there's open country to the north, so I've heard, and leagues and leagues of ruins in the south, where no one lives. But now, look between those poplars. Do you see the inn?"

I did not, and said so.

"Under the tree. You've promised me a meal, and that's where I want it. We should just have time to eat before you have to meet the Septentrion."

"Not now," I said. "I'll be happy to feed you when my duel is over. I'll make the arrangements now, if you like." I could still find no building, but I had come to see that there was something strange about the tree: a stair of rustic wood twined up the trunk.

"Do so. If you're killed, I'll invite the Septentrion—or if he won't come, that broken sailor who is forever inviting me. We'll drink to you."

A light kindled high in the branches of the tree, and now I saw that a path led up to the stair. Before it, a painted sign showed a weeping woman dragging a bloody sword. A monstrously fat man in an apron stepped out of the shadow and stood beside it, rubbing his hands while he waited our coming. Faintly now, I could hear the clinking of pots.

"Abban at your command," said the fat man when we reached him. "What is your wish?" I noticed he kept a nervous eye on my avern

"We'll have dinner for two, to be served at . . ." I looked at Agia.

"The new watch."

"Good, good. But it cannot be so soon, sieur. It will take longer to prepare. Unless you'll settle for cold meats, a salad, and a bottle of wine?"

Agia looked impatient. "We'll have a roast fowl—a young one."

"As you wish. I'll have the cook begin his preparations now, and you can amuse yourselves with baked stuff after the sieur's victory until the bird is done." Agia nodded, and a look flashed between the two that made me feel certain they had met previously. "Meanwhile," the innkeeper continued, "if you've yet time, I could provide a basin of warm water and a sponge for this other young lady, and perhaps you might all enjoy a glass of Medoc and some biscuits?"

I was suddenly conscious of having fasted since my breakfast at dawn with Baldanders and Dr. Talos, and conscious too that Agia and Dorcas might have had nothing all day. When I nodded, the innkeeper conducted us up the broad, rustic stair; the trunk it circled was a full ten paces around.

"Have you visited us before, sieur?"

I shook my head. "I was about to ask you what manner of inn this is. I've never seen anything like it."

"Nor will you, sieur, except here. But you ought to have come before—we keep a famous kitchen, and dining in the open air gives one the best appetite."

I thought that it must indeed if he maintained such a girth in a place where every room was reached by steps, but I kept the reflection to myself.

"The law, you see, sieur, forbids all buildings so near the Wall. We are permitted, having neither walls nor a roof. Those who attend the Sanguinary Field come here, the famous combatants and heroes, the spectators and physicians, even the ephors. Here's your chamber now."

It was a circular and perfectly level platform. Around and above it, pale green foliage shut out sight and sound. Agia sat in a canvas chair, and I (very tired, I confess) threw myself down beside Dorcas on a couch made of leather and the linked horns of lechwes and waterbucks. When I had laid the avern behind it, I drew *Terminus Est* and began to clean her blade. A scullion brought water and a sponge for Dorcas and, when she saw what I was doing, rags and oil for me. I was soon tapping at the pommel so I could strip the blade from its furniture for a real cleaning.

"Can't you wash yourself?" Agia asked Dorcas.

"I'd like a bath, yes, but not with you watching me."

"Severian will turn his head if you ask him. He did very well in a place where we' were this morning."

"And you, madame," Dorcas said softly. "I'd rather you didn't watch. I'd like a private place, if I might have one."

Agia smiled at that, but I called the scullion again and gave her an orichalk to bring a folding screen. When it was set up, I told Dorcas I would buy her a gown if there were one to be had at the inn.

"No," she said. In a whisper, I asked Agia what she thought was the matter with her.

"She likes what she has, clearly. I must walk with a hand up to hold my bodice if I wouldn't be shamed for life." She let her hand fall, so that her high breasts gleamed in the dying sunlight. "But those rags let her show just leg and chest enough. There's a rent at the groin too, though I dare say you haven't noticed it."

The innkeeper interrupted us, leading in a waiter who carried a plate of pastries, a bottle, and glasses. I explained that my clothing was wet, and he had a brazier brought in—then proceeded to warm himself by it, for all the world as if he stood in his private apartment. "Feels good, this time of year," he said. "The sun's dead and don't know it yet, but we do. If you're killed, you'll get to miss next winter, and if you're hurt bad, you'll get to stay inside. That's what I always tell them. Of course, most of the fights are around midsummer's eve, so it's more appropriate then, so to speak. I don't know if it comforts them or not, but it does no harm."

I took off the brown mantle and my guild cloak, put my boots on a stool near the brazier, and stood beside him to dry my breeches and hose, asking if all those who came this way on monomachy stopped to refresh themselves with him. Like every man who feels himself likely to die, I would have been happy to know that I was taking part in some established tradition.

"*All?* Oh, no," he said. "May moderation and St. Amand bless you, sieur. If everyone who came tarried at my inn, why it wouldn't be my inn—I'd have sold it, and be living comfortable in a big, stone house with atroxes at the door and a few young fellows with knives hanging about me to settle my enemies. No, there's many a one goes by here without a glance, never thinking that when he comes past next time, it may be too late to drink my wine."

"Speaking of which," said Agia, and handed me a glass. It was full to the brim with a dark, crimson vintage. Not a good wine, perhaps—it made my tongue prickle, and carried with its delicious taste something of harshness. But a wonderful wine, a wine better than good, in the mouth of someone as fatigued and cold as I. Agia held a full glass of her own, but I saw by her flaming cheeks and sparkling eyes that she had already downed one other at least. I told her to save something for Dorcas, and she said, "That milk and water virgin? She won't drink it, and it's you who'll need courage—not she."

Not quite honestly, I said I was not afraid.

The innkeeper exclaimed, "That's the way! Don't you be feared, and don't fill your head with no noble thoughts about death and last days and all that. The ones that do is the ones that never come back, you may be sure. Now you was going to order a meal, I think, for you and your two young women afterward?"

"We have ordered it," I said.

"Ordered, but not paid nothing toward, that was my meaning. Also there's the wine and these here *gâteaux secs*. Those must be paid for here and now as they're eaten here and now, and drank up too. For the dinner I'll require a deposit of three orichalks, with two more to be paid when you come to eat it."

"And if I don't come?"

"Then there's no more charge, sieur. That's how I'm able to offer my dinners at such low prices."

The man's complete insensibility disarmed me; I handed over the money and he left us. Agia peeped around the side of the screen behind which Dorcas was cleansing herself with the aid of the scullion, and I sat down again on the couch and took a pastry to go with what remained of my wine.

"If we could make the hinges in this thing lock, Severian, we might enjoy ourselves for a few moments without interruption. We could put a chair against it, but no doubt those two would choose the worst possible moment to squall and knock everything over."

I was about to make some bantering reply when I noticed a scrap of paper, folded many times, that had been put beneath the waiter's tray in such a fashion that it could be seen only by someone sitting where I was. "This is really too much," I said. "A challenge, and now the mysterious note."

Agia came to look. "What are you talking about? Are you drunk already?"

I put my hand on the rounded fullness of her hip, and when she made no objection, used that pleasant handle to draw her toward me until she could see the paper. "What do you suppose it says? 'The Commonwealth has need of you—ride at once . . .' 'Your friend is he who shall say to you, camarilla . . .' 'Beware of the man with pink hair . . .'"

Falling in with the joke, Agia offered, "'Come when you hear three pebbles tap the window . . .' The *leaves*, I should say here. 'The rose hath stabbed the iris, who nectar affords . . .' That's your avern killing me, clearly. 'You will know your true love by her red pagne . . .'" She bent to kiss me, then sat in my lap. "Aren't you going to look?"

"I *am* looking." Her torn bodice had fallen again.

"Not there. Cover that with your hand, and then you can look at the note."

I did as she told me, but left the note where it was. "It's really too much, as I said a moment ago. The mysterious Septentrion and his challenge, then Hildegrin, and now this. Have I mentioned the Chatelaine Thecla to you?"

"More than once, while we were walking."

"I loved her. She read a great deal—there was really nothing for her to do when I was gone but read and sew and sleep—and when I was with her we used to laugh at the plots of some of the stories. This sort of thing was always happening to the people in them, and they were incessantly involved in high and melodramatic affairs for which they had no qualifications."

Agia laughed with me and kissed me again, a lingering kiss. When our lips parted, she said, "What's this about Hildegrin? He seemed ordinary enough."

I took another pastry, touched the note with it, then put a corner into her mouth. "Some time ago I saved the life of a man called Vodalus—"

Agia pulled away from me, spewing crumbs. "Vodalus? You're joking!"

"Not at all. That's what his friend called him. I was still hardly more than a boy, but I held back the haft of an ax for a moment. The blow would have killed him, and he gave me a chrisos."

"Wait. What has this to do with Hildegrin?"

"When I first saw Vodalus, he had a man and a woman with him. Enemies came upon them, and Vodalus remained behind to fight while the other man took the woman to safety." (I had decided it was wiser to say nothing about the corpse, or my killing of the axman.)

"I'd have fought myself—then there'd have been three fighters instead of one. Go on."

"Hildegrin was the man with Vodalus, that's all. If we had met him first, I would have had some idea, or thought I had some idea, of why a hipparch of the Septentrion Guard would want to fight me. And for that matter why someone has chosen to send me some sort of furtive message. You know, all the things the Chatelaine Thecla and I used to laugh about, spies and intrigue, masked trysts, lost heirs. What's the matter, Agia?"

"Do I revolt you? Am I so ugly?"

"You're beautiful, but you look as if you're about to be sick. I think you drank too fast."

"Here." A quick twist took Agia out of her pavonine gown; it lay about her brown, dusty feet like a heap of precious stones. I had seen her naked in the cathedral of the Pelerines, but now (whether because of the wine I had drunk or the wine she had drunk, because the light was dimmer now, or brighter, or only because she had been frightened and shamed then, covering her breasts and hiding her womanhood between her thighs) she drew me far more. I felt stupid with desire, thick-headed and thick-tongued as I pressed her warmth against my own cold flesh.

"Severian, wait. I'm not a strumpet, whatever you may think. But there's a price."

"What?"

"You must promise me you won't read that note. Throw it into the brazier."

I let go of her and stepped back.

Tears appeared in her eyes, rising as springs do among rocks. "I wish you could see the way you're looking at me now, Severian. No, I don't know what it says. It's just that—have you never heard of some women having supernatural knowledge? Premonitions? Knowing things they could not possibly have learned?"

The longing I had felt was nearly gone. I was frightened as well as angry, though I did not know why. I said, "We have a guild of such women, our sisters, in the Citadel. Neither their faces nor their bodies are like yours."

"I know I'm not like that. But that's why you must do what I advise. I've never in my life had a premonition of any strength, and I have one now. Don't you see that must mean it's something so true and so important to you that you can't and mustn't ignore it? Burn the note."

"Someone is trying to warn me, and you don't want me to see it. I asked you if the Septentrion was your lover. You told me he was not, and I believed you."

She started to speak, but I silenced her.

"I believe you still. Your voice had truth in it. Yet you are laboring to betray me in some way. Tell me now that isn't so. Tell me you are acting in my best interests, and nothing beyond."

"Severian . . ."

"Tell me."

"Severian, we met this morning. I hardly knew you and you hardly know me. What can you expect, and what would you expect if you had not just left the shelter of your guild? I've tried to help you from time to time. I'm trying to help you now."

"Put on your dress." I took the note from under the tray. She rushed at me, but it was not difficult to hold her off with one hand. The note had been penned with a crow quill, in a straggling scrawl; in the dim light I could decipher only a few words.

"I could have distracted you, and thrown it into the fire. That's what I ought to have done. Severian, let me go—"

"Be quiet."

"I had a knife, only last week. A misericorde with an ivy-root handle. We were hungry, and Agilus put it in pawn. If I had it still, I could stab you now!"

"It would be in your gown, and your gown is over there on the floor." I gave her a push that sent her staggering backward (there was wine enough in her stomach that it was not entirely from the violence of my motion) into the canvas chair, and carried the note to a spot where the last light of the sun penetrated the crowding leaves.

The woman with you has been here before.
Do not trust her. Trudo says the man is
a torturer. You are my mother come again.

XXVI

Sennet

I HAD JUST HAD TIME to absorb the words when Agia jumped from her chair, snatched the note from my hand, and threw it over the edge of the platform. For a moment she stood before me, looking from my face to *Terminus Est*, which by this time leaned, reassembled, against an arm of the couch. I think she feared I was going to strike off her head and throw it after the note. When I did nothing, she said, "Did you read it? Severian, say you didn't!"

"I read it, but I don't understand it."

"Then don't think about it."

"Be calm for a moment. It wasn't even meant for me. It may have been for you, but if it was, why was it put where no one but I could see it? Agia, have you had a child? How old are you?"

"Twenty-three. That's plenty old enough, but no, I haven't. I'll let you look at my belly if you don't believe me."

I tried to make a mental calculation and discovered I did not know enough about the maturation of women. "When did you menstruate first?"

"Thirteen. If I'd got pregnant, I would have been fourteen when the baby came. Is that what you're trying to find out?"

"Yes. And the child would be nine now. If it were bright, it might be able to write a note like that. Do you want me to tell you what it said?"

"No!"

"How old would you say Dorcas is? Eighteen? Nineteen, perhaps?"

"You shouldn't think about it, Severian. Whatever it was."

"I won't play games with you now. You're a woman—how old?"

Agia pursed her full lips. "I'd say your drab little mystery's sixteen or seventeen. Hardly more than a child."

Sometimes, as I suppose everyone has noticed, talking of absent persons seems to summon them up like eidolons. So it was now. A panel of the screen swung back and Dorcas came out, no longer the muddy creature we had become accustomed to, but a round-breasted, slender girl of singular grace. I have seen skin whiter than hers, but that was not a healthy whiteness. Dorcas seemed to glow. Freed of filth, her hair was pale gold; her eyes were as they had always been: the deep blue of the world-river Uroboros in my dream. When she saw that Agia was naked, she tried to return to the shelter of the screen, but the thick body of the scullion prevented her.

Agia said, "I had better put my rags on again before your pet faints."

Dorcas murmured, "I won't look."

"I don't care if you do," Agia told her, but I noticed she turned her back to us while she put on her gown. Speaking to the wall of leaves, she added, "Now we really must go, Severian. The trumpet will sound at any moment."

"And what will that mean?"

"You don't know?" She swung about to face us. "When the machinations of the City Wall appear to touch the edge of the solar disc, a trumpet—the first—is sounded on the Sanguinary Field. Some think it's only to regulate the combats there, though that's not so. It is a signal to the guards inside the Wall to close the gates. It's also the signal to begin the fighting, and if you're there when it blows, that's when your contest will start. When the sun is below the horizon and true night comes, a trumpeter on the Wall sounds tattoo. That means the gates will not be opened again even for those who carry special passes and also that anyone who, having given or received a challenge, has not yet come to the Field is assumed to have refused satisfaction. He can be assulted wherever he is found, and an armiger or an exultant can engage assassins without soiling his honor."

The scullion, who had been standing by the stair listening to all this and nodding, moved aside for her master, the innkeeper. "Sieur," he said, "if you indeed have a mortal appointing, I—"

"That is just what my friend was saying," I told him. "We must go."

Dorcas asked then if she might have some wine. Somewhat surprised, I nodded; the innkeeper poured her a glass, which she held in both hands like a child. I asked him if he supplied writing implements for his guests.

"You wish to make a testament, sieur? Come with me—we have a bower reserved for that purpose. There's no charge, and if you like, I will engage a boy who'll carry the document to your executor."

I picked up *Terminus Est* and followed him, leaving Agia and Dorcas to keep watch on the avern. The bower our host boasted of was perched on a small limb and hardly big enough to hold a desk, but there was a stool there, several crow-quill pens, paper, and a pot of ink. I sat down and wrote out the words of the note; so far as I could judge, the paper was the same as that on which it had been written, and the ink gave the same faded black line. When I had sanded my scribble, folded it, and tucked it away in a compartment of my sabretache I seldom used, I told the innkeeper no messenger would be required, and asked if he knew anyone named Trudo.

"Trudo, sieur?" He looked puzzled.

"Yes. It's a common enough name."

"Surely it is, sieur, I know that. It's just that I was trying to think of somebody that might be known to me and somebody, if you understand me, sieur, in your exalted position. Some armiger or—"

"Anyone," I said. "Anyone at all. It would not, for example, be the name of the waiter who served us, would it?"

"No, sieur. His name's Ouen. I had a neighbor once named Trudo, sieur, but that was years ago, before I bought this place. I don't suppose it would be him you're after? Then there's my ostler here—his name's Trudo."

"I'd like to speak to him."

The innkeeper nodded, his chin vanishing in the fat that circled his neck. "As you wish, sieur. Not that he's likely to be able to tell you much." The steps creaked beneath his weight. "He's from far south, I warn you." (He meant the southern regions of the city, not the wild and largely treeless lands abutting on the ice.) "And from across the river to boot. You're not likely to get much sense from him, though he's a hard-working fellow."

I said, "I suspect I know what part of the city he comes from."

"Do you now? Well, that's interesting, sieur. Very interesting. I've heard one or two say they could tell such things by the way a man dressed or how he spoke, but I wasn't aware you'd laid eyes on Trudo, as the saying is." We were nearing the ground now, and he bawled, "*Trudo! Tr-u-u-do!*" And then, "REINS!"

No one appeared. A single flagstone the size of a large tabletop had been laid at the foot of the stair, and we stepped out upon it.

It was just at that moment when lengthening shadows cease to be shadows at all and become instead pools of blackness, as if some fluid darker even than the waters of the Lake of Birds was rising from the ground. Hundreds of people, some alone, some in small groups, were hurrying over the grass from the direction of the city. All seemed intent, bowed by an eagerness they carried upon their backs and shoulders like a pack. Most bore no weapons I could see, but a few had cases of rapiers, and at some distance off I made out the white blossom of an avern, carried, it seemed, on a pole or staff just as mine was.

"Pity they won't stop here," the innkeeper said. "Not that I won't get some of them coming back, but a dinner before is where the money is. I speak frankly, for I can see that young as you are, sieur, you're too sensible not to know that every business is run to make a profit. I try to give good value, and as I've said, we've a famous kitchen. *Tr-u-do!* I have to have one, for no other sort of food will agree with me—I'd starve, sieur, if I had to eat what most do. *Trudo you louse farm, where are you?*"

A dirty boy appeared from somewhere behind the trunk, wiping his nose on his arm. "He's not back there, Master."

"Well, where is he? Go look for him."

I was still watching the streaming hundreds. "They are all going to the Sanguinary Field then?" For the first time, I think, I fully realized that I was liable to die before the moon shone. Accounting for the note seemed futile and childish.

"Not all to fight, you understand. Most are only going to watch, there's some come only once, because somebody they know's fighting, or just because they were told about it, or read about it, or heard a song. Usually those get taken ill, because they come here and generally put away a bottle or so when they're getting over it.

"But there's others that come every night, or anyway four or five nights out of the week. They're specialists, and only foller one weapon, or perhaps two, and they pretend to know more about those than them that use them, which perhaps some do. After your victory, sieur, two or three will want to buy you a round. If you let them, they'll tell you what you did wrong and what the other man did wrong, but you'll find they don't agree."

I said, "Our dinner is to be private," and as I spoke I heard the whisper of bare feet on the steps behind us. Agia and Dorcas were coming down, Agia carrying the avern, which seemed to me to have grown larger in the failing light.

I have already told how strongly I desired Agia. When we are talking to women, we talk as though love and desire are two separate entities; and women, who often love us and sometimes desire us, maintain the same fiction. The fact is that they are aspects of the same thing, as I might have talked to the innkeeper of the north side of his tree and the south. If we desire a woman, we soon come to love her for her condescension in submitting to us (this, indeed, had been the original foundation of my love for Thecla), and since if we desire her she always submits in imagination at least, some element of love is ever present. On the other hand, if we love her, we soon come to desire her, since attraction is one of the attributes a woman should possess, and we cannot bear to think she is without any of them; in this way men come to desire even women whose legs are locked in paralysis, and women to desire those men who are impotent save with men like themselves.

But no one can say from what it is that what we call (almost at our pleasure) *love* or *desire* is born. As Agia came down the stair, one side of her face was lit by the last light of day, and the other thrown into shadow; her skirt, split nearly to the waist, permitted a flash of silken thigh. And all I had lost in feeling for her a few moments before when I had pushed her away came back doubled and doubled again. She saw that in my face, I know, and Dorcas, hardly a step behind her, saw it too and looked away. But Agia was angry with me still (as perhaps she had a right to be), so although she smiled for policy's sake and could not have concealed the ache in her loins if she would, yet she withheld much.

I think it is in this that we find the real difference between those women to whom if we are to remain men we must offer our lives, and those who (again—if we are to remain men) we must overpower and outwit if we can, and use as we never would a beast: that the second will never permit us to give them what we give the first. Agia enjoyed my admiration and would have been moved to ecstasy by my caresses; but even if I were to pour myself into her a hundred times, we would part strangers. I understood all this as she descended the last few steps, one hand closing the bodice of her gown, the other upholding the avern, whose pole she used as a staff and carried like a baculus. And yet I loved her still, or would have loved her if I could.

The boy came running up. "Trudo's gone, cook says. She was out fetchin' water 'cause the girl was gone, and seen him runnin' off, and his things is gone from the mews too."

"Gone for good, then," the innkeeper said. "When did he go? Just now?"

The boy nodded.

"He heard you were looking for him, sieur, that's what I'm afraid of. One of the others must have heard you asking me about the name, and run and told him. Did he steal from you?"

I shook my head. "He did me no harm, and I suspect he was trying to do good in whatever he did do. I'm sorry I cost you a servant."

The innkeeper spread his hands. "He'd some wages coming, so I won't lose by it."

As he turned away, Dorcas whispered. "And I am sorry to have taken your joy from you upstairs. I would not have deprived you. But, Severian, I love you."

From somewhere not far off, the silver voice of a trumpet called to the renascent stars.

XXVII

Is He Dead?

THE SANGUINARY FIELD, of which all my readers will have heard, though some, I hope, will never have visited it, lies northwest of the built sections of our capital of Nessus, between a residential enclave of city armigers and the barracks and stables of the Xenagie of the Blue Dimarchi. It is near enough the Wall to seem very near to someone like myself, who had never been near it at all, yet still leagues of hard walking by twisted avenues from the actual base. How many combats can be accommodated I do not know. It may be that the railings that delimit the grounds of each—upon which the spectators lean or sit as the fancy takes them—can be moved, and are adjusted to suit the evening's needs. I have only visited the spot once, but it seemed to me, with its trampled grass and silent, languid watchers, a strange and melancholy one.

During the brief time I have occupied the throne, many issues have been of more immediate concern than monomachy. Whether it is good or evil (as I am inclined to think), it is surely ineradicable in a society such as ours, which must for its own survival hold the military virtues higher than any others, and in which so few of the armed retainers of the state can be spared to police the populace.

Yet is it evil?

Those ages that have outlawed it (and many hundreds have, by my reading) have replaced it largely with murder—and with just such murders, by and large, as monomachy seems designed to prevent: murders resulting from quarrels among families, friends, and acquaintances. In these cases two die instead of one, for the law tracks down the slayer (a person not by disposition a criminal but by chance) and slays him, as though his death would restore his victim's life. Thus if, say, a thousand legal combats between individuals resulted in a thousand deaths (which is very unlikely, since most such combats do not terminate in death) but prevented five hundred murders, the state would be no worse.

Further, the survivor of such a combat is likely to be the individual most suited to defending the state, and also the most suited to engendering healthy children; while there is no survivor of most murders, and the murderer (were he to survive) is likely to be only vicious, and not strong, quick, or intelligent.

And yet how readily this practice lends itself to intrigue.

We heard the shouted names when we were still a hundred strides away, loudly and formally announced above the trilling of the hylas.

"*Cadroe of the Seventeen Stones!*"

"*Sabas of the Parted Meadow!*"

"*Laurentia of the House of the Harp!*" (This in a woman's voice.)

"*Cadroe of the Seventeen Stones!*"

I asked Agia who it was who thus called.

"They have given challenges, or have been challenged themselves. By bawling their names—or having a servant do it for them—they advertise that they have come, and to the world that their opponent has not."

"*Cadroe of the Seventeen Stones!*"

The vanishing sun, whose disc was now a quarter concealed behind the impenetrable blackness of the Wall, had dyed the sky with gamboge and cerise, vermillion and lurid violet. These colors, falling upon the throng of monomachists and loungers much as we see the aureate beams of divine favor fall on hierarchs in art, lent them an appearance insubstantial and thaumaturgic, as though they had all been produced a moment before by the flourish of a cloth and would vanish into the air again at a whistle.

"*Laurentia of the House of the Harp!*"

"Agia," I said, and from somewhere nearby we heard the choking death makes in a man's throat. "Agia, you are to call out, 'Severian of the Matachin Tower.'"

"I'm not your servant. Bawl it yourself if you want it bawled."

"*Cadroe of Seventeen Stones!*"

"Don't look at me like that, Severian. I wish we hadn't come! *Severian! Severian of the Torturers! Severian of the Citadel! Of the Tower of Pain! Death! Death is come!*" My hand caught her just below the ear and she went sprawling, the avern on its pole beside her.

Dorcas gripped my arm. "You ought not have done that, Severian."

"It was only the flat of my hand. She'll be all right."

"She will hate you even more."

"Then you think she hates me now?"

Dorcas did not answer, and a moment later I myself forgot for the time being that I had asked the question—some distance away among the crowd, I had seen an avern.

The ground was a level circle some fifteen strides across, railed off save for an entrance at either end.

The ephor called: "The adjudication of the avern has been offered and accepted. Here is the place. The time is now. It only remains to be decided whether you will engage as you are, naked, or otherwise. How say you?"

Before I could speak, Dorcas called, "Naked. That man is in armor."

The Septentrion's grotesque helm swung from side to side in

negation. Like most cavalry helmets it left the ears bare to better hear the graisle and the shouted orders of the wearer's superiors; in the shadow behind the cheekpiece I thought I saw a narrow band of black, and tried to recall where I had seen such a thing before.

The ephor asked, "You refuse, hipparch?"

"The men of my country do not go naked save in the presence of women alone."

"He wears armor," Dorcas called again. "This man has not even a shirt." Her voice, always so soft before, rang in the twilight like a bell.

"I will remove it." The Septentrion threw back his cape and raised a gauntleted hand to the shoulder of his cuirass. It slipped from him and fell at his feet. I had expected a chest as massive as Master Gurloes's, but the one I saw was narrower than my own.

"The helmet also."

Again the Septentrion shook his head, and the ephor asked, "Your refusal is absolute?"

"It is." There was a barely perceptible hesitation. "I can only say that I am instructed not to remove it."

The ephor turned to me. "We none of us would desire, I think, to embarrass the hipparch, and still less the personage—I do not say whom it may be—that he serves. I believe the wisest course would be to allow you, sieur, some compensating advantage. Have you one to suggest?"

Agia, who had been silent since I had struck her, said, "Refuse the combat, Severian. Or reserve your advantage until you need it."

Dorcas, who was loosening the strips of rag that bound the avern, said also, "Refuse the combat."

"I've come too far to turn back now."

The ephor asked pointedly, "Have you decided, sieur?"

"I think I have." My mask was in my sabretache. Like all those used in the guild it was of thin leather stiffened with strips of bone. Whether it would keep out the thrown leaves of the

avern I had no way of knowing—but it was satisfying to hear the
lookers-on draw breath when I snapped it open.

"You are ready now? Hipparch? Sieur? Sieur, you must give
that sword to someone to hold for you. No weapon but the avern
may be carried."

I looked about for Agia, but she had vanished into the crowd.
Dorcas handed me the deadly blossom, and I gave her *Terminus
Est*.

"Begin!"

A leaf whizzed close to my ear. The Septentrion was
advancing with an irregular motion, his avern gripped beneath
the lowest leaves by his left hand, and his right thrust forward as
though to wrestle mine from me. I recalled that Agia had warned
me of the danger of this, and clasped it as close as I dared.

For the space of five breaths we circled. Then I struck at his
outstretched hand. He countered with his plant. I raised my own
above my head like a sword, and as I did so realized the position
was an ideal one—it put the vulnerable stem out of my
opponent's reach, permitted me to slash downward with the
whole plant at will, yet allowed me to detach leaves with my
right hand.

This last discovery I put to the test at once, snapping off a leaf
and sending it skimming toward his face. Despite the protection
his helm gave him he ducked, and the crowd behind him
scattered to avoid the missile. I followed it with another. And
then another, which struck his own in flight.

The result was remarkable. Instead of absorbing the other's
momentum and clattering down together as inanimate blades
would, the leaves appeared to writhe and wind their edged
lengths about each other, slashing and striking with their points
so rapidly that before they had fallen a cubit they were no more
than ragged strips of blackish-green that turned to a hundred
colors and spun like a child's top . . .

Something, or someone, was pressing against my back. It was
as though an unknown stood close behind me, his spine against

mine, exerting a slight pressure. I felt cold, and was grateful for the warmth of his body.

"Severian!" The voice was Dorcas's, but she seemed to have wandered away.

"Severian! Won't anyone help him? Let me go!"

The peal of a carillon. The colors, which I had taken to be those of the struggling leaves, were in the sky instead, where a rainbow unrolled beneath the aurora. The world was a great paschal egg, crowded with all the colors of the palette. Near my head a voice inquired, "Is he dead?" and someone answered matter-of-factly, "That's it. Those things always kill. Unless you want to see them drag him off?"

The Septentrion's voice (oddly familiar) said, "I claim victor right to his clothing and weapons. Give me that sword."

I sat up. The leaves were still faintly struggling wisps a few paces from my boots. The Septentrion stood beyond them, still holding his avern. I drew breath to ask what had happened, and something fell from my chest to my lap; it was a leaf with a bloodstained tip.

Seeing me, the Septentrion whirled and lifted his avern. The ephor stepped between us, arms extended. From the railings some spectator called, "Gentle right! Gentle right, soldier! Let him stand up and get his weapon."

My legs would hardly bear me. I looked around stupidly for my own avern, and found it at last only because it lay near the feet of Dorcas, who was struggling with Agia. The Septentrion shouted, "He should be dead!" The ephor said, "He is not, hipparch. When he regains his weapon, you may pursue the combat."

I touched the stem of my avern, and for an instant felt I had grasped the tail of some cold-blooded but living animal. It seemed to stir in my hand, and the leaves rattled. Agia was shouting, "Sacrilege!" and I paused to look at her, then picked up the avern and turned to face the Septentrion.

His eyes were shadowed by his helmet, but there was terror in every line of his body. For a moment he seemed to look from me to Agia. Then he turned and fled toward the opening in the rails at his end of the arena. The spectators blocked his way and he used his avern like a scourge, striking to right and left. There was a scream, then a crescendo of screams. My own avern was pulling me backward, or rather, my avern was gone and someone gripped me by the hand. Dorcas. Somewhere far away Agia shrieked, "*Agilus!*" and another woman called, "*Laurentia of the House of the Harp!*"

XXVIII

Carnifex

I WOKE THE NEXT MORNING in a lazaret, a long, high-ceilinged room where we, the sick, the injured, lay upon narrow beds. I was naked, and for a long time, while sleep (or perhaps it was death) tugged at my eyelids, I moved my hands slowly over my body, searching it for injuries while I wondered, as I might have wondered of someone in a song, how I would live without clothing or money, how I should explain to Master Palaemon the loss of the sword and cloak he had given me.

For I was sure they were lost—or rather, that I was myself in some way lost from them. An ape with the head of a dog ran down the aisle, paused at my bed to look at me, then ran on. That seemed no stranger to me than the light that, passing through a window I could not see, fell upon my blanket.

I woke again, and sat up. For a moment I truly thought I was in our dormitory again, that I was captain of apprentices, that everything else, my masking, the death of Thecla, the combat of the averns, had been only a dream. This was not the last time this was to happen. Then I saw that the ceiling was of plaster and not our familiar metal one, and that the man in the bed next to my own was swathed in bandages. I threw back the blanket and swung my feet to the floor. Dorcas sat, asleep, with her back to the wall at the head of my bed. She had wrapped herself in the brown mantle; *Terminus Est* lay across her lap, the hilt and scabbard-tip protruding from either side of my heaped belongings. I managed to get my boots and hose, my breeches, my cloak, and my belt with its sabretache without waking her, but when I tried to take my sword she murmured and clung to it, so I left it with her.

Many of the sick were awake and stared at me, but none spoke. A door at the end of the room opened onto a flight of steps, and these descended to a courtyard where destriers stamped. For a moment I thought I was dreaming still: the cynocephalus was climbing upon the crenelations of the wall. But it was an animal as real as the champing steeds, and when I threw a bit of rubbish at it, it bared teeth as impressive as Triskele's.

A trooper in a hauberk came out to get something from his saddlebag, and I stopped him and asked where I was. He supposed that I meant in what part of the fortress, and pointed out a turret behind which, he said, was the Hall of Justice; then told me that if I would come with him I could probably get something to eat.

As soon as he spoke, I realized I was famished. I followed him down a dark hallway into a room much lower and darker than the lazaret, where two or three score dimarchi like himself were bent over a midday meal of fresh bread, beef, and boiled greens. My new friend advised me to take a plate and tell the cooks I had been instructed to come here for my dinner. I did so, and though they looked a trifle surprised at my fuligin cloak, they served me without objection.

If the cooks were incurious, the soldiers were curiosity itself. They asked my name, and where I came from, and what my rank was (for they assumed our guild was organized like the military). They asked where my ax was, and when I told them we used the sword, where that was; and when I explained that I had a woman with me who was watching it, they cautioned me that she might run away with it, and then counseled me to carry out bread for her under my cloak, since she would not be permitted to come where we were to eat. I discovered that all the older men had supported women—camp followers of what is perhaps the most useful and least dangerous kind—at one time or another, though few had them now. They had spent the summer before in fighting in the north and had been sent to winter in Nessus, where they served to maintain order. Now they expected to go north again within a week. Their women had returned to their own villages to live with parents or relatives. I asked if the women would not have preferred to follow them south.

"Prefer it?" said my friend, "Of course they'd prefer it. But how would they do it? It's one thing to follow cavalry that's fighting its way north with army, for that doesn't make more than a league or two on the best days, and if it clears three in a week, you can bet it will lose two the next. But how would they keep up on the way back to the city? Fifteen leagues a day. And what would they eat on the way? It's better for them to wait. If a new xenagie comes to our old sector, they'll have some new men. Some new girls will come too, and some of the old ones drop out, and it gives everyone a chance to change off if they want. I heard they brought in one of you carnifexes last night, but he was nearly dead himself. Have you been to see him?"

I said I had not.

"One of our patrols reported him, and when the chiliarch heard of it he sent them back to bring him, seeing we were sure to need one in a day or so. They swear they didn't touch him, but they had to bring him back on a litter. I don't know if he's one of your comrades, but you might want to take a look."

I promised I would, and after thanking the soldiers for their hospitality, left them. I was worried about Dorcas, and their questioning, though it was clearly well meant, had made me uneasy. There were too many things I could not explain—how I had come to be injured, for example, if I had admitted I was the man who had been carried in the night before, and where Dorcas had come from. Not really understanding those things myself bothered me at least as much, and I felt, as we always feel when there is a whole sector of our lives that cannot bear light, that no matter how far the last question had been from one of the forbidden subjects, the next would pierce to the heart of it.

Dorcas was awake and standing by my bed, where someone had left a cup of steaming broth. She was so delighted to see me that I felt happy myself, as though joy were as contagious as a pestilence. "I thought you were dead," she told me. "You were gone, and your clothes were gone, and I thought they had taken them to bury you in."

"I'm all right," I said. "What happened last night?"

Dorcas became serious at once. I made her sit on the bed with me and eat the bread I had brought and drink the broth while she answered. "You remember fighting with the man who wore that strange helmet, I'm sure. You put on a mask and went into the arena with him, although I begged you not to. Almost at once he hit you in the chest, and you fell. I remember seeing the leaf, a horrible thing like a flatworm made of iron, half in your body and turning red as it drank your blood.

"Then it fell away. I don't know how to describe it. It was as though everything I had seen had been *wrong*. But it wasn't wrong—I remember what I saw. You got up again, and you looked . . . I don't know. As if you were lost, or some part of you was far away. I thought he was going to kill you at once, but the ephor protected you, saying he had to allow you to get your avern. His was quiet, the way ours had been when you pulled it up in that awful place, but yours had begun to writhe and open its flower—I thought it had been open before, the white thing with the swirl of petals, only now I believe I was thinking too much of roses, and it had not been open at all. There was something underneath, something else, a face like the face poison would have, if poison had a face.

"You didn't notice. You picked it up and it began to curl toward you, slowly, as though it were only half awake. But the other man, the hipparch, couldn't believe what he had seen. He was staring at you, and that woman Agia was shouting to him. And all at once he turned and ran away. The people who were watching didn't want him to, they wanted to see someone killed. So they tried to stop him, and he . . ."

Her eyes were brimming with tears; she turned her head to keep me from seeing them. I said, "He struck several of them with his avern, and I suppose killed them. Then what happened?"

"It wasn't just that he struck them. It struck *at* them, after the first two, like a snake. The ones who were cut with the leaves didn't die at once, they screamed, and some of them ran and fell and got up and ran again, as if they were blind, knocking other people down. And at last a big man struck him from behind and a woman who had been fighting somewhere else came with a braquemar. She cut the avern—not sidewise but down the stem so it split. Then some of the men held the hipparch and I heard her blade clash on his helmet.

"You were just standing there. I wasn't sure you even knew he was gone, and your avern was bending back toward your face. I thought of what the woman had done and hit at it with your sword. It was heavy, so very heavy at first, and then it was hardly heavy at all. But when I slashed down with it I felt as if I could have struck the head from a bison. Only I had forgotten to take off the sheath. But it knocked the avern out of your hand, and I took you and led you away . . ."

"Where?" I asked.

She shivered and dipped a piece of bread in the steaming broth. "I don't know. I didn't care. It was just so good to be walking with you, to know I was taking care of you the way you had taken care of me before we got the avern. But I was cold, terribly cold, when night came. I put your cloak all around you and fastened it in front, and you didn't seem to be cold, so I took this mantle and wrapped myself in it. My dress was falling to pieces. It still is."

I said, "I wanted to buy you another one when we were at the inn."

She shook her head, chewing the tough crust. "Do you know, I think this is the first food I've had in a long, long time. I have pains in my stomach—that's why I drank the wine there—but this makes it feel better. I hadn't realized how weak I was getting.

"But I didn't want a new dress from there because I would have had to wear it for a long time, and it would always have reminded me of that day. You can buy me a dress now, if you like, because *it* will remind me of this day, when I thought you were dead when you were really well.

"Anyway, we got back into the city somehow. I was hoping to find a place to stop where you could lie down, but there were only big houses with terraces and balustrades. That sort of thing. Some soldiers came galloping up and asked if you were a carnifex. I didn't know the word, but I remembered what you had told me and so I told them you were a torturer, because soldiers have always seemed to me to be a kind of torturer and I knew they would help us. They tried to get you to ride, but you fell off. So some of them tied their capes between two lances and laid you on that, and put the ends of the lances in the stirrup straps of two destriers. One of them wanted to take me up into his saddle, but I wouldn't do it. I walked beside you all the way and sometimes I talked to you, but I don't think you heard me."

She drained the last of the broth. "Now I want to ask you a question. When I was washing myself behind the screen, I could hear you and Agia whispering about a note. Later you were looking for someone in the inn. Will you tell me about that?"

"Why didn't you ask before?"

"Because Agia was with us. If you had found out anything, I didn't want her to hear what it was."

"I'm sure Agia could discover anything I discovered," I said. "I don't know her well, and in fact I don't feel I know her as well as I know you. But I know her well enough to realize that she's much cleverer than I am."

Dorcas shook her head again. "She's the sort of woman who's good at making puzzles for other people, but not at solving ones she didn't make herself. I think she thinks—I don't know—sidewise. So no one else can follow it. She's the kind of woman people say thinks like a man, but those women don't think like real men at all, in fact, they think less like real men than most women do. They just don't think like women. The way they do think is hard to follow, but that doesn't mean it's clear, or deep."

I told her about the note, and what it said, and mentioned that although it had been destroyed I had copied it out on the inn's paper and found it to be the same paper, and the same ink.

"So someone wrote it there," she said pensively. "Probably one of the inn servants, because he called the ostler by name. But what does it mean?"

"I don't know."

"I can tell you why it was put where it was. I sat there, on that horn settee, before you sat down. It made me happy, I recall, because you sat beside me. Do you remember if the waiter—he must have carried the note, whether he wrote it or not—put the tray there before I got up to bathe?"

"I can remember everything," I said, "except last night. Agia sat in a folding canvas chair, you sat on the couch, that's right, and I sat down beside you. I had been carrying the avern on the pole as well as my sword, and I laid the avern flat behind the couch. The kitchen girl came in with water and towels for you, then she went out and got oil and rags for me."

Dorcas said, "We ought to have given her something."

"I gave her an orichalk to bring the screen. That's probably as much as she's paid for a week. Anyway, you went behind it, and a moment later the host led the waiter in with the tray and wine."

"That's why I didn't see it, then. But the waiter must have known where I was sitting, because there was no place else. So he left it under the tray, hoping I'd see it when I came out. What was the first part again?"

"'The woman with you has been here before. Do not trust her.'"

"It must have been for me. If it had been for you, it would have distinguished between Agia and me, probably by hair color. And if it had been meant for Agia, it would have been out on the other side of the table where she would have seen it instead."

"So you reminded someone of his mother."

"Yes." Once more there were tears in her eyes.

"You're not old enough to have had a child who could have written that note."

"I don't remember," she said, and buried her face in the loose folds of the brown mantle.

XXIX

Agilus

When the physician in charge had examined me and found I had
no need of treatment, he asked us to leave the lazaret, where my
cloak and sword were, as he said, upsetting to his patients.

On the opposite side of the building in which I had eaten with
the troopers, we found a shop that catered to their needs. Together
with false jewelry and trinkets of the sort such men give their
paramours, it carried a certain amount of women's clothing; and
though my money had been much depleted by the dinner we had
never returned to the Inn of Lost Loves to enjoy, I was able to buy
Dorcas a simar.

The entrance to the Hall of Justice was not far from this shop. A
crowd of a hundred or so was milling before it, and since the people
pointed and elbowed one another when they caught sight of my
fuligin, we retreated again to the courtyard where the destriers were
tethered. A portreeve from the Hall of Justice found us there—an
imposing man with a high, white forehead like the belly of a
pitcher. "You are the carnifex," he said. "I was told you are well
enough to perform your office."

I told him I could do whatever was necessary today, if his master
required it.

"Today? No, no, that's not possible. The trial won't be over until this afternoon."

I remarked that since he had come to make certain I was well enough to carry out the execution, he must have felt certain the prisoner would be found guilty.

"Oh, there's no question of that—not the least. Nine persons died, after all, and the man was apprehended on the spot. He's of no consequence, so there's no possibility of pardon or appeal. The tribunal will reconvene at midmorning, but you won't be required until noon."

Because I had had no direct experience with judges or courts (at the Citadel, our clients had always been sent to us, and Master Gurloes dealt with those officials who occasionally came to inquire about the disposition of some case or other), and because I was eager to actually perform the act in which I had been drilled for so long, I suggested that the chiliarch might wish to consider a torchlight ceremony that same night.

"That would be impossible. He must meditate his decision. How would it look? A great many people feel already that the military magistrates are hasty and even capricious. And to be frank, a civil judge would probably have waited a week, and the case would be all the better for it, since there would have been ample time, then, for someone to come forward with fresh evidence, which of course no one will actually do."

"Tomorrow afternoon then," I said. "We'll require quarters for the night. Also I'll want to examine the scaffold and block, and ready my client. Will I need a pass to see him?"

The portreeve asked if we could not stay in the lazaret, and when I shook my head, we—the portreeve, Dorcas, and I—went there to permit him to argue with the physician in charge, who, as I had predicted, refused to have us. That was followed by a lengthy discussion with a noncommissioned officer of the xenagie, who explained that it was impossible for us to stay in the barracks with the troopers, and that if we were to use one of the rooms set aside for the higher ranks, no one would want to occupy it in the future.

In the end a little, windowless storeroom was cleared out for us, and two beds and some other furniture (all of which had seen hard use) brought in. I left Dorcas there, and after assuring myself that I was unlikely to step through a rotten board at the critical moment, or to have to saw the client's head off while I held him across my knee, I went to the cells to make the call that our traditions demand.

Subjectively at least, there is a great difference between detention facilities to which one has become accustomed and those to which one has not. If I had been entering our own oubliette, I would have felt I was, quite literally, coming home—perhaps coming home to die, but coming home nevertheless. Although I would have realized in the abstract that our winding metal corridors and narrow gray doors might hold horror for the men and women confined there, I would have felt nothing of that horror myself, and if one of them had suggested I should, I would have been quick to point out their various comforts—clean sheets and ample blankets, regular meals, adequate light, privacy that was scarcely ever interrupted, and so on.

Now, going down a narrow and twisted stone stair into a facility a hundredth the size of ours, my feelings were precisely the reverse of what I would have felt there. I was oppressed by the darkness and stench as if by a weight. The thought that I might myself be confined there by some accident (a misunderstood order, for example, or some unsuspected malice on the part of the portreeve) recurred no matter how often I pushed it aside.

I heard the sobbing of a woman, and because the portreeve had spoken of a man, assumed that it came from a cell other than the one that held my client. That, I had been told, was the third from the right. I counted: one, two, and three. The door was merely wood bound with iron, but the locks (such is military efficiency!) had been oiled. Within, the sobbing hesitated and almost ceased as the bolt fell back.

Inside a naked man lay upon straw. A chain ran from the iron collar about his neck to the wall. A woman, naked too, bent over him, her long, brown hair falling past her face and his so that it seemed to unite them. She turned to look at me, and I saw that it was Agia.

She hissed, "Agilus!" and the man sat up. Their faces were so nearly alike that Agia might have been holding a mirror to her own.

"It was you," I said. "But that isn't possible." Even while I spoke, I was recalling the way Agia had behaved at the Sanguinary Field, and the strip of black I had seen by the hipparch's ear.

"You," Agia said. "Because you lived, he has to die."

I could only answer, "Is it really Agilus?"

"Of course." My client's voice was an octave lower than his twin's, though less steady. "You still don't understand, do you?"

I could only shake my head.

"It was Agia in the shop. In the Septentrion costume. She came in through the rear entrance while I was speaking to you, and I made a sign to her when you wouldn't even talk of selling the sword."

Agia said, "I couldn't speak—you would have known it for a woman's voice—but the cuirass hid my breasts and the gauntlets my hands. Walking like a man isn't as hard as men think."

"Have you ever *looked* at that sword? The tang should be signed." Agilus's hands lifted for a moment, as though he would have taken it still if he could. Agia added in a toneless voice, "It is. By Jovinian. I saw it in the inn."

There was a tiny window high up in the wall behind them, and from it, suddenly, as though the ridge of a roof, or a cloud, had now fallen below the sun, a beam of light came to bathe them both. I looked from one aureate face to the other. "You tried to kill me. Just for my sword."

Agilus said, "I hoped you would leave it—don't you remember? I tried to persuade you to leave, to flee in disguise. I would have given the clothes to you, and as much money as I could."

"Severian, don't you understand? It was worth ten times more than our shop, and the shop was all we had."

"You've done this before. You must have. Everything went too smoothly. A legal murder, with no body to weight for Gyoll."

"You're going to kill Agilus, aren't you? That must be why you're here—but you didn't know it was us until you opened the door. What have we done that you're not going to do?"

Less stridently, her brother's voice followed Agia's. "It was a fair combat. We were equally armed, and you agreed to the conditions. Will you give me such a fight tomorrow?"

"You knew that when evening came the warmth of my hands would stimulate the avern, and that it would strike at my face. You wore gloves and you only had to wait. In reality, you didn't even have to do that, because you had thrown the leaves often before."

Agilus smiled. "So the business of the gauntlets was a side issue after all." He spread his hands. "I won. But in reality you won, by some concealed art neither my sister nor I understand. I have been wronged by you three times now, and the old law said that a man three times wronged might claim any boon of his oppressor. I grant that the old law is no longer in force, but my darling tells me you have an attachment to times past, when your guild was great and your fortress the center of the Commonwealth. I claim the boon. Set me free."

Agia rose, brushing the straw from her knees and rounded thighs. As though she realized only now that she was naked, she picked up the blue-green brocade gown I remembered so well and clasped it to her.

I said, "How have I wronged you, Agilus? It seems to me that you have wronged me, or tried to."

"First by entrapment. You carried an heirloom worth a villa about the city without knowing what it was you had. As owner it was your duty to know, and your ignorance threatens to cost me my life tomorrow unless you free me tonight. Secondly, by refusing to entertain any offer to buy. In our commercial society, one may set one's price as high as one wishes, but to refuse to sell at any price is treason. Agia and I wore the gaudy armor of a barbarian—you wore his heart. Thirdly, by the sleight with which you won our combat. Unlike you, I found myself contesting powers greater than I could comprehend. I lost my nerve, as any man would, and here I am. I call on you to free me."

Laughter came unwished-for, carrying with it the taste of gall.

"You're asking me to do for you, whom I have every reason to despise, what I wouldn't do for Thecla, whom I loved almost more than my own life. No. I'm a fool, and if I was not one before, surely your darling sister has made one of me. But not such a fool as that."

Agia dropped her gown and threw herself toward me with such violence that I thought for an instant she was attacking me. Instead she covered my mouth with kisses, and seizing my hands put one on her breast and the other upon her velvet hip. There were bits of rotten straw there still, and on her back, to which I shifted both hands a moment later.

"Severian, I love you! I longed for you when we were together, and tried to give myself to you a score of times. Don't you remember the Garden of Delectation? How much I wanted to take you there? It would have been rapture for us both, but you wouldn't go. For once be honest." (She spoke as if honesty were an abnormality like mania.) "Don't you love me? Take me now . . . here. Agilus will turn his face away, I promise you." Her fingers had slid between my waistband and my belly, and I was not aware that her other hand had lifted the flap of my sabretache until I heard the rustle of paper there.

I slapped her wrist, perhaps harder than I should, and she flew at me, clawing for my eyes as Thecla used sometimes to do when she could no longer bear the thoughts of imprisonment and pain. I pushed her away—not into a chair this time but against the wall. Her head struck the stone, and though it must have been padded by her abundant hair, the sound was as sharp as the tap of a mason's hammer. All the strength seemed to leave her knees; she slid down until she was sitting on the straw. I would never have guessed that Agia was capable of weeping, but she wept.

Agilus asked, "What did she do?" There was no emotion beyond curiosity in the question.

"You must have seen her. She tried to reach into my sabretache." I scooped what coins I possessed out of their compartment: two brass orichalks and seven copper aes. "Or perhaps she wanted to steal the letter I have to the archon of Thrax. I told her about that once, but I don't carry it in here."

"She wanted the coins, I am sure. They've fed me, but she must be dreadfully hungry."

I picked Agia up and thrust her torn gown into her arms, then opened the door and led her out. She was still dazed, but when I gave her an orichalk she threw it down and spat at it.

When I reentered the cell, Agilus was sitting cross-legged, his back propped by the wall. "Don't ask me about Agia," he said. "Everything you suspect is true—is that enough? I will be dead tomorrow, and she will wed the old man who dotes on her, or someone else. I wanted her to do it sooner. He couldn't have prevented her from seeing me, her brother. Now I will be gone, and she won't have even that to worry about."

"Yes," I said, "you will die tomorrow. That's what I've come to talk to you about. Do you care how you look on the scaffold?"

He stared at his hands, slender and rather soft, where they lay in the narrow beam of sunlight that had given his head, and Agia's, an aureole a few moments before. "Yes," he said. "She may come. I hope she won't, but yes, I care."

I told him then (as I had been taught) to eat little in the morning so that he would not be ill when the time came, and cautioned him to empty his bladder, which relaxes at the stroke. I drilled him too in that false routine we teach to all who must die, so they will think the moment is not quite come when in fact it has come, the false routine that lets them die with something less of fear. I do not know if he believed me, though I hope he did; if ever a lie is justified in the sight of the Pancreator, it is that one.

When I left him, the orichalk was gone. In its place—and no doubt with its edge—a design had been scratched on the filthy stones. It might have been the snarling face of Jurupari, or perhaps a map, and it was wreathed with letters I did not know. I rubbed it away with my foot.

X X X

Night

THERE WERE FIVE of them, three men and two women. They waited outside the door, in a sense, but not near it, grouped a dozen strides away. Waiting, they talked among themselves, two or three talking together, almost shouting, laughing, waving arms, nudging one another. I watched them from the shadows for a time. They could not see me there, or did not, wrapped as I was in my fuligin cloak, and I was able to pretend I did not know what they were; they might have been at a party, all a little drunk.

They came eagerly yet hesitantly, afraid of being repulsed and determined to make the advance. One man was taller than I, surely the illegitimate son of some exultant, fifty or more, and nearly as fat as the host at the Inn of Lost Loves. A thin woman of twenty or so walked beside him, almost pressing against him; she had the hungriest eyes I have ever seen. When the fat man stepped in front of me, blocking my way with his bulk, she nearly (yet not quite) embraced me, coming so close it seemed almost magical that we did not touch, her long-fingered hands moving at the opening of my cloak with the desire to stroke my chest, but never quite doing so, so that I felt I was about to fall prey to some blood-drinking ghost, a succubus or lamia. The others crowded around me, hemming me against the building.

"It's tomorrow, isn't it? How does it feel?" "What's your real name?" "He's a bad one, isn't he? A monster?" None of them waited for answers to their questions, or, so far as I could see, expected or wanted any. They sought propinquity, and the experience of having spoken to me. "Will you break him first? Will there be a branding?" "Have you ever killed a woman?"

"Yes," I said. "Yes, I did, once."

One of the men, short and slight, with the high, bumpy forehead of an intellectual, was putting an asimi into my hand. "I know you fellows don't get much, and I hear he's a pauper, can't tip." A woman, gray hair straggling over her face, tried to make me take a lace-trimmed handkerchief. "Get blood on it. As much as you want, or even only a little. I'll pay you afterward."

All of them stirred me to pity even as they revolted me; but one man most of all. He was even smaller than the one who had given me the money, grayer than the gray-haired woman; and there was a madness in his dull eyes, a shadow of some half-supressed concern that had worn itself out in the prison of his mind until all its eagerness was gone and only its energy remained. He seemed to be waiting until the other four had finished speaking, and since that time clearly would never come, I quieted them with a gesture and asked him what he wanted.

"M-m-master, when I was on the *Quasar* I had a paracoita, a doll, you see, a genicon, so beautiful with her great pupils as dark as wells, her i-irises purple like asters or pansies blooming in summer, Master, whole beds of them, I thought, had b-been gathered to make those eyes, that flesh that always felt sun-warmed. Wh-wh-where is she now, my own scopolagna, my poppet? Let h-h-hooks be buried in the hands that took her! Crush them, master, beneath stones. Where has she gone from the lemon-wood box I made for her, where she never slept at all, for she lay with me all night, not in the box, the lemon-wood box where she waited all day, watch-

and-watch, Master, smiling when I laid her in so she might smile when I drew her out. How soft her hands were, her little hands. Like d-d-doves. She might have flown with them about the cabin had she not chosen instead to lie with me. W-w-wind their guts about your w-windlass, stuff their eyes into their mouths. Unman them, shave them clean below so their doxies may not know them, their lemans may rebuke them, leave them to the brazen laughter of the brazen mouths of st-st-strumpets. Work your will upon those guilty. Where was their mercy on the innocent? When did they tremble, when weep? What kind of men could do as they have done—thieves, false friends, betrayers, bad shipmates, no shipmates, murderers and kidnappers. W-without you, where are their nightmares, where are their restitutions, so long promised? Where are their chains, fetters, manacles, and cangues? Where are their abacinations, that shall leave them blind? Where are the defenestrations that shall break their bones, where is the estrapade that shall grind their joints? Where is she, the beloved whom I lost?"

Dorcas had found a daisy for her hair; but as we walked about outside the walls (I wrapped in my cloak, so that to anyone more than a few paces off it must have seemed that she walked alone), it folded its petals in sleep, and she plucked instead one of those white, trumpet-shaped blossoms that are called moonflowers because they appear green in the moon's green light. Neither of us had much to say other than that we would be utterly alone save for the other. Our hands spoke of that, clasping each other tightly.

Victuallers came and went, for the soldiers were making ready to depart. To north and east the Wall hemmed us round, making the wall that enclosed the barracks and administrative buildings seem no more than children's work, a wall of sand that might be trodden down by accident. To south and west extended the Sanguinary Field. We heard the trumpet blown there, and the cries of the new monomachists who sought their foes. Both of us, I think, for a time dreaded that the other would suggest we walk there and watch the combats. Neither did.

When the last curfew had come drifting down from the Wall, we returned, with a borrowed candle, to our windowless and fireless room. There was no bolt for the door, but we put the table against it and stood the candlestick on that. I had told Dorcas she was free to go, and that forever afterward it would be said of her that she was a torturer's woman, who gave herself under the scaffold for money spotted with blood.

She had said, "That money has clothed and fed me." Now she drew off the brown mantle (which hung to her heels—and beyond, when she was not careful of it, so the hem dragged in the dust) and smoothed the raw, yellow-brown linen of her simar.

I asked if she were frightened.

"Yes," she said. Then quickly, "Oh, not of you."

"Of what then?" I was taking off my clothes. If she had asked me, I would not have touched her throughout the night. But I wanted her to ask—indeed, I wanted her to beg; and the pleasure I would have had in abstinence would then have been at least as great (as I thought) as I would have had in possession, with the additional pleasure of knowing that on the next night she would feel the more obliged because I had spared her.

"Of myself. Of what thoughts may return to me when I lie again with a man."

"Again? Do you remember a time before?"

Dorcas shook her head. "But I am certain I am no virgin. I have desired you often, yesterday and today. For whom did you believe I washed myself? Last night I held your hand while you slept, and I dreamed we sated ourselves and lay in each other's arms. But I know satiety as well as desire—so I have known one man at least. Do you wish me to remove this before I blow out the candle?"

She was slender, high-breasted and narrow-hipped, strangely childlike to me, though fully a woman. "You seem so small," I said, and held her to me.

"And you are so big."

I knew then that however much I tried not to I would hurt her, that night and afterward. I knew too that I was incapable of sparing her. A moment before I would have refrained if she had asked. Now I could not; and just as I would have thrust forward though it had plunged my body on a spike, I would follow her later and try to cleave her to me.

But it was not my body that was impaled, but hers. We had been standing while I ran my hands over her and kissed her breasts, that were like round fruits sliced in two. Now I lifted her, and together we fell on one of the beds. She cried out, half in delight, half in pain, and pushed me away before she clutched at me. "I'm glad," she said. "I'm so glad," and bit me on the shoulder. Her body bent backward like a bow.

Later we pushed the beds together so we could lie side by side. Everything was slower the second time; she would not agree to a third. "You'll need your strength tomorrow," she said.

"Then you don't care."

"If we could have our way, no man would have to go roving or draw blood. But women did not make the world. All of you are torturers, one way or another."

It rained that night, so hard we could hear it drumming on the tiles over our heads, a cleansing, crashing, unending downpour of water. I dozed, and dreamed that the world had been turned upside down. Gyoll was overhead now, decanting all its flood of fish and filth and flowers over us. I saw the great face I had seen under the water when I had nearly drowned—a portent of coral and white seen in the sky, smiling with needle teeth.

Thrax is called the City of Windowless Rooms. This windowless room of ours, I thought, is a preparation for Thrax. Thrax will be like this. Or perhaps Dorcas and I are already there, it was not so far north as I thought, so far north as I was led to believe . . .

Dorcas got up to go out, and I went with her, knowing it would not be safe for her to go alone at night in a place where there were so many soldiers. The corridor outside our room ran along an outer wall pierced with embrasures; water splashed through each in a fine spray. I wanted to keep *Terminus Est* in her sheath, but so large a sword is slow to draw. When we were back in our room again, with the table against the door, I took out the whetstone and sharpened the man-side of the blade, honing its edge until the endmost third, the part I would use, would divide a thread tossed into the air. Then I wiped and oiled the whole blade and stood the sword against the wall near my head.

Tomorrow would be my first appearance on the scaffold, unless the chiliarch decided at the last moment to exercise clemency. That was always a possibility, always a risk. History shows that every age has some unquestioned neurosis, and Master Palaemon had taught me that clemency is ours, a way of saying that one less one is more than nothing, that since human law need not be self-consistent, justice need not be so either. There is a dialogue in the brown book somewhere between two mystes, in which one argues that culture was an outgrowth of the vision of the Increate as logical and just, bound by interior consistency to fulfill his promises and threats. If that was the case, I thought, surely we will perish now, and the invasion from the north, that so many have died to resist, is no more than the wind that topples a tree already rotten.

Justice is a high thing, and that night, when I lay beside Dorcas listening to the rain, I was young, so that I desired high things only. That, I think, was why I so desired that our guild regain the position and regard it had once possessed. (And I still desired that, even then, when I had been cast out of it.) Perhaps it was for the same reason that the love of living things, which I had felt so strongly as a child, had declined until it was hardly more than a memory when I found poor Triskele bleeding outside the Bear Tower. Life, after all, is not a high thing, and in many ways is the reverse of purity. I am wise now, if not much older, and I know it is better to have all things, high and low, than to have the high only.

Unless the chiliarch decided, then, to grant clemency, tomorrow I would take Agilus's life. No one can say what that means. The body is a colony of cells (I used to think of our oubliette when Master Palaemon said that). Divided into two major parts, it perishes. But there is no reason to mourn the destruction of a colony of cells: such a colony dies each time a loaf of bread goes into the oven. If a man is no more than such a colony, a man is nothing; but we know instinctively that a man is more. What happens, then, to that part that is more?

It may be that it perishes as well, though more slowly. There are a great many haunted buildings, tunnels, and bridges; yet I have heard that in those cases in which the spirit is that of a human being and not an elemental, its appearances grow less and less frequent and at last cease. Historiographers say that in the remote past men knew only this one world of Urth, and had no fear of such beasts as were on it then, and traveled freely from this continent to the north; but no one has ever seen even the ghosts of such men.

It may be that it perishes at once—or that it wanders among the constellations. This Urth, surely, is less than a village in the immensity of the universe. And if a man lives in a village and his neighbors burn his house, he leaves the place if he does not die in it. But then we must ask how he came.

Master Gurloes, who has performed a great many executions, used to say that only a fool worried about making some failure of ritual: slipping in the blood, or failing to perceive that the client wore a wig and attempting to lift the head by the hair. The greater dangers were a loss of nerve that would make one's arms tremble and give an awkward blow and a feeling of vindictiveness that would transform the act of justice into mere revenge. Before I slept again, I tried to steel myself against both.

The Shadow of the Torturer

IT IS A PART of our office to stand uncloaked, masked, sword bared, upon the scaffold for a long time before the client is brought out. Some say this is to symbolize the unsleeping omnipresence of justice, but I believe the real reason is to give the crowd a focus, and the feeling that something is about to take place.

A crowd is not the sum of the individuals who compose it. Rather it is a species of animal, without language or real consciousness, born when they gather, dying when they depart. Before the Hall of Justice, a ring of dimarchi surrounded the scaffold with their lances, and the pistol their officer carried could, I suppose, have killed fifty or sixty before someone could snatch it from him and knock him to the cobblestones to die. Still it is better to have a focus, and some open symbol of power.

The people who had come to see the execution were by no means all, or even mostly, poor. The Sanguinary Field is near one of the better quarters of the city, and I saw plenty of red and yellow silk, and faces that had been washed with scented soap that morning. (Dorcas and I had splashed ourselves at the well in the courtyard.) Such people are much slower to violence than the poor, but once roused are far more dangerous because they are not accustomed to being overawed by force, and despite the dema-gogues, have a good deal more courage.

And so I stood with my hands resting on the quillions of *Terminus Est*, and turned this way and that, and adjusted the block so that my shadow would fall across it. The chiliarch was not visible, though I discovered later that he was watching from a window. I looked for Agia in the crowd but could not find her; Dorcas was on the steps of the Hall of Justice, a position reserved for her at my request by the portreeve.

The fat man who had waylaid me the day before was as near the scaffold as he could get, with a lance-fire threatening his bulging coat. The woman of the hungry eyes was on his right and the gray-haired woman on his left; I had her handkerchief in my boot top. The short man who had given me an asimi and the dull-eyed man who stammered and talked so strangely were nowhere to be seen. I looked for them on the rooftops where they could have had a good view despite their small stature, and though I did not find them, perhaps they were there.

Four sergeants in high dress helmets led Agilus forth. I saw the crowd opening for them like the water behind Hildegrin's boat before I could see them at all. Then came the scarlet plumes, then the flash of armor, and at last Agilus's brown hair and his wide, boyish face held uptilted because the chains that bound his arms forced his shoulder blades together. I remembered how elegant he had looked in the armor of a guards officer, with the golden chimera splashed across his chest. It seemed tragic that he could not be accompanied now by men of the unit that had in some sense been his, instead of these scarred regulars in laboriously polished steel. He had been stripped of all his finery now, and I waited to receive him wearing the fuligin mask in which I had fought him. Silly old women believe the Panjudicator punishes us with defeats and rewards us with victory: I felt I had been given more reward than I desired.

A few moments later he mounted the scaffold and the brief

ceremony began. When it was over, the soldiers forced him to his knees and I lifted my sword, forever blotting out the sun.

When the blade is as sharp as it should be, and the stroke is given correctly, one feels only a slight hesitation as the spinal column parts, then the solid bite of the edge into the block. I would take an oath that I smelled Agilus's blood on the rain-washed air before his head banged into the basket. The crowd drew back, then surged forward against the leveled lances. I heard the fat man's exhalation distinctly, precisely the sound he might have made at climax when he sweated over some hired woman. From far away came a scream, Agia's voice as unmistakable as a face seen by lightning. Something in its timbre made me feel she had not been watching at all, but had known nevertheless when her twin died.

The aftermath is often more troublesome than the act itself. As soon as the head has been exhibited to the crowd, it can be dropped back into the basket. But the headless body (which remains capable of losing a good deal of blood for a long time after the action of the heart has ceased) must be taken away in a manner dignified yet dishonorable. Furthermore, it must be not just taken "away," but taken to some specific spot where it will be safe from molestation. An exultant can, by custom, be laid across the saddle of his own destrier, and his remains are surrendered to his family at once. Persons of lesser rank, however, must be provided with some resting place secure from the eaters of the dead; and at least until they are safely out of sight, they must be dragged. The executioner cannot perform this task because he is already burdened with the head and with his weapon, and it is rare for anyone else involved—soldiers, officers of the court, and so on—to be willing to do so. (At the Citadel it was done by two journeymen and thus presented no difficulty.)

The chiliarch, a cavalryman by training and no doubt by inclination, had solved the problem by ordering that the body should be pulled behind a baggage sumpter. The animal had not been consulted, however, and being more of the laborer than the warrior kind, took fright at the blood and tried to bolt. We had an interesting time of it before we were able to get poor Agilus into a quadrangle from which the public was excluded.

I was cleaning off my boots when the portreeve met me there. When I saw him I supposed he had come to give me my fee, but he indicated that the chiliarch wished to pay me himself. As I told him, it was an unexpected honor.

"He watched everything," the portreeve said. "And he was quite pleased. He instructed me to tell you that you and the woman who travels with you are welcome to spend the night here, if you wish."

"We'll leave at twilight," I told him. "I believe that will be safer."

He took thought for a moment, then nodded, showing more intelligence than I would have anticipated. "The miscreant will have a family, I suppose, and friends—though no doubt you know no more of them than I. Still, it's a difficulty you must face frequently."

"I have been warned by more experienced members of my guild," I said.

I had said that we would leave at twilight, but in the event we waited until it was fully dark, in part for safety's sake and in part because it seemed wise to eat the evening meal before we left.

We could not, of course, make directly for the Wall and Thrax. The gate (of whose location I had only a vague idea in any event) would be shut, and I had been told by everyone that there were no inns between the barracks and the Wall. What we had to do, then, was first to lose ourselves, and then to find a place where we could spend the night and from which we could go without difficulty to the gate the next day. I had gotten detailed directions from the portreeve, and though we missed our way, it was some time before we realized it, and we began our walk quite cheerfully. The chiliarch had tried to hand me my fee instead of casting it on the ground at my feet (as is customary), and I had had to dissuade him for the sake of his own reputation. I gave Dorcas a detailed account of this incident, which had amused me nearly as much as it had flattered me. When I had finished, she asked practically, "He paid you well then, I suppose?"

"More than twice what he should have given for the services of a single journeyman. A master's fee. And of course I got a few tips in connection with the ceremony. Do you know, despite all I spent while Agia was with me, I have more money now than I did when I left our tower? I'm beginning to think that by practicing the mystery of our guild while you and I are traveling, I'll be able to support us."

Dorcas seemed to draw the brown mantle closer about her. "I was hoping you wouldn't have to practice it again at all. At least, not for a long time. You were so ill afterward, and I don't blame you."

"It was only nerves—I was afraid that something would go wrong."

"You pitied him. I know you did."

"I suppose so. He was Agia's brother, and like her, I think, in everything except sex."

"You miss Agia, don't you? Did you like her so much?"

"I only knew her for a day—much less time than I have known you already. If she had had her way, I'd be dead now. One of those two averns would have been the end of me."

"But the leaf didn't kill you."

I still recall the tone she used when she told me that; indeed, if I close my eyes now, I can hear her voice again and renew the shock I felt as I realized that ever since I had sat up to see Agilus still grasping his plant, I had been avoiding the thought. The leaf had not killed me, but I had turned my mind from my survival just as a man suffering from a deadly sickness manages by a thousand tricks never to look at death squarely; or rather, as a woman alone in a large house refrains from looking into mirrors, and instead busies herself with trivial errands, so that she may catch no glimpse of the thing whose feet she hears at times on the stairs.

I had survived, and I should be dead. I was haunted by my own life. I thrust one hand into my cloak and stroked my flesh, gingerly at first. There was something like a scar, and a little caked blood still adhered to the skin; but there was no bleeding and no pain. "They don't kill," I said. "That's all."

"She said they did."

"She told a great many lies." We were mounting a gentle hill bathed in pale green moonlight. Ahead of us, seeming as mountains do to be nearer than it was or could possibly be, was the pitch-black line of the Wall. Behind us the lights of Nessus created a false dawn that died bit by bit as the night advanced. I stopped at the top of the hill to admire them, and Dorcas took my arm. "So many homes. How many people are there in the city?"

"No one knows."

"And we will be leaving them all behind. Is it far to Thrax, Severian?"

"A long way, as I've told you already. At the foot of the first cataract. I'm not compelling you to go. You know that."

"I want to. But suppose . . . Severian, just suppose I wanted to go back later. Would you try and stop me?"

I said, "It would be dangerous for you to try to make the trip alone, so I might try to persuade you not to. But I wouldn't bind or imprison you, if that's what you mean."

"You told me you'd written out a copy of the note someone left for me in that inn. Do you remember? But you never showed it to me. I'd like to see it now."

"I told you exactly what it said, and it's not the real note, you know. Agia threw that away. I'm sure she thought that someone— Hildegrin, perhaps—was trying to warn me." I had already opened my sabretache; as I grasped the note, my fingers touched something else as well, something cold and strangely shaped.

Dorcas saw my expression and asked, "What is it?"

I drew it out. It was larger than an orichalk, but not by much, and only a trifle thicker. The cold material (whatever it was) flashed celestine beams back at the frigid rays of the moon. I felt I held a beacon that could be seen all over the city, and I thrust it back and dropped the closure of my sabretache.

Dorcas was clasping my arm so tightly that she might have been a bracelet of ivory and gold grown woman-sized. "What was that?" she whispered.

I shook my head to clear my thoughts. "It isn't mine. I didn't even know I had it. A gem, a precious stone . . ."

"It couldn't be. Didn't you feel the warmth? Look at your sword there—that's a gem. But what was that thing you just took out?"

I looked at the dark opal on the pommel of *Terminus Est*. It glowed in the moonlight, but it was no more like the object I had drawn from my sabretache than a lady's glass is like the sun. "The Claw of the Conciliator," I said. "Agia put it there. She must have, when we broke the altar, so it would not be found on her person if she were searched. She and Agilus would have got it again when Agilus claimed victor-right, and when I didn't die, she tried to steal it in his cell."

Dorcas was no longer staring at me. Her face was lifted and turned toward the city and the sky-glow of its myriad lamps. "Severian," she said. "It can't be."

Hanging over the city like a flying mountain in a dream was an enormous building—a building with towers and buttresses and an arched roof. Crimson light poured from its windows. I tried to speak, to deny the miracle even as I saw it; but before I could frame a syllable, the building had vanished like a bubble in a fountain, leaving only a cascade of sparks.

XXXII

The Play

IT WAS ONLY after the vision of that great building hanging, then vanishing, above the city, that I knew I had come to love Dorcas. We walked down the road—for we had found a new road just over the top of the hill—into darkness. And because our thoughts were entirely of what we had seen, our spirits embraced without hindrance, each passing through those few seconds of vision as if through a door never previously opened and never to be opened again.

I do not know just where it was we walked. I recall a winding road down the hillside, an arched bridge at the bottom, and another road, bordered for a league or so by a vagabond wooden fence. Wherever it was we went, I know we talked about ourselves not at all, but only of what we had seen and what its meaning might be. And I know that at the beginning of that walk I looked on Dorcas as no more than a chance-met companion, however desirable, however to be pitied. And at the end of it I loved Dorcas in a way that I have never loved another human being. I did not love her because I had come to love Thecla less—rather by loving Dorcas I loved Thecla more, because Dorcas was another self (as Thecla was yet to become in a fashion as terrible as the other was beautiful), and if I loved Thecla, Dorcas loved her also.

"Do you think," she asked, "that anyone saw it but us?"

I had not considered that, but I said that although the suspension of the building had endured for only a moment, yet it had taken place above the greatest of cities; and that if millions and tens of millions had failed to see it, yet hundreds must still have seen.

"Isn't it possible it was only a vision, meant only for us?"

"I have never had a vision, Dorcas."

"And I don't know whether I've had any or not. When I try to recall the time before I helped you out of the water, I can only remember being in the water myself. Everything before that is like a vision shattered to pieces, only small bright bits, a thimble I saw laid on velvet once, and the sound of a small dog barking outside a door. Nothing like this. Nothing like what we've seen."

What she said made me remember the note, which I had been searching for when my fingers touched the Claw, and that in turn suggested the brown book, which lay in the pleat of my sabretache next to it. I asked Dorcas if she would not like to see the book that had once been Thecla's, when we found a place to stop.

"Yes," she said. "When we are seated by a fire again, as we were for a moment at that inn."

"Finding that relic—which of course I will have to return before we can leave the city—and what we have been saying too remind me of something I read there once. Do you know of the key to the universe?"

Dorcas laughed softly. "No, Severian, I who scarcely know my name do not know anything about the key to the universe."

"I didn't say that as well as I should have. What I meant was, are you familiar with the idea that the universe has a secret key? A sentence, or a phrase, some say even a single word, that can be wrung from the lips of a certain statue, or read in the firmament, or that an anchorite on a world across the seas teaches his disciples?"

"Babies know it," Dorcas said. "They know it before they learn to speak, but by the time they're old enough to talk, they have forgotten most of it. At least, someone told me that once."

"That's what I mean, something like that. The brown book is a

collection of the myths of the past, and it has a section listing all the
keys of the universe—all the things people have said were The
Secret after they had talked to mystagogues on far worlds or studied
the *popul vuh* of the magicians, or fasted in the trunks of holy trees.
Thecla and I used to read them and talk about them, and one of
them was that everything, whatever happens, has three meanings.
The first is its practical meaning, what the book calls, 'the thing the
plowman sees.' The cow has taken a mouthful of grass, and it is
real grass, and a real cow—that meaning is as important and as true
as either of the others. The second is the reflection of the world
about it. Every object is in contact with all others, and thus the wise
can learn of the others by observing the first. That might be called
the soothsayers' meaning, because it is the one such people use
when they prophesy a fortunate meeting from the tracks of serpents
or confirm the outcome of a love affair by putting the elector of one
suit atop the patroness of another."

"And the third meaning?" Dorcas asked.

"The third is the transsubstantial meaning. Since all objects have
their ultimate origin in the Pancreator, and all were set in motion
by him, so all must express his will—which is the higher reality."

"You're saying that what we saw was a sign."

I shook my head. "The book is saying that everything is a sign.
The post of that fence is a sign, and so is the way the tree leans
across it. Some signs may betray the third meaning more readily
than others."

For perhaps a hundred paces we were both silent. Then Dorcas
said, "It seems to me that if what the Chatelaine Thecla's book says
is true, then people have everything backward. We saw a great
structure leap into the air and fall to nothing, didn't we?"

"I only saw it suspended over the city. Did it leap?"

Dorcas nodded. I could see the glimmer of her pale hair in the
moonlight. "It seems to me that what you call the third meaning is
very clear. But the second meaning is harder to find, and the first,
which ought to be the easiest, is impossible."

I was about to say I understood her—at least about the first meaning—when I heard from some distance off a rumbling roar that might have been a long roll of thunder. Dorcas exclaimed, "What's that?" and took my hand in her own small, warm one, which I found very pleasant.

"I don't know, but I think it came from the copse up ahead."

She nodded. "Now I hear voices."

"Your hearing is better than mine then."

The rumbling sounded again, louder and more prolonged; and this time, perhaps only because we were a trifle nearer, I thought I saw the gleam of lights through the trunks of the grove of young beeches ahead of us.

"There!" Dorcas said, and pointed in a direction somewhat to the north of the trees. "That can't be a star. It's too low and too bright, and moves too quickly."

"It's a lantern, I think. On a wagon, perhaps, or carried in someone's hand."

The rumble came once more, and this time I knew it for what it was, the rolling of a drum. I could hear voices now myself, very faintly, and particularly one voice that sounded deeper than the drum and almost as loud.

As we rounded the edge of the copse, we saw about fifty people gathered around a small platform. On it, between flaring torches, stood a giant who held a kettledrum beneath one arm like a tom-tom. A much smaller man, richly dressed, stood on his right, and on his left, nearly naked, the most sensuously beautiful woman I have ever seen.

"Everyone is here," the small man was saying, loudly and very rapidly. "Everyone is here. What would you have? Love and beauty?" He pointed to the woman. "Strength? Courage?" He waved the stick he carried toward the giant. "Deception? Mystery?" He tapped his own chest. "Vice?" He pointed toward the giant again. "And look here—see who's just come! It's our old enemy Death, who always comes sooner or later." With this he pointed to me, and every face in the audience turned to stare.

It was Dr. Talos and Baldanders; their presence seemed

inevitable as soon as I had recognized them. So far as I knew, I had never seen the woman.

"Death!" Dr. Talos said. "Death has come. I doubted you these past two days, old friend; I ought to have known better."

I expected the audience to laugh at this grim humor, but they did not. A few muttered to themselves, and a crone spat into her palm and pointed two fingers toward the ground.

"And who is it he has brought with him?" Dr. Talos leaned forward to peer at Dorcas in the torchlight. "Innocence, I believe it is. Yes, it's Innocence. Now everyone is here! The show will begin in a moment or two. Not for the faint of heart! You have never seen anything like it, anything at all! Everyone is here now."

The beautiful woman was gone, and such was the magnetism of the doctor's voice that I had not noticed when she left.

If I were to describe Dr. Talos's play now, as it appeared to me (a participant), the result could only be confusion. When I describe it as it appeared to the audience (as I intend to do at a more appropriate point in this account), I will not, perhaps, be believed. In a drama with a cast of five, of whom two on this first night had not learned their parts, armies marched, orchestras played, snow fell, and Urth trembled. Dr. Talos demanded much from the imagination of his audience; but he assisted that imagination with narration, simple yet clever machinery, shadows cast upon screens, holographic projectors, recorded noises, reflecting backdrops, and every other conceivable sleight, and on the whole he succeeded admirably, as evidenced by the sobs, shouts, and sighs that floated toward us from time to time out of the dark.

Triumphing in all this, he yet failed. For his desire was to communicate, to tell a great tale that had being only in his mind and could not be reduced to common words; but no one who ever witnessed a performance—and still less we who moved across his stage and spoke at his bidding—ever left it, I think with any clear understanding of what that tale was. It could only (Dr. Talos said) be expressed in the ringing of bells and the thunder of explosions, and sometimes by the postures of ritual. Yet as it proved in the end it could not be expressed even by these. There was a scene in which Dr. Talos fought Baldanders until the blood ran down both their faces; there was another in which Baldanders searched for a terrified Jolenta (that was the name of the most beautiful woman in the world) in a room of an underground palace, and at last seated himself on the chest where she lay hidden. In the final part I held the center of the stage, presiding over a chamber of inquiry in which Baldanders, Dr. Talos, Jolenta, and Dorcas were bound in various apparatuses. As the audience watched, I inflicted the most bizarre and ineffective (had they been real) torments on each in turn. In this scene, I could not help but notice how strangely the audience began to murmur while I was preparing, as it seemed, to wrench Dorcas's legs from their sockets. Though I was unaware of it, they had been permitted to see that Baldanders was freeing himself. Several women screamed when his chain clattered to the stage; I looked covertly toward Dr. Talos for directions, but he was already springing toward the audience, having freed himself with far less effort.

"Tableau," he called. "Tableau, everyone." I froze in position, having learned that was what was meant. "Gracious people, you have watched our little show with admirable attention. Now we ask a bit of your purse as well as your time. At the conclusion of the play you will see what occurs now that the monster has freed himself at last." Dr. Talos was holding out his tall hat to the audience, and I heard several coins clink into it. Unsatisfied, he leaped from the stage and began to move among the people. "Remember that once he is free, nothing stands between him and the consummation of his brutal desires. Remember that I, his tormentor, am bound now and at his mercy. Remember that you have never as yet learned—thank you, sieur—the identity of the mysterious figure seen by the Contessa through the curtained windows. Thank you. That above the dungeon you see now the weeping statue—thank you—still digs under the rowan tree. Come now, you have been very generous with your time. We ask only that you will not be penurious with your money. A few, truly, have treated us well, but we will not perform for a few. Where are the shining asimi that should have showered into my poor hat long ago from the rest of you? The few shall not pay for the multitude! If you've no asimis, then orichalks; if you have none, surely there is no one here without an aes!"

Eventually a sufficient sum was gathered, and Dr. Talos vaulted back into his place and deftly reaffixed the fastenings that seemed to hold him in an embrace of spikes. Baldanders roared and stretched forth his long arms as though to grasp me, allowing the audience to observe that a second chain, unnoticed previously, still constrained him. "See him," Dr. Talos prompted me *sotto voce*. "Hold him off with one of the flambeaux."

I pretended to discover for the first time that Baldanders's arms were free, and plucked one of the torches from its socket at the corner of the stage. At once both torches guttered; the flames, which had been of clear yellow above scarlet, now burned blue and pale green, spitting sparks and sputtering, doubling and tripling in size with a fearful hiss, only to sink at once as if on the point of going out. I thrust the one I had uprooted at Baldanders, shouting, "No! No! Back! Back!" prompted again by Dr. Talos. Baldanders responded by roaring more furiously than ever. He strained at the chain in a way that made the scenery wall to which he was bound creak and snap, and his mouth began quite literally to foam, a thick white liquid running from the corners of his lips to bedew his huge chin and fleck his rusty black clothes as though with snow. Someone in the audience screamed, and the chain broke with a report like the snapping of a drover's whip. By this time the giant's face was hideous in its madness, and I would no more have attempted to stand in his way than to stop an avalanche; but before I could move a step to escape him, he had wrested the torch from me and knocked me down with its iron shaft.

I got my head up in time to see him jerk the other torch from its place and make for the audience with both. The shrieking of men drowned the shrilling of women—it sounded as if our guild were exercising a hundred clients together. I pulled myself up and was about to seize Dorcas and dash for the cover of the copse when I saw Dr. Talos. He seemed filled with what I can only call malignant good humor, and though he was freeing himself from his fastenings, he was taking his time about it. Jolenta was setting herself free as well, and if there were any expression at all on that perfect face, it was one of relief.

"Very well!" Dr. Talos exclaimed. "Very well indeed. You may come back now, Baldanders. Don't leave us in the dark." To me: "Did you enjoy your maiden experience of the boards, Master Torturer? For a beginner acting without rehearsal, you played nicely enough."

I managed to nod.

"Except when Baldanders knocked you down. You must forgive him, he could see you didn't know enough to drop. Come with me now. Baldanders has his talents, but a fine eye for minutiae lost in grass isn't one of them. I have some lights backstage, and you and Innocence shall help us pick up."

I did not understand what he meant, but in a few moments the torches were back in place and we were hunting through the trampled area in front of the stage with dark lanterns. "It's a gambling proposition," Dr. Talos explained. "And I confess to loving them. The money in the hat is a sure thing—by the close of the first act I can predict to an orichalk how much it will be. But the dropsies! They may be no more than two apples and a turnip, or as much as the imagination can encompass. We have found a baby pig. Delicious, so Baldanders told me when he ate it. We have found a baby baby. We have found a gold-headed stick, and I retain it. Antique brooches. Shoes . . . We frequently find shoes of all kinds. Just now I have found a woman's parasol." He held it up. "This will be just the thing to keep the sun from our fair Jolenta when we go strolling tomorrow."

Jolenta straightened up as people do who are straining not to stoop. Above the waist her creamy amplitude was such that her spine must have been curved backward to balance the weight. "If we're going to an inn tonight, I'd like to go now," she said. "I'm very tired, Doctor."

I was exhausted myself.

"An inn? Tonight? A criminal waste of funds. Look at it this way, my dear. The nearest is a league away at the very least, and it would take Baldanders and me a watch to pack the scenery and properties, even with the help of this friendly Angel of Torment. By the time we reached the inn at that rate the horizon would be under the sun, the cocks would be crowing, and like as not a thousand fools would be rising, banging their doors and throwing their slops."

Baldanders grunted (I thought in confirmation), then struck with his boot as if at some venomous thing he had discovered in the grass.

Dr. Talos threw wide his arms to embrace the universe. "While here, my dear, beneath stars that are the personal and cherished property of the Increate, we have all anyone could wish for the most salubrious rest. There's just chill enough in the air tonight to make sleepers grateful for the warmth of their coverings and the heat of the fire, and not a hint of rain. Here we will camp, here we will break our fast in the morning, and from here we will walk renewed in the joyful hours when the day is young."

I said, "You mentioned something about breakfast. Is there any food now? Dorcas and I are hungry."

"Of course there is. I see Baldanders has just picked up a basket of yams."

Several members of our erstwhile audience must have been farm people returning from a market with whatever produce they had been unable to sell. Besides the yams we had, eventually, a pair of squabs and several stalks of young sugar cane. There was not much bedding, but there was some, and Dr. Talos himself used none of it, saying he would sit up and watch the fire, and perhaps nap, later, in the chair that had been the Autarch's throne and the Inquisitor's bench a short time before.

XXXIII

Five Legs

FOR PERHAPS A WATCH I lay awake. I soon realized that Dr. Talos was not going to sleep, but I clung to the hope that he would leave us for one reason or another. He sat for a time as if deep in thought, then stood and began to pace up and down before the fire. His was an immobile yet expressive face—a slight movement of one eyebrow or the cocking of his head could change it utterly, and as he passed back and forth before my half-closed eyes I saw sorrow, glee, desire, ennui, resolution, and a score of other emotions that have no names flicker across that vulpine mask.

At last he began to swing his cane at the blossoms of wild flowers. In a short time he had decapitated all those within a dozen steps of the fire. I waited until I could no longer see his erect, energetic figure and only faintly hear the whistling strokes of his cane. Then slowly I drew forth the gem.

It was as if I held a star, a thing that burned in the night. Dorcas was asleep, and though I had hoped that we could examine the gem together, I forbore from waking her. The icy blue radiance waxed until I was afraid Dr. Talos would see it, far off as he was. I held the gem to my eye with some childish idea of viewing the fire through it as through a lens, then snatched it away—the familiar world of grass and sleepers had become no more than a dance of sparks, slashed by a scimitar blade.

I am not sure how old I was when Master Malrubius died. It was a number of years before I became captain, so I must have been quite a small boy. I remember very well, however, how it was when Master Palaemon succeeded him as master of apprentices; Master Malrubius had held that position ever since I had been aware that such a thing existed, and for weeks and perhaps months it seemed to me that Master Palaemon (though I liked him as well or better) could not be our real master in the sense that Master Malrubius had been. The atmosphere of dislocation and unreality was heightened by the knowledge that Master Malrubius was not dead or even away . . . that he was, in fact, merely lying in his cabin, lying in the same bed he had slept in each night when he was still teaching and disciplining us. There is a saying that unseen is as good as unbeen; but in this case it was otherwise—unseen, Master Malrubius was more palpably present than ever before. Master Palaemon refused to assert that he would never return, and so every act was weighed in double scales: "*Would Master Palaemon permit it?*" and "*What would Master Malrubius say?*"

(In the end he said nothing. Torturers do not go to the Tower of Healing, no matter how ill; there is a belief—whether true or not I cannot say—that old scores are settled there.)

If I were writing this history to entertain or even to instruct, I would not digress here to discuss Master Malrubius, who must, at the moment when I thrust away the Claw, have been dust for long years. But in a history, as in other things, there are necessities and necessities. I know little of literary style; but I have learned as I have progressed, and find this art not so much different from my old one as might be thought.

Many scores and sometimes many hundreds of persons come to watch an execution, and I have seen balconies torn from their walls by the weight of the watchers, killing more in their single crash than I in my career. These scores and hundreds may be likened to the readers of a written account.

But there are others besides these spectators who must be satisfied: the authority in whose name the carnifex acts; those who have given him money so that the condemned may have an easy (or a hard) death; and the carnifex himself.

The spectators will be content if there are no long delays, if the condemned is permitted to speak briefly and does it well, if the upraised blade gleams in the sun for a moment before it descends, thus giving them time to catch breath and nudge one another, and if the head falls with a satisfactory gout of blood. Similarly you, who will some day delve in Master Ultan's library, will require of me no long delays; personages who are permitted to speak only briefly yet do it well; certain dramatic pauses which shall signal to you that something of import is about to occur; excitement; and a sating quantity of blood.

The authorities for whom the carnifex acts, the chiliarchs or archons (if I may be permitted to prolong my figure of speech), will have little complaint if the condemned is prevented from escaping, or much inflaming the mob; and if he is undeniably dead at the conclusion of the proceedings. That authority, as it seems to me, in my writing is the impulse that drives me to my task. Its requirements are that the subject of this work must remain central to it—not escaping into prefaces or indexes or into another work entirely; that the rhetoric not be permitted to overwhelm it; and that it be carried to a satisfactory conclusion.

Those who have paid the carnifex to make the act a painless or a painful one may be likened to the literary traditions and accepted models to which I am compelled to bow. I recall that one winter day, when cold rain beat against the window of the room where he gave us our lessons, Master Malrubius—perhaps because he saw we were too dispirited for serious work, perhaps only because he was dispirited himself—told us of a certain Master Werenfrid of our guild who in olden times, being in grave need, accepted remuneration from the enemies of the condemned and from his friends as well; and who by stationing one party on the right of the block and the other on the left, by his great skill made it appear to each that the result was entirely satisfactory. In just this way, the contending parties of tradition pull at the writers of histories. Yes, even at autarchs. One desires ease; the other, richness of experience in the execution . . . of the writing. And I must try, in the dilemma of Master Werenfrid but lacking his abilities, to satisfy each. This I have attempted to do.

There remains the carnifex himself; I am he. It is not enough for him to earn praise from all. It is not enough, even, for him to perform his function in a way he knows to be entirely creditable and in keeping with the teaching of his masters and the ancient traditions. In addition to all this, if he is to feel full satisfaction at the moment when Time lifts his own severed head by the hair, he must add to the execution some feature however small that is entirely his own and that he will never repeat. Only thus can he feel himself a free artist.

When I shared a bed with Baldanders, I dreamed a strange dream; and in composing this history I did not hesitate to relate it, the relation of dreams being entirely in the literary tradition. At the time I write of now, when Dorcas and I slept under the stars with Baldanders and Jolenta, and Dr. Talos sat by, I experienced what may have been less or greater than a dream; and that is outside that tradition. I give warning to you who will later read this that it has little bearing on what will soon follow; I give it only because it puzzled me at the time and it will provide me with satisfaction to relate it. Yet it may be that insofar as it entered my mind and has remained there from that time to this, it affected my actions during the latter part of my narrative.

With the Claw safely hidden away, I lay stretched on an old blanket near the fire. Dorcas lay with her head near mine; Jolenta with her feet to mine; Baldanders on his back on the opposite side of the fire, his thick-soled boots among the embers. Dr. Talos's chair stood near the giant's hand, but it was turned away from the fire. Whether or not he did sit in it with his face to the night I cannot say; for parts of the time I am going to relate I seemed conscious of his presence in the chair, at other times I sensed that he was absent. The sky was growing lighter, I believe, than it is at full dark.

Footfalls reached my ears yet hardly disturbed my rest, heavy, yet softly pattering; then the sound of breath, the snuffling of an animal. If I was awake, my eyes were open; but I was still so nearly in sleep that I did not turn my head. The animal approached me and sniffed at my clothes and my face. It was Triskele, and Triskele lay down with his spine pressed against my body. It did not seem odd then that he had found me, though I recall feeling a certain pleasure at seeing him again.

Once more I heard footsteps, now the slow, firm tread of a man; I knew at once that it was Master Malrubius—I could recall his step in the corridors under the tower on the days when we made the rounds of the cells; the sound was the same. He came into the circle of my vision. His cloak was dusty, as it always was save on the most formal occasions; he drew it about him in the old way as he seated himself on a box of properties. "Severian. Name for me the seven principles of governance."

It was an effort for me to speak, but I managed (in my dream, if it was a dream) to say, "I do not recall that we have studied such a thing, Master."

"You were always the most careless of my boys," he told me, and fell silent.

A foreboding grew on me; I sensed that if I did not reply, some tragedy would occur. At last I began weakly, "Anarchy . . ."

"That is not governance, but the lack of it. I taught you that it precedes all governance. Now list the seven sorts."

"Attachment to the person of the monarch. Attachment to a bloodline or other sequence of succession. Attachment to the royal state. Attachment to a code legitimizing the governing state. Attachment to the law only. Attachment to a greater or lesser board of electors, as framers of the law. Attachment to an abstraction conceived as including the body of electors, other bodies giving rise to them, and numerous other elements, largely ideal."

"Tolerable. Of these, which is the earliest form, and which the highest?"

"The development is in the order given, Master," I said. "But I do not recall that you ever asked before which was highest."

Master Malrubius leaned forward, his eyes burning brighter than the coals of the fire. "Which is highest, Severian?"

"The last, Master?"

"You mean attachment to an abstraction conceived as including the body of electors, other bodies giving rise to them, and numerous other elements, largely ideal?"

"Yes, Master."

"Of what kind, Severian, is your own attachment to the Divine Entity?"

I said nothing. It may have been that I was thinking; but if so, my mind was too much filled with sleep to be conscious of its thought. Instead, I became profoundly aware of my physical surroundings. The sky above my face in all its grandeur seemed to have been made solely for my benefit, and to be presented for my inspection now. I lay upon the ground as upon a woman, and the very air that surrounded me seemed a thing as admirable as crystal and as fluid as wine.

"Answer me, Severian."

"The first, if I have any."

"To the person of the monarch?"

"Yes, because there is no succession."

"The animal that rests beside you now would die for you. Of what kind is his attachment to you?"

"The first?"

There was no one there. I sat up. Malrubius and Triskele had vanished, yet my side felt faintly warm.

XXXIV

Morning

"YOU ARE AWAKE," Dr. Talos said. "I trust you slept well?"

"I had a strange dream." I stood and looked about.

"There's no one here but ourselves." As though he were reassuring a child, Dr. Talos gestured toward Baldanders and the sleeping women.

"I dreamed my dog—he has been lost for years now—came back and lay beside me. I could still feel the warmth of his body when I woke."

"You were lying beside a fire," Dr. Talos pointed out. "There has been no dog here."

"A man, dressed much as I am."

Dr. Talos shook his head. "I could not have failed to see him."

"You might have dozed."

"Only earlier in the evening. I have been awake for the past two watches."

"I'll guard the stage and properties for you," I said, "if you'd like to sleep now." The truth was that I was afraid to lie down again.

Dr. Talos seemed to hesitate, then said, "That's very kind of you," and stiffly lowered himself onto my now dew-soaked blanket.

I took his chair, turning it so I could watch the fire. For some time I was alone with my thoughts, which were at first of my dream, then of the Claw, the mighty relic chance had dropped into my hands. I felt very glad when Jolenta began to stir and at last rose and stretched her lush limbs against the scarlet-shot sky. "Is there water?" she asked. "I want to wash."

I told her that I thought Baldanders had carried the water for our supper from the direction of the copse, and she nodded and went off to look for a stream. Her appearance, at least, distracted my thoughts; I found myself glancing from her retreating figure to Dorcas's prone one. Jolenta's beauty was perfect. No other woman I have ever seen could approach it—Thecla's towering stateliness made her seem coarse and mannish in comparison, Dorcas's blond delicacy as meager and childlike as Valeria, the forgotten girl I had encountered in the Atrium of Time.

Yet I was not attracted to Jolenta as I had been to Agia; I did not love her as I had loved Thecla; and I did not desire the intimacy of thought and feeling that had sprung up between Dorcas and me, or think it possible. Like every man who ever saw her I desired her, but I wanted her as one wants a woman in a painting. And even while I admired her, I could not help but notice (as I had on the stage the night before) how clumsily she walked, she who appeared so graceful in repose. Those round thighs chafed one another, that admirable flesh weighed her until she carried her voluptuousness as another woman would have carried a child in her belly. When she returned from the copse with drops of clear water shining in her lashes, and her face as pure and perfect as the curve of the rainbow, I felt still almost as though I were alone.

". . . I said, there's fruit if you want it. The doctor had me save some last night so we'd have something for breakfast." Her voice was husky and slightly breathless. One listened as if to music.

"I'm sorry," I told her. "I was thinking. Yes, I'd like some fruit. That's very kind of you."

"I won't get it for you, you'll have to fetch it yourself. It's there, behind that stand of armor."

The armor to which she pointed was actually of cloth stretched over a wire frame and painted silver. Behind it I found an old basket containing grapes, an apple, and a pomegranate.

"I'd like something too," Jolenta said. "Those grapes, I think."

I gave her the grapes, and considering that Dorcas would probably prefer the apple, put it near her hand and took the pomegranate for myself.

Jolenta held up her grapes. "Grown under glass by some exultant's gardener—it's too soon for natural ones. I don't think this strolling life's going to be too bad. And I get a third of the money."

I asked if she had not trouped with the doctor and his giant before.

"You don't remember me, do you? I didn't think so." She popped a grape into her mouth and so far as I could see swallowed it whole. "No, I haven't. I did have a rehearsal, although with that girl thrust into the story so suddenly we had to change everything."

"I must have disturbed things more than she did. She was on stage much less."

"Yes, but you were supposed to be there. Dr. Talos took your roles when we practiced as well as his own, and told me what you were supposed to say."

"He depended on my meeting him, then."

The doctor himself sat up at that, almost with a snap. He looked wide awake. "Of course, of course. We told you where we'd be when we were at breakfast, and if you hadn't appeared last night, we would've presented 'Great Scenes From' and waited another day. Jolenta, you won't be getting a third of the receipts now, but a quarter—it's only fair that we share with the other woman."

Jolenta shrugged and swallowed another grape.

"Wake her now, Severian. We should be going. I'll rouse Baldanders, and we can divide the money and pack."

"I won't be going with you," I said.

Dr. Talos looked at me quizzically.

"I have to return to the city. I have business with the Order of Pelerines."

"You can remain with us until we reach the main road, then. It will be your most expeditious route back." Perhaps because he refrained from questioning me, I felt he knew more than what he had said indicated.

Ignoring our talk, Jolenta smothered a yawn. "I'll have to have more sleep before tonight, or my eyes won't look as good as they should."

I said, "I will, but when we reach the road, I must go."

Dr. Talos had already turned away to wake the giant, shaking him and striking his shoulders with his slender cane. "As you wish," he said, and I could not be sure whether he was addressing Jolenta or me. I stroked Dorcas's forehead and whispered that we would have to move on now.

"I wish you hadn't done that. I was having the most wonderful dream . . . Very detailed, very real."

"So was I—before I woke, I mean."

"You've been awake a long time then? Is this apple mine?"

"All the breakfast you'll get, I'm afraid."

"All I need. Look at it, how round it is, how red. What is it they say? 'Red as the apples of . . .' I can't think of it. Would you like a bite?"

"I've eaten already. I had a pomegranate."

"I should have known from the stains on your mouth. I thought you'd been sucking blood all night." I must have looked shocked when she said this, because she added, "Well, you did look like a black bat bending over me."

Baldanders was sitting up now, rubbing his eyes with his hands like an unhappy child. Dorcas called across the fire, "Terrible to have to rise so early, isn't it, goodman? Were you dreaming too?"

"No dreams," Baldanders answered. "I never dream." (Dr. Talos looked toward me and shook his head as if to say, *Most unhealthy.*)

"I'll give you some of mine then. Severian says he has plenty of his own."

Though he seemed thoroughly awake, Baldanders stared at her. "Who are you?"

"I'm . . ." Dorcas turned toward me, frightened.

"Dorcas," I said.

"Yes, Dorcas. Don't you remember? We met behind the curtain last night. You . . . your friend introduced us, and said I shouldn't be afraid of you, because you would only pretend to hurt people. In the show. I said I understood, because Severian does terrible things but is really so kind." Dorcas looked to me again. "You remember, Severian, don't you?"

"Of course. I don't think you have to be anxious about Baldanders just because he's forgotten. He's big, I know, but his size is like my fuligin clothes—it makes him look much worse than he is."

Baldanders told Dorcas, "You have a wonderful memory. I wish I could recall everything like that." His voice was like the rolling of heavy stones.

While we were talking, Dr. Talos had produced the money box. He jingled it now to interrupt us. "Come, friends, I have promised you a fair and equitable distribution of the proceeds of our performance, and when that is complete, it will be time to be moving. Turn around, Baldanders, and spread your hands in your lap. Sieur Severian, ladies, will you gather around me as well?"

I had observed, of course, that when the doctor spoke earlier of dividing the contributions he had collected the night before, he had specified division into four parts; but I had assumed it was Baldanders, who seemed to be his slave, who would receive nothing. Now, however, after rummaging in the box, Dr. Talos dropped a shining asimi into the giant's hands, gave another to me, a third to Dorcas, and a fistful of orichalks to Jolenta; then he began to distribute orichalks singly. "You will notice that everything thus far is good money," he said. "I regret to report that there are a fair number of dubious coins here as well. When the undoubted specie is exhausted, you will each come in for a share of them."

Jolenta asked, "Have you already taken yours, Doctor? I think the rest of us ought to have been present."

For a moment Dr. Talos's hands, which had been darting

from one of us to another as he counted out the coins, paused. "I take no share from this," he said.

Dorcas glanced toward me as if to confirm her judgment and whispered, "That doesn't seem fair."

I said, "It isn't fair. Doctor, you took as large a part in the show last night as any of us, and collected the money, and from what I have seen, you provided the stage and scenery as well. If anything, you should have a double share."

"I take nothing," Dr. Talos said slowly. It was the first time I had seen him abashed. "It is my pleasure to direct what I may now call the company. I wrote the play we perform, and like . . ." (he looked around as if at a loss for a simile) ". . . that armor there I play my part. These things are my pleasure, and all the reward I require.

"Now, friends, you will have observed that we are reduced to single orichalks, and there are not enough to make the circle again. To be specific, only two are left. Whoever wishes may have both by renouncing claim to the aes and doubtful stuff remaining. Severian? Jolenta?"

Somewhat to my surprise, Dorcas announced, "I'll take them."

"Very good. I will not presume to judge among the rest, but simply hand it out. I warn you who receive it to be careful in passing it. There are penalties for such things, though outside the Wall— What's this?"

I followed the direction of his eyes and saw a man in shabby gray advancing toward us.

X X X V

Hethor

I DO NOT KNOW why it should be humiliating to receive a stranger while sitting on the ground, but it is so. Both the women stood as the gray figure approached, and so did I. Even Baldanders lumbered to his feet, so that by the time the newcomer was within speaking distance, only Dr. Talos, who had reoccupied our one chair, remained seated.

Yet a less impressive figure would have been difficult to imagine. He was small of stature, and because his clothes were too large for him, seemed smaller still. His weak chin was covered with stubble; as he approached, he pulled a greasy cap away to show a head on which the hair had retreated at either side to leave a single wavering line like the crest of an old and dirty burginot. I knew I had seen him elsewhere, but it was a moment before I recognized him.

"Lords," he said. "O lords and mistresses of creation, silken-capped, silken-haired women, and man commanding empires and the armies of the F-f-foemen of our Ph-ph-photosphere! Tower strong as stone is strong, strong as the o-o-oak that puts forth leaves new after the fire! And my master, dark master, death's victory, viceroy over the n-night! Long I signed on the silver-sailed ships, the hundred-masted whose masts reached out to touch the st-st-

stars, I, floating among their shining jibs with the Pleiades burning beyond the top-royal sp-sp-spar, but never have I seen ought like you! He-he-hethor am I, come to serve you, to scrape the mud from your cloak, whet the great sword, c-c-carry the basket with the eyes of your victims looking up at me, Master, eyes like the dead moons of Verthandi when the sun has gone out. When the sun has g-g-gone out! Where are they then, the bright players? How long will the torches burn? The f-f-freezing hands grope toward them, but the torch bowls are colder than any ice, colder than the moons of Verthandi, colder than the dead eyes! Where is the strength then that beats the lake to foam? Where is the empire, where the Armies of the Sun, long-lanced and golden-bannered? Where are the silken-haired women we loved only l-l-last night?"

"You were in our audience, I take it," said Dr. Talos. "I can well sympathize with your desire to see the performance again. But we won't be able to oblige you until evening, and by then we hope to be some distance from here."

Hethor, whom I had met outside Agilus's prison with the fat man, the hungry-eyed woman and the others, did not seem to have heard him. He was staring at me, with occasional glances toward Baldanders and Dorcas. "He hurt you, didn't he? Writhing, writhing. I saw you with the blood running, red as pentecost. Wh-wh-what honor for you! You serve him too, and your calling is higher than mine."

Dorcas shook her head and turned her face away. The giant only stared. Dr. Talos said, "Surely you understand that what you saw was a theatrical performance." (I remember thinking that if most of the audience had had a firmer grip on that idea, we would have found ourselves in an embarrassing dilemma when Baldanders jumped from the stage.)

"I u-understand more than you think, I the old captain, the old lieutenant, the old c-c-cook in his old kitchen, cooking soup, cooking broth for the dying pets! My master is real, but where are your armies? Real, and where are your empires? Sh-shall false blood run from a true wound? Where is your strength when the bb-blood is gone, where is the luster of the silken hair? I w-will catch it in a cup of glass, I, the old c-captain of the old limping sh-ship, with its crew black against the silver sails, and the C-c-coalstack behind it."

Perhaps I should say here that at the time I paid little attention to the rush and stumble of Hethor's words, though my ineradicable memory enables me to recreate them on paper now. He spoke a gobbling singsong, with a fine spray of spittle flying through the gaps in his teeth. In his slow way, Baldanders may have understood him. Dorcas, I feel sure, was too repelled by him to hear much of what he said. She turned aside as one turns from the mutterings and cracking bones when an alzabo savages a carcass, and Jolenta listened to nothing that did not concern herself.

"You can see for yourself that the young woman is unharmed." Dr. Talos rose and put away his money box. "It's always a pleasure to speak to someone who has appreciated our performance, but I'm afraid we've work to do. We must pack. If you'll excuse us?"

Now that his conversation had become one with Dr. Talos exclusively, Hethor put his cap on again, pulling it down until it nearly covered his eyes. "Stowage? There's no one better for it than I, the old s-supercargo, the old chandler and steward, the old st-stevedore. Who else shall put the kernels back on the cob, fit the f-fledgling into the egg again? Who shall fold the solemn-winged m-moth, with w-wings each like stuns'ls, into the broken cocoon left h-hanging like a s-s-sarcophagus? And for the love of the M-master, I'll do it, for the sake of the M-master, I'll do it. And f-f-f-follow anywhere, anywhere he goes."

I nodded, not knowing what to say. Just at the moment, Baldanders—who had apparently caught the references to packing if he had caught nothing else—scooped a backdrop from the stage and began to wind it on its pole. Hethor vaulted up with unexpected agility to fold the set for the Inquisitor's chamber and reel in the projector wires. Dr. Talos turned to me as if to say, *He's your responsibility after all, just as Baldanders is mine.*

"There are a good many of them," I told him. "They find

pleasure in pain, and want to associate with us just as a normal man might want to be around Dorcas and Jolenta."

The doctor nodded. "I wondered. One can imagine an ideal servant who serves out of pure love for his master, just as one can an ideal rustic who remains a ditcher from a love of nature, or an ideal fricatrice who spreads her legs a dozen times a night from a love of copulation. But one never encounters these fabulous creatures in reality'."

In about a watch we were on the road. Our small theater packed itself quite neatly into a huge barrow formed from parts of the stage, and Baldanders, who wheeled this contraption, also carried a few odds and ends on his back. Dr. Talos, with Dorcas, Jolenta, and me behind him, led the way, and Hethor followed Baldanders at a distance of perhaps a hundred paces.

"He's like me," Dorcas said, glancing back. "And the doctor is like Agia, only not as bad. Do you remember? She couldn't make me go away, and eventually you made her stop trying."

I did remember, and asked why she had followed us with such determination.

"You were the only people I knew. I was more afraid of being alone than I was of Agia."

"Then you *were* afraid of Agia."

"Yes, very much. I still am. But . . . I don't know where I've been, but I think I've been alone, wherever I was. For a long time. I didn't want to do that anymore. You won't understand this—or like it—but . . ."

"Yes?"

"If you had hated me as much as Agia did, I would have followed you anyway."

"I don't think Agia hated you."

Dorcas stared up at me, and I can see that piquant face now as well as if it were reflected in the quiet well of vermillion ink. It was, perhaps, a trifle pinched and pale, too childlike for great beauty; but the eyes were bits of the azure firmament of some hidden world waiting for Man; they could have vied with Jolenta's own. "She hated me," Dorcas said softly. "She hates me more now. Do you remember how dazed you were after the fight? You never looked back when I led you away. I did, and I saw her face."

Jolenta had been complaining to Dr. Talos because she had to walk. Baldanders's deep, dull voice came from behind us now. "I will carry you."

She glanced back at him. "What? On top of all the rest?"

He did not reply.

"When I say I want to ride, I don't mean, as you seem to think, like a fool at a flogging."

In my imagination, I saw the giant's sad nod.

Jolenta was afraid of looking foolish, and what I am going to write now will sound foolish indeed, though it is true. You, my reader, may enjoy yourself at my expense. It struck me then how fortunate I was, and how fortunate I had been since leaving the Citadel. Dorcas I knew was my friend—more than a lover, a true companion, though we had been together only a few days. The giant's heavy tread behind me reminded me of how many men there are who wander Urth utterly alone. I knew then (or thought I did) why Baldanders chose to obey Dr. Talos, bending his mighty strength to whatever task the red-haired man laid on him.

A touch at my shoulder took me from my revery. It was Hethor, who must have come up silently from his position in the rear. "Master," he said.

I told him not to call me that, and explained that I was only a journeyman of my guild, and would probably never attain to mastership.

He nodded humbly. Through his open lips I could glimpse the broken incisors. "Master, where do we go?"

"Out the gate," I said, and told myself I said it because I wanted him to follow Dr. Talos and not me; the truth was that I was thinking of the preternatural beauty of the Claw, and how sweet it would be to carry it to Thrax with me, instead of retracing my steps to the center of Nessus. I gestured toward the Wall, which now rose in the distance as the walls of a common fortress must rise before a mouse. They were black as thunderheads, and held certain clouds captive at their summit.

"I will carry your sword, Master."

The offer seemed honestly made, though I was reminded that the plot Agia and her brother had conceived against me had been born of their desire for *Terminus Est*. As firmly as I could, I said, "No. Not now or ever."

"I feel pity for you, Master, seeing you walk with it on your shoulder so. It must be very heavy."

I was explaining, quite truthfully, that it was not as burdensome as it appeared, when we rounded the side of a gentle hill and saw half a league off a straight highway running toward an opening in the Wall. It was crowded with carts and wagons and traffic of all kinds, all dwarfed by the Wall and the towering gate until the people looked like mites and the beasts like ants pulling at little crumbs. Dr. Talos turned until he was walking backward and waved at the Wall as proudly as if he had built it himself.

"Some of you, I think, have never seen this. Severian? Ladies? Have you been this near before?"

Even Jolenta shook her head, and I said, "No. I've spent my life so near the middle of the city that the wall was no more than a dark line on the northern horizon when we looked from the glass-roofed room at the top of our tower. I am astounded, I admit."

"The ancients built well, did they not? Think—after so many millennia, all the open area through which we have passed today yet remains for the growth of the city. But Baldanders is shaking his head. Don't you see, my dear patient, that all these bosquets and pleasant meadows among which we have journeyed this morning will one day be displaced by buildings and streets?"

Baldanders said, "They were not for the growing of Nessus."

"Of course, of course. I'm sure you were there, and know all about it." The doctor winked at the rest of us. "Baldanders is older than I, and so believes he knows everything. Sometimes."

We were soon within a hundred paces or so of the highway, and Jolenta's attention became fixed on its traffic. "If there's a litter for hire, you must get it for me," she told Dr. Talos. "I won't be able to perform tonight if I have to walk all day."

He shook his head. "You forget, I have no money. Should you see a litter and wish to engage it, you are of course free to do so. If you cannot appear tonight, your understudy will take your role."

"My understudy?"

The doctor gestured toward Dorcas. "I'm certain she is eager to try the starring part, and that she will do famously. Why do you think I permitted her to join us and share in the proceeds? Less rewriting will be necessary than if we have two women."

"She will go with Severian, you fool. Didn't he say this morning he was going back to look for—" Jolenta wheeled on me, more beautiful than ever for being angry. "What did you call them? Pelisses?"

I said, "Pelerines." And at this a man riding a merychip at the edge of the concourse of people and animals reined his diminutive mount over. "If you're looking for the Pelerines," he said, "your way lies with mine—out the gate, not toward the city. They passed along this road last night."

I quickened my step until I could grasp the cantle of his saddle, and asked if he were sure of his information.

"I was disturbed when the other patrons of my inn rushed into the road to receive their blessing,". the man on the merychip said. "I looked out the window and saw their procession. Their servants carried deeses illuminated with candles but reversed, and the priestesses themselves had torn their habits." His face, which was long and worn and humorous, split in a wry grin. "I don't know what was wrong, but believe me, their departure was impressive and unmistakable—that's what the bear said, you know, about the picnickers."

Dr. Talos whispered to Jolenta, "I think the angel of agony there, and your understudy, will remain with us a while longer."

As it proved, he was half in error. No doubt you, who have perhaps seen the Wall many times, and perhaps passed often through one or another of its gates, will be impatient with me; but before I continue this account of my life, I find I must for my own peace spend a few words on it.

I have already spoken of its height. There are few sorts of birds, I think, that would fly over it. The eagle and the great mountain teratornis, and possibly the wild geese and their allies; but few others. This height I had come to expect by the time we reached the base: the Wall had been in plain view then for many leagues, and no one who saw it, with the clouds moving across its face as ripples do across a pond, could fail to realize its altitude. It is of black metal, like the walls of the Citadel, and for this reason it seemed less terrible to me than it would have otherwise—the buildings I had seen in the city were of stone or brick, and to come now on the material I had known from earliest childhood was no unpleasant thing.

Yet to enter the gate was to enter a mine, and I could not suppress a shudder. I noticed too that everyone around me except for Dr. Talos and Baldanders seemed to feel as I did. Dorcas clasped my hand more tightly, and Hethor hung his head. Jolenta seemed to consider that the doctor, with whom she had been quarreling a moment before, might protect her; but when he paid no heed to her touch at his arm and continued to swagger forward and pound the pavement with his stick just as he had in the sunlight, she left him and to my astonishment took the stirrup strap of the man on the merychip.

The sides of the gate rose high above us, pierced at wide intervals by windows of some material thicker, yet clearer, than glass. Behind these windows we could see the moving figures of men and women, and of creatures that were neither men nor women. Cacogens, I think, were there, beings to whom the avern was but what a marigold or a marguerite is to us. Others seemed beasts with too much of men about them, so that horned heads watched us with eyes too wise, and mouths that appeared to speak showed teeth like nails or hooks. I asked Dr. Talos what these creatures were.

"Soldiers," he said. "The pandours of the Autarch."

Jolenta, whose fear made her press the side of one full breast against the thigh of the man on the merychip, whispered, "Whose perspiration is the gold of his subjects."

"Within the Wall itself, Doctor?"

"Like mice. Although it is of immense thickness, it's honeycombed everywhere—so I am given to understand. In its passages and galleries there dwell an innumerable soldiery, ready to defend it just as termites defend their ox-high earthen nests on the pampas of the north. This is the fourth time Baldanders and I have passed through, for once, as we told you, we came south, entering Nessus by this gate and going out a year afterward through the gate called Sorrowing. Only recently we returned from the south with what little we had won there, passing in at the other southern gate, that of Praise. On all these passages we beheld the interior of the Wall as you see it now, and the faces of these slaves of the Autarch looked out at us. I do not doubt that there are among them many who search for some particular miscreant, and that if they were to see the one they seek, they would sally out and lay hold of him."

At this the man on the merychip (whose name was Jonas, as I learned later) said, "I beg your pardon, optimate, but I could not help overhearing what you said. I can enlighten you further, if you wish."

Dr. Talos glanced at me, his eyes sparkling. "Why that would be pleasant, but we must make one proviso. We will speak only of the Wall, and those who dwell in it. Which is to say, we will ask you no questions concerning yourself. And you, likewise, will return that courtesy to us."

The stranger pushed back his battered hat, and I saw that in place of his right hand he wore a jointed contrivance of steel. "You have understood me better than I wanted, as the man said when he looked in the mirror. I admit I'd hoped to ask you why you traveled with the carnifex, and why this lady, the loveliest I've ever seen, is walking in the dust."

Jolenta released his stirrup strap and said, "You're poor, goodman, from the look of you, and no longer young. It hardly suits you to inquire of me."

Even in the shadow of the gate, I saw the flush of blood creep into the stranger's cheeks. All she had said was true. His clothes were worn and travel-stained, though not so dirty as Hethor's. His face had been lined and coarsened by the wind. For perhaps a dozen steps he did not reply, but at last he began. His voice was flat and neither high nor deep, but possessed of a dry humor.

"In the old times, the lords of this world feared no one but their own people, and to defend themselves against them built a great fortress on a hilltop to the north of the city. It was not called Nessus then, for the river was unpoisoned.

"Many of the people were angry at the building of that citadel, holding it to be their right to slay their lords without hindrance if they so desired. But others went out in the ships that ply between the stars, returning with treasure and knowledge. In time there returned a woman who had gained nothing among them but a handful of black beans."

"Ah," said Dr. Talos. "You are a professional tale-teller. I wish you had informed us of it from the beginning, for we, as you must have seen, are something the same."

Jonas shook his head. "No, this is the only tale I know—or nearly so." He looked down at Jolenta. "May I continue, most marvelous of women?"

My attention was distracted by the sight of daylight ahead of us, and by the disturbance among the vehicles that clogged the road as many sought to turn back, flailing their teams and trying to clear a path with their whips.

"—she displayed the beans to the lords of men, and told them that unless she were obeyed she would cast them into the sea and so put an end to the world. They had her seized and torn to bits, for they were a hundred times more complete in their domination than our Autarch."

"May he endure to see the New Sun," Jolenta murmured.

Dorcas tightened her grip on my arm and asked, "Why are they so frightened?" Then screamed and buried her face in her hands as the iron tip of a lash flicked her cheek. I pressed past the merychip's head, seized the ankle of the wagoneer who had struck her, and pulled him from his seat. By that time all the gate was ringing with bawling and swearing, and the cries of the injured, and the bellowings of frightened animals; and if the stranger continued his tale I could not hear it.

The driver I pulled down must have died at once. Because I had wished to impress Dorcas, I had hoped to perform the excruciation we call *two apricots*; but he had fallen under the feet of the travelers and the heavy wheels of the carts. Even his screams were lost.

Here I pause, having carried you, reader, from gate to gate— from the locked and fog-shrouded gate of our necropolis to this gate with its curling wisps of smoke, this gate which is perhaps the largest in existence, perhaps the largest ever to exist. It was by entering that first gate that I set my feet upon the road that brought me to this second gate. And surely when I entered this second gate, I began again to walk a new road. From that great gate forward, for a long time, it was to lie outside the City Imperishable and among the forests and grasslands, mountains and jungles of the north.

Here I pause. If you wish to walk no farther with me, reader, I cannot blame you. It is no easy road.

APPENDIX

A Note on the Translation

IN RENDERING this book—originally composed in a tongue that has not yet achieved existence—into English, I might easily have saved myself a great deal of labor by having recourse to invented terms; in no case have I done so. Thus in many instances I have been forced to replace yet undiscovered concepts by their closest twentieth-century equivalents. Such words as *peltast*, *androgyn*, and *exultant* are substitutions of this kind, and are intended to be suggestive rather than definitive. *Metal* is usually, but not always, employed to designate a substance of the sort the word suggests to contemporary minds.

When the manuscript makes reference to animal species resulting from biogenetic manipulation or the importation of extrasolar breeding stock, the name of a similar extinct species has been freely substituted. (Indeed, Severian sometimes seems to assume that an extinct species has been restored.) The nature of the riding and draft animals employed is frequently unclear in the original text. I have scrupled to call these creatures *horses*, since I am certain the word is not strictly correct. The "destriers" of *The Book of the New Sun* are unquestionably much swifter and more enduring animals than those we know, and the speed of those used for military purposes seems to permit the delivering of cavalry charges against enemies supported by high-energy armament.

Latin is once or twice employed to indicate that inscriptions and the like are in a language Severian appears to consider obsolete. What the actual language may have been, I cannot say.

To those who have preceded me in the study of the posthistoric world, and particularly to those collectors—too numerous to name here—who have permitted me to examine artifacts surviving so many centuries of futurity, and most especially to those who have allowed me to visit and photograph the era's few extant buildings, I am truly grateful.

G.W.

THE CLAW OF
THE CONCILIATOR

But strength still goes out from your thorns,
   and from your abysses the sound of music.
Your shadows lie on my heart like roses
   and your nights are like strong wine.

I

The Village of Saltus

MORWENNA'S FACE FLOATED in the single beam of light, lovely and framed in hair dark as my cloak; blood from her neck pattered to the stones. Her lips moved without speech. Instead I saw framed within them (as though I were the Increate, peeping through his rent in Eternity to behold the World of Time) the farm, Stachys her husband tossing in agony upon his bed, little Chad at the pond, bathing his fevered face.

Outside, Eusebia, Morwenna's accuser, howled like a witch. I tried to reach the bars to tell her to be quiet, and at once became lost in the darkness of the cell. When I found light at last, it was the green road stretching from the shadow of the Piteous Gate. Blood gushed from Dorcas's cheek, and though so many screamed and shouted, I could hear it pattering to the ground. Such a mighty structure was the Wall that it divided the world as the mere line between their covers does two books; before us now stood such a wood as might have been growing since the founding of Urth, trees as high as cliffs, wrapped in pure green. Between them lay the road, grown up in fresh grass, and on it were the bodies of men and women. A burning cariole tainted the clean air with smoke.

Five riders sat destriers whose hooked tushes were encrusted with lazulite. The men wore helmets and capes of indanthrene blue and carried lances whose heads ran with blue fire; their faces were more akin than the faces of brothers. On these riders, the tide of travelers broke as a wave on a rock, some turning left, some right. Dorcas was torn from my arms, and I drew *Terminus Est* to cut down those between us and found I was about to strike Master Malrubius, who stood calmly, my dog Triskele at his side, in the midst of the tumult. Seeing him so, I knew I dreamed, and from that knew, even while I slept, that the visions I had had of him before had not been dreams.

I threw the blankets aside. The chiming of the carillon in the Bell Tower was in my ears. It was time to rise, time to run to the kitchen pulling on my clothes, time to stir a pot for Brother Cook and steal a sausage—a sausage bursting, savory, and nearly burned—from the grill. Time to wash, time to serve the journeymen, time to chant lessons to myself before Master Palaemon's examination.

I woke in the apprentices' dormitory, but everything was in the wrong place: a blank wall where the round port should have been, a square window that should have been a bulkhead. The row of hard, narrow cots was gone, and the ceiling too low.

Then I was awake. Country smells—much like the pleasant odors of flower and tree that used to float across the ruined curtain wall from the necropolis, but mixed now with the hot reek of a stable—drifted through the window. The bells began again, ringing in some campanile not far away, calling the few who retained their faith to beseech the coming of the New Sun, though it was very early still, the old sun had hardly dropped Urth's veil from his face, and save for the bells the village lay silent.

As Jonas had discovered the night before, our water-ewer held wine. I used some to rinse my mouth, and its astringency made it better than water; but I still wanted water to splash on my face and smooth my hair. Before sleeping I had folded my cloak, with the Claw at the center, to use for a pillow. I spread it now, and remembering how Agia had once tried to slip her hand into the sabretache on my belt, thrust the Claw into my boot top.

Jonas still slept. In my experience, people asleep look younger than they do awake, but Jonas seemed older—or perhaps only ancient; he had the face, with straight nose and straight forehead, that I have often noted in old pictures. I buried the smoldering fire in its own ashes and left without waking him.

By the time I had finished refreshing myself from the bucket of the innyard well, the street before the inn was no longer silent, but alive with hooves that splashed through the puddles left by the previous night's rain, and the clacking of scimitar horns. Each animal was taller than a man, black or piebald, rolling-eyed and half blinded by the coarse hair that fell across its face. Morwenna's father, I remembered, had been a drover; it was possible this herd was his, though it seemed unlikely. I waited until the last lumbering beast had passed and watched the men ride by. There were three, dusty and common looking, flourishing iron-tipped goads longer than themselves; and with them, their hard, watchful, low-bred dogs.

Inside the inn once more, I ordered breakfast and got bread warm from the oven, newly churned butter, pickled duck's eggs, and peppered chocolate beaten to a froth. (This last a sure sign, though I did not know it then, that I was among people who drew their customs from the north.) Our hairless gnome of a host, who had no doubt seen me in conversation with the alcalde the night before, hovered over my table wiping his nose on his sleeve, inquiring about the quality of each dish as it was served—though they were all, in truth, very good—promising better food at supper, and condemning the cook, who was his wife. He called me *sieur*, not because he thought as they sometimes had in Nessus that I was an exultant incognito, but because a torturer here, as the efficient arm of the law, was a great person. Like most peons, he could conceive of no more than one social class higher than his own.

"The bed, it was comfortable? Plenty of quilts? We will bring more."

My mouth was full, but I nodded.

"Then we shall. Will three be enough? You and the other sieur, are you comfortable together?"

I was about to say that I would prefer separate rooms (I thought Jonas no thief, but I was afraid the Claw might be too much of a temptation for any man, and I was unused, moreover, to sleeping double) when it occurred to me that he might have difficulty paying for a private accommodation.

"You will be there today, sieur? When they break through the wall? A mason could take down the ashlars, but Barnoch's been heard moving inside and may have strength left. Perhaps he's found a weapon. Why, he could bite the masons' fingers, if nothing else!"

"Not in an official capacity. I may watch if I can."

"Everyone's coming." The bald man rubbed his hands, which slithered together as if they had been oiled. "There's to be a fair, you know. The alcalde announced it. He's got a good head for business, our alcalde has. You take the average man—he'd see you here in my parlor and never think of a thing. Or at least, no more than to have you put an end to Morwenna. Not ours! He sees things. He sees the possibilities of them. You might say that in the wink of an eye the whole fair sprang up out of his head, colored tents and ribbons, roast meat and spun sugar, all together. Today? Why today we'll open the sealed house and pull Barnoch out like a badger. That will warm them up, that will draw them for leagues around. Then we'll watch you do for Morwenna and that country fellow. Tomorrow you'll begin on Barnoch—hot irons you start with usually, don't you? And everybody will want to be there. The day after, finish him off and fold the tents. It doesn't do to let them hang about too long after they've spent their money, or they begin to beg and fight and so on. All well planned, all well thought out! There's an alcalde for you!"

I went out again after breakfast and watched the alcalde's enchanted thoughts take shape. Countryfolk were stumping into the village with fruits and animals and bolts of home-woven cloth to sell; among them were a few autochthons carrying fur pelts and strings of black and green birds killed with the cerbotana. Now I wished I still had the mantle Agia's brother had sold me, for my fuligin cloak drew some odd looks. I was about to step inside once more when I heard the quickstep of marching feet, a sound familiar to me from the drilling of the garrison in the Citadel, but which I had not heard since I had left it.

The cattle I had watched earlier that morning had been going down to the river, there to be herded into barges for the remainder of their trip to the abattoirs of Nessus. These soldiers were coming the other way, up from the water. Whether that was because their officers felt the march would toughen them, or because the boats that had brought them were needed elsewhere, or because they were destined for some area remote from Gyoll, I had no way of knowing. I heard the shouted order to sing as they came into the thickening crowd, and almost together with it the thwacks of the vingtners' rods and the howls of the unfortunates who had been hit.

The men were kelau, each armed with a sling with a two-cubit handle and each carrying a painted leather pouch of incendiary bullets. Few looked older than I and most seemed younger, but their gilded brigandines and the rich belts and scabbards of their long daggers proclaimed them members of an elite corps of the erentarii. Their song was not of battle or women as most soldiers' songs are, but a true slingers' song. Insofar as I heard it that day, it ran thus:

> "When I was a lad, my mother said,
>   'You dry your tears and go to bed;
> I know my son will travel far,
>   Born beneath a shooting star.'
>
> "In after years, my father said,
>   As he pulled my hair and knocked my head,

'They mustn't whimper at a scar,
Who're born beneath a shooting star.'

"A mage I met, and the mage he said,
'I see for you a future red,
Fire and riot, raid and war,
O born beneath a shooting star.'

"A shepherd I met, and the shepherd said,
'We sheep must go where we are led,
To Dawn-Gate where the angels are,
Following the shooting star.'"

And so on, verse after verse, some cryptic (as it seemed to me), some merely comic, some clearly assembled purely for the sake of the rhymes, which were repeated again and again.

"A fine sight, aren't they?" It was the innkeeper, his bald head at my shoulder. "Southerners—notice how many have yellow hair and dotted hides? They're used to cold down there, and they'll need to be in the mountains. Still, the singing almost makes you want to join 'em. How many, would you say?"

The baggage mules were just coming into view, laden with rations and prodded forward with the points of swords. "Two thousand. Perhaps twenty-five hundred."

"Thank you, sieur. I like to keep track of them. You wouldn't believe how many I've seen coming up our road here. But precious few going back. Well, that's what war is, I believe. I always try to tell myself they're still there—I mean, wherever it was they went—but you know and I know there's a lot that have gone to stay. Still, the singing makes a man want to go with 'em."

I asked if he had news of the war.

"Oh, yes, sieur. I've followed it for years and years now, though the battles they fight never seem to make much difference, if you understand me. It never seems to get much closer to us, or much farther off either. What I've always supposed was that our Autarch and theirs appoints a spot to fight in, and when it's over they both go home. My wife, fool that she is, don't believe there's a real war at all."

The crowd had closed behind the last mule driver, and it thickened with every word that passed between us. Bustling men set up stalls and pavilions, narrowing the street and making the press of people greater still; bristling masks on tall poles seemed to have sprouted from the ground like trees.

"Where does your wife think the soldiers are going, then?" I asked the innkeeper.

"Looking for Vodalus, that's what *she* says. As if the Autarch—whose hands run with gold and whose enemies kiss his heel—would send his whole army to fetch a bandit!"

I scarcely heard a word beyond V*odalus.*

Whatever I possess I would give to become one of you, who complain every day of memories fading. My own do not. They remain always, and always as vivid as at their first impression, so that once summoned they carry me off spellbound.

I think I turned from the innkeeper and wandered into the crowd of pushing rustics and chattering vendors, but I saw neither them nor him. Instead I felt the bone-strewn paths of the necropolis under my feet, and saw through the drifting river fog the slender figure of Vodalus as he gave his pistol to his mistress and drew his sword. Now (it is a sad thing to have become a man) I was struck by the extravagance of the gesture. He who had professed in a hundred clandestine placards to be fighting for the old ways, for the ancient high civilization Urth has now lost, has discarded the effectual weapon of that civilization.

If my memories of the past remain intact, perhaps it is only because the past exists only in memory. Vodalus, who wished as I did to summon it again, yet remained a creature of the present. That we are capable only of being what we are remains our unforgivable sin.

No doubt if I had been one of you whose memories fade, I

would have rejected him on that morning as I elbowed my way through the crowd, and so in some fashion would have escaped this death in life that grips me even as I write these words. Or perhaps I would not have escaped at all. Yes, more likely not. And in any case, the old, recalled emotions were too strong. I was trapped in admiration for what I had once admired, as a fly in amber remains the captive of some long-vanished pine.

II

The Man in the Dark

THE BANDIT'S HOUSE had differed in no way from the common houses of the village. It was of broken mine-stone, single storied, with a flattish, solid-looking roof of slabs of the same material. The door and the only window I could see from the street had been closed with rough masonry. A hundred or so fair-goers stood before the house now, talking and pointing; but there was no sound from within, and no smoke issuing from the chimney.

"Is this commonly done hereabouts?" I asked Jonas.

"It's traditional. You've heard the saying, 'A legend, a lie, and a likelihood make a tradition'?"

"It seems to me it would be easy enough to get out. He could break through a window or the wall itself by night, or dig a passage. Of course, if he expected something like this—and if it's common and he was really engaged in spying for Vodalus, there's no reason he shouldn't—he could have supplied himself with tools as well as a quantity of food and drink."

Jonas shook his head. "Before they close the openings, they go through the house and take everything they can find in the way of food and tools and lights, besides whatever else may be of value."

A resonant voice said, "Having good sense, as we flatter

ourselves, we do indeed." It was the alcalde, who had come up behind us without either of us noticing his presence in the crowd. We wished him a good day, and he returned the courtesy. He was a solid, square-built man whose open face was marred by something too clever about the eyes. "I thought I recognized you, Master Severian, bright clothes or no. Are these new? They look it. If they don't give satisfaction, speak out to me about it. We try to keep the traders honest that come to our fairs. It's only good business. If he doesn't make them right for you, whoever he is, we'll duck him in the river, you may be sure. One or two ducked a year keep the rest from feeling too comfortable."

He paused to step back and examine me more carefully, nodding to himself as though greatly impressed. "They become you. I must say, you've a fine figure. A handsome face too, save perhaps for a bit too much pallor, which our hot northern weather will soon make right. Anyway, they become you and look to wear well. If you're asked where you had them, you might say Saltus Fair. Such talk does no harm."

I promised I would, though I was far more concerned about the safety of *Terminus Est*, which I had left hidden in our room at the inn, than about my own appearance or the durability of the lay clothes I had bought from a slopman.

"You and your assistant have come to see us draw out the miscreant, I suppose? We'll be at him as soon as Mesmin and Sebald bring the post. A battering ram is what we called it when we passed the word of what was intended, but I'm afraid the truth is that it's nothing more than a tree trunk, and not a big one either—otherwise the village would have had to fee too many men to handle it. Yet it should do the work. I don't suppose you've heard of the case we had here eighteen years gone?"

Jonas and I shook our heads.

The alcalde threw out his chest, as politicians do whenever they see an opportunity to speak for more than a couple of sentences. "I recall it well enough, though I wasn't more than a stripling. A woman. I've forgotten her name, but we called her Mother Pyrexia. The stones were put up on her, just like what you see here, for it's largely the same ones doing it, and they did it in the same way. But it was the other end of summer, just at apple-picking time, and that I recall very well because of the people drinking new cider in the crowd, and myself with a fresh apple to eat while I watched.

"Next year when the corn was up, someone wanted to buy the house. Property becomes the property of the town, you know. That's how we finance the work, the ones that do it take what they can find for their share, and the town takes the house and ground.

"To shorten a lengthy tale, we cut a ram and broke through the door in fine fashion, thinking to sweep up the old woman's bones and turn the place over to the new owner." The alcalde paused and laughed, throwing back his head. There was something ghostly in that laughter, possibly only because it blended with the noise of the crowd, and so seemed silent.

I asked, "Wasn't she dead?"

"It depends on what you mean by that. I'll say this—a woman sealed in the dark long enough can become something very strange, just like the strange things you find in rotten wood, back among the big trees. We're miners, mostly, here in Saltus, and used to things found underground, but we took to our heels and came back with torches. It didn't like the light, or the fire either."

Jonas touched me on the shoulder and pointed to a swirl in the crowd. A group of purposeful-looking men were shouldering their way down the street. None had helmets or body armor, but several carried narrow-headed piletes, and the rest had brass-bound staves. I was strongly reminded of the volunteer guards who had admitted Drotte, Roche, Eata, and me to the necropolis so long ago. Behind these armed men were four who carried the tree trunk the alcalde had mentioned, a rough log about two spans across and six cubits long.

A collective indrawn breath greeted them; it was followed by louder talk and some good-natured cheering. The alcalde left us to take charge, directing the men with staves to clear a space about the door of the sealed house and using his authority, when Jonas and I pushed forward to get a better view, to make the crowd give way for us.

I had supposed that when all the breakers-in were in position they would proceed without ceremony. In that, I had reckoned without the alcalde. At the last possible moment he mounted the doorstep of the sealed house, and waving his hat for silence, addressed the crowd.

"Welcome visitors and fellow villagers! In the time it takes to draw breath thrice, you will see us smash this barrier and drag out the bandit Barnoch. Whether he be dead, or, as we have good reason to believe—for he hasn't been in there that long—alive. You know what he has done. He has collaborated with the traitor Vodalus's cultellarii, informing them of the arrivals and departures of those who might become their victims! All of you are thinking now, and rightly!, that such a vile crime deserves no mercy. Yes, I say! Yes, we all say! Hundreds and maybe thousands lie in unmarked graves because of this Barnoch. Hundreds and maybe thousands have met a fate far worse!

"Yet for a moment, before these stones come down, I ask you to reflect. Vodalus has lost a spy. He will be seeking another. On some still night not long, I think, from now, a stranger will come to one of you. It is certain he will have much talk—"

"Like you!" someone shouted, to general laughter.

"Better talk than mine—I'm only a rough miner, as many of you know. Much smooth, persuasive talk, I ought to have said, and possibly some money. Before you nod your head at him, I want you to remember this house of Barnoch's the way it looks now, with those ashlars where the door should be. Think about your own house with no doors and no windows, but with you inside it.

"Then think about what you're going to see done to Barnoch

when we take him out. Because I'm telling you—you strangers particularly—what you're about to see here is only the beginning of what you'll be seeing at our fair in Saltus! For the events of the next few days we have employed one of the finest professionals from Nessus! You will see *at least* two persons executed here in the formal style, with the head struck off at a single blow. One's a woman, so we'll be using the chair! That's something a lot of people who boast of their sophistication and the cosmopolitan tincture of their educations have never seen. And you will see this man," pausing, the alcalde struck the sunlit door-stones with the flat of his hand, "this Barnoch, led to Death by an expert guide! It may be that he has made some sort of small hole in the wall by now. Frequently they do, and if so he may be able to hear me."

He lifted his voice to a shout. "If you can, Barnoch, cut your throat now! Because if you don't, you're going to wish you had starved long ago!"

For a moment there was silence. I was in agony at the thought that I should soon have to practice the Art on a follower of Vodalus's. The alcalde raised his right arm over his head, then brought it down in an emphatic gesture. "All right, lads, at it with a will!"

The four who had brought the ram counted *one, two, three* to themselves as if by prearrangement and ran at the walled-up door, losing some of their impetuosity when the two in front mounted the step. The ram struck the stones with a loud thump, but with no other result.

"All right, lads," the alcalde repeated. "Let's try it again. Show them the kind of men Saltus breeds."

The four charged a second time. At this attempt, those in front handled the step more skillfully; the stones plugging the doorway seemed to shudder under the impact, and a fine dust issued from the mortar. A volunteer from the crowd, a burly, black-bearded fellow, joined the original ramsmen, and all five charged; the thump of the ram was not noticeably louder, but it was accompanied by a cracking like the breaking of bones. "One more," the alcalde said.

He was right. The next blow sent the stone it struck into the house, leaving a hole the size of a man's head. After that, the ramsmen no longer bothered with a running start; they knocked the remaining stones out by swinging the ram with their arms until the aperture was large enough for a man to step through.

Someone I had not noticed previously had brought torches, and a boy ran to a neighboring house to kindle them at the kitchen fire. The men with piletes and staves took them from him. Showing more courage than I would have credited to those clever eyes, the alcalde drew a short truncheon from under his shirt and entered first. We spectators crowded after the armed men, and because Jonas and I had been in the forefront of the onlookers, we reached the opening almost at once.

The air was foul, far worse than I had anticipated. Broken furniture lay on every side, as though Barnoch had locked his chests and cupboards when the sealers came, and they had smashed them to get at his household goods. On a crippled table, I saw the guttered wax of a candle that had burned to the wood. The people behind me were pushing to go in farther; and I, as I discovered somewhat to my surprise, was pushing back.

There was a commotion at the rear of the house—hurried and confused footsteps—a shout—then a high, inhuman scream.

"They've got him!" someone behind me called, and I heard the news being passed to those outside.

A fattish man who might have been a smallholder came running out of the dark, a torch in one hand and a stave in the other. "Out of the way! Get back, all of you! They're bringing him out!"

I do not know what I expected to see. . . . Perhaps a filthy creature with matted hair. What came instead was a ghost. Barnoch had been tall; he was tall still, but stooped and very thin, with skin so pale it seemed to glow as decayed wood does. He was hairless, bald, and beardless; I learned that afternoon from his guards that he had formed the habit of plucking his hairs out. Worst of all were his eyes: protuberant, seemingly blind, and dark as the black abscess of his mouth. I turned away from him as he spoke, but I knew the voice was his. "I will be free," it said. "Vodalus! Vodalus will come!"

How I wished then that I had never been imprisoned myself, for his voice brought back to me all those airless days when I waited in the oubliette beneath our Matachin Tower. I too had dreamed of rescue by Vodalus, of a revolution that would sweep away the animal stench and degeneracy of the present age and restore the high and gleaming culture that was once Urth's.

And I had been saved not by Vodalus and his shadowy army, but by the advocacy of Master Palaemon—and no doubt of Drotte and Roche and a few other friends—who had persuaded the brothers that it would be too dangerous to kill me and too disgraceful to bring me before a tribunal.

Barnoch would not be saved at all. I, who should have been his comrade, would brand him, break him on the wheel, and at last sever his head. I tried to tell myself that he had acted, perhaps, only to get money; but as I did so some metal object, no doubt the steel head of a pilete, struck stone, and I seemed to hear the ringing of the coin Vodalus had given me, the ringing as I dropped it into the space beneath the floor-stone of the ruined mausoleum.

Sometimes when all our attention is thus focused on memory, our eyes, unguided by ourselves, will distinguish from a mass of detail some single object, presenting it with a clarity never achieved by concentration. So it was with me. Out of all the struggling tide of faces beyond the doorway, I saw one, upturned, illuminated by the sun. It was Agia's.

III

The Showman's Tent

THE INSTANT WAS frozen as though we two, and all those about us, stood in a painting. Agia's uptilted face, my own wide eyes; so we remained amid the cloud of countryfolk with their bright clothes and bundles. Then I moved, and she was gone. I would have run to her if I could; but I could only push my way through the onlookers, taking perhaps a hundred poundings of my heart to reach the spot where she had stood.

By then she had vanished utterly, and the crowd was swirling and changing like the water under the bow of a boat. Barnoch had been led forth, screaming at the sun. I took a miner by the shoulder and shouted a question to him, but he had paid no attention to the young woman beside him and had no notion of where she might have gone. I followed the throng who followed the prisoner until I was sure she was not among them, then, knowing nothing better to do, began to search the fair, peering into tents and booths, and making inquiries of the farmwives who had come to sell their fragrant cardamom-bread, and of the hot-meat vendors.

All this, as I write it, slowly convoluting a thread of the vermilion ink of the House Absolute, sounds calm and even methodical. Nothing could be further from the truth. I was gasping and sweating as I did these things, shouting questions to which I hardly stayed for an answer. Like a face seen in dream, Agia's floated before my imagination: wide, flat cheeks and softly rounded chin, freckled, sun-browned skin and long, laughing, mocking eyes. Why she had come, I could not imagine; I only knew she had, and that my glimpse of her had reawakened the anguish of my memory of her scream.

"*Have you seen a woman so tall, with chestnut hair?*" I repeated it again and again, like the duelist who had called out "Cadroe of Seventeen Stones," until the phrase was as meaningless as the song of the cicada.

"Yes. Every country maid who comes here."

"Do you know her name?"

"A woman? Certainly I can get you a woman."

"Where did you lose her?"

"Don't worry, you'll soon find her again. The fair's not big enough for anybody to stay lost long. Didn't the two of you arrange a place to meet? Have some of my tea—you look so tired."

I fumbled for a coin.

"You don't have to pay, I sell enough as it is. Well, if you insist. It's only an aes. Here."

The old woman rummaged in her apron pocket and produced a flood of little coins, then splashed the tea, hissing hot, from her kettle into an earthenware cup and offered me a straw of some dimly silver metal. I waved it away.

"It's clean. I rinse everything after each customer."

"I'm not used to them."

"Watch the rim then—it'll be hot. Have you looked by the judging? There'll be a lot of people there."

"Where the cattle are? Yes." The tea was maté, spicy and a trifle bitter.

"Does she know you're looking for her?"

"I don't think so. Even if she saw me, she wouldn't have recognized me. I . . . am not dressed as I usually am."

The old woman snorted and pushed a straggling lock of gray

hair back under her kerchief. "At Saltus Fair? Of course not! Everybody wears his best to a fair, and any girl with sense would know that. How about down by the water where they've got the prisoner chained?"

I shook my head. "She seems to have disappeared."

"But you haven't given up. I can tell from the way you look at the people going past instead of me. Well, good for you. You'll find her yet, though they do say all manner of strange things have been happening round and about of late. They caught a green man, do you know that? Got him right over there where you see the tent. Green men know everything, people say, if you can but make them talk. Then there's the cathedral. I suppose you've heard about that?"

"The cathedral?"

"I've heard tell it wasn't what cityfolk call a real one—I know you're from the city by the way you drink your tea—but it's the only cathedral most of us around Saltus ever saw, and pretty too, with all the hanging lamps and the windows in the sides made of colored silk. Myself, I don't believe—or rather, I think that if the Pancreator don't care nothing for me, I won't care nothing for him, and why should I? Still, it's a shame what they did, if they did what's told against them. Set fire to it, you know."

"Are you talking about the Cathedral of the Pelerines?"

The old woman nodded sagely. "There, you said it yourself. You're making the same mistake they did. It wasn't the Cathedral of the Pelerines, it was the Cathedral of the Claw. Which is to say, it wasn't theirs to burn."

To myself I muttered, "They rekindled the fire."

"I beg pardon." The old woman cocked an ear. "I didn't hear that."

"I said they burned it. They must have set fire to the straw floor."

"That's what I heard too. They just stood back and watched it burn. It went up to the Infinite Meadows of the New Sun, you know."

A man on the opposite side of the alleyway began to pound a drum. When he paused I said, "I know that certain persons have claimed to have seen it rise into the air."

"Oh, it rose all right. When my grandson-in-law heard about it, he was fairly struck flat for half a day. Then he pasted up a kind of hat out of paper and held it over my stove, and it went up, and then he thought it was nothing that the cathedral rose, no miracle at all. That shows what it is to be a fool—it never came to him that the reason things were made so was so the cathedral would rise just like it did. He can't see the Hand in nature."

"He didn't see it himself?" I asked. "The cathedral, I mean."

She failed to understand. "Oh, he's seen it when they've been through here, at least a dozen times."

The chant of the man with the drum, similar to that I had once heard Dr. Talos use, but more hoarsely delivered and bereft of the doctor's malicious intelligence, cut through our talk. *"Knows everything! Knows everybody! Green as a gooseberry! See for yourself!"*

(The insistent voice of the drum: BOOM! BOOM! BOOM!)

"Do you think the green man would know where Agia is?"

The old woman smiled. "So that's her name, is it? Now I'll know, if anybody should mention her. He might. You've money, why not try him?"

Why not indeed, I thought.

"Brought from the jun-gles of the North! Never eats! A-kin to the bush-es and the grass-es!" BOOM! BOOM! *"The fu-ture and the re-mote past are one to him!"*

When he saw me approaching the door of his tent, the drummer stopped his clamor. "Only an aes to see him. Two to speak with him. Three to be alone with him."

"Alone for how long?" I asked as I selected three copper aes. A wry grin crossed the drummer's face. "For as long as you wish." I handed him his money and stepped inside.

It had been plain he had not thought I would want to stay

long, and I expected a stench or something equally unpleasant. There was nothing beyond a slight odor as of hay curing. In the center of the tent, in a dust-spangled shaft of sunlight admitted by a vent in the canvas roof, was chained a man the color of pale jade. He wore a kilt of leaves, now fading; beside him stood a clay pot filled to the brim with clear water.

For a moment we were silent. I stood looking at him. He sat looking at the ground. "That's not paint," I said. "Nor do I think it dye. And you have no more hair than the man I saw dragged from the sealed house."

He looked up at me, then down again. Even the whites of his eyes held a greenish tint.

I tried to bait him. "If you are truly vegetable, I would think your hair should be grass."

"No." He had a soft voice, saved from womanishness only by its depth.

"You *are* vegetable then? A speaking plant?"

"You are no countryman."

"I left Nessus a few days ago."

"With some education."

I thought of Master Palaemon, then of Master Malrubius and my poor Thecla, and I shrugged. "I can read and write."

"Yet you know nothing about me. I am not a talking vegetable, as you should be able to see. Even if a plant were to follow the one evolutionary way, out of some many millions, that leads to intelligence, it is impossible that it should duplicate in wood and leaf the form of a human being."

"The same thing might be said of stones, yet there are statues."

For all his aspect of despair (and his was a sadder face by far than my friend Jonas's), something tugged at the corners of his lips. "That is well put. You have no scientific training, but you are better taught than you realize."

"On the contrary, all my training has been scientific—

although it had nothing to do with these fantastic speculations. What are you?"

"A great seer. A great liar, like every man whose foot is in a trap."

"If you'll tell me what you are, I'll endeavor to help you."

He looked at me, and it was as if some tall herb had opened eyes and shown a human face. "I believe you," he said. "Why is it that you, of all the hundreds who come to this tent, know pity?"

"I know nothing of pity, but I have been imbued with a respect for justice, and I am well acquainted with the alcalde of this village. A green man is still a man; and if he is a slave, his master must show how he came to that state, and how he himself came into possession of him."

The green man said, "I'm a fool, I suppose, to put any confidence in you. And yet I do. I am a free man, come from your own future to explore your age."

"That is impossible."

"The green color that puzzles your people so much is only what you call pond scum. We have altered it until it can live in our blood, and by its intervention have at last made our peace in humankind's long struggle with the sun. In us, the tiny plants live and die, and our bodies feed from them and their dead and require no other nourishment. All the famines, and all the labor of growing food, are ended."

"But you must have sun."

"Yes," the green man said. "And I have not enough here. Day is brighter in my age."

That simple remark thrilled me in a way that nothing had since I had first glimpsed the unroofed chapel in the Broken Court of our Citadel. "Then the New Sun comes as prophesied," I said, "and there is indeed a second life for Urth—if what you say is the truth."

The green man threw back his head and laughed. Much later

I was to hear the sound the alzabo makes as it ranges the snow-swept tablelands of the high country; its laughter is horrible, but the green man's was more terrible, and I drew away from him. "You're not a human being," I said. "Not now, if you ever were."

He laughed again. "And to think I hoped in you. What a poor creature I am. I thought I had resigned myself to dying here among a people who are no more than walking dust; but at the tiniest gleam, all my resignation fell from me. I am a true man, friend. You are not, and in a few months I will be dead."

I remembered his kin. How often I had seen the frozen stalks of summer flowers dashed by the wind against the sides of the mausoleums in our necropolis. "I understand you. The warm days of sun are coming, but when they are gone, you will go with them. Grow seed while you can."

He sobered. "You do not believe me or even understand that I am a man like yourself, yet you still pity me. Perhaps you are right, and for us a new sun has come, and because it has come we have forgotten it. If I am ever able to return to my own time, I will tell them there of you."

"If you are indeed of the future, why cannot you go forward to your home, and so escape?"

"Because I am chained, as you see." He held out his leg so that I could examine the shackle about his ankle. His berylline flesh was swollen about it, as I have seen the bark of a tree swollen that had grown through an iron ring.

The tent flap opened, and the drummer thrust his head through. "Are you still here? I have others outside." He looked significantly at the green man and withdrew.

"He means that I must drive you off, or he will close the vent through which my sunlight falls. I drive away those who pay to see me by foretelling their futures, and I will foretell yours. You are young now, and strong. But before this world has wound itself ten times more about the sun you shall be less strong, and you shall never regain the strength that is yours now. If you breed sons, you will engender enemies against yourself. If—"

"Enough!" I said. "What you are telling me is only the fortune of all men. Answer one question truthfully for me, and I will go. I am looking for a woman called Agia. Where will I find her?"

For a moment his eyes rolled upward until only a narrow crescent of pale green showed beneath their lids. A faint tremor seized him; he stood and extended his arms, his fingers splayed like twigs. Slowly he said, "Above ground."

The tremor ceased, and he sat again, older looking and paler than before.

"You are only a fraud then," I told him as I turned away. "And I was a simpleton to believe in you even by so little."

"No," the green man whispered. "Listen. In coming here, I have passed through all your future. Some parts of it remain with me, no matter how clouded. I told you only the truth—and if you are indeed a friend of the alcalde of this place, I will tell you something further that you may tell him, something I have learned from the questions of those who have come to question me. Armed men are seeking to free a man called Barnoch."

I took my whetstone from the sabretache at my belt, broke it on the top of the chain-stake, and gave half to him. For a moment he did not comprehend what it was he held. Then I saw the knowledge growing in him, so that he seemed to unfold in his great joy, as though he were already basking in the brighter light of his own day.

IV

The Bouquet

AS I LEFT the showman's tent, I glanced up at the sun. The western horizon had already climbed more than half up the sky; in a watch or less it would be time for me to make my appearance. Agia was gone, and any hope of overtaking her had been lost in the frantic time I had spent dashing from one end of the fair to the other; yet I took comfort from the green man's prophecy, which I took to mean that Agia and I should meet again before either of us died, and from the thought that since she had come to watch Barnoch drawn into the light, so, equally, might she come to observe the executions of Morwenna and the cattle thief.

These speculations occupied me at first as I made my way back to the inn. But before I reached the room I shared with Jonas, they had been displaced by recollections of Thecla and my elevation to journeyman, both occasioned by the need to change from my new lay clothes into the fuligin of the guild. So strong is the power of association that it could be exercised by that habit while it was still out of sight on the pegs in the room, and by *Terminus Est* while she remained concealed beneath the mattress.

It used to entertain me, while I was still attendant upon Thecla, to find that I could anticipate much of her conversation, and particularly the first of it, from the nature of the gift I carried when I entered her cell. If it were some favorite food thieved from the kitchen, for example, it would elicit a description of a meal at the House Absolute, and the kind of food I brought even governed the nature of the repast described: flesh, a sporting dinner with the shrieking and trumpeting of game caught alive drifting up from the abattoir below and much talk of brachets, hawks, and hunting leopards; sweets, a private repast given by one of the great Chatelaines for a few friends, deliciously intimate, and soaked in gossip; fruit, a twilit garden party in the vast park of the House Absolute, lit by a thousand torches and enlivened by jugglers, actors, dancers, and pyrotechnic displays.

She ate standing as often as sitting, walking the three strides that took her from one end of her cell to the other, holding the dish in her left hand while she gestured with her right. "Like this, Severian, they all spring into the ringing sky, showering green and magenta sparks, while the maroons boom like thunder!"

But her poor hand could hardly show the rockets rising higher than her towering head, for the ceiling was not much taller than she.

"But I'm boring you. A moment ago, when you brought me these peaches, you looked so happy, and now you won't smile. It's just that it does me good, here, to remember those things. How I'll enjoy them when I see them again."

I was not bored, of course. It was only that it saddened me to see her, a woman still young and endowed with a terrible beauty, so confined. . . .

Jonas was uncovering *Terminus Est* for me when I came into our room. I poured myself a cup of wine. "How do you feel?" he asked.

"What of you? It's your first time, after all."

He shrugged. "I only have to fetch and carry. You've done it before? I wondered, because you look so young."

"Yes, I've done it before. Never to a woman."

"You think she's innocent?"

I was taking off my shirt; when I had my arms freed I mopped my face with it and shook my head. "I'm sure she's not. I went down and talked to her last night—they have her chained at the edge of the water, where the midges are bad. I told you about it."

Jonas reached for the wine himself, his metal hand clinking when it met the cup. "You told me that she was beautiful, and that she had black hair like—"

"Thecla. But Morwenna's is straight. Thecla's curled."

"Like Thecla, whom you seem to have loved as I love your friend Jolenta. I confess you had a great deal more time to fall in love than I did. And you told me she said her husband and child had died of some sickness, probably from bad water. The husband had been quite a bit older than she."

I said, "About your age, I think."

"And there was an older woman there who had wanted him too, and now she was tormenting the prisoner."

"Only with words." Among the guild, apprentices alone wear shirts. I drew on my trousers and put my cloak (which was of fuligin, the color darker than black) around my bare shoulders. "Clients who have been exposed by the authorities like that have usually been stoned. When we see them they're bruised, and often they've lost a few teeth. Sometimes they have broken bones. The women have been raped."

"You say she's beautiful. Perhaps people think she's innocent. Perhaps they took pity on her."

I picked up *Terminus Est*, drew her, and let the soft sheath fall away. "The innocent have enemies. They are afraid of her."

We went out together.

When I had entered the inn, I had to push my way through the mob of drinkers. Now it opened before me. I wore my mask and carried *Terminus Est* unsheathed across my shoulder. Outside, the sounds of the fair stilled as we went forward until nothing remained but a whispering, as though we strode through a wilderness of leaves.

The executions were to take place at the very center of the festivities, and a dense crowd had already gathered there. A caloyer in red stood beside the scaffold clutching his little formulary; he was an old man, as most of them are. The two prisoners waited beside him, surrounded by the men who had taken forth Barnoch. The alcalde wore his yellow gown of office and his gold chain.

By ancient custom, we must not use the steps (although I have seen Master Gurloes assist his vault to the scaffold with his sword, in the court before the Bell Tower). I was, very possibly, the only person present who knew of the tradition; but I did not break it, and a great roar, like the voice of some beast, escaped the crowd as I leaped up with my cloak billowing about me.

"*Increate*," read the caloyer, "*it is known to us that those who will perish here are no more evil in your sight than we. Their hands run with blood. Ours also.*"

I examined the block. Those used outside the immediate supervision of the guild are notoriously bad: "Wide as a stool, dense as a fool, and dished, as a rule." This one fulfilled the first two specifications in the proverbial description only too well, but by the mercy of Holy Katharine it was actually slightly convex, and though the idiotically hard wood would be sure to dull the male side of my blade, I was in the fortunate position of having before me one subject of either sex, so that I could use a fresh edge on each.

"*. . . by thy will they may, in that hour, have so purified their spirits as to gain thy favor. We who must confront them then, though we spill their blood today . . .*"

I posed, legs wide as I leaned upon my sword as if I were in complete control of the ceremony, though the truth was that I did not know which of them had drawn the short ribbon.

"*You, the hero who will destroy the black worm that devours the sun; you for whom the sky parts as a curtain; you whose breath shall wither vast Erebus, Abaia, and Scylla who wallow beneath the wave; you that equally live in the shell of the smallest seed in the farthest forest, the seed that hath rolled into the dark where no man sees."*

The woman Morwenna was coming up the steps, preceded by the alcalde and followed by a man with an iron spit who used it to prod her. Someone in the crowd shouted an obscene suggestion.

". . . have mercy on those who had no mercy. Have mercy on us, who shall have none now."

The caloyer was finished, and the alcalde began. "Most hatefully and unnaturally . . ."

His voice was high, quite different both from his normal speaking voice and the rhetorical tone he had adopted for the speech outside Barnoch's house. After listening absently for a few moments (I was looking for Agia in the crowd), it struck me that he was frightened. He would have to witness everything that was done to both prisoners at close range. I smiled, though my mask concealed it.

". . . of respect for your sex. But you shall be branded on the right cheek and the left, your legs broken, and your head struck from your body."

(I hoped they had had sense enough to remember that a brazier of coals would be required.)

"Through the power of the high justice laid upon my unworthy arm by the condescension of the Autarch—whose thoughts are the music of his subjects—I do now declare . . . I do now declare . . ."

He had forgotten it. I whispered the words: "That your moment has come upon you."

"I do now declare that your moment has come on you, Morwenna."

"If you have pleas for the Conciliator, speak them in your heart."

"If you have pleas for the Conciliator, speak them."

"If you have counsels for the children of women, there will be no voice for them after this."

The alcalde's self-possession was returning, and he got it all: "If you have counsels for the children of women, there will be no voice for them after this."

Clearly but not loudly, Morwenna said, "I know that most of you think me guilty. I am innocent. I would never do the horrible things you have accused me of."

The crowd drew closer to hear her.

"Many of you are my witnesses that I loved Stachys. I loved the child Stachys gave me."

A patch of color caught my eye, purple-black in the strong spring sunshine. It was such a bouquet of threnodic roses as a mute might carry at a funeral. The woman who held them was Eusebia, whom I had met when she tormented Morwenna at the riverside. As I watched her, she inhaled their perfume rapturously, then employed their thorny stems to open a path for herself through the crowd, so that she stood just at the base of the scaffold. "These are for you, Morwenna. Die before they fade."

I hammered the planks with the blunt tip of my blade for silence. Morwenna said, "The good man who read the prayers for me, and who has talked to me before I was brought here, prayed that I would forgive you if I achieved bliss before you. I have never until now had it in my power to grant a prayer, but I grant his. I forgive you now."

Eusebia was about to speak again, but I silenced her with a look. The gap-toothed, grinning man beside her waved, and with something of a start I recognized Hethor.

"Are you ready?" Morwenna asked me. "I am."

Jonas had just set a bucket of glowing charcoal on the scaffold. From it thrust what was presumably the handle of a suitable inscribed iron; but there was no chair. I gave the alcalde a glance I intended to be significant.

I might have been looking at a post. At last I said, "Have we a chair, Your Worship?"

"I sent two men to fetch one. And some rope."

"When?" (The crowd was beginning to stir and murmur.)

"A few moments ago."

The evening before he had assured me that everything would be in readiness, but there was no point in reminding him of that now. There is no one, as I have since found, so liable to fluster on the scaffold as the average rural official. He is torn between an ardent desire to be the center of attention (a position closed to him at an execution) and the quite justified fear that he lacks the ability and training that might enable him to comport himself well. The most cowardly client, mounting the steps in the full knowledge that his eyes are to be plucked out, will in nineteen cases from a score conduct himself better. Even a shy cenobite, unused to the sounds of men and diffident to the point of tears, can be better relied on.

Someone called, "Get it over with!"

I looked at Morwenna. With her famished face and clear complexion, her pensive smile and large, dark eyes, she was a prisoner likely to arouse quite undesirable feelings of sympathy in the crowd.

"We could seat her on the block," I told the alcalde. I could not resist adding, "It's more suited to that anyway."

"There's nothing to tie her with."

I had permitted myself a remark too many already, so I forbore giving my opinion of those who require their prisoners bound.

Instead, I laid *Terminus Est* flat behind the block, made Morwenna sit down, lifted my arms in the ancient salute, took the iron in my right hand, and, gripping her wrists with my left, administered the brand to either cheek, then held up the iron still glowing almost white. The scream had silenced the crowd for an instant; now they roared.

The alcalde straightened himself and seemed to become a new man. "Let them see her," he said.

I had been hoping to avoid that, but I helped Morwenna to rise. With her right hand in mine, as though we were taking part in a country dance, we made a slow, formal circuit of the platform. Hethor was beside himself with delight, and though I tried to shut out the sound of his voice, I could hear him boasting of his acquaintance with me to the people around him. Eusebia held up her bouquet to Morwenna, calling, "Here, you'll need these soon enough."

When we had gone once around, I looked at the alcalde, and after the pause necessitated by his wondering at the occasion for the delay, received the signal to proceed.

Morwenna whispered, "Will it be over soon?"

"It is almost over now." I had seated her on the block again, and was picking up my sword. "Close your eyes. Try to remember that almost everyone who has ever lived has died, even the Conciliator, who will rise as the New Sun."

Her pale, long-lashed eyelids fell, and she did not see the upraised sword. The flash of steel silenced the crowd again, and when the full hush had come, I brought the flat of the blade down upon her thighs; over the smack of it on flesh, the sound of the femurs breaking came as clear as the *crack*, *crack* of a winning boxer's left-hand, right-hand blows. For an instant Morwenna remained poised on the block, fainted but not fallen; in that instant I took a backward step and severed her neck with the smooth, horizontal stroke that is so much more difficult to master than the downward.

To be candid, it was not until I saw the up-jetting fountain of blood and heard the thud of the head striking the platform that I knew I had carried it off. Without realizing it, I had been as nervous as the alcalde.

That is the moment when, again by ancient tradition, the customary dignity of the guild is relaxed. I wanted to laugh and caper. The alcalde was shaking my shoulder and babbling as I wished to myself; I could not hear what he said—some happy nonsense. I held up my sword, and taking the head by the hair held it up too, and paraded the scaffold. Not a single circuit this time, but again and again, three times, four times. A breeze had

sprung up; it dotted my mask and arm and bare chest with
scarlet. The crowd was shouting the inevitable jests: "Will you
cut my wife's (husband's) hair too?" "Half a measure of sausage
when you're done with that." "Can I have her hat?"

I laughed at them all and was feigning to toss the head to them
when someone plucked at my ankle. It was Eusebia, and I knew
before her first word that she was under that compulsion to speak
I had often observed among the clients in our tower. Her eyes
were sparkling with excitement, and her face was twisted by her
attempt to get my attention, so that she looked simultaneously
older and younger than she had appeared before. I could not
make out what she was shouting and bent to listen.

"*Innocent! She was innocent!*"

This was no time to explain that I had not been Morwenna's
judge. I only nodded.

"*She took Stachys—from me! Now she's dead. Do you
understand? She was innocent after all, but I am so glad!*"

I nodded again and made another circuit of the scaffold,
holding up the head.

"*I killed her!*" Eusebia screamed. "*Not you—!*"

I called down to her: "If you like!"

"*Innocent! I knew her—so careful. She would have kept
something back—poison for herself! She would have died before
you got her.*"

Hethor grasped her arm and pointed to me. "*My master!
Mine! My own!*"

"*So it was somebody else. Or sickness after all—*"

I shouted: "To the Demiurge alone belongs all justice!" The
crowd was still noisy, though it had quieted a trifle by this time.

"*But she stole my Stachys, and now she's gone.*" Louder than
ever: "*Oh, wonderful! She's gone!*" With that, Eusebia plunged
her face into the bouquet as though to fill her lungs to bursting
with the roses' cloying perfume. I dropped Morwenna's head
into the basket that awaited it and wiped my sword blade with the

piece of scarlet flannel Jonas handed me. When I noticed Eusebia again she was lifeless, sprawled among a circle of onlookers.

At the time I thought little of it, only supposing that her heart had failed in her excess of joy. Later that afternoon the alcalde had her bouquet examined by an apothecary, who found among the petals a strong but subtle poison he could not identify. Morwenna must, I suppose, have had it in her hand when she mounted the steps, and must have cast it into the blossoms when I led her around the scaffold after the branding.

Allow me to pause here and speak to you as one mind to another, though we are separated, perhaps, by the abyss of eons. Though what I have already written—from the locked gate to the fair at Saltus—embraces most of my adult life, and what remains to be recorded concerns a few months only, I feel I am less than half concluded with my narrative. In order that it shall not fill a library as great as old Ultan's, I will (I tell you now plainly) pass over many things. I have recounted the execution of Agia's twin brother Agilus because of its importance to my story, and that of Morwenna because of the unusual circumstances surrounding it. I will not recount others unless they hold some special interest. If you delight in another's pain and death, you will gain little satisfaction from me. Let it be sufficient to say that I performed the prescribed operations on the cattle thief, which terminated in his execution; in the future, when I describe my travels, you are to understand that I practiced the mystery of our guild where it was profitable to do so, though I do not mention the specific occasions.

V

The Bourne

THAT EVENING, JONAS and I dined alone in our room. It is a very pleasant thing, I found, to be popular with the mob and known to everyone; but it is tiring too, and after a time one grows weary of answering the same simple-minded questions again and again, and of politely refusing invitations to drink.

There had been a slight disagreement with the alcalde concerning the compensation I was to receive for my work, my understanding having been that in addition to the quarter-payment made when I was engaged, I would receive full payment for each client upon death, while the alcalde had intended, so he said, that full payment should be made only after all three were attended to. I would never have agreed to that, and liked it less than ever in the light of the green man's warning (which out of loyalty to Vodalus I had kept to myself). But after I had threatened not to appear on the following afternoon I was paid, and everything peaceably resolved.

Now Jonas and I were settled over a smoking platter and a bottle of wine, the door was shut and bolted, and the innkeeper had been instructed to deny that I was in his establishment. I would have been completely at ease if the wine in my cup had not recalled to me so vividly the much better wine Jonas had discovered in our ewer the night before, after I had examined the Claw in secret.

Jonas, observing me, I think, as I stared at the pale red fluid, poured a cup of his own and said, "You must remember that you are not responsible for the sentences. If you had not come here, they would have been punished eventually anyway, and probably would have suffered worse in less skilled hands."

I asked him what he thought he was talking about.

"I can see it troubles you . . . what happened today."

"I thought it went well," I said.

"You know what the octopus remarked when he got out of the mermaid's kelp bed: 'I'm not impugning your skill—quite the opposite. But you look as if you could use a little cheering up.'"

"We're always a little despondent afterward. That's what Master Palaemon always said, and I've found it true in my own case. He called it a purely mechanical psychological function, and at the time that seemed to me an oxymoron, but now I'm not sure he wasn't right. Could you see what happened, or did they keep you too busy?"

"I was standing on the steps behind you most of the time."

"You had a good view then, so you must have seen how it was—everything proceeded smoothly after we decided not to wait for the chair. I exercised my skills to applause, and I was the focus of admiration. There's a feeling of lassitude afterward. Master Palaemon used to talk of crowd melancholy and court melancholy, and said that some of us have both, some have neither, and some have one but not the other. Well, I have crowd melancholy; I don't suppose I'll ever have the chance, in Thrax, of discovering whether I also have court melancholy or not."

"And what is that?" Jonas was looking down into his wine cup.

"A torturer, let's say a master at the Citadel, is occasionally brought into contact with exultants of the highest degree. Suppose there's some exceedingly sensitive prisoner who's thought to possess important information. An official of lofty standing is likely to be delegated to attend such a prisoner's examination. Very often he will have had little experience with the more delicate operations, so he will ask the master questions and perhaps confide in him certain fears he has concerning the subject's temperament or health. A torturer under those circumstances feels himself to be at the center of things—"

"Then feels let down when it's over with. Yes, I suppose I can see that."

"Have you ever seen one of these affairs when it was badly botched?"

"No. Aren't you going to eat any of this meat?"

"Neither have I, but I've heard about them, and that's why I was tense. Times when the client has broken away and fled into the crowd. Times when several strokes were needed to part the neck. Times when a torturer lost all confidence and was unable to proceed. When I vaulted onto that scaffold, I had no way of knowing that none of those things was going to happen to me. If they had, I might have been finished for life."

"'Still, it's a terrible way to earn a living.' That's what the thorn-bush said to the shrike, you know."

"I really don't—" I broke off because I had seen something move on the farther side of the room. At first I thought it was a rat, and I have a pronounced dislike of them; I have seen too many clients bitten in the oubliette under our tower.

"What is it?"

"Something white." I walked around the table to see. "A sheet of paper. Someone has slipped a note under our door."

"Another woman wanting to sleep with you," Jonas said, but by that time I had already picked it up. It was indeed a woman's delicate script, written in grayish ink upon parchment. I held it close to the candle to read.

Dearest Severian:
    From one of the kind men who are assisting me, I have learned you are in the village of Saltus, not far away. It seems too

good to be true, but now I must discover whether you can forgive me.

I swear to you that any suffering you have endured for my sake was not by my choice. From the first, I wanted to tell you everything, but the others would not hear of it. They judged that no one should know but those who had to know (which meant no one but themselves), and at last told me outright that if I did not obey them in *everything* they would forgo the plan and leave me to die. I knew you would die for me, and so I dared to hope that you would have chosen, if you could choose, to suffer for me too. Forgive me.

But now I am away and almost free—my own mistress so long as I obey the simple and humane instructions of good Father Inire. And so I will tell you everything, in the hope that when you have heard it all you will indeed forgive me.

You know of my arrest. You will remember too how anxious your Master Gurloes was for my comfort, and how frequently he visited my cell to talk to me, or had me brought to him so that he and the other masters might question me. That was because my patron, the good Father Inire, had charged him to be strictly attentive to me.

At length, when it became clear that the Autarch would not free me, Father Inire arranged to do so himself. I do not know what threats were made to Master Gurloes, or what bribes were offered him. But they were sufficient, and a few days before my death—as you thought, dearest Severian—he explained to me how the matter was to be arranged. It was not enough, of course, that I be freed. I must be freed in such a way that no search should be made for me. That meant it needs appear that I was dead; yet the instructions Master Gurloes had received had charged him strictly not to let me die.

You will now be able to fathom for yourself how we cut through this tangle of obstructions. It was arranged that I should be subjected to a device whose action was internal only, and Master Gurloes first so disarmed it that I should suffer no real harm. When you thought me in agony, I was to ask you for means of terminating my wretched life. All went as planned.

You provided the knife, and I made a shallow cut on my arm, crouched near the door so some blood would run beneath it, then smeared my throat and fell across the bed for you to see when you looked into my prison.

Did you look? I lay as still as death. My eyes were closed, but I seemed to feel your pain when you saw me there. I nearly wept, and I recall how frightened I was that you might see the tears welling up. At last I heard your footsteps, and I bandaged my arm and washed my face and neck. After a time Master Gurloes came and took me away. Forgive me.

Now I would see you again, and if Father Inire wins a pardon for me as he has solemnly pledged himself to do, there is no reason why we need ever part again. But come to me at once—I am awaiting his messenger, and if he arrives I must fly to the House Absolute to cast myself at the feet of the Autarch, whose name be thrice-blessed balm upon the scorched brows of his slaves.

Speak to *no one* of this, but go northeast from Saltus until you encounter a brook that winds its way to Gyoll. Trace it against the current, and you will find it to issue from the mouth of a mine.

Here I must impart to you a grave secret, which you must by no means reveal to others. This mine is a treasure house of the Autarch's, and in it he has stored great sums of coined money, bullion, and gems against a day in which he may be forced from the Phoenix Throne. It is guarded by certain servitors of Father Inire's, but you need have no fear of them. They have been instructed to obey me, and I have told them of you, and ordered them to permit you to pass without challenge. Entering the mine, then, follow the water-course until you reach the end, where it issues from a stone. Here I wait, and here I write, in the hope that you will forgive your

THECLA

I cannot describe the surge of joy I felt as I read and reread this letter. Jonas, who saw my face, at first leaped from his chair—I think he supposed I was on the point of fainting—then drew away as he might have from a lunatic. When at last I folded the letter and thrust it in my sabretache, he asked no questions (for Jonas was indeed a friend) but showed by his look that he stood ready to help me.

"I nead your animal," I said. "May I take her?"

"Gladly. But—"

I was already unbolting the door. "You cannot come. If all goes well, I'll see that she is returned to you."

As I raced down the stair and into the innyard, the letter spoke in my mind in Thecla's very voice; and by the time I entered the stable I was a lunatic indeed. I looked for Jonas's merychip, but instead saw before me a great destrier, his back higher than my eyes. I had no notion who might have ridden him into this peaceful village, and I gave it no thought. Without hesitating an instant I sprang onto his back, drew *Terminus Est*, and with a stroke severed the reins that tethered him.

I have never seen a better mount. He was out of the stable in one bound, and in two, lunging into the village street. For the space of a breath I feared he would trip on some tent rope, but he was sure-footed as a dancer. The street ran east toward the river; as soon as we were clear of the houses, I urged him to the left. He leaped a wall as a boy might skip across a stick, and I found myself galloping full tilt over a meadow where bulls lifted their horns in the green moonlight.

I am no great rider now, and was still less one then. Despite the high saddle, I think I would have tumbled from the back of an inferior animal before we had covered half a league; but my stolen destrier moved, for all his speed, as smoothly as a shadow. A shadow indeed we must have appeared, he with his black hide, I in my fuligin cloak. He had not slacked his pace before we splashed across the brook mentioned in the letter. I checked him there—partly by grasping his halter, more by speech, to which he harkened as a brother might. There was no path on either side of the water, and we had not traced it far before trees rimmed the banks. I guided him into the brook then (though he was loath to go) where we made our way up foaming races as a man climbs steps, and swam deep pools.

For more than a watch, we waded this brook through a forest much like the one through which Jonas and I had passed after being separated from Dorcas, Dr. Talos, and the rest at the Piteous Gate. Then the banks grew higher and more rugged, the trees smaller, and twisted. There were boulders in the stream; from their squared edges I knew they were the work of hands, and that we were in the region of the mines, with the wreck of some great city below us. Our way was steeper, and for all his mettle he faltered sometimes on sliding stones, so that I was forced to dismount and lead him. In this way we passed through a series of little, dreaming hollows, each dark in the shadows of its high sides, but each flecked in places with green moonlight, each ringing with the sound of water—but with that sound only, and otherwise wrapped in silence.

At last we entered a vale smaller and narrower than any of the others; and at the end of it, a chain or so off where the moonlight spilled upon a sheer elevation, I saw a dark opening. The brook had its origin there, flooding out like saliva from the lips of petrified titan. I found a patch of ground beside the water sufficiently level for my mount to stand and contrived to tie him there, knotting what remained of his reins around a dwarfish tree.

Once, no doubt, a timber trestle had provided access to the mine, but it had rotted away long ago. Though the climb looked impossible in the moonlight, I was able to find a few footholds in the ancient wall and scaled it to one side of the descending jet.

I had my hands inside the opening when I heard, or thought I heard, some sound from the vale behind me. I paused, and turned my head to look back. The rush of the water would have drowned any noise less commanding than a bugle call or an explosion, and it had drowned this, yet still I had sensed something—the note of stone falling upon stone, perhaps, or the splash of something plunging into the water.

The vale seemed peaceful and silent. Then I saw my destrier shift his stance, his proud head and forward-cocked ears coming for an instant into the light. I decided that what I had heard was nothing more than the striking of his steel-shod feet against the rock as he stamped in discontent at being so closely tethered. I drew my body into the mine entrance, and by doing so, as I later learned, saved my life.

A man of any wit, setting out as I had and knowing he must enter such a place, would have brought a lantern and a plentiful supply of candles. I had been so wild at the thought that Thecla still lived that I had none. Thus I crept forward in the dark, and had not taken a dozen steps before the moonlight of the vale had vanished behind me. My boots were in the stream, so I walked as I had when I had led the destrier up it. *Terminus Est* was slung over my left shoulder, and I had no fear that the tip of her sheath might be wet by the stream, for the ceiling of the tunnel was so low that I walked bent double. So I proceeded for a long time, fearing always that I had come wrong, and that Thecla waited for me elsewhere, and would wait in vain.

VI

Blue Light

I GREW SO accustomed to the sound of the icy water that had you asked me I should have said I walked in silence; but it was not so, and when, most suddenly, the constricted tunnel opened into a large chamber equally dark, I knew it at once from the change in the music of the stream. I took another step, and then another, and raised my head. There was no ragged stone now to strike it. I lifted my arms. Nothing. I grasped *Terminus Est* by her onyx hilt and waved her blade, still in the protection of its sheath. Nothing still.

Then I did something that you, reading this record, will find foolish indeed, though you must recall that I had been told that such guards as might be in the mine had been warned of my arrival and instructed to do me no harm. I called Thecla's name.

And the echoes answered: *"Thecla . . . Thecla . Thecla . . ."*

Then silence again.

I remembered that I was to have followed the water until it welled from a rock, and that I had not done so. Possibly it trickled through as many galleries here beneath the hill as it had through dells outside it. I began to wade again, feeling my way at each step for fear I might plunge over my head with the next.

I had not taken five strides when I heard something, far off yet distinct, above the whispering of the now smoothly flowing water. I had not taken five more when I saw light.

It was not the emerald reflection of the fabled forests of the moon, nor was it such a light as guards might carry with them—the scarlet flame of a torch, the golden radiance of a candle, or even the piercing white beam I had sometimes glimpsed by night when the fliers of the Autarch soared over the Citadel. Rather, it was a luminous mist, sometimes seeming of no color, sometimes of an impure yellowish green. It was impossible to say how far it was, and it seemed to possess no shape. For a time it shimmered before my sight; and I, still following the stream, splashed toward it. Then it was joined by another.

It is difficult for me to concentrate on the events of the next few minutes. Perhaps everyone holds in his subconscious certain moments of horror, as our oubliette held, in its lowest inhabited level, those clients whose minds had long ago been destroyed or transformed into consciousness no longer human. Like them, these memories shriek and lash the walls with their chains, but are seldom brought high enough to see the light.

What I experienced under the hill remains with me as they remained with us, something I endeavor to lock within the furthest recesses of my mind but am from time to time made conscious of. (Not long ago, when the *Samru* was still near the mouth of Gyoll, I looked over the sternrail by night; there I saw each dipping of the oars appear as a spot of phosphorescent fire, and for a moment imagined that those from under the hill had come for me at last. They are mine to command now, but I have small comfort in that.)

The light I had seen was joined by a second, as I have described, then the first two by a third, and the first three by a fourth, and still I went on. Soon there were too many of the lights to count; but not knowing what they were, I was actually comforted and encouraged by the sight of them, imagining each perhaps to be a spark from a torch of some kind not known to me, a torch held by one of the guards mentioned in the letter. When I had taken a dozen more steps, I saw that these flecks of light were coalescing into a pattern, and that the pattern was a dart or arrowhead pointed toward myself. Then I heard, very faintly, such a roaring as I used to hear from the tower called the Bear when the beasts were given their food. Even then, I think, I might have escaped if I had turned and fled.

I did not. The roaring grew—not quite any noise of animals, yet not the shouting of the most frenzied human mob. I saw that the flecks of light were not shapeless, as I had imagined before. Rather, each was of that figure called in art a star, having five unequal points.

It was then, much too late, that I halted.

By this time the uncertain, hueless light these stars shed had increased enough for me to see as looming shadows the shapes about me. To either side were masses whose angular sides suggested that they were works of men—it seemed I walked in the buried city (here not collapsed under the weight of the overlaying soil) from which the miners of Saltus delved their treasures. Among these masses stood squat pillars of an ordered irregularity such as I have sometimes noticed in ricks of firewood, from which every stick protrudes yet goes to make the whole. These glinted softly, throwing back the corpse light of the moving stars as something less sinister, or at least more beautiful, then they had received.

For a moment I wondered at these pillars; then I looked at the star-shapes again, and for the first time saw them. Have you ever toiled by night toward what seemed a cottage window, and found it to be the balefire of a great fortress? Or climbing, slipped, and caught yourself, and looked below, and seen the fall a hundred times greater than you had believed? If you have, you will have some notion of what I felt. The stars were not sparks of light, but shapes like men, small only because the cavern in which I stood was more vast than I had ever conceived that such a place could be. And the men, who seemed not men, being thicker of shoulder and more twisted than men, were rushing toward me. The roar I heard was the sound of their voices.

I turned, and when I found I could not run through the water mounted the bank where the dark structures stood. By that time they were almost upon me, and some were moving wide to my right and left and cut me off from the outer world.

They were terrible in a fashion I am not certain I can explain—like apes in that they had hairy, crooked bodies, long-armed, short-legged, and thick-necked. Their teeth were like the fangs of smilodons, curved and saw-edged, extending a finger's length below their massive jaws. Yet it was not any of these things, nor the noctilucent light that clung to their fur, that brought the horror I felt. It was something in their faces, perhaps in the huge, pale-irised eyes. It told me they were as human as I. As the old are imprisoned in rotting bodies, as women are locked in weak bodies that make them prey for the filthy desires of thousands, so these men were wrapped in the guise of lurid apes, and knew it. As they ringed me, I could see that knowledge, and it was the worse because those eyes were the only part of them that did not glow.

I gulped air to shout *Thecla* once more. Then I knew, and closed my lips, and drew *Terminus Est*.

One, larger or at least bolder than the rest, advanced on me. He carried a short-hafted mace whose shaft had once been a thigh bone. Just out of sword-reach he threatened me with it, roaring and slapping the metal head of his weapon in a long hand.

Something disturbed the water behind me, and I turned in time to see one of the glowing man-apes fording the stream. He leaped backward as I slashed at him, but the square blade-tip caught him below the armpit. So fine was that blade, so magnificently tempered and perfectly edged, that it cut its way out through the breastbone.

He fell and the water carried his corpse away, but before the stroke went home I had seen that he waded in the stream with distaste, and that it had slowed his movements at least as much as it had slowed mine. Turning to keep all my attackers in view, I backed into it and began slowly to move toward the point where it ran to the outside world. I felt that if I could once reach the constricted tunnel I would be safe; but I knew too that they would never permit me to do so.

They gathered more thickly around me until there must have been several hundred. The light they gave was so great then that I could see that the squared masses I had glimpsed earlier were indeed buildings, apparently of the most ancient construction, built of seamless gray stone and soiled everywhere by the dung of bats.

The irregular pillars were stacks of ingots in which each layer was laid across the last. From their color I judged them to be silver. There were a hundred in each stack, and surely many hundreds of stacks in the buried city.

All this I saw while taking a half-dozen steps. At the seventh they came for me, twenty at least, and from all sides. There was no time for clean strokes through the neck. I swung my blade in circles, and its singing filled that underground world and echoed from the stony walls and ceiling, audible over the bellowing and the screams.

One's sense of time goes mad at such moments. I recall the rush of the attack and my own frantic blows, but in retrospect everything seems to have happened in a breath. Two and five and ten were down, until the water around me was blood-black in the corpse light, choked with dying and dead; but still they came. A blow on my shoulder was like the smash of a giant's fist. *Terminus Est* slipped out of my hand, and the weight of the bodies bore me down until I was grappling blind under water. My enemy's fangs slashed my arm as two spikes might, but he feared drowning too much, I think, to fight as he would have otherwise. I thrust fingers into his wide nostrils and snapped his neck, though it seemed tougher than a man's.

If I could have held my breath then until I worked my way to the tunnel, I might have escaped. The man-apes seemed to have lost sight of me, and I drifted underwater some small distance downstream. By then my lungs were bursting; I lifted my face to the surface, and they were upon me.

No doubt there comes a time for every man when by rights he should die. This, I have always felt, was mine. I have counted all the life I have held since as pure profit, an undeserved gift. I had no weapon, and my right arm was numbed and torn. The man-apes were bold now. That boldness gave me a moment more of life, for so many crowded forward to kill me that they obstructed one another. I kicked one in the face. A second grasped my boot; there was a flash of light, and I (moved by what instinct or inspiration I do not know) snatched at it. I held the Claw.

As though it gathered to itself all the corpse light and dyed it with the color of life, it streamed forth a clear azure that filled the cavern. For one heartbeat the man-apes halted as though at the stroke of a gong, and I lifted the gem overhead; what frenzy of terror I hoped for (if I really hoped at all) I cannot say now.

What happened was quite different. The man-apes neither fled shrieking nor resumed their attack. Instead they retreated until the nearest were perhaps three strides off, and squatted with their faces pressed against the floor of the mine. There was silence again as there had been when I had first entered it, with no sound but the whispering of the stream; but now I could see everything, from the stacks of tarnished silver ingots near to which I stood, to the very end where the man-apes had descended a ruined wall, appearing to my sight then like flecks of pale fire.

I began to back away. The man-apes looked up at that, and their faces were the faces of human beings. When I saw them thus, I knew of the eons of struggles in the dark from which their fangs and saucer eyes and flap ears had come to be. We, so the mages say, were apes once, happy apes in forests swallowed by deserts so long ago they have no names. Old men return to childish ways when at last the years becloud their minds. May it not be that mankind will return (as an old man does) to the decayed image of what once was, if at last the old sun dies and we are left scuffling over bones in the dark? I saw our future— one future at least—and I felt more sorrow for those who had triumphed in the dark battles than for those who had poured out their blood in that endless night.

I took a step backward (as I have said), and then another, and still none of the man-apes moved to stop me. Then I remembered *Terminus Est*. Were I to have made my escape from the most frantic battle, I would have despised myself if I had left her behind. To walk out unmolested without her was more than I could bear. I began to advance again, watching by the light of the Claw for her gleaming blade.

At this the faces of those strange, twisted men seemed to brighten, and I saw by their looks that they hoped I meant to remain with them, so that the Claw and its blue radiance would be theirs always. How terrible it seems now when I set the words on paper; yet it would not, I think, have been terrible in fact. Bestial though they appeared, I could see adoration on every brute face, so that I thought (as I think now) that if they are worse in many ways than we are, these people of the hidden cities beneath Urth are better in others, blessed with an ugly innocence.

From side to side I searched, from bank to bank; but I saw nothing, though it seemed to me that the light shone from the Claw more brightly, and more brightly still, until at last each tooth of stone that hung from the ceiling of that cavernous space cast behind it a sharp-sided shadow of pitch black. At last I called out to the crouching men, "My sword . . . Where is my sword? Did one of you take her?"

I would not have spoken to them if I had not been half frantic with the fear of losing her; but it seemed they understood. They began to mutter among themselves and to me, and to make signs to me—without rising—to show they would fight no more, extending their bludgeons and spears of pointed bone for me to take.

Then above the murmuring of the water and the muttering of the man-apes, I heard a new sound, and at once they fell silent. If an ogre were to eat of the very legs of the world, the grinding of his teeth would make just such a noise. The bed of the stream (where I still stood) trembled under me, and the water, which had been so clear, received a fine burden of silt, so that it looked as though a ribbon of smoke wound through it. From far below I heard a step that might have been the walking of a tower on the Final Day, when it is said all the cities of Urth will stride forth to meet the dawn of the New Sun.

And then another.

At once the man-apes rose, and crouching low fled toward the farther end of the gallery, silent now and swift as so many flitting bats. The light went with them, for it seemed, as I had somehow feared, that the Claw had flamed for them and not for me.

A third step came from underground, and with it the last gleam winked out; but at that instant, in that final gleam, I saw *Terminus Est* lying in the deepest water. In the dark I bent, and putting the Claw back into the top of my boot, took up my sword; and in so doing I discovered that the numbness had left my arm, which now seemed as strong as it had before the fight.

A fourth step sounded and I turned and fled, groping before me with the blade. What creature it was we had called from the roots of the continent I think I now know. But I did not know then, and I did not know whether it was the roaring of the man-apes, or the light of the Claw, or some other cause that had waked it. I only knew that there was something far beneath us before which the man-apes, with all the terror of their appearance and their numbers, scattered like sparks before a wind.

VII

The Assassins

WHEN I RECALL my second passage through the tunnel that led to the outer world, I feel it occupied a watch or more. My nerves have never, I suppose, been fully sound, tormented as they have always been by a relentless memory. Then they were keyed to the highest pitch, so that to take three strides seemed to exhaust a lifetime. I was frightened, of course. I have never been called a coward since I was a small boy, and on certain occasions various persons have commented on my courage. I have performed my duties as a member of the guild without flinching, fought both privately and in war, climbed crags, and several times nearly drowned. But I believe there is no other difference between those who are called courageous and those who are branded craven than that the second are fearful before the danger and the first after it.

No one can be much frightened, certainly, during a period of great and immanent peril—the mind is too much concentrated on the thing itself, and on the actions necessary to meet or avoid it. The coward is a coward, then, because he has brought his fear with him; persons we think cowardly will sometimes amaze us by their bravery, if they have had no forewarning of their danger.

Master Gurloes, whom I had supposed to be of the most

dauntless courage when I was a boy, was unquestionably a coward. During the period when Drotte was captain of apprentices, Roche and I used to alternate, turn and turn about, in serving Master Gurloes and Master Palaemon; and one night, when Master Gurloes had retired to his cabin but instructed me to stay to fill his cup for him, he began to confide in me.

"Lad, do you know the client Ia? An armiger's daughter and quite good-looking."

As an apprentice I had few dealings with clients; I shook my head.

"She is to be abused."

I had no idea what he meant, so I said, "Yes, Master."

"That's the greatest disgrace that can befall a woman. Or a man either. To be abused. By the torturer." He touched his chest and threw back his head to look at me. He had a remarkably small head for so large a man; if he had worn a shirt or jacket (which of course he never did), one would have been tempted to believe it padded.

"Yes, Master."

"Aren't you going to offer to do it for me? A young fellow like you, full of juice. Don't tell me you're not hairy yet."

At last I understood what he meant, and I told him that I had not realized it would be permissible, since I was still an apprentice; but that if he gave the order, I would certainly obey.

"I imagine you would. She's not bad, you know. But tall, and I don't like them tall. There's an exultant's bastard in that family a generation or so back, you may be sure. Blood will confess itself, as they say, though only we know all that means. Want to do it?"

He held out his cup and I poured. "If you wish me to, Master." The truth was that I was excited at the thought. I had never possessed a woman.

"You can't. I must. What if I were to be questioned? Then too, I must certify it—sign the papers. A master of the guild for twenty years, and I've never falsified papers. I suppose you think I can't do it."

The thought had never crossed my mind, just as the opposite

thought (that he might still retain some potency) had never occurred to me with regard to Master Palaemon, whose white hair, stooped shoulders, and peering lens made him seem like one who had been decrepit always.

"Well, look here," Master Gurloes said, and heaved himself out of his chair.

He was one of those who can walk well and speak clearly even when they are very drunk, and he strode over to a cabinet quite confidently, though I thought for a moment that he was going to drop the blue porcelain jar he took down.

"This is a rare and potent drug." He took the lid off and showed me a dark brown powder. "It never fails. You'll have to use it someday, so you ought to know about it. Just take as much as you could get under your fingernail on the end of a knife, you follow me? If you take too much, you won't be able to appear in public for a couple of days."

I said, "I'll remember, Master."

"Of course it's a poison. They all are, and this is the best—a little more than *that* would kill you. And you mustn't take it again until the moon changes, understand?"

"Perhaps you'd better have Brother Corbinian weigh the dose, Master." Corbinian was our apothecary; I was terrified that Master Gurloes might swallow a spoonful before my eyes.

"Me? I don't need it." Contemptuously, he put the lid on the jar again and banged it down on its shelf in the cabinet.

"That's well, Master."

"Besides" (he winked at me), "I'll have this." From his sabretache he took an iron phallus, It was about a span and a half long and had a leather thong through the end opposite the tip.

It must seem idiotic to you who read this, but for an instant I could not imagine what the thing was for, despite the somewhat exaggerated realism of its design. I had a wild notion that the wine had rendered him childish, as a little boy is who supposes there is no essential difference between his wooden mount and a real animal. I wanted to laugh.

"'Abuse,' that's their word. That, you see, is where they've left us an out." He had slapped the iron phallus against his palm— the same gesture, now that I think of it, that the man-ape who had threatened me had made with his mace. Then I had understood and had been gripped by revulsion.

But even that revulsion was not the emotion I would feel now in the same situation. I did not sympathize with the client, because I did not think of her at all; it was only a sort of repugnance for Master Gurloes, who with all his bulk and great strength was forced to rely on the brown powder, and still worse, on the iron phallus I had seen, an object that might have been sawed from a statue, and perhaps had been. Yet I saw him on another occasion, when the thing had to be done immediately for fear the order could not otherwise be carried out before the client died, act at once, and without powder or phallus, and without difficulty.

Master Gurloes was a coward then. Still, perhaps his cowardice was better than the courage I would have possessed in his position, for courage is not always a virtue. I had been courageous (as such things are counted) when I had fought the man-apes, but my courage was no more than a mixture of foolhardiness, surprise, and desperation; now, in the tunnel, when there was no longer any cause for fear, I was afraid and nearly dashed my brains out against the low ceiling; but I did not pause or even slacken speed before I saw the opening before me, made visible by the blessed sheen of moonlight. Then, indeed, I halted; and considering myself safe wiped my sword as well as I might with the ragged edge of my cloak, and sheathed her.

That done, I slung her over my shoulder and swung myself out and down, feeling with the toes of my sodden boots for the ledges that had supported me in the ascent. I had just gained the third when two quarrels struck the rock near my head. One must have wedged its point in some flaw in the ancient work, for it remained in place, blazing with white fire. I recall how astonished I was, and also how I hoped, in the few moments before the next struck nearer still and nearly blinded me, that the arbalests were not of the kind that bring a new projectile to the string when cocked, and thus are so swift to shoot again.

When the third exploded against the stone, I knew they were, and dropped before the marksmen who had missed could fire yet again.

There was, as I ought to have known there would be, a deep pool where the stream fell from the mouth of the mine. I got another ducking, but since I was already wet it did no harm, and in fact quenched the flecks of fire that had clung to my face and arms.

There could be no question here of cannily remaining below the surface. The water seized me as if I were a stick and flung me to the top where it willed. This, by the greatest good luck, was some distance from the rock face, and I was able to watch my attackers from behind as I clambered onto the bank. They and the woman who stood between them were staring at the place where the cascade fell.

As I drew *Terminus Est* for the final time that night, I called, "Over here, Agia."

I had guessed earlier that it was she, but as she turned (more swiftly than either of the men with her) I glimpsed her face in the moonlight. It was a terrible face to me (though for all her self-depreciation so lovely) because the sight of it meant that Thecla was surely dead.

The man nearest me was fool enough to try to bring his arbalest to his shoulder before he pulled the trigger. I ducked and cut his legs from under him, while the other's quarrel whizzed over my head like a meteor.

By the time I had straightened up again, the second man had dropped his arbalest and was drawing his hanger. Agia was quicker, making a cut at my neck with an athame before his weapon was free of the scabbard. I dodged her first stroke and parried her second, though *Terminus Est*'s blade was not made for fencing. My own attack made her bound back.

"Get behind him," she called to the second arbalestier. "I can front him."

He did not answer. Instead, his mouth swung open and his point swung wide. Before I realized that it was not at me that he was looking, something feverishly gleaming bounded past me. I heard the ugly sound of a breaking skull. Agia turned as gracefully as any cat and would have spitted the man-ape, but I struck the poisoned blade from her hand and sent it skittering into the pool. She tried to flee then; I caught her by the hair and jerked her off her feet.

The man-ape was mumbling over the body of the arbalestier he had killed—whether he sought to loot it or was merely curious about its appearance I have never known. I set my foot on Agia's neck, and the man-ape straightened and turned to face me, then dropped in the crouching posture I had seen in the mine and held up his arms. One hand was gone; I recognized the clean cut of *Terminus Est*. The man-ape mumbled something I could not understand.

I tried to reply. "Yes, I did that. I am sorry. We are at peace now."

The beseeching look remained, and he spoke again. Blood still seeped from the stump, though his kind must possess a mechanism for pinching shut the veins, as thylacodons are said to do; without the attentions of a surgeon, a man would have bled to death from that wound.

"I cut it," I said. "But it was while we were still fighting, before you people saw the Claw of the Conciliator." Then it came to me that he must have followed me outside for another glimpse of the gem, braving the fear engendered by whatever we had waked below the hill. I thrust my hand into the top of my boot and pulled out the Claw, and the instant I had done so realized what a fool I had been to put the boot and its precious cargo so close to Agia's reach, for her eyes went wide with cupidity at the moment that the man-ape abased himself further and stretched forth his piteous stump.

For a moment we were posed, all three, and a strange group we must have looked in that eerie light. An astonished voice—Jonas's—called "Severian!" from the heights above. Like the trumpet note in a shadow play that dissolves all feigning, that shout ended our tableau. I lowered the Claw and concealed it in my palm. The man-ape bolted for the rock face, and Agia began to struggle and curse beneath my foot.

A rap with the flat of my blade quieted her, but I kept my boot on her until Jonas had joined me and there were two of us to prevent her escape.

"I thought you might need help," he said. "I perceive I was mistaken." He was looking at the corpses of the men who had been with Agia.

I said, "This wasn't the real fight."

Agia was sitting up, rubbing her neck and shoulders. "There were four, and we would have had you, but the bodies of those things, those firefly tiger-men, started pitching out of the hole, and two were afraid and slipped away."

Jonas scratched his head with his steel hand, a sound like the currying of a charger. "I saw what I thought I saw, then. I had begun to wonder."

I asked what he thought he had seen.

"A glowing being in a fur robe making an obeisance to you. You were holding up a cup of burning brandy, I think. Or was it incense? What's this?" He bent and picked up something from the edge of the bank, where the man-ape had crouched.

"A bludgeon."

"Yes, I see that." There was a loop of sinew at the end of the bone handle, and Jonas slipped it over his wrist. "Who are these people who tried to kill you?"

"We would have," Agia said, "if it hadn't been for that cloak. We saw him coming out of the hole, but it covered him when he started to climb down, and my men couldn't see the target, only the skin of his arms."

I explained as briefly as I could how I had become involved with Agia and her twin, and described the death of Agilus.

"So now she's come to join him." Jonas looked from her to the crimson length of *Terminus Est* and gave a little shrug. "I left my merychip up there, and perhaps I ought to go and look after her. That way I can say afterward that I saw nothing. Was this woman the one who sent the letter?"

"I should have known. I had told her about Thecla. You don't know about Thecla, but she did, and that was what the letter was about. I told her while we were going through the Botanic Gardens in Nessus. There were mistakes in the letter and things Thecla would never have said, but I didn't stop to think of them when I read it."

I stepped away and replaced the Claw in my boot, thrusting it deep. "Maybe you had better attend to your animal, as you say. My own seems to have broken loose, and we may have to take turns riding yours."

Jonas nodded and began to climb back the way he had come.

"You were waiting for me, weren't you?" I asked Agia. "I heard something, and the destrier cocked his ears at the sound. That was you. Why didn't you kill me then?"

"We were up there." She gestured toward the heights. "And I wanted the men I'd hired to shoot you when you came wading up the brook. They were stupid and stubborn as men always are, and said they wouldn't waste their quarrels—that the creatures inside would kill you. I rolled down a stone, the biggest I could move, but by then it was too late."

"They had told you about the mine?"

Agia shrugged, and the moonlight turned her bare shoulders to something more precious and more beautiful than flesh. "You're going to kill me now, so what does it matter? All the local people tell stories about this place. They say those things come out at night during storms and take animals from the cowsheds, and sometimes break into the houses for children.

There's also a legend that they guard treasure inside, so I put that in the letter too. I thought if you wouldn't come for your Thecla, you might for that. Can I stand with my back to you, Severian? If it's all the same, I don't want to see it coming."

When she said that, I felt as though a weight had been lifted from my heart: I had not been certain I could strike her if I had to look into her face.

I raised my own iron phallus, and as I did so felt there was one more thing I wanted to ask Agia; but I could not recall what it might be.

"Strike," she said. "I am ready."

I sought good footing, and my fingers found the woman's head at one end of the guard, the head that marked the female edge.

And a little later, again, "Strike!"

But by that time I had climbed out of the vale.

VIII

The Cultellarii

WE RETURNED TO the inn in silence, and so slowly that the eastern sky was gray before we reached the town. Jonas was unsaddling the merychip when I said, "I didn't kill her."

He nodded without looking at me. "I know."

"Did you watch? You said you wouldn't."

"I heard her voice when you were practically standing beside me. Will she try again?"

I waited, thinking, while he carried the little saddle into the tack room. When he came out, I said, "Yes, I'm sure she will. I didn't exact a promise from her, if that's what you mean. She wouldn't have kept one in any case."

"I would have killed her then."

"Yes," I said. "That would have been the right thing to do."

We walked out of the stable together. There was light enough in the innyard now for us to see the well, and the wide doors that led into the inn.

"I don't think it would have been right—I'm only saying that I would have done it. I would have imagined myself stabbed in my sleep, dying on a dirty bed somewhere, and I would have swung that thing. It wouldn't have been right." Jonas lifted the mace the man-ape had left behind, and chopped with it in a parody, brutal and graceless, of a sword cut. The head caught the light and both of us gasped.

It was of pounded gold.

Neither of us felt any desire to join the festivities the fair still proffered to those who had caroused all night. We retired to the room we shared, and prepared for sleep. When Jonas offered to share his gold with me, I refused. Earlier, I had had money in plenty and the advance on my fee, and he had been living, as it were, upon my largess. Now I was happy that he would no longer feel himself in my debt. I was ashamed, too, when I saw how completely he trusted me with his gold, and remembered how carefully I had concealed (in fact, still concealed) the existence of the Claw from him. I felt bound to tell him of it; but I did not, and contrived instead to slip my foot from my wet boot in such a way that the Claw fell into the toe.

I woke about noon, and after satisfying myself that the Claw was still there, roused Jonas as he had asked me. "There should be jewelers at the fair who'll give me some sort of price for this," he said. "At least, I can bargain with them. Want to come with me?"

"We should have something to eat, and by the time we're through, I'll be due at the scaffold."

"Back to work then."

"Yes." I had picked up my cloak. It was sadly torn, and my boots were dull and still slightly damp.

"One of the maids here can sew that for you. It won't be as good as new, but it will be a lot better than it is now." Jonas swung open the door. "Come along, if you're hungry. What are you looking so thoughtful about?"

In the inn's parlor, with a good meal between us, and the innkeeper's wife exercising her needle on my cloak in another room, I told him what had happened under the hill, ending with the steps I had heard far below ground.

"You're a strange man," was all he said.

"You are stranger than I. You don't want people to know it, but you're a foreigner of some kind."

He smiled. "A cacogen?"

"An outlander."

Jonas shook his head, then nodded. "Yes, I suppose I am. But you—you have this talisman that lets you command nightmares, and you have discovered a hoard of silver. Yet you talk about it to me as someone else might talk about the weather."

I took a bit of bread. "It is strange, I agree. But the strangeness resides in the Claw, the thing itself, and not in me. As for talking about it to you, why shouldn't I? If I were to steal your gold, I could sell it and spend the money, but I don't think things would go well for someone who stole the Claw. I don't know why I think that, but I do, and of course Agia stole it. As for the silver—"

"And she put it in your pocket?"

"In the sabretache that hangs from my belt. She thought her brother would kill me, remember. Then they were going to claim my body—they had planned that already, so they'd get *Terminus Est* and my habit. She would have had my sword and clothes and the gem too, and meanwhile, if it were found, I would be blamed and not she. I remember . . ."

"What?"

"The Pelerines. They stopped us as we were trying to get out. Jonas, do you think it's true that some people can read the thoughts of others?"

"Of course."

"Not everyone is so sure. Master Gurloes used to speak favorably of the idea, but Master Palaemon wouldn't hear of it. Still, I think the chief priestess of the Pelerines could, at least to some degree. She knew Agia had taken something, and that I had not. She made Agia strip so they could search her, but they didn't search me. Later they destroyed their cathedral, and I think that must have been because of the loss of the Claw—it was the Cathedral of the Claw, after all."

Jonas nodded thoughtfully.

"But none of this is what I wanted to ask you about. I'd like your opinion of the footsteps. Everyone knows about Erebus and Abaia and the other beings in the sea who will come to land someday. Nevertheless, I think you know more about them than most of the rest of us."

Jonas's face, which had been so open before, was closed and guarded now. "And why do you think that?"

"Because you've been a sailor, and because of the story about the beans—the story you told at the gate. You must have seen my brown book when I was reading it upstairs. It tells all the secrets of the world, or at least what various mages have said they were. I haven't read it all or even half of it, though Thecla and I used to read an entry every few days and spend the time between readings arguing about it. But I've noticed that all the explanations in that book are simple, and seemingly childish."

"Like my story."

I nodded. "Your story might have come out of the book. When I first carried it to Thecla, I supposed it was intended for children, or for adults who enjoyed childish things. But when we had talked about some of the thoughts in it, I understood that they had to be expressed in that way or they couldn't be expressed at all. If the writer had wanted to describe a new way to make wine or the best way to make love, he could have used complex and accurate language. But in the book he really wrote he had to say, 'In the beginning was only the hexaemeron,' or 'It is not to see the icon standing still, but to see the still standing.' The thing I heard underground . . . was that one of them?"

"I didn't see it." Jonas rose. "I'm going out now to sell the mace, but before I go I'm going to tell you what all housewives sooner or later tell their husbands: 'Before you ask more questions, think about whether you really want to know the answers.'"

"One last question," I said, "and then I promise I won't ask you anything more. When we were going through the Wall, you said the things we saw in there were soldiers, and you implied they had been stationed there to resist Abaia and the others. Are the man-apes soldiers of the same kind? And if they are, what good can human-sized fighters do when our opponents are as large as mountains? And why didn't the old autarchs use human soldiers?"

Jonas had wrapped the mace in a rag and stood now shifting it from one hand to the other. "That's three questions, and the only one I can answer for certain is the second. I'll guess at the other two, but I'm going to hold you to your promise; this is the last time we're going to speak of these things.

"The last question first. The old autarchs, who were not autarchs or called so, did use human soldiers. But the warriors they had created by humanizing animals, and perhaps, in secret by bestializing men, were more loyal. They had to be, since the populace—who hated their rulers—hated these inhuman servitors more still. Thus the servitors could be made to endure things that human soldiers would not. That may have been why they were used in the Wall. Or there may be some other explanation entirely."

Jonas paused and walked to the window, looking not into the street but up at the clouds. "I don't know whether your man-apes are the same kind of hybrid. The one I saw looked quite human to me except for his pelt, so I would be inclined to agree with you that they are human beings who have undergone some change in their essential nature as a result of their life in the mines and their contact with the relics of the city buried there. Urth is very old now. It's very old, and no doubt there have been many treasures hidden in bygone times. Gold and silver do not alter, but their guardians can suffer metamorphoses stranger than those that turn grapes to wine and sand to pearls."

I said, "But we outside endure the dark each night, and the treasures carried up from the mines are brought to us. Why haven't we changed too?"

Jonas did not answer, and I remembered my promise to ask

him nothing more. Still, when he turned to face me there was something in his eyes that told me I was being a fool, that we *had* changed. He turned away again and stared out and up once more.

"All right," I conceded, "you don't have to answer that. But what about the other question you pledged yourself to answer? How can human soldiers resist the monsters from the seas?"

"You were correct when you said Erebus and Abaia are as great as mountains, and I admit that I was surprised you knew it. Most people lack the imagination to conceive of anything so large, and think them no bigger than houses or ships. Their actual size is so great that while they remain on this world they can never leave the water—their own weight would crush them. You mustn't think of them battering at the Wall with their fists, or tossing boulders about. But by their thoughts they enlist servants, and they fling them against all rules that rival their own."

Jonas opened the inn's door then and slipped out into the bustle of the street; I remained where I was, resting an elbow on what had been our breakfast table, and recalled the dream I had experienced when I had shared Baldanders's bed. *The land could not hold us*, the monstrous women had said.

Now I am come to a part of my story where I cannot help but write of something I have largely avoided mentioning before. You that read it cannot but have noticed that I have not scrupled to recount in great detail things that transpired years ago, and to give the very words of those who spoke to me, and the very words with which I replied; and you must have thought this only a conventional device I had adopted to make my story flow more smoothly. The truth is that I am one of those who are cursed with what is called perfect recollection. We cannot, as I have sometimes heard foolishly alleged, remember everything. I cannot recall the ordering of the books on the shelves in the library of Master Ultan, for example. But I can remember more than many would credit: the position of each object on a table I walked past when I was a child, and even that I have recalled some scene to mind previously, and how that remembered incident differed from the memory of it I have now.

It was my power of recollection that made me the favorite pupil of Master Palaemon, and so I suppose it can be blamed for the existence of this narrative, for if he had not favored me, I would not have been sent to Thrax bearing his sword.

Some say this power is linked to weak judgement—of that I am no judge. But it has another danger, one I have encountered many times. When I cast my mind into the past, as I am doing now and as I did then when I sought to recall my dream, I remember it so well that I seem to move again in the bygone day, a day old-new, and unchanged each time I draw it to the surface of my mind, its eidolons as real as I. I can even now close my eyes and walk into Thecla's cell as I did one winter evening; and soon my fingers will feel the heat of her garment while the perfume of her person fills my nostrils like the perfume of lilies warmed before a fire. I lift her gown from her and embrace that ivory body, feeling her nipples pressed to my face. . . .

You see? It is very easy to waste hours and days in such rememberings, and sometimes I fall so deeply into them that I am drugged and drunken. So it was now. The footfalls I had heard in the man-apes' cavern still echoed in my mind, and seeking some explanation I returned to my dream, certain now that I knew from whom it had come, and hoping it had revealed more than its shaper apprehended.

Again I bestride the mitred, leather-winged steed. Pelicans fly below us with stiffly formal strokes, and gulls wheel and keen.

Again I fall, tumbling through the abyss of air, whistling toward the sea, yet suspended, for a time, between wave and cloud. I arch my body, bring down my head, let my legs trail behind me like a banner, and so cleave the water and see floating in clear azure the head with hair of snakes and the many-headed beast, and then the swirling sand-garden far below. The giantesses lift arms like the trunks of sycamores, each finger tipped with an amaranthine talon. Then very suddenly, I who had been blind before understood why it was that Abaia had sent me this dream, and had sought to enlist me in the great and final war of Urth.

But now the tyranny of memory overwhelmed my will. Though I could see the titan odalisques and their garden and knew them to be no more than dream-stuff recalled, I could not escape from their fascination and the memory of the dream. Hands grasped me like a doll, and as I dandled thus between the meretrices of Abaia, I was lifted from my broad-armed chair in the inn of Saltus; yet still, for perhaps a hundred heartbeats more, I could not rid my mind of the sea and its green-haired women.

"He sleeps."

"His eyes are open."

A third voice: "Shall we bring the sword?"

"Bring it—there may be work for it."

The titanesses faded. Men in deerskin and rough wool held me on either side, and one with a scarred face held the point of his dirk at my throat. The man on my right had picked up *Terminus Est* with his free hand; he was the black-bearded volunteer who had helped break open the sealed house.

"Someone's coming."

The man with the scarred face glided away. I heard the door rattle, and Jonas's exclamation as he was drawn inside.

"This is your master, isn't it? Well, don't move, my friend, or cry out. We'll kill you both."

IX

The Liege of Leaves

THEY FORCED US to stand with our faces to the wall while they bound our hands. Our cloaks were draped over our shoulders afterward to hide the thongs, so that we appeared to walk with our hands clasped behind us, and we were led out into the innyard, where a huge baluchither shifted from foot to foot under a plain howdah of iron and horn. The man who held my left arm reached up and struck the beast at the hollow of the knee with the shaft of a goad to make him kneel, and we were driven onto his back.

When Jonas and I had come to Saltus, our path had threaded hills of debris from the mines, hills composed largely of broken stone and brick. When I had ridden on the false errand of Agia's letter, I had galloped past more of these, though my route had lain chiefly through the forest at its nearest approach to the village. Now we went among the heaps of tailings where there was no path. Here, in addition to much rubble, the miners had cast all they had brought forth from the buried past that might otherwise have defamed their village and occupation. Everything foul lay in tumbled heaps ten times and more the height of the baluchither's lofty back—obscene statues, canted and crumbling, and human bones to which strips of dry flesh and hanks of hair still clung. And with them ten thousand men and women; those who, in seeking a private resurrection, had rendered their corpses forever imperishable lay here like drunkards after their debauch, their crystal sarcophagi broken, their limbs relaxed in grotesque disarray, their clothing rotted or rotting, and their eyes blindly fixed upon the sky.

At first Jonas and I had attempted to question our captors, but they had silenced us with blows. Now that the baluchither wound his way among this desolation, they seemed easier of mind, and I asked again where they were taking us. The man with the scarred face replied, "To the wild, the home of free men and lovely women."

I thought of Agia and asked if he served her; he laughed and shook his head. "My master is Vodalus of the Wood."

"Vodalus!"

"Ah," he said. "You know him then." And he nudged the black-bearded man, who rode in the howdah with us. "Very kindly Vodalus will treat you, no doubt, for offering so blithely to rack one of his servants."

"I know him indeed," I said, and was about to tell the scarred man of my connection with Vodalus, whose life I had preserved in the last year before I became captain of apprentices. But then I came to doubt if Vodalus would remember it, and only said that if I had known Barnoch to be a servant of Vodalus, I would on no account have agreed to perform his excruciation. I lied, of course; for I had known, and had justified accepting my fee by the thought that I would be able to spare Barnoch some suffering. The lie did me no good; all three chortled, even the trainer who bestrode the baluchither's neck.

When their merriment had subsided, I said, "Last night I rode out of Saltus to the northeast. Are we going that way now?"

"So that's where you were. Our master came seeking you, and came back empty-handed." The scarred man smiled, and I could see that it was not an unpleasant thought that he returned now successful where Vodalus himself had failed.

Jonas whispered, "We go north, as you can see by the sun."

"Yes," said the scarred man, who must have been sharp-eared. "North, but not for long." And then, to pass the time, he described to me the means by which his master dealt with captives, most of which were primitive in the extreme, and more productive of theatrical effects than of true agony.

As if some invisible hand had spread a curtain over us, the shadows of the trees fell upon the howdah. The glitter of billions of shards of glass was left behind with the staring of the dead eyes, and we entered into the coolness and green shade of the high forest. Among those mighty trunks even the baluchither, though he stood three times the height of a man, seemed no more than a little, scurrying beast; and we who rode his back might have been pygmies from some children's tale, bound for the anthill stronghold of a pixie monarch.

And it came to me that these trees had been hardly smaller when I was yet unborn, and had stood as they stood now when I was a child playing among the cypresses and peaceful tombs of our necropolis, and that they would stand yet, drinking in the last light of the dying sun, even as now, when I had been dead as long as those who rested there. I saw how little it weighed on the scale of things whether I lived or died, though my life was precious to me. And of those two thoughts I forged a mood by which I stood ready to grasp each smallest chance to live, yet in which I cared not too much whether I saved myself or not. By that mood, as I think, I did live; it has been so good a friend to me that I have endeavored to wear it ever since, succeeding not always, but often.

"Severian, are you all right?"

It was Jonas who spoke. I looked at him, I think, in some wonder. "Yes. Did I seem ill?"

"For a moment."

"I was only reflecting on the familiarity of this place, seeking to understand it. I think it recalls to me many summer days in our Citadel. These trees are nearly as large as the towers there, and many of the towers are wrapped in ivy, so that in quiet summer weather the light between them has this emerald quality. Too, it is quiet here, as there. . . ."

"Yes?"

"You must have ridden many times in boats, Jonas."

"Occasionally, yes."

"It is something I had long wanted to do, and did for the first time only when Agia and I were ferried to the island where the Botanic Gardens stands, and then later when we crossed the Lake of Birds. The motion is much like the motion of this beast, and it is as silent, save for a splashing, sometimes, when the oar goes into the water. I feel now that I'm traveling through the Citadel in a flood, solemnly rowed."

At that Jonas looked so grave that I burst out laughing at the sight of his face, and stood up, meaning (I think) to look over the side of the howdah and show by some remark about the forest floor that I was merely indulging my fancy.

I had no sooner stood, however, than the scarred man rose too, and holding his dirk's point within a thumb of my throat told me to sit again. To spite him I shook my head.

He flourished his weapon. "Get down or I'll rip your belly open!"

"And lose the glory of bringing me back? I don't think so. Wait until the others tell Vodalus that you had me, and you stabbed me when my hands were tied."

Now came the turn of fate. The bearded man who held *Terminus Est* tried to draw her, and not being acquainted with the proper way to bare so long a sword—which is to grip the quillons in one hand and the throat of the sheath with the other, and by opening the arms to the right and left draw the blade clear—sought to free it by pulling up, as if he were jerking a weed from a field. In this clumsy business he was taken off guard by one of the baluchither's rolling steps, and lurched against the man with the scarred face. The edges of the blade, keen enough to part a hair, cut them both; the man with the scarred face threw himself backward, and Jonas, by hooking one of his feet behind the scarred man's and pressing his leg with the sole of the other, managed to tumble him over the railing of the howdah.

Meantime, the black-bearded man had dropped *Terminus Est* and was staring at his wound, which was very long, though no doubt shallow. I knew that weapon as I know my own hand, and it took only a moment to turn and crouch and grasp the hilt, and then, wedging it between my heels, to cut the thongs that bound my wrists. The black-bearded man drew a dagger then and might have killed me had not Jonas kicked him between the legs.

He bent double, and long before he could straighten himself I was up, with *Terminus Est* ready.

The contraction of his muscles snapped him erect, as often happens when the subject is not made to kneel; I think the spray of blood was the first sign the trainer had (so swiftly had it all taken place) that something was amiss. He looked back at us, and I was able to take him very neatly, swinging the blade one-handed in the horizontal stroke, as I leaned out of the howdah.

His head had no more than struck the ground when the baluchither stepped between two great trees growing so close together that he seemed to squeeze himself like a mouse through a crevice in a wall. Beyond lay a glade more open than anything I had seen in that forest—where grass grew as well as fern, and spots of sunlight, unshaded with green and rich as orpiment, played over the turf. Here Vodalus had caused to be erected his throne, beneath a canopy woven of flowering vines; and here, as it chanced, he sat with the Chatelaine Thea beside him just as we entered, judging and rewarding his followers.

Jonas saw nothing of that, being still sprawled on the floor of the howdah, where he was cutting his hands free with the dagger. I made up for him, for I beheld everything as I stood upright, balanced against the pitching of the baluchither's back and holding up my sword, red now to the hilt. A hundred faces turned toward us, with the face of the exultant on the throne among them, and the heart-shaped face of his consort; and in their eyes I saw what they must have seen at that moment: the great animal bestridden by a headless man, its forequarters dyed with his blood; myself standing erect upon its back, with my sword and fuligin cloak.

Had I slipped down and sought to flee, or tried to goad the baluchither to greater speed, I would have died. Instead, by the virtue of the spirit that had entered me when I saw the long-dead bodies among the refuse of the mines and the eternal trees, I remained as I was; and the baluchither, with no one to guide him, trod forward steadily (Vodalus's followers dodging aside to make a path for him) until the dais supporting the throne and canopy were before him. Then he halted, and the dead man pitched forward and fell on the dais at Vodalus's feet; and I, leaning far out of the howdah, struck the beast behind one leg and the other with the flat of my blade, and he knelt.

Vodalus smiled a thin smile that held many things, but amusement was one of them, and perhaps the foremost. "I sent my men to fetch the headsman," he said. "I perceive they succeeded."

I saluted with my sword, holding the hilt before my eyes as we were taught to do when an exultant came to observe an execution in the Grand Court. "Sieur, they have brought you the anti-headsman—there was a time when your own would have rolled on fresh-turned soil if it had not been for me."

He looked at me more closely then, at my face instead of at my sword and cloak, and after a moment he said, "Yes, you were the youth. Has it been that long?"

"Just long enough, sieur."

"We will talk of this in private, but I have public business to do now. Stand here." He pointed to the ground at the left of the dais.

I climbed from the baluchither with Jonas following me, and two grooms led the beast away. There we waited and heard Vodalus give his orders and transmit his plans, reward and punish, for perhaps a watch. All the boasted human panoply of pillars and arches is no more than an imitation in sterile stone of the boles and vaulting branches of the forest, and here it seemed to me that there was scarcely any difference between the two except that the one was gray or white, and the other brown and pale green. Then I believed I understood why all the soldiers of the Autarch and all the thronging retainers of the exultants could not subdue Vodalus—he occupied the mightiest fortress of Urth, greater far than our Citadel, to which I had likened it.

At length he dismissed the crowd, each man and woman to his or her own place, and came down from the dais to talk to me, bending over me as I might have bent above a child.

"You served me once," he said. "For that I will spare your life whatever else befalls, though it may be necessary that you remain my guest for a time. Knowing that your life is no longer in danger, will you serve me again?"

The oath to the Autarch I had taken on the occasion of my elevation had not the strength to resist the memory of that misty evening with which I have begun this account of my life. Oaths are only mere weak things of honor compared to the benefits we give to others, which are things of the spirit; let us once save another, and we are his for life. I have often heard it said that gratitude is not to be found. That is not true—those who say so have always looked in the mistaken place. One who truly benefits another is for a moment at a level with the Pancreator, and in gratitude for that elevation will serve the other all his days; and so I told Vodalus.

"Good!" he said, and clapped me on the shoulder. "Come. Not far from here we have a meal prepared. If you and your friend will sit with me and eat, I will tell you what must be done."

"Sieur, I have disgraced my guild once. I only ask that I may not be made to disgrace it again."

"Nothing you do will be known," Vodalus said. And that satisfied me.

X

Thea

WITH A DOZEN or so others we left the glade on foot, and half a league away found a table set among the trees. I was placed at Vodalus's left hand, and while the others ate, I feigned to and feasted my eyes on him and his lady, whom I had so often recalled as I lay on my cot among the apprentices in our tower.

When I had saved him, mentally at least I had still been a boy, and to a boy all grown men appear lofty unless they are of very low stature indeed. I saw now that Vodalus was as tall as Thecla or taller, and that Thecla's half-sister Thea was as tall as she. Then I knew them to be truly of the exalted blood, and not armigers merely, such as Sieur Racho had been.

It was with Thea that I had first fallen in love, worshipping her because she belonged to the man I had saved. Thecla I had loved, in the beginning, because she recalled Thea. Now (as autumn dies, and winter and spring, and summer comes again, the end of the year as it is its beginning) I loved Thea once more—because she recalled Thecla.

Vodalus said, "You are an admirer of women," and I lowered my eyes.

"I have been little in polite company, sieur. Please forgive me."

"I share your admiration, so there is nothing to forgive. But you were not, I hope, studying that slender throat with the thought of parting it?"

"Never, sieur."

"I am delighted to hear it." He picked up a platter of thrushes, selected one, and put it upon my plate. It was a sign of special favor. "Still, I own I am a trifle surprised. I would have thought that a man in your profession would look on us poor human beings much as a butcher does on cattle."

"Of that I cannot inform you, sieur. I have not been bred a butcher."

Vodalus laughed. "A touch! I am almost sorry now that you have consented to serve me. If you had only elected to remain my prisoner, we would have had many delightful conversations while I used you—as I had intended to—to cheap for the unfortunate Barnoch's life. As it is, you will be away by morning. Yet I think I have an errand for you that will consort well with your own inclinations."

"If it is your errand, sieur, it must."

"You are wasted on the scaffold." He smiled. "We will find better work for you before long. But if you are to serve me well, you must understand something of the position of the pieces on the board, and the goal of the game we play. Call the sides white and black, and in honor of your garments—so that you shall know where your interests lie—we shall be black. No doubt you have been told that we blacks are mere bandits and traitors, but have you any notion of what it is we strive to do?"

"To checkmate the Autarch, sieur?"

"That would be well enough, but it is only a step and not our final goal. You have come from the Citadel—I know, you see, something of your journeyings and history—that great fortress of bygone days, so you must possess some feeling for the past. Has it never struck you that mankind was richer by far, and happier too, a chiliad gone than it is now?"

"Everyone knows," I said, "that we have fallen far from the brave days of the past."

"As it was then, so shall it be again. Men of Urth, sailing between the stars, leaping from galaxy to galaxy, the masters of the daughters of the sun."

The Chatelaine Thea, who must have been listening to Vodalus though she had showed no sign of it, looked across him to me and said in a sweet, cooing voice, "Do you know how our world was renamed, torturer? The dawn-men went to red Verthandi, who was then named War. And because they thought that had an ungracious sound that would keep others from following them, they renamed it, calling it Present. That was a jest in their tongue, for the same word meant *Now* and *The Gift*. Or so one of our tutors once explained the matter to my sister and me, though I do not see how any language could endure such confusion."

Vodalus listened to her as though he were impatient to speak himself, yet was too well mannered to interrupt her.

"Then others—who would have drawn a people to the innermost habitable world for their own reasons—took up the game as well, and called that world Skuld, the World of the Future. Thus our own became Urth, the World of the Past."

"You are wrong in that, I fear," Vodalus told her. "I have it on good authority that this world of ours has been called by that name from the utmost reaches of antiquity. Still, your error is so charming that I would rather have it that you are correct and I mistaken."

Thea smiled at that, and Vodalus turned again toward me. "Though it does not explain why Urth is called as she is, my dear Chatelaine's tale makes the vital point well, which is that in those times mankind traveled by his own ships from world to world, and mastered each, and built on them the cities of Man. Those were the great days of our race, when our fathers' fathers' fathers strove for the mastery of the universe."

He paused, and because he seemed to expect some comment from me, I said, "Sieur, we are much diminished in wisdom from that age."

"Ah, now you strike to the heart. Yet with all your perspicacity, you mistake it. No, we are not diminished in wisdom. We are diminished in power. Study has advanced without letup, but even as men have learned all that is needful for mastery, the strength of the world has been exhausted. We exist now, and precariously, upon the ruin of those who preceded us. While some skim the air in their fliers, ten thousand leagues in a day, we others creep upon the skin of Urth, unable to go from one horizon to the next before the westernmost has lifted itself to veil the sun. You spoke a moment ago of checkmating that mewling fool the Autarch. I want you to conceive now of two autarchs— two great powers striving for mastery. The white seeks to maintain things as they are, the black to set Man's foot on the road to domination again. I called it the black by chance, but it would be well to remember that it is by night that we see the stars strongly; they are remote and all but invisible in the red light of day. Now, of those two powers, which would you serve?"

The wind was stirring in the trees, and it seemed to me that everyone at the table had fallen silent, listening to Vodalus and waiting for my reply. I said, "The black, surely."

"Good! But as a man of sense you must understand that the way to reconquest cannot be easy. Those who wish no change may sit hugging their scruples forever. We must do everything. We must dare everything!"

The others had begun to talk and eat again. I lowered my voice until only Vodalus could hear me. "Sieur, there is something I have not told you. I dare not conceal it longer for fear you should think me faithless."

He was a better intriguer than I, and turned away before he answered, pretending to eat. "What is it? Out with it."

"Sieur," I said, "I have a relic, the thing they say is the Claw of the Conciliator."

He was biting the roasted thigh of a fowl as I spoke. I saw him pause; his eyes turned to look at me, though he did not move his head.

"Do you wish to see it, sieur? It is very beautiful, and I have it in the top of my boot."

"No," he whispered. "Yes, perhaps, but not here. . . . No, better not at all."

"To whom should I give it, then?"

Vodalus chewed and swallowed. "I had heard from friends I have in Nessus that it was gone. So you have it. You must keep it until you can dispose of it. Do not try to sell it—it would be identified at once. Hide it somewhere. If you must, throw it into a pit."

"But surely, sieur, it is very valuable."

"It is beyond value, which means it is worthless. You and I are men of sense." Despite his words, there was a tinge of fear in his voice. "But the rabble believe it to be sacred, a performer of all manner of wonders. If I were to possess it, they would think me a desecrator and an enemy of the Theologoumenon. Our masters would think me turned traitor. You must tell me—"

Just at that moment, a man I had not seen previously came running up to the table with a look that indicated he bore urgent news. Vodalus rose and walked a few paces away with him, looking very much, I thought, like a handsome schoolmaster with a boy, for the messenger's head was no higher than his shoulder.

I ate, thinking he would soon return; but after a long questioning of the messenger he walked away with him, disappearing among the broad trunks of the trees. One by one the others rose too, until no one remained but the beautiful Thea, Jonas and me, and one other man.

"You are to join us," Thea said at last in her cooing voice. "Yet you do not know our ways. Have you need of money?"

I hesitated, but Jonas said, "That's something that's always welcome, Chatelaine, like the misfortunes of an older brother."

"Shares will be set aside for you, from this day, of all we take. When you return to us, they will be given to you. Meanwhile I have a purse for each of you to speed you on your way."

"We are going, then?" I asked.

"Were you not told so? Vodalus will instruct you at the supper."

I had supposed the meal we were eating would be the final one of the day, and the thought must have been reflected in my face.

"There will be a supper tonight, when the moon is bright," Thea said. "Someone will be sent to fetch you." Then she quoted a scrap of verse:

> "Dine at dawn to open your eyes,
> Dine at noon that you be strong.
> Dine at eve, and then talk long,
> Dine by night, if you'd be wise. . . .

But now my servant Chuniald will take you to a place where you can rest for your journey."

The man, who had been silent until now, stood and said, "Come with me."

I told Thea, "I would speak with you, Chatelaine, when we have more leisure. I know something that concerns your schoolmate."

She saw that I was serious in what I said, and I saw that she had seen. Then we followed Chuniald through the trees for a distance, I suppose, of a league or more, and at length reached a grassy bank beside a stream. "Wait here," he said. "Sleep if you can. No one will come until after dark."

I asked, "What if we were to leave?"

"There are those all through this wood who know our liege's will concerning you," he said, and turning on his heel, walked away.

Then I told Jonas what I had seen beside the opened grave, just as I have written it here.

"I see," he remarked when I was finished, "why you will join this Vodalus. But you must realize that I am your friend, not his. What I desire is to find the woman you call Jolenta. You want to serve Vodalus, and to go to Thrax and begin a new life in exile, and to wipe out the stain you say you have made on the honor of your guild—though I confess I don't understand how such a thing can be stained—and to find the woman called Dorcas, and to make peace with the woman called Agia while returning something we both know of to the women called Pelerines."

He was smiling by the time he finished this list, and I was laughing.

"And though you remind me of the old man's kestrel, that sat on a perch for twenty years and then flew off in all directions, I hope you achieve these things. But I trust you realize that it is possible—just barely possible, perhaps, but possible—that one or two of them may get in the way of four or five of the others."

"What you're saying is very true," I admitted. "I'm striving to do all those things, and although you won't credit it, I am giving all my strength and as much of my attention as can be of any benefit to all of them. Yet I have to admit things aren't going as well as they might. My divided ambitions have landed me in no better place than the shade of this tree, where I am a homeless wanderer. While you, with your single-minded pursuit of one all-powerful objective . . . look where you are."

In such talk we passed the watches of late afternoon. Birds twittered overhead, and it was very pleasant to have such a friend as Jonas, loyal, reasonable, tactful, and filled with wisdom, humor, and prudence. At that time I had no hint of his history, but I sensed that he was being less than candid about his background, and I sought, without venturing direct questions, to draw him out. I learned (or rather, I thought I did) that his father had been a craftsman; that he had been raised by both parents in what he called the usual way, though it is, in fact, rather rare; and that his home had been a seacoast town in the south, but that when he had last visited it he had found it so much changed that he had no desire to remain.

From his appearance, when I had first encountered him beside the Wall, I had supposed him to be about ten years my elder. From what he said now (and to a lesser extent from some earlier talks we had had) I decided he must be somewhat older; he seemed to have read a good deal of the chronicles of the past, and I was still too naive and unlettered myself, despite the attention Master Palaemon and Thecla had given my mind, to think that anyone much below middle age could have done so. He had a slightly cynical detachment from mankind that suggested he had seen a great deal of the world.

We were still talking when I glimpsed the graceful figure of the Chatelaine Thea moving among the trees some distance away. I nudged Jonas, and we fell silent to watch her. She was coming toward us without having seen us, so that she moved in the blind way people do who are merely following directions. At times a shaft of sunlight fell upon her face, which, if it chanced to be in profile, suggested Thecla's so strongly that the sight of it seemed to tear at my chest. She had Thecla's walk as well, the proud phororhacos stalk that should never have been caged.

"It must be a truly ancient family," I whispered to Jonas. "Look at her! Like a dryad. It might be a willow walking."

"Those ancient families are the newest of all," he answered. "In ancient times there was nothing like them."

I do not believe she was near enough to make out our words, but she seemed to hear his voice, and looked toward us. We waved and she quickened her pace, not running yet coming very rapidly because of the length of her stride. We stood, then sat again when she had reached us and seated herself upon her scarf with her face toward the brook.

"You said you had something to tell me about my sister?" Her voice made her seem less formidable, and seated she was hardly taller than we.

"I was her last friend," I said. "She told me they would try to make you persuade Vodalus to give himself up to save her. Did you know she was imprisoned?"

"Were you her servant?" Thea seemed to weigh me with her eyes. "Yes, I heard they took her to that horrible place in the slums of Nessus, where I understand she died very quickly."

I thought of the time I had spent waiting outside Thecla's door before the scarlet thread of blood came trickling from under it, but I nodded.

"How was she arrested—do you know?"

Thecla had told me the details, and I recounted them just as I had got them from her, omitting nothing.

"I see," Thea said, and was silent for a moment, staring at the moving water. "I have missed the court, of course. Hearing about those people and that business of muffling her with a tapestry—that's so very characteristic—calls up the reasons I left it."

"I think she missed it sometimes too," I said. "At least, she talked of it a great deal. But she told me that if she were ever freed she would not go back. She spoke about the country house from which she took her title, and told me how she would refurnish it and give dinners there for the leading persons of the region, and hunt."

Thea's face twisted in a bitter smile. "I have had enough of hunting now for ten lifetimes. But when Vodalus is Autarch, I will be his consort. Then I shall walk beside the Well of Orchids again, this time with the daughters of fifty exultants in my train to amuse me with their singing. Enough of that; it is some months off at least. For the present I have—what I have."

She looked somberly at Jonas and me, and rose very gracefully, indicating by a gesture that we were to remain where we were. "I was happy to hear something now of my half-sister. That house you spoke of is mine now, you know, though I can't claim it. To recompense you, I warn you of the supper we will soon share. You didn't seem receptive of the hints Vodalus flung you. Did you understand them?"

When Jonas said nothing, I shook my head.

"If we, and our allies and masters who wait in the countries beneath the tides, are to triumph, we must absorb all that can be learned of the past. Do you know of the analeptic alzabo?"

I said, "No, Chatelaine, but I have heard tales of the animal of that name. It is said it can speak, and that it comes by night to house where a child has died, and cries to be let in."

Thea nodded. "That animal was brought from the stars long ago, as were many other things for the benefit of Urth. It is a beast having no more intelligence than a dog, and perhaps less. But it is a devourer of carrion and a clawer at graves, and when it has fed upon human flesh it knows, at least for a time, the speech and ways of human beings. The analeptic alzabo is prepared from a gland at the base of the animal's skull. Do you understand me?"

When she had gone, Jonas would not look at me, nor I at his face; we both knew what feast it was we were to attend that night.

XI

Thecla

AFTER WE HAD sat, so it seemed to me, for a long time (though it was probably no more than a few moments), I could tolerate what I felt no longer. I went to the margin of the brook, and kneeling there on the soft earth spewed out the dinner I had eaten with Vodalus; and when there was nothing more to come forth, I remained where I was, retching and shivering, and rinsing my face and mouth, while the cold, clear water washed away the wine and half-digested meat I had brought up.

When at last I was able to stand, I returned to Jonas and told him, "We must go."

He looked at me as though he pitied me, and I suppose he did. "Vodalus's fighting men are all around us."

"You were not sick, I see, the way I was. But you heard who their allies are. Perhaps Chuniald was lying."

"I've heard our guards walking among the trees—they're not as silent as all that. You have your sword, Severian, and I have a knife, but Vodalus's men will have bows. I noticed that most of those who sat with us at table did. We can try to hide behind the trunks like alouattes. . . ."

I understood what he meant, and said, "Alouattes are shot every day."

"Still, no one hunts them by night. It would be dark in a watch or less."

"You will go with me if we wait until then?" I thrust out my hand.

Jonas clasped it. "Severian, my poor friend, you told me of seeing Vodalus—and this Chatelaine Thea and another man— beside a violated grave. Didn't you know what it was they planned to do with what they got there?"

I had known, of course, but it had been a remote and seemingly irrelevant knowledge then. Now I found I had nothing to say, and indeed almost no thoughts at all outside the hope that night would come quickly.

The men Vodalus sent for us came more quickly still: four burly fellows who might have been peasants and carried berdiches, and a fifth, with something of the armiger about him, who wore an officer's spadroon. Perhaps these men were in the crowd before the dais who had watched us arrive; at any rate, they seemed determined to take no risks with us and surrounded us with their weapons at the ready even while they hailed us as friends and comrades in arms. Jonas put as brave a face on it as a man could, and chatted with them while they escorted us down the forest paths; I could think of nothing but the ordeal ahead, and walked as I might have to the end of the world.

Urth turned her face from the sun's as we traveled. No glimmer of starlight seemed to penetrate the thronging leaves, yet our guides knew the way so well they hardly slowed. With each step I took, I wanted to ask if we would be forced to join in the meal to which we were led, but I knew without asking that to refuse—or even to seem to wish to refuse—would destroy whatever confidence Vodalus had in me, endangering my freedom and perhaps my life.

Our five guards, who had talked only reluctantly at first in response to Jonas's jests and queries, grew more cheerful as I became more desperate, gossiping as if they were on the way to a drinking bout or a brothel. Yet though I recognized the note of anticipation in their voices, the gibes they made were as unintelligible to me as the banter of libertines is to a little child: "Going far this time? Going to drown yourself again?" (This from the man at the back of our party, a mere disembodied voice in the dark.)

"By Erebus, I'm going to sink so far you won't see me until winter."

A voice I recognized as belonging to the armiger asked, "Have any of you seen her yet?" The others had sounded merely boastful, but there was hunger of a kind I had never heard before behind his simple words. He might have been some lost traveler asking about his home.

"No, Waldgrave."

(Another voice.) "Alcmund says a good one, not old or too young."

"Not another tribade, I hope."

"I don't . . ."

The voice broke off, or perhaps I only stopped attending to what it said. I had seen a glimmer through the trees.

After a few strides more, I could make out torches, and hear the sound of many voices. Someone ahead called for us to halt, and the armiger went forward and gave a password softly.

Soon I found myself sitting on forest duff, with Jonas on my right and a low chair of carved wood at my left. The armiger had taken a position on Jonas's right, and the rest of the people present (almost as though they had been waiting for our arrival) had formed a circle whose center was a smokey orange lantern suspended from the boughs of a tree.

No more than a third of those who had been at the audience in the glade were there, but from their dress and weapons it seemed to me that they were largely those of highest rank, together, perhaps, with members of certain favored fighting cadres. There were four or five men to every woman; but the women seemed as warlike as the men, and if anything more eager for the feast to begin.

We had been waiting for some time when Vodalus stepped dramatically out of the darkness and strode across the circle. All present stood, then resumed their seats as he dropped into the carved chair beside me.

Almost at once, a man in the livery of an upper servant in some great house came forward to stand in the center of the circle beneath the orange light. He carried a salver with a large and a small bottle on it, and a crystal goblet. A murmuring began—not a thing for words, I thought, but the sound of a hundred little noises of satisfaction, of quick breathings and tongues on lips. The man with the salver stood motionless until this had run its course, then advanced toward Vodalus with measured steps.

Behind me the cooing voice of Thea said, "The alzabo, of which I told you, is in the smaller bottle. The other holds a compound of herbs that soothe the stomach. Take one full swallow of the mixture."

Vodalus turned to look at her with an expression of surprise.

She entered the circle, passing between Jonas and me, and then between Vodalus and the man who bore the salver, and at last took a place at Vodalus's left. Vodalus leaned toward her and would have spoken, but the man with the salver had begun to mix the contents of the bottles in the goblet, and he seemed to think the moment inappropriate.

The salver was moved in circles to impart a gentle swirling motion to the liquid. "Very good," Vodalus said. He took the goblet from the salver with both hands and raised it to his lips, then passed it to me. "As the Chatelaine told you, you must take one full swallow. If you take less, the amount will be insufficient, and there will be no sharing. If you take more, it will be of no benefit to you, and the drug, which is very precious, will be wasted."

I drank from the goblet as he had directed. The mixture was as bitter as wormwood and seemed cold and fetid, recalling a winter day long before when I had been ordered to clean the exterior drain that carried wastes away from the journeymen's quarters. For a moment I felt that my gorge would rise as it had beside the brook, though in truth nothing remained in my stomach to come up. I choked and swallowed and passed the goblet to Jonas, then discovered that I was salivating rapidly.

He had as much difficulty as I, or more, but he managed it at last and passed the goblet to the Waldgrave who had captained our guards. After that I watched it make its slow way around the circle. It appeared to hold enough for ten drinkers; when it was emptied, the man in livery wiped the rim, filled the goblet again from the bottles on the salver, and started it once more.

Gradually, he seemed to lose the solid form natural to a rounded object and become a silhouette only, a mere colored figure sawn from wood. I was reminded of the marionettes I had seen in my dream on the night I had shared Baldanders's bed.

The circle, too, in which we sat, though I knew it to contain thirty or forty persons, seemed to have been cut from paper and bent like a toy crown. Vodalus on my left and Jonas at my right were normal; but the armiger appeared already half pictured, as did Thea.

As the man in livery reached her, Vodalus rose, and moving so effortlessly that he might have been propelled by the night breeze, floated toward the orange lantern. In the orange light he seemed far away, yet I could feel his gaze as one feels the heat from the brazier that readies the irons.

"There is an oath to be sworn before the sharing," he said, and the trees above us nodded solemnly. "By the second life you are to receive, do you swear you will never betray those gathered here? And that you will consent to obey, without hesitation or scruple, to death if need be, Vodalus as your chosen leader?"

I tried to nod with the trees, and when that seemed insufficient I said, "I consent," and Jonas, "Yes."

"And that you will obey as you would Vodalus, any person whatsoever whom Vodalus sets over you?"

"Yes."

"Yes."

"And that you will put this oath above all other oaths, whether sworn before this time or after it?"

"We will," said Jonas.

"Yes," I said.

The breeze was gone. It was as if some unquiet spirit had haunted the gathering, then suddenly vanished. Vodalus was once more in his chair beside me. He leaned toward me. If his voice was slurred, I did not observe it; but something in his eyes told me he was under the influence of the alzabo, perhaps as deeply as I was myself.

"I am no scholar," he began, "but I know it has been said that the greatest causes are often joined by the basest means. Nations are united by trade, the fair ivory and rare woods of altars and reliquaries by the boiled offal of ignoble animals, men and women by the organs of elimination. So we are joined—you and I. So will we both be joined, a few moments hence, to a fellow mortal who will live again—strongly, for a time—in us, by the effluvia pressed from the sweetbreads of one of the filthiest beasts. So blossoms spring from muck."

I nodded.

"This was taught us by our allies, those who wait until man is purified again, ready to join with them in the conquest of the universe. It was brought by the others for foul purposes they hoped to keep secret. I mention this to you because you, when you go to the House Absolute, may meet them, whom the common people call cacogens and the cultured Extrasolarians or Hierodules. You must be careful in no way to bring yourself to their notice, because if they observe you closely they will know by certain signs that you have used alzabo."

"The House Absolute?" Though only for an instant, the thought dispersed the mists of the drug.

"Indeed. I've a fellow there to whom I must transmit certain instructions, and I have learned that the troupe of players to which you once belonged will be admitted there for a thiasus a few days hence. You will rejoin them and take the opportunity to give what I shall give you," he fumbled in his tunic, "to the one who shall say to you, 'The pelagic argosy sights land.' And should he give you any message in return, you may entrust it to whoever says to you, 'I am from the quercine penetralia.'"

"Liege," I said, "my head is swimming." (Then, lying,) "I cannot remember those words—truly, I have forgotten them already. Did I hear you say that Dorcas and the other will be in the House Absolute?"

Vodalus now pressed into my hand a small object that was not a knife, yet was shaped something like one. I stared at it; it was a steel, such as flint is struck against to kindle fire. "You will remember," he said. "And you will never forget your oath to me. Many of those you see here came, as they believed, only once."

"But, sieur, the House Absolute . . ."

The fluting notes of a upanga sounded from the trees behind the farther side of the circle.

"I must go soon to escort the bride, but have no fear. Some time past you encountered a certain badger of mine—"

"Hildegrin! Sieur, I understand nothing."

"He uses that name among others, yes. He thought it sufficiently unusual to see a torturer so far from the Citadel—and talking of me—as to make it worthwhile to have you watched, though he had no notion you had saved me that night. Unfortunately, the watchers lost you at the Wall; since then they have observed the movements of your traveling companions in the hope you would rejoin them. I supposed that an exile might choose to side with us and so save my poor Barnoch long enough for us to free him. Last night I myself rode into Saltus to speak with you, but I had my mount stolen for my pains and accomplished not a straw. Today, then, it was necessary that we take you by whatever means to prevent you from exercising your skills on my servant; but I still hoped you would make cause with us, and for that reason instructed the men I sent for you to bring you living to me. That cost me three and gained two. The question now is whether the two will outweigh the three."

Vodalus stood then, a little unsteadily; I thanked Holy Katharine that I did not have to stand as well, for I was sure my legs would not hold me. Something dim and white and twice the height of a man was sailing among the trees to the twittering of the upanga. Every neck craned to look at it, and Vodalus drifted to meet it. Thea leaned across his empty chair to speak to me. "Lovely, is she not? They have accomplished wonders."

It was a woman seated on a silver litter borne on the shoulders of six men. For a moment I thought it was Thecla—it looked so like her in the orange light. Then I realized that it was rather her image, made, perhaps, of wax.

"It is said to be perilous," Thea cooed, "when one has known the shared in life; memories held together may amaze the mind. Yet I who loved her will risk that confusion, and knowing from your look when you spoke of her that you would desire it as well, I said nothing to Vodalus."

He had reached up to touch the figurine's arm as it was borne through the circle; with it entered a sweet and unmistakable odor. I recalled the agoutis served at our masking banquets, with their fur of spiced coconut and their eyes of preserved fruits, and knew that what I saw was just such a re-creation of a human being in roasted flesh.

I think I would have gone mad at that moment if it had not been for the alzabo. It stood between my perception and reality like a giant of mist, through which everything could be seen but nothing apprehended. I had another ally as well: it was the knowledge growing in me, the certainty that if I were to consent now and swallow some part of Thecla's substance, the traces of her mind that must otherwise soon fade in decay would enter me and endure, however attenuated, as long as I.

Consent came. What I was about to do no longer seemed filthy or frightening. Instead I opened every part of myself to Thecla, and decked the essence of my being with welcome. Desire came too, born of the drug, a hunger no other food could satisfy, and when I looked around the circle I saw that hunger on every face.

The liveried servant, who I think must have been one of Vodalus's old household gone into exile with him, joined the six who had borne Thecla into the circle and helped lower the litter to the ground. For the space of a few breaths their backs blocked my view. When they parted, she was gone; nothing remained but smoking meats laid upon what might have been a white tablecloth. . . .

I ate and waited, begging forgiveness. She deserved the most magnificent sepulcher, priceless marble of exquisite harmony. In its place she was to be entombed in my torturer's workroom, with the floor scrubbed and the devices half disguised under garlands of flowers. The night air was cool, but I was sweating. I waited for her to come, feeling the drops roll down my bare chest and staring at the ground because I was afraid I would see her in the faces of the others before I felt her presence in myself.

Just when I despaired—she was there, filling me as a melody fills a cottage. I was with her, running beside the Acis when we were a child. I knew the ancient villa moated by a dark lake, the view through the dusty windows of the belvedere, and the secret space in the odd angle between two rooms where we sat at noon to read by candlelight. I knew the life of the Autarch's court, where poison waited in a diamond cup. I learned what it was for one who had never seen a cell or felt a whip to be a prisoner of the torturers, what dying meant, and death.

I learned that I had been more to her than I had ever guessed, and at last fell into a sleep in which my dreams were all of her.

Not memories merely—memories I had possessed in plenty before. I held her poor, cold hands in mine, and I no longer wore the rags of an apprentice, nor the fuligin of a journeyman. We were one, naked and happy and clean, and we knew that she was no more and that I still lived, and we struggled against neither of those things, but with woven hair read from a single book and talked and sang of other matters.

XII

The Notules

I CAME FROM my dreams of Thecla directly to the morning. At one instant we walked mutely together in what surely must have been the paradise the New Sun is said to open to all who, in their final moments, call upon him; and though the wise teach that it is closed to those who are their own executioners, yet I cannot but think that he who forgives so much must sometimes forgive that as well. At the next, I was aware of cold and unwelcome light, and the piping of birds.

I sat up. My cloak was soaked with dew, and dew lay like sweat upon my face. Beside me, Jonas had just begun to stir. Ten paces off two great destriers—one the color of white wine, one of unspotted black—champed their bits and stamped with impatience. Of feast and feasters there was no more sign than of Thecla, whom I have never seen again and now no longer hope to see in this existence.

Terminus Est lay beside me in the grass, secure in her tough, well oiled sheath. I picked her up and made my way downhill until I found a stream, where I did what I might to refresh myself. When I returned, Jonas was awake. I directed him to the water, and while he was gone I made my farewell to dead Thecla.

Yet some part of her is with me still; at times I who remember am not Severian but Thecla, as though my mind were a picture framed behind glass, and Thecla stands before that glass and is reflected in it. Too, ever since that night, when I think of her without thinking also of a particular time and place, the Thecla who rises in my imagination stands before a mirror in a shimmering gown of frost-white that scarcely covers her breasts but falls in ever changing cascades below her waist. I see her poised for a moment there; both hands reach up to touch our face.

Then she is whirled away in a room whose walls and ceiling and floor are all of mirrors. No doubt it is her own memory of her image in those mirrors that I see, but after a step or two she vanishes into the dark and I see her no more.

By the time Jonas returned I had mastered my grief and was able to make a show of examining our mounts. "The black for you," he said, "and the cream for me, obviously. Both of them look like they outvalue either of us, though, as the sailor told the surgeon who took off his legs. Where are we going?"

"To the House Absolute." I saw the incredulity in his face. "Did you overhear me talking with Vodalus last night?"

"I caught the name, but not that we were to go there."

I am no rider, as I have said before, but I got one foot into the black's stirrup and swung myself up. The mount I had stolen from Vodalus two nights before had worn a lofty war saddle, fiendishly uncomfortable but very difficult to fall out of; this black carried a nearly flat affair of padded velvet that was both luxurious and treacherous. I had no sooner got my legs around him than he began to dance with eagerness.

It was the worst possible time, perhaps; but it was also the only time. I asked, "How much do you remember?"

"About the woman last night? Nothing." Jonas dodged the black, loosed the cream's reins, and vaulted up. "I didn't eat. Vodalus was watching you, but after they had swallowed the drug, no one was watching me, and anyway I have learned the art of appearing to eat without actually doing it."

I looked at him in astonishment.

"I've practiced several times with you—at breakfast yesterday, for example. I don't have much appetite, and I find it socially useful." As he urged the cream down a forest path, he called over his shoulder, "As it happens, I know the route fairly well, at least for most of the way. But would you mind telling me why we're going?"

"Dorcas and Jolenta will be there," I said. "And I have to do an errand for our liege, Vodalus." Because we were almost certainly watched, I thought it better not to say that I had no intention of performing it.

Here, lest this account of my career run forever, I must pass very quickly over the events of several days. As we rode, I told Jonas all that Vodalus had told me, and much more. We halted at villages and towns as we found them, and where we halted I practiced such of my craft as was in demand—not because the money I earned was strictly necessary to us (for we had the purses the Chatelaine Thea had given us, much of my fee from Saltus, and the money Jonas had obtained for the man-ape's gold) but in order to allay suspicion.

Our fourth morning found us still pressing northward. Gyoll sunned itself to our right like a sluggish dragon guarding the forbidden road that returned to grass upon its bank. The day before, we had seen uhlans on patrol, men mounted much as we were and bearing lances like those that had killed the travelers at the Piteous Gate.

Jonas, who had been ill at ease since we had set out, muttered, "We must hurry if we're to be near the House Absolute tonight. I wish Vodalus had given you the date that celebration begins and some indication of how long it's to last."

I asked, "Is the House Absolute still far off?"

He pointed out an isle in the river. "I think I recall that, and when I was two days from it, some pilgrims told me the House Absolute was nearby. They warned me of the praetorians, and seemed to know what they were talking about."

Following his example, I had allowed my mount to break into a trot. "You were walking."

"Riding my merychip—I suppose I'll never see the poor creature again. She was slower at her best than these animals at their worst, I'll grant you. But I'm not certain they're twice as fast."

I was about to say I did not believe Vodalus would have dispatched us when he did if he had not thought it possible for us to reach the House Absolute in time, when something that at first seemed a great bat came skimming within a handsbreadth of my head.

If I did not know what it was, Jonas did. He shouted words I could not understand and lashed my destrier with the ends of his reins. It bounded forward and nearly threw me, and in an instant we were galloping madly. I remember shooting between two trees with not a span to spare on either side and seeing the thing silhouetted against the sky like a fleck of soot. A moment later it was rattling among the branches behind us.

When we cleared the margin of the wood and entered the dry gully beyond, it was not to be seen; but as we reached the bottom and began to climb the farther side, it emerged from the trees, more ragged than ever.

For the space of a prayer it seemed to have lost sight of us, soaring at an angle to our own path, then swooping toward us again in a long, flat glide. I had *Terminus Est* clear of her sheath, and I neck-reined the black between the flying thing and Jonas.

Swift though our destriers were, it came far more swiftly. If I had possessed a pointed blade, I think I could have spitted it as it dove; had I done so I would surely have perished. As it was, I caught it with a two-handed stroke. It was like cutting air, and I thought the thing too light and tough for even that bitter edge. An instant later it parted like a rag; I felt a brief sensation of warmth, as though the door of an oven had been opened, then soundlessly shut.

I would have dismounted to examine it, but Jonas shouted and waved. We had left the lofty forest about Saltus far behind, and were entering a broken country of steep hills and ragged cedars. A grove of these stood at the top of the slope; we plunged into their tangled growth like madmen, flattened against the necks of our mounts.

Soon the foliage grew so thick they could move no faster than a walk. Almost at once we reached a sheer rock face and were forced to halt. When we were no longer smashing through the tangled limbs, I could hear something else behind us—a dry rustling, as though a wounded bird were fluttering among the treetops. The medicinal fragrance of the cedars oppressed my lungs.

"We must get out," Jonas panted, "or at least keep moving." The splintered end of a branch had gouged his cheek; a trickle of blood coursed down it as he spoke. After looking in both directions he chose the right, toward the river, and lashed his mount to force it into what appeared to be an impenetrable thicket.

I let him break a trail for me, reflecting that if the dark thing caught us I might be able to make some sort of defense against it. Soon I saw it through the gray-green foliage; a few moments later there was another, much like the first and only a short distance behind it.

The wood ended, and we were able to flog our mounts to a gallop again. The fluttering scraps of night came after us, but though their smaller size made them appear swifter, they were slower than the single large entity had been.

"We have to find a fire," Jonas shouted above the drumming of the destriers' hooves. "Or a big animal we can kill. If you slashed the belly of one of these beasts, that would probably do it. But if it didn't, we couldn't get away."

I nodded to show that I also opposed killing one of the destriers, though it crossed my mind that my own might soon drop from exhaustion. Jonas was having to allow his to slow now to keep from distancing me. I asked, "Is it blood they want?"

"No. Heat."

Jonas swung his destrier to the right and slapped its flank with his steel hand. It must have been a good blow, for the animal leaped ahead as though stung. We jumped a dry water course, careened sliding and stumbling down a dusty hillside, then struck open, rolling ground where the destriers could show their best speed.

Behind us fluttered the rags of black. They flew at twice the height of a tall tree and seemed to be blown along by the wind, though the rippling of the grass showed that they faced it.

Ahead, the lay of the ground changed as subtly and yet as abruptly as cloth alters at a seam. A sinuous ribbon of green lay as flat as if it had been rolled, and I swung the black down it, shouting in his ears and belaboring him with the flat of my blade. He was drenched with sweat now and streaked with blood from the broken twigs of the cedars. Behind us I could hear Jonas's shouted warnings, but I gave them no heed.

We rounded a curve, and through a break in the trees I saw the gleam of the river. Another curve, with the black beginning to flag again—then, far off, the sight I had been waiting for. Perhaps I should not tell it, but I lifted my sword to Heaven then, to the diminished sun with the worm in his heart; and I called, "His life for mine, New Sun, by your anger and my hope!"

The uhlan (and there was only one alone) must surely have thought me threatening him, as indeed I was. The blue radiance at the tip of his lance increased as he spurred toward us.

Winded though he was, the black swerved for me like a hunted hare. A twitch of the reins, and he was sliding and turning, his hooves scarring the green verdure of the road. In no more than a breath, we had reversed our track and were pounding back toward the things that pursued us. Whether Jonas understood my plan then I do not know, but he fell in with it as though he did, never slackening his own pace.

One of the fluttering creatures swooped, looking for all Urth like a hole torn in the universe, for it was true fuligin, as lightless as my own habit. It was trying for Jonas, I believe, but it came within sword reach, and I parted it as I had before, and again felt a gust of warmth. Knowing from where that heat came, it seemed more evil to me than any vile odor could; the mere sensation on my skin made me ill. I reined sharply away from the river, fearing a bolt from the uhlan's lance at any moment. We had no more than left the road when it came, searing the ground and setting a dead tree ablaze.

I pulled my mount's head up, making him rear and roar. For a moment I looked for the three dark things around the burning tree. They were not there. I glanced toward Jonas then, fearing they had overtaken him after all and were attacking him in some way I could not comprehend.

They were not there either, but his eyes showed me where they had gone: they flitted about the uhlan, and he, as I watched, sought to defend himself with his lance. Bolt after bolt split the air, so that there was a continual crashing like thunder. With each bolt the brightness of the sun was washed away, but the very energies with which he sought to destroy them seemed to give them strength. To my eyes they no longer flew, but flickered as beams of darkness might, appearing first in one place then in another, and always nearer the uhlan, until in less time than I have taken to write of it all three were at his face. He tumbled from his saddle, and the lance fell from his hand and went out.

XIII

The Claw of the Conciliator

I CALLED, "IS he dead?", and saw Jonas nod in reply. I would have ridden away then, but he motioned for me to join him and dismounted. When we met by the uhlan's body, he said, "We may be able to destroy those things so they can't be flown against us again or be used to harm anyone else. They're sated now, and I think we might handle them. We need something to put them in—something water-tight, of metal or glass."

I had nothing of that kind and told him so.

"Neither have I." He knelt beside the uhlan and turned out his pockets. Aromatic smoke from the blazing tree wreathed everything like incense, and I had the sensation of being once more in the Cathedral of the Pelerines. The litter of twigs and last summer's leaves on which the uhlan lay might have been the straw-strewn floor; the trunks of the scattered trees, the supporting poles.

"Here," Jonas said, and picked up a brass vasculum. Unscrewing the lid he emptied it of herbs, then rolled the dead uhlan on his back.

"Where are they?" I asked. "Has the body absorbed them?"

Jonas shook his head, and after a moment began, very carefully and delicately, to draw one of the dark things from the uhlan's left nostril. Save for being absolutely opaque, it was like the finest tissue paper.

I wondered at his caution. "If you tear it, won't it just become two?"

"Yes, but it is sated now. Divided, it would lose energy and might be impossible to handle. A lot of people have died, by the way, because they found they could cut these creatures, and chose to stand their ground doing it until they were surrounded by too many to fend off."

One of the uhlan's eyes was half open. I had seen corpses often before, but I could not escape the eerie feeling that he was in some sense watching me, the man who had killed him to save himself. To turn my mind to other things, I said, "After I cut the first one, it seemed to fly more slowly."

Jonas had placed the horror he had drawn out in the vasculum and was extracting a second from the right nostril; he murmured, "The speed of any flying thing depends on its wing area. If that weren't the case, the adepts who use these creatures would tear them into scraps before they sent them forth, I suppose."

"You sound as though you've encountered them before."

"We docked once at a port where they're used in ritual murders. I suppose it was inevitable that someone would bring them home, but these are the first I've seen here." He opened the brass lid and laid the second fuligin thing on the first, which stirred sluggishly. "They'll recombine in there—this is what the adepts do to get them back together. I doubt if you noticed it, but they were torn somewhat in going through the wood and healed themselves in flight."

"There's one more," I said.

He nodded and used his steel hand to force open the dead man's mouth; instead of holding teeth and livid tongue and gums it appeared to be a bottomless gulf, and for a moment my stomach churned. Jonas drew out the third creature, streaked with the dead man's saliva.

"Wouldn't he have had a nostril open, or his mouth, if I hadn't cut the thing a second time?"

"Until they worked their way into his lungs. We're lucky, actually, to have been able to get to him so quickly. Otherwise you would have had to slice the body open to get them out."

A wisp of smoke called to mind the burning cedar. "If it was heat they wanted . . ."

"They prefer life's heat, though they can sometimes be distracted by a fire of living vegetable matter. It's something more than heat, I think, really. Perhaps some radiant energy characteristic of growing cells." Jonas stuffed the third creature into the vasculum and snapped it shut. "We called them notules, because they usually came after dark, when they could not be seen, and the first warning we had was a breath of warmth; but I have no idea what the natives call them."

"Where is this island?"

He looked at me curiously.

"Is it far from the coast? I've always wanted to see Uroboros, though I suppose it is dangerous."

"Very far," Jonas said in a flat voice. "Very far indeed. Wait a moment."

I waited, watching, as he strode to the riverbank. He threw the vasculum hard—it had almost reached midstream when it dropped into the water. When he returned I asked, "Couldn't we have used those things ourselves? It doesn't seem likely that whoever sent them is going to give up now, and we might have need of them."

"'They would not obey us, and the world is better without them anyway,' as the butcher's wife told him when she cut away his manhood. Now we'd best be going. There's somebody coming down the road."

I looked where Jonas had pointed, and saw two figures on foot. He had caught his destrier by the halter as it drank and was ready to climb into the saddle. "Wait," I said. "Or go on a chain or two and wait for me there." I was thinking of the man-ape's bleeding stump, and I seemed to see the dim votive lights of the cathedral hanging, crimson and magenta, among the trees. I reached into my boot, far down where I had pushed it for safety, and drew out the Claw.

It was the first time I had seen it by full daylight. It caught the sun and flashed like a New Sun itself, not blue only but with every color from violet to cyan. I laid it on the uhlan's forehead, and for an instant tried to will him alive.

"Come on," Jonas called. "What are you doing?"

I did not know how to answer him.

"He's not quite dead," Jonas called. "Get off the road before he finds his lance!" He lashed his mount.

Faintly, a voice I seemed to recognize called, "Master!" I turned my head to look down the grass-grown highway.

"Master!" One of the travelers waved an arm, and both began to run.

"It's Hethor," I said; but Jonas had gone. I looked back at the uhlan. Both his eyes were open now, and his chest rose and fell. When I took the Claw from his forehead and thrust it back into my boot top, he sat up. I shouted to Hethor and his companion to leave the road, but they did not appear to understand.

"Who are you?"

"A friend," I said.

Though the uhlan was feeble, he tried to rise. I gave him my hand and pulled him up. For a moment he stared at everything—myself, the two men running toward him, the river, and the trees. The destriers appeared to frighten him, even his own, which stood patiently awaiting its rider. "What is this place?"

"Only a stretch of the old road beside Gyoll."

He shook his head and pressed it with his hands.

Hethor came panting up, like an ill-bred dog that has run when called and now expects a petting for it. His companion, whom he had outreached by a hundred strides or so, wore the gaudy clothes and greasy look of a small trader.

"M-m-master," Hethor said, "you can have no idea how much t-t-trouble, how much deadly loss and difficulty we have had in overtaking you across the mountains, across the wide-blown seas and c-c-creaking plains of this fair world. What am I, your s-slave, but an abandoned sh-shell, the sport of a thousand tides, cast up here in this lonely place because I cannot r-r-rest without you? H-how could you, the red-clawed master, know of the endless labor you've cost us?"

"Since I left you in Saltus afoot and have been well mounted these past few days, I should think a good deal."

"Exactly," he said. "Exactly." He looked significantly at his companion as if my remark had confirmed something he had told him earlier, and sank down to rest upon the ground.

The uhlan said slowly, "I am Cornet Mineas. Who are you?"

Hethor bobbed his head as though he would have bowed. "M-m-master is the noble Severian, servant of the Autarch—whose urine is the wine of his subjects—in the Guild of the Seekers for Truth and Penitence. H-h-hethor is his humble servant. Beuzec is also his humble servant. I suppose the man who rode away is his servant too."

I gestured for him to be quiet. "We are all only poor travelers, Cornet. We saw you lying here stunned and sought to help you. A moment ago, we thought you dead; it must have been a near thing."

"What is this place?" the uhlan asked again.

Hethor answered eagerly. "The road north of Quiesco. M-m-master, we were on a boat, sailing the wide waters of Gyoll in the blind night. We di-d-disembarked at Quiesco. On her deck and at her sails we worked our p-passage, Beuzec and me. So slowly upriver, while the lucky ones whizzed above on their way to the H-h-house Absolute, but she m-m-made h-h-headway whether we woke or slept, and thus we caught up to you."

"The House Absolute?" the uhlan muttered.

I said, "It's not far from here, I think."

"I am to be especially vigilant."

"I feel sure one of your comrades will be along soon." I caught my mount and clambered onto his lofty back.

"M-m-master, you're not going to l-l-leave us again? Beuzec has seen you perform but twice."

I was about to answer Hethor when I caught sight of a flash of white among the trees across the highway. Something huge was moving there. At once, the thought that the sender of the notules might have other weapons at hand filled my mind, and I dug my heels into the black's flanks.

He sprang away. For half a league or more we raced along the narrow strip of ground that separated the road from the river. When at last I saw Jonas, I galloped across to warn him, and told him what I had seen.

While I spoke he seemed lost in reflection. When I had finished, he said, "I know of nothing like the being you describe, but there may be many importations I know nothing of."

"But surely such a thing wouldn't be wandering free like a strayed cow!"

Instead of replying, Jonas pointed toward the ground a few strides ahead.

A graveled path hardly more than a cubit wide wound among the trees. It was bordered with more wild flowers than I have ever seen growing naturally in company, and it was of pebbles so uniform in size, and of such shining whiteness, that they must surely have been carried from some secret and far off beach.

After riding a bit closer to examine it, I asked Jonas what such a path here could possibly mean.

"Only one thing, surely—that we are already on the grounds of the House Absolute."

Quite suddenly, I recalled the spot. "Yes," I said. "Once Josepha and I, with some others, made up a fishing party and came here. We crossed by the twisted oak . . ."

Jonas looked at me as though I were mad, and for a moment I

felt that I was. I had ridden hunting often before, but this was a charger I sat, and no hunter. My hands raised themselves like spiders to pluck out my eyes—and would have done so if the ragged man beside me had not struck them down with his own hand, which was of steel. "You are not the Chatelaine Thecla," he said. "You are Severian, a journeyman of the torturers, who was unfortunate enough to love her. See yourself!" He held up the steel hand so that I could see a stranger's face, narrow, ugly, and bewildered, reflected in its work-polished balm.

I remembered our tower then, the curved walls of smooth, dark metal. "I am Severian," I said.

"That is correct. The Chatelaine Thecla is dead."

"Jonas . . ."

"Yes?"

"The uhlan is alive now—you saw him. The Claw gave him life again. I laid it on his forehead, but perhaps it was just that he saw it with his dead eyes. He sat up. He breathed and spoke to me, Jonas."

"He was not dead."

"You saw him," I said again.

"I am much older than you are. Older than you think. If there is one thing I have learned in so many voyages, it is that the dead do not rise, nor the years turn back. What has been and is gone does not come again."

Thecla's face was before me still, but it was blown by a dark wind until it fluttered and went out. I said, "If I had only used it, called on the power of the Claw when we were at the banquet of the dead . . ."

"The uhlan had nearly suffocated, but was not quite dead. When I got the notules away from him he was able to breathe, and after a time he regained consciousness. As for your Thecla, no power in the universe could have restored her to life. They must have dug her up while you were still imprisoned in the Citadel and stored her in an ice cave. Before we saw her, they had gutted her like a partridge and roasted her flesh." He gripped my arm. "Severian, don't be a fool!"

At that moment I wanted only to perish. If the notule had reappeared, I would have embraced it. What did appear, far down the path, was a white shape like that I had seen nearer the river. I tore myself away from Jonas and galloped toward it.

XIV

The Antechamber

THERE ARE BEINGS—and artifacts—against which we batter our intelligence raw, and in the end make peace with reality only by saying, "It was an apparition, a thing of beauty and horror."

Somewhere among the swirling worlds I am so soon to explore, there lives a race like and yet unlike the human. They are no taller than we. Their bodies are like ours save that they are perfect, and that the standard to which they adhere is wholly alien to us. Like us they have eyes, a nose, a mouth; but they use these features (which are, as I have said, perfect) to express emotions we have never felt, so that for us to see their faces is to look upon some ancient and terrible alphabet of feeling, at once supremely important and utterly unintelligible.

Such a race exists, yet I did not encounter it there at the edge of the gardens of the House Absolute. What I had seen moving among the trees, and what I now—until I at last saw it clearly—flung myself toward, was rather the giant image of such a being kindled to life. Its flesh was of white stone, and its eyes had the smoothly rounded blindness (like sections cut from eggshells) we see in our own statues. It moved slowly, like one drugged or sleeping, yet not unsteadily. It seemed sightless, yet it gave the impression of awareness, however slow.

I have just paused to reread what I have written of it, and I see that I have failed utterly to convey the essence of the thing. Its spirit was that of sculpture. If some fallen angel had overheard my conversation with the green man, he might have contrived such an enigma to mock me. In its every movement it carried the serenity and permanency of art and stone; I felt that each gesture, each position of the head and limbs and torso, might be the last. Or that each might be repeated interminably, as the poses of the gnomens of Valeria's many-faceted dial were repeated down the curving corridors of the instants.

My initial terror, after the white statue's strangeness had washed away my will toward death, was the instinctive one that it would do me hurt.

My second was that it would not attempt to. To be as frightened of something as I was of that silent, inhuman figure, and then to discover that it meant no harm, would have been unbearably humiliating. Forgetting for a moment the ruin it would bring her blade to strike that living stone, I drew *Terminus Est* and reined in the black. The breeze itself seemed to pause as we stood there, the black hardly quivering, myself with sword upraised, as still almost ourselves as statues. The real statue came toward us, its three or four times life-size face stamped with inconceivable emotion and its limbs wrapped in terrible and perfect beauty.

I heard Jonas shout, and the sound of a blow. I had just time to see him on the ground grappling with men in tall, crested helmets that vanished and reappeared even as I looked at them, when something whizzed past my ear; another struck my wrist, and I found myself struggling in a web of cords that constricted like little boas. Someone seized my leg and pulled, and I fell.

*   *   *

When I had recovered enough to be aware of what was taking place, I had a wire noose about my neck, and one of my captors was rummaging through my sabretache. I could see his hands clearly, darting like brown sparrows. His face was visible too, an impassive mask that might have been suspended above me on a conjuror's thread. Once or twice, as he moved, the extraordinary armor he wore gleamed; then I saw it as one sees a crystal beaker immersed in clear water. It was reflective, I think, burnished beyond any merely human skill, so that its own material was invisible and only the greens and browns of the wood could be seen, twisted by the shapes of cuirass, gorget, and greaves.

Despite my protest that I was a member of the guild, the praetorian took all the money I had (though he left me Thecla's brown book, my fragment of whetstone, oil and flannel, and the other miscellaneous objects in my sabretache). Then he skillfully drew off the cords that entangled me and thrust them (as nearly as I could tell) into the armhole of his breastplate, though not before I had seen them. They reminded me of the whip we used to call a "cat," and were a bundle of thongs joined at one end and weighted at the other; I have learned since that this weapon is called the *achico*.

My captor now lifted the wire noose until I stood. I was conscious, as I have been on several similar occasions, that we were in some sense playing a game. We were pretending that I was totally in his power, when in fact I might have refused to rise until he had either strangled me or called over some of his comrades to carry me. I could have done several other things as well—seized the wire and tried to wrest it from him, struck him in the face. I might have escaped, been killed, been rendered unconscious, or plunged into agony; but I could not actually be forced to do as I did.

At least I knew it was a game, and I smiled as he sheathed *Terminus Est* and led me to where Jonas stood.

Jonas said, "We've done no harm. Return my friend's sword and give us back our animals, and we will go."

There was no reply. In silence two praetorians (four fluttering sparrows, as it seemed) caught our destriers and led them away. How like us those animals were, walking patiently they knew not where, their massive heads following thin strips of leather. Nine-tenths of life, so it seems to me, consists of these surrenders.

We were made to go with our captors out of the wood and onto a rolling meadow that soon became a lawn. The statue walked after us, and others of his kind joined him until there were a dozen or more, all huge, all different, and all beautiful. I asked Jonas who the soldiers were and where they were taking us; but he did not answer, and I was nearly throttled for my pains.

So far as I could tell, they were armored from head to foot, yet the perfect polish of the metal imparted to it a seeming softness, an almost liquid yielding, that was profoundly disturbing to the eye and that permitted it to fade into sky and grass at a distance of a few paces. When we had walked half a league across the sward, we entered a grove of flowering plums, and at once the crested helms and flaring pauldrons danced with pink and white.

There we struck a path that curved and curved again. Just as we were on the point of emerging from the grove we halted, and Jonas and I were pushed violently back. I heard the feet of the stony figures that followed us grate on the gravel as they too stopped short; one of the soldiers warned them off with what seemed to me a wordless cry. I peered through the blossoms as well as I could to see what lay ahead.

Before us was a walk much broader than the one we trod. It was, in fact, a garden path grown until it had become a magnificent processional way. The pavement was of white stone, and marble balustrades flanked it to either side. Down it marched a motley company. Most were on foot, but some rode beasts of various sorts. One led a shaggy arctother; another perched upon the neck of a ground sloth greener than the lawns. No sooner had this group passed than other groups followed them. While they were still too far for me to distinguish their faces, I noticed one in which the bowed head of a single individual was lifted above the rest by at least three cubits. A moment later I had recognized another as Dr. Talos, strutting along with his chest thrown out and his head well back. My own dear Dorcas followed close behind him, looking more than ever like a forlorn child wandered from some higher sphere. Fluttering with veils and sparkling with bijoux under her parasol, Jolenta rode a diminutive jennet sidesaddle; and behind them all, patiently wheeling such properties as he could not shoulder, lumbered he whom I had identified first, the giant, Baldanders.

If it was painful for me to see them pass without being able to call out, it must have been torment for Jonas. When Jolenta was nearly opposite us, she turned her head. To me, at that moment, it seemed she must have winded his desire, as among the mountains certain unclean spirits are said to be attracted by the odor of meat that has been cast upon a fire for them. No doubt it was really only the flowering trees among which we stood that caught her attention. I heard the inhalation of Jonas's breath; but the first syllable of her name was cut short by the thud of the blow that followed, and he pitched at my feet. When I recall that scene now, the rattle of his metal hand on the gravel of the path is as vivid as the perfume of the plum blossoms.

After all the troupes of performers had gone, two praetorians picked up poor Jonas and carried him. They did it as easily as they might have carried a child; but I at the time attributed that only to their strength. We crossed the road down which the performers had come and penetrated a hedge of roses higher than a man, covered with immense white blossoms and filled with nesting birds.

Beyond it lay the gardens proper. If I should try to describe them, I should seem only to have borrowed the mad, stammering eloquence of Hethor. Every hill and tree and flower seemed to have been arranged by some master intelligence (which I have since learned is that of Father Inire) to form a breathtaking vision. The observer feels that he is at the center, that everything he sees has been directed toward the point at which he stands; but after he has walked a hundred paces, or a league, he finds himself at the center still; and every vision seems to convey some incommunicable truth, like one of the unutterable insights granted eremites.

So beautiful were these gardens that we had been in them for some time before I realized that no towers were lifted above them. Only the birds and the clouds, and beyond them the old sun and the pale stars, rose higher than their treetops; we might have been wandering through some divine wilderness. Then we reached the crest of a wave of land more lovely than any cobalt wave of Uroboros's, and with breathtaking suddenness a pit opened at our feet. I have called it a pit, but it was not at all like the dark abyss usually associated with that word. Rather, it was a grotto filled with fountains and night flowers, and dotted with people more brilliant than any flowers, people who loitered beside its waters and gossiped among its shades.

At once, as though a wall had collapsed to let light into a tomb, many of the memories of the House Absolute, mine by absorption now from the life of Thecla, coalesced. I understood something that had been implicit in the doctor's play and in many of the stories Thecla had told me as well, though she had never mentioned it directly: The whole of this great palace lay underground—or rather, its roofs and walls were heaped with soil planted and landscaped, so that we had been walking all this time over the seat of the Autarch's power, which I had thought still some distance away.

We did not go down into that grotto, which no doubt opened onto chambers quite unsuited to the detention of prisoners, or into any of the next score or so we passed. At last, however, we came upon one far more grim, though no less beautiful. The stair by which we entered it had been carved to resemble a natural formation of dark rock, irregular and sometimes treacherous. Water dripped from above, and ferns and dark ivy grew in the upper parts of this artificial cavern, where a little sunlight still found its way. In the lower regions, a thousand steps down, the walls were studded with blind fungi; some of these were luminous; some strewed the air with strange, musty odors; some suggested fantastic phallic fetishes.

In the center of this dark garden, supported by scaffolding and green with verdigris, hung a set of gongs. It appeared to me that they were intended to be rung by the wind; yet it seemed impossible that any wind should ever reach them.

So I thought, at least, until one of the praetorians opened a heavy door of bronze and worm-scarred wood in one of the dark stone walls. Then a draft of cold, dry air blew through that doorway and set the gongs to swaying and clashing, so well tuned that their chiming seemed the purposeful composition of some musician, whose thoughts were now in exile here.

In looking up at the gongs (which the praetorians did not prevent me from doing) I saw the statues, forty at least, who had followed us all the way across the gardens. They now rimmed the pit, motionless at last, and looked down on us like a frieze of cenotaphs.

I had expected to be the only occupant of a small cell, I suppose because I unconsciously transferred the practices of our own oubliette to this unknown place. Nothing more different from the actual arrangement could have been imagined. The entrance opened on no corridor of narrow doors, but to a spacious and carpeted one with a second entrance opposite. Hastarii with flaming spears stood as sentries before this second set of doors. At a word from one of the praetorians, they swung them open; beyond lay a vast, shadowy, bare room with a very low ceiling. Several dozen persons, men and women and a few children, were scattered in diverse parts of it—most singly, but some in couples or groups. Families occupied alcoves, and in some places screens of rags had been erected to provide privacy.

Into this we were thrust. Or rather, I was thrust and the unfortunate Jonas was thrown. I tried to catch him as he fell, and I at least prevented his head from striking the floor; as I did so, I heard the doors slam shut behind me.

XV

Fool's Fire

I WAS RINGED by faces. Two women took Jonas from me, and promising to care for him carried him away. The rest began to ply me with questions. What was my name? What clothes were those I wore? Where had I come from? Did I know such a one, or such a one, or such a one? Had I ever been to this town or that? Was I of the House Absolute? Of Nessus? From the east bank of Gyoll or the west? What quarter? Did the Autarch still live? What of Father Inire? Who was archon in the city? How went the war? Had I news of so-and-so, a commander? Of so-and-so, a trooper? Of so-and-so, a chiliarch? Could I sing, recite, play an instrument?

As may be imagined, in such a welter of inquiries I was able to answer almost none. When the first flurry was spent, an old, gray-bearded man and a woman who seemed almost equally old silenced the others and drove them away. Their method, which would surely have succeeded nowhere but here, was to clap each by the shoulder, point to the most remote part of the room, and say distinctly, *"Plenty of time."* Gradually the others fell silent and walked to what seemed the limits of hearing, until at last the low room was as still as it had been when the doors opened.

"I am Lomer," the old man said. He cleared his throat noisily. "This is Nacarete."

I told him my name, and Jonas's.

The old woman must have heard the concern in my voice. "He will be safe, rest assured. Those girls will treat him as well as they can, in the hope that he'll soon be able to talk to them." She laughed, and something in the way she threw back her well shaped head told me she had once been beautiful.

I began to question them in my turn, but the old man interrupted me. "Come with us," he said, "to our corner. We will be able to sit at ease there, and I can offer you a cup of water."

As soon as he pronounced the word, I realized that I was terribly thirsty. He led us behind the rag screen nearest the doors and poured water for me from an earthenware jug into a delicate porcelain cup. There were cushions there, and a little table not more than a span high.

"Question for question," he said. "That's the old rule. We have told you our names and you have told us yours, and so we begin again. Why were you taken?"

I explained that I did not know, unless it were merely for violating the grounds.

Lomer nodded. His skin was of that pale color peculiar to those who never see the sun; with his straggling beard and uneven teeth, he would have been repulsive in any other setting; but he belonged here as much as the half-obliterated tiles of the floor did. "I am here by the malice of the Chatelaine Leocadia. I was seneschal to her rival the Chatelaine Nympha, and when she brought me here to the House Absolute with her in order that we might review the accounts of the estate while she attended the rites of the philomath Phocas, the Chatelaine Leocadia entrapped me by the aid of Sancha, who—"

The old woman, Nicarete, interrupted him. "Look!" she exclaimed. "He knows her."

And so I did. A chamber of pink and ivory had risen in my mind, a room of which two walls were clear glass exquisitely framed. Fires burned there on marble hearths, dimmed by the sunbeams streaming through the glass but filling the room with a dry heat and the odor of sandalwood. An old woman wrapped in many shawls sat in a chair that was like a throne; a decanter of cut crystal and several brown phials stood on an inlaid table at her side. "An elderly woman with a hooked nose," I said. "The Dowager of Fors."

"You do know her then." Lomer's head nodded slowly, as though it were answering the question put by its own mouth. "You are the first in many years."

"Let us say that I remember her."

"Yes." The old man nodded. "They say she is dead now. But in my day she was a fine, healthy young woman. The Chatelaine Leocadia persuaded her to it, then caused us to be discovered, as Sancha knew she would. She was but fourteen, and no crime was charged to her. We had done nothing in any case; she had only begun to undress me."

I said, "You must have been quite a young man yourself."

He did not answer, so Nicarete replied for him. "He was twenty-eight."

"And you," I asked. "Why are you here?"

"I am a volunteer."

I looked at her in some surprise.

"Someone must make amends for the evil of Urth, or the New Sun will never come. And someone must call attention to this place and the others like it. I am of an armiger family that may yet remember me, and so the guards must be careful of me, and of all the others while I remain here."

"Do you mean that you can leave, and will not?"

"No," she said, and shook her head. Her hair was white, but she wore it flowing about her shoulders as young women do. "I will leave, but only on my own terms, which are that all those who have been here so long that they have forgotten their crimes be set free as well."

I remembered the kitchen knife I had stolen for Thecla, and

the ribbon of crimson that had crept from under the door of her cell in our oubliette, and I said, "Is it true that prisoners really forget their crimes here?"

Lomer looked up at that. "Unfair! Question for question— that's the rule, the old rule. We still keep the old rules here. We're the last of the old crop, Nicarete and me, but while we last, the old rules still stand. Question for question. Have you friends who may strive for your release?"

Dorcas would, surely, if she knew where I was. Dr. Talos was as unpredictable as the figures seen in clouds, and for that very reason might seek to have me freed, though he had no real motive for doing so. Most importantly, perhaps, I was Vodalus's messenger, and Vodalus had at least one agent in the House Absolute—him to whom I was supposed to deliver his message. I had tried to cast away the steel twice while Jonas and I were riding north, but had found that I could not; the alzabo, it seemed, had laid yet another spell upon my mind. Now I was glad of that.

"Have you friends? Relations? If you have, you may be able to do something for the rest of us."

"Friends, possibly," I said. "They may try to help me if they ever learn what has happened to me. Is it likely they may succeed?"

In that way we talked for a long time; if I were to write it all here, there would be no end to this history. In that room, there is nothing to do but talk and play a few simple games, and the prisoners do those things until all the savor has gone out of them, and they are left like gristle a starving man has chewed all day. In many respects, these prisoners are better off than the clients beneath our own tower; by day they have no fear of pain, and none is alone. But because most of them have been there so long, and few of our clients had been long confirmed, ours were, for the most part, filled with hope, while those in the House Absolute are despairing.

After what must have been ten watches or more, the glowing

lamps in the ceiling began to fade, and I told Lomer and Nicarete I could remain awake no longer. They led me to a spot far from the door, where it was very dark, and explained that it would be mine until one of the other prisoners died and I succeeded to a better position.

As they left, I heard Nicarete say, "Will they come tonight?" Lomer made some reply, but I could not say what that reply was, and I was too fatigued to ask. My feet told me there was a thin pallet on the floor; I sat down and had begun to stretch myself full length when my hand touched a living body.

Jonas's voice said, "You needn't jerk back. It's only me."

"Why didn't you say something? I saw you walking about, but I couldn't break away from the two old people. Why didn't you come over?"

"I didn't say anything because I was thinking. And I didn't come over because I couldn't break away from the women who had me, at first. Afterward, those people couldn't break away from me. Severian, I must escape from here."

"Everyone wants to, I suppose," I told him. "Certainly I do."

"But I *must*." His thin, hard hand—his left hand of flesh—gripped mine. "If I don't, I will kill myself or lose my reason. I've been your friend, haven't I?" His voice dropped to the faintest of whispers. "Will the talisman you carry . . . the blue gem . . . set us free? I know the praetorians didn't find it; I watched while they searched you."

"I don't want to take it out," I said. "It gleams so in the dark."

"I'll turn one of these mats on its side and hold it to shield us."

I waited until I could feel the pallet in position, then drew out the Claw. Its light was so faint I might have shaded it with my hand.

"Is it dying?" Jonas asked.

"No, it's often like this. But when it is active—when it transmuted the water in our carafe and when it awed the man-apes—it shines brightly. If it can procure our escape at all, I don't believe it will do so now."

"We must take it to the door. It might spring the lock." His voice was shaking.

"Later, when the others are all asleep. I'll free them if we can get free ourselves; but if the door doesn't open—and I don't think it will—I don't want them to know I have the Claw. Now tell me why you must escape at once."

"While you were talking to the old people I was being questioned by a whole family," Jonas began. "There were several old women, a man of about fifty, another about thirty, three other women, and a flock of children. They had carried me to their own little niche in the wall, you see, and the other prisoners couldn't come there unless they were invited, which they weren't. I expected that they'd ask me about friends on the outside, or politics, or the fighting in the mountains. Instead I seemed to be only a kind of amusement for them. They wanted to hear about the river, and where I had been, and how many people dressed the way I did. And the food outside—there were a great many questions about food, some of them quite ludicrous. Had I ever seen butchering? And did the animals plead for their lives? And was it true that the ones who make sugar carried poisoned swords and would fight to defend it? . . .

"They had never seen bees, and seemed to think they were about the size of rabbits.

"After a time I began to ask questions of my own and found that none of them, not even the oldest woman, had ever been free. Men and women are put into this room alike, it seems, and in the course of nature they produce children. And though some are taken away, most remain here throughout their lives. They have no possessions and no hope of release. Actually, they don't know what freedom is, and although the older man and one girl told me seriously that they would like to go outside, I don't think they meant to stay. The old women are seventh-generation prisoners, so they said—but one let it slip that her mother had been a seventh-generation prisoner as well.

"They are remarkable people in some respects. Externally

they have been shaped completely by this place where they have spent all their lives. Yet beneath that are . . ." Jonas paused, and I could feel the silence pressing in all about us. "Family memories, I suppose you could call them. Traditions from the outside world that have been handed down to them, generation to generation, from the original prisoners from whom they are descended. They don't know what some of the words mean any longer, but they cling to the traditions, to the stories, because those are all they have; the stories and their names."

He fell silent. I had thrust the tiny spark of the Claw back into my boot, and we were in perfect darkness. His labored breathing was like the pumping of the bellows at a forge.

"I asked them the name of the first prisoner, the most remote from whom they counted their descent. It was Kimlee-soong. . . . Have you heard that name?"

I told him I had not.

"Or anything like it? Suppose it were three words."

"No, nothing like that," I said. "Most of the people I have known have had one-world names like you, unless a part of the name was a title, or a nickname of some sort that had been attached to it because there were too many Bolcans or Altos or whatever."

"You told me once that you thought I had an unusual name. Kim Lee Soong would have been a very common kind of name when I was . . . a boy. A common name in places now sunk beneath the sea. Have you ever heard of my ship, Severian? She was the *Fortunate Cloud*."

"A gambling ship? No, but—"

My eye was caught by a gleam of greenish light so faint that even in that darkness it was scarcely visible. At once there came a murmur of voices echoing and reechoing throughout the wide, low, crooked room. I heard Jonas scrambling to his feet. I did the same, but I was no sooner up than I was blinded by a flash of blue fire. The pain was as severe as I have ever felt; it seemed as though my face were being torn away. I would have fallen if it had not been for the wall.

Somewhere farther off the blue fire flashed again, and a woman cried out.

Jonas was cursing—at least, the tone of his voice told me he was cursing, though the words came in tongues unknown to me. I heard his boots on the floor. There was another flash, and I recognized the lightning-like sparks I had seen the day Master Gurloes, Roche, and I administered the revolutionary to Thecla. No doubt Jonas screamed as I had, but by that time there was such bedlam I could not distinguish his voice.

The greenish light grew stronger, and while I watched, still more than half paralyzed with pain and wracked by as much fear as I can recall ever having experienced, it gathered itself into a monstrous face that glared at me with saucer eyes, then quickly faded to mere dark.

All this was more terrifying than my pen could ever convey, though I were to slave over this part of my account forever. It was the fear of blindness as well as of pain, but we were all, for all that mattered, already blind. There was no light, and we could make none. There was not one of us who could light a candle or so much as strike fire to tinder. All around that cavernous room, voices screamed, wept, and prayed. Over the wild din I heard the clear laughter of a young woman; then it was gone.

XVI

Jonas

I HUNGERED THEN for light as a starving man for meat, and at last I risked the Claw. Perhaps I should say that it risked me; it seemed I had no control of the hand that slid into my boot top and grasped it.

At once the pain faded, and there came a rush of azure light. The hubbub redoubled as the other wretched inhabitants of the place, seeing that radiance, feared some new terror was to be thrust among them. I pushed the gem down into my boot once more, and when its light was no longer visible began to grope for Jonas.

He was not unconscious, as I had supposed, but lay writhing, some twenty steps from where we had rested. I carried him back (finding him astonishingly light) and when I had covered us both with my cloak touched his forehead with the Claw.

In a short time he was sitting up. I told him to rest, that whatever it was that had been in the prison chamber with us was gone.

He stirred and muttered, "We must get power to the compressors before the air goes bad."

"It's all right," I told him. "Everything is all right, Jonas." I despised myself for it, but I was talking to him as if he were the youngest of apprentices, just as, years before, Master Malrubius had spoken to me.

Something hard and cold touched my wrist, moving as if it were alive. I grasped it, and it was Jonas's steel hand; after a moment I realized he had been trying to clasp my own hand with it. "I feel weight!" His voice was growing louder. "It must be only the lights." He turned, and I heard his hand ring and scrape as it struck the wall. He began talking to himself in a nasal, monosyllabic language I did not understand.

Greatly daring, I drew out the Claw again and touched him with it once more. It was as dull as it had been when we had first examined it that evening, and Jonas became no better; but in time I was able to calm him. At last, long after the remainder of the room had grown quiet, we lay down to sleep.

When I woke, the dim lamps were burning again, though I somehow felt that it was yet night outside, or at least no more than earliest morning.

Jonas lay beside me, still asleep. There was a long tear in his tunic, and I saw where the blue fire had branded him. Recalling the man-ape's severed hand, I made certain no one was observing us and began to trace the burn with the Claw.

It sparkled in the light much more brightly than it had the evening before; and though the black scar did not vanish, it seemed narrower, and the flesh to either side less inflamed. To reach the lower end of the wound, I lifted the cloth a trifle. When I thrust in my hand, I heard a faint note; the gem had struck metal. Drawing back the cloth more, I saw that my friend's skin ended as abruptly as grass does where a large stone lies, giving way to shining silver.

My first thought was that it was armor; but soon I saw that it was not. Rather, it was metal standing in the place of flesh, just as metal stood in the place of his right hand. How far it continued I could not see, and I was afraid to touch his legs for fear of waking him.

Concealing the Claw again, I rose. And because I wanted to be alone and think for a few moments, I walked away from Jonas and into the center of the room. It had been a strange enough place the day before, when everyone was awake and active. Now it seemed stranger still, a ragged blot of a room, frayed with odd corners and crushed under its lowering ceiling. Hoping that exercise would set my mind in motion (as it often does), I decided to pace off the room's length and width, treading softly so as not to wake the sleepers.

I had not gone forty paces when I saw an object that seemed completely out of place in that collection of ragged people and filthy canvas pallets. It was a woman's scarf woven of some rich, smooth material the color of a peach. There is no describing the scent of it, which was not that of any fruit or flower that grows on Urth, but was very lovely.

I was folding this beautiful thing to put in my sabretache when I heard a child's voice say, "It's bad luck. Terrible luck. Don't you know?"

Looking around, then down, I saw a little girl with a pale face and sparkling midnight eyes that seemed too large for it; and I asked, "What's bad luck, Mistress?"

"Keeping findings. They come back for them later. Why do you wear those black clothes?"

"They're fuligin, the hue that is darker than black. Hold out your hand and I'll show you. Now, do you see how it seems to disappear when I trail the edge of my cloak across it?"

Her little head, which small though it was seemed much too big for the shoulders below it, nodded solemnly. "Burying people wear black. Do you bury people? When the navigator was buried there were black wagons and people in black clothes walking. Have you ever seen a burying like that?"

I crouched to look more easily into the solemn face. "No one wears fuligin clothes at funerals, Mistress, for fear they might be mistaken for members of my guild, which would be a slander of the dead—in most cases. Now here is the scarf. See how pretty it is? Is it what you call a finding?"

She nodded. "The whips leave them, and what you ought to do is push them out through the space under the doors. Because they'll come and take their things back." Her eyes were no longer on mine. She was looking at the scar that ran across my right cheek.

I touched it. "These are the whips? The ones who do this? Who are they? I saw a green face."

"So did I." Her laughter held the notes of little bells. "I thought it was going to eat me."

"You don't sound frightened now."

"Mama says the things you see in the dark don't mean anything—they're different almost every time. It's the whips that hurt, and she held me behind her, between her and the wall. Your friend is waking up. Why are you looking so funny?"

(I recalled laughing with other people; three were young men, two were women of about my own age. Guibert handed me a scourge with a heavy handle and a lash of braided copper. Lollian was preparing the firebird, which he would twirl on a long cord.)

"*Severian!*" It was Jonas, and I hurried over. "I'm glad you're here," he said when I was squatting beside him. "I . . . thought you'd gone away."

"I could hardly do that, remember?"

"Yes," he said. "I remember now. Do you know what this place is called, Severian? They told me yesterday. It's the antechamber. I see you already knew."

"No."

"You nodded."

"I recalled the name when you pronounced it, and I knew it was the right one. I . . . Thecla was here, I think. She never considered it a strange place for a prison, I suppose because it was the only one she had seen before she was taken to our tower, but I find I do. Individual cells, or at least several separate rooms, seem more practical to me. Perhaps I'm only prejudiced."

Jonas pulled himself up until he was sitting with his back to the wall. His face had gone pale under the brown, and it shone with perspiration as he said, "Can't you imagine how this place came to be? Look around you."

I did so, seeing no more than I had seen before: the sprawling room with its dim lamps.

"This used to be a suite—several suites, probably. The walls have been torn away, and a uniform floor laid over all the old ones. I'm sure that's what we used to call a drop ceiling. If you were to lift one of those panels, you'd see the original structure above it."

I stood and tried; but though the tips of my fingers brushed the rectangular panes, I was not tall enough to exert much force on them. The little girl, who had been watching us from a distance of ten paces or so, and listening, I feel sure, to every word, said, "Hold me up and I'll do it."

She ran toward us. I lifted her and found that with my hands around her waist I could easily raise her over my head. For a few seconds her small arms struggled with the square of ceiling above her. Then it went up, showering dust. Beyond it I saw a network of slender metal bars, and through them a vaulted ceiling with many moldings and a flaking painting of clouds and birds. The girl's arms weakened, the panel sunk again, with more dust, and my view was cut off.

When she was safely down, I turned back to Jonas. "You're right. There was an old ceiling above this one, for a room much smaller than this. How did you know?"

"Because I talked to those people. Yesterday." He raised his hands, the hand of steel as well as the hand of flesh, and appeared to rub his face with both. "Send that child away, will you?"

I told the little girl to go to her mother, though I suspect she only crossed the room, then made her way back along the wall until she was within earshot of us.

"I feel as if I were waking up," Jonas said. "I think I said yesterday that I was afraid I would go mad. I think perhaps I'm going sane, and that is as bad or worse." He had been sitting on the canvas pad where we had slept. Now he slumped against the wall just as I have since seen a corpse sit with its back to a tree. "I used to read, aboard ship. Once I read a history. I don't suppose you know anything about it. So many chiliads have elapsed here."

I said, "I suppose not."

"So different from this, but so much like it too. Queer little customs and usages . . . some that weren't so little. Strange institutions. I asked the ship and she gave me another book."

He was still perspiring, and I thought his mind was wandering. I used the square of flannel I carried to wipe my sword blade to dry his forehead.

"Hereditary rulers and hereditary subordinates, and all sorts of strange officials. Lancers with long, white mustaches." For an instant the ghost of his old humorous smile appeared. "The White Knight is sliding down the poker. He balances very badly, as the King's notebook told him."

There was a disturbance at the farther end of the room. Prisoners who had been sleeping, or talking quietly in small groups, were rising and walking toward it. Jonas seemed to assume that I would go as well, and gripped my shoulder with his left hand; it felt as weak as a woman's. "None of it began so." There was a sudden intensity in his quavering voice. "Severian, the king was elected at the Marchfield. Counts were appointed by the kings. That was what they called the dark ages. A baron was only a freeman of Lombardy."

The little girl I had lifted to the ceiling appeared as if from nowhere and called to us, "There's food. Aren't you coming?" and I stood up and said, "I'll get us something. It might make you feel better."

"It became ingrained. It all endured too long." As I walked toward the crowd, I heard him say, "The people didn't know."

Prisoners were walking back with small loaves cradled in one arm. By the time I reached the doorway the crowd had thinned, and I was able to see that the doors were open. Beyond it, in the corridor, an attendant in a miter of starched white gauze watched over a silver cart. The prisoners were actually leaving the antechamber to circle around this man. I followed them, feeling for a moment that I had been set free.

The illusion was dispelled soon enough. Hastarii stood at either end of the corridor to bar it, and two more crossed their weapons before the door leading to the Well of Green Chimes.

Someone touched my arm, and I turned to see the white-haired Nicarete. "You must get something," she said. "If not for yourself, then for your friend. They never bring enough."

I nodded, and by reaching over the heads of several persons I was able to pick up a pair of sticky loaves. "How often do they feed us?"

"Twice a day. You came yesterday just after the second meal. Everyone tries not to take too much, but there is never quite enough."

"These are pastries," I said. The tips of my fingers were coated with sugar icing flavored with lemon, mace, and turmeric.

The old woman nodded. "They always are, though they vary from day to day. That silver biggin holds coffee, and there are cups on the lower tier of the cart. Most of the people confined here don't like it and don't drink it. I imagine a few don't even know about it."

All the pastries were gone now, and the last of the prisoners, save for Nicarete and me, had drifted back into the low-ceilinged room. I took a cup from the lower tier and filled it. The coffee was very strong and hot and black, and thickly sweetened with what seemed to me thyme honey.

"Aren't you going to drink it?"

"I'm going to carry it back to Jonas. Will they object if I take the cup?"

"I doubt it," Nicarete said, but as she spoke she jerked her head toward the soldiers.

They had advanced their spears to the position of guard, and the fires at the spearheads burned more brightly. With her I stepped back into the antechamber, and the doors swung closed behind us.

I reminded Nicarete that she had told me the day before that she was here by her will, and asked if she knew why the prisoners were fed on pastries and southern coffee.

"You know yourself," she said. "I hear it in your voice."

"No. It's only that I think Jonas knows."

"Perhaps he does. It is because this prison is not supposed to be a prison at all. Long ago—I believe before the reign of Ymar—it was the custom for the Autarch himself to judge anyone accused of a crime committed within the precincts of the House Absolute. Perhaps the autarchs felt that by hearing such cases they would be made aware of plots against them. Or perhaps it was only that they hoped that by dealing justly with those in their immediate circle they might shame hatred and disarm jealousy. Important cases were dealt with quickly, but the offenders in less serious ones were sent here to wait—"

The doors, which had closed such a short time ago, were opening again. A little, ragged, gap-toothed man was pushed inside. He fell sprawling, then picked himself up and threw himself at my feet. It was Hethor.

Just as they had when Jonas and I had come, the prisoners swarmed around him, lifting him up and shouting questions. Nicarete, soon joined by Lomer, forced them away and asked Hethor to identify himself. He clutched his cap (reminding me of the morning when he had found me camping on the grass by Ctesiphon's Cross) and said, "I am the slave of my master, far-traveled, m-m-map-worn Hethor am I, dust-choked and doubly deserted," looking at me all the while with bright, deranged eyes, like one of the Chatelaine Lelia's hairless rats, rats that ran in circles and bit their own tales when one clapped one's hands.

I was so disgusted by the sight of him, and so concerned about Jonas, that I left at once and went back to the spot where we had slept. The image of a shaking, gray-fleshed rat was still vivid as I sat down; then, as though it had itself recalled that it was no more than an image purloined from the dead recollections of Thecla, it flicked out of existence like Domnina's fish.

"Something wrong?" Jonas asked. He appeared to be a trifle stronger.

"I'm troubled by thoughts."

"A bad thing for a torturer, but I'm glad of the company."

I put the sweet loaves in his lap and set the cup by his hand. "City coffee—no pepper in it. Is that the way you like it?"

He nodded, picked up the cup, and sipped. "Aren't you having any?"

"I drank mine there. Eat the bread; it's very good."

He took a bit of one of the loaves. "I have to talk to somebody, so it has to be you even though you'll think I'm a monster when I'm done. You're a monster too, do you know that, friend Severian? A monster because you take for your profession what most people only do as a hobby."

"You're patched with metal," I said. "Not just your hand. I've known that for some time, friend monster Jonas. Now eat your bread and drink your coffee. I think it will be another eight watches or so before they feed us again."

"We crashed. It had been so long, on Urth, that there was no port when we returned, no dock. Afterward my hand was gone, and my face. My shipmates repaired me as well as they could, but there were no parts anymore, only biological material." With the steel hand I had always thought scarcely more than a hook, he picked up the hand of muscle and bone as a man might lift a bit of filth to cast it away.

"You're feverish. The whip hurt you, but you'll recover and we'll get out and find Jolenta."

Jonas nodded. "Do you remember how, when we neared the end of the Piteous Gate, in all that confusion, she turned her head so that the sun shone on one cheek?"

I told him I did.

"I have never loved before, never in all the time since our crew scattered."

"If you can't eat anything more, you ought to rest now."

"Severian." He gripped my shoulder as he had before, but this time with his steel hand; it felt as strong as a vise. "You must talk to me. I cannot bear the confusion of my own thoughts."

For some time I spoke of whatever came into my head, without receiving any reply. Then I remembered Thecla, who had often been oppressed in much the same way, and how I had read to her. Taking out her brown book, I opened it at random.

XVII

The Tale of the Student and His Son

Part I

The Redoubt of the Magicians

ONCE, UPON THE margin of the unpastured sea, there stood a city of pale towers. In it dwelt the wise. Now that city had both law and curse. The law was this: That for all who dwelt there, life held but two paths: they might rise among the wise and walk clad with hoods of myriad colors, or they must leave the city and go into the friendless world.

Now one there was who had studied long all the magic known in the city, which was most of the magic known in the world. And he grew near the time at which he must choose his path. In high summer, when flowers with yellow and careless heads thrust even from the dark walls overlooking the sea, he went to one of the wise who had shaded his face with myriad colors for longer than most could remember, and for long had taught the student whose time was come. And he said to him: "How may I—even I who know nothing—have a place among the wise of the city? For I wish to study spells that are *not* sacred all my days, and not go into the friendless world to dig and carry for bread."

Then the old man laughed and said, "Do you recall how, when you were hardly more than a boy, I taught you the art by which we flesh sons from dream stuff? How skillful you were in those days, surpassing all the others! Go now, and flesh such a son, and I will show it to the hooded ones, and you will be as we."

But the student said: "Another season. Let pass another season, and I will do everything you advise."

Autumn came, and the sycamores of the city of pale towers, that were sheltered from the sea winds by its high wall, dropped leaves like the gold manufactured by their owners. And the wild salt geese streamed among the pale towers, and after them the ossifrage and the lammergeir. Then the old man sent again for him who had been his student, and said: "Now, surely, you must flesh for yourself a creation of dream as I have instructed you. For the others among the hooded ones grow impatient. Save for us, you are the eldest in the city, and it may be that if you do not act now they will turn you out by winter."

But the student answered: "I must study further, that I may achieve what I seek. Can you not for one season protect me?" And the old man who had taught him thought of the beauty of the trees that had for so many years delighted his eyes like the white limbs of women.

At length the golden autumn wore away, and Winter came stalking into the land from his frozen capital, where the sun rolls along the edge of the world like a trumpery gilded ball and the fires that flow between the stars and Urth kindle the sky. His touch turned the waves to steel, and the city of the magicians welcomed him, hanging banners of ice from its balconies and heaping its roofs with glaces of snow. The old man summoned his student again, and the student answered as before.

Spring came and with it gladness to all nature, but at spring the city was hung with black; and hatred, and the loathing of one's own powers—that eats like a worm at the heart—fell on the magicians. For the city had but one law and one curse, and though the law held sway all the year, the curse ruled the spring. In spring, the most beautiful maidens of the city, the daughters of the magicians, were clothed in green; and while the soft winds of spring teased their golden hair, they walked unshod through the portal of the city, and down the narrow path that led to the quay, and boarded the black-sailed ship that waited them. And because of their golden hair, and their gowns of green faille, and because it seemed to the magicians that they were reaped like grain, they were called Corn Maidens.

When the man who had long been the student of the old man but was yet unhooded heard the dirges and laments, and looking from his window saw the maidens filing by, he set aside all his books and began to draw such figures as no man had ever seen, and to write in many languages, as his master had taught him aforetime.

Part II

The Fleshing of the Hero

DAY AFTER DAY he labored. When the first light came at the window, his pen had been a drudge already many hours; and when the moon tangled her crooked back among the pale towers, his lamp shone bright. At first it seemed to him that all the skill his master had taught him of old had deserted him, for from the first light to the moonlight he was alone in his chambers save for the moth that fluttered sometimes to show the insignia of Death at his undaunted candle flame.

Then there crept into his dreams, when sometimes he nodded over the table, another; and he, knowing who that other was, welcomed him, though the dreams were fleeting and soon forgotten.

He labored on, and that which he strove to create gathered about him as smoke collects about the new fuel thrown upon a fire almost dead. At times (and particularly when he worked early or late, and when having at long last laid aside all the implements of his art, he stretched himself at length upon the narrow bed provided for those who had not yet earned the many colored hood) he heard the step, always in another room, of the man he hoped to call into life.

In time these manifestations, originally rare, and, indeed, at first limited almost entirely to those nights when thunder rumbled among the pale towers, became common, and there were unmistakable signs of the other's presence: a book he had not unshelved in decades lying beside a chair; windows and doors that unlocked, as it seemed, of themselves; an ancient alfange, for years past an ornament hardly more deadly than a trompe l'œil picture, found cleansed of its patina, gleaming and newly sharp.

One golden afternoon, when the wind played the innocent games of childhood with the fresh-fledged sycamores, there came a knock at the door of his study. Not daring to turn or express even the smallest part of what he felt by his voice, or even to desist from his work, he called: "Enter."

As doors open at midnight though no living thing stirs, the door began, a thread's width at a time, to swing back. Yet as it moved it seemed to gather strength, so that when it was open (as he judged by the sound) enough that a hand might have been thrust into the room, it seemed that the playful breeze had come in by the window to push life into its wooden heart. And when it was open, as he judged again, wider still, so much so that a diffident helot might have entered with a tray, it seemed a very sea storm seized it and flung it back against the wall. Then he heard strides behind him—quick and resolute—and a voice respectful and youthful, yet deep with a cleanly manhood, addressed him, saying: "Father, I little like to vex you when you are deep in your art. But my heart is sorely troubled and has been so these several days, and I beg you by the love you have for me to suffer my intrusion and counsel me in my difficulties."

Then the student dared turn himself where he sat, and he saw standing before him a youth haughty of port, wide of shoulder, and mighty of thew. Command was in his firm mouth, knowing wit in his bright eyes, and courage in all his face. Upon his brow sat that crown that is invisible to every eye, but can be seen even by the blind; the crown beyond price that draws brave men to a paladin, and makes weak men brave. Then the student said: "My son, have no fear of disturbing me, now or ever, for there is nothing under Heaven that I should rather see than your face. What is it that troubles you?"

"Father," the young man said, "every night for many nights my sleep has been rent with the screams of women, and often I have seen, like a green serpent called by the notes of a pipe, a column of green slip down the cliff below our city to the quay. And sometimes it is vouchsafed me in my dream to go near, and then I see that all who walk in that column are fair women, and that they weep and scream and stagger as they walk, so that I might think them a field of young grain beaten by a moaning wind. What is the meaning of this dream?"

"My son," said the student, "the time has come when I must tell you what I have concealed from you until now, fearing that in the rashness of your youth you might dare too much before the time was ripe. Know that this city is oppressed by an ogre, who each year demands of it its fairest daughters, even as you have seen in your dream."

At this the young man's eyes flashed, and he demanded: "Who is this ogre, and what form has he, and where does he dwell?"

"His name no man knows, for no man can approach near enough. His form is that of a naviscaput, which is to say that to men he appears a ship having upon its deck—which is in truth his shoulders—a single castle, which is his head, and in the castle a single eye. But his body swims in the deep waters with the skate and the shark, with arms longer than the most lofty masts and legs like pilings that reach even to the floor of the sea. His harbor is an isle to the west, where a channel with many a twist and bend, dividing and redividing, reaches far inland. It is on this isle, so my lore teaches me, that the Corn Maidens are made to dwell; and there he rides at anchor in the midst of them, turning his eye ever to left and right to watch them in their despair."

Part III

The Encounter with the Princess

THEN THE YOUNG man fared forth and gathered to him other young men of the city of the magicians to be his crew, and from those who wore the colored hoods he obtained a stout ship, and all that summer he and the young men he had gathered to him armored her, and mounted on her sides the mightiest artillery, and a hundred times practiced the making of sail, and the reefing of sail, and the firing of the guns, until she answered as a blooded mare does to the rein. For the pity they felt for the Corn Maidens, they christened her *Land of Virgins*.

At last, when the golden leaves fell from the sycamores (even as the gold manufactured by magicians falls at last from the hands of men), and the gray salt geese streamed among the pale towers of the city with the lammergeir and the ossifrage screaming after them, the youths set sail. Much befell them on the whale road to the isle of the ogre that has no place here; but at the end of those adventures the lookouts saw before them a country of tawny hills dotted with green; and even as they shaded their eyes to see it, the green grew greater, and greater still. Then the young man whom the student had fleshed from dreams knew that it was indeed the isle of the ogre, and that the Corn Maidens were hastening to the shore for the sight of his sail.

Then were the great guns readied, and the flags of the city of the magicians, that are all of yellow and black, were hung in the rigging. Near they came and nearer, until fearing to run aground they put about and beat along the coast. The Corn Maidens followed them, and following attracted more of their sisterhood until they covered all the land like grain indeed. But the young man did not forget what he had been told: that the ogre lived among the Corn Maidens.

After a half day's sailing, they rounded a point and saw that the coast fell away as a deep channel that did not end, but wound its way among the low hills of the country until it was lost to sight. At the entrance to this channel stood a calotte of white marble surrounded by gardens, and here the young man ordered his companions to cast anchor; and went ashore.

He had no more than set foot on the soil of the isle than there came to meet him a woman of great beauty, swart of skin, black of hair, and luminous of eye. He bowed before her, saying: "Princess or Queen, I see that you are not of the Corn Maidens. Their robes are green; yours is sable. Yet were you to wear a dress of green, I should know you still, for your eyes sorrow not, and the light that is in them is not of Urth."

"You speak truly," the princess said. "For I am Noctua, the daughter of the Night, and the daughter too of him whom you have come to slay."

"Then we cannot be friends, Noctua," said the young man. "But let us not be enemies." For though he did not know why, being of the stuff of dreams he was drawn to her; and she, whose eyes held starlight, to him.

At this the princess spread her hands and declared: "Know that my father took my mother by force, and here holds me against my wishes where I would soon go mad were it not that she comes to me at each day's end. If you do not see sorrow in my eyes, it is only because it lies upon my heart. That I may be free, I shall willingly counsel you how you may engage my father and triumph."

All the young men of the city of the magicians grew quiet and gathered to listen to her.

"First you must understand that the waterways of this isle turn and turn again, in such a way that they can never be charted. You can by no means use sail as you wander them, but must kindle your furnaces ere you go farther."

"I have no fear of that," said the young man fleshed from dreams. "Half a forest was laid waste to fill our bins, and those great wheels you see shall walk these waters with the tread of giants."

At that the princess trembled and said: "Oh, speak not of giants, for you know not what you say. Many ships have come as you have, until the oozy bottoms of all these measureless channels are white with skulls. For it is the custom of my father to allow them to wander among the islets and straits until their fuel is spent—however much it may be—and then, coming upon them by night when he can see them by the glow of their dying fires and they not see him, slay them."

Then the heart of the young man fleshed from dreams was troubled, and he said: "We will seek him as we are sworn, but is there no way in which we may escape the fate of those others?"

At this the princess took pity on him, for all who have the stuff of dreams about them seem fair in some degree at least to the daughters of Night, and he fairest of all. Thus she said: "To find my father before your last stick is burned, you need only search out the darkest water, for wherever he passes his great body raises a foul mud, and by observing it you may discover him. But each day you must begin the search at dawn, and at noon desist; for otherwise you may come upon him by twilight, and it will go evilly with you."

"For this counsel I would have given my life," said the young man, and all his companions who had come ashore with him raised a cheer. "For now we will surely overcome the ogre."

At this the solemn face of the princess became more sober yet, and she said: "No, not surely, for he is a dread antagonist in any sea fight. But I know a stratagem that may aid you. You have said that you came well supplied. Have you tar to pay your ship, should she leak?"

"Many barrels," said the young man.

"Then when you fight, see that the wind blows from yourself to him. And when the fight is hottest—which will not be long after you have joined—have your men cast tar into your furnaces. I cannot promise that it will give you the victory, but it will aid you greatly."

At this all the young men thanked her most extravagantly, and the Corn Maidens, who had stood shyly by while the young man fleshed from dreams and the daughter of Night spoke, raised such a cheer as maidens raise, a cheer not strong, but filled with joy.

Then the young men made ready to depart, kindling the fires in the great furnaces amidships until the white specter was born that drives good ships ahead no matter what wind may blow. And the princess watched them from the strand and gave them her blessing.

But just as the great wheels began to turn, so slowly at first that they appeared scarcely to move, she called the young man fleshed from dreams to the railing, saying: "It may be that you shall find my father. Should you find him, it may be that you shall defeat him, laying low even such prowess as his. Yet even so, you may be sorely vexed to find your way to the sea once more, for the channels of this isle are most wondrously wrought. Yet there is a way. From my father's right hand you must flay the tip of the first finger. There you will see a thousand tangled lines. Be not discouraged, but study it closely; for it is the map he followed in webbing the waterways, that he himself might always have it by him."

Part IV

The Battle with the Ogre

INLAND THEY TURNED their bow, and even as the princess had foretold, the channel they followed soon divided, and divided again, until there were a thousand forking channels and ten thousand islets. When the shadow of the mainmast was no larger than a hat, the young man fleshed from dreams gave orders that the anchors be cast, and the fires banked, and there, for a long afternoon, they waited, oiling the guns, and readying the powder, and preparing all that might be needful in the hardest fought battle.

At length Night came, and they saw her striding from islet to islet with her bats about her shoulders and her dire wolves dogging her steps. No more than an easy carronade shot from their anchorage she seemed, yet they all observed that she passed not before Hesperus or even Sirius; but they before her. For a moment only she turned her face toward them, and none could be certain what her look conveyed. But all of them wondered if indeed the ogre had taken her without her will as her daughter had said; and if so, if she had not lost the resentment she might be imagined to have felt.

With the first light, the trumpet sounded from the quarterdeck and the banked fires were fed new fuel; but as the dawn breeze stood fair for the channel they held, the young man ordered all plain sail set before the great wheels were ready to take their first step. And when the white specter wakened, the ship pressed forward at double speed.

For many leagues that channel ran, not straight, but near enough that there was no need to furl the sails or even put about. A hundred others crossed it, and at each they studied the water; but each was translucent as crystal. To tell the strange sights they beheld on the islets they passed would require a dozen tales as long as this—women stem-grown like flowers overhung the ship, and in kissing them sought to smear their faces with the powder from their cheeks; men to whom wine had brought death long before lay by springs of wine and drank still, too stupefied to know their lives were past; beasts that would be omens to future times, with twisted limbs and fur of colors never seen, waited the nearer approach of battles, earthquakes, and the murders of kings.

At last the youth who stood first mate to the young man fleshed from dreams approached him where he waited near the steersman, saying: "Far we have traveled on this channel already, and the sun, that had not shown his face when we bent our sails, approaches his zenith. Following it, we have crossed a thousand others, and none has shone a trace of the ogre. May it not be that it is an unlucky course we take? Would not it be wiser to turn aside soon and try another?"

Then the young man answered: "Even now we pass a channel to starboard. Look down, and tell me if its waters are more soiled than our own."

The youth did as he was bid, and said: "Nay, clearer."

"Soon now, another opens to port. To what depth can you see?"

The youth waited until the ship stood opposite the channel of which the young man spoke, and then he answered: "To the utmost. I see the wreck of a ship of long time past, many a fathom down."

"And can you see so far in this channel we sail now?"

Then the youth looked at the waters they cleaved, and they were become as ink; and the very splatters that flew from the laboring wheels might have been rooks and ravens. At once understanding came to him, and he shouted to all the others to stand by the guns, for he could not tell them to make ready, who had made ready so long before.

Ahead lay an islet higher than most, crowned with tall and

somber trees; and here the channel bent gently, so that the wind, that had been dead astern, was at the quarter. The steersman shifted his grip on the wheel, and the watch payed out certain sheets and tightened others, and the ship's prow came around the quick curve of the cliff, and there before them lay a long hull of narrow beam, with a single castle of iron amidships and a single gun larger than any they carried thrusting from its one embrasure.

Then the young man fleshed from dreams opened his lips to shout to the bow-chaser crews that they should fire. Before the words could be spoken, the great gun of their enemy roared, and its sound was not as thunder or as any other sound familiar to the ears of men; but rather, it seemed that they had stood in a tall tower of stone, and it had fallen all around them in a moment.

And the ball of that shot struck the breech of the first gun of their starboard battery, and striking it broke it to pieces and shattered itself as well, so that the fragments of the breaking of both scattered through the ship like dark leaves before a great wind, and many died thereby.

Then the steersman, waiting no order, swung the ship about until her port battery bore, and the guns fired each by the will of the man that pointed it, as wolves howl at the moon. And their shots flew about the single castle of the enemy to either side, and some struck it so that it tolled knells for those who had perished a moment before, and some struck the water before the hull that bore it, and some struck the deck (which was of iron also) and at that contact fled shrieking into the sky.

Then the single gun of their enemy spoke again.

And so it continued, in moments that seemed whole years of time. At last the young man bethought him of the advice of the princess, the daughter of Night; but through the wind blew strong, it was hardly more than astern of his ship, and if he were to shift until it blew from him to his enemy (as the princess had counseled) for many moments no gun would bear but the bow chasers, and then when a battery might be brought to bear, it would be the starboard, of which one gun was destroyed and so many men dead.

But it came to him in that moment that they fought as a hundred others had fought, and that these hundred others were all dead, their ships sunk and their bones scattered among the myriad channels that whorled and tangled the face of the isle of the ogre. Then he gave his order to the steersman; but none answered, for he was dead, and the wheel he had held, held him. So seeing, the young man fleshed from dreams took the spokes in his own hands and presented to their enemy the ship's narrow bow. Then it was seen how the three sisters favor the bold, for the next shot from their enemy, that might have raked her from stem to stern, went to port by the length of an oar. And the next, to starboard by the width of a boat.

Now their enemy, who had stood fast before, neither seeking to fly nor to close, swung about. Seeing that he would escape them if he could, the crew raised a great shout as though already they had won the victory. But marvelous to see, the single castle, which all had until then believed fixed, swung about the other way, so that its great gun, that was greater than any of their own, still bore.

A moment later and its ball had struck them amidships, dashing a gun of the starboard battery from its truck as a drunken man might fling an infant from its cradle and sending it skittering across the deck and smashing everything in its path. Then the guns of the battery—those that remained—spoke all in a chorus of fire and iron. And because the distance was now less than half what it had been (or perhaps only because their enemy, having shown fear, had weakened the fabric of his being), their shot no longer struck his castle with an empty clanging, but with a cracking as though the bell that will toll the end of the world were breaking; and ragged flaws sprang to life on the oiled blackness of the iron.

Then the young man shouted into the gosport to those who had remained faithfully in the engine room feeding the furnaces with tree-wrack, telling them to cast tar into the flames as the princess had counseled them. At first he feared that all there were dead, then that the order was not understood in the din of battle. But a shadow fell upon the sun-brightened water that stretched between their enemy and himself, and he looked upward.

In ancient times, so it is said, a tattered child, the daughter of a fisherman, found on the sand a stoppered flask, and by breaking the seal and drawing forth the cork became queen from ice to ice. Just so, it seemed, an elemental being, strong with the strength of the forging of creation, debouched from the tall smokestacks of their ship, tumbling over himself in dark joy and growing with a rush, as the wind comes.

And the wind came indeed, and it seized him with its uncounted hands and bore him as a solid mass down upon their enemy. Even when nothing more could be seen—neither the long, dark hull with its deck of iron, nor the single guns whose mouth had spoken words to doom them—they wasted no moment, but fell to their guns and fired into the blackness. And from time to time they heard the gun of their enemy also firing; but no flash did they see, and where those shots struck they could not say.

It may be they have struck nothing yet, and still circle round the world seeking their target.

They fired until the barrels shone like ingots newly come from the crucible. Then the smoke that had poured forth so long diminished, and those below shouted by the gosport that all the tar was consumed, and the young man fleshed from dreams ordered that firing cease, and the men who had worked the guns fell upon the deck like so many corpses, too exhausted even to beg water.

The black cloud melted. Not as fog melts in the sun, but as an army strong to evil dissolves before repeated charges, giving here, stubbornly standing there, still mustering a wisp of skirmishers when it seems all has given way.

In vain then they searched the new-polished waves for their enemy. Nothing could they see: not his hull, nor his castle, nor his gun, nor any plank or spar.

Slowly, so cautiously it might have been thought they feared an unseen foe, they advanced to the very spot where he had lain at anchor, noting the shattered trees and furrowed ground of the islet beyond, where their shot had spent its energies. When they were over the point at which that long iron hull had lain, the young man fleshed from dreams ordered the great wheels reversed, and at last halted, so that they rested as quietly as their opponent had. Then he strode to the rail and looked down; but with such an expression that no one, not even the most brave, dared to look at him.

When he lifted his eyes at last, his face was set and grim, and with no word to any man he took himself to his cabin and barred the door. Then the youth that was second to him ordered the ship put about, that they might return to the white calotte of the princess; and he ordered also that wounds be bandaged, and pumps set in motion, and such repairs as could be made begun. But the dead he kept with them, that they might be buried on the high sea.

Part V

The Death of the Student

IT MAY BE that the channel was not so straight as they believed. Or that they had lost their bearings in the fight, without being aware thereof. Or that the channels twisted (as some alleged) like worms in a litch, when no eye was upon them. Whatever the truth might be, all day they steamed—for the wind had died away—and by the last light saw only that they cruised among islets unknown.

All night they lay to. When morning came, the youth called to him such others as he felt might offer the most valuable counsel; but none of them could suggest anything save calling upon the young men fleshed from dreams (which they were loath to do) or pressing onward until they reached open waters or the calotte of the princess.

That they did all day, striving to hold a straight course, but winding against their will among the many turnings of the channels. And when night came again, their position was no better than before.

But on the morning of the third day, the young man fleshed from dreams came out of his cabin and began to walk up and down the decks as he was wont to do, examining such repairs as they had made to their damage and asking those wounded who by the pain of their wounds were awake early how they fared. Then the youth and those who had advised him came to him, and they explained all that they had done and asked how they might find the sea again, that they might bury the dead and return to their homes in the city of the magicians.

At this he looked up into the very vault of the firmament. And some thought he prayed, and some that he sought to restrain the anger he felt against them, and some only that he hoped to gain inspiration there. But so long did he stare that they waxed afraid, even as they had when he had peered into the water, and one or two began to creep away. Then he said to them: "Behold! Do you not see the sea birds? From every corner of the sky they stream. Follow them."

Until morning was nearly done, they followed the birds insofar as the winding channels permitted. And at last they saw them wheeling and diving at the water ahead, so their white wings and ebon heads seemed a cloud low hung in their course, a cloud fair without but thunderous within. Then the young man fleshed from dreams told them to load a carronade with powder only, and to fire it; and at the crash of the gun all those sea birds rose mewing and crying. And where they had been, the crew saw a great piece of carrion floating, which seemed to them to have been a beast of the land, for it had, as they thought, a head and legs four. But it was greater than many elephants.

When they were near, the young man ordered the boat put into the water, and when he climbed aboard they saw that he had thrust into his belt a great alfange whose blade caught the sun. For a time he labored over the carrion, and when he returned he carried a chart, the largest any of them had seen, drawn upon untanned hide.

By dark they reached the calotte of the princess. All waited on board while her mother visited her; but when that terrible woman was gone, all who could walk went ashore, and the Corn Maidens crowded about them, a hundred to each youth, and the young man fleshed from dreams took the daughter of Night into his arms and led them all in dances. None of them ever forgot that night.

The dew found them beneath the trees of the princess' garden, half smothered in flowers. For a time they slept so, but when afternoon threw backward the shadows of their masts they were awake. Then the princess bade farewell to the isle and swore that though she might visit every country over which her mother strode, she never would return there; and the Corn Maidens swore likewise. Too many of them there were, perhaps, for the ship to hold; yet it held them, so that all the decks were green with their gowns and gold with their hair. Many adventures they had in making their way back to the city of the magicians. This tale might tell how they cast their dead into the sea with prayers, yet afterward saw them in the rigging by night; or how certain of the Corn Maidens wed those princes who, having spent years so long enchanted that they are loath to leave that life (and have in that time learned much of gramary), build palaces on lily pads and are seldom seen by men.

But all those things have no place here. Be it sufficient to say that as they neared the cliff at whose top stands the city of the magicians, the student who had fleshed the young man from dreams stood on the battlements, watching for them over the sea. And when he beheld their dark sails, smutted by the burning tar that had blinded their enemy, he believed them blackened in mourning for the young man, and he threw himself down, and so perished. For no man lives long when his dreams are dead.

XVIII

Mirrors

AS I READ this idle tale I looked at Jonas from time to time, but I never saw the least flicker of expression on his face, though he did not sleep. When it was complete, I said, "I'm not certain I understand why the student at once assumed his son was dead when he saw the black sails. The ship the ogre sent had black sails, but it came only once a year, and had already come."

"I know," Jonas said. His voice held a flatness I had not heard before.

"Do you mean you know the answers to those questions?"

He did not reply, and for a time we sat in silence, I with the brown book (so insistently evocative of Thecla and the evenings we had shared) still held open by a forefinger, he with his back to the cold wall of the prison room, and his hands, one of metal, one of flesh, lying to either side as though he had forgotten them.

At last a small voice ventured to say, "That must be a really old story." It was the little girl who had lifted the ceiling tile for me.

I was so concerned for Jonas that for a moment I was angry at her for interrupting us; but Jonas muttered, "Yes, it is a very old story, and the hero had told the king, his father, that if he failed he would return to Athens with black sails." I am not sure what that remark meant, and it may have been delirium; but since it was almost the last thing I heard Jonas say, I feel I should record it here, as I have transcribed the wonder-tale that prompted it.

For a time both the girl and I endeavored to persuade him to speak again. He would not, and at last we desisted. I spent the remainder of the day sitting beside him, and after a watch or so Hethor (whose small store of wit—as I supposed—had soon been exhausted by the prisoners) came to join us. I had a word with Lomer and Nicarete, and they arranged that his sleeping place should be on the opposite side of the room.

Whatever we may say, all of us suffer from disturbed sleep at times. Some in truth hardly sleep, though some who sleep copiously swear that they do not. Some are disquieted by incessant dreams, and a fortunate few are visited often by dreams of delightful character. Some will say they were at one time troubled in sleeping but have "recovered" from it, as though awareness were a disease, as perhaps it is.

My own case is that I usually sleep without memorable dreams (though I sometimes have them, as the reader who has gone this far with me will know) and seldom wake before morning. But on this night my sleep was so different from its usual nature that I have sometimes wondered if it should be called sleep at all. Perhaps it was some other state posing as sleep, as alzabos, when they have eaten of men, pose as men.

If it was the result of natural causes, I attribute it to a combination of unfortunate circumstances. I, who had all my life been accustomed to hard work and violent exercise, had for that day been confined without either. The tale from the brown book had affected my imagination—which was still more stimulated by the book itself and its associations with Thecla, and by the knowledge that I was now within the walls of the House Absolute itself, of which I had heard her speak so often. Possibly most important, my thoughts were oppressed by worry for Jonas, and by the feeling (which had been growing on me all day) that this place was the end of my journey; that I would never reach Thrax; that I would never rejoin poor Dorcas; that I would never restore the Claw, or even rid myself of it; that in fact the Increate, whom the owner of the Claw had served, had decreed that I who had seen so many prisoners die should end my own life as one.

I slept, if it may be called sleep, only for a moment. I had the sensation of falling; a spasm, the instinctive stiffening of a victim cast from a high window, wrenched all my limbs. When I sat up, I could see nothing but darkness. I heard Jonas's breathing, and my fingers told me he was still sitting as I had left him, his back propped by the wall. I lay down and slept again.

Or rather, I tried to sleep, and passed into that vague state that is neither sleeping nor waking. At other times I have found it pleasant, but it was not so now—I was conscious of the need for sleep, and conscious that I was not sleeping. Yet I was not "conscious" in the usual meaning of that term. I heard faint voices in the innyard, and felt, somehow, that soon the bells of the campanile would chime, and it would be day. My limbs jerked again, and I sat up.

For a moment I imagined I had seen a flash of green fire, but there was nothing. I had covered myself with my cloak; I threw it off, and in the instant it took to do so remembered that I was in the antechamber of the House Absolute, and that I had left the inn of Saltus far behind, though Jonas lay beside me still, on his back, his good hand behind his head. The pale blur I saw was the white of his right eye, though the sighing of his breath was that of one who slept. I was still too much asleep myself to wish to talk, and I had a presentiment that he would not answer me in any case.

Lying down again, I surrendered myself to my irritation at being unable to sleep. I thought of the herd driven through Saltus and counted them from memory: one hundred and thirty-seven. Then there were the soldiers who had come singing up from Gyoll. The inkeeper had asked me how many there were and I had guessed at a figure, but I had never counted them until now. He might, or might not, have been a spy.

Master Palaemon, who had taught us so much, had never taught us how to sleep—no apprentice had ever needed to learn that after a day of errands and scrubbing and kitchen work. We had rioted each night for half a watch in our quarters, then slept like the citizens of the necropolis until he came to wake us to polishing floors and emptying slops.

There is a rack of knives over the table where Brother Aybert slices meat. One, two, three, four, five, six, seven knives, all with plainer blades than Master Gurloes's. One with a rivet missing from its handle. One with a handle a little burned because Brother Aybert had once laid it on the stove. . . .

I was wide awake again, or thought I was, and I did not know why. Beside me Drotte slumbered undisturbed. I closed my eyes once more and tried to sleep as he did.

Three hundred and ninety steps from the ground to our dormitory. How many more to the room where the guns throbbed at the top of the tower? One, two, three, four, five, six guns. One, two, three levels of cells in use in the oubliette. One, two, three, four, five, six, seven, eight wings on each level. One, two, three, four, five, six, seven, eight wings on each level. One, two, three, four, five, six, seven, eight, nine, ten, eleven, twelve, thirteen, fourteen, fifteen, sixteen, seventeen cells in each wing. One, two, three bars on the little window of my cell's door.

I woke with a start and a sensation of cold, but the sound that had disturbed me was only the slamming of one of the hatches far down the corridor. Beside me, my boy lover, Severian, lay in the easy sleep of youth. I sat up thinking I would light my candle and look for a moment at the fresh coloring of that chiseled face. Each time he returned to me, he carried a speck of freedom glowing on that face. Each time I took it and blew upon it, and held it to my breast, and each time it pined and died; yet sometime it would not, and then instead of sinking deeper under this load of earth and metal, I would rise through metal and earth to the wind and the sky.

Or so I told myself. If it was not true, still the only joy remaining to me was to gather in that speck.

But when I groped for the candle it was gone, and my eyes and my ears and the very skin of my face told me that my cell itself had vanished with it. There was dim light here—very dim, but not the light from the candle of the torturer in the corridor, the light that filtered through the three bars of my cell's hatch. Faint echoes proclaimed that I was in an area larger than a hundred such cells; my cheeks and forehead, which had worn themselves away in signaling the nearness of my walls, confirmed it.

I stood and smoothed my gown, and began to walk almost as a somnambulist might. . . . One, two, three, four, five, six, seven strides, then the odor of close-kept bodies and confined air told me where I was. It was the antechamber! I felt a wrench of dislocation. Had the Autarch ordered me carried here while I slept? Would the others spare their lashes when they saw me? The door! The door!

My confusion was so great I nearly fell, borne down by the jumble of my mind.

I wrung my hands, but the hands I wrung were not my own. My right hand felt a hand too large and too strong, and at the same instant my left hand felt a similar hand.

Thecla fell from me like a dream. Or I should say, dwindled to nothing, and in dwindling vanished within me until I was myself again, and nearly alone.

Yet I had caught it. The location of the door, the secret door through which the young exultants came by night with their energized lashes of braided wire, was still in my memory. With everything else I have seen or thought. I could escape tomorrow. Or now.

"Please," a voice beside me said, "where did the lady go?"

It was the child again, the little girl with the dark hair and the staring eyes. I asked her if she had seen a woman.

She took my hand in her own tiny one. "Yes, a tall lady, and I'm scared. There's a horrible thing in the dark. Did it find her?"

"You're not afraid of horrible things, remember? You laughed at the green face."

"This is different, a black thing that snuffles in the dark." There was real terror in her voice, and the hand that held mine shook.

"What did the lady look like?"

"I don't know. I could only see her because she was darker than the shadows, but I could tell she was a lady by the way she walked. When I came to see who it was, there was nobody here but you."

"I understand," I told her, "though I doubt that you ever will. Now you must return to your mother and go to sleep."

"It's coming along the wall," she said. Then she released my hand and vanished, but I am sure she did not do as I told her. Instead, she must have followed Jonas and me, for I have glimpsed her twice since I returned here to the House Absolute, where no doubt she exists on stolen food. (It is possible she used to return to the antechamber to eat, but I have ordered that all the people confined there are to be freed, even if it is necessary— as I think it will be—to drive most of them forth at pike point. I have also ordered that Nicarete be brought to me, and when I was writing of our capture, a moment ago, my chamberlain entered to say she waited my pleasure.)

Jonas lay as I had left him, and again I saw the whites of his eyes in the dark. "You said it was necessary to go if you were to remain sane," I told him. "Come. The sender of the notules,

whoever that may be, has laid his hands upon another weapon. I
have found the way out, and we are going now."

He did not move, and at last I had to take him by the arm and
lift him up. Many of those parts of him that were metal must
have been forged from those white alloys that deceive the hand
by their lightness, for it was like lifting a boy; but the metal parts,
and his flesh as well, had been wetted with some thin slime. My
foot found the same filthy dampness on the floor nearby and on
the wall itself. Whatever it was the child had warned me of had
come and gone while I spoke with her, and it had not been for
Jonas that it had searched.

The door by which the tormentors entered was not far from
our sleeping place, in the center of the rearmost wall of the
antechamber. It was unlocked by a word of power, as such
ancient things almost always are. I whispered, and we passed
through the hidden portal and left it standing open, poor Jonas
striding beside me like a thing wholly metal.

A narrow stairway, festooned with the webs of pale spiders and
carpeted with dust, led by circuitous turnings downward. That
much I recalled, but beyond the stair I could remember nothing.
Whatever might come, the stale air tasted of freedom, so that
merely to breathe it was pleasure. Worried though I was, I could
have laughed aloud.

Secret doors opened at many landings, but there seemed a
chance and more than a chance that we might encounter
someone as soon as we entered one, and the stair seemed
deserted. Before I was seen by any resident of the House
Absolute, I wished to be as far from the antechamber as possible.

We had descended perhaps a hundred steps when we reached
a door painted with a crimson teratoid sign that appeared to me
to be a glyph from some tongue beyond the shores of Urth. At
that moment I heard a tread upon the stair. There was neither
knob nor latch, but I threw myself against the door, and after an
initial resistance it flew open. Jonas followed me; it shut behind

us so quickly that it seemed it should have made a great noise, though there was none.

The chamber beyond the door was dim, but the light grew brighter when he had entered. After I had made certain there was no one present but ourselves, I made use of this light to examine him. His face was still fixed, as it had been when he sat with the wall of the antechamber at his back, yet it was not the lifeless thing I had feared. It was the face, almost, of a man about to wake, and tears had left moist furrows down his cheeks.

"Do you know me?" I asked, and he nodded without speaking. "Jonas, I must recover *Terminus Est*, if I can. I've run like any coward, but now that I've had a chance to think, I see I must go back for her. My letter to the archon of Thrax is in her scabbard pocket, and I couldn't bear to part with her anyway. But if you want to try to escape this place, I'll understand. You're not bound to me."

He did not appear to have heard. "I know where we are," he said, and raised one arm stiffly to point toward something I had taken to be a folding screen.

I was delighted to hear his voice, and largely in the hope that he would speak again, I asked, "Where are we, then?"

"On Urth," he answered, and strode across the room to the folded panels. Their backs were set with clustered diamonds, as I now saw, and enameled with such twisted signs as had been on the door. Yet these signs were no stranger than the actions of my friend Jonas when he threw the panels open. The rigidity I had remarked in him only a moment before was gone—yet he had not returned to his old self.

It was then that I knew. We have all watched someone who has lost one hand (as he had) and replaced it with a hook or some other artificial contrivance perform some task that involves both his real hand and the artificial one. So it was with Jonas when I watched him pull back the panels; but the prosthetic hand was the hand of flesh. When I understood that, I understood what he had said much earlier: that in the wreck of his ship his face had been destroyed.

I said, "The eyes . . . They could not replace your eyes. Is that right? And so they gave you that face. Was he killed too?"

He looked about at me in a way that told me he had forgotten I was present. "He was on the ground," he said. "We killed him by accident, coming in. I needed his eyes and larynx, and I took some other parts."

"That was why you were able to tolerate me, a torturer. You are a machine."

"You are no worse than the rest of your kind. Remember that for years before I met you, I had become one of you. Now I am worse than you. You would not have left me, but I am leaving you. Now I have the chance, and it is the chance I sought for years as I went up and down the seven continents of this world seeking the Hierodules and tinkering with clumsy mechanisms."

I thought of all that had happened since I had carried the knife to Thecla; and though I did not follow everything he had said, I told him, "If it is your only chance, then go, and good luck. If I ever see Jolenta, I will tell her you once loved her, and nothing more."

Jonas shook his head. "Don't you understand? I will come back for her when I have been repaired. When I am sane and whole."

Then he stepped into the circle of panels, and a brilliant light kindled in the air above his head.

How foolish to call them mirrors. They are to mirrors as the enveloping firmament is to a child's balloon. They reflect light indeed; but that, I think, is no part of their true function. They reflect reality, the metaphysical substance that underlies the material world.

Jonas closed the circle and moved to its center. For perhaps the time of the briefest prayer, something of wires and flashing, metallic dust danced above the tops of the panels before all was gone and I was alone.

XIX

Closets

I WAS ALONE, and I had not been truly alone since I had entered his room in the tumbledown city inn and seen Baldanders's broad shoulders above the blankets. There had been Dr. Talos, then Agia, then Dorcas, then Jonas. The disease of memory gained upon me, and I saw the sharp silhouette of Dorcas, the giant, and the others as I had seen them when Jonas and I were being led through the plum grove. There had been men with animals as well and performers of other kinds, all of them no doubt going to that part of the grounds where (as Thecla had often told me) the outdoor entertainments were held.

I began to search the room with some vague hope of finding my sword. It was not there, and it struck me that there was probably some repository near the antechamber where the goods of the prisoners were kept—most likely on the same level. The stair I had come down would only lead me into the antechamber itself again; the exit from the room of the mirrors took me only to another room, one in which curious objects were stored. Eventually I found a door that opened onto a dark and quiet corridor, carpeted and hung with paintings. I put on my mask and drew my cloak about me, thinking that though the guards who had seized us in the wood had not seemed to know of the existence of the guild, those I might encounter in the halls of the House Absolute itself might not be so ignorant.

In the event, I was never challenged. A man in rich and elaborate clothing drew aside, and several lovely women stared at me curiously; I felt Thecla's memories stirring at the sight of their faces. At last I found another stair—not narrow and secretive like the one that had taken Jonas and me to the chamber of mirrors, but a broad, open flight of wide steps.

I ascended some distance, reconnoitered the corridor there until I was certain I was still lower than the antechamber, then began to climb again when I saw a young woman hurrying down the stair toward me.

Our eyes met.

In that moment, I feel sure, she was as conscious as I that we had exchanged glances thus before. In memory I heard her say again, "My dearest sister," in that cooing voice, and the heart-shaped face sprang into place. It was not Thea, the consort of Vodalus, but the woman who looked like her (and no doubt borrowed her name) whom I had passed on the stair in the House Azure—she descending and I climbing, just as we were now. Harlots then, as well as entertainers, had been summoned for whatever fete was being organized.

Almost purely by chance, I discovered the level of the antechamber. I had no sooner left the stair than I realized I was standing almost precisely where the hastarii had stood while Nicarete and I talked beside the silver cart. This was the point of greatest danger, and I was careful to walk slowly. The wall on my right held a dozen or more doors, each framed in carved woodwork, and each (as I saw when I stopped to examine them) spiked to its frame and sealed with the varnish of years. On my left, the only door was the great one of worm-gnawed oak through which the soldiers had dragged Jonas and me. Opposite it was the entrance to the antechamber, and beyond that stretched another row of spiked doors like the first, at the end of which was another stair. It appeared that the antechamber had grown to occupy all of this level of this wing of the House Absolute.

If there had been anyone in sight, I would not have dared to pause; but since the corridor was empty, I ventured to lean for a moment against the newel post of the second stair. While two soldiers had guarded me, a third had carried *Terminus Est*. It was reasonable to suppose that as Jonas and I were being put through the doorway of the antechamber, this third man would have taken the first few steps at least toward wherever it was that such captured weapons were kept. But I could remember nothing; the soldier had dropped behind when we descended the steps of the grotto, and I had not seen him again. It was possible, even, that he had not come in with us.

In desperation, I returned to the worm-gnawed door and opened it. The musty odor of the well entered the corridor at once, and I heard the song of the green gongs begin. Outside, the world was plunged in night. Save for the corpse candles of the fungi, the rugged walls were invisible, and only a circle of stars overhead showed where the well dropped into the earth.

I closed the door; no sooner had it grated shut than I heard the sound of footsteps on the stair up which I myself had come. There was no place to hide, and if I had darted for the second stair I would have had little chance of reaching it before I was seen. Rather than attempt to duck out through the heavy oak door and close it once more, I decided to remain where I was.

The newcomer was a plump man of fifty or so dressed in livery. Even down the length of the corridor, I saw his face pale at the sight of me. He came hurrying toward me, however, and when he was still twenty or thirty paces off he began to bow, saying, "Can I help you, your honor? I am Odilo, the steward here. You, I can see, are on a mission of some confidence to . . . Father Inire?"

"Yes," I said. "But first I must require my sword of you."

I had hoped that he had seen *Terminus Est* and would produce her for me, but he looked blank.

"I was escorted here earlier. At that time I was told that I would have to surrender my sword, but that it would be restored to me before Father Inire required me to use it."

The little man was shaking his head. "I assure you, in my position I would have been informed if any of the other servants—"

"I was told this by a praetorian," I said.

"Ah, I ought to have known. They've been everywhere, answering to no one. We have an escaped prisoner, your honor, as I suppose you've heard."

"No."

"A man called Beuzec. They say he's not dangerous, but he and another fellow were found lurking in an arbor. This Beuzec made a dash for it before they locked him up, and got away. They say they'll take him soon; I don't know. I'll tell you, I've lived in our House Absolute all my life, and it has some strange corners—some very strange corners."

"Possibly my sword is in one of them. Will you look?"

He took a half step back, as though I had raised my hand to him. "Oh, I will, Your Honor, I will. I was only trying to make a bit of conversation. It's probably down here. If you'll just follow me . . ."

We walked toward the other stair, and I saw that in my hasty search I had overlooked one door, a narrow one beneath the staircase. It was painted white, so that it was almost of the same shade as the stone.

The steward produced a heavy ring of keys and opened this door. The triangular room inside was much larger than I would have guessed, reaching far back beneath the steps and boasting a sort of loft, accessible by a shaky ladder, toward the rear. Its lamp was of the same type as those I had noticed in the antechamber, but dimmer.

"Do you see it?" the steward asked. "Wait, there's a candle about here somewhere, I think. That one light's not much use, the shelves throw such heavy shadows."

I was examining the shelves as he spoke. They were piled with clothing, with here and there a pair of shoes, a pocket fork, a pen case, a pommander ball.

"When I was just a lad myself, the kitchen boys used to pick the lock and come in here to rummage about. I put a stop to that—got a good lock—but I'm afraid the best things disappeared long ago."

"What is this place?"

"A closet for petitioners, originally. Coats, hats, and boots— you know. Those places always fill up with the things the lucky ones forget to take with them when they go, and then this wing has always been Father Inire's, and I suppose there's always been some that came to see him that never came back out, as well as the ones that come out what never came in." He paused and glanced around. "I had to give the soldiers keys to keep them from kicking down the doors when they were searching for this Beuzec, so I suppose they might have put your sword in here. If they didn't, they probably took it up to their guardroom. This wouldn't be it, I don't imagine?" From a corner he drew out an ancient spadone.

"Hardly."

"It seems to be the only sword here, I'm afraid. I can give you directions for getting to the guardroom. Or I can wake up one of the pages to go and ask, if you like."

The ladder to the loft was shaky, but I scrambled up it after borrowing the steward's candle. Though it seemed exceedingly improbable that the soldier had put *Terminus Est* there, I wanted a few moments to think over the courses of action open to me.

As I climbed I heard a slight noise from above that I supposed was the scurrying of some rodent; but when I thrust my head and the candle above the level of the loft's floor, I saw the small man who had been with Hethor on the road kneeling in an attitude of intense supplication. That was Beuzec, of course; I had failed to recall the name until I saw him.

"Anything up there, your honor?"

"Rags. Rats."

"Just as I thought," the steward said as I stepped from the last rung. "I should have a look myself sometime, but one isn't anxious to climb a thing like that at my age. Would you like to go to the guardroom yourself, or shall I rouse one of the boys?"

"I'll go."

He nodded sagaciously. "That's best, I think. They might not hand it over to a page, or even admit they had it. You're in the Hypogeum Apotropaic now, as I suppose you know. If you don't want to be stopped by the patrols, you had better go indoors, so the best plan would be to go up this stairway we're standing under for three flights, then left. Follow the gallery around for about a thousand paces until you come to the hypethral. With it dark out you might miss it, so keep an eye open for the plants. Turn right in there and go another two hundred paces. There's always a sentry at the door."

I thanked him and managed to get ahead of him on the stair by leaving while he was still fumbling with the lock, then stepped into a corridor off the first landing I reached and allowed him to go past me. When he was well out of the way, I went down again to the corridor of the antechamber.

It seemed to me that if my sword had indeed been carried off to some guardroom, it was very unlikely that I could recover it save by stealth or violence, and I wished to assure myself that it had not been left in some more accessible place before I attempted either. Then too, it seemed possible that Beuzec had seen it in the course of his creeping and hiding, and I wanted to question him about it.

At the same time, I was very much concerned about the prisoners of the antechamber. By that time (as I imagined) they would have discovered the door Jonas and I had left open for them, and would be spreading through this wing of the House

Absolute. It could not be long before one was recaptured and a search began for the others.

When I reached the door of the closet beneath the stair, I pressed my ear to the panel hoping to hear Beuzec moving about. There was no sound. I called him softly by name without eliciting a response, then tried to push the door open with my shoulder. It would not budge, and I was afraid to make noise by running against it. At last I managed to wedge the steel Vodalus had given me between the door and the jamb, and so split out the lock.

Beuzec was gone. After a short search I discovered a hole in the back of the closet that opened into the hollow center of some wall. From there he must have crept into the closet looking for a place large enough for him to stretch his limbs, and to there he had fled again. It is said that in the House Absolute such recesses are inhabited by a species of white wolf that slunk in from the surrounding forests long ago. Perhaps he fell prey to these creatures; I have not seen him since.

That night I did not seek to follow him, but pulled the closet door into place and concealed the damage to the lock as well as I could. It was only then that I noticed the symmetry of the corridor: the entrance to the antechamber in the center, the sealed doors to either side of it, the staircases at either end. If this hypogeum had been set aside for Father Inire (as the steward had said and its name indicated) its selection might have been due, at least in part, to this mirror-image quality. If that were so, then there should certainly be a second closet beneath the other stair.

XX

Pictures

THE QUESTION WAS why Odilo the steward had not taken me there; but I did not pause to think on it while I sprinted along the corridor, and when I arrived the answer was plain enough. That door had been broken long before—not just the socket of the lock, but the entire thing smashed so that only two discolored fragments of wood clinging to the hinges showed there had ever been a door there. The lamp within had gone out, leaving the interior to darkness and spiders.

I had actually turned away from it and taken a step or two before I stopped, under the influence of that consciousness of error that often comes to us before we understand in the least in what the error consists. Jonas and I had been thrust into the antechamber late in the afternoon. That night the young exultants had come with their whips. The next morning Hethor had been taken, and at that time, it seemed, Beuzec had bolted from the praetorians, who had been given keys by the steward so they might search the hypogeum for him. When the same steward, Odilo, had met me a few moments before, and I had told him that *Terminus Est* had been taken from me by a praetorian, he had assumed I had come during the day, after Beuzec's escape.

In point of fact, I had not; and therefore, the praetorian who had been carrying *Terminus Est* could not have put her in the locked closet beneath the second stair.

I went back to the closet with the broken door again. By the scant light that filtered in from the corridor, it was apparent that it had once been lined with shelves like its twin; its interior was bare now, the shelving having been stripped away to serve some new use, leaving the shelf brackets to thrust fruitlessly from the walls. I could see no other object of any kind, but I could also see that no guardsman who had to stand inspection would willingly have set foot among its dust and cobwebs. Without bothering to thrust my own head inside, I reached around the jamb of the broken door, and—with an indescribable mingling of triumph and familiarity—felt my hand close upon the beloved hilt.

I was a whole man again. Or rather, more than a man: a journeyman of the guild. There in the corridor I verified that my letter remained in the pocket of the sheath, then drew the shining blade, wiped it, oiled it, and wiped it again, testing its edges with finger and thumb as I walked along. Now let the hunter in the dark appear.

My next objective was to rejoin Dorcas, but I knew nothing of the location of Dr. Talos's company except that they were to perform at a thiasus held in a garden—no doubt one of many gardens. If I went outside now, by night, it would perhaps be as difficult for the praetorians to see me in my fuligin as for me to see them. But I was unlikely to find any aid; and when the eastern horizon dropped below the sun, I would no doubt be apprehended as promptly as Jonas and I had been when we rode onto the grounds. If I stayed within the House Absolute itself, my experience with the steward indicated I might well pass unchallenged, and I might even come across someone who would give me information; indeed, I hit upon the plan of telling anyone I met that I had been summoned to the celebration myself (I supposed it was not unlikely that an excruciation would be a part of the festivities) and that I had left the sleeping quarters assigned to me and lost my way. In that fashion, I might discover where Dorcas and the rest were staying.

Thinking upon this plan I mounted the stair, and at the second landing turned off down a corridor I had not seen previously. It was far longer and more sumptuously furnished than the one before the antechamber. Dark pictures in gold frames hung on the walls, and urns and busts and objects for which I knew no names stood on pedestals between them. The doors opening off the corridor were a hundred or more paces apart, indicating huge rooms beyond; but all were locked, and when I tried their handles I found that they were of a form and metal unknown to me, not shaped to be grasped by human fingers.

When I had walked down this corridor for what seemed at least half a league, I saw someone ahead of me sitting (as I first thought) upon a high stool. As I drew nearer, I found that what I had taken to be a stool was a stepladder, and that the old man perched on it was cleaning one of the pictures. "Excuse me," I said.

He turned and peered down at me in puzzlement. "Know your voice, don't I?"

Then I knew his, and his face as well. It was Rudesind the curator, the old man I had met so long before, when Master Gurloes had first sent me to fetch books for the Chatelaine Thecla.

"While ago you come looking for Ultan. Didn't you find him?"

"Yes, I found him," I said. "But it wasn't a short time ago."

He seemed to grow angry at that. "I didn't mean today! But it wasn't long. Why, I recollect the landscape I was working on, so it couldn't have been that long."

"So do I," I told him. "Brown desert reflected in the gold visor of a man in armor."

He nodded, and his anger seemed to melt away. Gripping the

sides of the ladder, he began to descend, his sponge still in his hand. "Exactly. Exactly the one. Want me to show it to you? It come out very nice."

"We're not in the same place, Master Rudesind. That was in the Citadel. This is the House Absolute."

The old man ignored that. "Come out nice . . . It's down here a ways, somewhere. Those old artists—you couldn't beat 'em for drawing, though their colors has gone off now. And let me tell you, I know art. I've seen armigers, and exultants too, that come and look at them and say this and that, but they don't know a thing. Who's looked at every little bit of these pictures up close?" He thumped his own bosom with the sponge, then bent close to me, whispering though there was no one but ourselves in the long corridor. "Now I'll tell you a secret they don't none of them know—one of these is me!"

To be polite, I said I would like to see it.

"I'm looking for it, and when I find it I'll tell you where. They don't know, but that's why I clean them all the time. Why, I could have retired. But I'm still here, and I work longer than any, except maybe Ultan. He can't see the watchglass." The old man gave a long, cracked laugh.

"I wonder if you could help me. There are performers here who have been summoned for the thiasus. Do you know where they're quartered?"

"I've heard tell of it," he said doubtfully. "The Green Room is what they call it."

"Can you take me there?"

He shook his head. "There's no picturers there, so I've never been, though there's a picture of it. Come and walk a ways with me. I'll find the picture and point it out to you."

He pulled the edge of my cloak, and I followed him.

"I'd rather you took me to someone who could guide me there."

"I can do that too. Old Ultan has a map somewhere in his library. That boy of his will get it for you."

"This isn't the Citadel," I reminded him again. "How did you come to be here, anyway? Did they bring you here to clean these?"

"That's right. That's right." He leaned on my arm. "There's a logical explanation for everything, and don't you forget it. That must have been the way. Father Inire wanted me to clean his, so here I am." He paused, considering. "Wait a bit, I've got it wrong. I had talent as a boy, that's what I'm supposed to say. My parents, you know, always encouraged me, and I'd draw for hours. I recollect one time I spent all one sunny day sketching in chalk on the back of our house."

A narrower corridor had opened to our left, and he pulled me down it. Though it was less well lit (nearly dark, in fact) and so cramped that one could not stand at anything like the proper distance from them, it was lined with pictures much larger than those in the main corridor, pictures that stretched from floor to ceiling, and that were far wider than my outstretched arms. From what I could see of them, they appeared very bad—mere daubs. I asked Rudesind who it was who had told him he must tell me about his childhood.

"Why, Father Inire," he said, cocking his head up to look at me. "Who do you suppose?" He dropped his voice. "Senile. That's what they say. Been vizier to I don't know how many autarchs since Ymar. Now you be quiet and let me talk. I'll find old Ultan for you.

"An artist—a real one—came by where we lived. My mother, being so proud of me, showed him some of the things I'd done. It was Fechin, Fechin himself, and the portrait he made of me hangs here to this day, looking out at you with my brown eyes. I'm at a table with some brushes and a tangerine on it. I'd been promised them when I was through sitting."

I said, "I don't think I have time to look at it right now."

"So I became an artist myself. Pretty soon, I took to cleaning and restoring the works of the great ones. Twice I've cleaned my own picture. It's strange, I tell you, for me to wash my own little face like that. I keep wishing somebody would wash mine now, make the dirt of the years come off with his sponge. But that's not what I'm taking you to see—it's the Green Room you're after, ain't it?"

"Yes," I said eagerly.

"Well, we've a picture of it right here. Have a look. Then when you see it, you'll know it."

He indicated one of the wide, coarse paintings. It was not of a room at all, but seemed to show a garden, a pleasance bordered by high hedges, with a lily pond and some willows swept by the wind. A man in the fantastic costume of a llanero played a guitar there, as it appeared for no ear but his own. Behind him, angry clouds raced across a sullen sky.

"After this you can go to the library and see Ultan's map," the old man said.

The painting was of that irritating kind which dissolves into mere blobs of color unless it can be seen as a whole. I took a step backward to get a better perspective of it, then another. . . .

With the third step, I realized I should have made contact with the wall behind me, and that I had not. I was standing instead inside the picture that had occupied the opposite wall: a dark room of ancient leather chairs and ebony tables. I turned to look at it, and when I turned back, the corridor where I had stood with Rudesind had vanished, and a wall covered with old and faded paper stood in its place.

I had drawn *Terminus Est* without consciously willing to do so, but there was no enemy to strike. Just as I was on the point of trying the room's single door, it opened and a figure in a yellow robe entered. Short, white hair was brushed back from his rounded brow, and his face might almost have served a plump woman of forty; about his neck, a phallus-shaped vial I remembered hung on a slender chain.

"Ah," he said. "I wondered who had come. Welcome, Death."

With as much composure as I could muster, I said, "I am the

Journeyman Severian—of the guild of torturers, as you see. My entrance was entirely involuntary, and to be truthful, I would be very grateful to you if you could explain just how it happened. When I was in the corridor outside, this room appeared to be no more than a painting. But when I took a step or two back to view the one on the other wall, I found myself in here. By what art was that done?

"No art," the man in the yellow robe said. "Concealed doors are scarcely an original invention, and the constructor of this room did no more than devise a means of concealing an open door. The room is shallow, as you see; indeed, it is shallower than you perceive even now, unless you're already aware that the angles of the floor and ceiling converge, and that the wall at the end is not so high as the one through which you came."

"I see," I said, and in fact I did. As he spoke that crooked room, which my mind, accustomed always to ordinary ones, had tricked me into believing of normal shape, became itself, with a slanted and trapezoidal ceiling and a trapezoidal floor. The very chairs that faced the wall through which I had come were things of little depth, so that one could hardly have sat on them; the tables were no wider than boards.

"The eye is deceived in a picture by such converging lines," the man in the yellow robe continued. "So that when it encounters them in reality, with little actual depth and the additional artificiality of monochromatic lighting, it believes it sees another picture—particularly when it has been conditioned by a long succession of true ones. Your entrance with that great weapon caused a real wall to rise behind you to detain you until you had been examined. I need hardly add that the other side of the wall is painted with the picture you believed you saw."

I was more astounded than ever. "But how could the room know I carried my sword?"

"That is more complex than I can well explain . . . far more so than this poor room. I can only say that the door is wrapped with metal strands, and that these know when the other metals, their brothers and sisters, pass their circle."

"Did you do all this?"

"Oh, no. All these things . . ." He paused. "And a hundred more like them, make up what we call the Second House. They are the work of Father Inire, who was called by the first Autarch to create a secret palace within the walls of the House Absolute. You or I, my son, would no doubt have built a mere suite of concealed rooms. He contrived that the hidden house should be everywhere coextensive with the public one."

"But you aren't he," I said. "Because now I know who you are! Do you recognize me?" I drew off my mask so he could see my face.

He smiled and said, "You came but once. The khaibit did not please you, then."

"She pleased me less than the woman she counterfeited—or rather, I loved the other more. Tonight I have lost a friend, yet it seems to be a time for meeting old acquaintants. May I ask how you've come here from your House Azure? Were you summoned for the thiasus? I saw one of your women earlier tonight."

He nodded absently. An oddly angled mirror set above a trumeau at one side of the strange, shallow room caught his profile, delicate as a cameo, and I decided he must be an androgyne. Pity welled up in me, with a sense of helplessness, as I thought of him opening the door to men, night after night, at his establishment in the Algedonic Quarter. "Yes," he said. "I will remain here for the celebration, then go."

My mind was full of the picture old Rudesind had shown me in the corridor outside, and I said, "Then you can show me where the garden is."

I sensed at once that he had been caught off guard, possibly for the first time in many years. There was pain in his eyes, and his left hand moved (though only slightly) toward the vial at his throat. "So you have heard of that . . ." he said. "Even supposing that I knew the way, why should I reveal it to you? Many will seek to flee by that road if the pelagic argosy sights land."

XXI

Hydromancy

SEVERAL SECONDS PASSED before I rightly understood what it was the androgyne had said. Then the remembered scent of Thecla's roasted flesh rose sickening-sweet in my nostrils, and I seemed to feel the unquiet of the leaves. Forgetting in the stress of the moment how futile such precautions must be in that deception-filled room, I looked about, seeking to assure myself that no one could overhear us, then found that without my having willed it (consciously, I had intended to question him before betraying my connection with Vodalus) my hand had taken the knife-shaped steel from the innermost compartment of my sabretache.

The androgyne smiled. "I felt you might be the one. For days now I have been expecting you, and I have kept the old man outside and many others under instructions to bring promising strangers to me."

"I was imprisoned in the antechamber," I said. "And so lost time."

"But you escaped, I see. It isn't likely you'd be released before my man came to search it. It's well you did—there isn't much time left . . . the three days of the thiasus, then I must go. Come, and I will

show you the way to the Garden, though I am by no means sure
you will be permitted to enter."

He opened the door by which he had come in, and this time I
saw that it was not truly rectangular. The room beyond was hardly
larger than the one we had left; but its angles seemed normal, and it
was richly furnished.

"You came to the correct part of the Secret House at least," the
androgyne said. "Otherwise we would have had to walk a weary
way. Your pardon, while I read the message you brought."

He crossed to what I at first supposed was a glass-topped table,
and put the steel under it on a shelf. At once a light kindled,
shining down from the glass, though there was no light above it.
The steel grew until it seemed a sword, and its striations, in place of
mere teeth on which to strike sparks from a flint, I saw to be lines of
flowing script.

"Stand back," the androgyne said. "If you have not read this
before, you must not read it now."

I did as he bid, and for some time watched him bending over the
little object I had carried away from Vodalus's glade. At last he said,
"There is no help for it then . . . we must fight on two flanks. But
this is none of your affair. Do you see that cabinet with the eclipse
carved in its door? Open it and lift down the book you find there.
Here, you may put it on this stand."

Although I feared some trap, I opened the door of the cabinet
he had indicated. It held one monstrous book—a thing nearly as
tall as I and a good two cubits wide—that stood with its cover of
mottled blue-green leather facing me much as a corpse might
had I opened the lid of an upright casket. Sheathing my sword, I
gripped this great volume with both hands and placed it on the
stand. The androgyne asked if I had seen it previously, and I told
him I had not.

"You looked fearful of it, and tried . . . as it appeared to me
. . . to keep your face from it when you carried it." He threw
back the cover as he spoke. The first page, thus revealed, was

written in red in a character I did not know. "This is a warning to the seekers of the path," he said. "Shall I read it to you?"

I blurted, "It seemed to me that I saw a dead man in the leather, and that he was myself."

He closed the cover again and ran his hand over it. "These pavonine dyeings are but the work of craftsmen long gone . . . the lines and swirls beneath them, only the scars of the suffering animals' back, the marks of ticks and whips. But if you are fearful, you need not go."

"Open it," I said. "Show me the map."

"There is no map. This is the thing itself," he said, and with that he threw back the cover and the first page as well.

I was blinded, almost, as I have been on dark nights by a discharge of lightning. The inner pages seemed of pure silver, beaten and polished, that caught every wisp of illumination in the room and flung it back amplified a hundred times. "They're mirrors," I said, and in saying it realized that they were not, but those things for which we have no word but *mirrors*, those things that less than a watch before had returned Jonas to the stars. "But how can they have power, when they do not face each other?"

The androgyne answered, "Consider how long they faced each other when the book was closed. Now the field will withstand the tension we put on it for some time. Go, if you dare."

I did not dare. As he spoke, something shaped itself in shining air above the open pages. It was neither a woman nor a butterfly, but it partook of both, and just as we know when we look at the painted figure of a mountain in the background of some picture that it is in reality as huge as an island, so I knew that I saw the thing only from far off—its wings beat, I think, against the proton winds of space, and all Urth might have been a mote disturbed by their motion. Then as I had seen it, so it saw me, much as the androgyne a moment before had seen the swirls and loops of writing on the steel through his glass. It paused and turned to me and opened its wings that I might observe them. They were marked with eyes.

The androgyne closed the book with a crash, like a door slammed shut. "What did you see?" he asked.

I could think only that I no longer had to look into the pages, and said, "Thank you, sieur. Whoever you may be, I am your servant from this time forward."

He nodded. "Perhaps sometime I may remind you of that. But I will not ask you again what it was you saw. Here, wipe your forehead. The sight has marked you."

He handed me a clean cloth as he spoke, and I wiped my brow with it as he told me, because I could feel the moisture running down my face. When I looked at the cloth, it was crimson with blood.

As though he had read my thoughts, he said, "You are not wounded. The physicians' term is haematidrosis, I believe. Under the stress of strong emotion, minute veins in the skin of the afflicted part . . . of the skin everywhere, sometimes . . . rupture during a profuse sweating. You will have a nasty bruise there, I'm afraid."

"Why did you do that?" I asked. "I thought you were going to show me a map. I only want to find the Green Room, as old Rudesind out there says it's called, where the players are quartered. Did Vodalus's message say you were to kill the bearer?" I was fumbling for my sword as I spoke, but when my hands gripped the familiar hilt, I found I was too weak to draw the blade.

The androgyne laughed. It was pleasant laughter at first, wavering somewhere between a woman's and a boy's, but it trailed off into tittering, as a drunken man's sometimes does. Thecla's memories stirred in me; almost, they woke. "Was that all you wished?" he said when he had control of himself again. "You asked me for a light for your candle, and I tried to give you the sun, and now you are burned. The fault was mine . . . I sought, perhaps, to postpone my time, yet even so I would not have let you travel so far had I not read in the message that you have carried the Claw. And now I am most truly sorry, but I cannot help but laugh. Where will you go, when you have found the Green Room, Severian?"

"Where you send me. As you remind me, I have sworn service to Vodalus." (In fact, I feared him, and feared that the androgyne would inform him if I professed disobedience.)

"But if I have no orders for you? Have you already disposed of the Claw?"

"I could not," I said.

There was a pause. He did not speak.

"I'll go to Thrax," I said. "I have a letter to the archon there; he's supposed to have work for me. For the honor of my guild, I would like to go."

"That is well. How great, in truth, is your love of Vodalus?"

Again I felt the haft of the ax in my hand. For you others, as I am told, memory dies; mine scarcely dims. The mist that shrouded the necropolis that night blew against my face again, and everything I had felt when I received the coin from Vodalus and watched him walk away to a place where I could not follow returned to me. "I saved him once," I said.

The androgyne nodded. "Then here is what you are to do. You must go to Thrax as you planned, telling everyone . . . even yourself . . . that you are going to fill the position that waits you there. The Claw is perilous. Are you aware of it?"

"Yes. Vodalus told me that if it became known we possess it, we might lose the support of the populace."

For a moment the androgyne stood silent again. Then he said, "The Pelerines are in the north. If you are given the opportunity, you must restore the Claw to them."

"That is what I had hoped to do."

"Good. There is something else you must do as well. The Autarch is here, but long before you reach Thrax he will be in the north too, with the army. If he comes near Thrax, you are able to go to him. In time you will discover the way in which you must take his life."

His tone betrayed him as much as Thecla's thoughts. I wanted to kneel, but he clapped his hands, and a bent little man slipped silently into the room. He wore a cowled habit like a cenobite's. The Autarch spoke to him, something I was too distracted to understand.

In all the world, there can be few sights more beautiful than that of the sun at dawn seen through the thousand sparkling waters of the Vatic Fountain. I am no esthete, but my first sight of its dance (of which I had so often heard), must have acted as a restorative. I still recall it for my pleasure, just as I saw it when the cowled servitor opened a door for me—after so many leagues of the contrived corridors of the Second House—and I watched the silver streams trace ideographs across the solar disc.

"Straight ahead," the cowled figure murmured. "Follow the path through the Gate of Trees. You will be safe among the players." The door shut behind me and became the grassy slope of a hillock.

I stumbled toward the fountain, which refreshed me with windblown spray. I was surrounded by a pavement of serpentine; for a time I stood there, seeking to read my fortune in the dancing shapes, and at last I fumbled in my sabretache for an offering. The praetorians had taken all my money, but while I felt among the few possessions I yet carried there (a flannel, the fragment of whetstone, and a flask of oil for *Terminus Est*; a comb and the brown book for myself) I spied a coin wedged between the green blocks at my feet. After only a little effort I was able to draw it out—a single asimi, worn so thin that hardly a trace of the imprint remained. With a whispered wish, I threw it into the very center of the fountain. A jet caught it there and tossed it skyward, so that it flashed for a moment before it fell. I began to read the symbols the water made against the sun.

A sword. That seemed clear enough. I would continue a torturer.

A rose then, and beneath it a river. I would climb Gyoll as I had planned, since that was the road to Thrax.

Now angry waves, becoming soon a long, sullen swell. The sea, perhaps; but one could not reach the sea, I thought, by climbing toward the source of the river.

A rod, a chair, a multitude of towers, and I began to think the oracular powers of the fountain, in which I had never greatly believed, to be wholly false. I turned away; but as I turned, I glimpsed a many-pointed star, growing ever larger.

Since I have returned to the House Absolute, I have twice revisited the Vatic Fountain. Once I came at the first light, approaching it through the same door through which I first glimpsed it. But I have never again dared to ask it questions.

My servants, who confess one and all that they have dropped their orichalks into it when the garden was clear of guests, tell me one and all that they have received no true prophecy for their money. Yet I am unsure, recalling the green man, who drove off his visitors with his accounts of their futures. May it not be that these servants of mine, seeing only a lifetime of trays and brooms and ringing bells, reject it? I have asked my ministers as well, who doubtless cast in chrisos by the handful, but their answers are doubtful and mixed.

It was hard indeed to keep my back to the fountain and its lovely, cryptic messages and walk toward the old sun. Huge as a giant's face and darkly red it showed as the horizon dropped away. The poplars of the grounds were silhouetted against it, making me think of the figure of Night atop the khan on this western bank of Gyoll, which I had so often seen with the sun behind it at the close of one of our swimming parties.

Not realizing that I was now deep within the bounds of the House Absolute and well away from the patrols about the periphery, I feared I might be stopped at any moment, and perhaps cast back into the antechamber—whose secret door, I felt sure, would have been discovered and sealed by now. Nothing of the kind occurred. So far as I could see, no one stirred in all the leagues of hedge and velvet lawn, flower and trickling water, except myself. Lilies far taller than I, their star-shaped faces spangled with unshaken dew, overhung the path; its perfect surface showed behind me only the disturbance of my own feet. Nightingales, some free, some suspended from the branches of trees in golden cages, were singing still.

Once I saw before me, with something of the old feeling of horror, one of the walking statues. Like a colossal man (though it was not a man) too graceful and too slow to be human, it came across a small secretive lawn as if moving to the inaudible notes of some strange processional. I confess I hung back until it had passed, wondering if it could sense me where I stood in the shadow, and if it cared that I stood so.

Just when I had despaired of finding the Gate of Trees, I saw it. There was no mistaking it. Even as lesser gardeners espalier pears against a wall, the greater gardeners of the House Absolute, who have generations in which to complete their work, had molded the huge limbs of oaks until every twig conformed to an inspiration wholly architectural, and I, walking on the rooftops of the greatest palace of Urth, with not a stone in sight, saw looming to one side that great, green entranceway built of living wood as if of masonry.

I ran then.

XXII

Personifications

THROUGH THE WIDE, dripping arch of the Gate of Trees I ran, and out onto a broad expanse of grass, now spangled with tents. Somewhere a megathere roared and shook its chain. There seemed to be no other sound. I halted and listened, and the megathere, no longer disturbed by my footfalls, settled back into the death-like sleep of its kind. I could hear the dew running from the leaves, and the faint, interrupted twitter of birds.

Something else there was as well. A faint *whick, whick*, quick and irregular, that grew louder as I listened for it. I began to thread a path among the silent tents, following the sound. I must have misjudged it, however, for Dr. Talos saw me before I saw him.

"My friend! My partner! They are all asleep—your Dorcas and the rest. All but you and I. Over here!"

He flourished his cane as he spoke; the *whick, whick* had been his chopping at the heads of flowers.

"You have rejoined us just in time. Just in time! We perform tonight, and I would have been forced to hire one of these fellows to take your part. I'm delighted to see you! I owe you some money—do you recall? Not much, and between you and I, I think it false. But it is owed just the same, and I always pay."

"I'm afraid I don't recall," I said, "so it can't be a great sum. If Dorcas is all right I'm quite willing to forget it, provided you'll give me something to eat and show me where I can sleep for a couple of watches."

The doctor's sharp nose dipped for an instant to express regret. "Sleep you may have in plenty until the others wake you. But I'm afraid we've no food. Baldanders, you know, eats like a fire. The Thiasus Marshal has promised to bring something today for all of us." He waved his stick vaguely at the irregular city of tents. "But I'm afraid that won't be before midmorning at the earliest."

"It's probably just as well. I'm really too tired to eat, but if you'll show me where I can lie down—"

"What got your head? Never mind—we'll mask it with grease-paint. This way!" He was already trotting before me. I followed him through a maze of tent ropes to a heliotrope dome. Baldanders's barrow stood at the door, and at last I felt certain I had found Dorcas again.

When I woke, it was as though we had never been separated. Dorcas's delicate loveliness was unchanged; Jolenta's radiance threw it into shadow as always, yet made me wish, when the three of us were together, that she would leave so that I might rest my eyes on Dorcas. I took Baldanders to one side, an hour or so after we were all awake, and asked him why he had left me in the forest beyond the Piteous Gate.

"I was not with you," he said slowly. "I was with my Dr. Talos."

"And so was I. We might have sought him together and been of help to each other."

There was a long hesitation; I seemed to feel the weight of those dull eyes on my face, and thought in my ignorance what a terrible thing it would be if Baldanders possessed energy and the will to anger. At last he said, "Were you with us when we left the city?"

"Of course. Dorcas and Jolenta and I were all with you."

Another hesitation. "We found you there, then."

"Yes, don't you remember?"

He shook his head slowly, and I noticed that his thatch of coarse black hair was touched with gray. "I woke one morning and there you were. I was thinking. You left me soon."

"The circumstances were different then—we had arranged to meet again." (I felt a pang of guilt when I recalled that I had never intended to honor that promise.)

"We have met again," Baldanders said dully; and then, seeing that the answer failed to satisfy me, added, "There is nothing here real to me but Dr. Talos."

"Your loyalty is very commendable, but you might have remembered that he wanted me with him as well as yourself." I found it impossible to be angry with this dim, gentle giant.

"We will collect money here in the south, and then we will build again, as we have built before, when they have forgotten."

"This is the north. But that's right, your house was destroyed, wasn't it?"

"Burned," Baldanders said. I could almost see the flames reflected in his eyes. "I am sorry if you came to harm. For so long I have thought only of the castle and my work."

I left him sitting there and went to inspect the properties of our theater—not that they seemed in need of it, or that I could have detected any but the most obvious lacks. A number of showmen were gathered around Jolenta, and Dr. Talos drove them away and ordered her to go into the tent. A moment later, I heard the smack of his cane on flesh; he came out grinning but still angry.

"It isn't her fault," I said. "You know how she looks."

"Too gaudy. Too gaudy by far. Do you know what I like about you, Sieur Severian? You prefer Dorcas. Where is she, by the way? Have you seen her since you came back?"

"I warn you, Doctor. Don't strike her."

"I wouldn't think of it. I'm only afraid she may be lost."

His surprised expression convinced me that he was telling the truth. I told him, "We only got to talk for a moment. She's gone to fetch water."

"That's courageous of her," he said, and when I looked puzzled he added, "She's afraid of it. Surely you've noticed. She's clean, but even when she washes, the water is only thumb deep; when we cross bridges, she holds onto Jolenta and trembles."

Dorcas returned then, and if the doctor said anything more I did not hear it. When she and I had met that morning, neither of us had been able to do much more than smile, and touch with incredulous hands. Now she came to me, putting down the pails she carried, and seemed to devour me with her eyes. "I have missed you so," she said. "I've been so lonely without you."

I laughed to think of anyone missing me, and held up the edge of my fuligin cloak. "You missed this?"

"Death, you mean. Did I miss death? No, I missed you." She took the cloak from my hand and used it to draw me toward the line of poplars that formed one wall of the Green Room. "There is a bench I found where there are beds of herbs. Come and sit with me. They can spare us for a while after so many days, and eventually Jolenta will come out and find the water, which was for her anyway."

As soon as we were away from the bustle of the tents, where jugglers tossed their knives and acrobats their children, we were wrapped in the stillness of the gardens. They are perhaps the largest tract of land anywhere planned and planted for beauty, save for those wildernesses that are the gardens of the Increate and whose cultivators are invisible to us. Overlapping hedges formed a narrow door. We passed into a grove of trees with white, perfumed boughs that reminded me sadly of the flowering plums through which the praetorians had dragged Jonas and me, though those had seemed planted for ornament, and these, I thought, for the sake of their fruit. Dorcas had broken a twig bearing half a dozen of the blossoms and thrust it into her pale golden hair.

Beyond the orchard was a garden so old that I felt sure it had been forgotten by everyone save the servants who tended it. The stone seat there had been carved with heads, but they had worn away until they were almost featureless. A few beds of simple flowers remained, and with them fragrant rows of kitchen herbs—rosemary, angelica, mint, basil, and rue, all growing in a soil black as chocolate from the labor of countless years.

There was a little stream too, where Dorcas had no doubt drawn her water. Its source may once have been a fountain—now it was only a species of spring, rising in a shallow stone bowl to splash over the lip and eventually wind its way through little canals lined with rough masonry to water the fruit trees. We sat in the stone seat, I leaned my sword against its arm, and she took my hands in hers.

"I am afraid, Severian," she said. "I have such terrible dreams."

"Since I've been gone?"

"All the time."

"When we slept side by side in the field, you told me you had awakened from a good dream. You said it was very detailed and seemed real."

"If it was good, I have forgotten it now."

I had already noticed that she was careful to keep her eyes away from the water spilling from the ruined fountain.

"Every night, I dream I am walking through streets of shops. I am happy, or at least content. I have money to spend, and there is a long list of things I wish to buy. Again and again I recite the list to myself, and I try to decide in what parts of the quarter I can get each in the best quality for the lowest price.

"But gradually, as I go from shop to shop, I grow aware that everyone who sees me hates me and holds me in contempt, and I am aware that it is because they believe me to be an unclean spirit who has wrapped itself in the woman's body they see. At last I enter a tiny shop conducted by an old man and an old woman. She sits making lace while he spreads their wares on the counter for me. I hear the sound her thread makes behind me as it is pulled through the work."

I asked, "What is it you have come to buy?"

"Tiny clothes." Dorcas held her small, white hands half a span apart. "Doll's clothing, perhaps. I particularly remember little shirts of fine wool. At last I choose one and hand the old man money. But it is not money at all—only a lump of filth."

Her shoulders were shaking, and I put my arm about her to comfort her.

"I want to scream then that they are wrong, that I am not the foul specter they take me for. Yet I know that if I do, whatever I may say will be taken as the final proof that they are right, and the words choke me. The worst part is that just then the hissing of the thread stops." She had taken my free hand again, and now she gripped it as though to drive her meaning into me. "I know that no one could understand who has not had the same dream, but it is terrible. Terrible."

"Perhaps now that I am here with you again, these dreams will end."

"And then I sleep, or at least fall into blackness. If I do not wake then, there is a second dream. I am in a boat poled across a spectral lake—"

"There is no mystery in that, at least," I said. "You rode in such a boat with Agia and me. It belonged to a man named Hildegrin. Surely you must remember that trip."

Dorcas shook her head. "It is not that boat but a much smaller one. An old man poles it, and I lie at his feet. I am awake, but I cannot move. My arm trails in the black water. Just as we are about to touch shore, I fall from the boat, but the old man does not see me, and as I sink through the water I know that he has never known I was there at all. Soon the light is gone, and I am very cold. Far above me, I hear a voice I love calling my name, but I cannot remember whose voice it is."

"It's my voice, calling to wake you."

"Perhaps." The whip mark Dorcas had carried from the Piteous Gate burned on her cheek like a brand.

For a while we sat without speaking. The nightingales were

silent now, but linnets were singing in all the trees, and I saw a parrot, clad in scarlet and green like a little messenger in livery, flash among the branches.

At last Dorcas said, "What a frightful thing water is. I should not have brought you here, but it was the only place nearby where I could think to go. I wish we had sat on the grass under those trees."

"Why do you hate it? It seems beautiful to me."

"Because it is here in the sunshine, but by its own nature it runs down and down forever, away from the light."

"But it rises again," I said. "The rain we see in spring is the same water we saw running the gutters the year before. Or so Master Malrubius taught us."

Dorcas's smile flashed like a star. "That is good to believe, whether it's true or not. Severian, it's silly for me to say you're the best person I know, because you're the only good person I know. But I think if I met a thousand others, you would still be the best. That was what I wanted to talk to you about."

"If you need my protection, you have it. You know that."

"It isn't that at all," Dorcas said. "In a way I want to give you mine. Now *that* sounds silly, doesn't it? I have no family, I have no one except you, and yet I think I can protect you."

"You know Jolenta, and Dr. Talos and Baldanders."

"They are no one. Don't you feel that, Severian? Even I am no one, but they are less than I. The five of us were in the tent last night, and yet you were alone. You told me once that you don't have much imagination, but you must have sensed that."

"Is that what you want to protect me from—loneliness? I would welcome such protection."

"Then I will give you all I can, for as long as I can. But most of all, I want to protect you from the opinion of the world. Severian, do you remember what I told you of my dream? How all the people in the shops, and on the street, believed that I was only some hideous ghost? They may be right."

She was shaking, and I held her.

"That is part of the reason the dream is so painful. The other part comes from knowing that in some other way they are wrong. The foul specter is in me. It is me. But there are other things in me too, and they are what I am as much as it is."

"You could never be a foul specter, or anything foul."

"Oh, yes," she said seriously, and looked up at me. Her small, tilted face was never more beautiful than it was then in the sunlight, or more pure. "Oh, yes I could, Severian. Just as you can be what they call you. What you sometimes are. Do you remember how we saw the cathedral leap into the sky and burn away in an instant? And how we went walking down a road between trees until we saw a light ahead, and it was Dr. Talos and Baldanders, ready to put on their show with Jolenta?"

"You held my hand," I said. "And we talked about philosophy. How could I forget?"

"When we came to the light and Dr. Talos saw us—do you remember what he said?"

I cast my mind back to that evening, the end of the day on which I had executed Agilus. In memory I heard the roar of the crowd, Agia's scream, and then the roll of Baldanders's drum. "He said that everyone had come now, and that you were Innocence, and I was Death."

Dorcas nodded solemnly. "That's right. But you're not really Death, you know, no matter how often he calls you that. You're no more death than a butcher is because he cuts the throats of steers all day. To me you're Life, and you're a young man named Severian, and if you wanted to put on different clothes and become a carpenter or a fisherman, no one could stop you."

"I have no desire to leave my guild."

"But you could. Today. That's the thing to remember. People don't want other people to be people. They throw names over them and lock them in, but I don't want you to let them lock you in. Dr. Talos is worse than most. In his own way, he's a liar . . ."

She left the accusation unfinished, and I ventured, "I once heard Baldanders say he seldom lied."

"In his own way, I said. Baldanders is right, Dr. Talos doesn't lie the way other people understand lying. Calling you Death wasn't a lie, it was a . . . a . . ."

"Metaphor," I suggested.

"But it was a dangerous, *bad* metaphor, and it was aimed at you like a lie."

"Do you think Dr. Talos hates me, then? I would have said he was one of the few people who've showed me real kindness since I left the Citadel. You, Jonas—who's gone now—an old woman I met while I was imprisoned, a man in a yellow robe—who also called me Death, by the way—and Dr. Talos. It's a short list, actually."

"I don't think he hates in the way we understand it," Dorcas replied softly. "Or for that matter, that he loves. He wants to manipulate everything he comes upon, to change it with his will. And since tearing down is easier than building, that's what he does most often."

"Baldanders seems to love him, though," I said. "I used to have a crippled dog, and I've seen Baldanders look at the doctor the way Triskele used to look at me."

"I understand you, but it doesn't strike me that way. Have you ever thought of how you must have looked, when you looked at your dog? Do you know anything about their past?"

"Only that they lived together near Lake Diurturna. The people there appear to have set fire to their house to drive them away."

"Do you think Dr. Talos could be Baldanders's son?"

The idea was so absurd that I laughed, happy to have the release from tension.

"Just the same," Dorcas said, "that's how they act. Like a slow-thinking, hard-working father with a brilliant, erratic son. At least so it seems to me."

It was not until we had left the bench and were walking back to the Green room (which no more resembled the picture Rudesind had shown me than any other garden would have) that it occurred to me to wonder whether Dr. Talos's calling Dorcas "Innocence" had not been a metaphor of the same kind.

XXIII

Jolenta

THE OLD ORCHARD and the herb garden beyond it had been so silent, so freighted with oblivion, that they had recalled to me the Atrium of Time, and Valeria with her exquisite face framed in furs. The Green Room was pandemonium. Everyone was awake now, and sometimes it seemed that everyone was shouting. Children climbed the trees to free the caged birds, pursued by their mothers' brooms and their fathers' missiles. Tents were being struck even while rehearsals continued, so that I saw a seemingly solid pyramid of striped canvas collapse like a flag thrown down and reveal beyond it the grass-green megathere rearing on his hind legs while a dancer pirouetted on his forehead.

Baldanders and our tent were gone, but in a moment Dr. Talos came rushing up and hurried us away down twisted walks, past balustrades and waterfalls and grottoes filled with raw topazes and flowering moss, to a bowl of clipped lawn where the giant labored to erect our stage under the eyes of a dozen white deer.

It was to be a much more elaborate stage than the one I had played upon within the Wall of Nessus. Servants from the House Absolute, it seemed, had brought timbers and nails, tools and paint and cloth in quantities much greater than we could possibly make use of. Their generosity had waked the doctor's bent toward the grandiose (which never slumbered deeply) and he alternated between assisting Baldanders and me with the heavier constructions and making frantic additions to the manuscript of his play.

The giant was our carpenter, and though he moved slowly, he worked so steadily, and with such great strength—driving a spike as thick as my forefinger with a blow or two and cutting a timber it would have taken me a watch to saw through with a few strokes of his ax—that he might have been ten slaves toiling under the whip.

Dorcas found a talent for painting that I at least was surprised by. Together, we erected the black plates that drink the sun, not only to gather energy for the night's performance, but to power the projectors now. These contrivances can provide a backdrop of a thousand leagues as easily as the interior of a hut, but the illusion is complete only in total darkness. It is best, therefore, to strengthen it with painted scenes behind, and Dorcas created those with skill, standing waist high in mountains as she thrust her brushes through the daylight-faded images.

Jolenta and I were of less value. I had no painter's hand, and too little understanding of the necessities of the play even to assist the doctor in arranging our properties. Jolenta, I think, rebelled physically and psychically against any kind of work, and certainly against this. Those long legs, so slender below the knees, so rounded to bursting above them, were inadequate to bear much weight beyond that of her own body; her jutting breasts were in constant danger of having their nipples crushed between lumber or smeared with paint. Nor had she any of that spirit that animates the members of a group forwarding the group's purpose. Dorcas had said that I had been alone the night before, and perhaps she had been more nearly correct than I supposed, but Jolenta was more solitary still. Dorcas and I had each other, Baldanders and the doctor their crooked friendship, and we came together in the performance of the play. Jolenta had only herself, the incessant performance whose sole goal was to garner admiration.

She touched my arm, and without speaking rolled enormous emerald eyes to indicate the edge of our natural amphitheater, where a grove of chestnuts lifted white candles among their pale leaves.

I saw that none of the others were looking at us and nodded. After Dorcas, Jolenta walking beside me seemed nearly as tall as Thecla, though she took small steps instead of Thecla's swinging strides. She was a head taller than Dorcas at least, her coiffure made her seem taller still, and she wore boots with high, riding heels.

"I want to see it," she said. "It's the only chance I shall ever have."

That was a palpable lie, but as though I believed it I said, "The opportunity is symmetric. Today and only today the House Absolute has the opportunity to see you."

She nodded; I had enunciated a profound truth. "I need someone—someone the ones I don't want to talk to will be afraid of. I mean all these showmen and mummers. When you were gone, no one but Dorcas would go with me, and no one is afraid of her. Could you draw that sword and carry it over your shoulder?"

I did so.

"If I don't smile, make them leave. Understand?"

Grass much longer than that in the natural amphitheater, but softer than fern, grew among the chestnuts; the path was of quartz pebbles shot with gold.

"If only the Autarch saw me, he would desire me. Do you think he will come to our play?"

To please her I nodded, but added, "I have heard he has little use for women, however beautiful, save as advisors, spies, and shield maids."

She stopped and turned, smiling. "That's just it. Don't you

see? I can make anyone desire me, and so he, the One Autarch, whose dreams are our reality, whose memories are our history, will desire me too, unmanned or not. You have wanted women other than me, haven't you? Wanted them badly?"

I admitted I had.

"And so you think you desire me as you wished for them." She turned and began to walk again, hobbling a little, as it seemed she always did, but invigorated for the moment by her own argument. "But I make every man stiffen and every woman itch. Women who have never loved women wish to love me— did you know that? The same ones come to our performances again and again, and send me their food and their flowers, scarfs, shawls, and embroidered kerchiefs with oh, such sisterly, motherly notes. They're going to *protect* me, protect me from my physician, from his giant, from their husbands and sons and neighbors. And the *men!* Baldanders has to throw them in the river."

I asked if she were lame, and as we emerged from the chestnuts, I looked about for some conveyance for her, but there was nothing.

"My thighs are chafed and it hurts to walk. I have an unguent for them that helps a bit, and a man bought a jennet for me to ride, but I don't know where it's pastured now. I'm really only comfortable when I can keep my legs apart."

"I could carry you."

She smiled again, displaying perfect teeth. "We'd both enjoy that, wouldn't we? But I'm afraid it wouldn't look dignified. No, I'll walk—I just hope I don't have to walk far. I *won't* walk far, in fact, no matter what happens. No one seems to be about but the mummers anyway. Perhaps the important people are sleeping late to prepare for the night's festivities. I'll have to sleep myself, four watches at least, before I go on."

I heard the sound of water sliding over stones, and having no better goal to seek made for it. We passed through a hawthorn hedge whose spotted white blossoms seemed from a distance to present an insurmountable barrier, and saw a river hardly wider than a street, on which swans sailed like sculptures of ice. There was a pavilion there, and beside it three boats, each shaped like the wide flower of the nenuphar. Their interiors were lined with the thickest silk brocade, and when I stepped into one I found that they exuded the odor of spices.

"Wonderful," Jolenta said. "They won't mind if we take one, will they? Or if they do, I'll be brought before someone important, just as it is in the play, and when he sees me he'll never let me leave. I'll make Dr. Talos stay with me, and you if you want. They'll have some use for you."

I told her I would have to continue my journey north and lifted her into the boat, putting my arm about a waist quite as slender as Dorcas's.

She lay down at once upon the cushions, where the uplifted petals gave her perfect complexion shade. It made me think of Agia, laughing in the sun as we descended the Adamnian Steps and boasting of the wide-brimmed hat she would wear next year. Agia had no feature that was not inferior to Jolenta's; she had been hardly taller than Dorcas, with hips over-wide and breasts that would have seemed meager beside Jolenta's overflowing plenitude; her long, brown eyes and high cheekbones were more expressive of shrewdness and determination than passion and surrender. Yet Agia had engendered a healthy rut in me. Her laughter, when it came, was often tinged with spite; but it was real laughter. She had sweated with her heat; Jolenta's desire was no more than the desire to be desired, so that I wished, not to comfort her loneliness as I had wished to comfort Valeria's, nor to find expression for an aching love like the love I had felt for Thecla, nor to protect her as I wished to protect Dorcas; but to shame and punish her, to destroy her self-possession, to fill her eyes with tears and tear her hair as one burns the hair of corpses to torment the ghosts that have fled them. She had boasted that she made tribadists of women. She came near to making an algophilist of me.

"This is my last performance, I know. I feel it. The audience is sure to hold someone . . ." She yawned and stretched. It appeared so certain her straining bodice would be unable to contain her that I averted my eyes. When I looked again, she was sleeping.

A slender oar trailed behind the boat. I took it and found that despite the circularity of the hull above the water, there was a keel below. In the center of the river the current ran strongly enough that I needed only to steer our slow progress along a series of gracefully sweeping meanders. Just as the hooded servant and I had passed unseen through suites and alcoves and arcades when he had escorted me along the hidden ways of the Second House, so now the sleeping Jolenta and I passed without noise or effort, almost completely unobserved, through leagues of garden. Couples lay on the soft grass beneath the trees and in the more refined comfort of summerhouses and seemed to think our craft hardly more than a decoration sent idly downstream for their delectation, or if they saw my head above the curved petals assumed us intent upon our own affairs. Lone philosophers meditated on rustic seats, and parties, not invariably erotic, proceeded undisturbed in clerestories and arboriums.

Eventually I came to resent Jolenta's sleep. I abandoned the oar and knelt beside her on the cushions. There was a purity in her sleeping face, however artificial, that I had never observed when she was awake. I kissed her, and her large eyes, hardly open, seemed almost Agia's long eyes, as her red-gold hair appeared almost brown. I loosened her clothing. She seemed half drugged, whether by some soporific in the heaped cushions or merely by the fatigue induced by our walk in the open and the burden of so great a quantity of voluptuous flesh. I freed her breasts, each nearly as large as her own head, and those wide thighs, which seemed to hold a new-hatched chick between them.

*   *   *

When we returned, everyone knew where we had been, though I doubt that Baldanders cared. Dorcas wept in private, vanishing for a time only to emerge with inflamed eyes and a heroine's smile. Dr. Talos, I think, was simultaneously enraged and delighted. I received the impression (which I hold to this day) that he had never enjoyed Jolenta, and that it was only to him, of all the men of Urth, that she would have given herself entirely willingly.

We spent the watches that remained before nightfall in listening to Dr. Talos chaffer with various officials of the House Absolute, and in rehearsal. Since I have already said something of what it was to act in Dr. Talos's play, I propose to give an approximation of the text here—not as it existed on the fragments of soiled paper we passed from hand to hand that afternoon, which often contained no more than hints for improvisations, but as it might have been recorded by some diligent clerk in the audience; and as it was, in fact, recorded by the demonic witness who dwells behind my eyes.

But first you must visualize our theater. Urth's laboring margin has climbed once more above the red disc; long-winged bats flit overhead, and a green quarter moon hangs low in the eastern sky. Imagine the slightest of valleys, a thousand paces or more from lip to lip, set among the gentlest turf-covered rolling hills. There are doors in these hills, some no wider than the entrance to an ordinary private room, some as wide as the doors of a basilica. These doors are open, and a mist-tinged light spills from them. Flagged paths wind down toward the tiny arch of our proscenium; they are dotted with men and women in the fantastic costumes of a masque—costumes drawn largely from remote ages, so that I, with no more than the smattering of history furnished me by Thecla and Master Palaemon, scarcely recognize one of them. Servants move among these masquers carrying trays loaded with cups and tumblers, heaped with delicious-smelling meats and pastries. Black seats of velvet and ebony, as delicate as crickets, face our stage, but many in the audience prefer to stand, and throughout our performance the spectators come and go without interruption, many remaining to hear no more than a dozen lines. Hylas sing in the trees, the nightingales trill, and atop the hills the walking statues move slowly through many poses. All the parts in the play are taken by Dr. Talos, Baldanders, Dorcas, Jolenta, or me.

XXIV

Dr. Talos's Play:
Eschatology and Genesis

*Being a dramatization (as he claimed) of certain parts
of the lost* Book of the New Sun

Persons in the Play:	A Statue
Gabriel	A Prophet
The Giant Nod	The Generalissimo
Meschia, the First Man	Two Demons (disguised)
Meschiane, the First Woman	The Inquisitor
Jahi	His Familiar
The Autarch	Angelic Beings
The Contessa	The New Sun
Her Maid	The Old Sun
Two Soldiers	The Moon

The back of the stage is dark. GABRIEL *appears bathed in golden
light and carrying a crystal clarion.*

GABRIEL: Greetings. I have come to set the scene for you—after
all, that is my function. It is the night of the last day, and
the night before the first. The Old Sun has set. He will
appear in the sky no more. Tomorrow the New Sun will

> rise, and my siblings and I will greet him. Tonight . . .
> tonight no one knows. Everyone sleeps.

Footsteps, heavy and slow. Enter NOD.

GABRIEL: Omniscience! Defend your servant!

NOD: Do you serve him? So do we Nephilim. I will not harm
you, then, unless he suggests it.

GABRIEL: You are of his household? How does he communicate
with you?

NOD: To tell the truth, he doesn't. I'm forced to guess at what he
wishes me to do.

GABRIEL: I was afraid of that.

NOD: Have you seen Meschia's son?

GABRIEL: Have I seen him? Why, you great ninny, he isn't even
born yet. What do you want with him?

NOD: He is to come and dwell with me, in my land east of this
garden. I will give him one of my daughters to wife.

GABRIEL: You have the wrong creation, my friend—you're fifty
million years too late.

NOD: *(Nods slowly, not understanding.)* If you should see him—

Enter MESCHIA *and* MESCHIANE, *with* JAHI *following. All are
naked, but* JAHI *wears jewelry.*

MESCHIA: What a lovely place! Delightful! Flowers, fountains,
and statues—isn't it wonderful?

MESCHIANE: *(Timidly.)* I saw a tame tiger with fangs longer than
my hand. What shall we call him?

MESCHIA: Whatever he wants. *(To* GABRIEL:*)* Who owns this
beautiful spot?

GABRIEL: The Autarch.

MESCHIA: And he permits us to live here. That's very gracious
of him.

GABRIEL: Not exactly. There's someone following you, my
friend. Do you know it?

MESCHIA: *(Not looking.)* There's something behind you too.

GABRIEL: *(Flourishing the clarion that is his badge of office.)*
Yes, *He* is behind me!

MESCHIA: Close, too. If you're going to blow that horn to call help, you'd better do it now.

GABRIEL: Why, how perceptive of you. But the time is not quite ripe.

The golden light fades, and GABRIEL *vanishes from the stage.* NOD *remains motionless, leaning on his club.*

MESCHIANE: I'll start a fire, and you had better begin to build us a house. It must rain often here—see how green the grass is.

MESCHIA: (*Examining* NOD.) Why, it's only a statue. No wonder he wasn't afraid of it.

MESCHIANE: It might come to life. I heard something once about raising sons from stones.

MESCHIA: Once! Why you were only born just now. Yesterday, I think.

MESCHIANE: Yesterday! I don't remember it. . . . I'm such a child, Mescia. I don't remember anything until I walked out into the light and saw you talking to a sunbeam.

MESCHIA: That wasn't a sunbeam! It was . . . to tell the truth, I haven't thought of a name for what it was yet.

MESCHIANE: I fell in love with you then.

Enter the AUTARCH.

AUTARCH: Who are you?

MESCHIA: As far as that goes, who are *you?*

AUTARCH: The owner of this garden.

MESCHIA *bows, and* MESCHIANE *curtsies, though she has no skirt to hold.*

MESCHIA: We were speaking to one of your servants only a moment ago. Now that I come to think of it, I am astonished at how much he resembled your august Self. Save that he was . . . ah . . .

AUTARCH: Younger?

MESCHIA: In appearance, at least.

AUTARCH: Well, it is inevitable, I suppose. Not that I am attempting to excuse it now. But I was young, and

though it would be better to confine oneself to women
nearer one's own station, still there are times—as you
would understand, young man, if you had ever been in
my position—when a little maid or country girl, who can
be wooed with a handful of silver or a bolt of velvet, and
will not demand, at the most inconvenient moment, the
death of some rival or an ambassadorship for her
husband . . . Well, when a little person like that becomes a most enticing proposition.

While the AUTARCH *has been speaking,* JAHI *has been
creeping up behind* MESCHIA. *Now she lays a hand on his
shoulder.*

JAHI: Now you see that he, whom you have esteemed your
           divinity, would countenance and advise all I have
           proposed of you. Before the New Sun rises, let us make a
           new beginning.

AUTARCH: Here's a lovely creature. How is it, child, that I see
           the bright flames of candles reflected in each eye, while
           your sister there still puffs cold tinder?

JAHI: She is no sister of mine!

AUTARCH: Your adversary then. But come with me. I will give
           these two my leave to camp here, and you shall wear a
           rich gown this night, and your mouth shall run with
           wine, and that slender figure shall be rendered a shade
           less graceful, perhaps, by larks stuffed with almonds and
           candied figs.

JAHI: Go away, old man.

AUTARCH: What! Do you know who I am?

JAHI: I am the only one here who does. You are a ghost and
           less, a column of ashes upheld by the wind.

AUTARCH: I see, she is mad. What does she want you to do,
           friend?

MESCHIA: *(Relieved.)* You hold no resentment toward her?
           That is good of you.

AUTARCH: None at all! Why, a mad mistress should be a most interesting experience—I am looking forward to it, believe me, and there are few things to look forward to when you've seen and done all I have. She doesn't bite, does she? I mean, not hard?

MESCHIANE: She does, and her fangs run with venom.

JAHI springs forward to claw her. MESCHIANE *darts offstage, pursued.*

AUTARCH: I shall have my piquenaires search the garden for them.

MESCHIA: Don't worry, they'll both be back soon. You'll see. Meanwhile I am, actually, glad to have a moment alone with you like this. There are some things I've been wanting to ask you.

AUTARCH: I grant no favors after six—that's a rule I've had to make to keep my sanity. I'm sure you understand.

MESCHIA: *(Somewhat taken aback.)* That's good to know. But I wasn't going to ask *for* something, really. Only for information, for divine wisdom.

AUTARCH: In that case, go ahead. But I warn you, you must pay a price. I mean to have that demented angel for my own tonight.

MESCHIA drops to his knees.

MESCHIA: There is something I have never understood. Why must I talk to you when you know my every thought? My first question was: Knowing her to be of that brood you have banished, should I not still do what she proposes? For she knows I know, and it is in my heart to believe that she puts forward right action in the thought that I will spurn it because it comes from her.

AUTARCH: *(Aside.)* He is mad too, I see, and because of my yellow robes thinks me divine. *(To* MESCHIA:*)* A little adultery never hurt any man. Unless of course it was his wife's.

MESCHIA: Then mine would hurt her? I—

Enter the CONTESSA *and her* MAID.

CONTESSA: My Sovereign Lord! What do you do here?

MESCHIA: I am at prayer, daughter. Take off your shoes at least, for this is holy ground.

CONTESSA: Liege, who is this fool?

AUTARCH: A madman I found wandering with two women as mad as he.

CONTESSA: Then they outnumber us, unless my maid be sane.

MAID: Your grace—

CONTESSA: Which I doubt. This afternoon she laid out a purple stole with my green capote. I was to look like a post decked with morning-glories, it would seem.

MESCHIA, *who has been growing angrier as she speaks, strikes her, knocking her down. Unseen behind him, the* AUTARCH *flees.*

MESCHIA: Brat! Don't trifle with holy things when I am near, or dare do anything but what I tell you.

MAID: Who are you, sir?

MESCHIA: I am the parent of the human race, my child. And you *are* my child, as she is.

MAID: I hope you will forgive her—and me. We had heard you were dead.

MESCHIA: That requires no apology. Most are, after all. But I have come round again, as you see, to welcome the new dawn.

NOD: (*Speaking and moving after his long silence and immobility.*) We have come too early.

MESCHIA: (*Pointing.*) A giant! A giant!

CONTESSA: Oh! Solange! Kyneburga!

MAID: I'm here, Your Grace. Lybe is here.

NOD: Too early for the New Sun by some time still.

CONTESSA: (*Beginning to weep.*) The New Sun is coming! We shall melt like dreams.

MESCHIA: *(Seeing that NOD intends no violence.)* Bad dreams. But it will be the best thing for you. you understand that, don't you?

CONTESSA: *(Recovering a little.)* What I don't understand is how you, who suddenly seem so wise, could mistake the Autarch for the Universal Mind.

MESCHIA: I know that you are my daughters in the old creation. You must be, since you are human women, and I have had none in this.

NOD: His son will take my daughter to wife. It is an honor our family has done little to deserve—we are only humble people, the children of Gea—but we will be exulted. I will be . . . What will I be, Meschia? The father-in-law of your son. It may be, if you don't object, that someday my wife and I will visit our daughter on the same day you come to see him. You wouldn't refuse us, would you, a place at the table? We would sit on the floor, naturally.

MESCHIA: Of course not. The dog does that already—or will, when we see him. *(To the CONTESSA:)* Has it not struck you that I may know more of him you call the Universal Mind than your Autarch does of himself? Not only your Universal Mind, but many lesser powers wear our humanity like a cloak when they will, sometimes only as concerns two or three of us. We who are worn are seldom aware that, seeming ourselves to ourselves, we are yet Demiurge, Paraclete, or Fiend to another.

CONTESSA: That is wisdom I have gained late, if I must fade with the New Sun's rising. Is it past midnight?

MAID: Nearly so, Your Grace.

CONTESSA: *(Pointing to the audience.)* All these fair folk—what will befall them?

MESCHIA: What befalls leaves when their year is past, and they are driven by the wind?

CONTESSA: If—

MESCHIA *turns to watch the eastern sky, as though for the first sign of dawn.*

CONTESSA: If—

MESCHIA: If what?

CONTESSA: If my body held a part of yours—drops of liquescent tissue locked in my loins . . .

MESCHIA: If it did, you might wander Urth for a time longer, a lost thing that could never find its way home. But I will not bed you. Do you think that you are more than a corpse? You are less.

MAID *faints.*

CONTESSA: You say you are the father of all things human. It must be so, for you are death to woman.

The stage darkens. When the light returns, MESCHIANE *and* JAHI *are lying together beneath a rowan tree. There is a door in the hillside behind them.* JAHI'*s lip is split and puffed, giving her a pouting look. Blood trickles from it to her chin.*

MESCHIANE: How strong I would be still to search for him, if only I knew you would not follow me.

JAHI: I move with the strength of the World Below, and will follow you to the second ending of Urth, if need be. But if you strike me again you will suffer for it.

MESCHIANE *lifts her fist, and* JAHI *cowers back.*

MESCHIANE: Your legs were shaking worse than mine when we decided to rest here.

JAHI: I suffer far more than you. But the strength of the World Below is to endure past endurance—even as I am more beautiful than you, I am a more tender creature by far.

MESCHIANE: We've seen that, I think.

JAHI: I warn you again, and there will be no third warning. Strike me at your peril.

MESCHIANE: What will you do? Summon up Erinys to destroy me? I have no fear of that. If you could, you would have done it long before.

JAHI: Worse. If you strike me again, you will come to enjoy it.
Enter FIRST SOLDIER *and* SECOND SOLDIER, *armed with pikes.*

FIRST SOLDIER: Look here!

SECOND SOLDIER: *(To the women:)* Down, down! Don't stand,
or like a heron I'll skewer you. You're coming with us.

MESCHIANE: On our hands and knees?

FIRST SOLDIER: None of your insolence!

*He prods her with his pike, and as he does there is a groaning
almost too deep for hearing. The stage vibrates in sympathy with
it, and the ground shakes.*

SECOND SOLDIER: What was that?

FIRST SOLDIER: I don't know.

JAHI: The end of Urth, you fool. Go ahead and spear her. It's
the end of you anyway.

SECOND SOLDIER: Little you know! It's the beginning for us.
When the order came to search the garden, special
mention was made of you two, and orders given to
bring you back. Ten chrisos you'll be worth, or I'm a
cobbler.

He seizes JAHI, *and as soon as he does so,* MESCHIANE *darts off
into the darkness.* FIRST SOLDIER *runs after her.*

SECOND SOLDIER: Bite me, will you!

He strikes JAHI *with the shaft of his weapon. They struggle.*

JAHI: Fool! She's escaping!

SECOND SOLDIER: That's Ivo's worry. I've got my prisoner, and
he let his escape, if he doesn't catch her. Come on, we're
going to see the chiliarch.

JAHI: Will you not love me before we leave this winsome spot?

SECOND SOLDIER: And have my manhood cut off and shoved
into my mouth? Not I!

JAHI: They'd have to find it first.

SECOND SOLDIER: What's that? *(Shakes her.)*

JAHI: You take the office of Urth, who will not trouble herself for me. But wait—release me only for a moment and I will show you wonderful things.

SECOND SOLDIER: I can see them now, for which I give all thanks to the moon.

JAHI: I can make you rich. Ten chrisos will be as nothing to you. But I have no power while you grasp my body.

SECOND SOLDIER: Your legs are longer than the other woman's, but I've seen that you don't move so readily on them. Indeed, I think that you can scarcely stand.

JAHI: No more can I.

SECOND SOLDIER: I'll hold your necklace—the chain looks stout enough. If that's sufficient, show me what you can do. If it's not, come with me. You'll be no freer while I have you.

JAHI raises both hands, with the little fingers, index fingers, and thumbs extended. For a moment there is silence, then a strange, soft music filled with trillings. Snow falls in gentle flakes.

SECOND SOLDIER: Stop that!

He seizes one arm and jerks it down. The music stops abruptly. A few last snowflakes settle on his head.

SECOND SOLDIER: That was not gold.

JAHI: Yet you saw.

SECOND SOLDIER: There's an old woman in my home village who can work the weather too. She's not as quick as you, I admit, but then she's a lot older, and feeble.

JAHI: Whoever she may be, she is not a thousandth part as old as I.

Enter the STATUE, moving slowly and as though blind.

JAHI: What is that thing?

SECOND SOLDIER: One of Father Inire's little pets. It can't hear you or make a sound. I'm not even sure it's alive.

JAHI: Why, neither am I, for all of that.

As the STATUE passes near her, she strokes its cheek with her free hand.

JAHI: Lover . . . lover . . . lover. Have you no greeting for me?

STATUE: E-e-e-y!

SECOND SOLDIER: What's this? Stop! Woman, you said you had no power while I held you.

JAHI: Behold my slave. Can you fight him? Go ahead—break your spear on that broad chest.

The STATUE kneels and kisses JAHI's foot.

SECOND SOLDIER: No, but I can outrun him.

He throws JAHI across his shoulder and runs. The door in the hill opens. He enters, and it slams shut behind him. The STATUE hammers it with mighty blows, but it does not yield. Tears stream down his face. At last he turns away and begins to dig with his hands.

GABRIEL: *(Offstage.)* Thus stone images keep faith with a departed day, Alone in the desert when man has fled away.

As the STATUE continues to dig, the stage grows dark. When the lights come up again, the AUTARCH is seated on his throne. He is alone on stage, but silhouettes projected on screens to either side of him indicate that he is surrounded by his court.

AUTARCH: Here I sit as though the lord of a hundred worlds. Yet not master even of this.

The tramp of marching men is heard offstage. There is a shouted order.

AUTARCH: Generalissimo!

Enter a PROPHET. He wears a goat skin and carries a staff whose head has been rudely carved into a strange symbol.

PROPHET: A hundred portents are abroad. At Incusus, a calf was dropped that had no head, but mouths in its knees. A woman of known propriety has dreamed she is with child by a dog, last night a shower of stars fell hissing onto the southern ice, and prophets walk abroad in the land.

AUTARCH: You yourself are a prophet.

PROPHET: The Autarch himself has seen them!

AUTARCH: My archivist, who is most learned in the history of this spot, once informed me that over a hundred prophets have been slain here—stoned, burned, torn by beasts, and drowned. Some have even been nailed like vermin to our doors. Now I would learn of you something of the coming of the New Sun, so long prophesied. How is it to come about? What does it mean? Speak, or we shall give the old archivist another mark for his tally, and train the pale moonflower to climb that staff.

PROPHET: I despair of satisfying you, but I shall attempt it.

AUTARCH: Do you not know?

PROPHET: I know. But I know you for a practical man, concerned with the affairs of this universe alone, who seldom looks higher than the stars.

AUTARCH: For thirty years I have prided myself on that.

PROPHET: Yet even you must know that cancer eats the heart of the old sun. At its center, matter falls in upon itself, as though there were there a pit without bottom, whose top surrounds it.

AUTARCH: My astronomers have long told me so.

PROPHET: Think on an apple rotten from the bud. Fair still without, until it collapses into foulness at last.

AUTARCH: Every man who finds himself still strong in the latter half of life has thought on that fruit.

PROPHET: So much then for the old sun. But what of its cancer? What know we of that, save that it deprives Urth of heat and light, and at last of life?

Sounds of struggle are heard offstage. There is a scream of pain, and a crash as though a large vase had been knocked from its pedestal.

AUTARCH: We will learn what that commotion is soon enough, Prophet. Continue.

PROPHET: We know it to be far more, for it is a discontinuity in our universe, a rent in its fabric bound by no law we know. From it nothing comes—all enters in, nought escapes. Yet from it anything may appear, for it alone of all the things we know is no slave to its own nature.

Enter NOD, *bleeding, prodded by pikes held offstage.*

AUTARCH: What is this miscreation?

PROPHET: The very proof of those portents I spoke to you. In future times, so it has long been said, the death of the old sun will destroy Urth. But from its grave will rise monsters, a new people, and the New Sun. Old Urth will flower then as a butterfly from its dry husk, and the New Urth shall be called Ushas.

AUTARCH: Yet all we know will be swept aside? This ancient house in which we stand? Yourself? Me?

NOD: I have no wisdom. Yet I heard a wise man—soon to be a relative of marriage—say not long ago that all that is for the best. We are but dreams, and dreams possess no life by their own right. See, I am wounded. *(Holds out his hand.)* When my wound heals, it will be gone. Should it with its bloody lips say it is sorry to heal? I am only trying to explain what another said, but that is what I think he meant.

Deep bells toll offstage.

AUTARCH: What's that? You, Prophet, go and see who's ordered that clamor, and why. *Exit* PROPHET

NOD: I feel sure your bells have begun the welcome of the New Sun. It is what I came to do myself. It is our custom, when an honored guest arrives, to roar and beat our chests, and pound the ground and the trunks of trees all about with gladness, and lift the greatest rocks we can, and send them down the gorges in honor of him. I will do that this morning, if you will set me free, and I feel sure Urth herself will join me. The very mountains will leap into the sea when the New Sun rises up today.

AUTARCH: And from where did you come? Tell me, and I'll release you.

NOD: Why, from my own country, to the east of Paradise.

AUTARCH: And where is that?

NOD *points to the east.*

AUTARCH: And where is Paradise? In the same direction?

NOD: Why, this is Paradise—we are in Paradise, or at least under it.

Enter the GENERALISSIMO, *who marches to the throne and salutes.*

GENERALISSIMO: Autarch, we have searched all the land above this House Absolute, as you ordered. The Contessa Carina has been found, and, her injuries not being serious, escorted to her apartments. We have also found the colossus you see before you, the bejeweled woman you described, and two merchants.

AUTARCH: What of the other two, the naked man and his wife?

GENERALISSIMO: There is no trace of them.

AUTARCH: Repeat your search, and this time look well.

GENERALISSIMO: *(Salutes.)* As my Autarch wills.

AUTARCH: And have the jeweled woman sent to me.

NOD *begins to walk offstage, but is stopped by pikes. The* GENERALISSIMO *draws his pistol.*

NOD: Am I not free to leave?

GENERALISSIMO: By no means!

NOD: *(To* AUTARCH.*)* I told you where my country lies. Just east of here.

GENERALISSIMO: More than your country lies. I know that area well.

AUTARCH: *(Fatigued.)* He has told the truth as he knows it. Perhaps the only truth there is.

NOD: Then I am free to go.

AUTARCH: I think that he whom you came to welcome will arrive whether you are free or not. Yet there is a chance—and such creatures as you cannot be allowed to roam abroad in any case. No, you are not free, nor ever again will be.

NOD *rushes from the stage, pursued by the* GENERALISSIMO.

Shots, screams, and crashes. The figures around the AUTARCH
fade. In the midst of the uproar, the bells toll again. NOD
REENTERS WITH A LASER BURN ACROSS ONE CHEEK. THE
AUTARCH *strikes him with his scepter; each blow produces an
explosion and a burst of sparks.* NOD *seizes the* AUTARCH *and is
about to dash him to the stage when two* DEMONS *disguised as
merchants enter, throw him down, and restore the* AUTARCH *to
his throne.*

AUTARCH: Thank you. You will be richly rewarded. I had
given up hope of being rescued by my guards, and I see I
thought rightly. May I ask who you are?

FIRST DEMON: Your guards are dead. That giant has smashed
their skulls against your walls and broken their spines
upon his knees.

SECOND DEMON: We are two traders merely. Your soldiers
took us up.

AUTARCH: Would that they were traders, and in their places I
had such soldiers as you! And yet, you are in appearance
so slight I would think you incapable of even ordinary
strength.

FIRST DEMON: *(bowing).* Our strength is inspired by the master
we serve.

SECOND DEMON: You will wonder why we—two commonplace traders in slaves—should have been found
wandering your grounds by night. The fact is that we
came to warn you. Our travels but lately took us to the
northern jungles, and there, in a temple older than man,
a shrine overgrown with rank vegetation until it seemed
hardly more than a leafy mound, we spoke to an ancient
shaman who foretold great peril to your realm.

FIRST DEMON: With that intelligence we hastened here to give
you the alarm before it should be too late, arriving at the
very wince of time.

AUTARCH: What must I do?

SECOND DEMON: This world that you and we treasure has now

been driven round the sun so often that the warp and woof of its space grow threadbare and fall as dust and feeble lint from the loom of time.

FIRST DEMON: The continents themselves are old as raddled women, long since stripped of beauty and fertility. The New Sun comes—

AUTARCH: I know!

FIRST DEMON: —and he will send them crashing into the sea like foundered ships.

SECOND DEMON: And from the sea lift new—glittering with gold, silver, iron, and copper. With diamonds, rubies, and turquoises, lands wallowing in the soil of a million millennia, so long ago washed down to the sea.

FIRST DEMON: To people these lands, a new race is prepared. The humankind you know will be shouldered aside even as the grass, that has prospered on the plain so long, yields to the plow and so gives way to wheat.

SECOND DEMON: But what if the seed were burned? What then? The tall man and the slight woman you met not long ago are such seed. Once it was hoped that it might be poisoned in the field, but she who was dispatched to accomplish it has lost sight of the seed now among the dead grass and broken clods, and for a few sleights of hand has been handed over to your Inquisitor for strict examination. Yet the seed might be burned still.

AUTARCH: The thought you suggest has already passed through my own mind.

FIRST & SECOND DEMON: (In chorus). Of course!

AUTARCH: But would the death of those two truly halt the coming of the New Sun?

FIRST DEMON: No. But would you wish it? The new lands shall be yours.

The screens grow radiant. Wooded hills and cities of spires appear. The AUTARCH *turns to face them. There is a pause. He draws a communicator from his robes.*

AUTARCH: May never the New Sun see what we do here. . . .
         Ships! Sweep over us with flame till all is sere.

As the two DEMONS *vanish,* NOD *sits up. The cities and hills
fade, and the screens show the image of the* AUTARCH *multiplied
many times. The stage goes dark.*

When the lights go up again, the INQUISITOR *sits at a high desk
in the center of the stage. His* FAMILIAR, *dressed as a torturer and
masked, stands beside the desk. To either side are various
instruments of torment.*

INQUISITOR: Bring in the woman said to be a witch, Brother.

FAMILIAR: The Contessa waits outside, and as she is of exalted
         blood, and a favorite of our sovereign's, I beg you see her
         first.

Enter the CONTESSA.

CONTESSA: I heard what was said, and as I could not think you
         would be deaf, Inquisitor, to such an appeal, I have
         made bold to come in at once. Do you think me bold for
         that?

INQUISITOR: You toy with words. But yes, I own I do.

CONTESSA: Then you think wrongly. Eight years since my
         girlhood have I abode in this House Absolute. When first
         the blood seeped from out my loins and my mother
         brought me here, she warned me never to come near
         these apartments of yours, where the blood has trickled
         from so many, caring nothing for the phases of the fickle
         moon. And never have I come till now, and now,
         trembling.

INQUISITOR: Here the good need have no fear. Yet even so, I
         think you grown bold by your own testimony.

CONTESSA: And am I good? Are you? Is he? My confessor
         would tell you I am not. What does yours tell you, or is
         he in fear? And is your familiar a better man than you?

FAMILIAR: I would not wish to be.

CONTESSA: No, I am not bold—nor safe here, as I know. It is
         fear that drives me to these grim chambers. They have

told you of the naked man who struck me. Has he been taken?

INQUISITOR: He has not been brought before me.

CONTESSA: Scarcely a watch ago some soldiers found me moaning in the garden, where my maid sought to comfort me. Because I feared to be outside by dark, they carried me to my own suite by way of that gallery called the Road of Air. Do you know it?

INQUISITOR: Well.

CONTESSA: Then you know too that it is everywhere overhung with windows, so that all the chambers and corridors that abut on it may receive the benefit. As we passed by, I saw in one the figure of a man, tall and clean-limbed, wide of shoulder and slender of waist.

INQUISITOR: There are many such men.

CONTESSA: So I thought. But in a little time, the same figure appeared in another window—and another. Then I appealed to the soldiers who carried me to fire upon it. They thought me mad and would not, but the party they sent to take that man returned with empty hands. Still he looked at me through the windows, and appeared to sway.

INQUISITOR: And you believe this man you saw to be the man who struck you?

CONTESSA: Worse. I fear it was not he, though it resembled him. Besides, he would be kind to me, I am sure, if only I treated his madness with respect. No, on this strange night, when we, who are the winter-killed stalks of man's old sprouting, find ourselves so mixed with next year's seed, I fear that he is something more we do not know.

INQUISITOR: That may be so, but you will not find him here, nor the man who struck you. *(To his FAMILIAR:)* Bring in the witch-woman, Brother.

FAMILIAR: Such are they all—though some are worse than others.

He exits and returns leading MESCHIANE *by a chain.*

INQUISITOR: It is alleged against you that you so charmed seven of the soldiers of our sovereign the Autarch that they betrayed their oath and turned their weapons upon their comrades and their officers. *(He rises, and lights a large candle at one side of his desk.)* I now most solemnly adjure you to confess this sin, and if you have so sinned, what power aided you to accomplish it, and the names of those who taught you to call upon that power.

MESCHIANE: The soldiers only saw I meant no harm, and were afraid for me. I—

FAMILIAR: Silence!

INQUISITOR: No weight is given to the protestations of the accused unless they are made under duress. My familiar will prepare you.

FAMILIAR *seizes* MESCHIANE *and straps her into one of the contrivances.*

CONTESSA: With so little time left to the world, I shall not waste it in watching this. Are you a friend to the naked man of the garden? I am going to seek him, and I will tell him what has become of you.

MESCHIANE: Oh, do! I hope that he will come before it is too late.

CONTESSA: And *I* hope he will accept me, in your stead. No doubt both hopes are equally forlorn, and we shall soon be sisters in despair.

Exit the CONTESSA.

INQUISITOR: I go too, to speak to those that were her rescuers. Prepare the subject, for I shall return shortly.

FAMILIAR: There is another, Inquisitor. Of similar crimes, but less, perhaps, in potency.

INQUISITOR: Why did you not tell me? I might have instructed both together. Bring her in.

FAMILIAR *exits and returns leading* JAHI. *The* INQUISITOR *searches among the papers on his desk.*

INQUISITOR: It is alleged against you that you so charmed seven
of the soldiers of our sovereign the Autarch that they
betrayed their oath and turned their weapons upon their
comrades and their officers. I now most solemnly adjure
you to confess this sin, and if you have so sinned, what
power aided you to accomplish it, and the names of those
who taught you to call upon that power.

JAHI: *(Proudly.)* I have done all you accuse me of and more
than you know. The power I dare not name lest this
upholstered rathole be blasted to bits. Who taught me?
Who teaches a child to call upon her father?

FAMILIAR: Her mother?

INQUISITOR: I would not know. Prepare her. I shall return
soon.

Exit the INQUISITOR.

MESCHIANE: They fought for you too? How sad that so many
had to die!

FAMILIAR: *(Locking JAHI in a contrivance on the other side of
the desk.)* He had your paper again. I'll point his error
out to him—diplomatically, you may be sure—when he
comes back.

JAHI: You charmed the soldiers? Then charm this fool, and free
us.

MESCHIANE: I have no chant of power, and I charmed but
seven of fifty.

Enter NOD, bound, driven by FIRST SOLDIER with a pike.

FAMILIAR: What's this?

FIRST SOLDIER: Why, such a prisoner as you've never had
before. He's killed a hundred men as we might puppies.
Have you shackles big enough for him?

FAMILIAR: I'll have to link several pairs together, but I'll
contrive something.

NOD: I am no man, but less and more—being born of the clay,
of Mother Gea, whose pets are the beasts. If your
dominion is over men, then you must let me go.

JAHI: We're not men either. Let us go too!

FIRST SOLDIER: *(Laughing.)* We can see you're not. I wasn't in
   doubt for a moment.

MESCHIANE: She's no woman. Don't let her trick you.

FAMILIAR: *(Snapping the last fetter on NOD.)* She won't.
   Believe me, the time of tricks is over.

FIRST SOLDIER: You'll have some fun, won't you, when I'm
   gone.

He reaches for JAHI, who spits like a cat.

FIRST SOLDIER: I don't suppose you'd be a good fellow and turn
   your back for a moment?

FAMILIAR: *(Preparing to torture MESCHIANE.)* If I were such a
   good fellow as that, I'd find myself broken on my own
   wheel soon enough. But if you wait here until my master
   the Inquisitor returns, you may find yourself lying beside
   her as you wish.

*FIRST SOLDIER hesitates, then realizes what is meant, and hurries
out.*

NOD: That woman will be the mother of my son-in-law. Do
   not harm her. *(He strains at his chains).*

JAHI: *(Stifling a yawn.)* I've been up all night, and though the
   spirit is as willing as ever, this flesh is ready for rest. Can't
   you hurry with her and get to me?

FAMILIAR: *(Not looking.)* There is no rest here.

JAHI: So? Well, it's not quite as homelike as I would expect.

*JAHI yawns again, and when she moves a hand to cover her
mouth, the shackle falls away.*

MESCHIANE: You have to hold her—don't you understand?
   The soil has no part in her, so iron has no power over
   her.

FAMILIAR: *(Still looking at MESCHIANE, whom he is torturing.)*
   She is held, never fear.

MESCHIANE: Giant! Can you free yourself? The world depends
   on it!

NOD strains at his bonds, but cannot break them.

JAHI: *(Walking out of her shackles.)* Yes! It is I who answer, because in the world of reality I am far larger than any of you. *(She walks around the desk and leans over the FAMILIAR's shoulder.)* How interesting! Crude, but interesting.

The FAMILIAR turns and gapes at her, and she flees, laughing. He runs clumsily after her, and a moment later returns crestfallen.

FAMILIAR: *(Panting.)* She's gone.

NOD: Yes. Free.

MESCHIANE: Free to pursue Meschia and ruin everything, as she did before.

FAMILIAR: You don't realize what this means. My master will return soon, and I am a dead man.

NOD: The world is dead. So she has told you.

MESCHIANE: Torturer, you have one chance yet—listen to me. You must free the giant as well.

FAMILIAR: And he will kill me and release you. I will consider it. At least it will be a quick death.

MESCHIANE: He hates Jahi, and though he isn't clever he knows her ways, and he is very strong. What's more, I can tell you an oath that he will never break. Give him the key to his shackles, then stand by me with your sword at my neck. Make him swear to find Jahi, return her here, and bind himself again.

The FAMILIAR hesitates.

MESCHIANE: You've nothing to lose. Your master doesn't even know he's supposed to be here. But if she's gone when he returns . . .

FAMILIAR: I'll do it! *(He detaches a key from the ring at his belt.)*

NOD: I swear as I hope to be linked by marriage to the family of Man, so that we giants may be called the Sons of the Father, that I will capture the succubus for you, and return her here, and hold her so that she shall not escape again, and bind myself as I am bound now.

FAMILIAR: Is that the oath?

MESCHIANE: Yes!

The FAMILIAR *throws the key to* NOD, *then draws his sword and holds it ready to strike* MESCHIANE.

FAMILIAR: Can he find her?

MESCHIANE: He *must* find her!

NOD: (*Unlocking himself.*) I will catch her. That body weakens, as she said. She may whip it far, but she will never learn that whipping will not do everything. (*Exits.*)

FAMILIAR: I must continue with you. I hope you understand. . . .

The FAMILIAR *tortures* MESCHIANE, *who screams.*

FAMILIAR: (*Sotto voce.*) How fair she is! I wish that we . . . were met when better things might be.

The stage darkens; JAHI's *running feet are heard. After a time, a faint light shows* NOD *loping through the corridors of the House Absolute. Moving images of urns, pictures, and furniture behind him show his progress.* JAHI *appears among them, and he exits stage right in pursuit.* JAHI *enters stage left, with* SECOND DEMON *walking in lockstep behind her.*

JAHI: Where can he have gone? The gardens are burned black. You have no flesh beyond a seeming—cannot you make yourself an owl and seek him out for me?

SECOND DEMON: (*Mocking.*) Who-o-o?

JAHI: Meschia! Wait until the Father hears how you have treated me, and betrayed all our efforts.

SECOND DEMON: From you? It was you who left Meschia, lured away by the woman. What will you say? "The woman tempted me?" We have done with that so long ago that no one remembers it save you and I, and now you have spoiled the lie by making it come true.

JAHI: (*Turning on him.*) You little foul sniveler! You scrabbler at windows!

SECOND DEMON: (*Jumping back.*) And now you are exiled to the land of Nod, east of Paradise.

NOD's *footfalls are heard offstage.* JAHI *hides behind a clepsydra, and* SECOND DEMON *produces a pike and stands with it in the attitude of a soldier as* NOD *enters.*

NOD: How long have you been standing there?

SECOND DEMON: *(Saluting.)* As long as you want, sieur.

NOD: What news is there?

SECOND DEMON: All you want, sieur. A giant as high as a steeple has killed the throne-guards, and the Autarch's missing. We've searched the gardens so often that if only we'd been carrying dung instead of spears, the daisies'd be as big as umbrellas. Ducks' clothes is down and hopes is up—so's the turnips. Tomorrow should be fair, warm, and bright . . . *(looks significantly toward the clepsydra)* and a woman with no clothes on has been running through the halls.

NOD: What is that thing?

SECOND DEMON: A water clock, sieur. See, you, knowing what time it is, can tell by that how much water's flowed.

NOD: *(Examining the clepsydra.)* There is nothing like this in my land. Do these puppets move by water?

SECOND DEMON: Not the big one, sieur.

JAHI *bolts offstage, pursued by* NOD, *but before he is fully out of sight of the audience, she dives between his legs, reentering. He continues off, giving her time to hide in a chest. Meanwhile,* SECOND DEMON *has disappeared.*

NOD: *(Reentering.)* Ho! Stop! *(Runs to opposite side of stage and returns.)* My fault! My fault! In the garden there— she passed close by me once. I could have reached out and crushed her like a cat—a worm—a mouse—a snake. *(Turns on audience.)* Don't laugh at me! I could kill you all! The whole poisoned race of you! Oh, to strew the valleys with your white bones! But I am done—I am done! And Meschaine, who trusted in me, is undone!

NOD *strikes the clepsydra, sending brass pans and water flying across the stage.*

NOD: What good is this gift of speech, except that I can curse

myself. Good mother of all the beasts, take it from me. I
would be as I was, and shout wordless among the hills.
Reason shows reason can only bring pain—how wise to
forget and be happy again!

NOD *seats himself on the chest in which* JAHI *hides, and buries his
face in his hands. As the lights dim, the chest begins to splinter
beneath his weight.*

When the lights come up again, the scene is once more the
INQUISITOR's *chamber.* MESCHIANE *is on the rack. The*
FAMILIAR *is turning the wheel. She screams.*

FAMILIAR: That made you feel better, didn't it? I told you it
would. Besides, it lets the neighbors know we're awake in
here. You wouldn't believe it, but this whole wing is full
of empty rooms and sinecures. Here the master and I do
our business still. We do it still, and that's why the
Commonwealth stands. And we want them to know it.

Enter the AUTARCH. *His robes are torn and stained with blood.*

AUTARCH: What place is this? *(He sits on the floor, his head in
his hands in an attitude reminiscent of* NOD's.*)*

FAMILIAR: What place? Why, the Chambers of Mercy, you
jackass. Can you come here without knowing where you
are?

AUTARCH: I have been so hunted through my house this night
that I might be anywhere. Bring me some wine—or
water, if you've no wine here—and bar the door.

FAMILIAR: We have claret, but no wine. And I can hardly bar
the door, since I expect my master back.

AUTARCH: *(More forcefully.)* Do as I tell you.

FAMILIAR: *(Very softly.)* You are drunk, friend. Go out.

AUTARCH: I am— What does it matter? The end is here. I am a
man neither worse nor better than you.

NOD's *heavy tread is heard in the distance.*

FAMILIAR: He has failed—I know it!

MESCHIANE: He has succeeded! He would not come back so
soon with empty hands. The world may yet be saved!

AUTARCH: What do you mean?

Enter NOD. *The madness he prayed for is upon him, but he drags* JAHI *behind him. The* FAMILIAR *runs forward with shackles.*

MESCHIANE: Someone must hold her, or she will escape as she
        did before.

The FAMILIAR *drapes chains on* NOD *and snaps closed the locks, then chains one of* NOD's *arms across his body in such a way that he holds* JAHI. NOD *tightens the grip.*

FAMILIAR: He's killing her! Let go, you great booby!

The FAMILIAR *snatches up the bar with which he has been tightening the rack and belabors* NOD *with it.* NOD *roars, tries to grasp him, and lets the unconscious* JAHI *slip down. The* FAMILIAR *seizes her by the foot and pulls her to where the* AUTARCH *sits.*

FAMILIAR: Here, you, you'll do.

He jerks the AUTARCH *erect and swiftly imprisons him in such a way that one hand is clamped about* JAHI's *wrist, then returns to torture* MESCHIANE. *Unseen behind him,* NOD *is freeing himself of his chains.*

XXV

The Attack on the Hierodules

THOUGH WE WERE outdoors, where sounds are so easily lost against the immensity of the sky, I could hear the clatter Baldanders made as he feigned to struggle with his bonds. There were conversations in the audience, and I could hear those as well—one about the play, which discovered in it significances I had never guessed and which Dr. Talos, I would say, had never intended; and another about some legal case that a speaker with the drawling intonation of an exultant seemed certain the Autarch was about to judge wrongly. As I turned the windlass of the rack, letting the pawl drop with a satisfying clack, I risked a sidelong look at those who watched us.

No more than ten chairs were in use, but lofty figures stood at the sides of the seating area, and behind it. There were a few women in court dresses much like the ones I had once seen in the House Azure, dresses with very low décolletages and full skirts that were often slit, or relieved with panels of lace. Their hair was simply dressed, but it was set off with flowers, jewels, or brilliantly luminous larvae.

Most of those in our audience seemed men, and more arrived momentarily. Many were as tall as or taller than Vodalus. They stood wrapped in their cloaks as though they were chilled by the soft spring air. Their faces were shadowed beneath broad-brimmed, low-crowned petasoses.

Baldanders's chains fell with a crash, and Dorcas shrieked to let me know he was free. I turned toward him, then cowered away, wrenching the nearest flambeau from its socket to fend him off. It guttered as the oil in its bowl nearly drowned the flame, sputtering to renewed life when the brimstone and mineral salts Dr. Talos had gummed around the rim took fire.

The giant was feigning madness, as his role required. His coarse hair hung about his eyes; and they, behind its screen, blazed so wildly I could see them despite it. His mouth hung slack, drooling spittle and showing his yellowed teeth. Arms twice the length of my own groped toward me.

What frightened me—and I was frightened, I admit, and wished heartily I had *Terminus Est* in my hands instead of the iron flambeau—was what I can only call the expression beneath the lack of expression on his face. It was there like the black water we sometimes glimpse moving beneath the ice when the river freezes. Baldanders had found a terrible joy now in being as he was; and when I faced him I realized for the first time that he was not so much feigning madness on the stage as feigning sanity and his dim humility off it. I wondered then how much he had influenced the writing of the play, though it may be only that Dr. Talos had (as he surely had) understood his patient better than I.

We were not, of course, to terrify the Autarch's courtiers as we had the country people. Baldanders would wrest the flambeau from me, pretend to break my back, and end the scene. He did not. Whether he was as mad as he pretended or was genuinely enraged at our growing audience, I cannot say. Perhaps both those explanations are correct.

However that might be, he jerked the flambeau from me and turned on them, flourishing it so the burning oil flew about him in a shower of fire. My sword, with which I had threatened Dorcas's head a few moments before, lay near my feet, and I stooped for it instinctively. By the time I had straightened up again, Baldanders was in the midst of the audience. The flambeau had gone out, and he swung it like a mace.

Someone fired a pistol. The bolt set his costume afire, but must have missed his body. Several exultants had drawn their swords, and someone—I could not see who—possessed that rarest of all weapons, a dream. It moved like tyrian smoke, but very much faster, and in an instant it had enveloped the giant. It seemed then that he stood wrapped in all that was past and much that had never been: a gray-haired woman sprouted from his side, a fishing boat hovered just over his head, and a cold wind whipped the flames that wreathed him.

Yet the visions, which are said to leave soldiers dazed and helpless, a burden to their cause, did not seem to affect Baldanders. He strode forward still, and the flambeau smashed clear a path for him.

Then, in the moment more that I watched (for I soon recovered enough self-command to flee that mad fight) I saw several figures throw aside their capes and—as it appeared—their faces too. Under those faces, which when they were no longer worn seemed of a tissue as insubstantial as that of the notules, were such monstrosities as I had not thought existence could support: a circular mouth rimmed with needle teeth; eyes that were themselves a thousand eyes, clustered like the scales of a pine cone; jaws like tongs. These things have remained in my memory as everything remains, and I have stared again at them in the dark watches of the night. I am very glad, when at last I rouse myself to turn my face toward the stars and moon-drenched clouds instead, that I could see only those nearest our footlights.

I have already said that I fled. But that slight delay, during which I picked up *Terminus Est* and stood observing Baldanders's mad attack, almost cost me dearly; by the time I turned to take Dorcas to safety, she was gone.

I ran then not so much from Baldanders's fury, or from the

cacogens in the audience, or from the Autarch's praetorians
(who I felt would surely arrive soon), but in pursuit of Dorcas.
Searching for her and calling her name as I went, I found
nothing but the groves and fountains and abrupt wells of that
endless garden; and at last, winded and with aching legs, I
slowed to a walk.

It is impossible for me to set down on paper all the bitterness I
felt then. To have found Dorcas and lost her so soon seemed
more than I could bear. Women believe—or at least often
pretend to believe—that all our tenderness for them springs from
desire; that we love them when we have not for a time enjoyed
them, and dismiss them when we are sated, or to express it more
precisely, exhausted. There is no truth in this idea, though it
may be made to appear true. When we are rigid with desire, we
are apt to pretend a great tenderness in the hope of satisfying that
desire; but at no other time are we in fact so liable to treat
women brutally, and so unlikely to feel any deep emotion but
one. As I wandered through the nighted gardens, I felt no
physical need for Dorcas (though I had not enjoyed her since we
had slept in the fortress of the dimarchi, beyond the Sanguinary
Fields) because I had poured out my manhood again and again
with Jolenta in the nenuphar boat. Yet if I had found Dorcas I
would have smothered her with kisses; and for Jolenta, whom I
had been prone to dislike, I now had conceived a certain
affection.

Neither Dorcas nor Jolenta appeared, nor did I see hastening
soldiers or even the revelers we had come to entertain. The
thiasus, it seemed clear, had been confined to some certain part
of the grounds; and I was now far from that part. Even now, I am
unsure how far the House Absolute extends. There are maps,
but they are incomplete and contradictory. There are no maps of
the Second House, and even Father Inire tells me that he has
long ago forgotten many of its mysteries. In wandering its narrow
corridors, I have seen no white wolves; but I have found stairs
leading to domes beneath the river, and hatches opening into

what appears to be untouched forest. (Some of these are marked above ground by ruinous, half-overgrown marble steles; some are not.) When I have closed such hatches and retreated regretfully into an artificial air still laced with the odors of vegetable growth and decay, I have often wondered whether some passage or other does not reach the Citadel. Old Ultan hinted once that his library stacks extended to the House Absolute. What is that but to say that the House Absolute extended to his library stacks? There are parts of the Second House that are not unlike the blind corridors in which I searched for Triskele; perhaps they are the same corridors, though if they are, I ran a greater risk than I then knew.

Whether these speculations of mine are rooted in fact or not, I had no notion of them at the time of which I write now. In my innocence I supposed that the borders of the House Absolute, which extended both in space and in time so much further than the uninformed would guess, could be strictly delimited; and that I was approaching, or would soon approach, or had already passed them. Thus I walked all that night, directing my course northward by the stars. And as I walked, I reviewed my life in just the way I have so often attempted to prevent myself from doing while I waited for sleep. Again Drotte and Roche and I swam in the clammy cistern beneath the Bell Keep; again I replaced Josephina's toy imp with the stolen frog; again I stretched forth my hand to grasp the haft of the ax that would have slain the great Vodalus and so saved a Thecla not yet imprisoned; again I saw the ribbon of crimson creep from under Thecla's door, Malrubius bending over me, Jonas vanishing into the infinity between dimensions. I played again with pebbles in the courtyard beside the fallen curtain wall, as Thecla dodged the hooves of my father's mounted guard.

Long after I had seen the last balustrade, I feared the soldiers of the Autarch; but after some time, when I had not so much as glimpsed a distant patrol, I grew contemptuous of them, believing their ineffectiveness to be a part of that general disorganization I had observed in the Commonwealth so often. With or without my help, Vodalus, I felt, would surely destroy such bunglers—indeed, could do so now, if he would only strike.

And yet the androgyne in the yellow robe, who had known Vodalus's password and received his message as if expecting it, was unquestionably the Autarch, the master of those soldiers and in fact of the entire Commonwealth insofar as it recognized a master. Thecla had seen him often; those memories of Thecla's were now my own, and it was he. If Vodalus had won already, why did he remain in hiding? Or was Vodalus merely a creature of the Autarch's? (If so, why did Vodalus refer to the Autarch as though he were a servitor?) I tried to persuade myself that everything that had passed in the chamber of the picture and the rest of the Second House had been a dream; but I knew it was not so, and the steel was gone.

Thinking of Vodalus reminded me of the Claw, which the Autarch himself had urged me to return to the order of priestesses called Pelerines. I drew it out. Its light was soft now, neither flashing as it had been in the mine of the man-apes nor dull as it had been when Jonas and I had examined it in the antechamber. Though it lay upon the palm of my hand, it seemed to me now a great pool of blue water, purer than the cistern, purer far than Gyoll, into which I might dive . . . though in doing so I should in some incomprehensible fashion be diving *up*. It was at once comforting and disquieting, and I pushed it into my boot top again and walked on.

Dawn found me on a narrow path that straggled through a forest more sumptuous in its decay even than that outside the Wall of Nessus. The cool fern arches I had seen there were absent here, but fleshy-fingered vines clung to the great mahoganies and rain-trees like hetaerae, turning their long limbs to clouds of floating green and lowering rich curtains spangled with flowers. Birds unknown to me called overhead, and once a monkey who might, save for his four hands, have been a wizened, red-bearded man in fur, spied on me from a fork as high as a spire. When I could walk no farther, I found a dry, well shaded spot between pillar-thick roots and wrapped myself in my cloak.

Often I have had to hunt down sleep as though it were the most elusive of chimeras, half legend and half air. Now it sprang upon me. I had no sooner closed my eyes than I faced the maddened giant again. This time I held *Terminus Est*, but she seemed no more than a wand. Instead of the stage, we stood upon a narrow parapet. To one side flamed the torches of an army. On the other a sheer drop terminated in a spreading lake that at once was and was not the azure pool of the Claw. Baldanders lifted his terrible flambeau, and I had somehow become the childish figure I had seen beneath the sea. The gigantic women, I felt, could not be far away. The mace crashed down.

It was broad afternoon, and flame-colored ants were making a caravan across my chest. After two or three watches spent in walking among the pale leaves of that noble yet doomed forest, I struck a broader path, and in another watch (when the shadows were lengthening) I halted, sniffed the air, and found that the odor I had detected was indeed the reek of smoke. I was wracked with hunger by that time, and I hurried forward.

XXVI

Parting

WHERE THE PATH crossed another, four people sat on the ground around a tiny fire. I recognized Jolenta first—her aura of beauty made the clearing seem a paradise. At almost the same moment, Dorcas recognized me and came running to kiss me, and I glimpsed Dr. Talos's fox-like face over Baldanders's massive shoulder.

The giant, whom I ought to have known at once, was changed almost out of recognition. His head was swathed in dirty bandages, and in place of the baggy black coat he had worn, his wide back was covered with a sticky ointment that resembled clay and smelled like stagnant water.

"Well met, well met," Dr. Talos called. "We've all been wondering what became of you." Baldanders indicated with a slight inclination of his head that it was actually Dorcas who had been wondering, which I think I might have guessed without the hint.

"I ran," I said. "So did Dorcas, I know. I'm surprised the rest of you weren't killed."

"We very nearly were," the doctor admitted, nodding.

Jolenta shrugged, making the simple movement seem an exquisite ceremony. "I ran away too." She cupped her huge breasts with her hands. "But I don't think I'm well suited to running, do you? Anyway, in the dark I soon bumped against an exultant who told me I would have to run no farther, that he would protect me. But then some spahis came—I would like to have their animals harnessed to my carriage someday, they were very fine—and they had with them a high official of the sort that cares nothing for women. I hoped then that I would be taken to the Autarch—whose pores outshine the stars themselves—the way it nearly happens in the play. But they made my exultant leave, and instead it was back to the theater where he," she gestured toward Baldanders, "and the doctor were. The doctor was putting salve on him, and the soldiers were going to kill us, although I could see they didn't really want to kill me. Then they let us go, and here we are."

Dr. Talos added, "We found Dorcas at daybreak. Or rather, she found us, and we have been traveling slowly toward the mountains ever since. Slowly, because ill though he is, Baldanders is the only one of us with the strength to carry our baggage, and though we have discarded much of it, there remain certain items we must keep."

I said I was surprised to hear Baldanders was merely ill, since I had been certain he was dead.

"Dr. Talos stopped him," Dorcas said. "Isn't that right, Doctor? That's how he was captured. It's surprising that both of them weren't killed."

"Yet as you see," Dr. Talos said, smiling, "we yet walk among the living. And though we are somewhat the worse for wear, we are rich. Show Severian our money, Baldanders."

Painfully, the giant shifted his position and took out a bulging leather purse. After looking at the doctor as though for additional instructions, he loosened the strings and poured into his huge hand a shower of new-minted chrisos.

Dr. Talos took one of the coins and held it up so it caught the light. "How long do you think a man from one of the fishing villages about Lake Diuturna would build walls for that?"

I said, "At least a year, I should imagine."

"Two! Every day, winter and summer, rain or shine, provided we dole it out in bits of copper, as we shall. We'll have fifty such men to help rebuild our home. Wait until you see it next!"

Baldanders added in his heavy voice, "If they will work."

The red-haired doctor whirled on him. "They'll work! I've learned something since last time, let me tell you!"

I interposed. "I assume that a part of that money is mine, and that a part belongs to these women—does it not?"

Dr. Talos relaxed. "Oh, yes. I had forgotten. The women have already had their shares. Half of this is yours. After all, we wouldn't have had it without you." He scooped the coins out of the giant's hand and began to create two stacks on the ground before him.

I supposed that he meant only that I had contributed to the success of his play, such as it was. But Dorcas, who must have sensed that something more lay behind the credit he had given me, asked, "Why do you say that, Doctor?"

The fox-face smiled. "Severian has friends in high places. I own I have thought so for some time—a torturer wandering the roads like a vagrant was a bit too much even for Baldanders to swallow, and I have, I fear, an excessively narrow throat."

"If I have such friends," I said, "I am unaware of them."

The stacks were level now, and the doctor pushed one toward me and the other back to the giant. "At first, when I found you abed with Baldanders, I thought you might have been sent to warn us against performing my play—in some respects it is, as you may have observed, at least in appearance critical of the Autarchy."

"Somewhat," Jolenta lisped sarcastically.

"Yet surely, to send a torturer from the Citadel to frighten a couple of strolling mountebanks would be an absurd overreaction. Then I realized that we, by the very fact that we were staging the play, served to conceal you. Few would suspect that a servant of the Autarch would associate himself with such an enterprise. I wrote in the Familiar's part so that we should hide you better by giving your habit a reason for existence."

"I know nothing of this," I said.

"Of course. I have no desire to force you to violate your trust. But as we were setting up our theater yesterday, a highly placed servant from the House Absolute—an agamite, I think, and they are always close to the ear of authority—came asking if our troupe was the one in which you performed, and if you were with us. You and Jolenta had absented yourselves, but I answered in the affirmative. He asked then how great a share you had of what we made, and when I told him, said that he was instructed to pay us now for the night's performance. Very fortunate that proved, since this great ninny went charging out into our audience."

It was one of the few times I saw Baldanders appear hurt by his physician's jibes. Though it clearly cost him pain to do so, he swung his big body about until he faced away from us.

Dorcas had told me that when I had slept in Dr. Talos's tent, I had slept alone. Now I sensed that the giant felt so; that for him the clearing held only himself and certain small animals, pets of whom he was tiring.

"He has paid for his rashness," I said. "He looks badly burned."

The doctor nodded. "Actually, Baldanders was fortunate. The Hierodules dialed down their beams and tried to turn him back instead of killing him. He lives now through their forbearance, and will regenerate."

Dorcas murmured, "Heal, you mean? I trust so. I feel more pity for him than I can say."

"Yours is a tender heart. Too tender, perhaps. But Baldanders is still growing, and growing children have great recuperative powers."

"Still growing?" I asked. "His hair is partly gray."

The doctor laughed. "Then perhaps he is growing grayer. But

now, dear friends," he rose and dusted his trousers, "now we have come, as some poet aptly puts it, to the place where men are pulled apart by their destinations. We had halted here, Severian, not only because we were fatigued, but because it is here that the route toward Thrax, where you are going, and that toward Lake Diuturna and our own country diverge. I was loath to pass this point, the last at which I had hopes of seeing you, without making a fair division of our gains—but that is accomplished now. Should you communicate again with your benefactors in the House Absolute, will you own that you have been equitably dealt with?"

The stack of chrisos was still on the ground before me. "There is a hundred times more here than I ever expected to receive," I said. "Yes. Certainly." I picked up the coins and put them into my sabretache.

A glance passed between Dorcas and Jolenta, and Dorcas said, "I am going to Thrax with Severian, if that is where Severian is going."

Jolenta held up a hand to the doctor, obviously expecting that he would help her to rise.

"Baldanders and I will be traveling alone," he said, "and we will walk all night. We will miss all of you, but the time of parting is upon us. Dorcas, my child, I am delighted that you will have a protector." (Jolenta's hand was by this time on his thigh.) "Come, Baldanders, we must be away."

The giant lumbered to his feet, and though he made no moan, I could see how much he suffered. His bandages were wet with mingled sweat and blood. I knew what I had to do, and said, "Baldanders and I must speak privately for a moment. Could I ask the rest of you to move off a hundred paces or so?"

The women began to do as I had asked, Dorcas walking down one path and Jolenta (whom Dorcas had helped up) down another; but Dr. Talos remained where he was until I repeated my request that he go.

"You wish me to leave as well? It's quite useless. Baldanders will tell me anything you tell him as soon as we are together again. Jolenta! Come here, dear."

"She is leaving at my request, just as I asked you to."

"Yes, but she's going the wrong way, and I cannot have it. Jolenta!"

"Doctor, I only wish to help your friend—or your slave, or whatever he is."

Quite unexpectedly, Baldanders's deep voice issued from beneath his swirl of bandages. "I am his master."

"Exactly so," said the doctor, as taking up the stack of chrisos he had pushed toward Baldanders, he dropped it into the giant's trousers pocket.

Jolenta had hobbled back to us with tears streaking her lovely face. "Doctor, can't I go with you?"

"Of course not," he said as coolly as if a child had asked for a second slice of cake. Jolenta collapsed at his feet.

I looked up at the giant. "Baldanders, I can help you. A friend of mine was burned as much as you are not long ago, and I was able to help him. But I won't do it while Dr. Talos and Jolenta look on. Will you come with me, only a short way, back down the path toward the House Absolute?"

Slowly, the giant's head swung from side to side.

"He knows the lenitive you offer," Dr. Talos said, laughing. "He himself has provided it to many, but he loves life too much."

"Life is what I offer—not death."

"Yes?" The doctor raised an eyebrow. "Where is your friend?"

The giant had picked up the handles of his barrow. "Baldanders," I said, "do you know who the Conciliator was?"

"That was long ago," Baldanders answered. "It does not matter." He started down the path Dorcas had not taken. Dr. Talos followed him for a few strides, with Jolenta clinging to his arm, then stopped.

"Severian, you have guarded a good many prisoners, according to what you've told me. If Baldanders were to give you another chrisos, would you hold this creature until we are well gone?"

I was still sick with the thought of the giant's pain and my own failure; but I managed to say, "As a member of the guild, I can accept commissions only from the legally constituted authorities."

"We will kill her then, when we are out of your sight."

"That is a matter between you and her," I said, and started· after Dorcas.

I had hardly caught up with her before we heard Jolenta's screams. Dorcas halted and grasped my hand more tightly, asking what the sound was; I told her of the doctor's threat.

"And you let her go?"

"I didn't believe he meant it."

As I said that, we had turned and were already retracing our way. We had not gone a dozen strides before the screams were succeeded by a silence so profound we could hear the rustling of a dying leaf. We hurried on; but by the time we reached the crossing, I felt certain we were too late, and so I was, if the truth be known, only hurrying because I knew Dorcas would be disappointed in me if I did not.

I was wrong in thinking Jolenta dead. As we rounded a turn in the path we saw her running toward us, her knees together as if her legs were hampered by her generous thighs, her arms crossed over her breasts to steady them. Her glorious red-gold hair fell across her eyes, and the thin organza shift she wore had been slashed to tatters. She fainted when Dorcas embraced her. "Those devils, they've beaten her," Dorcas said.

"A moment ago we were afraid they would kill her." I looked at the welts on the beautiful woman's back. "These are the marks of the doctor's cane, I think. She's lucky he didn't set Baldanders on her."

"But what can we do?"

"We can try this." I fished the Claw from my boot top and showed it to her. "Do you remember the thing we found in my sabretache? That you said was no true gem? This is what it was, and I seems to help injured people, sometimes. I wanted to use it on Baldanders, but he wouldn't let me."

I held the Claw over Jolenta's head, then ran it along the bruises on her back, but it flamed no brighter and she seemed no better. "It isn't working," I said. "I'll have to carry her."

"Put her over your shoulder, or you'll be holding her just where she's been hurt worst."

Dorcas carried *Terminus Est*, and I did as she suggested, finding Jolenta nearly as heavy as a man. For a long while we trudged thus beneath the pale green canopy of the leaves before Jolenta's eyes opened. Even then she could hardly walk or stand without help, however, or so much as comb back that extraordinary hair with her fingers to let us better see the tear-stained oval of her face.

"The doctor won't let me come with him," she said.

Dorcas nodded. "It seems not." She might have been talking to someone far younger than herself.

"I will be destroyed."

I asked why she said that, but she only shook her head. After a time she said, "May I go with you, Severian? I don't have any money. Baldanders took away what the doctor had given me." She shot a sidelong glance at Dorcas. "She has money too— more than I got. As much as the doctor gave you."

"He knows that," Dorcas said. "And he knows any money I have is his, if he wants it."

I changed the subject. "Perhaps both of you should know that I may not be going to Thrax, or at least, not directly. Not if I can discover the whereabouts of the order of Pelerines."

Jolenta looked at me as if I were mad. "I've heard they roam the whole world. Besides, they accept only women."

"I don't want to join them, only to find them. The last news I had was that they were on the way north. But if I can find out where they are, I'll have to go there—even if it means turning south again."

"I'm going where you go," Dorcas declared. "Not to Thrax."

"And I'm going nowhere," Jolenta sighed.

As soon as we no longer had to support Jolenta, Dorcas and I drew somewhat ahead of her. When we had been walking for some time, I turned to look back at her. She was no longer weeping, but I hardly recognized the beauty who had once accompanied Dr. Talos. She had held her head proudly, and even arrogantly. Her shoulders had been thrown back and her magnificent eyes had flashed like emeralds. Now her shoulders drooped with weariness and she looked at the ground.

"What was it you spoke of with the doctor and the giant?" Dorcas asked as we walked.

"I've already told you," I said.

"Once you called out so loudly that I could hear what you said. It was 'Do you know who the Conciliator was?' But I couldn't tell if you didn't know yourself, or were only seeking to discover if they knew."

"I know very little—nothing, really. I've seen pictures that are supposed to be of him, but they differ so much they can hardly be of the same man."

"There are legends."

"Most of them I've heard sound very foolish. I wish Jonas were here; he would take care of Jolenta, and he would know about the Conciliator. Jonas was the man we met at the Piteous Gate, the man who rode the merychip. For a time he was a good friend to me."

"Where is he now?"

"That's what Dr. Talos wanted to know. I don't know, and I don't wish to speak of it. Tell me about the Conciliator, if you want to talk."

No doubt it was foolish, but as soon as I mentioned that name, I felt the silence of the forest like a weight. The sighing of a little wind somewhere among the uppermost branches might have been the sigh from a sickbed; the pale green of the light-starved leaves suggested the pallid faces of starved children.

"No one knows much about him," Dorcas began, "and I probably know less than you do. I don't even remember now how I learned what I know. Anyway some people say he was hardly more than a boy. Some say he was not a human being at all—not a cacogen, but the thought, tangible to us, of some vast intelligence to whom our actuality is no more real than the paper theaters of the toy sellers. The story goes that he once took a dying woman by the hand and a star by the other, and from that time forward he had the power to reconcile the universe with humanity, and humanity with the universe, ending the old breach. He had a way of vanishing, then reappearing when everyone thought he was dead—reappearing sometimes after he had been buried. He might be encountered as an animal, speaking the human tongue, and he appeared to some pious woman or other in the form of roses."

I recalled my masking. "Holy Katharine, I suppose, at her execution."

"There are darker legends, too."

"Tell them to me."

"They frightened me," Dorcas said. "Now I don't even remember them. Doesn't that brown book you carry with you make any mention of him?"

I drew it out and saw that it did, and then, since I could not comfortably read while we walked, I thrust it back in my sabretache again, resolving to read that section when we camped, as we would have to soon.

XXVII

Toward Thrax

OUR PATH RAN through the stricken forest for as long as the light lasted; a watch after dark we reached the edge of a river smaller and swifter than Gyoll, where by moonlight we could see broad cane fields on the farther side waving in the night wind. Jolenta had been sobbing with weariness for some distance, and Dorcas and I agreed to halt. Since I would never have risked *Terminus Est's* honed blade on the heavy limbs of the forest trees, we would have had little firewood there; such dead branches as we had come across had been soaked with moisture and were already spongy with decay. The riverbank provided an abundance of twisted, weathered sticks, hard and light and dry.

We had broken a good many and laid our fire before I remembered I no longer had my striker, having left it with the Autarch, who must also, I felt certain, have been the "highly placed servant" who had filled Dr. Talos's hands with chrisos. Dorcas had flint, steel, and tinder among her scant baggage, however, and we were soon comforted by a roaring blaze. Jolenta was fearful of wild beasts, though I labored to explain to her how unlikely it was that the soldiers would permit anything dangerous to live in a forest that ran up to the gardens of the House Absolute.

For her sake we burned three thick brands at one end only, so that if need arose we could snatch them from the fire and threaten the creatures she dreaded.

No beasts came, our fire drove off the mosquitoes, and we lay upon our backs and watched the sparks mount into the air. Far higher, the lights of fliers passed to and fro, filling the sky for a moment or two with a ghostly false dawn as the ministers and generals of the Autarch returned to the House Absolute or went forth to war. Dorcas and I speculated about what they might think when they looked down—for only an instant as they were whirled away—and saw our scarlet star; and we decided that they must wonder about us much as we wondered about them, pondering who we might be, and where we went, and why. Dorcas sang a song for me, a song about a girl who wanders through a grove in spring, lonely for her friends of the year before, the fallen leaves.

Jolenta lay between our fire and the water, I suppose because she felt safer there. Dorcas and I were on the opposite side of the fire, not only because we wanted to be out of her sight as nearly as possible, but because Dorcas, as she told me, disliked the sight and sound of the cold, dark stream slipping by. "Like a worm," she said. "A big ebony snake that is not hungry now, but knows where we are and will eat us by and by. Aren't you afraid of snakes, Severian?"

Thecla had been; I felt the shade of her fear stir at the question and nodded.

"I've heard that in the hot forests of the north, the Autarch of All Serpents is Uroboros, the brother of Abaia, and that hunters who discover his burrow believe they have found a tunnel under the sea, and descending it enter his mouth and all unknowing climb down his throat, so that they are dead while they still believe themselves living; though there are others who say that Uroboros is only the great river there that flows to its own source, or the sea itself, that devours its own beginnings."

Dorcas edged closer as she recounted all this, and I put my arm about her, knowing that she wanted me to make love to her, though we could not be sure Jolenta was asleep on the other side of the fire. Indeed, from time to time she stirred, seeming because of her full hips, narrow waist, and billowing hair, to undulate like a serpent herself. Dorcas lifted her small, tragically clean face to mine, and I kissed her and felt her press herself to me, trembling with desire.

"I am so cold," she whispered.

She was naked, though I had not seen her undress. When I put my cloak about her, her skin felt flushed—as my own was— from the heat of the blaze. Her little hands slipped under my clothes, caressing me.

"So good," she said. "So smooth." And then (though we had coupled before), "Won't I be too small?", like a child.

When I woke, the moon (it was almost beyond belief that it was the same moon that had guided me through the gardens of the House Absolute) had nearly been overtaken by the mounting horizon of the west. Its berylline light streamed down the river, giving to every ripple the black shadow of a wave.

I felt uneasy without knowing why. Jolenta's fears of beasts no longer seemed so foolish as they had, and I got up and, after making certain she and Dorcas were unharmed, found more wood for our dying fire. I remembered the notules, which Jonas had told me were often sent forth by night, and the thing in the antechamber. Night birds sailed overhead—not only owls, such as we had in plenty nesting in the ruined towers of the Citadel, birds marked by their round heads and short, broad, silent wings, but birds of other kinds with two-forked and three-forked tails, birds that stooped to skim the water and twittered as they flew. Occasionally, moths vastly larger than any I had seen before passed from tree to tree. Their figured wings were as long as a man's arms, and they spoke among themselves as men do, but in voices almost too high for hearing.

After I had stirred the fire, made sure of my sword, and looked for a time on Dorcas's innocent face with its great, tender eyelashes closed in sleep, I lay down again to watch the birds voyage among the constellations and enter that world of memory that, no matter how sweet or how bitter it may be, is never wholly closed to me.

I sought to recall that celebration of Holy Katharine's day that fell the year after I became captain of apprentices; but the preparations for the feast were hardly begun before other memories came crowding unbidden around it. In our kitchen I lifted a cup of stolen wine to my lips—and found it had become a breast running with warm milk. It was my mother's breast then, and I could hardly contain my elation (which might have wiped the memory away) at having reached back at last to her, after so many fruitless attempts. My arms sought to clasp her, and I would, if only I could, have lifted my eyes to look into her face. My mother certainly, for the children the torturers take know no breasts. The grayness at the edge of my field of vision, then, was the metal of her cell wall. Soon she would be led away to scream in the Apparatus or gasp in Allowin's Necklace. I sought to hold her back, to mark the moment so I might return to it when I chose; she faded even as I tried to bind her to me, dissolving as mist does when the wind rises.

I was a child again . . . a girl . . . Thecla. I stood in a magnificent chamber whose windows were mirrors, mirrors that at once illuminated and reflected. Around me were beautiful women twice my height or more, in various stages of undress. The air was thick with scent. I was searching for someone, but as I looked at the painted faces of the tall women, lovely and indeed perfect, I began to doubt if I should know her. Tears rolled down my cheeks. Three women ran to me and I stared from one to another. As I did, their eyes narrowed to points of light, and a heart-shaped patch beside the lips of the nearest spread web-fingered wings.

"*Severian.*"

I sat up, uncertain of the point at which memory had become dream. This voice was sweet, yet very deep, and though I was conscious of having heard it before, I could not at once recall where. The moon was nearly behind the western horizon now, and our fire was dying a second death. Dorcas had thrown aside her ragged bedding, so that she slept with her sprite's body exposed to the night air. Seeing her thus, her pale skin rendered more pale still by the waning moonlight, save where the glow of the embers flushed it with red, I felt such desire as I had never known—not when I had clasped Agia to me on the Adamnian Steps, not when I had first seen Jolenta on Dr. Talos's stage, not even on the innumerable occasions when I had hastened to Thecla in her cell. Yet it was not Dorcas I desired; I had enjoyed her only a short time ago, and though I fully believed she loved me, I could not be certain she would have given herself so readily if she had not more than suspected I had entered Jolenta on the afternoon before the play, and if she had not believed Jolenta to be watching us across the fire.

Nor did I desire Jolenta, who lay upon her side and snored. Instead I wanted them both, and Thecla, and the nameless meretrix who had feigned to be Thecla in the House Azure, and her friend who had taken the part of Thea, the woman I had seen on the stair in the House Absolute. And Agia, Valeria, Morwenna, and a thousand more. I recalled the witches, their madness and their wild dancing in the Old Court on nights of rain; the cool, virginal beauty of the red-robed Pelerines.

"*Severian.*"

It was no dream. Sleepy birds, perched on branches at the margin of the forest, had stirred at the sound. I drew *Terminus Est* and let her blade catch the cold dawn light, so that whoever had spoken should know me armed.

All was quiet again—quieter now than it had ever been by night. I waited, turning my head slowly in my attempt to locate the one who had called my name, though I was conscious it would have been better if I could have appeared to know the correct direction already. Dorcas stirred and moaned, but neither she nor Jolenta woke; there was no other sound but the crackling of the fire, the dawn wind among the leaves, and the lapping water.

"Where are you?" I whispered, but there was no reply. A fish jumped with a silver splash, and all was silent again.

"Severian."

However deep, it was a woman's voice, throbbing with passion, moist with need; I remembered Agia and did not sheathe my sword.

"The sandbar . . ."

Though I feared it was merely a trick to make me turn my back on the trees, I let my eyes search the river until I saw it, about two hundred paces from our fire.

"Come to me."

It was no trick, or at least not the trick I had at first feared. It was from downstream that the voice spoke.

"Come. Please. I cannot hear you where you stand."

I said, "I did not speak," but there was no reply. I waited, reluctant to leave Dorcas and Jolenta alone.

"Please. When the sun reaches this water, I must go. There may be no other chance."

The little river was wider at the sandbar than below or above it, and I could walk upon the yellow sand itself, dryshod, nearly to the center. To my left the greenish water gradually narrowed and deepened. To my right lay a deep pool perhaps twenty paces wide, from which water flowed swiftly yet smoothly. I stood on the sand with *Terminus Est* gripped in both hands, her square point buried between my feet. "I'm here," I said. "Where are you? Can you hear me now?"

As though the river itself were replying, three fish leaped at once, then leaped again, making a series of soft explosions on the surface. A moccasin, his brown back marked with linked rings of gold and black, glided up almost at my boot toes, turned as if to menace the jumping fish and hissed, then entered the ford on the upper side of the bar and swam away in long undulations. Through the body, he had been as thick as my forearm.

"*Do not fear. Look. See me. Know that I will not harm you.*"

Green though the water had been, it grew greener still. A thousand jade tentacles writhed there, never breaking the surface. As I watched, too fascinated to be afraid, a disc of white three paces across appeared among them, rising slowly toward the surface.

It was not until it was within a few spans of the ripples that I understood what it was—and then only because it opened eyes. A face looked through the water at me, the face of a woman who might have dandled Baldanders like a toy. Her eyes were scarlet, and her mouth was bordered by full lips so darkly crimson I had not at first thought them lips at all. Behind them stood an army of pointed teeth; the green tendrils that framed her face were her floating hair.

"*I have come for you, Severian,*" she said. "*No, you are not dreaming.*"

XXVIII

The Odalisque of Abaia

I SAID," ONCE before I dreamed of you." Dimly, I could see her naked body in the water, immense and gleaming.

"We watched the giant, and so found you. Alas, we lost sight of you too soon, when you and he separated. You believed then that you were hated, and did not know how much you were loved. The seas of the whole world shook with our mourning for you, and the waves wept salt tears and threw themselves despairing upon the rocks."

"And what is it you want of me?"

"Only your love. Only your love."

Her right hand came to the surface as she spoke, and floated there like a raft of five white logs. Here, truly, was the hand of the ogre, whose fingertip held the map of his domain.

"Am I not fair? Where have you beheld skin clearer than mine, or redder lips?"

"You are breathtaking," I said truthfully. "But may I ask why you were observing Baldanders when I met him? And why you were not observing me, though it seems you wished to?"

"We watch the giant because he grows. In that he is like us, and like our father-husband, Abaia. Eventually he must come to

the water, when the land can bear him no longer. But you may come now, if you will. You will breathe—by our gift—as easily as you breathe the thin, weak wind here, and whenever you wish you shall return to the land and take up your crown. This river Cephissus flows to Gyoll, and Gyoll to the peaceful sea. There you may ride dolphin-back through current-swept fields of coral and pearl. My sisters and I will show you the forgotten cities built of old, where a hundred trapped generations of your kin bred and died when they had been forgotten by you above."

"I have no crown to take up," I said. "You mistake me for someone else."

"All of us will be yours there, in the red and white parks where the lionfish school."

As the undine spoke, she slowly lifted her chin, allowing her head to fall back until the whole plane of face lay at an equal depth, and only just submerged. Her white throat followed, and crimson-tipped breasts broke the surface, so that little lapping waves caressed their sides. A thousand bubbles sparkled in the water. In the space of a few breaths she lay at full length upon the current, forty cubits at least from alabaster feet to twining hair.

No one who reads this, perhaps, will understand how I could be drawn to so monstrous a thing; yet I wanted to believe her, to go with her, as a drowning man wants to gasp air. If I had fully credited her promises, I would have plunged into the pool at that moment, forgetting everything else.

"You have a crown, though you know not of it yet. Do you think that we, who swim in so many waters—even between the stars—are confined to a single instant? We have seen what you will become, and what you have been. Only yesterday you lay in the hollow of my palm, and I lifted you above the clotted weed lest you die in Gyoll, saving you for this moment."

"Give me the power to breathe water," I said, "and let me test it on the other side of the sandbar. If I find you have told the truth, I will go with you."

I watched those huge lips part. I cannot say how loudly she spoke in the river that I should hear her where I stood in air; but again fish leaped at her words.

"*It is not so easily done as that. You must come with me, trusting, though it is only a moment. Come.*"

She extended her hand toward me, and at the same moment I heard Dorcas's agonized voice crying for help.

I turned to run to her. Yet if the undine had waited, I think I might have turned back. She did not. The river itself seemed to heave from its bed with a roar like breaking surf. It was as though a lake had been flung at my head, and it struck me like a stone and tumbled me in its wash like a stick. A moment later, when it receded, I found myself far up the bank, soaked and bruised and swordless. Fifty paces away the undine's white body rose half out of the river. Without the support of the water her flesh sagged on bones that seemed ready to snap under its weight, and her hair hung lank to the soaking sand. Even as I watched, water mingled with blood ran from her nostrils.

I fled, and by the time I reached Dorcas at our fire, the undine was gone save for a swirl of silt that darkened the river below the sandbar.

Dorcas's face was nearly as white. "What was that?" she whispered. "Where were you?"

"You saw her then. I was afraid . . ."

"How horrible." Dorcas had thrown herself into my arms, pressing her body to mine. "Horrible."

"That wasn't why you called, though, was it? You couldn't have seen her from here until she rose out of the pool."

Dorcas pointed mutely toward the farther side of the fire, and I saw the ground was soaked with blood where Jolenta lay.

There were two narrow cuts in her left wrist, each about the length of my thumb; and though I touched them with the Claw, it seemed the blood that welled from them would not clot. When we had soaked several bandages torn from Dorcas's scant store of clothing, I boiled thread and needle in a little pan she had and sewed the edges of the wounds shut. Through all this Jolenta seemed less than half conscious; from time to time her eyes opened, but they closed again almost immediately, and there was no recognition in them. She spoke only once, saying, "Now you see that he, whom you have esteemed your divinity, would countenance and advise all I have proposed to you. Before the New Sun rises, let us make a new beginning." At the time, I did not recognize it as one of her lines.

When her wound no longer bled, and we had shifted her to clean ground and washed her, I went back to the place where I had found myself when the water receded, and after some searching discovered *Terminus Est* with only her pommel and two fingers' width of hilt protruding from the wet sand.

I cleaned and oiled the blade, and Dorcas and I discussed what we should do. I told her of my dream, the night before I met Baldanders and Dr. Talos, and then about hearing the undine's voice while she and Jolenta slept, and what she had said.

"Is she still there, do you think? You were down there when you found your sword. Could you have seen her through the water if she were near the bottom?"

I shook my head. "I don't believe she is. She injured herself in some way when she tried to leave the river to stop me, and from the pallor of her skin, I doubt she would stay long in any water shallower than Gyoll's under the sun of a clear day. But no, if she had been there I don't think I would have seen her—the water was too roiled."

Dorcas, who had never looked more charming than at this moment, sitting on the ground with her chin propped on one knee, was silent for a time, and seemed to watch the eastern clouds, dyed cerise and flame by the eternal mysterious hope of dawn. At length she said, "She must have wanted you very badly."

"To have come up out of the water like that? I think she must have been on land before she had become so large, and she forgot for a moment at least that she could no longer do it."

"But before that she swam up filthy Gyoll, and then up this narrow little river. She must have been hoping to seize you when we crossed, but she found she could not get above the sandbar, and so she called you down. Altogether, it can't have been a pleasant trip for someone accustomed to swimming between the stars."

"You believe her, then?"

"When I was with Dr. Talos and you were gone, he and Jolenta used to tell me what a simple-minded person I was for believing people we met on the road, and things that Baldanders said, and things they said themselves, too. Just the same, I think that even the people who are called liars tell the truth much more often than they lie. It's so much easier! If that story about saving you wasn't true, why tell it? It could only frighten you when you thought back on it. And if she *doesn't* swim between stars, what a useless thing to say. Something's bothering you, though. I can see it. What is it?"

I did not want to describe my meeting with the Autarch in detail, so I said, "Not long ago I saw a picture—in a book—of a being who lives in the gulf. She was winged. Not like birds' wings, but enormous continuous planes of thin, pigmented material. Wings that could beat against the starlight."

Dorcas looked interested. "Is it in your brown book?"

"No, another book. I don't have it here."

"Just the same, it reminds me that we were going to see what your brown book has to say about the Conciliator. Do you still have it?"

I did, and I drew it out. It was damp from my wetting, so I opened it and laid it where the sun would strike its leaves, and the breezes that had sprung up as Urth's face looked on his again would play over them. After that, the pages turned gently as we talked, so that pictures of men and women and monsters took my eye between our words, and thus engraved themselves on my mind, so that they are there yet. Occasionally too, phrases, and even short passages, glowed and faded as the light caught, then released, the sheen of the metallic ink: "soulless warrior!" "lucid yellow," "by noyade." Later: "These times are the ancient times, when the world is ancient." And: "Hell has no limits, nor is circumscribed; for where we are is Hell, and where Hell is, there we must be."

"You don't want to read it now?" Dorcas asked.

"No. I want to hear what happened to Jolenta."

"I don't know. I was sleeping and dreaming of . . . the kind of thing I always do. And I went into a toy shop. There were shelves along the wall with dolls on them, and a well in the center of the floor with dolls sitting on the coping. I remember thinking that my baby was too young for dolls, but they were so pretty, and I had not had one since I was a little girl, so I would buy one and keep it for the baby, and meanwhile I could take it out sometimes and look at it, and perhaps make it stand before the mirror in my room. I pointed to the most beautiful one, which was one of those on the coping, and when the shopman picked it up fo rme I saw it was Jolenta, and it slipped from his hands. I saw it falling down very far, toward the black water. Then I woke up. Naturally I looked to see if she was all right . . ."

"And you found her bleeding?"

Dorcas nodded, her pale golden hair glinting in the light. "So I called for you—twice—and then I saw you down by the sandbar, and that thing came out of the water after you."

"There's no reason for you to look so pale," I told her. "Jolenta was bitten by an animal, that's clear. I've no idea of what kind, but judging from the bite it was a fairly small one, and no more to be feared than any other little animal with sharp teeth and a bad disposition."

"Severian, I remember being told that there were blood bats farther north. When I was just a child, someone used to frighten me by telling me about them. And then when I was older, once a common bat got into the house. Somebody killed it, and I asked my father if it were a blood bat, and if there were really any such things. He said there were, but they lived in the north, in the steaming forests at the center of the world. They bit sleeping people and grazing animals by night, and their spittle was poisoned so that the wounds of their teeth bled on."

Dorcas paused, looking up into the trees. "My father said that the city had been creeping northward along the river for all of history, having begun as an autochthon village where Gyoll joins the sea, and how terrible it would be when it entered the region where the blood bats fly and they could roost in the derelict buildings. It must be terrible already for the people of the House Absolute. We cannot have walked so very far from there."

"The Autarch has my sympathy," I said. "But I don't think I have ever heard you talk so much about your past life before. Do you remember your father now, and the house where the bat was killed?"

She stood; though she tried to look brave, I could see that she was trembling. "I remember more each morning, after my dreams. But, Severian, we must go now. Jolenta will be weak. She must have food, and clean water to drink. We can't stay here."

I was ravenously hungry myself. I put the brown book back into my sabretache and sheathed *Terminus Est*'s freshly oiled blade. Dorcas packed her little bundle of belongings.

Then we set out, fording the river well above the sandbar. Jolenta was unable to walk alone; we had to support her on either side. Her face was drawn, and though she had regained consciousness when we lifted her, she seldom spoke. When she did it was only a word or two. For the first time, I noticed how thin her lips were, and now the lower lip had lost its firmness and hung away from her teeth, showing the livid gums. It seemed to me that her entire body, yesterday so opulent, had softened like wax, so that instead of appearing (as she once had) a woman to Dorcas's child, she seemed a flower too long blown, the very end of summer to Dorcas's spring.

As we walked thus along a narrow, dusty track with sugarcane already higher than my head to either side, I found myself thinking over and over of how I had desired her in the short time I had known her. Memory, so perfect and vivid as to be more compelling than any opiate, showed me the woman as I had believed I had seen her first, when Dorcas and I had come around a grove of trees by night to find Dr. Talos's stage gleaming with lights in a pasture. How strange it had seemed to see her by daylight as perfect as she had appeared in the flattering glow of the flambeaux the night before, when we set off northward on the most glorious morning I can remember.

Love and desire are said to be no more than cousins, and I had found it so until I walked with Jolenta's flaccid arm about my neck. But it is not really true. Rather, the love of women was the dark side of a feminine ideal I had nourished for myself on dreams of Valeria and Thecla and Agia, of Dorcas and Jolenta and Vodalus's leman of the heart-shaped face and cooing voice, the woman I now knew to be Thecla's half-sister Thea. So that as we trudged between the walls of cane, when desire had fled and I could only look at Jolenta with pity, I found that though I had believed I cared only for her importunate, rose-flushed flesh and the awkward grace of her movements, I loved her.

XXIX

The Herdsmen

FOR MOST OF the morning we walked through the cane, meeting no one. Jolenta grew neither stronger nor weaker, so far as I could judge; but it seemed to me that hunger, and the fatigue of supporting her, and the pitiless glare of the sun were telling upon me, for twice or thrice, when I glimpsed her from the corner of an eye, it seemed that I was not seeing Jolenta at all, but someone else, a woman I recalled but could not identify. If I turned my head to look at her, this impression (which was always very slight) vanished altogether.

So we walked, talking little. It was the only time since I had received her from Master Palaemon that *Terminus Est* seemed burdensome to me. My shoulder grew raw under the baldric.

I cut cane for us, and we chewed it for the sweet juice. Jolenta was always thirsty, and since she could not walk unless we aided her, and could not hold her stalk of cane when we did, we were forced to stop often. It was strange to see those long legs, so beautifully molded, with their slender ankles and ripe thighs, so useless.

In a day we reached the end of the cane and emerged onto the edge of the true pampa, the sea of grass. Here there were still a few trees, though they were so widely scattered that each was in sight of no more than two or three others. To each of these trees the body of some beast of prey was lashed with rawhide, its forepaws outspread like arms. They were mostly the spotted tigers common in that part of the country; but I saw atroxes too, with hair like man's, and sword-toothed smilodons. Most were hardly more than bones, but some lived and made those sounds that, as the people believe, serve to frighten other tigers, atroxes, and smilodons which, if they were not so frightened, would prey upon the cattle.

These cattle represented a far greater danger to us than the cats did. The herd bulls will charge anything that comes near them, and we were forced to give each herd we came across as much room as would prevent their short-sighted eyes from seeing us, and to move downwind of each. On these occasions, I was forced to let Dorcas prop Jolenta's weight as best she could, so I could walk ahead of them and somewhat nearer the animals. Once I had to leap aside and strike off the head of a bull as it charged. We built a fire of dry grass and roasted some of the meat.

The next time I recalled the Claw, and the way in which it had ended the attack of the man-apes. I drew it out, and the fierce black bull trotted to me and nuzzled my hand. We put Jolenta on his back with Dorcas to hold her on, and I walked beside his head, holding the gem where he could see its blue light.

A living smilodon was bound to the next tree we reached, which was nearly the last we saw, and I was afraid he would frighten the bull. Yet when we passed him I seemed to feel his eyes upon my back, yellow eyes as large as pigeon's eggs. My own tongue was swollen with his thirst. I gave Dorcas the gem to hold and went back and cut him down, thinking all the while that he would surely attack me. He fell to the ground too weak to stand, and I, who had no water to give him, could only walk away.

A little after noon, I noticed a carrion bird circling high above us. It is said they smell death, and I remembered that once or twice when the journeymen were very busy in the examination room, it was necessary for us apprentices to turn out to throw stones at those who settled on the ruined curtain wall, lest they give the Citadel a reputation more evil than it already possessed. The thought that Jolenta might die was repugnant to me, and I would have given much for a bow, so that I might perhaps pick the bird out of the air; but I had nothing of the kind, and could only wish.

After an interminable time, this first bird was joined by two much smaller ones, and from their bright head color, occasionally visible even from so far below, I knew them to be Cathartidae. Thus the first, whose wings had three times the spread of theirs, was a mountain teratornis, the breed that is said to attack climbers, raking their faces with poisoned talons and striking them with the elbows of its great pinions until they fall to their deaths. From time to time the other two approached it too closely, and it turned upon them. When that occurred, we sometimes heard a shrill cry come drifting down from the ramparts of their castle of air. Once, in a macabre mood, I gestured for the birds to join us. All three dove, and I brandished my sword at them and gestured no more.

When the western horizon had climbed nearly to the sun, we reached a low house, scarcely more than a hut, built of turf. A wiry man in leather leggings sat on a bench before it, drinking maté and pretending to watch the colors in the clouds. In truth, he must have seen us long before we saw him, for he was small and brown and blended well with his small, brown home, while we had been silhouetted against the sky.

I thrust away the Claw when I saw this herdsman, though I was not certain what the bull would do when it was no longer in his sight. In the event he did nothing, plodding ahead with the two women on his back as before. When we reached the sod house I lifted them down, and he raised his muzzle and sniffed the wind, then looked at me from one eye. I waved toward the undulating grass, both to show him I had no more need of him and to let him see that my hand was empty. He wheeled and trotted away.

The herdsman took his pewter straw from between his lips. "That was an ox," he said.

I nodded. "We needed him to carry this poor woman, who is ill, and so we borrowed him. Is he yours? We hoped you wouldn't mind, and after all, we did him no harm."

"No, no." The herdsman made a vaguely deprecating gesture. "I only asked because when I first saw you I thought he was a destrier. My eyes are not as good as they once were." He told us how good they once were, which was very good indeed. "But as you say, it was an ox."

This time Dorcas and I nodded together.

"You see what it is to become old. I would have licked the blade of this knife," he slapped the metal hilt that protruded above his broad belt, "and pointed it to the sun to swear that I saw something between the ox's legs. But if I were not such a fool I would know that no one can ride the bulls of the pampas. The red panther does it, but then he holds on with his claws, and sometimes he dies even so. No doubt it was an udder the ox inherited from his mother. I knew her, and she had one."

I said I was a city man, and very ignorant of everything that concerned cattle.

"Ah," he said, and sucked his maté. "I am a man more ignorant than you. Everyone around here but me is one ignorant eclectic. You know these people they call eclectics? They don't know anything—how can a man learn with neighbors like that?"

Dorcas said, "Please, won't you let us take this woman inside where she can lie down? I am afraid she's dying."

"I told you I don't know nothing. You should ask this man here—he can lead an ox—I almost said a bull—like a dog."

"But he can't help her! Only you can."

The herdsman cocked an eye at me, and I understood that he had established to his own satisfaction that it was I, and not Dorcas, who had tamed the bull. "I'm very sorry for your friend," he said, "who I can see must have been a lovely woman once. But even though I've been sitting here cracking jokes with you, I have a friend of my own, and right now he's lying inside. You're afraid your friend is dying. I know mine is, and I'd like to let him go with no one to bother him."

"We understand, but we won't disturb him. We may even be able to help him."

The herdsman looked from Dorcas to me and back again. "You are strange people—what do I know? No more than one of those ignorant eclectics. Come in, then. But be quiet, and remember you're my guests."

He rose and opened the door, which was so low I had to stoop to get through it. A single room constituted the house, and it was dark and smelled of smoke. A man much younger and, I thought, much taller than our host lay on a pallet before the fire. He had the same brown skin, but there was no blood beneath the pigment; his cheeks and forehead might have been smeared with dirt. There was no bedding beyond that on which the sick man lay, but we spread Dorcas's ragged blanket on the earthen floor and laid Jolenta on it. For a moment her eyes opened. There was no consciousness in them, and their once clear green had faded like shoddy cloth left in the sun.

Our host shook his head and whispered, "She won't last longer than that ignorant eclectic Manahen. Maybe not as long."

"She needs water," Dorcas told him.

"In back, in the catch barrel. I'll get it."

When I heard the door shut behind him, I drew out the Claw. This time it flashed with such searing, cyaneous flame that I feared it would penetrate the walls. The young man who lay on the pallet breathed deeply, then released his breath with a sigh. I put the Claw away again at once.

"It hasn't helped her," Dorcas said.

"Perhaps the water will. She's lost a great deal of blood."

Dorcas reached down to smooth Jolenta's hair. It must have

been falling out, as the hair of old women and of people who
suffer high fevers often does; so much clung to Dorcas's damp
palm that I could see it plainly despite the dimness of the light.
"I think she's always been ill," Dorcas whispered. "Ever since
I've known her. Dr. Talos gave her something that made her
better for a time, but now he has driven her away—she used to
be very demanding, and he has had his revenge."

"I can't believe he meant it to be as severe as this."

"Neither can I, really. Severian, listen; he and Baldanders will
surely stop to perform and spy out the land. We might be able to
find them."

"To spy?" I must have looked as surprised as I felt.

"At least, it always seemed to me that they wandered as much
to discover what passed in the world as to get money, and once
Dr. Talos as much as admitted that to me, though I never
learned just what they were looking for."

The herdsman came in with a gourd of water. I lifted Jolenta
to a sitting position, and Dorcas held it to her lips. It spilled and
soaked Jolenta's tattered shift, but some of it went down her
throat as well, and when the gourd was empty and the herdsman
filled it again, she was able to swallow. I asked him if he knew
where Lake Diuturna lay.

"I am only an ignorant man," he said. "I have never ridden so
far. I have been told that way," pointing, "to the north and the
west. Do you wish to go there?"

I nodded.

"You must pass through a bad place, then. Perhaps through
many bad places, but surely through the stone town."

"There is a city near here, then?"

"There is a city, yes, but no people. The ignorant eclectics
who live near there believe that no matter which way a man
goes, the stone town moves itself to wait in his path." The
herdsman laughed softly, then sobered. "That is not so. But the
stone town bends the way a man's mount walks, so he finds it

before him when he thinks he will go around it. You understand? I think you do not."

I remembered the Botanic Gardens and nodded. "I understand. Go on."

"But if you are going north and west, you must pass through the stone town anyway. It will not even have to bend the way you walk. Some find nothing there but the fallen walls. I have heard that some find treasures. Some come back with fresh stories and some do not come back. Neither of these women are virgins, I think."

Dorcas gasped. I shook my head.

"That is well. It is they who most often do not return. Try to pass through by day, with the sun over the right shoulder by morning and later in the left eye. If night comes, do not stop or turn to one side. Keep the stars of the Ihuaivulu before you when they first grow bright."

I nodded and was about to ask for further information when the sick man opened his eyes and sat up. His blanket fell away, and I saw there was a bloodstained bandage over his chest. He started, stared at me, and shouted something. Instantly, I felt the cold blade of the herdsman's knife at my throat. "He won't harm you," he told the sick man. He used the same dialect, but because he spoke more slowly I was able to understand him. "I don't believe he knows who you are."

"I tell you, Father, it is the new lictor of Thrax. They have sent for one, and the clavigers say he's coming. Kill him! He'll kill all of them who haven't died already."

I was astounded to hear him mention Thrax, which was still so far away, and wanted to question him about it. I believe I could have talked to him and his father and made some sort of peace, but Dorcas struck the older man on the ear with the gourd—a futile, woman's blow that did nothing more than smash the gourd and cause little pain. He slashed at her with his crooked, two-edged knife, but I caught his arm and broke it, then broke the knife too under the heel of my boot. His son, Manahen, tried to rise; but if the Claw had restored his life it had, at least, not made him strong, and Dorcas pushed him down on his pallet again.

"We will starve," the herdsman said. His brown face was twisted by the effort he made not to cry out.

"You cared for your son," I told him. "Soon he will be well enough to care for you. What was it he did?"

Neither man would tell.

I set the bone and splinted it, and Dorcas and I ate and slept outside that night after telling father and son that we woud kill them if we so much as heard the door open, or if any harm was done Jolenta. In the morning, while they were still asleep, I touched the herdsman's broken arm with the Claw. There was a destrier picketed not far from the house, and riding him I was able to catch another for Dorcas and Jolenta. As I led it back, I noticed the sod walls had turned green overnight.

X X X

The Badger Again

DESPITE WHAT THE herdsman had told me, I hoped for some place like Saltus, where we might find pure water and a few aes would buy us food and rest. What we found instead was scarcely the remnant of a town. Coarse grass grew between the enduring stones that had been its pavements, so that from a distance it seemed hardly different from the surrounding pampa. Fallen columns lay among this grass like the trunks of trees in a forest devastated by some frenzied storm; a few others still stood, broken and achingly white beneath the sun. Lizards with bright, black eyes and serrated backs lay frozen in the light. The buildings were mere hillocks from which more grass sprouted in soil caught from the wind.

There was no reason I could see to turn from our course, and so we continued northwest, urging our destriers forward. For the first time I became conscious of the mountains ahead. Framed in a ruined arch, they were no more than a faint line of blue on the horizon; yet they were a presence, as the mad clients on the third level of our oubliette were a presence though they were never taken up a single step, or even out of their cells. Lake Diuturna lay somewhere in those mountains. So did Thrax; the Pelerines, so far as I had been able to discover, wandered somewhere among their peaks and chasms, nursing the wounded of the endless war against the Ascians. That too lay in the mountains. There hundreds of thousands perished for the sake of a pass.

But now we had come to a town where no voice sounded but the raven's. Although we had carried water in skin bags from the herdsman's house, it was nearly gone. Jolenta was weaker, and Dorcas and I agreed that if we did not find more by nightfall, it was likely she would die. Just as Urth began to roll across the sun, we came upon a broken sacrificial table whose basin still caught rain. The water was stagnant and stinking, but in our desperation we allowed Jolenta to drink a few swallows, which she immediately vomited. Urth's turning revealed the moon, now well past the full, so that we gained her weak greenish gleam as we lost the sunlight.

To have come upon a simple campfire would have seemed a miracle. What we actually saw was stranger but less startling. Dorcas pointed to the left. I looked, and a moment later beheld, as I thought, a meteor. "It's a falling star," I said. "Did you see one before? They come in showers sometimes."

"No! That's a building—can't you see it? Look for the dark place against the sky. It must have a flat roof, and someone's up there with flint and steel."

I was about to tell her that she imagined too much, when a dull red glow no bigger, it seemed, than the head of a pin, appeared where the sparks had fallen. Two breaths more, and there was a tiny tongue of flame.

It was not far, but the dark and the broken stones we rode over made it seem so, and by the time we reached the building the fire was bright enough for us to see that three figures crouched about it. "We need your help," I called. "This woman is dying."

All three raised their heads, and a crone's screech asked, "Who speaks? I hear a man's voice, but I see no man. Who are you?"

"Here," I called, and threw back my fuligin cloak and hood. "On your left. I've dark clothes, that's all."

"So you do . . . so you do. Who's dying? Not little pale hair

. . . big red-gold. We've wine here and a fire, but no other physic. Go around, that's where the stair is."

I led our animals around the corner of the building as she had indicated. The stone walls cut off the low moon and left us in blind darkness, but I stumbled on rough steps that must have been made by piling stones from fallen structures against the side of the building. After hobbling the two destriers, I carried Jolenta up, Dorcas going before us to feel the way and warn me of danger.

The roof, when we reached it, was not flat; and the pitch was great enough for me to fear falling at every step. Its hard, uneven surface seemed to be of tiles—once one loosened, and I heard it grating and clattering against the others until it fell over the edge and smashed on the uneven slabs below.

When I was an apprentice and too young to be entrusted with any but the most elementary tasks, I was given a letter to take to the witches' tower, across the Old Court from our own. (I learned much later that there was a good reason for selecting only boys well below the age of puberty to carry the messages our proximity to the witches required.) Now, when I know of the horror our own tower inspired not only in the people of the quarter but to an equal or greater degree in the other residents of the Citadel itself, I find a flavor of quaint naïveté in the recollection of my own fear; yet to the small and unattractive boy I was, it was very real. I had heard terrible stories from the older apprentices, and I had seen that boys unquestionably braver than I were afraid. In that most gaunt of all the Citadel's myriad towers, strangely colored lights burned by night. The screams we heard through the ports of our dormitory came not from some underground examination room like our own, but from the highest levels; and we knew that it was the witches themselves who screamed thus and not their clients, for in the sense we used that word, they had none. Nor were those screams the howlings of lunacy and the shrieks of agony, as ours were.

I had been made to wash my hands so they would not soil the

envelope, and I was very conscious of their dampness and their redness as I picked my way among the puddles of freezing water that dotted the courtyard. My mind conjured up a witch who should be immensely dignified and humiliating, who would not shrink from punishing me in some particularly repulsive way for daring to carry a letter to her in red hands and would send me back with a scornful report to Master Malrubius as well.

I must have been very small indeed: I had to jump to reach the knocker. The smack of the witches' deeply worn doorstep against the thin soles of my shoes remains with me still.

"Yes?" The face that looked into mine was hardly higher than my own. It was one of those—outstanding of its kind among all the hundreds of thousands of faces I have seen—that are at once suggestive of beauty and disease. The witch to whom it belonged seemed old to me and must actually have been about twenty or a little less; but she was not tall, and she carried herself in the bent-backed posture of extreme age. Her face was so lovely and so bloodless that it might have been a mask carved in ivory by some master sculptor.

Mutely, I held up my letter.

"Come with me," she said. Those were the words I had feared, and now that they had actually been given voice, they seemed as inevitable as the procession of the seasons.

I entered a tower very different from our own. Ours was oppressively solid, of plates of metal so closely fitted that they had, ages ago, diffused into one another to become one mass, and the lower floors of our tower were warm and dripping. Nothing seemed solid in the witches' tower, and few things were. Much later, Master Palaemon explained to me that it was far older than most other parts of the Citadel, and had been built when the design of towers was still little more than the imitation in inanimate materials of human physiology, so that skeletons of steel were used to support a fabric of flimsier substances. With the passing of the centuries, that skeleton had largely corroded away—until at last the structure it had once stiffened was held up only by the piecemeal repairs of past generations. Oversized rooms were separated by walls not much thicker than draperies; no floor was level, and no stair straight; each bannister and railing I touched seemed ready to come off in my hand. Gnostic designs in white, green, and purple had been chalked on the walls, but there was little furniture, and the air seemed colder than that outside.

After climbing several stairs and a ladder lashed together from the unpeeled saplings of some fragrant tree, I was ushered into the presence of an old woman who sat in the only chair I had yet seen there, staring through a glass tabletop at what appeared to be an artificial landscape inhabited by hairless, crippled animals. I gave her my letter and was led away; but for a moment she had glanced at me, and her face, like the face of the young-old woman who had brought me to her, has of course remained graven in my mind.

I mention all this now because it seemed to me, as I laid Jolenta on the tiles beside the fire, that the women who crouched over it were the same. It was impossible; the old woman to whom I had handed my letter was almost certainly dead, and the young one (if she were still living) would be changed beyond recognition, as I was myself. Yet the faces that turned toward me were the faces I recalled. Perhaps there are but two witches in the world, who are born into it again and again.

"What is the matter with her?" the younger woman asked, and Dorcas and I explained as well as we could.

Long before we finished, the older one had Jolenta's head in her lap and was forcing wine from a clay bottle into her throat. "It would harm her if it were strong to harm," she said. "But this is three parts pure water. Since you do not wish to see her die, you are fortunate, possibly, to have come across us so. Whether she is also fortunate, I cannot say."

I thanked her, and inquired where the third person who had been at their fire had gone.

The old woman sighed, and stared at me for a moment before returning her attention to Jolenta.

"There were only the two of us," the younger woman said. "You saw three?"

"Very clearly, in the firelight. Your grandmother—if that is who she is—looked up and spoke to me. You and whoever was with you lifted your heads, then bowed them again."

"She is the Cumaean."

I had heard the word before, but for a moment I could not remember where, and the younger woman's face, immobile as an oread's in a picture, gave me no clue.

"The seeress," Dorcas supplied. "And who are you?"

"Her acolyte. My name is Merryn. It is significant, possibly, that you, who are three, saw three of us at the fire, while we who are two at first saw but two of you." She looked to the Cumaean as if for confirmation, and then, as if she had received it, back to us, though I saw no glance pass between them.

"I'm quite sure I saw a third person who was larger than either of you," I said.

"This is a strange evening, and there are those who ride the night air who sometimes choose to borrow a human seeming. The question is why such a power would wish to show itself to you."

The effect of her dark eyes and serene face was so great that I think I might have believed her if it had not been for Dorcas, who suggested with an almost imperceptible movement of her head that the third member of the group about the fire might have escaped our observation by crossing the roof and hiding on the farther side of the ridge.

"She may live," the Cumaean said without lifting her gaze from Jolenta's face. "Though she does not wish it."

"It's a good thing for her that the two of you had so much wine," I said.

The old woman did not rise to the bait, saying only, "Yes, it is. For you and possibly even for her."

Merryn picked up a stick and stirred the fire. "There is no death."

I laughed a little, mostly, I think, because I was no longer quite so worried about Jolenta. "Those of my trade think otherwise."

"Those of your trade are mistaken."

Jolenta murmured, *"Doctor?"* It was the first time she had spoken since morning.

"You do not need a physician now," Merryn said. "Someone better is here."

The Cumaean muttered, "She seeks her lover."

"Who is not this man in fuligin then, Mother? I thought he seemed too common for her."

"He is but a torturer. She seeks a worse."

Merryn nodded to herself, then said to us, "You will not wish to move her farther tonight, but we must ask that you do. You will find a hundred better camping places on the other side of the ruins, and it would be dangerous for you to stay here."

"A danger of death?" I asked. "But you tell me there is none— so if I believe you, why should I fear? And if I cannot believe you, why should I believe you now?" Nevertheless, I rose to go.

The Cumaean looked up. "She's right," she croaked. "Though she does not know it, and only speaks by rote like a starling in a cage. Death is nothing, and for that reason you must fear it. What is more to be feared?"

I laughed again. "I can't argue with someone as wise as you. And because you gave us what help you could, we will go now because you wish it."

The Cumaean permitted me to take Jolenta from her, but said, "I do not wish it. My acolyte still believes the universe hers to command, a board where she can move counters to form whatever patterns suit her. The Magi see fit to number me among themselves when they write their short roll, and I should lose my place on it if I did not know that people like ourselves are only little fish, who must swim with unseen tides if we are not to exhaust ourselves without finding sustenance. Now you must wrap this poor creature in your cloak and lay her by my fire. When this place passes out of the shadow of Urth, I will look to her wound again."

I remained standing, holding Jolenta, uncertain whether we should go or stay. The Cumaean's intentions seemed friendly enough, but her metaphor had carried an unpleasant reminder of the undine; and as I studied her face I had come to doubt that she was an old woman at all, and to recall only too clearly the hideous faces of the cacogens who had removed their masks when Baldanders had rushed among them.

"You shame me, Mother," Merryn said. "Shall I call to him?"

"He has heard us. He will come without your call."

She was right. I already detected the scrape of boots on the tiles of the other side of the roof.

"You are alarmed. Would it not be better to put down the woman as I instructed you, so you might take up your sword to defend your paramour? But there will be no need."

By the time she had finished speaking, I could see a tall hat and a big head and broad shoulders silhouetted against the night sky. I laid Jolenta near Dorcas and drew *Terminus Est*.

"No need of that," a deep voice said. "No need at all, young fellow. I'd have come out sooner to renew our acquaintance, but I didn't know the Chatelaine here wanted it. My master—and yours—sends his greetings." It was Hildegrin.

XXXI

The Cleansing

"YOU MAY TELL your master I delivered his message," I said.

Hildegrin smiled. "And have you a message to return, armiger? Remember, I'm from the quercine penetralia."

"No," I said. "None."

Dorcas looked up. "I do. A person I met in the gardens of the House Absolute told me I would encounter someone who identified himself thus, and that I was to say to him, 'When the leaves are grown, the wood is to march north.'"

Hildegrin laid a finger beside his nose. "*All* the wood? Is that what he said?"

"He gave me the words I have already recited to you, and nothing more."

"Dorcas," I asked, "why didn't you tell me this?"

"I've hardly had an opportunity to talk to you alone since we met at the crossing of the paths. And besides, I could see it was a dangerous thing to know. I couldn't see any reason to put that danger on you. It was the man who gave Dr. Talos all that money who told me. But he didn't give Dr. Talos the message—I know because I listened when they talked. He only said that he was your friend, and told me."

"And told you to tell me."

Dorcas shook her head.

Hildegrin's thick-throated chuckle might almost have come from underground. "Well, it don't hardly matter now, does it? It's been delivered, and for myself I don't mind tellin' you I wouldn't have minded if it had waited a little longer. But we're all friends here, except maybe for the sick girl, and I don't think she can hear what's said, or understand what we're talkin' about if she could. What did you say her name was? I couldn't hear you too clear when I was over there on the other side."

"That was because I didn't say it at all," I told him. "But her name is Jolenta." As I pronounced *Jolenta*, I looked at her, and seeing her in the firelight realized she was Jolenta no longer— nothing of the beautiful woman Jonas had loved remained in that haggard face.

"And a bat bite did it? They've grown uncommon strong lately then. I've been bit a couple of times myself." I looked at Hildegrin sharply, and he added, "Oh yes, I've seen her before, young sieur, as well as yourself and little Dorcas. You didn't think I let you and that other gal leave the Botanic Gardens alone, did you? Not with you talkin' of goin' north and fightin' a officer of the Septentrions. I saw you fight and saw you take that fellow's head off—I helped to catch him, by the bye, because I thought he might be from the House Absolute for true—and I was in the back of the people that watched you on the stage that night. I didn't lose you till the affair at the gate the next day. I seen you and I seen her, though there's not much left of her now except the hair, and I think even that's changed."

Merryn asked the Cumaean, "Shall I tell them, Mother?"

The old woman nodded. "If you can, child."

"She has been imbued with a glamour that rendered her beautiful. It is fading fast now because of the blood she lost, and because she has had a great deal of exercise. By morning only traces will remain."

Dorcas drew back. "Magic, you mean?"

"There is no magic. There is only knowledge, more or less hidden."

Hildegrin was staring at Jolenta with a thoughtful expression. "I didn't know looks could be changed so much. That might be useful, that might. Can your mistress do it?"

"She could do much more than this, if she willed it."

Dorcas whispered, "But how was this done?"

"There have been substances drawn from the glands of beasts added to her blood, to change the pattern in which her flesh was deposited. Those gave her a slender waist, breasts like melons, and so on. They may have been used to add calf to her legs as well. Cleaning and the application of healthening broths to the skin freshened her face. Her teeth were cleaned too, and some were ground down and given false crowns—one has fallen away now, if you'll look. Her hair was dyed, and thickened by sewing threads of colored silk into her scalp. No doubt much body hair was killed as well, and that at least will remain so. Most important, she was promised beauty while entranced. Such promises are believed with faith greater than any child's, and her belief compelled yours."

"Can nothing be done for her?" Dorcas asked.

"Not by me, and it is a not a task of the kind the Cumaean undertakes, save in great need."

"But she will live?"

"As the Mother told you—though she will not wish it."

Hildegrin cleared his throat and spat over the side of the roof. "That's settled then. We've done what we can for her, and it's all we can do. So what I say is let's get on with what we come for. Like you said, Cumaean, it's good these others showed up. I got the message I was supposed to, and they're friends of the Liege of Leaves, just like me. The armiger here can help me fetch up this Apu-Punchau, and what with my two fellows bein' killed on the road, I'll be glad to have him. So what's to keep us from goin' ahead?"

"Nothing," the Cumaean murmured. "The star is in the ascendant."

Dorcas said, "If we're going to assist you with something, shouldn't we know what it is?"

"Bringin' back the past," Hildegrin told her grandly. "Divin' back into the time of old Urth's greatness. There was somebody who used to live in this here place we're sittin' on that knew things that could make a difference. I intend to have him up. It'll be the high point, if I may say it, of a career that's already considered pretty spectacular in knowin' circles."

I asked, "You're going to open the tomb? Surely, even with alzabo—"

The Cumaean reached out to smooth Jolenta's forehead. "We may call it a tomb, but it was not his. His house, rather."

"You see what with me workin' so near," Hildegrin explained, "I've been in the way to do this Chatelaine a favor now and again. More than one, if I may say it, and more than two. Finally I figured the time had come for me to collect. I mentioned my little plan to the Master of the Wood, you may be sure. And here we are."

I said, "I had been given to understand that the Cumaean served Father Inire."

"She pays her debts," Hildegrin announced smugly. "Quality always does. And you don't have to be a wise woman to know it might be wise to have a few friends on the other side, just in case that's the side that wins."

Dorcas asked the Cumaean, "Who was this Apu-Punchau, and why is his palace still standing when the rest of the town is only tumbled stones?"

When the old woman did not reply, Merryn said, "Less than a legend, for not even scholars now remember his story. The Mother has told us that his name means the Head of Day. In the earliest eons he appeared among the people here and taught them many wonderful secrets. Often he vanished, but always he returned. At last he did not return, and invaders laid waste to his cities. Now he shall return for the last time."

"Indeed. Without magic?"

The Cumaean looked up at Dorcas with eyes that seemed as bright as the stars. "Words are symbols. Merryn chooses to delimit magic as that which does not exist . . . and so it does not exist. If you choose to call what we are about to do here magic, then magic lives while we do it. In ancient days, in a land far off, there stood two empires, divided by mountains. One dressed its soldiers in yellow, the other in green. For a hundred generations they struggled. I see that the man with you knows the tale."

"And after a hundred generations," I said, "an eremite came along them and counseled the emperor of the yellow army to dress his men in green, and the master of the green army that he should clothe it in yellow. But the battle continued as before. In my sabretache, I have a book called *The Wonders of Urth and Sky*, and the story is told there."

"That is the wisest of all the books of men," the Cumaean said. "Though there are few who can gain any benefit from reading it. Child, explain to this man, who will be a sage in time, what we do tonight."

The young witch nodded. "All time exists. That is the truth beyond the legends the epopts tell. If the future did not exist now, how could we journey toward it? If the past does not exist still, how could we leave it behind us? In sleep the mind is encircled by its time, which is why we so often hear the voices of the dead there, and receive intelligence of things to come. Those who, like the Mother, have learned to enter the same state while waking live surrounded by their own lives, even as the Abraxas perceives all of time as an eternal instant."

There had been little wind that night, but I noticed now that such wind as there had been had died utterly. A stillness hung in the air, so that despite the softness of Dorcas's voice her words seemed to ring. "Is that what this woman you call the Cumaean will do, then? Enter that state, and speaking with the voice of the dead tell this man whatever it is he wishes to know?"

"She cannot. She is very old, but this city was devastated whole ages before she came to be. Only her own time rings her, for that is all her mind comprehends by direct knowledge. To restore the city, we must make use of a mind that existed when it was whole."

"And is there anyone in the world that old?"

The Cumaean shook her head. "In the world? No. Yet such a mind exists. Look where I point, child, just above the clouds. The red star there is called the Fish's Mouth, and on its one surviving world there dwells an ancient and acute mind. Merryn, take my hand, and you, Badger, take the other. Torturer, take the right hand of your sick friend, and Hildegrin's. Your paramour must take the sick woman's other hand, and Merryn's. . . . Now we are linked, men to one side, women to the other."

"And we'd best do somethin' quick," Hildegrin grumbled. "There's a storm comin', I would say."

"We shall, as quickly as may be. Now I must use all your minds, and the sick woman's will be of little help. You will feel me guiding your thought. Do as I bid you."

Releasing Merryn's hand for a moment, the old woman (if she were in truth a woman at all) reached into her bodice and drew out a rod whose tips vanished into the night as if they were at the borders of my field of vision, though it was hardly longer than a dagger. She opened her mouth; I thought she meant to hold the rod between her teeth, but she swallowed it. A moment later I could detect its glowing image, muted and tinged with crimson, below the sagging skin of her throat.

"Close eyes, all of you. . . . There is a woman here I do not know, a high woman chained . . . never mind, Torturer, I know her now. Do not shrink from my hand. . . . None of you shrink from my hand. . . ."

In the stupor that had followed Vodalus's banquet, I had

known what it was to share my mind with another. This was different. The Cumaean did not appear as I had seen her, or as a young version of herself, or (as it seemed to me) as anything. Rather, I found my thought surrounded by hers, as a fish in a bowl floats in a bubble of invisible water. Thecla was there with me, but I could not see her whole; it was as if she were standing behind me and I saw her hand over my shoulder at one moment, and felt her breath on my cheek at the next.

Then she was gone and everything with her. I felt my thought hurled off into the night, lost among the ruins.

When I recovered, I was lying on the tiles near the fire. My mouth was wet with the foam of my spittle mixed with my own blood, for I had bitten my lips and tongue. My legs were too weak to stand, but I raised myself to a sitting posture again.

At first I thought the others were gone. The roof was solid under me, but they had become, to my sight, as vaporous as ghosts. A phantom Hildegrin sprawled on my right—I thrust my hand into his chest and felt his heart beat against it like a moth that struggled to escape. Jolenta was dimmest of all, hardly present. More had been done to her than Merryn had guessed; I saw wires and bands of metal beneath her flesh, though even they were dim. I looked to myself then, at my legs and feet, and found I could see the Claw burning like a blue flame through the leather of my boot. I grasped it, but there was no strength in my fingers; I could not take it forth.

Dorcas lay as if in sleep. There was no foam flecking her lips, and she was more solid in appearance than Hildegrin. Merryn had collapsed into a black-clad doll, so thin and dim that slender Dorcas seemed robust beside her. Now that intelligence no longer animated that ivory mask, I saw that it was no more than parchment over bone.

As I had suspected, the Cumaean was not a woman at all; yet neither was she one of the horrors I had beheld in the gardens of the House Absolute. Something sleekly reptilian coiled about the glowing rod. I looked for the head but found none, though each of the patternings on the reptile's back was a face, and the eyes of each face seemed lost in rapture.

Dorcas woke while I looked from one to another. "What has happened to us?" she said. Hildegrin was stirring.

"I think we are seeing ourselves from a perspective longer than a single instant's."

Her mouth opened, but there was no cry.

Although the threatening clouds had brought no wind, dust was swirling through the streets below us. I do not know how to describe it except by saying that it seemed as if an uncountable host of minute insects a hundredth the size of midges had been concealed in the crevices of the rough pavement, and now were drawn by the moonlight to their nuptial flight. There was no sound, and no regularity in their motions, but after a time the undifferentiated mass formed swarms that swept to and fro, growing always larger and more dense, and at last sank again to the broken stones.

It seemed then that the insects no longer flew, but crawled over one another, each trying to reach the center of the swarm. "They are alive," I said.

But Dorcas whispered, "Look, they are dead."

She was correct. The swarms that had seethed with life a moment before now showed bleached ribs; the dust motes, linking themselves just as scholars piece together shards of ancient glass to re-create for us a colored window shattered thousands of years before, formed skulls that gleamed green in the moonlight. Beasts—aelurodons, lumbering spelaeae, and slinking shapes to which I could put no name, all fainter than we who watched from the rooftop—moved among the dead.

One by one they rose, and the beasts vanished. Feebly at first, they began to rebuild their town; stones were lifted again, and timbers molded of ashes were laid into sockets in the restored walls. The people, who had seemed hardly more than ambulant corpses when they rose, gathered strength from their work and became a bandylegged race who walked like sailors and rolled cyclopean stones with the might of their wide shoulders. Then the town was complete, and we waited to see what would happen next.

Drums broke the stillness of the night; by their tone I knew that when they had last beat a forest had stood about the town, for they reverberated as sounds only reverberate among the boles of great trees. A shaman with a shaven head paraded the street, naked and painted with pictographs in a script I had never seen, so expressive that the mere shapes of the words seemed to shout their meanings.

Dancers followed him, a hundred or more capering in lockstep, single file, the hands of each on the head of the dancer before him. Their faces were upturned, making me wonder (as I wonder still) if they did not dance in imitation of the hundred-eyed serpent we called the Cumaean. Slowly they coiled and twined, up and down the street, around the shaman and back again until at last they reached the entrance to the house from which we watched them. With a crash like thunder, the stone slab of the door fell. There was an odor as of myrrh and roses.

A man came forth to greet the dancers. If he had possessed a hundred arms, or had worn his head beneath his hands, I could not have been more astonished, for his was a face I had known since childhood, the face of the funeral bronze in the mausoleum where I played as a boy. There were massive gold bracelets on his arms, bracelets set with jacinths and opals, carnelians and flashing emeralds. With measured strides he advanced until he stood in the center of the procession, with the dancers swaying about him. Then he turned toward us and lifted his arms. He was looking at us, and I knew that he, alone of all the hundreds there, truly saw us.

I had been so entranced by the spectacle below me that I had not noticed when Hildegrin left the roof. Now he darted—if so large a man can be said to dart—into the crowd and laid hold of Apu-Punchau.

What followed I hardly know how to describe. In a way it was like the little drama in the house of yellow wood in the Botanic Gardens; yet it was far stranger, if only because I had known then that the woman and her brother, and the savage, were chant-caught. And now it seemed almost that it was Hildegrin, Dorcas, and I who were wrapped in magic. The dancers, I am sure, could not see Hildegrin; but they were somehow aware of him, and cried out against him, and slashed the air with stone-toothed cudgels.

Apu-Punchau, I felt certain, *did* see him, just as he had seen us on the rooftop and as Isangoma had seen Agia and me. Yet I do not believe he saw Hildegrin as I saw him, and it may be that what he saw seemed as strange to him as the Cumaean had to me. Hildegrin held him, but he could not subdue him. Apu-Punchau struggled, but he could not break free. Hildegrin looked up to me and shouted for help.

I do not know why I responded. Certainly I no longer consciously desired to serve Vodalus and his purposes. Perhaps it was the lingering effect of the alzabo, or only the memory of Hildegrin's rowing Dorcas and me across the Lake of Birds.

I tried to push the bandylegged men away, but one of their random blows caught the side of my head and knocked me to my knees. When I rose again, I seemed to have lost sight of Apu-Punchau among the leaping, shrieking dancers. Instead there were two Hildegrins, one who grappled with me, one who fought something invisible. Wildly, I threw off the first and tried to come to the aid of the second.

"Severian!"

Rain beating upon my upturned face awakened me—big drops of cold rain that stung like hail. Thunder rolled across the pampas. For a moment I thought I had gone blind; then a flash of lightning showed me wind-lashed grass and tumbled stones.

"Severian!"

It was Dorcas. I started to rise, and my hand touched cloth as well as mud. I seized it and pulled it free—a long, narrow strip of silk tipped with tassels.

"Severian!" There was terror in the cry.

"Here!" I called. "I'm down here!" Another flash showed me the building and Dorcas's frantic figure silhouetted on the roof. I circled the blind walls and found the steps. Our mounts were gone. On the roof, so were the witches; Dorcas, alone, bent over the body of Jolenta. By lightning, I saw the dead face of the waitress who had served Dr. Talos, Baldanders, and me in the café in Nessus. It had been washed clean of beauty. In the final reckoning there is only love, only that divinity. That we are capable only of being what we are remains our unforgivable sin.

Here I pause again, having taken you, reader, from town to town—from the little mining village of Saltus to the desolate stone town whose very name had long ago been lost among the whirling years. Saltus was for me the gateway to the world beyond the City Imperishable. So too, the stone town was a gateway, a gateway to the mountains I had glimpsed through its ruined arches. For a long way thereafter, I was to journey among their gorges and fastnesses, their blind eyes and brooding faces.

Here I pause. If you wish to walk no farther with me, reader, I do not blame you. It is no easy road.

Appendixes

Social Relationships in the Commonwealth

ONE OF THE translator's most difficult tasks is the accurate expression of matter concerned with caste and position in terms intelligible to his own society. In the case of *The Book of the New Sun*, the lack of supportive material renders it doubly difficult, and nothing more than a sketch is presented here.

So far as can be determined from the manuscripts, the society of the Commonwealth appears to consist of seven basic groups. Of these, one at least seems completely closed. A man or woman must be born an *exultant*, and if so born, remains an exultant throughout life. Although there may well be gradations within this class, the manuscripts indicate none. Its women are called "Chatelaine," and its men by various titles. Outside the city I have chosen to call Nessus, it carries on the administration of day-to-day affairs. Its hereditary assumption of power is deeply at variance with the spirit of the Commonwealth, and sufficiently accounts for the tension evident between the exultants and the autarchy; yet it is difficult to see how local governance might be better arranged under the prevailing conditions—democracy would inevitably degenerate into mere haggling, and an appointive bureaucracy is impossible without a sufficient pool of educated but relatively unmoneyed executives to fill its offices. In any case, the wisdom of the autarchs no doubt includes the principle that an entire sympathy with the ruling class is the most deadly disease of the state. In the manuscripts, Thecla, Thea, and Vodalus are unquestionably exultants.

The *armigers* seem much like exultants, though on a lesser scale. Their name indicates a fighting class, but they do not appear to have monopolized the major roles in the army; no doubt their position could be likened to that of the samurai who served the daimyos of feudal Japan. Lomer, Nicarete, Racho, and Valeria are armigers.

The *optimates* appear to be more or less wealthy traders. Of all the seven, they make the fewest appearances in the manuscripts, though there are some hints that Dorcas originally belonged to this class.

As in every society, the *commonality* constitute the vast bulk of the population. Generally content with their lot, ignorant because their nation is too poor to educate them, they resent the exultants' arrogance and stand in awe of the Autarch, who is, however, in the final analysis their own apotheosis. Jolenta, Hildegrin, and the villagers of Saltus all belong to this class, as do countless other characters in the manuscripts.

Surrounding the Autarch—who appears to distrust the exultants, and no doubt with good reason—are the *servants of the throne*. They are his administrators and advisors, both in military and civil life. They appear to be drawn from the commonality, and it is noteworthy that they treasure such education as they have obtained. (For contrast, see Thecla's contemptuous rejection of it.) Severian himself and the other inhabitants of the Citadel, with the exception of Ultan, might be said to belong to this class.

The *religious* are almost as enigmatic as the god they serve, a god that appears fundamentally solar, but not Apollonian. (Because the Conciliator is given a Claw, one is tempted to make the easy association of the eagle of Jove with the sun; it is perhaps too pat.) Like the Roman Catholic clergy of our own day, they appear to be members of various orders, but unlike them they seem subject to no uniting authority. At times there is something suggestive of Hinduism about them, despite their obvious monotheism. The Pelerines, who play a larger part in the manuscripts than any other holy community, are clearly a sisterhood of priestesses, accompanied (as such a roving group would have to be in their place and time) by armed male servants.

Lastly, the *cacogens* represent, in a way we can hardly more than sense, that foreign element that by its very foreignness is most universal, existing in nearly every society of which we have knowledge. Their common name seems to indicate that they are feared, or at least hated, by the commonality. Their presence at the Autarch's festival would seem to show that they are accepted (though perhaps under duress) at court. Although the populace of Severian's time appears to consider them a homogeneous group, it appears likely that they are in fact diverse. In the manuscripts, the Cumaean and Father Inire represent this element.

The honorific I have translated as *sieur* would seem to belong only to the highest classes, but to be widely misapplied at the lower levels of society. *Goodman* properly indicates a householder.

Money, Measures, and Time

I HAVE FOUND it impossible to derive precise estimates of the values of the coins mentioned in the original of *The Book of the New Sun*. In the absence of certainty, I have used *chrisos* to designate any piece of gold stamped with the profile of an autarch; although these no doubt differ somewhat in weight and purity, it appears they are of roughly equal value.

The even more various silver coins of the period I have lumped together as *asimi*.

The large brass coins (which appear from the manuscripts to furnish the principal medium of exchange among the common people) I have called *orichalks*.

The myriad small brass, bronze, and copper tokens (not struck by the central government, but by the local archons at need, and intended only for provincial circulation) I have called *aes*. A single aes buys an egg; an orichalk, a day's work from a common laborer; an asimi, a well made coat suitable for an optimate; a chrisos, a good mount.

It is important to remember that measures of length or distance are not, strictly speaking, commensurable. In this book, *league* designates a distance of about three miles; it is the correct measure for distances between cities, and within large cities such as Nessus.

The *span* is the distance between the extended thumb and forefinger—about eight inches. A *chain* is the length of a measuring chain of 100 links, in which each link measures a span; it is thus roughly 70 feet.

An *ell* represents the traditional length of the military arrow; five spans, or about 40 inches.

The *pace*, as used here, indicates a single step, or about two and a half feet. The *stride* is a double step.

The most common measure of all, the distance from a man's elbow to the tip of his longest finger (about 18 inches), I have given as a *cubit*. (It will be observed that throughout my translation I have preferred modern words that will be understandable to every reader in attempting to reproduce—in the Roman alphabet—the original terms.)

Words indicative of duration seldom occur in the manuscripts; one sometimes intuits that the writer's sense of the passage of time, and that of the society to which he belongs, has been dulled by dealings with intelligences who have been subjected to, or have surmounted, the Einsteinian time paradox. Where they occur, a *chiliad* designates a period of 1,000 years. An *age* is the interval between the exhaustion of some mineral or other resource in its naturally occurring form (for example, sulfur) and the next. The *month* is the (then) lunar one of 28 days, and the *week* is thus precisely equal to our own week: a quarter of the lunar month, or seven days. A *watch* is the duty period of a sentry: one-tenth of the night, or approximately one hour and 15 minutes.

G.W.